Ruth Rendell

NO MORE DYING THEN

MURDER BEING ONCE DONE

A GUILTY THING SURPRISED

CRESSET
EDITIONS

This edition published in 1998 by Cresset Editions,
an imprint of Random House UK Ltd,
20 Vauxhall Bridge Road, London SW1V 2SA

No More Dying first published in 1991 by Hutchinson
Murder Being Once Done first published in 1992 by
Hutchinson
A Guilty Thing Surprised first published in 1970 by
Hutchinson

Printed and bound in Germany

ISBN 0 0918 6678 2

NO MORE DYING THEN

For Gerald Austin

So shalt thou feed on death that feeds on men,
And death, once dead, there's no more dying then.

Shakespeare, Sonnet 146

1

THE spell of fine weather which so often occurs in the middle of October is known as St Luke's Little Summer. The 'little summer' part needs no explanation; the St Luke bit derives from its coincidence with the eighteenth, which is that saint's day. Basking in the warm autumn sunlight, Station Sergeant Camb delivered this piece of interesting but useless information to Harry Wild and smiled sententiously.

'Is that so? Maybe I'll do a diary note on it.' Wild sucked at his smelly old pipe and rested leather-patched elbows on the counter top. He yawned. 'Haven't you got anything more exciting for me?'

Camb caught the yawn and yawned himself. He remarked for the third time on the closeness of the weather and then he opened his book.

'Two vehicles in collision at the junction of Kingsmarkham High Street and Queen Street,' he read. 'Nobody hurt. That was Sunday. Nothing in that for the *Courier*, is there? Girl of seventeen missing, but we know where she is all right. Oh, and there's a baboon got lost from the pet shop . . .' Wild looked up, lazily enquiring. '. . . Only they found it up on their balcony, tucking in to the waste bin.'

'What a dump,' said Wild. He put away his notebook. 'Still, I opted for the quiet life. I could be up in Fleet Street tomorrow if I fancied it. Only got to say the word and I'd be up there where it's all happening.'

'Sure you would.' Camb knew very well that Wild remained as chief reporter of the *Kingsmarkham Courier* because idleness and general ineptitude, as well now as his advancing years, made him unfit for any more illustrious newspaper. Wild had been coming into the police station for

7

more years than Camb cared to remember and every time he came he talked about Fleet Street as if he had rejected it and not it him. But they sustained the fiction for the sake of peace and pleasantness. 'Much the same for me,' he said. 'Many a time in the old days Mr Wexford begged me to consider the C.I.D. but I wouldn't. I'm not ambitious. I don't say I wouldn't have had the ability, mind.'

'Of course you would've.' Playing fair, Wild returned praise for praise. 'Where does it get you, though, ambition? Look at Inspector Burden, just to take an example. Worn out, and not forty yet, I daresay.'

'Well, he's had a lot of trouble, hasn't he? Losing his wife like that and two kids to bring up.'

Wild gave a heavy lugubrious sigh. 'That,' he said, 'was a tragic business. Cancer, wasn't it?'

'That's right. Fit as a fiddle this time last year and dead by Christmas. Only thirty-five. It makes you think.'

'In the midst of life. Looks to me as if he's taken it hard. I suppose they were a devoted couple?'

'More like sweethearts than man and wife.' Camb cleared his throat and stood up straighter as the lift opened and Chief Inspector Wexford marched out.

'Gossiping again, Sergeant? Good afternoon, Harry.' Wexford just glanced at the two empty teacups on the counter. 'This place,' he said, 'gets more like a Mothers' Union bun fight every week.'

'I was just telling Mr Wild,' said Camb with dignity, 'about our escaped baboon.'

'My God, that's hot news. There's a story in that, Harry. Terrorising the populace, mothers afraid to let their kids out of their sight. Is any woman safe while this wild beast roams our meadows?'

'It's been found, sir. In a dustbin.'

'Sergeant, if I didn't know you to be incapable of it, I should say you were mocking me.' Wexford quivered with silent laughter. 'When Inspector Burden comes in, tell him I've gone, will you? I want a few hours to enjoy our Indian Summer.'

'St Luke's Little Summer, sir.'

'Indeed? I stand corrected. I wish I had the time to devote

8

to digging up these fascinating pieces of meteorological lore. I'll give you a lift, Harry, if you've finished your monkey business.'

Camb sniggered. 'Thanks very much,' said Wild.

It was gone five but still very warm. The sergeant stretched and wished Constable Peach would appear so that he could send him to the canteen for another cup of tea. Half an hour and he would knock off.

Presently the phone rang.

A woman's voice, low and rich. Actressy, Camb thought. 'I'm sorry to trouble you, but my little boy . . . He's—well, hc was out playing and he's—he's disappeared. I don't . . . Am I making a fuss over nothing?'

'Not at all, madam,' said Camb soothingly. 'That's what we're here for, to be troubled. What name is it?'

'Lawrence. I live at 61 Fontaine Road, Stowerton.'

Camb hesitated for a second. Then he remembered Wexford had told him all cases of missing children must be reported to C.I.D. They didn't want another Stella Rivers . . .

'Don't worry, Mrs Lawrence. I'm going to put you through to someone who will help you.' He got the switchboard and heard Sergeant Martin's voice, put down the receiver.

Sergeant Camb sighed. It was a pity Harry had gone like that, just when the only piece of news had come in for weeks. He could give poor old Harry a ring . . . Tomorrow would do. The kid would be found, come to that, like that monkey had been. Missing people and things usually were found in Kingsmarkham and in more or less good order. Camb turned his head in the sunlight like someone turning a piece of toast in the red light of a fire. It was twenty past five. By six he'd be sitting down to his dinner in Severn Court, Station Road; then a little jaunt out with the wife to the Dragon, then telly . . .

'Having a nice little kip, Sergeant?' said a cold voice with an edge to it like a freshly unwrapped razor blade. Camb nearly jumped out of his skin.

'Sorry, Mr Burden. It's the heat, makes you sleepy. St Luke's Little Summer, they call it, on account of . . .'

'Are you off your bloody head?' Burden had never sworn in the old days. It had been quite a joke in the police station

9

the way he never took the name of the Lord in vain or said bloody or any of the things everyone else said. Camb liked the old days better. He felt his face reddening and it wasn't the sun. 'Any messages for me?' Burden snapped.

Camb looked at him sadly. He was terribly sorry for Inspector Burden, his heart ached for his bereaved colleague, and that was why he forgave Burden for humiliating him and showing him up in front of Martin and Gates and even Peach. Camb couldn't imagine what it must be like to lose one's wife, the mother of one's children, and be alone and desolate. Burden was so thin. The sharp high cheekbones jutted out of his taut skin and his eyes glittered nastily when you glanced at them but they were unbearable when you looked deeper. Once he had been rather a handsome man, English-looking, blond and ruddy, but now all the colour and life had gone out of him and he was a sort of grey. He still wore a black tie, pulled so tight you thought it would choke him.

Once, when it had first happened, the sergeant had expressed his sympathy along with everyone else, and that was all right, that was expected. And then, later, he had tried to say something more sincere and more personal, and Burden had swung on him like a man drawing a sword. He had said terrible things. It was more terrible to hear them coming from those mild cool lips than from the mouths of the Kingsmarkham roughs who used them habitually. It was like opening a nice book written by someone whose books you liked and asked the library to keep for you, opening it and reading a word that used to be printed with an f and a dash.

So, although Camb wanted at this moment to say something kind—wasn't he old enough to be this man's father?—he only sighed and replied in a blank official voice, 'Mr Wexford went home, sir. He said he . . .'

'That's all?'

'No, sir. There's a child missing and . . .'

'Why the hell didn't you say so before?'

'It's all taken care of,' Camb stammered. 'Martin knows and he's bound to have phoned Mr Wexford. Look, sir, it's not for me to interfere, but—well, why don't you just go home, sir?'

'When I require your instructions, Sergeant, I'll ask for

10

them. The last child that went missing here was never found. *I am not going home.*' I have nothing to go home for. He didn't say it, but the words were there and the sergeant heard them. 'Get me an outside line, will you?'

Camb did so and Burden said, 'My home.' When Grace Woodville answered, Camb gave the phone to her brother-in-law. 'Grace? Mike. Don't wait dinner for me. There's a child missing. I should be in by ten.'

Burden crashed down the receiver and made for the lift. Camb watched the doors blankly for ten minutes and then Sergeant Mathers came down to take over the desk.

The bungalow in Tabard Road looked exactly as it had done in Jean Burden's lifetime. The floors gleamed, the windows shone and there were flowers—chrysanthemums at this season —in the Poole pottery vases. Plain English food was served at regular times and the children had the cared-for look of children who have a loving mother. The beds were made by eight-thirty, the washing was on the line by nine and a pleasant cheerful voice sounded a greeting to those who came home.

Grace Woodville had seen to all this. It had seemed to her the only way, to keep the house as her sister had done, to act with the children as her sister had done. She already looked as much like her sister as is possible for two women who are not twins. And it had worked. Sometimes she thought John and Pat almost forgot. They came to her when they were hurt or in trouble or had something interesting to tell just as they had gone to Jean. They seemed happy, recovered from the wound of Christmas. It had worked for them and the house and the practical business of running things, but it hadn't worked for Mike. Of course it hadn't. Had she really thought it would?

She put down the phone and looked into the glass where she saw Jean's face looking back at her. Her own face had never seemed like Jean's while Jean was alive, but quite different, squarer and stronger and more fulfilled and—well, why not say it?—more intelligent. It was like Jean's now. The liveliness had gone out of it, the sharp wit, and that wasn't surprising when she thought how she spent her days,

11

cooking and cleaning and comforting and waiting at home for a man who took it all for granted.

She called out, 'John? That was your father. He won't be home till ten. I think we'll eat, shall we?' His sister was in the garden, gathering caterpillars for the collection she kept in the garage. Grace was more afraid of caterpillars than most women are of mice or spiders, but she had to pretend to like them, even to gloat over them, because she was all Pat had for a mother. 'Pat! Food, darling. Don't be long.'

The little girl was eleven. She came in and opened the matchbox she was holding. Grace's heart squeezed and chilled at the sight of the fat green thing inside. 'Lovely,' she said faintly. 'A lime hawk?' She had done her home-work, and Pat, like all children, valued adults who bothered.

'Look at his sweet face.'

'Yes, I am. I hope he'll grow into a chrysalis before the leaves die off. Daddy won't be home for dinner.'

Pat gave an indifferent shrug. She didn't love her father much at present. He had loved her mother more than her, she knew that now, and she also knew that he ought to love her to make up for what she had lost. One of the teachers at school had told her that he would, that all fathers did that. She had waited and he hadn't. He had always stayed out late working but now he stayed out nearly all the time. She transferred her simple animal-like love to her Aunt Grace. Privately she thought it would be nice if John and her father went away and left her with her aunt and then the two of them would have a lovely time collecting better and rarer caterpillars and reading books on natural history and science and the Bolshoi Ballet.

She sat down at the table next to her aunt and then began to eat the chicken-and-ham pie which was just like the ones Jean used to make.

Her brother said, 'We had a debate at school today on the equality of the sexes.'

'That was interesting,' said Grace. 'What did you have to say?'

'I left most of the talking to the others. One thing I did say, women's brains don't weigh as much as men's.'

'They do,' said Pat.

12

'No, they don't. They don't, do they, Auntie Grace?'

'I'm afraid they don't,' said Grace, who had been a nurse. 'But that doesn't mean they aren't as good.'

'I bet,' said Pat with a vindictive look at her brother, 'I bet mine weighs more than yours. My head's bigger. Anyway, it's all boring, discussions and stuff. A lot of talk.'

'Come along, darling, eat your pie.'

'When I am grown up,' said Pat, beginning on a perennial theme, 'I'm not going to talk and argue and do boring things. I'm going to get my degree—no, maybe I'll wait till I've got my doctorate—and then I'm going to go to Scotland and make a big investigation of the lochs, all the very deep lochs, and discover the monsters that live in them, and then I'm . . .'

'There aren't any monsters. They looked and they never found one.'

Pat ignored her brother. 'I'll have divers and a special boat and a whole staff and Auntie Grace will be at the station looking after us and cooking for us.'

They began to argue fiercely. It could happen, Grace thought. That was the horrible thing, it could just happen. Sometimes she could see herself staying here until they were grown up and she was old and then tagging along after Pat, being her housekeeper. What else would she be fit for then? And what did it matter whether her brain weighed less than a man's or more or the same when it was stuck in a little house in the depths of Sussex, atrophying away?

She had been a sister in a big London teaching hospital when Jean died and she had taken the six weeks' leave that was owing to her to come here and care for Mike and Mike's children. Just six weeks she was going to stay. You didn't spend years of your life studying, taking cuts in salary, to study for more qualifications, going to the States for two years to learn the latest obstetric methods at a Boston clinic, and then just give it all up. The hospital board had told her not to and she had laughed at the very idea. But the six weeks had lengthened into six months, into nine, ten, and now her post at the hospital had been filled by someone else.

She looked thoughtfully at the children. How could she leave them now? How could she even think of leaving them

13

for five years? And then Pat would be only sixteen.

It was all Mike's fault. A hard thing to think, but true. Other men lost their wives. Other men adjusted. On Mike's salary and with his allowances he could afford a housekeeper. And it wasn't only that. A man as intelligent as Mike ought to realise what he was doing to her and the children. She had come at his invitation, his passionate plea, thinking that she would have his support in her task, certain that he would make an effort to be home in the evenings, take the children out at weekends, compensate them in some measure for the loss of their mother. He had done none of this. How long was it now since he'd spent one evening at home? Three weeks? Four? And he wasn't always working. One night when she could no longer stand the sight of John's bitter rebellious face she had phoned Wexford and the chief inspector had told her Mike went off duty at five. A neighbour had told her later where Mike went. She had seen him sitting in his car on one of the paths in Cheriton Forest, just sitting still and staring at the straight, parallel, endless trees.

'Shall we have some television?' she said, trying to keep the weariness out of her voice. 'There's quite a good film on, I believe.'

'Too much homework,' John said, 'and I can't do the maths till my father comes. Did you say he'd be back at ten?'

'He said about ten.'

'I think I'll go into my room, then.'

Grace and Pat sat on the sofa and watched the film. It was all about the domestic lives of policemen and bore little relation to reality.

Burden drove to Stowerton, through the new part and into the old High Street. Fontaine Road was parallel with Wincanton Road, and there, years and years ago when they were first married, he and Jean had for six months rented a flat. Wherever he went in Kingsmarkham and its environs he kept coming on places that he and Jean had been to or visited on some special occasion. He couldn't avoid them, but the sight of them brought fresh hurt every time and the pain did not diminish. Since her death he had avoided Wincanton Road, for there they had been especially happy, young lovers

14

learning what love was. Today had been a bad day, bad in that for some reason he was ultra-sensitive and prickly, and he felt that the sight of the house where their flat had been would be the last straw. Control might go utterly and he would stand at the gate and weep.

He didn't even look at the street name as he passed it but kept his eyes fixed straight ahead. He turned left into Fontaine Road and stopped outside number 61.

It was a very ugly house, built about eighty years ago, and surrounded by a wild untended garden full of old fruit trees whose leaves lay in drifts on the grass. The house itself was built of khaki-coloured bricks with a shallow, almost flat, slate roof. Its windows were the sash kind and very small, but the front door was enormous, quite out of proportion, a great heavy thing with inset panels of red and blue stained glass. It was slightly ajar.

Burden didn't go into the house at once. Wexford's car, among other police cars, was parked against the fence which divided the end of the street from the field Stowerton Council had turned into a children's playground. Beyond this came more fields, woods, the rolling countryside.

Wexford was sitting in his car, studying an ordnance survey map. He looked up as Burden approached and said:

'Good of you to get here so fast. I've only just arrived myself. Will you talk to the mother or shall I?'

'I will,' said Burden.

There was a heavy knocker on the front door of number 61, shaped like a lion's head with a ring in its mouth. Burden touched it lightly and then he pushed open the door.

2

A YOUNG woman was standing in the hall, holding her hands clasped in front of her. The first thing Burden noticed about her was her hair which was the same colour as the dead apple leaves that had blown in on to the tiled passage floor. It was fiery copper hair, neither straight nor curly but massy and glittering like fine wire or thread spun on a distaff, and it stood out from her small white face and fell to the middle of her back.

'Mrs Lawrence?'

She nodded.

'My name is Burden, Inspector Burden, C.I.D. Before we talk about this I'd like a photograph of your son and some article of clothing he's recently worn.'

She looked at him, wide-eyed, as if he were a clairvoyant who could sense the missing boy's whereabouts from handling his garments.

'For the dogs,' he said gently.

She went upstairs and he heard her banging about feverishly, opening drawers. Yes, he thought, it would be an untidy house with nothing in its place, nothing to hand. She came back, running, with a dark green school blazer and an enlarged snapshot. Burden looked at the photograph as he hurried up the road. It was of a big sturdy child, neither very clean nor very tidy, but undeniably beautiful, with thick light hair and large dark eyes.

The men who had come to search for him stood about in groups, some in the swings field, some clustered around the police cars. There were sixty or seventy of them, neighbours, friends and relatives of neighbours, and others who had arrived on bicycles from further afield. The speed with which news of this kind travels always amazed Burden. It was

16

scarcely six o'clock. The police themselves had only been alerted half an hour before.

He approached Sergeant Martin, who seemed to be involved in some kind of altercation with one of the men, and handed him the photograph.

'What was all that about?' said Wexford.

'Chap told me to mind my own business because I advised him he'd need thicker shoes. That's the trouble with getting the public in, sir. They always think they know best.'

'We can't do without them, Sergeant,' Wexford snapped. 'We need every available man at a time like this, police and public.'

The two most efficient and experienced searchers belonged, properly speaking, in neither category. They sat a little apart from the men and viewed them with wary scorn. The labrador bitch's coat gleamed like satin in the last of the sun, but the alsatian's thick pelt was dull and rough and wolf-like. With a quick word to the man Sergeant Martin had admonished not to go near the dogs—he appeared to be about to caress the alsatian—Wexford passed the blazer over to the labrador's handler.

While the dogs explored the blazer with expert noses, Martin formed the men into parties, a dozen or so in each and each with its leader. There were too few torches to go round and Wexford cursed the season with its deceptive daytime heat and its cold nights that rushed in early. Already dark fingers of cloud were creeping across the redness of the sky and a sharp bite of frost threatened. It would be dark before the search parties reached the wood that crouched like a black and furry bear over the edges of the fields.

Burden watched the small armies enter the wide swings field and begin the long hunt that would take them to Forby and beyond. A frosty oval moon, just beginning to wane from the full, showed above the woods. If only it would shine bright, unobscured by that blue-black floating cloud, it would be a greater asset than all their torches.

The women of Fontaine Road who had hung over their gates to see the men go now strayed lingeringly back into their houses. Each one of them would have to be questioned. Had she seen anything? Anyone? Had anything at all out of

17

the way happened that day? On Wexford's orders, Loring and Gates were beginning a house-to-house investigation. Burden went back to Mrs Lawrence and followed her into the front room, a big room full of ugly Victorian furniture to match the house. Toys and books and magazines were scattered everywhere and there were clothes about, shawls and scarves draped over the furniture. A long patchwork dress on a hanger hung from a picture rail.

The place looked even dirtier and frowstier when she switched on the standard lamp, and she looked stranger. She wore jeans, a satin shirt and strings of tarnished chains around her neck. He didn't need to admire her, but he would have liked to be able to feel sympathy. This woman with her wild hair and her strange clothes made him immediately feel that she was no fit person to be in charge of a child and even that her appearance and all he associated with it had perhaps contributed to that child's disappearance. He told himself not to jump to conclusions, not yet.

'Now, what is the boy's name and how old is he?'

'John. He's five.'

'Not at school today?'

'It's half-term for the primary schools,' she said. 'I'll tell you about this afternoon, shall I?'

'Please.'

'Well, we had our lunch, John and I, and after lunch at about two his friend from next door came to call for him. He's called Gary Dean and he's five too.' She was very composed, but now she swallowed and cleared her throat.' 'They were going to play in the street on their tricycles. It's quite safe. They know they have to stay on the pavement.

'When John goes out to play I look out of the window every half-hour or so to see he's all right and I did that today. You can see all the street and the field where the swings are from my landing window. Well, for a bit they played on the pavement with the other boys, all boys from around here, but when I looked out at half past three they'd gone into the swings field.'

'You could make out your son from this distance?'

'He's wearing a dark blue sweater and he's got fair hair.'

'Go on, Mrs Lawrence.'

18

She took a deep breath and clasped the fingers of one hand tightly in the other.

'They'd left their tricycles in a sort of huddle on the pavement. The next time I looked they were all on the swings and I could pick out John by his hair and his sweater. Or—or I thought I could. There were six boys there, you see. Anyway, when I looked out again they'd all gone and I went down to open the front door for John. I thought he must be coming in for his tea.'

'But he wasn't?'

'No, his tricycle was on the pavement by itself.' She bit her lip, her face very white now. 'There weren't any children in the street. I thought John must have gone into someone else's house—he does that sometimes although he's not supposed to without telling me so I waited—oh, five minutes, not more—and then I went into the Deans to see if he was there. It gave me a shock,' she said, half-whispering. 'That was when I first started getting frightened. Gary was there, having his tea, and there was a boy with him in a blue sweater and with fair hair, but it wasn't John. It was his cousin who'd come over for the afternoon. You see, I realised then that the boy I'd been thinking was John ever since half past three was this cousin.'

'What did you do next?'

'I asked Gary where John was and he said he didn't know. He'd gone some hours ago, he said—that was how he put it, hours ago—and they thought he was with me. Well, I went to another boy's house then, a boy called Julian Crantock at 59, and Mrs Crantock and I, we got it out of Julian. He said Gary and the cousin had started on John, just silly children's teasing, but you know what they're like, how they hurt each other and get hurt. They picked on John about his sweater, said it was a girl's because of the way the buttons do up at the neck, and John—well, Julian said he sat on the roundabout by himself for a bit and then he just walked off towards the road.'

'This road? Fontaine Road?'

'No. The lane that runs between the swings field and the farm fields. It goes from Stowerton to Forby.'

'I know it,' Burden said, 'Mill Lane. There's a drop into

19

it from those fields, down a bank, and there are trees all along the top of the bank.'

She nodded. 'But why would he go there? Why? He's been told again and again he's never to leave the street or the swings field.'

'Little boys don't always do as they are told, Mrs Lawrence. Was it after this that you phoned us?'

'Not at once,' she said. She lifted her eyes and met Burden's. They were greenish-grey eyes and they held a terrified bewilderment, but she kept her voice low and even. 'I went to the houses of all the boys. Mrs Crantock came with me and when they all said the same, about the quarrel and John going off, Mrs Crantock got out her car and we drove along Mill Lane all the way to Forby and back, looking for John. We met a man with cows and we asked him, and a postman and someone delivering vegetables, but nobody had seen him. And then I phoned you.'

'So John has been missing since about three-thirty?'

She nodded. 'Nearly three hours. It's getting dark. He's afraid of the dark.'

Her composure remained and yet Burden felt that the wrong word or gesture from him, perhaps even a sudden sound, would puncture it and release a scream of terror. He didn't quite know what to make of her. She looked peculiar, the kind of woman who belonged to a world he knew of only through newspapers. He had seen pictures of her, or of women who closely resembled her, leaving London courts after being found guilty of possessing cannabis. Such as she were found dead in furnished rooms after an overdose of barbiturates and drink. Such as she? The face was the same, pinched and pale, and the wild hair and the repellent clothes. It was her control which puzzled him and the sweet soft voice which didn't fit the image he had made for her of eccentric conduct and an unsound life.

'Mrs Lawrence,' he began, 'we get dozens of cases of missing children in the course of our work and more than ninety per cent of them are found safe and sound.' He wasn't going to mention the girl who hadn't been found at all. Someone else probably would, some interfering neighbour, but perhaps by then the boy would be back with his mother. 'Do you know

20

what happens to most of them? They wander away out of
pique or bravado and get lost and exhausted, so they lie down
in some warm hole and—sleep.'

Her eyes dismayed him. They were so large and staring
and she hardly seemed to blink at all. Now he saw in them
a faint gleam of hope. 'You are very kind to me,' she said
gravely. 'I trust you.'

Burden said awkwardly, 'That's good. You trust us and
let us do the worrying, eh? Now what time does your husband get home?'

'I'm divorced. I live alone.'

He wasn't surprised. She would be divorced. She couldn't
be more than twenty-eight and by the time she was thirty-
eight she would probably have been married and divorced
twice more. God knew what combination of circumstances
had brought her to the depths of Sussex from London where
she rightly belonged, to live in squalour and cause untold
trouble to the police by her negligence.

Her quiet voice, grown rather shaky, broke into his harsh
and perhaps unjust reverie. 'John's all I've got. I've no one
in the world but John.'

And whose fault was that? 'We'll find him,' said Burden
firmly. 'I'll find a woman to be with you. Perhaps this Mrs
Crantock?'

'Would you? She's very nice. Most of the people around
here are nice, although they're not . . .' She paused and considered. 'They're not quite like any people I've known
before.'

I'll bet they're not, thought Burden. He glanced at the
patchwork dress. For what respectable social occasion would
any woman choose to wear a thing like that?

She didn't come to the door with him. He left her staring
into space, playing with the long chain of beads that hung
round her neck. But when he was outside he looked back
and saw her white face at the window, a smeared dirty window that those thin hands had never polished. Their eyes
met for a moment and convention forced him to grin uneasily.
She gave no answering smile but only stared, her face as
pale and wan as the moon between clouds of heavy hair.

21

Mrs Crantock was a neat and cheerful woman who wore her greying black hair in crisp curls and a string of cultured pearls against her pink twinset. At Burden's request she left immediately to keep Mrs Lawrence company. Her husband had already gone off with the search parties and only Julian and his fourteen-year-old sister remained in the house.

'Julian, when you saw John walk off towards Mill Lane, did you see anything else? Did anyone speak to him?'

The boy shook his head. 'He just went off.'

'And then what did he do? Did he stand under the trees or go down the lane?'

'Don't know.' Julian fidgeted and looked down. 'I was on the swings.'

'Did you look over towards the lane? Didn't you look to see where he was?'

'He'd gone,' said Julian. 'Gary said he'd gone and a jolly good thing because we didn't want babies.'

'I see.'

'Honestly, he doesn't know,' said the sister. 'We've been on and on at him but he really doesn't know.'

Burden gave up and went to the Deans at 63.

'I'm not having Gary hounded,' said Mrs Dean, a hard-looking young woman with an aggressive manner. 'Children quarrel all the time. Gary's not to be blamed because John Lawrence is so sensitive that a bit of teasing makes him run off. The child's disturbed. That's what's at the root of the trouble. He comes from a broken home, so what can you expect?'

These were Burden's own sentiments. 'I'm not blaming Gary,' he said. 'I just want to ask him some questions.'

'I'm not having him bullied.'

These days the least bit of opposition was liable to set him off.

'You're at liberty,' he said sharply, 'to report me to the Chief Constable, madam, if I bully him.'

The boy was in bed but not asleep. He came down in his dressing-gown, his eyes sulky and his lip stuck out.

'Now, Gary, I'm not angry with you. No one's angry. We just want to find John. You understand that, don't you?'

The boy didn't answer.

'He's tired,' said his mother. 'He's told you he didn't see anyone and that ought to be enough.'

Burden ignored her. He leant towards the boy. 'Look at me, Gary.' The eyes which met his were full of tears. 'Don't cry. You could help us, Gary. Wouldn't you like everyone to think of you as the boy who helped the police to find John? All I want you to tell me is if you saw anyone at all, any grown-up, by the lane when John went away.'

'I didn't see them today,' said Gary. He screamed and threw himself on his mother. 'I didn't see them, I didn't!'

'I hope you're satisfied,' said Mrs Dean. 'I'm warning you, I shall take this further.'

'I didn't see that person,' Gary sobbed.

'Well, Mike?' said Wexford.

'It looks as if a man's been hanging about that playing field. I thought I might have a go at the people in the end houses overlooking the swings field.'

'All right, and I'll try the two end ones in Wincanton.'

Did Wexford remember that he and Jean had once lived there? Burden wondered if he was attributing an excess of sensitivity to the chief inspector. Probably. A policeman has no private life when on a case. He made his way to the bottom of Fontaine Road. The fields were dark now but occasionally in the far distance, he could make out the gleam from a torch.

The last two houses faced each other. One was a detached bungalow, vintage 1935, the other a tall narrow Victorian place. Both had side windows facing the field. Burden knocked at the bungalow and a girl came to the door.

'I'm out at work all day,' she said. 'I've only just got in and my husband isn't home yet. What's happened? Has something awful happened?'

Burden told her.

'You can see the field from my window,' she said, 'but I'm never here.'

'I won't waste your time, then.'

'I hope you find him,' the girl said.

The door of the Victorian house was opened before he reached it. As soon as he saw the face of the woman who

23

was waiting for him he knew she had something to tell him. She was elderly, sharp-eyed and spry.

'It wasn't that man, was it? I'll never forgive myself if it was him and I . . .'

'Perhaps I could come in a minute? And may I have your name?'

'Mrs Mitchell.' She took him into a neat, newly decorated room. 'I ought to have gone to the police before but you know how it is. He never did anything, he never even spoke to any of the children. I did mention it to young Mrs Rushworth because her Andrew plays there, but she's always so busy, out at work all day, and I expect she forgot to tell the other mothers. And then when he didn't come back and the children went back to school . . .'

'Let's begin at the beginning, shall we, Mrs Mitchell? You saw a man hanging about the swings field. When did you first see him?'

Mrs Mitchell sat down and took a deep breath. 'It was in August, during the school holidays. I always clean my upstairs windows on a Wednesday afternoon and one Wednesday I was doing the landing window and I saw this man.'

'Where did you see him?'

'Over by the Forby road, Mill Lane, under the trees. He was standing there, looking at the children. Let me see, there was Julian Crantock and Gary Dean and poor little John Lawrence and Andrew Rushworth and the McDowell twins, and they were all playing on the swings and this man was looking at them. Oh, I should have gone to the police!'

'You spoke to one of the mothers, Mrs Mitchell. You mustn't reproach yourself. I take it you saw this man again?'

'Oh, yes, the next Wednesday, and I made a point of looking the next day, the Thursday, and he was there again, and it was then I spoke to Mrs Rushworth.'

'So, in fact, you saw him often throughout the August holiday?'

'We had a spell of bad weather after that and the children couldn't go into the field, and then it was time to go back to school. I forgot all about the man after that. Until yesterday.'

'You saw him *yesterday*?'

24

Mrs Mitchell nodded. 'It was Wednesday and I was doing the landing window. I saw the children come into the field and then this man appeared. It gave me a shock, seeing him again after two months. I thought to myself, I'm going to stand at this window and watch you and see what you do. But he didn't do anything. He walked around the field and he picked some leaves, branches of autumn leaves, you know, and then he stood still for a bit, looking at the boys. He was there for about half an hour and when I was just thinking, I'll have to get a chair because my legs won't hold me up, he went down over the bank.'

'Had he a car?' Burden asked quickly. 'In the lane?'

'I couldn't see. I *think* I heard a car start up but it mightn't have been his, might it?'

'Did you see him today, Mrs Mitchell?'

'I should have looked, I know that. But I *had* told Mrs Rushworth and it was her responsibility. Besides, I'd never seen this man do anything.' She sighed. 'I went out at two today,' she said. 'I went to see my married daughter in Kingsmarkham.'

'Describe this man to me, Mrs Mitchell.'

'I can do that,' she said, pleased. 'He was young, hardly more than a boy himself. Very slim, you know, and sort of slight. Not as tall as you, not nearly. About five feet six. He always wore the same clothes, one of those—what d'you call them?—duffel coats, black or very dark grey, and those jeans they all wear. Dark hair, not long for these days, but a lot longer than yours. I couldn't see his face, not from this distance, but he had very little hands. And he limps.'

'*Limps?*'

'When he was walking round the field,' said Mrs Mitchell earnestly, 'I noticed that he dragged one of his feet. Just slightly. Just a slight little limp.'

3

THE next parallel street was called Chiltern Avenue and access to it was by a footpath which ran along the side of Mrs Mitchell's house between her garden and the field. Burden went down Chiltern Avenue, calling at every house. The McDowell family lived at number 38 and the twins, Stewart and Ian, were still up.

Stewart had never seen the man, for during most of August he had been confined indoors with tonsillitis and today he had been with his mother to the dentist. But Ian had seen him and had even discussed him with Gary Dean, his special friend.

'He kept right under the trees all the time,' said Ian. 'Gary said he was a spy. Gary went to talk to him one day but he ran into Mill Lane.'

Burden asked the boy to describe him, but Ian lacked Mrs Mitchell's powers of observation.

'Just a man,' he said. 'About as big as my brother.' The brother in question was fifteen. Burden asked about the limp.

'What's limp?'

Burden explained. 'Dunno,' said Ian.

Further down, in a house of the same vintage as Mrs Lawrence's, he encountered the Rushworth family. Rushworth, it appeared, was an estate agent in Kingsmarkham, and he had gone off with the search parties, but his wife was at home with her four unruly children, all of whom were still up. Why hadn't she come to the police when Mrs Mitchell had first warned her back in August?

A little blonde woman whose stilt heels and long fingernails combined with a bouncing crest of hair gave her the look of a delicate game bird, Mrs Rushworth burst into tears.

'I meant to.' She choked. 'I had every intention. I work

26

so hard. I work in my husband's office, you know. There's never a moment to do *anything*!'

It was almost eight and John Lawrence had been missing for four and a half hours. Burden shivered a little less from the frosty chill of the night than from the sense of impending tragedy, of coming events casting a long cold shadow before them. He went over to the car and got in beside Wexford.

The chief inspector's driver had left him alone and he sat in the back of the black official car, not making notes, no longer studying his map, but pondering deeply. There was very little light—he hadn't switched on the interior light—and in the shadows he might have been a figure of stone. From head to foot he was grey—grey sparse hair, old grey raincoat, shoes that were always a little dusty. His face was deeply lined and in the half-dark it too looked grey. He turned slightly as Burden came in and fixed on him a pair of grey eyes which were the only brilliant sharp thing about him. Burden said nothing and for a few moments the two men were silent. Then Wexford said:

'A penny for them, Mike.'

'I was thinking of Stella Rivers.'

'Of course you were. Aren't we all?'

'It was her half-term holiday too,' Burden said. 'She was an only child of divorced parents. She also disappeared in Mill Lane. There are a good many similarities.'

'And a good many dissimilarities too. For one thing, she was a girl and older. You don't know much about the Stella Rivers case. You were off sick when it happened.'

They had thought he was going to have a breakdown. Back in February it had been when the first shock of Jean's death had abated, leaving grief and panic and the horror of his situation to pour in. He had lain in bed, sleeping when Dr Crocker drugged him, shouting out when he was conscious that it was only the flu he had, that he must get up and go back to work. But he had been off work for three weeks and when at last he was better he had lost nearly two stone. Still, he had been alive, while Stella Rivers was dead or vanished from the face of her small earth.

'She also lived with her mother,' said Wexford, 'and her

27

stepfather. On Thursday, February 25th, she had a riding lesson at Equita, the riding school in Mill Lane near Forby. She had her regular lessons on Saturdays, but this was an extra one, arranged to take advantage of her half-term holiday. The stepfather, Ivor Swan, drove her to Equita from their home at Hall Farm in Kingsmarkham, but there was some doubt as to how she was to get home again.'

'What d'you mean, doubt?'

'After she disappeared both Ivor and Rosalind Swan said Stella had told them she would get a lift home in a friend's car, as she sometimes did as far as Kingsmarkham, but it appeared that Stella had had no such idea and expected Swan to pick her up. When it got to six o'clock—the lesson ended at four-fifteen—Rosalind Swan, having checked with the friend, phoned us.

'We went first to Equita, saw Miss Williams who runs the school and her assistant, a Mrs Fenn, and were told that Stella had left alone at four-thirty. By now it was raining hard and the rain had begun at about four-forty. Eventually we made contact with a man who had passed Stella at four-forty and offered her a lift to Stowerton. At this time she was walking along Mill Lane towards Stowerton. She refused his offer which made us think she was a sensible girl who wouldn't take lifts from strangers.'

'She was twelve, wasn't she?' Burden put in.

'Twelve, slight and fair-haired. The man who offered her the lift is called Walter Hill and he's the manager of that little branch of the Midland Bank in Forby. If misguided, he's perfectly respectable and had nothing to do with her disappearance. We checked and double-checked him. No one else ever came forward to say he had seen Stella. She walked out of Equita, apparently believing she would meet her stepfather, and vanished into thin air.

'I can't go into all the details now, but of course we investigated Ivor Swan with the utmost care. Apart from the fact that he had no real alibi for that afternoon, we had no real reason to believe he wished harm to Stella. She liked Swan, she even seemed to have had a sort of crush on him. Not one relative or friend of the Swans could tell of any trouble whatsoever in their household. And yet...'

'And yet what?'

Wexford hesitated. 'You know those feelings I get, Mike, those almost supernatural sensations that something isn't, well—well, quite right?'

Burden nodded. He did.

'I felt it there. But it was only a feeling. People boast of their intuition because they only care to remember the times they've been proved right. I never let myself forget the numberless times my premonitions have been wrong. We never found the least thing to pin on Swan. We shall have to resurrect the case tomorrow. Where are you going?'

'Back to Mrs Lawrence,' said Burden.

An anxious-looking Mrs Crantock admitted him to the house.

'I don't think I've been much help,' she whispered to him in the hall. 'We aren't very close, you see, just neighbours whose children play with each other. I didn't know what to say to her. I mean, normally we'd discuss our little boys, but now—well, I didn't feel . . .' She gave a helpless shrug. 'And you can't talk to her about ordinary things, you know. You never can. Not about the house or what goes on in the neighbourhood.' Her forehead wrinkled as she made a mammoth effort to explain the inexplicable. 'Perhaps if I could talk about books or—or something. She just isn't like anyone else I know.'

'I'm sure you've done very well,' said Burden. He thought he knew very well what Mrs Lawrence would like to talk about. Her idea of conversation would be an endless analysis of the emotions.

'Well, I tried.' Mrs Crantock raised her voice. 'I'm going now, Gemma, but I'll come back later if you want me.'

Gemma. A curious name. He didn't think he had ever come across it before. She *would* have an outlandish name, either because her equally eccentric parents had labelled her with it or—more likely—she had adopted it herself on the grounds of its originality. Suddenly impatient with himself, he wondered why he kept speculating about her in this irritating way, why every new piece of knowledge of her he acquired gave immediate rise to enquiry. Because she is, or soon will be, involved in a murder case, he told himself. He pushed open the living-room door, his mind full of the flamboyant, wild and outrageous image he had made, and stopped, taken aback at what he saw. Yet it was only what he had left behind, a white-faced frightened girl, crouched in a chair, waiting, waiting . . .

She had switched on an electric fire, but it had done little to warm the room and she had wrapped herself in one of the shawls he had seen, a heavy black-and-gold thing with a long fringe. He found he couldn't picture her with a child or imagine her reading bedtime stories or pouring out corn-flakes. Sitting in some club, yes, singing and playing a guitar.

'Would you like some tea?' she said, turning to him. 'Some sandwiches? I can easily make sandwiches.'

'Don't bother for me.'

'Will your wife have something for you when you get home?'

'My sister-in-law,' he said. 'My wife's dead.'

He didn't like having to say it. People immediately became embarrassed, blushing or even recoiling slightly as if he had some infectious disease. Then came the rush of awkward insincere sympathy, meaningless words to be gabbled through and then as soon forgotten. No one ever looked as if they really cared, or no one had until now.

Gemma Lawrence said quietly and slowly, 'I am so sorry. She must have been quite young. That was a great tragedy for you. Now I can see what has taught you to be kind to other people who are in trouble.'

He felt ashamed of himself and shame made him stammer. 'I—well . . . I think I would like those sandwiches if it isn't any trouble.'

'How could it be?' she asked wonderingly, as if the polite conventional phrase was new to her. 'Naturally I want to do something in return for all you're doing for me.'

She brought the sandwiches in a very short time. It was evident they hadn't taken long to make. Ham had been roughly placed between two doorsteps of bread and the tea was in mugs without saucers.

Women had been spoiling Burden all his life, serving him food on dainty china from trays covered with lace cloths, and he took a sandwich without much enthusiasm, but when

30

he bit into it he found that the ham was tasty and not too salty and the bread fresh.

She sat on the floor and rested her back against the armchair opposite to him. He had told Wexford there were many more questions he wanted to ask her and he hazarded a few of them, routine enquiries as to John's adult acquaintances, the parents of his school friends, her own friends. She responded calmly and intelligently and the policeman's part of his mind registered her answers automatically. But something strange had happened to him. He was absorbing with a curious unease a fact which the average man would have observed as soon as he laid eyes on her. She was beautiful. Thinking the word made him look away, yet carry with him, as if imprinted on his retina, a brilliant impression of that white face with its good bones and, more disturbingly, her long legs and full firm breasts.

Her hair was vermilion in the red firelight, her eyes the clear water-washed green of jewels that are found under the sea. The shawl gave her an exotic look as if she were set within the frame of a Pre-Raphaelite portrait, posed, unreal, unfitted for any ordinary daily task. And yet there was about her something entirely natural and impulsive. Too natural, he thought, suddenly alarmed, too real. She is more real and more aware and more natural than any woman has a right to be.

Quickly he said, 'Mrs Lawrence, I'm sure you told John never to speak to strange men.'

The face whitened. 'Oh, yes.'

'But did he ever tell you that a man had spoken to him?'

'No, never. I take him to school and fetch him home. He's only alone when he goes out to play and then the other boys are with him.' She lifted her face and now there was no guard on it. 'What do you mean?'

Why did she have to ask so directly? 'No one has told me they saw any stranger speak to John,' he said truthfully, 'but I have to check.'

She said in the same uncompromising level voice, 'Mrs Dean told me a child was lost in Kingsmarkham last February and never found. She came in to tell me while Mrs Crantock was here.'

31

Burden forgot that he had ever allied himself with Mrs Dean. In savage, unpoliceman-like tones he burst out before he could stop himself, 'Why the hell don't these busybodies keep their mouths shut?' He bit his lip, wondering why what she had said brought out so much violence in him and the desire to go next door and strike the Dean woman. 'That child was a girl,' he said, 'and much older. The kind of—er— pervert who needs to attack girls isn't likely to be interested in a small boy.' But was that true? Who could yet understand the mysteries of a sane mind, let alone a diseased one?

She drew the shawl more closely about her and said, 'How shall I get through the night?'

'I shall get you a doctor.' Burden finished his tea and got up. 'Didn't I see a doctor's plate in Chiltern Avenue?'

'Yes. Dr Lomax.'

'Well, we'll get some sleeping pills out of this Lomax, and a woman to stay the night with you. I'll see you're not left alone.'

'I don't know how to thank you.' She bowed her head and he saw that at last she began to cry. 'You'll say it's only your job and your duty, but it's more than that. I—I do thank you. When I look at you I think, Nothing can happen to John while he's there.'

She was looking at him as a child should look at its father but as he could never remember his own children looking at him. Such trust was a terrible responsibility and he knew he shouldn't foster it. There was more than a fifty-fifty chance now that the child was dead and he wasn't God to bring the dead to life. He ought to say that she mustn't worry, mustn't think about it—how cruel and stupid and insensitive!—but all he could say in the face of those eyes was, 'I'll go for the doctor now and he'll see you get a good night.' There was no need to add anything but he added, 'Don't sleep too long. I'll be back with you by nine.'

Then he said good night. He didn't mean to look back. Something impelled him. She was standing in the doorway, framed in yellow light, a curious outlandish figure in that gypsy gilded shawl, her hair so bright that it seemed on fire. She waved to him tentatively, rather shyly, her other hand smoothing away the tears from under her eyes. He had seen

32

pictures of women like her but never known them, never spoken to them. Briefly he wondered if he wanted the child found, wanted it so passionately, because that would mean he need never see her again. He turned sharply towards the street and went to summon Dr Lomax.

A great moon drifted above the fields, pale and misty as if it drifted in a pool of water. Burden waited until the searchers got back at midnight. They had found nothing.

Grace had left a note for him: 'John waited up till eleven for you to help him with his maths. Could you just glance at it? He was in quite a state. G.'

It took Burden a couple of seconds to adjust to the fact that his own son was also called John. He glanced at the homework and, as far as he could see, the algebra was correct. A lot of fuss about nothing. These little nagging notes of Grace's were getting a bit much. He opened the door of his son's room and saw that he was fast asleep. Grace and Pat slept in the room that had been his and Jean's—impossible as his bedroom after her death—and he couldn't very well open that door. In his own room, once Pat's, a little room with ballet dancers cavorting on the walls as appropriate for an eleven-year-old, he sat on the bed and felt the tiredness ebb away, leaving him as alert as at eight in the morning. He could be weary to the point of collapse, but let him come in here, be alone with himself, and immediately he would be filled with this frightful, degrading urgency.

He put his head in his hands. They all thought he missed Jean as a companion, as someone to talk to and share trouble with. And so he did, terribly. But what assailed him most every day and every night, without respite, was sexual desire, which, because it had had no release in ten months, had become sealed-up, tormented sexual madness.

He knew very well how they all thought of him. To them he was a cold fish, stern when confronted by license, mourning Jean only because he had become used to marriage and was what Wexford called uxorious. Probably, if they had ever thought of it, they imagined him and Jean making love once a fortnight with the light out. It was the way people did think about you if you were the sort of man who shied away from

33

dirty jokes and found this permissive society foul.

They never seemed to dream that you could hate promiscuity and adultery because you knew what marriage could be and had experienced it to such a degree of excellence that anything else was a mockery, a poor imitation. You were lucky but . . . Ah, God, you were unlucky too!—cast adrift and sick when it was over. Jean had been a virgin when he married her and so had he. People said—stupid people and the stupid things they said—that it made it hard when you married, but it hadn't for him and Jean. They had been patient and giving and full of love and they had been so fulsomely rewarded that, looking back as from a desert, Burden could hardly believe it had been so good almost from the start, with no failures, no disappointments. But he could believe it because he knew and remembered and suffered.

And if they knew? He was aware what their advice would be. Get yourself a girl friend, Mike. Nothing serious. Just a nice easy girl to have a bit of fun with. Perhaps you could do that if you'd been used to kicking over the traces. He had never been any woman's lover but Jean's. Sex for him had been Jean. They didn't realise that telling him to get another woman would be like telling Gemma Lawrence to get another child.

He took off his clothes and lay face downwards, his fists carefully clenched and pushed under the pillow. There was no doubt in his mind how the night would be passed. All nights were the same. First the lying awake and the longing, the actual physical pain, as if his body was a great scream with no outlet for the scream to escape through; then at last sleep with the full, rich and orgiastic dream that would come to him just before the dawn.

4

IF MIKE made the slightest effort at an apology, Grace decided, she wouldn't say a word. Of course, he had to work and many times he couldn't get away without putting his job in jeopardy. She knew what that meant. Before she came to be his housekeeper she had had men friends, some who were just friends and some, a few, who were lovers, and often she had had to break a date because there was an emergency on at the hospital. But the next day she had always phoned or written a note to explain why.

Mike wasn't her lover but only her brother-in-law. Did that mean he owed her nothing, not even common politeness? And had you the right to stand up your children without a word, even when your son was trembling with nerves at nearly midnight because he couldn't believe he'd got his algebra right and old Parminter, the maths man, would put him in detention if he hadn't?

She cooked eggs and bacon for the lot of them and laid the dining table with a clean cloth. Not for the first time she wished her sister hadn't been such an excellent housekeeper, so correct and near-perfect in everything she did, but at least slackened to the extent of serving breakfast in the kitchen. Living up to Jean made life a bit of a burden.

She hadn't meant to make a pun and she didn't laugh. Her face hardened when Mike came down, grunted to the children and took his place at the table without a word. He wasn't going to mention last night. Well, she would.

'That algebra was perfectly O.K., John.'

The boy's face lit as it always did when Burden spoke to him.

'I reckoned it was. I don't really care about it, only old Mint Face will keep me in if it's not. I don't suppose you'd give me a lift to school.'

'Too busy,' said Burden. 'The walk does you good.' He smiled, but not too kindly, at his daughter. 'And you too, miss,' he said. 'Right, get going. It's nearly half past.'

Grace didn't usually see them to the door but she did today to make up for their father's hardness. When she came back Burden was on his second cup of tea and before she could stop herself she had burst into a long tirade all about John's nerves and Pat's bewilderment and the way he left them all alone.

He heard her out and then he said, 'Why is it that women' —he corrected himself, making the inevitable exception— 'most women—can't realise men have to work? If I didn't work God knows what would happen to the lot of you.'

'Were you working when Mrs Finch saw you sitting in the car in Cheriton Forest?'

'Mrs Finch,' he flared, 'can mind her own bloody business!'

Grace turned her back. She found she was slowly counting to ten. Then she said, 'Mike, I do understand. I can imagine how you feel.'

'I doubt that.'

'Well, I think I can. But John and Pat can't. John needs you and he needs you cheerful and matter-of-fact and—and like you used to be. Mike, couldn't you get home early tonight? There's a film they'd both like to see. It doesn't start till seven thirty, so you wouldn't have to be home till seven. We could all go. It would mean so much to them.'

'All right,' he said. 'I'll do my best. Don't look like that, Grace. I'll be home by seven.'

Her face lit up. She did something she hadn't done since his wedding. She bent over and kissed his cheek. Then she began quickly to clear the table. Her back was to him so that she didn't see the shiver he gave and the way he put his hand up to his face like a man who has been stung.

Gemma Lawrence had put on clean jeans and a clean thick sweater. Her hair was tied back in a bunch with a piece of ribbon and she smelt of soap like a good clean child.

'I slept all night.'

He smiled at her. 'Cheers for Dr Lomax,' he said.

'Are they still searching?'

'Of course. Didn't I promise you? We've borrowed a whole army of coppers from all the surrounding districts.'

'Dr Lomax was very kind. D'you know, he said that when he was living in Scotland before he came here his own little boy was missing and they found him in a shepherd's hut lying asleep, cuddling the sheep-dog. He'd wandered for miles and this dog had found him and looked after him like a lost lamb. It reminded me of Romulus and Remus and the wolf.'

Burden didn't know who Romulus and Remus were, but he laughed and said, 'Well, what did I tell you?' He wasn't going to spoil her hopes now by pointing out that this wasn't Scotland, a place of lonely mountains and friendly dogs. 'What are you going to do today? I don't want you to be alone.'

'Mrs Crantock's asked me to lunch and the neighbours keep coming in. People are very kind. I wish I had some closer friends here. All my friends are in London.'

'The best thing for worry,' he said, 'is work. Take your mind off things.'

'I don't have any work to do, unfortunately.'

He had meant housework, cleaning, tidying, sewing, tasks which he thought of as naturally a woman's work, and there was plenty of that to be done. But he could hardly tell her that.

'I expect I'll just sit and play records,' she said, shifting a dirty cup from the record player to the floor. 'Or read or something.'

'As soon as we have any news, I'll come to you. I won't phone, I'll come.'

Her eyes shone. 'If I were the Prime Minister,' she said, 'I'd make you a superintendent.'

He drove to Cheriton Forest where the search was now centred and found Wexford sitting on a log. It was misty this morning and the chief inspector was wrapped in an old raincoat, a battered felt hat pulled down over his eyes.

'We've got a lead on the car, Mike.'

'What car?'

'Last night when they were out in the fields one of the search party told Martin he'd seen a car parked in Mill Lane.

Apparently, he had a week off in August and he took his dog walking regularly up Mill Lane and three times he noticed a car parked near the spot where Mrs Mitchell saw the man. He noticed it because it was obstructing the lane, only leaving room for single-line traffic. A red Jaguar. Needless to say, he didn't get the number.'

'Did he see the man?'

'He didn't see anyone. What we want now is to find someone who regularly uses that road. A baker, for instance.'

'I'll see to that,' said Burden.

In the course of the morning he found a baker's roundsman who used the road every day and the driver of a van delivering soft drinks who used in only on Wednesdays and Fridays. The baker had seen the car because, coming round a corner one afternoon, he had almost hit it. A red Jaguar, he confirmed, but he hadn't taken the number either. And although he had been on the road the day before, he had passed the swings-field hedge at two and the car wasn't there then. At half-past four two women in a car had asked him if he had seen a little boy, but he was almost into Forby by then. The red Jaguar might have passed him, might have contained a child, but he couldn't remember.

The soft-drinks man was less observant. He had never noticed anything out of the way on that road, either recently or in August.

Burden went back to the station and had a quick lunch in Wexford's office. They spent the afternoon interviewing a sad little stream of men, all shifty and most undersized, who at some time or other had made overtures to children. There was the retarded nineteen-year-old whose speciality was waiting outside school gates; the middle-aged primary-school teacher, sacked by the authority years ago; the draper's assistant who got into train compartments that contained a solitary child; the schizophrenic who had raped his own little daughter and since been discharged from mental hospital.

'Lovely job, ours,' said Burden. 'I feel slimy all over.'

'There but for the grace of God . . .' said Wexford. 'You might have been one of them if your parents had rejected you. I might if I'd responded to the advances made to me in the school cloakroom. They sit in darkness, they're born, as

Blake or some clever sod said, to endless night. Pity doesn't cost anything, Mike, and it's a damn sight more edifying than shouting about flogging and hanging and castrating and what you will.'

'I'm not shouting, sir. I just happen to believe in the cultivation of self-control. And my pity is for the mother and that poor kid.'

'Yes, but the quality of mercy is not strained. The trouble with you is you're a blocked-up colander and your mercy strains through a couple of miserable little holes. Still, none of those wretched drop-outs was near Mill Lane yesterday and I don't see any of them living it up in a red Jaguar.'

If you haven't been out in the evening once in ten months the prospect of a trip to the cinema in the company of your brother-in-law and two children can seem like high living. Grace Woodville went to the hairdresser's at three and when she came out she felt more elated than she had the first day Pat came to kiss her of her own accord. There was a nice golden-brown sweater in Moran's window, and Grace, who hadn't bought a garment in months, decided on an impulse to have it.

Mike should have a special dinner tonight, curried chicken. Jean had never cooked that because she didn't like it, but Mike and the children did. She bought a chicken and by the time John and Pat came home the bungalow was filled with the rich scents of curry sauce and sweet-sour pineapple.

She had laid the table by six and changed into the new sweater. By five to seven they were all sitting in the living room, all dressed-up and rather self-conscious, more like people waiting to be taken to a party than a family off to the local cinema.

The telephone calls had begun. They came in to Kingsmarkham police station not only from people in the district, not only in Sussex, but from Birmingham and Newcastle and the north of Scotland. All the callers claimed to have seen John Lawrence alone or with a man or with two men or two women. A woman in Carlisle had seen him, she averred, with Stella Rivers; a shopkeeper in Cardiff had sold him an ice-

39

cream. A lorry-driver had given him and his companion, a middle-aged man, a lift to Grantham. All these stories had to be checked, though all seemed to be without foundation.

People poured into the station with tales of suspicious persons and cars seen in Mill Lane. By now not only red Jaguars were suspect but black ones and green ones, black vans, three-wheelers. And meanwhile the arduous search went on. Working without a break, Wexford's force continued a systematic house-to-house investigation, questioning most particularly every male person over sixteen.

Five to seven found Burden outside the Olive and Dove Hotel in Kingsmarkham High Street, facing the cinema, and he remembered his date with Grace and the children, remembered, too, that he must see Gemma Lawrence before he went off duty.

The phone box outside the hotel was occupied and a small queue of people waited. By the time they had all finished, Burden judged, a good ten minutes would have passed. He glanced again at the cinema and saw that whereas the last programme began at seven-thirty, the big picture didn't start until an hour later. No need to phone Grace when he could easily drive to Stowerton, find out how things were with Mrs Lawrence and be home by a quarter to eight. Grace wouldn't expect him on time. She knew better than that. And surely even his two wouldn't want to sit through a film about touring in East Anglia, the news and all the trailers.

For once the front door wasn't open. The street was empty, almost every house well-lit. It seemed for all the world as if nothing had happened yesterday to disturb the peace of this quiet country street. Time passed, men and women laughed and talked and worked and watched television and said, What can you do? That's life.

There were no lights on in her house. He knocked on the door and no one came. She must have gone out. When her only child was missing, perhaps murdered? He remembered the way she dressed, the state of her house. A good-time girl, he thought, not much of a mother. Very likely one of those London friends had come and she'd gone out with him.

He knocked again and then he heard something, a kind of shuffling. Footsteps dragged to the door, hesitated.

40

He called, 'Mrs Lawrence, are you all right?'

A little answering sound came to him, half a sob and half a moan. The door quivered, then swung inwards.

Her face was ravaged and swollen and sodden with crying. She was crying now, sobbing, the tears streaming down her face. He shut the door behind him and switched on a light.

'What's happened?'

She twisted away from him, threw herself against the wall and beat on it with her fists. 'Oh God, what shall I do?'

'I know it's hard,' he said helplessly, 'but we're doing everything that's humanly possible. We're ...'

'Your people,' she sobbed, 'they've been in and out all day, searching and—and asking me things. They searched this house! And people kept phoning, awful people. There was a woman—a *woman* . . . Oh my God! She said John was dead and she—she described how he died and she said it was my fault! I can't bear it, I can't bear it, I shall gas myself, I shall cut my wrists . . .'

'You must stop this,' he shouted. She turned to him and screamed into his face. He raised his hand and slapped her stingingly on the cheek. She gagged, gulped and crumpled, collapsing against him. To stop her falling, he put his arms round her and for a moment she clung to him, as in a lover's embrace, her wet face buried in his neck. Then she stepped back, the red hair flying as she shook herself.

'Forgive me,' she said. Her voice was hoarse with crying. 'I'm mad. I think I'm going mad.'

'Come in here and tell me. You were optimistic earlier.'

'That was this morning.' She spoke quietly now in a thin broken voice. Gradually and not very coherently she told him about the policeman who had searched her cupboards and tramped through the attics, how they had torn away the undergrowth that swamped the roots of old trees in that wild garden. She told him, gasping, of the obscene phone calls and of the letters, inspired by last night's evening-paper story, the second post had brought.

'You are not to open any letters unless you recognise the handwriting,' he said. 'Everything else we'll look at first. As to the phone calls . . .'

'Your sergeant said you'd have an arrangement to get my

41

phone monitored.' She sighed deeply, calmer now, but the tears were still falling.

'Have you got any brandy in this—er—place?'

'In the dining room.' She managed a damp, weak smile. 'It belonged to my great-aunt. This—er—place, as you call it, was hers. Brandy keeps for years and years, doesn't it?'

'Years and years make it all the better,' said Burden.

The dining room was cavernous, cold and smelling of dust. He wondered what combination of circumstances had brought her to this house and why she stayed. The brandy was in a sideboard that looked more like a wooden mansion than a piece of furniture, it was so ornamented with carved pillars and arches and niches and balconies.

'You have some too,' she said.

He hesitated. 'All right. Thank you.' He made his way back to the armchair he had occupied before going to the dining room, but she sat down on the floor, curling her legs under her and staring up at him with a curious blind trust. Only one lamp was alight, making a little golden glow behind her head.

She drank her brandy and for a long time they sat without talking. Then, warmed and calmed, she began to speak about the lost boy, the things he liked doing, the things he said, his little precocious cleverness. She spoke of London and of the strangeness of Stowerton to herself and her son. At last she fell silent, her eyes fixed on his face, but he had lost the embarrassment which this trusting childlike stare had at first occasioned in him and it didn't return even when, leaning forward with quick impulsiveness, she reached for his hand and held it tightly.

He wasn't embarrassed, but the touch of her hand electrified him. It brought him such a shock and such sudden turbulence that instead of the normal reactions of a normal man enclosing the hand of a pretty woman in his own he had the illusion that his whole body was holding her body. The effect of this was to make him tremble. He loosened his fingers and said abruptly, breaking the now heavy and languorous silence, 'You're a Londoner. You like London. Why do you live here?'

'It is rather ghastly, isn't it?' All the harshness and terror had gone from her voice and once more it was soft and rich. Although he had known she was bound to speak in answer to his question, the sound of her beautiful voice, quite normal now, disturbed him almost as much as the touch of her hand. 'A dreadful old white elephant of a house,' she said.

'It's no business of mine,' he muttered.

'But it's no secret either. I didn't even know I had this great-aunt. She died three years ago and left this house to my father, but he was dying himself of cancer.' With a peculiarly graceful but unstudied movement she raised her hand and pushed away the mass of hair from her face. The full embroidered sleeve of the strange tunic she wore fell away from her arm and the skin glowed whitely, faint golden down gleaming in the lamplight. 'I tried to sell it for my father, but no one wanted it, and then he died and Matthew—my husband—left me. Where else could I go but here? I couldn't afford the rent of our flat and Matthew's money had run out.' It seemed like hours since those eyes had first begun staring at him, but now at last she turned them away. 'The police,' she said very softly, 'thought Matthew might have taken John.'

'I know. It's something we always have to check on when the child of—er—estranged or divorced parents is missing.'

'They went to see him, or they tried to. He's in hospital, having his appendix out. I believe they talked to his wife. He married again, you see.'

Burden nodded. With more than a policeman's natural curiosity he passionately wanted to know whether this Matthew had divorced her or she him, what he did for a living, how it had all come about. He couldn't ask her. His voice felt strangled.

She edged a little closer towards him, not reaching out for his hand this time. Her hair curtained her face. 'I want you to know,' she said, 'how you've helped me. What a comfort you've been. I should have broken down completely tonight if you hadn't come. I should have done something dreadful.'

'You mustn't be alone.'

'I've got my sleeping tablets,' she said, 'and Mrs Crantock is coming in at ten.' Slowly she got to her feet, reached out and switched on the standard lamp. 'She'll be here in a minute. It's five to now.'

Her words and the sudden brightness brought Burden sharply back to reality. He blinked and shook himself.

'Five to ten? I've just remembered, I'm supposed to be taking my family to the pictures.'

'And I've stopped you? Would you like to phone? Please do. Use my phone.'

'Too late, I'm afraid.'

'I'm dreadfully sorry.'

'I think my being here was more important, don't you?'

'It was important to me. But you must go now. Will you come again tomorrow? I mean you yourself.'

He was standing in the doorway as she spoke. She put her hand lightly on his arm and they were close together, their faces only a foot apart. 'I—yes . . . Yes, of course.' He was stammering badly. 'Of course I'll come.'

'Inspector Burden . . . No, I can't keep calling you that. What's your first name?'

'I think it will be best if you . . .' he began, and then, almost desperately, 'It's Michael. People call me Mike.'

'Mike,' she said, and at that moment, as she dwelt on the name, repeating it softly, Mrs Crantock rang the bell.

Grace was curled up on the sofa and he could see that she had been crying. The enormity of what he had done for a moment overcame that other enormity, the urgency of his body.

'I'm terribly sorry,' he said, going over to her. 'The phone box was full and later . . .'

She lifted her head and faced him. 'We sat here and we waited for you. When you hadn't come by eight we had our meal, though it was ruined. I said, "Let's go just the same," and John said, "We can't go without Dad. We can't let him come home and find us gone.'

'I said I'm sorry,' said Burden.

'You could have phoned!' Grace said passionately. 'I wouldn't say a word if you'd phoned. Don't you realise, if you go on like this, you'll—you'll destroy those children!'

She went out and the door closed behind her, leaving Burden to thoughts that were neither of her nor his children.

5

BURDEN looked at the sheet of paper Wexford had handed him. Written on it in a bold, large but childlike hand were the names of every man, woman and child Gemma Lawrence had known during the past ten years.

'When did she write all that out?'

Wexford eyed him briefly and narrowly. 'This morning with Loring's help. You aren't her exclusive private eye, you know.'

Burden flushed. What hundreds of people she knew and what extraordinary names they had! Artists and models and theatre folk, he supposed, suddenly bad-tempered. 'Have we got to interview all this lot?'

'The Met are going to help us there. I asked Mrs Lawrence to write down every name because I want to show the list to the Swans.'

'You are connecting the two cases, then?'

Wexford didn't answer directly. He took the list from Burden, gave him another piece of paper and said, 'This came. It's been gone over for fingerprints, so you needn't worry about touching it. Of course there weren't any prints.'

'John Lawrence is safe and well with me,' Burden read. 'He is happy playing with my rabbits on the farm. To show you this is not a hoax, I am enclosing a lock of his hair.' The note, written in block capitals on a sheet of lined paper, was correctly spelt and punctuated. 'His mother can have him back on Monday. I will bring him to the southern end of Myfleet Ride in Cheriton Forest at 9 a.m. If anyone tries to collect him before nine-thirty, I will know and I will shoot John dead. This is a serious warning. I will not break my promise if you co-operate.'

Burden dropped it in disgust. Used as he was to such

45

things, he could still not read them without a shudder. 'Was there a lock of hair?' he asked.

'Here.'

It had been twisted into a smooth neat circle like a woman's pin curl. Burden lifted it in tweezers, noting the delicacy of each red-gold strand, the absence of those kinks and ridges which occur in adult hair.

'It's human,' said Wexford. 'I got Crocker on to it at once. He says it's the child's hair, but, of course, we shall have to have more expert tests.'

'Has Mrs Lawrence been told?'

'Thank God he's safe,' she said when she had read the first lines. She held the letter momentarily to her breast but she didn't cry. 'He's safe and well on a farm somewhere. Oh my God, and what agonies I've been through! Imagine, all that for nothing and he'll be back with me on Monday.'

Burden was appalled. He had already told her not to bank on the letter at all, that in ninety-nine cases out of a hundred such letters are cruel hoaxes. For all the notice she took, he might not have spoken.

'Let me see the hair,' she said.

Reluctantly he took the envelope which contained it from his briefcase. She gasped when she saw the small golden curl. So far it had been handled carefully with tweezers, but she took it, stroked it and pressed it to her mouth. 'Come upstairs.'

He followed her into John's bedroom, noticing that the child's bed hadn't been made since his disappearance. It was a nice bedroom, though, full of toys and with a beautiful expensive wallpaper of Dürer animals reproduced in line and wash. However much she might neglect the rest of the house, she had cared for this room and probably done the papering herself. Burden's opinion of her as a mother rose.

She went over to a small blue-painted chest of drawers and picked up John's hairbrush. A few fine blond hairs were caught in its bristles and, with an earnest concentrated expression, she compared them with the lock in her hand. Then she turned and smiled radiantly.

Burden had never seen her really smile before. Until then her smiles had been brief and watery, reminding him, he thought suddenly, of a faint sun coming out after rain. Such metaphors were very unusual with him, fanciful and not in his line. But he thought it now as he received the full force of her brilliant happy smile and saw again how beautiful she was.

'It is the same, isn't it?' she said, the smile fading as she almost pleaded, '*Isn't it?*'

'I don't know.' There was certainly a strong similarity, but Burden didn't know whether he wanted the hairs to be the same or not. If this man really had John and if he had really cut that lock from John's head, was it likely that he would let the boy go otherwise unharmed? Would he risk the boy's identifying him? On the other hand, he had demanded no money . . . 'You're his mother,' he murmured. 'I wouldn't like to say.'

'I know he's safe,' she said. 'I feel it. I've only got to get through two more days.

He hadn't the heart to say any more then. Only a brute, he thought, would destroy such shining happiness. So that she shouldn't read the last lines he wanted to take the letter from her, but she read it to the end.

'I've heard about cases like this,' she said, a little fear returning to her voice as she gazed at him, 'and what the police do. You wouldn't—you wouldn't do—do what he says you're not to do? You wouldn't try to trap him? Because then John . . .'

'I promise you,' he said, 'that we shall do nothing which might in any way endanger John's life.' She had said nothing vindictive about the writer of the letter, he noticed. Other women in her position would have raged and screamed for revenge. She had merely been filled with joy. 'We shall go there on Monday morning, at nine-thirty, and if he is there we shall bring him back to you.'

'He'll be there,' she said. 'I trust this man. I've got a feeling he's genuine. Really, I have, Mike.' Her use of his Christian name brought colour into his face. He felt his cheeks burn. 'He's probably dreadfully lonely,' she said gently. 'I know what it is to be lonely. If John has given him a few days' respite from his loneliness I don't grudge John to him.'

It was incredible and Burden couldn't understand. If it

47

had been his child, his John, he would have wanted to kill the man, to see him die a lingering death. As it was, his feelings towards the letter-writer were so violent that they frightened him. Let me get at him, he thought, give me five minutes alone in the cell with him and, by God, if I lose my job for it . . . He pulled himself up with a jerk and saw that her eyes were on him, kind, sweet and compassionate.

In his haste to see Gemma, Burden had forgotten the Swans, but now he remembered Wexford saying the note helped to establish a connection between the two cases. The chief inspector was still in his office.

'Swan lives on a farm,' he said. 'I phoned but he's out till three.'

'Does he keep rabbits?'

'Don't mention rabbits to me. I've only just got over an hour with the secretary of the local rabbit club. Rabbits! The place is crawling with them, Old English, Blue Beverens, you name 'em, we've got 'em. I tell you, Mike, it's like the Apocrypha says, "The coneys are a feeble folk, but they make their houses in the rocks"!'

'And every fancier being checked?' said Burden, unsmiling.

Wexford nodded. 'And I know the bloody thing's a hoax,' he said. 'I shall spend the best part of my weekend—and so will dozens of other policemen—chasing rabbits and farmers and checking shot-gun licences and being polite to human hair experts, but I know very well it's a hoax and what I'm doing is an utter waste of time.'

'But it has to be done.'

'Of course it has to be done. Let's go to lunch.'

At the Carousel Café only ham and salad was left on the menu. Wexford picked without enthusiasm at the salad in which lettuce leaves were economically eked out with shreds of cabbage and carrot. 'Can't get away from rabbits,' he muttered. 'Want me to tell you about Swan and his wife?'

'I suppose I ought to have a bit of background.'

'Usually,' Wexford began, 'you feel too much sympathy with the parents of a lost child. You find your emotions getting involved.' He shifted his gaze from his plate to Bur-

48

den's face and pursed his lips. 'Which doesn't help,' he said. 'I didn't feel particularly sorry for them. You'll see why not in a minute.' Clearing his throat, he went on, 'After Stella disappeared, we did more research into the life and background of Ivor Swan than I can ever remember doing with anyone. I could write his biography.

'He was born in India, the son of one General Sir Rodney Swan, and he was sent home to school and then to Oxford. Being in possession of what he calls small private means, he never took up any particular career but dabbled at various things. At one time he managed an estate for someone, but he soon got the sack. He wrote a novel which sold three hundred copies, so he never repeated that experiment. Instead he had a spell in P.R. and in three months lost his firm an account worth twenty thousand a year. Utter ingrained laziness is what characterises Ivor Swan. He is indolence incarnate. Oh, and he's good-looking, staggeringly so, in fact. Wait till you see.'

Burden poured himself a glass of water but said nothing. He was watching Wexford's expression warm and liven as he pursued his theme. Once he too had been able to involve himself as raptly in the characters of suspects.

'Swan rarely had any settled home,' Wexford said. 'Sometimes he lived with his widowed mother at her house in Bedfordshire, sometimes with an uncle who had been some sort of big brass in the Air Force. And now I come to an interesting point about him. Wherever he goes he seems to leave disaster behind him. Not because of what he does but because of what he *doesn't* do. There was a bad fire at his mother's house while he was staying there. Swan had fallen asleep with a cigarette burning in his fingers. Then there was the loss of the P.R. account because of what he didn't do; the sacking from the estate management job—he left a pretty mess behind him there—on account of his laziness.

'About two years ago he found himself in Karachi. At that time he was calling himself a free-lance journalist and the purpose of his visit was to enquire into the alleged smuggling of gold by airline staff. Any story he concocted would probably have been libellous, but, as it happened, it was never written or, at any rate, no newspaper printed it.

'Peter Rivers worked for an airline in Karachi, not as a pilot but among the ground staff, meeting aircraft, weighing baggage, that sort of thing, and he lived with his wife and daughter in a company house. In the course of his snooping Swan made friends with Rivers. It would be more to the point to say he made friends with Rivers' wife.'

'You mean he took her away from him?' Burden hazarded.

'If you can imagine Swan doing anything as active as taking anyone or anything away from anyone else. I should rather say that the fair Rosalind—"From the East to Western Ind, no jewel is like Rosalind"—fastened herself to Swan and held on tight. The upshot was that Swan returned to England plus Rosalind and Stella and about a year later Rivers got his decree.

'The three of them all lived in a poky flat Swan took in Maida Vale, but after they were married Swan, or more likely Rosalind, decided the place wasn't big enough and they came out here to Hall Farm.'

'Where did he get the money to buy a farm?'

'Well, in the first place it isn't a farm any more but a chichi tarted-up farm*house* with all the land let off. Secondly, he didn't buy it. It was part of the property held under a family trust. Swan put out feelers to his uncle and he let him have Hall Farm at a nominal rent.'

'Life's very easy for some people, isn't it?' said Burden, thinking of mortgages and hire purchase and grudgingly granted bank loans. 'No money worries, no housing problems.'

'They came here last October, a year ago. Stella was sent to the convent at Sewingbury—uncle paid the fees—and Swan let her have these riding lessons. He rides himself and hunts a bit. Nothing in a big way, but then he doesn't do anything in a big way.

'As to Rivers, he'd been having it off on the quiet with some air hostess and he also has married again. Swan, Rosalind and Stella plus an *au pair* girl settled down quite comfortably at Hall Farm, and then, bang in the middle of all this bliss, Stella disappears. Beyond a doubt, Stella is dead, murdered.'

'It seems clear,' said Burden, 'that Swan can have had nothing to do with it.'

Wexford said obstinately, 'He had no alibi. And there was something else, something less tangible, something in the personality of the man himself.'

'He sounds too lazy ever to commit an aggressive act.'

'I know, I know.' Wexford almost groaned the words 'And he had led, in the eyes of the law, a blameless life. No history of violence, mental disturbance or even bad temper. He hadn't even the reputation of a philanderer. Casual girl friends, yes, but until he met Rosalind he had never been married or engaged to be married or even lived with a woman. But he had a history of a sort, a history of disaster. There's a line in rather a sinister sonnet—"They that have power to hurt and will do none". I don't think that means they don't do any hurt but that they do *nothing*. That's Swan. If he didn't do this killing it happened because of him or through him or because he is what he is. D'you think that's all airy-fairy moonshine?'

'Yes,' said Burden firmly.

St Luke's Little Summer maintained its glory, at least by day. The hedges were a delicate green-gold and frost had not yet bitten into blackness the chrysanthemums and michaelmas daisies in cottage gardens. The year was growing old gracefully.

The farm was approached by a narrow lane scattered with fallen leaves and overhung by hedges of Old Man's Beard, the vapourish, thistledown seed heads of the wild clematis, and here and there, behind the fluffy masses, rose Scotch pines, their trunks a rich coral pink where the sun caught them. A long low building of stone and slate stood at the end of this lane, but most of its stonework was obscured by the flame and scarlet virginia creeper which covered it.

'*Du coté de chez Swan,*' said Wexford softly.

Proustian references were lost on Burden. He was looking at the man who had come round from the back of the house, leading a big chestnut gelding.

Wexford left the car and went up to him. 'We're a little early, Mr Swan. I hope we're not putting you out?'

51

'No,' said Swan. 'We got back sooner than we expected. I was going to exercise Sherry but that can wait.'

'This is Inspector Burden.'

'How do you do?' said Swan, extending a hand. 'Very pleasant, all this sunshine, isn't it? D'you mind coming round the back way?'

He was certainly an extremely handsome man. Burden decided this without being able to say in what his handsomeness lay, for Ivor Swan was neither tall nor short, dark nor fair, and his eyes were of that indeterminate colour men call grey for want of a more accurate term. His features had no special regularity, his figure, though lean, no sign of athletic muscular development. But he moved with an entirely masculine grace, exuded a vague lazy charm and had about him an air of attractiveness, of making himself immediately noticed.

His voice was soft and beautiful, the words he used slowly enunciated. He seemed to have all the time in the world, a procrastinator who would always put off till tomorrow what he couldn't bring himself to do today. About thirty-three or thirty-four, Burden thought, but he could easily pass for twenty-five to a less discerning observer.

The two policemen followed him into a kind of lobby or back kitchen where a couple of guns and an assortment of fishing tackle hung above neat rows of riding boots and wellingtons.

'Don't keep rabbits, do you, Mr Swan?' Wexford asked.

Swan shook his head. 'I shoot them, or try to, if they come on my land.'

In the kitchen proper two women were engaged on feminine tasks. The younger, an ungainly dark girl, was preparing —if the heaps of vegetables, tins of dried herbs, eggs and mincemeat spread on the counter in front of her were anything to go by—what Burden chauvinistically thought of as a continental mess. Well away from the chopping and splashing, a minute doll-like blonde was ironing shirts. Five or six had already been ironed. There were at least that number remaining. Burden noticed that she was taking extreme care not to cause a horizontal crease to appear under the yoke of the shirt she was at present attending to, an error into which hasty or careless women often fall and which makes the removal of a jacket by its wearer an embarrassment.

'Good afternoon, Mrs Swan. I wonder if I may trouble you for a few minutes?'

Rosalind Swan had a girlish air, a featherlight 'bovver' haircut and nothing in her face or manner to show that eight months before she had been deprived of her only child. She wore white tights and pink buckled shoes, but Burden thought she was as old as he.

'I like to see personally to all my husband's laundry,' she declared in a manner Burden could only describe as merry, 'and Gudrun can't be expected to give his shirts that little extra wifely touch, can she?'

From long experience Burden had learnt that if a man is having an affair with another woman and, in that woman's presence, his wife makes a more than usually coquettish and absurd remark, he will instinctively exchange a glance of disgust with his mistress. He had no reason to suppose Gudrun was anything more than an employee to Swan—she was no beauty, that was certain—but, as Mrs Swan spoke, he watched the other two. Gudrun didn't look up and Swan's eyes were on his wife. It was an appreciative, affectionate glance he gave her and he seemed to find nothing ridiculous in what she had said.

'You can leave my shirts till later, Rozzy.'

Burden felt that Swan often made remarks of this nature. Everything could be put off till another day, another time. Idleness or chat took precedence over activity always with him. He nearly jumped out of his skin when Mrs Swan said gaily:

'Shall we go into the lounge, my lover?'

Wexford just looked at him, his face impassive.

The 'lounge' was furnished with chintzy chairs, doubtful antiques, and, hanging here and there, brass utensils of no apparent use to a modern or, come to that, ancient household. It reflected no particular taste, had no individuality, and Burden remembered that Hall Farm, doubtless with all its contents, had been supplied to Swan by an uncle because he had nowhere else to live.

Linking her arm into her husband's, Mrs Swan led him

to a sofa where she perched beside him, disengaged arms and took his hand. Swan allowed himself to be thus manipulated in a passive fashion and seemed to admire his wife.

'None of these names mean anything to me, Chief Inspector,' he said when he had looked at the list. 'What about you, Roz?'

'I don't think so, my lover.'

Her lover said, 'I saw in the paper about the missing boy. You think the cases have some connection?'

'Very possibly, Mr Swan. You say you don't know any of the people on this list. Do you know Mrs Gemma Lawrence?'

'We hardly know anyone around here,' said Rosalind Swan. 'You might say we're still on our honeymoon, really.'

Burden thought this a tasteless remark. The woman was all of thirty-eight and married a year. He waited for her to say something about the child who had never been found, to show some feeling for her, but Mrs Swan was looking with voracious pride at her husband. He thought it time to put his own spoke in and he said flatly:

'Can you account for your movements on Thursday afternoon, sir?'

The man wasn't very tall, had small hands, and anyone could fake a limp. Besides, Wexford had said he hadn't had an alibi for that other Thursday afternoon ...

'You've quite cast me for the role of kidnapper, haven't you?' Swan said to Wexford.

'It was Mr Burden who asked you,' Wexford said imperturbably.

'I shall never forget the way you hounded me when we lost poor little Stella.'

'Poor little Stella,' Mrs Swan echoed comfortably.

'Don't get upset, Rozzy. You know I don't like it when you're upset. All right, what was I doing on Thursday afternoon? Every time you add anyone to your missing persons list I suppose I must expect this sort of inquisition I was here last Thursday. My wife was in London and Gudrun had the afternoon off. I was here all alone. I read for a bit and had a nap.' A flicker of temper crossed his face. 'Oh, and at about four I rode over to Stowerton and murdered a couple of tots that were making the streets look untidy.'

'Oh, Ivor, darling!'

'That sort of thing isn't amusing, Mr Swan.'

'No, and it's not amusing for me to be suspected of making away with two children, one of them my own wife's.'

No more could be got out of him. 'I've been meaning to ask,' said Burden as they drove back, 'did she go on calling herself Rivers after her mother re-married?'

'Sometimes she was one, sometimes the other, as far as I could gather. When she became a missing person she was Stella Rivers to us because that was her real name. Swan said he intended to have the name changed by deed poll, but he hadn't taken any steps towards it. Typical of him.'

'Tell me about this non-existent alibi,' said Burden.

6

MARTIN, Loring and their helpers were still interviewing rabbit-keepers, Bryant, Gates and half a dozen others continuing a house-to-house search of Stowerton. During the chief inspector's absence Constable Peach had brought in a child's plimsoll which he had found in a field near Flagford, but it was the wrong size, and, anyway, John Lawrence hadn't been wearing plimsolls.

Wexford read the messages which had been left on his desk, but most were negative and none needed immediate attention. He scanned the anonymous note again, then put it back in its envelope with a sigh.

'We had enough letters in the Stella Rivers case to paper the walls of this office,' he said, 'and we followed them all up. We had five hundred and twenty-three phone calls. The fantasies that go on in people's minds, Mike, the power of their imaginations! They were nearly all well intentioned. Ninety per cent of them really thought they had seen Stella and ...'

Burden interrupted him. 'I want to hear about Swan's alibi.'

'Swan drove Stella to Equita at two-thirty. Silly sort of name, isn't it? Whether it's supposed to mean all the pupils are equal or the only thing they teach is horse-riding, I wouldn't know.'

Burden was always impatient with these digressions. 'What kind of a car does he drive?'

'Not a red Jag. An oldish Ford shooting brake. He left Stella at the gates, believing, he said, that friends would bring her home, and went back home himself. At three-thirty he also got on a horse, that Sherry thing, and rode to Myfleet to see, believe it or not, a man about a dog.'

'You're joking.'

'Would I, about a thing like this? There's a fellow in Myfleet called Blain who breeds pointers. Swan went to look at some puppies with an eye to buying one for Stella. Of course, he didn't buy one, any more than he ever got her the pony he promised or got her name changed. Swan's always "just going to do something". One of the Four Just Men, he is.'

'But he did call on this man?'

'Blain told us Swan was with him from ten to four until four-fifteen, but he didn't get back to Hall Farm until five-thirty.'

'Where did he say he had been in that hour and a quarter?'

'Just riding round. The horse, he said, needed exercise. Maybe it also needed a wash, for both rider and mount must have been wet through when Swan got home. But odd though this sounds, it is the kind of thing Swan would do. He *would* moon about on horseback in the rain. His ride, he said, took him through Cheriton Forest, but he couldn't produce a single person to corroborate this. On the other hand, he could have got to Mill Lane in the time and killed Stella. But if he did, why did he? And what did he do with her body? His wife hasn't an alibi either. She says she was at Hall Farm and she can't drive. At any rate, she hasn't a driving licence.'

Burden digested all this carefully. Then, he decided, he wanted to know more about Stella's departure from Equita. He wanted the details Wexford hadn't had time to give him when they had sat together in the car in Fontaine Road.

'The children,' said Wexford, 'had an hour's riding lesson and a further hour they spent messing about with the horses. Miss Williams, the owner of Equita, who lives in that house adjoining the stables, saw Stella that afternoon but says she didn't speak to her and we have no reason to doubt her word. It was Mrs Margaret Fenn who took the children out for their ride. She's a widow of about forty and she lives in what used to be the lodge to Saltram House. Know it?'

Burden knew it. Ruined Saltram House and its grounds, now turned to wilderness, had been a favourite resort of his and Jean's. For them it had been a place of romance, a lost

57

domain, where they had gone for evening walks in the early days of their marriage and where they had later returned many times to bring their children on picnics.

All that day he had hardly thought about Jean and his happy past with her. His misery had been suspended by the present tumultuous events. But now again he saw her face before him and heard her call his name as they explored the gardens that time had laid waste and, hand in hand, entered the dark cold shell of the house. He shivered.

'You all right, Mike?' Wexford gave him a brief anxious glance and then he went on. 'Stella said good-bye to Mrs Fenn and said that as her step-father—incidentally, she always referred to him as her father—hadn't yet arrived, she would walk along Mill Lane to meet him. Mrs Fenn didn't much like letting the girl go alone, but it was still light and she couldn't go with her as she still had another hour and a half at Equita in which to clear up. She watched Stella go through the gates of Equita, thus becoming the last person but one to see her before she disappeared.'

'The last but one?'

'Don't forget the man who offered her a lift. Now for the houses in Mill Lane. There are only three between Equita and Stowerton, all widely separated, Saltram Lodge and two cottages. Before Hill offered her the lift she had passed one of these cottages, the one that is occupied only at week-ends, and, this being a Thursday, it was empty. We know no more of what happened to her after she was seen by Hill, but if she walked on unmolested she would next have come to the second cottage which has a tenant, not an owner occupier. This tenant, a single man, was out at work and didn't return until six. Again this was carefully checked because both this cottage and Saltram Lodge have telephones and one of the possibilities which occurred to me was that Stella might have called at a house and asked to phone Hall Farm. The third and last house, Saltram Lodge, was also empty until Mrs Fenn got home at six. She had had some relatives staying with her, but they had left for London by the three-forty-five train from Stowerton. A taxi-driver confirmed that he had picked them up at the lodge at twenty past three.'

'And was that all?' Burden said. 'No more leads?'

Wexford shook his head. 'Not what you'd call leads. The usual flock of people came forward with unhelpful evidence. A woman had picked up a child's glove outside one of the cottages but it wasn't Stella's. There was another of those free-lift merchants who said he had picked up an elderly man near Saltram Lodge at five-thirty and driven him into Stowerton, but this driver was a shifty sort of fellow and he impressed me as a sensation-monger rather than someone whose word you could rely on.

'A van-driver claimed to have seen a boy come out of the back door of the rented cottage and perhaps he did. They all leave their back doors unlocked in this part of the world. They think there's no crime in the country. But the van-driver also said he heard screams coming from behind the hedge just outside Equita, and we *know* Stella was alive and unharmed until she had refused Hill's offer. I doubt if we shall ever find out any more.'

Wexford looked tired, his jowly face heavier and more drooping than usual. 'I shall take a couple of hours off tomorrow morning, Mike, and I advise you to do the same. We're both dead-beat. Have a lie-in.'

Burden nodded abstractedly. He didn't say that there is no point in lying-in when there is no one to lie in with, but he thought it. Wearily he found himself recalling as he went out to his car those rare but delightful Sunday mornings when Jean, usually an early riser, consented to remain in bed with him until nine. Lying in each other's arms, they had listened to the sound of Pat making tea for them in the kitchen, and had sat bolt upright, jerking away from each other when she came in with the tray. Those had been the days, but he hadn't known it at the time, hadn't appreciated and treasured each moment as he should have done. And now he would have given ten years of his life for one of those mornings back again.

His memories brought him a dull misery, his only consolation that soon he would be in the company of someone as wretched as himself, but when he walked up to the always open door he heard her call out to him gaily and as intimately as if they were old friends, 'I'm on the phone, Mike. Go in and sit down. Make yourself at home.'

The telephone must be in the dining room, he thought. He sat down in the other room, feeling uncomfortable because untidiness always made him ill-at-ease. He wondered how anyone as beautiful and as charming as she could bear to live in such disorder and wondered more when she came in, for she was a changed woman, brilliantly smiling, almost elegant.

'You needn't have rung off on my account,' he said, trying not to stare too hard at the short kingfisher-blue dress she wore, the long silver chains, the silver comb in her high-piled hair.

'That was Matthew,' she said. 'They brought him a phone and he phoned me from his bed. He's terribly worried about John, but I told him it was all right. I told him everything would be all right on Monday. He has so many worries, poor boy. He's ill and his wife's expecting a baby and he's out of work and now this.'

'Out of work? What sort of work does he do?'

She sat down opposite him and crossed the best pair of legs Burden thought he had ever seen. He stared at a patch of floor some inches from her feet.

'He's a television actor, or he is when he can get work. He so terribly wants to be a household word. The trouble is his face is wrong. Oh, I don't mean he isn't good-looking. He was born too late. He looks just like Valentino and that won't do these days. John's going to be just like him. He's very like him now.'

Matthew Lawrence . . . it rang some sort of bell. 'I think I may have seen his picture in the papers,' said Burden.

She nodded earnestly. 'Squiring Leonie West about, I expect. She used to be photographed wherever she went.'

'I know her. She's a ballet dancer. My daughter's crazy about ballet. As a matter of fact, I think that's where I've seen your ex-husband, in pictures with Leonie West.'

'Matthew and Leonie were lovers for years. Then he met me. I was a drama student and I had a small part in a television series he was in. When we got married he said he wouldn't see Leonie any more, but he really only married me because he wanted a child. Leonie couldn't have children, otherwise he'd have married her.'

She had been speaking in a very cool practical voice, but

60

now she sighed and fell silent. Burden waited, no longer tired, even more interested than usual in other people's life stories, although this one perturbed him strangely.

After a while she went on. 'I tried to keep our marriage going and when John was born I thought we had a chance. Then I found out Matthew was still seeing Leonie. At last he asked me to divorce him and I did. The judge expedited the decree because there was a child on the way.'

'But you said Leonie West couldn't . . .'

'Oh, not Leonie. He didn't marry her. She was years older than he was. She must be well into her forties by now. He married a girl of nineteen he met at a party.'

'Good God,' said Burden.

'She had the baby, but it only lived two days. That's why I'm keeping my fingers crossed for them now. This one just must be all right.'

Burden couldn't keep his feelings to himself any longer. 'Don't you bear any malice?' he said. 'I should have thought you'd hate him and his wife and that West woman.'

She shrugged. 'Poor Leonie. She's too pathetic now to hate. Besides, I always rather liked her. I don't hate Matthew or his wife. They couldn't help themselves. They did what they had to do. You couldn't expect them all to spoil their lives for me.'

'I'm afraid I'm rather old-fashioned in these things,' said Burden. 'I believe in self-discipline. They spoiled your life, didn't they?'

'Oh, *no*! I've got John and he makes me very very happy.'

'Mrs Lawrence . . .'

'Gemma!'

'Gemma,' he said awkwardly. 'I must warn you not to bank too much on Monday. I don't think you should bank on it at all. My chief—Chief Inspector Wexford—has absolutely no faith in the veracity of this letter. He's sure it's a hoax.'

She paled a little and clasped her hands. 'No one would write a letter like that,' she said innocently, 'if it wasn't true. Nobody could be so cruel.'

'But people are cruel. Surely you must know that?'

'I won't believe it. I know John is going to be there on

Monday. Please—please don't spoil it for me. I'm holding on to it, it's made me so happy.'

He shook his head helplessly. Her eyes were beseeching. imploring him to give her one word of encouragement. And then, to his horror, she fell on her knees in front of him, seizing both his hands in hers.

'Please, Mike, tell me you think it'll be all right. Just say there's a chance. There could be, couldn't there? Please, Mike!'

Her nails dug into his wrists. 'There's always a chance . . .'

'More than that, more than that! Smile at me, show me there's a chance.' He smiled, almost desperately. She sprang up. 'Stay there. I'm going to make coffee.'

The evening was dying away. Soon it would be quite dark. He knew that he should go away now, follow her outside and say briskly, 'Well, if you're all right, I must be on my way.' Staying here was wrong, entirely overstepping the bounds of his duty. If she needed company it ought to be Mrs Crantock or one of those strange friends of hers.

He couldn't go. It was impossible. What a hypocrite he was with his talk of self-discipline. Jean? he said, savouring her name experimentally. If Jean had been at home there would have been no staying, no need for control.

She came back with the coffee and they drank it in the dusk. Soon he could hardly see her and yet somehow he felt her presence more forcefully. In one way he wanted her to turn on the light, but at the same time he prayed that she wouldn't and thus destroy the atmosphere, warm, dark and scented with her scent, a tension and yet a peace.

She poured him more coffee and their hands touched. 'Tell me about your wife,' she said.

He had never told anyone. He wasn't the kind of man to open his heart and relieve his soul. Grace had tried to draw him out. That idiot Camb had tried and, in a more subtle and tactful way, Wexford himself. And yet he would have liked to tell someone, if only the right listener could be found. This beautiful kind woman wasn't the right listener. What would she with her strange past, her peculiar permissiveness, understand of his notions of monogamy, his one-woman life? How could he talk to her of his simple gentle Jean, her quiet existence and her abominable death?

'It's all over now,' he said shortly. 'Best forgotten.' Too late he realised the impression his words had made.

'Even if you haven't been too happy,' she said, 'you don't just miss the person, you miss love.'

He saw the truth of it. Even for him it was true. But love wasn't quite the word. There was no love in those dreams of his and Jean never entered them. As if to deny his own thoughts, he said harshly, 'They say you can find a substitute, but you can't. I can't.'

'Not a substitute. That's the wrong word. But someone else for another way of love perhaps.'

'I don't know. I have to go now. Don't put on the light.' Light would show her too much, his face after suppressed pain had worked on it, and, worse than that, the hunger for her he could no longer hide. 'Don't put on the light!'

'I wasn't going to,' she said softly. 'Come here.'

It was a little light kiss on the cheek she gave him, such as a woman may give a man she has known for years, the husband of a friend perhaps, and, returning it, touching her cheek, he still meant to kiss her in the same way with a comradely reassurance. But he felt his heart beating and hers beside it as if he had two hearts of his own. Their mouths met and his long control broke.

He kissed her with everything he had, crushing her in his arms and forcing her back against the wall, his tongue thrusting down into her mouth.

When he let her go and moved away shivering, she stood still with her head bowed, saying nothing. He opened the front door and ran from her, not looking back.

7

SUNDAY, the morning of his lie-in. He had passed a horrible night, filled with dreams so disgusting that if he had read them in some work on psychology—the kind that Grace was always on about—he would have had no difficulty in believing they were the product of a diseased and perverted mind. Even thinking of them made him shudder with shame.

If you lie wakeful in bed when it is already light you have to think. But of what? Jean who was gone for ever? Dreams that made you wonder if inside you were as bad as all those local deviates? Gemma Lawrence? What a fool he had been to kiss her, to stay sitting there with her in the dark, to get involved!

He got up quickly. It was only seven-thirty when he came into the kitchen and no one else was about. He made a pot of tea and took a cup in to each of the others. It was another beautiful clear day.

Grace sat up in bed and took the teacup. She wore a nightgown just like Jean's. Her morning face was a little puffy with sleep, dreamy and vague just as Jean's had always been. He hated her.

'I have to go out,' he said. 'Work.'

'I didn't hear the phone,' said Grace.

'You were asleep.'

His children didn't stir when he put their teacups beside them. They were heavy sleepers and it was only natural. Burden knew all that, but it seemed to him that they no longer cared for him. Their mother was dead but they had a mother substitute, a mother facsimile. It was all one to them, he thought, whether their father was there or not.

He got out his car and drove off, but with no clear picture of where he was going. Perhaps to Cheriton Forest to sit and

64

think and torture himself. But instead of taking the Pomfret road he found himself heading towards Stowerton. All the control he had left was needed to stop him going towards Fontaine Road, but he kept his control and turned instead into Mill Lane.

It was here that the red Jaguar had been seen. Behind those trees the young duffel-coated man with the small hands had strolled picking leaves. Were they connected, the car and the youth? And was it possible in this wicked and cynical world that the leaf-picker kept rabbits—perhaps he had been picking leaves for his rabbits—and needed a child only for the pleasure of that child's company and the sight of its happy face when a small eager hand stroked thick smooth fur?

On such a morning even this improbable and Peter Pan-like notion seemed feasible. In the distance, ahead of him, he could hear the bells of St Jude, Forby, ringing for early Communion. He knew now where he was going. He rounded a bend in the road and Saltram House came suddenly and gloriously into view.

Who would have supposed, looking at it from this distance as it proudly crowned the hill, that those windows were not glazed, those rooms not inhabited, but that the great stone edifice was merely a shell, the skeleton, so to speak, of a palace? It was golden-grey in the morning sun, a palladian house, late eighteenth century, and in its splendid proportions it seemed both to smile and to frown on the valley below.

Fifty years old now, the tale of its destruction was known to everyone in Kingsmarkham. During the First World War it had been. Whoever had owned the house, and this was now forgotten, had given a house party and his guests had gone out on to a flat area of the roof to watch a Zeppelin pass over. One of them had dropped a cigar butt over the parapet and the butt had set fire to the shrubs below. There was nothing now behind those blank exquisite windows, nothing but trees and bushes which had grown up out of the burnt foundations to thrust their branches where once women in Paris gowns had walked, looking at pictures and trailing their fans.

He started the car again and drove slowly up to the iron gates where the drive to Saltram House began. On the left of the gates stood a small one-storey white house with a thatched roof. A woman was in the garden, picking mushrooms from the lawn. Mrs Fenn, he supposed. She hadn't lived there in the days when he and Jean used to come picnicking in the grounds. The lodge had stood empty for years.

Of course, these grounds would have been thoroughly searched back in February and then again by the search parties on Thursday night and Friday. But did the searchers know the place as he knew it? Would they know the secret places as he knew them?

Burden opened the gates and they creaked dully on their hinges.

Wexford and his friend Dr Crocker, the police doctor, sometimes played golf together on Sunday mornings. They had been friends since boyhood, these two, although Wexford was the senior by seven years and the doctor was a spry lean fellow who looked quite young when seen from a distance, whereas Wexford was a huge man, gone to seed and stout, with dangerously high blood pressure.

It was on account of this hypertension that Crocker had suggested the Sunday golf sessions and prescribed a rigorous diet. Wexford lapsed from his diet twice a week on average, but he didn't greatly object to the golf, although his handicap was disgracefully around thirty-six. It got him out of going to church with his wife.

'You wouldn't fancy a little drop of something?' he asked wistfully in the club bar.

'At this hour?' said Crocker, the disciplinarian.

'It's the effect that counts, not the hour.'

'If my sphyg wasn't about the best you can buy,' said the doctor, 'it would have busted last time I took your blood pressure. I kid you not, it would have snapped in sheer despair. You wouldn't put a thermometer under the hot tap now, would you? What you need isn't alcohol but a few brisk swings under the pro's eagle eye.'

'Not that,' Wexford pleaded. 'Anything but that.'

They went on to the first tee. His expression inscrutable,

Crocker watched his friend fumbling in his golf bag and then he handed him a five iron without a word.

Wexford drove. The ball disappeared, but nowhere in the direction of the first hole. 'It's so bloody unfair,' he said. 'You've been at this ridiculous pastime all your life and I'm a mere novice. It's giving me a hell of an inferiority complex. Now if we were to fetch someone else in on this, Mike Burden, for instance . . .'

'Do Mike good, I daresay.'

'I worry about him,' said Wexford, glad of a respite before having to witness one of the doctor's perfect drives. 'I wonder sometimes if he isn't heading for a nervous breakdown.'

'Men lose their wives. They get over it. D'you know what? Mike will marry his sister-in-law. It's right on the cards. She looks like Jean, she acts like Jean. Mike can marry her and almost stay monogamous. Enough of this nonsense. We're here to play golf, remember.'

'I mustn't go too far from the club-house. They may want to reach me at any time if anything comes up about that missing boy.'

It was a genuine anxiety on Wexford's part and not an excuse, but he had cried wolf on the golf course too often. The doctor grinned nastily. 'Then they can come and fetch you. Some members of this club can actually *run*, you know. Now watch me carefully.' He took his own well-seasoned five and drove with beautiful precision. 'On the green, I fancy,' he said complacently.

Wexford picked up his bag, sighed, and the strode manfully up the fairway. He murmured under his breath and with feeling towards the doctor's back, ' "Thou shalt not kill but needs't not strive, officiously to keep alive." '

The aspect of the house which faced the road and in front of which Burden now parked his car was the back or, more properly, the garden front. There could be no doubt from this distance that Saltram House was a shell. He went up to one of the stone-faced windows and stared through it into the still, dim and silent depths. Elder trees and young oaks—for how old is a mature oak?—thrust their way up out of sand

67

and rubble. The scars of the fire had long faded, their black ness washed away by fifty winters of rain. The leaves were golden now and rattling yellow, lying in their thousands on broken stone and massed rubble. The house had been like this when he and Jean had first come here and the only change was that the trees were taller, nature more rampant and more arrogant in her conquest, and yet it seemed to him that the ruin was personal, symbolic of his own.

He never read poetry. He seldom read anything. But like that of most people who don't read, his memory was good and sometimes he remembered the things Wexford had quoted to him. Under his breath, wonderingly, he whispered:

'Ruin hath taught me thus to ruminate
    That time will come and take my love away . . .'

He didn't know who had said it, but whoever it was knew all right. He swung away from the back of the house. There was no entering it this way. You entered by the front, clambering through what had once been an Italian garden.

To the right and left of him neglected parkland fell away. Whom did it belong to? Why did no one farm it? He didn't know the answers, only that this was a still and beautiful desert where grass grew long and wild and trees that man, not nature, had planted, cedars and ilexes and the tall slender *gingko biloba*, the Chinese maidenhair tree, raised proud trunks and prouder branches from an alien soil. It was a wilderness, desperately sad in that it should have been tended, was designed to be tended, but those who loved to tend it had been remove by ruining time. He thrust aside branches and brambles and came to the incomparably more beautiful front of Saltram House.

There was a great pediment crowning it with a frieze of classical figures and beneath this, above the front door, a vertical sun-dial, sky blue with figures of gold, which the wind and rain had scarred but not spoiled. From where he stood Burden could see the sky through the bones, as it were, of the house, pieces of sky as blue as the sun-dial.

It was no longer possible, and hadn't been for years, to walk into the Italian garden or up to the house without climbing. Burden scrambled over a five-foot-high wall of broken stone, through the cracks of which brambles and bryony had thrust their tendrils.

He had never seen the fountains playing, but he knew there had once been fountains here. Twelve years ago, when he and Jean had first penetrated as far as this, two bronze figures holding vases aloft had stood on either side of the overgrown drive. But vandals had come since then and torn the statues from their plinths, greedy perhaps for the lead from which the fountain pipes were made.

One figure had been that of a boy, the other of a girl in delicate drapery. The boy had disappeared, but the girl lay among the weeds, and the long-leaved grey mullion with its yellow flowers pushed its stalks between her arm and the curve of her body. Burden bent down and lifted the statue. It was broken and half-eaten away by verdigris and underneath it the ground was quite bare, a blank area of earth oddly and unpleasantly in the shape of a small human body.

He replaced the mass of metal which had once been a fountain and climbed the broken steps that led up to the door. But as soon as he stood on the threshold, at the point where in the past guests had entered and given their cloaks to a servant, he saw that there was no concealing a body here, not even the small body of a five-year-old.

For everything in Saltram House, cupboards, doors, staircase, even to a great extent dividing walls, was gone. There remained scarcely anything of the works of man. True, the towering and somewhat sinister walls of the house soared above him, but even these, which had once been painted and adorned with frescoes, were now hung everywhere with ivy, and they sheltered from the wind a young forest of rich growth. Elders and oaks, birch and beech saplings had forced their way from the rich burnt soil and some of them now rivalled the walls themselves in height. Burden was looking down into a copse which the breeze, entering by the window holes, ruffled gently. He could see the roots of these trees and see too that nothing lay amongst them.

He gazed and then he turned away. Down the steps he went and back into the Italian garden, remembering with a sudden pang how they had once eaten their tea on this very spot, and Pat, a little girl of six or so, had asked him why he couldn't make the fountains play. Because they were broken, because there was no water, he had said. He had never thought of it again, never wondered about it till now.

But those fountains had played once. Where had the water come from? Not directly from the main, surely, even if main water had ever reached Saltram House. For things like this, fountains and any ornamental water gadgets, you always had tanks. And whether there was main water or not at the time the house was burnt, there certainly wouldn't have been when the fountains were set up in seventeen something or other.

Therefore the water must have been stored somewhere. Burden felt a little thrill of dread. It was a stupid idea, he told himself. Fantastic. The searchers had been all over these grounds twice. Surely a notion like this would have occurred to one of them? Not if they didn't know the place like I do, he thought, not if they didn't know that statue was once a fountain.

He knew he wouldn't rest or have a moment's peace if he went now. He dropped down off the steps and stood knee-deep in weeds and brambles. The cisterns, if cisterns there were, wouldn't be up here by the house but as near as possible to the fountain plinths.

In the first place, these plinths were hard to find. Burden cut himself an elder branch with his penknife and pruned off its twigs. Then he began lifting away the dead and dying growth. In places the tangle seemed immovable and he had almost decided this was an impossible task when his stick struck something metallic and gave off a dull ring. Using his bare hands now, he tore away first ivy and under it a tenacious heathy plant to reveal a bronze disc with a hole in its centre. He closed his eyes, thought back and remembered that the boy had stood here, the girl in a similar position on the other side of the drive.

Now where would the cistern be? Not surely between the plinth and the drive, but on the other side. Again he used his stick. It hadn't rained for two or three weeks and the ground beneath the jungle of weeds was as hard as stone. No use going by feel, unless he felt with his feet. Accordingly, he shuffled slowly along the not very clear passage his stick was making.

He was looking down all the time, but still he stumbled when his left toe struck what felt like a stone ridge or step. Probing with the stick, he found the ridge and then traced a rectangular outline. He squatted down and worked with his hands until he had cleared away all the growth and revealed a slate slab the size and shape of a gravestone. Just as he had thought, the fountain cistern. Would it be possible to raise that slab? He tried and it came up easily before he had time to brace himself against the shock of what he might find inside.

The cistern was quite empty. Dry, he thought, for half a century. Not even a spider or a woodlouse had penetrated its stone fastness.

Well, there was another one, wasn't there? Another cistern to feed the fountain on the opposite side? No difficulty, at any rate, about finding it. He paced out the distance and cleared the second slab. Was it his imagination or did the growth seem newer here? There were no dense brambles, anyway, only the soft sappy weeds that die away entirely in winter. The slab looked just like its fellow, silvery black and here and there greened with lichen.

Burden's fingers were torn and bleeding. He wiped them on his handkerchief, raised the slab and, with a rasping intake of breath, looked down at the body in the cistern.

8

HARRY WILD knocked out his pipe into the ashtray on
Camb's counter. 'Well, are you going to tell me?'

'I don't know anything, Harry, and that's a fact. They
sent for Mr Wexford off the golf course and he just about
tore in here. You'll have to wait till he's got a moment to
spare. We're all at sixes and sevens. I don't remember a
Sunday like it all my time in the force.'

The phone rang. Camb lifted the receiver and said, 'You've
seen John Lawrence in Brighton, madam? One moment while
I put you through to the officers who are dealing with this
information.' He sighed. 'That,' he said to Wild, 'makes
thirty-two calls today from people who claim to have seen
that kid.'

'He's dead. My informant who's very reliable says he's
dead. Burden found his body this morning and that's why
I'm working on a Sunday.' Wild watched to see how this
affected Camb, and then added, 'I just want confirmation
from Wexford and then I'm off to interview the mother.'

'Rather you than me,' said Camb. 'By gum, I wouldn't
have your job for all the tea in China.'

Not at all abashed, Wild re-lit his pipe. 'Talking of tea, I
don't suppose there's any going?'

Camb didn't answer him. His phone was ringing again.
When he had dealt with a man who claimed to have found a
blue sweater answering to the description of the one John
Lawrence had been wearing he looked up and saw the lift
doors open. 'Here's Mr Wexford now,' he said, 'and Mr
Burden. On their way to the mortuary to see what Dr
Crocker's come up with, I daresay.'

'Ah, Mr Burden,' Wild said, 'the very man I want to see.

What's all this about finding the body of the lost kid?'

Burden gave him an icy stare, then turned on his heel, but Wexford snapped, 'What d'you want to know for, anyway? That rag of yours doesn't go to press till Thursday.'

'Excuse me, sir,' said Camb, 'but Mr Wild wants to send the stories to the London papers.'

'Oh, linage. I see. Well, far be it from me to keep a journalist from earning an honest penny on the Sabbath. Mr Burden did find a body this morning, in one of the fountain cisterns at Saltram House. You can say foul play is suspected. The body is that . . .' He paused and then went on more quickly, 'of a female child, aged about twelve, so far unidentified.'

'It's Stella Rivers, isn't it?' said Wild greedily. 'Come on, give a working man a break. This could be the biggest story of my career. Missing child found dead in ruins. No clue yet to lost boy. Is Kingsmarkham another Cannock Chase? I can see it all, I can . . .'

Wexford had great self-control. He also had two daughters and a grandson. He loved children with a passionate tenderness and his self-control broke down.

'Get out of here!' he roared. 'You back-street death reporter! You revolting ghoulish hack! Get out!'

Wild got out.

A gloom settles on policemen and on their police station when the body of a child has been found. Later they hunt for a child's killer with zeal, but at first, when the crime is discovered, they are aghast and sick at heart. For this is the crime most against nature, most life-denying and least forgivable.

Not at all ashamed of his castigation of Harry Wild, Wexford made his way to the mortuary where Dr Crocker and Burden stood on either side of the sheeted body.

'I've sent Loring to fetch Ivor Swan, sir,' said Burden. 'Better have him do it than the mother.'

Wexford nodded. 'How did she die?'

'The body's been there for God knows how many months,' said Crocker. 'The path experts will have to get working on it. I'd say, at a guess, asphyxiation. Violent pressure on the

73

windpipe. There are no wounds or anything like that and she wasn't strangled. No sexual interference.'

'We knew,' said Wexford quietly, 'that she must have been dead. It oughtn't to seem so horrible. It oughtn't to be such a shock. I hope she wasn't too frightened, that's all.' He turned away. 'I hope it was quick,' he said.

'That,' said Crocker, 'is the kind of thing you'd expect her parents to say, not a tough old nut like you, Reg.'

'Oh, shut up. Maybe it's because I know her parents won't say it that I'm saying it. Look at you, you bloody half-baked quack, you don't even *care*.'

'Now, steady on . . .'

'Here's Mr Swan,' said Burden.

He came in with Loring. Dr Crocker lifted the sheet. Swan looked and went white. 'That's Stella,' he said. 'The hair, the clothes . . . God, how horrible!'

'You're sure.'

'Oh, yes. I'd like to sit down. I've never seen a dead person before.'

Wexford took him into one of the interview rooms on the ground floor.

Swan asked for a glass of water and didn't speak again until he had drunk it.

'What a ghastly sight! I'm glad Roz didn't see it. I thought I was going to pass out in there.' He wiped his face with his handkerchief and sat staring at nothing but as if he were stil¹ seeing the child's body. Wexford thought his horror was occasioned only by the sight of what eight months underground had done to Stella Rivers and not by personal grief, an impression that wasn't much weakened when Swan said, 'I was fond of her, you know. I mean, it wasn't as if she was my own but I'd got quite attached to her.'

'We've been into all that before, Mr Swan. How well do you know the grounds of Saltram House?'

'That's where she was found, isn't it? I don't even know where it is.'

'And yet you must have passed the house every time you drove Stella to Equita.'

'D'you mean that ruin you can see from the road?'

Wexford nodded, watching the other man carefully. Swan

74

looked at the walls, the floor, anywhere but at the chief inspector. Then he said in the tone a man uses when his car keeps breaking down, 'I don't know why this sort of thing has to happen to me.'

'What d'you mean, "this sort of thing"?'

'Oh, nothing. Can I go now?'

'Nobody's detaining you, Mr Swan,' said Wexford.

Half an hour later he and Burden were sitting on the crumbling wall watching half a dozen men at work in the cistern, photographing, measuring, examining. The sun was still hot and its brilliance gave to the place an air of classical antiquity. Broken columns showed here and there among the long grass and the investigations had turned up fragments of pottery.

It might have been an archaeological dig they were supervising rather than a hunt for clues in a murder case. They had failed to find any trace of the male statue, but the figure of the girl lay as Burden had left her, lay like a dead thing, her face buried in ivy, her sculpted metal hair gleaming in the sun as gold as the hair of Stella Rivers in life.

'You'll think me a fanciful old fool,' said Wexford musingly, 'but I can't help seeing the analogy. It's like an omen.' He pointed to the statue and looked quizzically at Burden. 'The girl's dead. The boy has disappeared, someone has taken him away.' He shrugged. 'In life,' he said. 'In bronze. And somewhere maybe the thief has set the boy up in pleasant surroundings, taken care of him. I mean the statue, of course.'

'Well, sure, what else? More likely used what was useful and chucked the rest out.'

'Christ . . .' Wexford saw that the inspector had no idea what he had meant and gave up. He ought to have known, he reflected, that it was no use going into flights of fancy with Mike. 'Whoever put her in there,' he said more practically, 'knew the place better than you do. You didn't even know there were any cisterns.'

'I've only been here in summer. The slabs wouldn't be so overgrown in wintertime.'

'I wonder?' Wexford called Peach over. 'You were with

75

the search parties in February, Peach. Did you notice the cisterns?'

'We covered this ground the day after Stella went missing, sir. The Friday, it was. It poured with rain all the previous night and it was raining hard when we were here. The whole of this area was a sea of mud. I don't reckon you could have guessed the cistern slabs were there.'

'I think we'll go and have a word with Mrs Fenn.'

She was a small fair woman, anxious to help, appalled at the discovery which had been made less than a quarter of a mile from her home.

'She was the most promising pupil I had,' she said in a quiet voice with an edge of horror to it. 'I used to boast about her to my friends. Stella Rivers, I used to say—or Stella Swan, you never knew which was her right name— Stella Rivers will be a first-class show jumper one day. She won't will she? God, it's so *awful*. I'll never forgive myself for letting her go off on her own that day. I should have phoned Mr Swan. I knew he was a bit absent-minded. That wasn't the first time he'd let her down and forgotten to come.'

'You mustn't blame yourself,' said Wexford. 'Tell me, did you know those fountains had cisterns? If you knew, it means other local people would know.'

'Of course I knew.' Mrs Fenn looked puzzled. 'Oh you mean they get overgrown in summer?' Her brow cleared. 'I often ride up there in dry weather and take my guests for walks or on picnics. I know I've pointed out the fountains to people because the statues are so pretty, aren't they?' With a little tremor in her voice she said, 'I shan't feel like going there ever again.' She shook her head with a kind of shudder. 'After heavy rain the slabs might get covered, especially if a lot of earth got washed down from the side of the house.'

They were carrying the slab out to the waiting van now. It would go to the lab for extensive tests.

'If he left any prints,' said Wexford, 'all the mud and water will have got rid of them. The weather was on his side, wasn't it? What's the matter? Had an idea?'

'I'm afraid not.' Burden contemplated the quiet lane and the surrounding meadows. He didn't look back at the house but he felt its blind empty eyes on him. 'I was wondering about Mrs Lawrence,' he said. 'I mean, ought I to go and . . .'

Wexford snapped off the sentence in his scissors voice. 'Martin's been. I sent him to Fontaine Road as soon as we heard what you'd found. It wouldn't do for her to hear we'd found a body and not know whose.'

'That's what I thought.'

'So you needn't bother with her tonight. She won't want coppers hanging around her place all the time. Let her have a bit of peace. Besides, she said she'd got a friend coming down from London.'

He needn't bother with her tonight . . . Burden wondered who the friend was. Man or woman? Actress? Artist? Maybe someone who would listen avidly while Gemma told her about the kiss she had received from a sex-starved policeman. No, he needn't go there again tonight or any other night, come to that. The Stella Rivers case would take up all his time and it would be better that way. Far better, said Burden firmly to himself.

The national press had arrived in force on Sunday evening, and Wexford, most unwillingly, had held a conference. He didn't like reporters, but they had their uses. On the whole, he supposed, the publicity they gave to pain and horror did more good than harm. Their stories would be inaccurate, with most of the names spelt wrong—a national daily had once repeatedly referred to him as Police Chief Waterford—but the public would be alerted, someone might come up with something helpful. Certainly there would be hundreds of phone calls and, no doubt, more anonymous letters of the kind that this morning had sent Martin, Gates and Loring to keep a date in Cheriton Forest.

Wexford had left home before his morning paper arrived, and now, at nine, he entered Braddon's to buy all the dailies. The shop had only just opened, but there was someone ahead of him. Wexford sighed. He knew that round grizzled head, that short spare figure. Even now, when innocently purchasing sixty Number Six. the man had an air of lurking. 'Good morning, Monkey,' said Wexford softly.

Monkey Matthews didn't jump. He froze briefly and then turned round. It was easy to see when you regarded him full-face how he had acquired his nickname. He stuck out his prognathous jaw, wrinkled up his nose and said glumly. 'Small world. I come in here with Rube, just for the bus ride, minding my own business, and before I get me first fag on I've got the fuzz on me tail.'

'Don't be like that,' said Wexford pleasantly. He bought his papers and shepherded Monkey out on to the pavement.

'I haven't done nothing.'

Monkey always made this remark to policemen, even when he encountered one by chance, as on this present occasion. And Burden had once replied, Two negatives make an affirmative, so we know where we are, don't we?

'Long time no see.' Wexford abhorred the expression, but Monkey would understand it and find it irritating.

He did. To cover a slight confusion he lit a cigarette and inhaled voraciously. 'Been up north,' he said vaguely. 'Had a spell in the rag trade. Liverpool.'

Later, Wexford decided, he would check. For the present he made an inspired guess. 'You've been in Walton.'

At the name of the prison, Monkey removed the cigarette from his lip and spat. 'Me and my partner,' he said, 'as straight a feller as you'd wish to meet, we had this stall like and a dirty little bastard of a fuzz cadet planted fifty dozen pair of fishnet tights on us. Seconds, they was supposed to be, but half of them hadn't got no crotch. Bleeding little agent provoker.'

'I don't want to hear that sort of talk,' said Wexford, and then less severely, 'Back with Ruby, are you? Isn't it about time you made an honest woman of her?'

'Me with a wife living?' Unconsciously, Monkey echoed the Lear Limerick. 'Bigamy, sir, is a crime,' he said. 'Pardon me, but that's my bus coming. I can't stand about nattering all day.'

Grinning broadly, Wexford watched him scuttle off to the bus stop on the Kingsbrook bridge. He scanned the front page of the first of his papers, saw that Stella had been found by a Sergeant Burton in a cave not far from the tiny hamlet of Stowerton, and changed his grin to a scowl.

78

9

MONKEY MATTHEWS had been born during the First War in the East End of London and had been educated for the most past in Borstal institutions. His marriage at the age of twenty to a Kingsmarkham girl had brought him to her home town where he had lived—when not in gaol—with his wife in her parent's house. Violence was foreign to him, but only perhaps because he was a coward, not from principle. He stole mostly. He stole from private houses, from his own wife and her aged parents and from those few people who were foolish enough to employ him.

The second war absorbed him into the Army, where he stole stores, officers' uniforms and small electrical equipment. He went to Germany with the army of occupation; he became an expert in the black market and, on his return home, was probably Kingsmarkham's first spiv. Patiently, his wife took him back each time he came out of prison.

In spite of his looks, he was attractive to women. He met Ruby Branch in Kingsmarkham magistrates' court as she was leaving it after being put on probation and he entering between two policemen. They didn't, of course, speak. But Monkey sought her out when he was free again and became a frequent visitor to her house in Charteris Road, Stowerton, especially when Mr Branch was on night work. He suggested to her that she wasn't getting the most out of her job at the underwear factory and soon, on his advice, she was clocking out most Fridays wearing three bras, six slips and six suspender belts under her dress. An ardent lover, Monkey was waiting for her when she came back from Holloway.

Since those days Wexford had put Monkey away for shopbreaking, larceny as a servant, attempting to blow up one of Ruby's rivals with a home-made bomb, and stealing by finding. Monkey was nearly as old as Wexford, but there was as much life left in him as in the chief inspector, although he smoked sixty cigarettes a day, had no legitimate means of support and, since his wife had finally thrown him out, no fixed abode.

Returning to his office, Wexford wondered about him. Monkey could never be free for long without getting into trouble. Busy as he was, Wexford decided to do the checking he had resolved on outside the newsagent's.

His notion that Monkey had been in Walton was soon confirmed. He had been released in September. The conviction had been for receiving, knowing it to have been stolen, so huge a quantity of tights, nylon briefs, body stockings and other frippery which, had it ever been sold, would surely have supplied the entire female teenage population of Liverpool for months to come.

Shaking his head, but smiling rather wryly, Wexford dismissed Monkey from his mind and concentrated on the pile of reports that awaited his attention. He had read through three of them when Sergeant Martin came in.

'No one turned up, of course?' he said, looking up.

'I'm afraid not, sir. We separated, according to instructions. It's out of the question we could have been spotted, the forest's so thick there. The only person to come along the road was the receptionist at the Cheriton Forest Hotel. No one came down the ride. We stayed there till ten.'

'I knew it would be a dead loss,' said Wexford.

Burden shared his chief's antipathy to Ivor and Rosalind Swan but he found it impossible to view them with Wexford's cynicism. They had something, those two, the special relationship of two people who love each other almost exclusively and who mean their love to survive until death parts them. Would he ever again find a love like that for himself? Or was to have it once all that any man could expect, knowing that few ever found it at all? Rosalind Swan had lost her only child in a hideous way but she could bear that loss without too much pain while she had her husband. He felt that she would have sacrificed a dozen children to keep Swan. How had Stella fitted into this honeymoon life? Had either or both of them felt her a hindrance, a shadowy and undesired third?

Wexford had been questioning them for half an hour and Mrs Swan looked tired and pale, but she seemed to feel the enormity of her husband's interrogation more keenly than its cause. 'Ivor loved Stella,' she kept saying, 'and Stella loved him.'

'Come, Mr Swan,' Wexford said, ignoring this, 'you must often since then have thought about that ride of yours and yet you can't name to me a single person, apart from Mr Blain, who might have seen you.'

'I haven't thought about it much,' Swan said, holding his wife's hand closely in both his own. 'I wanted to forget it. Anyway, I do remember people, only not what they looked like or their car numbers. Why should I go about taking car numbers? I didn't know I'd have to give anyone an alibi.'

'I'll get you a drink, my lover.' She took as much trouble over it as another woman might over the preparation of her baby's feed. The glass was polished on a table napkin, Gudrun was applied to for ice. 'There. Have I put too much soda in?'

'You're good to me, Rozzy. I ought to be looking after you.'

Burden saw her grow pink with pleasure. She lifted Swan's hand and kissed it as if there was no one there to see. 'We'll go away somewhere,' she said. 'We'll go away tomorrow and forget all this beastliness.'

The little scene which had brought a pang of envy to Burden's heart had no softening effect on Wexford. 'I'd rather you didn't go anywhere until we've got a much clearer picture of this case,' he said. 'Besides, there will be an inquest which you must attend and, presumably,' he added with stiff sarcasm, 'a funeral.'

'An inquest?' Swan looked aghast.

'Naturally. What did you expect?'

'An inquest,' Swan said again. 'Will I have to attend it?'

Wexford shrugged impatiently. 'That's a matter for the coroner, but I should say, yes, certainly you will.'

'Drink up your drink, my lover. It won't be so bad if we're together, will it?'

81

'There's a mother for you!' Wexford exploded.

Burden said nothing for a moment. He was wondering if most of the ideas he held on mother lover were perhaps fallacious. Until now he had supposed that to a woman the death of her child would be an insupportable grief. But maybe it wouldn't. People were very resilient. They recovered fast from tragedy, especially when they had someone to love, especially when they were young. Rosalind Swan had her husband. Whom would Gemma Lawrence have when she was fetched away to view a body in a mortuary?

It was three days since he had seen her, but hardly an hour had passed without his thinking of her. He relived that kiss and each time he experienced it again in retrospect he felt a shivering thrill of excitement. Telling himself to stop dwelling on it and on her was useless, and there was no question for him of out of sight, out of mind. She was almost more vivid to him in her absence than her presence, her body softer and fuller, her hair more thick and brilliant, her childlike sweetness sweeter. But while he kept away he felt that he was safe. Time would dull the memory if only he had the strength to stay away.

In the back of the car Wexford's probing eyes were on him. He had to say something.

'What about the father, Rivers?' he managed at last. 'You must have got on to him way back in February.'

'We did. Immediately after the divorce he married again and his airline sent him to San Francisco. We did more than get on to him. We checked him very closely. There was always the chance that he had popped over and smuggled the child into the States.'

'What, just like that? Hopped on a plane, grabbed her and flown off again? He can't be a rich man.'

'Of course he isn't,' Wexford retorted, 'but he could have done it just as easily as if he were a millionaire with a private aircraft. Don't forget he works for an airline and like any of their employees travels at about a tenth of the usual rate. The same applies within reason to any dependent he might take with him. Also he'd have access to any aircraft, provided there was a vacant seat. Gatwick's only about thirty miles from here, Mike. If he had found out the girl's movements, fiddled a passport and a ticket, he could have done it all right.'

'Only he didn't.'

'No, he didn't. He was at work in San Francisco all day on February 25th. Naturally, he came over when he was told Stella had disappeared and, no doubt, he'll be over again now.'

Detailed reports from forensics had come in during Wexford's absence. They confirmed Crocker's diagnosis and, for all the expertise of those who had compiled them, added little to it. Eight months had elapsed since the child's death, but the conclusion was that she had died from manual pressure on her throat and mouth. Her mildewed and tattered clothes afforded no clues and neither did the slab which had covered the cistern.

More phone calls had come in from people who claimed to have seen John, to have seen Stella alive and well in September, to have seen them alive and well and together. A woman holidaying in the Isle of Mull wrote to say a girl answering Stella's description had spoken to her on a beach and asked to be shown the road to Tobermory. The little boy with her had fair hair and the girl said his name was John.

'I wish they wouldn't waste our time,' said Wexford, knowing it would have to be followed up, picking up the next envelope. 'What's this, then? Another communication from our rabbit-keeper, I think.'

'I warned you not to wait for me. Did you think I would not know what was in your minds? I know everything. Your men are not very skilful at hiding. John was disappointed at not going home on Monday. He cried all night. I will return him only to his mother. She must be waiting *alone* on Friday at twelve noon in the same place. Remember what I did to Stella Rivers and do not try any more tricks. I am sending a copy of this letter to John's mother.'

'She won't see it, that's one blessing. Martin's collecting all her mail unopened. If we don't catch this joker before Friday we'll have to dress one of the policewomen up in a red wig.'

The idea of this travesty of Gemma waiting for a boy who

wouldn't come made Burton feel rather sick. 'I don't like that bit about Stella Rivers,' he muttered.

'Doesn't mean a thing. He's just read the papers, that's all. My God, don't say you're going to fall for his line. He's just a hoaxer. Here's Martin now with Mrs Lawrence's mail. I'll take those, thank you, Sergeant. Ah, here's our joker's effusion in duplicate.'

Burden couldn't stop himself. 'How is she?' he said quickly.

'Mrs Lawrence, sir? She was a bit the worse for wear.'

Blood came into Burden's cheeks. 'What d'you mean, worse for wear?'

'Well, she'd been drinking, sir.' Martin hesitated, letting his face show as much exasperation as he dared. The inspector's eyes were cold, his face set, a prudish blush on his cheeks. Why did he always have to be so darned straitlaced? Surely a bit of sorrow-drowning was permitted in a woman as mad with anxiety as Mrs Lawrence? 'You can understand it. I mean to say . . .'

'I often wonder what you do mean to say, Martin,' Burden snapped. 'Believe me, it's not clear from your words.'

'I'm sorry, sir.'

'I suppose she's got someone with her?' Wexford raised his eyes from the letter and its copy which he had been perusing.

'The friend didn't turn up,' said Martin. 'Apparently, she took offence because the Met had been on to her, asking if she or some boy friend of hers had seen John lately. I gather they weren't too tactful, sir. The boy friend's got a record and he's out of work. This girl who was coming to stay with Mrs Lawrence teaches at drama school and acts a bit. She said that if it got about, the police questioning her, it wouldn't do her any good in her profession. I did offer to fetch a neighbour to be with Mrs Lawrence but she wouldn't have any. Shall I pop back and . . . ?'

'Pop anywhere as long as you get out of here!'

'Break it up,' said Wexford mildly. 'Thank you, Sergeant.' He turned to Burden when Martin had gone. 'You've been in a state, Mike, ever since we left Hall Farm. Why bite his head off? What's he done?'

If Burden had realised how haggard his own face was, how it mirrored all his pain and his turbulent feelings, he wouldn't have lifted it numbly to stare at the chief inspector. Thoughtfully, Wexford returned his gaze, but for a moment neither man spoke. Why don't you get yourself a woman? Wexford was thinking. D'you want to drive yourself into a nervous collapse? He couldn't say those things aloud, not to Mike Burden.

'I'm going out,' Burden muttered. 'See if they need any help searching the forest.'

Wexford let him go. He shook his head gloomily. Burden knew as well as he did that they had completed their search of Cheriton Forest on Monday afternoon.

10

THE inquest on Stella Rivers was opened and adjourned until further evidence should come to light. Swan and his wife were there and Swan stumbled brokenly through his evidence, impressing the coroner as a shattered parent. This was the first sign Wexford had seen of any real grief in Stella's stepfather and he wondered why it had taken the inquest to bring it out. Swan had heard the news of Burden's discovery stoically and had identified Stella's body with no more physical nausea. Why break down now? For he had broken down. Leaving the court, Wexford saw that Swan was weeping, a lost soul, clinging to his wife's arm.

Now, if ever, was the time to verify Rosalind Swan's statement that she couldn't drive. Wexford watched eagerly as they got into the shooting brake. And it was she, he saw, who got into the driving seat. But after a while, when they had whispered together and Rosalind had briefly laid her cheek against her husband's, they changed places. Odd that, Wexford thought.

Swan took the wheel wearily and they drove off in the direction of the Myfleet road.

She would get him home and comfort him with her drinks and her kisses and her love, Wexford thought. 'Come, come, come, come, give me your hand,' he said to himself. 'What's done cannot be undone. To bed, to bed, to bed.' But Rosalind Swan was no Lady Macbeth to counsel murder or even connive at it. As far as he knew. Certainly she would cover up any crime Swan might commit, even the killing of her own child, for the sake of keeping him with her.

The fine weather had broken. It was raining now, a fine drizzle dispersing the fog which had settled on Kingsmarkham since early morning. Pulling up his raincoat collar, Wexford walked the few yards that separated the court from the police station. No one at the inquest had mentioned John Lawrence, but the knowledge that a second child was missing had underlain, he felt, everything that was said. There was not a soul in Kingsmarkham or Stowerton who didn't connect the two cases, not a parent who doubted that a child killer stalked their countryside. Even the policemen who stood about the entrances to the court wore the grave aspect of men who believed a madman, a pathological criminal who killed children simply because they were children, went free and might attack again. He couldn't recall any inquest at which these hardened men had looked so dour and so downcast.

He stopped in his tracks and viewed the length of the High Street. The primary schools' half-term was over and all the younger children back at work. The big ones hadn't yet broken up. But was it imagination or fact that he could hardly see a single four-year-old out with its mother this morning, scarcely a toddler or a baby in its pram? Then he spotted a pram which its owner was parking outside the supermarket. He watched her lift out the baby and its older sister, take the one in her arms and propel the other, who could only just walk, ahead of her into the shop. That such care should have to be exercised in the town whose guardian he was brought him a deep depression.

Why not Ivor Swan? Why not? It meant nothing that the man had no record. He had no record perhaps because no one had ever found him out. Wexford decided that he would again review Swan's life with particular reference to the districts he had lived in since he left Oxford. He would find out if any children had disappeared while Swan was in their vicinity. If Swan had done this, he swore to himself, he would get Swan.

But before making further investigations into the antecedents of her stepfather he had to see Stella's father. Their appointment was for twelve and when Wexford reached his office Peter Rivers had already been shown in.

A woman is often attracted by the same type of man and Rivers was not unlike his supplanter. Here was the same dapper quality, the same groomed look, neat small head, finely cut, almost polished, features and womanish tapering hands. But Rivers lacked Ivor Swan's indolent air, the impression he gave that sexually he would be far from indolent. There was something bustling about him, a fussy restiveness combined with a nervous manner, that might not endear itself to a silly romantic woman like Rosalind Swan.

He jumped up when Wexford came into the room and embarked on a long explanation of why he hadn't attended the inquest followed by an account of the tiresomeness of his journey from America. Wexford cut him short.

'Will you be seeing your former wife while you are here?'

'I guess so.' Sponge-like, Rivers, although domiciled for less than a year in America, had already picked up a transatlantic phraseology. 'I guess I'll have to. Needless to say, I can't stand that Swan. I should never have let Stell go to him.'

'Surely you had no choice, Mr Rivers?'

'Where did you get that idea? I never opposed her mother's application for custody, that's all, on account of Lois—that's the present Mrs Rivers—not wanting to be lumbered with a big kid like that. Rosie wasn't keen on getting custody either, come to that. Swan egged her on. I can tell you why, if you want to know.'

Sickened by all this, Wexford merely looked his assent.

'Swan knew he wouldn't have a bean after he'd paid the costs, nowhere to live, nothing. The three of them were pigging it in a crumby furnished place in Paddington. His uncle told him he'd let him have that Hall Farm place if Rosie kept Stell. I know it for a fact. Rosie told me.'

'But why? Why should his uncle care?'

'He wanted Swan to settle down, raise a family and do a bit of good for himself. Some hopes! Swan was supposed to take an agricultural course at the college here so that he could farm the land. As soon as he got here he let the whole lot off to a farmer who had his eye on it. I don't know why the uncle doesn't kick them both out. He's got pots of money and no one to leave it to but Swan.'

'You seem to know a lot about it, Mr Rivers.'

'I made it my business to. Yes, sir! Rosie and me have corresponded regularly since Stell went missing. I'll tell you another thing. Before he came out to Karachi and messed up my married life Mr Ivor Swan was living with this uncle *and* the aunt. Only she died while he was there. You'll know what I mean when I say she died very suddenly.'

'Will I?'

'You're a detective. I'd have thought that'd make you sit up. Swan thought he was coming in for some money, but it all went to uncle.'

'I don't think I need detain you any longer, Mr Rivers,' said Wexford, who was beginning to think Rosalind Swan had decidedly bad taste in men. The dislike he felt for Swan was nothing to the loathing this man aroused in him. He watched Rivers buttoning his raincoat and waited for him to say something to the effect that he mourned the child whom nobody seemed to have wanted. The words came at last and in curious form.

'It was a bit of a shock hearing she was dead,' Rivers said briskly, 'but she'd been dead to me for a couple of years, anyway, in a manner of speaking. I guess I'd never have seen her again.' He made for the door, not at all abashed by Wexford's scowl. 'A newspaper's offered me two thousand for my exclusive story.'

'Oh, I should take it,' said Wexford in a level voice. 'It will be some recompense for your tragic loss.'

He went to the window. It was still raining. The children who went home to lunch were issuing from Queen Street where the primary school was. Usually on wet days they managed the journey as best they could. Today, the first day of the second half of term, not one went unaccompanied, not one lacked the shelter of an umbrella, which seemed to Wexford to have a deeper significance than that of protecting small heads from the drizzle.

Routine checking occupied Burden's afternoon. It was only just after six when he got home. For almost the first time since Jean's death he was anxious to be at home and with his children, particularly with his daughter. All day long he had been thinking of her, her image driving away Gemma's, and as he made himself more and more familiar with the circumstances of Stella's life and death, he kept seeing Pat alone and frightened and cruelly overpowered and—dead.

It was she who rushed to let him in almost before his key was in the lock. And Burden, thinking he saw in her eyes some special alarm, some unusual need for comfort, bent swiftly and put his arms round her. Had he only known it, Pat had quarrelled with her aunt and natural ally and was turning for support to the only other available grown-up.

'What is it, darling?' He saw a car stopping, a hand beckoning, a figure stepping out into the wet dusk. 'Tell me what's happened?'

'You've got to tell Auntie Grace she's not to meet me from school. I'm at the high school, I'm not an infant. I was *humiliated*.'

'Oh, is that all?' With relief came gratitude. He laughed at Pat's rebelliously pouting lower lip, tugged at her ponytail, and went out to the kitchen to thank Grace for her forethought. What a fool he had been to worry when he had such a guardian!

But he felt a need to stay close by his daughter that evening. All through their meal and afterwards, while he was helping John with his geometry—Pythagoras' theorem which 'old Mint-face' insisted on the third form knowing by the next day—his thoughts and his eyes wandered to Pat. He had failed in his duty to her, failed, through the indulgence of selfish grief, to watch over her and interest himself in her activities as he should have done. Suppose she were taken from him as Stella Rivers, her contemporary, had been taken?

'In a right-angled triangle,' he said mechanically, 'the square on the hypoteneuse is equal to the sum of the squares on the other two sides.'

Grace hadn't failed. He watched her covertly while John drew his diagram. She was sitting in a dark corner of the room, a table lamp throwing a small pool of light on to the letter she was writing. Suddenly it occurred to him that she must thousands of times have sat in just that attitude, at a lamplit desk in a long quiet hospital ward, writing the night's report and, while all the time aware that she was surrounded by people who depended on her, yet at the same time detached from them and contained. She wrote—indeed she did everything—with a beautiful economy of movement, an

90

absence of fuss or flutter. Her training had taught her this efficiency, this almost awe-inspiring reliability, but instead of spoiling her delicate feminine quality, had somehow enhanced it. They had had wisdom and prevision, he thought, those parents-in-law of his, when they named her Grace.

And now his gaze encompassed both his daughter and his sister-in-law, the child moving up to her aunt and standing beside her within the same circle of light. They were very alike, he saw, with the same strong gentle face and the same light gauzy hair. They were both like Jean. The image of Gemma Lawrence coarsened beside them, became harsh-coloured, red and white and strained. Then it dwindled away, leaving a vacant space for his daughter and her aunt to fill with the wholesome beauty he understood.

Grace, he realised, was just the type of woman he most admired. There was the delicate prettiness he loved combined with the competence he needed. Couldn't she, he asked himself, be Jean all over again? Why not? Couldn't she be his Rosalind Swan, as loving, as devoted, as all-in-all to him, without the other woman's silly affectations? Usually, when they parted for the night, Grace simply got up out of her chair, picked up her book and said, 'Well, good night, Mike. Sleep well,' and he said, 'Good night, Grace. I'll see that everything's locked up.' That was all. They never even touched hands, never stood close beside each other or let their eyes meet.

But tonight, when the time came for them to separate, why shouldn't he take her hand and, saying something of what her goodness had meant to him, take her gently in his arms and kiss her? He glanced at her again and this time both Grace and Pat turned to him and smiled. His heart seemed to swell with an easy warm happiness, very different from the storm of feelings Gemma Lawrence aroused in him. That had been a kind of madness, nothing more than lust brought about by frustration. How unimportant it seemed now!

Pat loved her aunt. If he married Grace she would return to him entirely. He put out his hand to his daughter and she, her earlier annoyance with him forgotten, skipped over to the sofa where he was sitting and snuggled close against him, her arms hard around his neck.

91

'Shall I show you my scrapbook?'

'What have you got in it?' said John, his eyes on the proof of his theorem. 'Pictures of caterpillars?'

'Caterpillars are my summer hobby.' Pat spoke with great dignity. 'You're so ignorant you wouldn't know, but in the winter they go into their chrysalises.'

'And even you couldn't collect pictures of chrysalises. Here, let's see.'

'You shan't! You're not to! It's mine!'

'Leave her alone, John. Put that book down.'

John said in disgust, 'It's only dancers, old ballet dancers.'

'Come and show me, love.'

Pat resumed her semi-suffocation of her father. 'Can I have ballet lessons, Daddy? I do want to. It's the great ambition of my life.'

'I don't see why not.'

Grace was smiling at him, her letter completed. They smiled at each other like fond parents, happy in conspiracy, in contemplation of what they would do for their children.

'You see,' said Pat, 'it'll be too late if I don't start now. I know I should have to work and work, but I don't mind that because it's my great ambition, and perhaps I could get a scholarship and be in the Bolshoi and be a *prima ballerina assoluta* like Leonie West.'

'I thought,' said her brother, 'you were going to be a research scientist.'

'Oh, *that*. That was ages ago, when I was a child.'

A cold shadow had touched Burden. 'Who did you say?'

'Leonie West. She's gone to live in *absolute retirement* in her flat and her house at the seaside. She broke her leg ski-ing and couldn't dance any more, but she was the most wonderful dancer *in the world*.' Pat considered. 'Anyway, I think so,' she said. 'I've got masses and masses of pictures of her. Shall I show you?'

'Yes, darling, if you like.'

There were indeed masses and masses of pictures. Pat had cut them out of magazines and newspapers. Not all of them were of Leonie West, but most were.

In the distant shots she was a beautiful woman, but time

and perhaps too the exigencies of continual strenuous dancing showed the toll they had taken in close-ups. For Burden that heavily painted heart-shaped face with its smoothly parted black hair held no magic, but he made appreciative comments to please his daughter as he turned the pages.

There were stills of ballet films, shots of the star at home, at social functions, dancing all the great classical roles. He was nearly at the end now.

He said, 'They're very nicely arranged, dear,' to Pat, and turned to the last photograph.

A fan of Leonie West would have seen only her, a magnificent figure in a floor-length cloak stiff with gold enbroidery. Burden hardly noticed her. He was looking, his heart knocking dully, at the crowd of friends from which she had emerged. Just behind the dancer, holding a man's arm and smiling listlessly with a kind of shy anxiety, was a red-haired woman swathed in a black-and-gold shawl.

He didn't need the caption to tell him anything, but he read it. 'Pictured at the first night of *La Fille Mal Gardée* at Covent Garden is Miss Leonie West with (right) actor Matthew Lawrence and his wife Gemma, 23.' He said nothing, but closed the book quickly and leaned back, shutting his eyes, as if he had felt a sudden pain.

No one took any notice of him. John was repeating the proof of his theorem, learning it by heart. Pat had taken her book away to restore it to some secret treasure chest. It was nine o'clock.

Grace said, 'Come along, my dears. Bed.'

The usual argument ensued. Burden put in the stern words which were expected of him, but he felt no enthusiasm, no real care whether his children got the required amount of sleep or not. He picked up the evening paper which he hadn't yet read. The words were just a black-and-white pattern, hieroglyphics as meaningless as they would be to someone who has never learned to read.

Grace came back from kissing Pat good night. She had combed her hair and put on fresh lipstick. He noticed and he felt a shrinking distaste. This was the same woman that, half an hour before, he had considered wooing with a view to making her his second wife. He must have been mad. Suddenly he saw clearly that all his imaginings of the evening had been madness, a fantasy of his own conjuring, and what they had made to appear as madness was his reality.

He could never marry Grace, for in gazing at her, studying and admiring her, he had forgotten what any happy marriage must have, what Rosalind Swan so evidently had. He liked Grace, was at ease with her. She was his ideal of what a woman should be, but he hadn't a particle of desire for her. The thought of attempting to kiss her, of going further than a kiss, caused a shrivelling in his flesh.

She had brought her chair closer to the sofa where he sat and, laying aside her book, looked expectantly at him, waiting for the conversation, the adult exchange of views, which all day long she was denied. His feeling for her was so slight, his acceptance of her as someone content with the world he had provided for her so great, that it hardly occurred to him she would be hurt by anything he did.

'I'm going out,' he said.

'What, *now*?'

'I've got to go out, Grace.'

He saw it now. Am I so boring? her eyes said. I have done everything for you, kept your house, cared for your children, borne with your moods. Am I so boring that you can't sit quietly with me for one single evening?

'Please yourself,' she said aloud.

11

THE rain had stopped and a thick mist settled on the countryside. Water clung to the trees in heavy drops and fell dully and regularly so that it seemed as if it were still raining. Burden swung the car into Fontaine Road and immediately made a U-turn out again. He was suddenly loth to let his car be seen outside her house at night. All the street would be on watch, ready to spread rumours and tell tales.

Finally he parked at the bottom of Chiltern Avenue. A footpath, skirting the swings field, joined this cul-de-sac with its neighbour, Fontaine Road. Burden left the car under a street lamp whose light the fog had dimmed to a faintly glowing nimbus and walked slowly towards the path. Tonight its entrance looked like the opening to a black tunnel. There were no lights on in the adjacent houses, no sound in the darkness but that of water dripping.

He walked along between bushes whose branches with their wet dying leaves splashed his face and dragged softly at his clothes. Half-way through he found the torch he always carried and switched it on. Then, just as he reached the point where a gate in Mrs Mitchell's fence opened into the path, he heard pounding feet behind him. He swung round, directing his torch beam back the way he had come and on to a white face framed in flying wet hair.

'What is it? What's the matter?'

The girl must have recognised him, for she almost threw herself into his arms. He recognised her too. It was Mrs Crantock's daughter, a child of about fourteen.

'Did something frighten you?' he asked.

'A man,' she said breathlessly. 'Standing by a car. He spoke to me. I got in a panic.'

'You shouldn't be out alone at night.' He shepherded her

95

into Fontaine Road, then thought better of it. 'Come with me,' he said. She hesitated. 'You're all right with me.'

Back through the black tunnel. Her teeth were chattering. He raised his torch and brought it like a searchlight on to the figure of a man who stood beside the bonnet of Burden's parked car. The duffel coat he wore with its raised hood gave him enough of a sinister air to alarm any child.

'Oh, it's Mr Rushworth.' She sounded shamefaced.

Burden had already recognised the man and saw he was recognised too. Frowning a little, he walked towards the husband of the woman who had failed to notify the police after Mrs Mitchell's warning.

'You gave this young lady a bit of a scare.'

Rushworth blinked in the glare of the torch. 'I said hallo to her and something about it being an awful night. She scooted off like all the devils in hell were after her. God knows why. She knows me by sight, at any rate.'

'Everyone round here is a bit nervous at present, sir,' said Burden. 'It's wiser not to speak to people you don't really know. Good night.'

'I suppose he was taking his dog out,' the girl said as they came into Fontaine Road. 'I didn't see his dog, though. Did you?'

Burden hadn't seen a dog. 'You shouldn't be out alone at this time of night.'

'I've been round to my friends. We were playing records. My friend's father said he'd see me home, but I wouldn't let him. It's only a couple of minutes' walk. Nothing could happen to me.'

'But something did, or you thought it did.'

She digested this in silence. Then she said, 'Are you going to see Mrs Lawrence?'

Burden nodded, and, realising she couldn't see his nod, said a bald, 'Yes.'

'She's in an awful state. My father says he wouldn't be surprised if she did something silly.'

'What does that mean?'

'Well, *you* know. Committed suicide. I saw her after school in the supermarket. She was just standing in the middle of the shop, crying.' A true daughter of the *bourgeoisie*, she

96

added with some disapproval, 'Everyone was looking at her.'

Burden opened the gate to the Crantocks' garden. 'Good night,' he said. 'Don't go out alone after dark any more.'

There were no lights in Gemma's house and for once the front door was shut. Very likely she had taken one of Lomax's sleeping tablets and gone to bed. He peered through the stained glass and made out a faint gleam of light coming from the kitchen. She was still up, then. He rang the bell.

When the gleam grew no brighter and still she didn't come, he rang the bell again and banged the lion's-head door knocker. Behind him, from the branches of the untended trees, came the incessant drip drip of water. He remembered what Martin had said about her drinking and then what the Crantock girl had said and, having rung the bell once more in vain, he made for the side entrance.

The path was nearly as overgrown as the gardens of Saltram House. He pushed away wet holly and slimy creeper, soaking his hair and his raincoat. His hands were so wet that he could hardly turn the handle on the back door, but the door wasn't locked and at last he got it open.

She was slumped at the kitchen table, her head on her outflung arms, and in front of her was an unopened bottle, labelled: 'Chianti-type wine, produce of Spain. This week's offer, 7p off.' He went up to her slowly and laid his hand on her shoulder.

'Gemma . . .'

She said nothing. She didn't move. He pulled up another chair, pulled it close to her, and took her gently in his arms. She rested against him, not resisting, breathing shallowly and fast, and Burden forgot all his agony of the past week, his battling against temptation, in an overwhelming selfish happiness. He could hold her like this for ever, he thought, warmly and wordlessly, without passion or desire or the need for any change.

She lifted her head. Her face was almost unrecognisable, it was so swollen with crying. 'You didn't come,' she said. 'For days and days I waited for you and you didn't come.' Her voice was thick and strange. 'Why didn't you?'

'I don't know.' It was true. He didn't know, for now his resistance seemed the height of pointless folly.

'Your hair's all wet.' She touched his hair and the rain-drops on his face. 'I'm not drunk,' she said, 'but I have been. That stuff is very nasty but it deadens you for a bit. I went out this afternoon to buy some food—I haven't eaten for days—but I didn't buy any, I couldn't. When I came to the sweet counter I kept thinking of how John used to beg me to buy chocolate and I wouldn't because it was bad for his teeth. And I wished I'd let him have it, all he wanted, because it wouldn't have made any difference now, would it?'

She stared at him blankly, the tears pouring down her face.

'You mustn't say that.'

'Why not? He's dead. You know he's dead. I keep thinking that sometimes I got cross with him and I smacked him and I wouldn't let him have the sweets he wanted . . . Oh, Mike! What shall I do? Shall I drink that wine and take all Dr Lomax's tablets? Or shall I go out in the rain and just walk and walk till I die? What's the use of living? I've got no one, no one.'

'You've got me,' said Burden.

For answer she clung to him again, but this time more tightly. 'Don't leave me. Promise you won't leave me.'

'You ought to go to bed,' he said. There was, he thought, a sickening irony here. Wasn't that what he had intended when he left the car in the next street? That he and she should go to bed? He had really imagined that this demented grief-stricken woman would welcome his love-making. You fool, he whispered harshly to himself. But he managed to say calmly, 'Go to bed. I'll make you a hot drink and you can take a tablet and I'll sit with you till you go to sleep.'

She nodded. He wiped her eyes on a handkerchief Grace had ironed as carefully as Rosalind Swan ironed her husband's shirts. 'Don't leave me,' she said again, and then she went, dragging her feet a little.

The kitchen was in a hideous mess. Nothing had been washed up or put away for days and there was a stale sweetish smell. He found some cocoa and some dried milk and did his best with these unsatisfactory ingredients, mixing them and heating them on a cooker that was black with burned-on fat.

She was sitting up in bed, the black-and-gold shawl around her shoulders, and that magic exotic quality, compounded of colour and strangeness and lack of inhibition, had to some extent returned to her. Her face was calm again, the large still eyes staring. The room was untidy, chaotic even, but its chaos was powerfully feminine, the scattered clothes giving off mingled sweet scents.

He tipped a sleeping pill out of the bottle and handed it to her with her drink. She gave him a wan smile and took his hand, lifting it first to her lips and then holding it tight.

'You won't ever stay away from me like that again?'

'I am a poor substitute, Gemma,' he said.

'I need,' she said softly, 'another kind of loving to make me forget.'

He guessed at what she meant but didn't know what reply to make, so he sat silently with her, holding her hand, until at last her hand grew limp and she sank back against the pillows. He switched off the bed lamp and stretched himself beside her but on top of the covers. Presently her steady regular breathing told him that she was asleep.

The luminous dial of his watch showed half past ten. It seemed much later, as if a lifetime had passed since he left Grace and drove out here through the damp, rain-filled mist. The room was cold, perfumed and thick-aired and cold. Her hand lay loosely in his. He slid his hand away and edged across the bed to get up and leave.

Wary, even in sleep, she murmured, 'Don't leave me, Mike.' Thick with sleep, her voice held a note of terror, of dread that she might again be abandoned.

'I won't leave you.' He made up his mind quickly and decisively. 'I'll stay all night.'

Shivering, he stripped off his clothes and got into bed beside her. It seemed quite natural to lie as he had lain beside Jean, his body curled about hers, his left arm around her waist, clasping the hand which again had grown possessive and demanding. Although cold to him, his body must have felt warm to her, for she sighed with a kind of happiness and relaxed against him.

He thought he would never sleep or, if he did, that he would fall immediately into one of those dreams of his. But the way they were lying, side by side, was what he had been used to in his happy years and had missed bitterly in the last wretched one. It brought him desire, but at the same time it lulled him. While wondering how he could bear this continuing continence, he fell asleep.

It was just beginning to get light when he awoke to find the other half of the bed empty but still warm. She was sitting by the window, wrapped in her shawl, a big album with gilt clasps open on her lap. He guessed that she was looking, in the first light of dawn, at pictures of her son, and he felt a powerful black jealousy.

For what seemed a long time he watched her, almost hating the child who came between them and drew his mother away with a ghostly subtle hand. She was slowly turning the pages, pausing sometimes to stare downwards with a passionate intensity. A resentment which he knew was totally unjust made him will her to look at him, to forget the child and remember the man who longed to be her lover.

At last she lifted her head and their eyes met. She said nothing and Burden didn't speak, for he knew that if he did it would be to say cruel indefensible things. They gazed at each other in the pale grey morning light, and then, getting up silently, she drew the curtains. They were of brocade, old and frayed but still retaining their rich plum colour and, filtering through them, the light in the room looked purplish. She dropped the shawl and stood still in this coloured shadow-light so that he might look at her.

Her red hair seemed to have grown purple, but the colour hardly touched her body, which was dazzling white. He gazed at her in a kind of wonder, content for the moment to do nothing but gaze. This ivory woman, still and smiling now, was nothing like his lascivious dream woman, nor did she resemble the distraught and weary creature he had comforted to sleep. The child had almost vanished from his jealousy and, he believed, from her thoughts. It was hardly possible to imagine that this exquisite firm body had ever borne a child.

Only a little stabbing doubt remained.

'Not out of gratitude, Gemma,' he said. 'Not to reward me.'

She moved then and came close to him. 'I never even thought of that. That would be to cheat.'

100

'To forget, then? Is that what you want?'

'Isn't all love about forgetting?' she said. 'Isn't it always a lovely escape from—from hatefulness?'

'I don't know.' He put out his arms to her. 'I don't care.' Gasping at the feel of her, here the slenderness and there the swell of flesh, he said breathlessly, 'I shall hurt you. I can't help it, it's been so long for me.'

'And for me,' she said. 'It will be like the first time. Oh, Mike, kiss me, make me happy. Make me happy for a little while. . . .'

12

'NOT bad news?' said Dr Crocker. 'About the Lawrence boy, I mean?'

Morosely eyeing the pile of papers on his desk, Wexford said, 'I don't know what you're on about.'

'You haven't got a lead, then? I was sure there must be something when I passed Mike driving out of Chiltern Avenue at seven-thirty this morning.' He breathed heavily on one of Wexford's window-panes and began drawing one of his recurrent diagrams. 'I wonder what he was doing?' he said thoughtfully.

'Why ask me? I'm not his keeper.' Wexford glared at the doctor and at his drawing of a human pancreas. 'I might ask you what you were doing, come to that.'

'A patient. Doctors always have an excuse.'

'So do policemen,' Wexford retorted.

'I doubt if Mike was ministering to a fellow who'd been struck down with stroke. Worst case I've come across since they called me out to that poor old boy who collapsed on Stowerton station platform back in February. Did I ever tell you about that? Chap had been staying here on holiday, got to the station and then found he'd left one of his cases behind in this hotel or whatever it was. Went back for it, got in a bit of a flutter and the next thing . . .'

Wexford let out an angry bellow. 'So what? Why tell me? I thought you were supposed to treat your patients in confidence. I'll have a stroke myself if you go on like that.'

'It was just that possibility,' said Crocker sweetly, 'that inspired my little narrative.' He dotted in the Islets of Langerhans with his little finger. 'Want a fresh prescription for those tablets of yours?'

'No, I don't. I've got hundreds of the damned things left.'

'Well, you shouldn't have,' said Crocker, pointing a damp finger at him. 'You can't have been taking them regularly.'

'Go away. Get lost. Haven't you anything better to do than deface my windows with your nasty anatomical studies?'

'Just going.' The doctor made a dancing exit, pausing in the doorway to favour the chief inspector with what seemed to Wexford a meaningless wink.

'Silly fool,' Wexford remarked to the empty room. But Crocker's visit had left him with an uneasy feeling. To rid himself of it, he began to read the reports the Metropolitan Police had sent him on Gemma Lawrence's friends.

For the most part they appeared to be in the theatrical profession or on its fringes, but hardly a name was familiar to him. His younger daughter had just left drama school and through her Wexford had heard of many actors and actresses whose names had never been in lights or the print of the *Radio Times*. None of them appeared in this list and he was aware of what they did only because 'actor' or 'assistant stage manager' or 'model' was written after almost every name.

They were an itinerant crowd, mostly—in Wexford's own official terminology—of no fixed abode. Half a dozen had been convicted on charges of possessing drugs or of allowing cannabis to be smoked on their premises; a further two or three fined for conduct likely to lead to a breach of the peace. Demonstrating or taking their clothes off in the Albert Hall, Wexford supposed. None were harbouring John Lawrence; none showed by their past histories or their present tendencies a propensity to violence or perverted inclination. From reading between the lines, he gathered that, rather than desire the company of a child, they would go to almost any lengths to avoid having one.

Only two names on the list meant anything to him. One was a ballet dancer, her name at one time a household word, the other a television character actor whose face appeared so monotonously on Wexford's screen that he was sick of the sight of him. He was called Gregory Devaux and he had been a friend of Gemma Lawrence's parents. Particular interest had been taken in him because once, five years ago, he had attempted to smuggle out of the country, and the care of his estranged wife, their six-year-old son. The report promised that a watch would be kept on Gregory Devaux.

According to the porter of the Kensington block where she had a flat, Leonie West, the dancer, had been in the South of France since August.

Nothing there. No hint of any of them taking more than a casual friendly interest in Mrs Lawrence and her son; no hint of a connection between any of them and Ivor Swan.

At ten Martin came in with Policewoman Polly Davies whom Wexford scarcely recognised under the red wig she wore.

'You look terrible,' he said. 'Where in God's name did you dig that up? A jumble sale?'

'Woolworth's, sir,' said Martin, rather offended. 'You're always telling us to go easy on expenses.'

'No doubt it would look better if Polly hadn't got black eyes and such a—well, Welsh complexion. Never mind. You'll have to cover it, anyway. It's pouring with rain.'

Sergeant Martin always took an old-womanish interest in the weather and its vagaries. Having first wiped off the doctor's pancreas diagram, he opened the window and stuck out one hand. 'I think it'll stop, sir. I see a gleam of light.'

'I only wish you did,' said Wexford. 'Pray cover your dismay as best you can. I've decided to come with you. I get sick of all this vicarious living.'

They went down the corridor in single file, to be stopped by Burden who opened the door of his own office. Wexford looked him up and down, looked him all over, hard.

'What's got into you? Your Ernie bonds come up?'

Burden smiled.

'I am glad,' said Wexford sarcastically, 'that someone sees fit to spread a little sunshine in this deluge, in this—er—town of terror. What d'you want, anyway?'

'I thought you might not have seen today's paper. There's an interesting story on the front page.'

Wexford took the paper from him and read the story as he went down in the lift. Under the headline. *Landowner Offers £2,000 reward. New Move in Stella Hunt*, he read: 'Group Captain Percival Swan, wealthy landowner and uncle of Mr Ivor Swan, Stella Rivers' stepfather, told me last night that he was offering a reward of £2,000 for information leading to the discovery of Stella's killer. "This is a devilish thing," he said as we chatted in the drawing room of his centuries-old mansion near Tunbridge Wells. "I was fond of Stella, though I had seen little of her. Two thousand pounds is a large sum, but not too large to sacrifice for the sake of seeing justice done." '

There was a good deal more in the same vein. Not so very interesting, Wexford thought, as he got into his car.

True to Sergeant Martin's prediction, the rain soon left off. Cheriton Forest was shrouded in thick white mist.

'You may as well take that thing off,' said Wexford to Polly Davies. 'He won't be able to see you if he does come.'

But nobody came. No car passed along the road and no one came down the Myfleet Ride which joined it. Only the mist moved sluggishly and the water which dripped from the boughs of the closely planted fir trees. Wexford sat on a damp log among the trees, thinking of Ivor Swan who rode in this forest and knew it well, who had ridden here on the day his stepdaughter died. Did he really suppose Swan would appear, walking on the wet sandy ride or mounted on the chestnut horse? With the child perched beside him or holding his hand? A hoax, a hoax, a cruel nonsense, he kept saying to himself, and at one, when the appointed time was an hour behind him and he was shivering with cold, he came out of his hiding place and whistled up the other two.

If Burden remained in his early mood he would, at any rate, have a cheerful lunch companion. There was no one behind the desk in the police-station foyer, an unheard-of dereliction of duty. With mounting rage Wexford stared at the empty stool on which Sergeant Camb should have been perched and was about to press a bell that had never, in all its years of existence, needed to be pressed before, when the Sergeant appeared, scuttling from the lift, the inevitable tea-cup in his hand.

'Sorry, sir. We're so short-handed what with all these crazy calls coming in that I had to fetch my own tea. I've only been away half a tick. You know me, sir, I perish without my tea.'

'Next time,' said Wexford, 'you perish. Remember, Sergeant, that the guard dies but it never surrenders.'

He went upstairs and looked for Burden.

'Mr Burden went to lunch ten minutes ago, sir,' said Loring.

Wexford cursed. He badly wanted to engage with Burden in one of those acrimonious but rewarding conferences which both cemented their friendship and contributed to their work. Lunch alone at the Carousel would be a dismal affair. He opened the door of his own office and stopped dead on the threshold.

Seated in the chief inspector's swivel chair at the chief inspector's rosewood desk, the cigarette in his fingers scattering ash all over the lemon-coloured carpet, was Monkey Matthews.

'They might have told me,' said Wexford distantly, 'that I'd been deposed. This kind of thing smacks of goings-on behind the Iron Curtain. What am I to do? Manage a power station?'

Monkey grinned. He had the grace to get up out of Wexford's chair. 'I'd never have believed,' he said, 'it was so easy to get into a nick. I reckon that old geezer Camb must have dropped dead at last and they've all gone off to bury him. Got in without a soul the wiser, I did. Bloody sight easier,' he added, 'to get in this nick than get out of it.'

'You won't find it hard today. You can get out now. And fast, before I do you for being found on enclosed premises for an unlawful purpose.'

'Ah, but my purpose *is* lawful.' Monkey surveyed the room with a pleased expression. 'This is the first time I've ever been in a nick of what you might call my own accord.' A dreamy smile spread across his face and was abruptly quenched by a fit of coughing.

Wexford stood half in the office, half in the corridor, waiting unsympathetically.

'You may as well shut the door,' said Monkey when he had recovered. 'We don't want the whole place to hear, do we? I've got some info. The Lawrence case.'

Wexford closed the door but gave no other sign that

Monkey's remark had interested him. '*You* have?' he said.

'Friend of mine has.'

'I didn't know you had any friends, Monkey, bar poor old Ruby.'

'You don't want to judge everybody by yourself,' said Monkey, stung. He coughed and stubbed out his cigarette, immediately lighting another and regarding the discarded stub with resentment, as if some peculiarity of its construction or fault in its make-up were responsible for his choking attack, rather than the tobacco it contained. 'I've got a lot of friends, picked up in me travels.'

'Picked up in cells, you mean,' said Wexford.

Monkey had long ago forgotten how to blush, but the wary look which crossed his face told Wexford the shot had gone home. 'My friend,' he said, 'come down here yesterday for a bit of a holiday with me and Rube. A bit of a rest, like. He's an old feller and his health's not what it was.'

'All those damp exercise yards, I daresay.'

'Oh, give over, will you? My friend has got some info as'll open your eyes all right, re the antecedents of Mr Ivor Bloody Swan.'

If Wexford was surprised, he didn't show it. 'He has no antecedents,' he said coldly, 'or not what you mean by the term.'

'Not wrote down, I daresay. Not all our misdemeanours is recorded, Mr Wexford, not by a long chalk. I've heard it said there's more murderers walking the streets free as ever got topped on account of them as they murdered being thought to have died natural.'

Wexford rubbed his chin and looked thoughtfully at Monkey. 'Let's see your friend,' he said, 'and hear what he's got to say. It might be worth a few bob.'

'He would want paying.'

'I'm sure he would.'

'He made a point of that,' said Monkey conversationally.

Wexford got up and opened a window to let some of the smoke out. 'I'm a busy man, Monkey. I can't hang about fencing with you all day. How much?'

'A monkey,' said Monkey succinctly.

In a pleasant but distant voice, tinged with incredulous

outrage, Wexford said, 'You must be off your nut if you seriously think the government is going to pay five hundred pounds to a clapped-out old lag for information it can get for nothing out of a file.'

'Five hundred,' Monkey repeated, 'and if it all works out nice, the two thou reward the uncle's putting up.' He coughed thickly but with no sign of distress. 'If you don't want nothing to do with it,' he said sweetly, 'my friend can always go to the chief constable. He's called Griswold, isn't he?'

'Don't you bloody threaten me!' said Wexford.

'Threaten? Who's threatening? This info's in the public interest, that's what it is.'

Wexford said firmly, 'You can bring your friend along here and then we'll see. Might be worth a couple of nicker.'

'He won't come here. He wouldn't go voluntary like into a fuzz box. Different to me, he is. But him and me, we'll be in the Pony six sharp tonight and I daresay he'd accept a friendly overture in the form of liquor.'

Was it possible that there was something in this story? Wexford wondered after Monkey had gone. And immediately he recalled Rivers' hints as to the death of Swan's aunt. Suppose, after all, that Swan *had* hastened the old lady's departure? Poison, maybe. That would be in Swan's line, a lazy, slow way of killing. And suppose this friend of Monkey's had been in service in the house, an odd-job man or even a butler? He might have seen something, extracted something, kept it hidden for years in his bosom . . .

Wexford came down to earth and, laughing, quoted to himself a favourite passage from Jane Austen: 'Consult your own understanding, your own sense of the probable, your own observation of what is passing around you. Does our education prepare us for such atrocities? Do our laws connive at them? Could they be perpetrated without being known in a country like this where social and literary intercourse is on such a footing; where every man is surrounded by a neighbourhood of voluntary spies and where roads and newspapers lay everything open?'

Long ago he had learned these lines by heart. They had been of constant service to him and, when inclined to sail away on flights of fancy, kept his feet firmly on the ground.

It was much too late now to go out for lunch. The staff of the Carousel looked askance at you if you arrived for your midday meal after one-thirty. Wexford sent to the canteen for sandwiches and had eaten the first half-round when the report on the lock of hair came in from the lab. The hair, Wexford read, was a child's but not John Lawrence's. Comparison had been made with the strands taken from John's hairbrush. Understanding only about twenty-five per cent of the technical jargon, Wexford did his best to follow just how they could be so certain the hairs in the brush differed from the hairs in the cut lock, and finally had to be content to know that they did differ.

His phone rang. It was Loring from the room where all the calls connected with the Lawrence and Rivers cases were received and checked.

'I think you'll want to take this one, sir.'

Immediately Wexford thought of Monkey Matthews and just as quickly dismissed the thought. Monkey had never been known to use a telephone.

'Record it, Loring,' he said, and then, 'Is it from a call box?'

'I'm afraid not, sir. We can't trace it.'

'Put him on,' said Wexford.

As soon as he heard the voice he knew an attempt was being made to disguise it. A couple of pebbles in the man's mouth, he decided. But some quality, the pitch perhaps, couldn't be disguised. Wexford recognised the voice. Not its owner, nor could he recall where he had seen the speaker, what he had said or anything about him. But he was sure he recognised the voice.

'I'm not prepared to give my name,' it said. 'I've written to you twice.'

'Your letters were received.' Wexford had stood up to take the call and from where he stood he could see the High Street and see a woman tenderly lifting a baby from a pram to take it with her into a shop. His anger was immense and he could feel the dangerous blood pounding in his head.

'You played around with me this morning. That's not going to happen tomorrow.'

'Tomorrow?' Wexford said evenly.

'I shall be in the grounds of Saltram House tomorrow by the fountains. I'll be there at six p.m. with John. And I want the mother to come for him. *Alone.*'

'Where are you speaking from?'

'My farm,' said the voice, growing squeaky. 'I've got a three-hundred-acre farm not so far from here. It's a fur farm, mink, rabbits, chinchillas, the lot. John doesn't know I keep them for their fur. That would only upset him, wouldn't it?'

Wexford caught the authentic note of derangement. He didn't know whether this comforted or distressed him. He was thinking about the voice which he had heard before, a thin high voice, its possessor quick to take offence, looking for insult where none existed.

'You haven't got John,' he said. 'That hair you sent me wasn't John's.' Scorn and rage made him forget caution. 'You are an ignorant man. Hair can be as precisely identified as blood these days.'

Heavy breathing at the other end of the line succeeded this statement. Wexford felt that he had scored. He drew breath to let loose vituperation, but before he could speak the voice said coldly:

'D'you think I don't know that? I cut that hair from Stella Rivers.'

13

THE Piebald Pony is not the kind of pub connoisseurs of rural England normally associate with her countryside. Indeed, if you approach it from the direction of Sparta Grove, and if you keep your eyes down so that you cannot see the green surrounding hills, you would not suppose yourself in the country at all. Sparta Grove and Charteris Road which it joins at a right angle—on this corner stands the Piebald Pony —resemble the back streets of an industrial city. A few of the houses have narrow front gardens, but most doors open directly on to the pavement, as do the entrances to the Pony's public and saloon bars.

One of these rooms fronts Sparta Grove, the other Charteris Road. They are the same shape and size and the saloon bar is distinguished from the public only in that drinks cost more in the former, about a third of its stone floor is covered with a square of brown Axminster and its seating includes a couple of settees, upholstered in battered black, of the kind that used to be seen in railway waiting rooms.

On one of the settees, under a poster recommending the Costa del Sol and displaying a photograph of a girl in a wet-look bikini leering at a bull in its death throes, sat Monkey Matthews with an old man. He looked, Wexford thought, very much by time's fell hand defaced and in nearly as bad case as the bull. It wasn't that he was thin or pale—in fact his squarish toad's face was purple—but there was an air about him of one who has been physically ruined by years of bad feeding, damp dwellings and nasty indulgences whose nature Wexford preferred not to dwell on.

Each man had an almost empty half-pint glass of the cheapest obtainable bitter and Monkey was smoking a miniscule cigarette.

' 'Evening,' said Wexford.

Monkey didn't get up but indicated his companion with an airy wave. 'This is Mr Casaubon.'

Wexford gave a tiny sigh, the outward and audible sign of an inward and outraged scream. 'I don't believe it,' he said thinly. 'Just enlighten me as to which one of you two intellectuals is acquainted with George Eliot.'

Far from living up to Monkey's image of a man intimidated by the police, Mr Casaubon had brightened as soon as Wexford spoke and now rejoined in thick hideous cockney, 'I see him once. Strangeways it was, 1929. They done him for a big bullion job.'

'I fear,' Wexford said distantly, 'that we cannot be thinking of the same person. Now what are you gentlemen drinking?'

'Port and brandy,' said Mr Casaubon almost before the words were out, but Monkey, to whom what could be inhaled always took priority over what could merely be imbibed, pushed forward his empty bitter glass and remarked that he would appreciate twenty Dunhill International.

Wexford bought the drinks and tossed the crimson and gold package into Monkey's lap. 'I may as well open the proceedings,' he said, 'by telling you two jokers you can forget about five hundred pounds or anything like it. Is that clear?'

Mr Casaubon received this in the manner of one used to frequent disappointment. The liveliness which had briefly appeared in his watery eyes died away and, making a low humming sound that might have been a long-drawn murmur of assent or just an attempt at a tune, he reached for his port and brandy. Monkey said, 'When all's said and done, me and my friend would settle for the reward.'

'That's very handsome of you,' said Wexford sarcastically. 'I suppose you realise that money will be paid only for information leading directly to the arrest of the murderer of Stella Rivers?'

'We wasn't born yesterday,' said Monkey. This remark was so obviously true, particularly in the case of Mr Casaubon, who looked as if he had been born in 1890, that the old man broke off from his humming to emit a cackle of laughter, showing Wexford the most hideous, dilapidated and rotting set of teeth he had ever seen in a human mouth. 'We

112

can read what's in the papers as well as you,' Monkey went on. 'Now then, cards on the table. If my friend tells you what he knows and what he's got papers to *prove*, are you going to do fair by us and see we get what's our right when Swan's under lock and key?'

'I can get a witness, if that's what you want. Mr Burden perhaps?'

Monkey puffed smoke out through his nostrils. 'I can't stomach that sarcastic devil,' he said. 'No, your word's good enough for me. When folks run down the fuzz I always say, Mr Wexford's hounded me, God knows, but he . . .'

'Monkey,' Wexford interrupted, 'are you going to tell me or aren't you?'

'Not here,' said Monkey, shocked. 'What, give you a load of info that'll put a man away for life here in what you might call the market place?'

'I'll drive you back to the station, then.'

'Mr Casaubon wouldn't like that.' Monkey stared at the old man, perhaps willing him to show some sign of terror, but Mr Casaubon, his eyelids drooping, simply continued to hum monotonously. 'We'll go to Rube's place. She's out baby-sitting.'

Wexford shrugged his agreement. Pleased, Monkey gave Mr Casaubon a poke. 'Come on, mate, wakey-wakey.'

It took Mr Casaubon quite a long time to get on to his legs. Wexford walked impatiently to the door, but Monkey, not usually renowned for his considerate manners, hovered with some solicitude at his friend's side, and then, giving him an arm, helped him tenderly out into the street.

Burden had never phoned her before. His heart palpitated lightly and fast as he listened to the ringing tone and imagined her running to answer, her heart beating quickly too because she would guess who it was.

The steadiness of her voice took the edge off his excitement. He spoke her name softly, on a note of enquiry.

'Yes, speaking,' she said. 'Who is it?'

'Mike.' She hadn't recognised his voice and his disappointment was profound.

But immediately he had identified himself she gasped and

113

said quickly, 'You've got some news for me? Something's happened at last?'

He closed his eyes momentarily. She could only think of that child. Even his voice, her lover's voice, was to her just the voice of someone who might have found her child. 'No, Gemma, no, there's nothing.'

'It was the first time you ever phoned me, you see,' she said quietly.

'Last night was a first time too.'

She said nothing. Burden felt that he had never known so long a silence, aeons of silence, time for twenty cars to drone past the phone box, time for the lights to change to green and back again to red, time for a dozen people to enter the Olive and leave the door swinging, swinging, behind them until it lapsed into stillness. Then at last she said, 'Come to me now, Mike. I need you so.'

There was another woman he had to have speech with first.

'I'm just going out on a job, Grace,' said Burden, too strait-laced, too innocent perhaps, to see a *double entendre* which would have had Wexford in stitches. 'I may be hours.'

They were given to pregnant, throbbing silences, his women. Grace broke the one she had created with a sharp ward sister's snap. 'Don't lie to me, Mike. I just phoned the station and they said you had a free evening.'

'You had no business to do that,' Burden flared. 'Even Jean never did that and she had the right, she was my wife.'

'I'm sorry, but the children asked and I thought . . . As a matter of fact, there's something special I want to discuss with you.'

'Can't it wait till tomorrow?' Burden thought he knew these discussions of Grace's. They were always about the children, more precisely about the children's psychological problems or what Grace imagined those problems to be: Pat's supposedly butterfly mind and John's mental block over his mathematics. As if all children didn't have their difficulties which were a part of growing up and which he in his day, and surely Grace in hers, had faced satisfactorily without daily analysis. 'I'll try to be in tomorrow night,' he said weakly.

'That,' said Grace, 'is what you always say.'

His conscience troubled him for about five minutes. It had

114

long ceased to do so before he reached the outskirts of Stowerton. Burden had yet to learn that the anticipation of sexual pleasure is the most powerful of all the crushers of conscience. He wondered why he felt so little guilt, why Grace's reproach had only momentarily stung him. Her words—or what he could recall of them—had become like the meaningless and automatic admonition of some schoolteacher spoken years ago. Grace was no longer anything to him but an impediment, an irritating force which conspired with work and other useless time-wasters to keep him from Gemma.

Tonight she came to the door to meet him. He was prepared for her to speak of the child and her anxieties and her loneliness, and he was ready with the gentle words and the tenderness which would come so easily to him after an hour in bed with her but which now his excitement must make strained and abrupt. She said nothing. He kissed her experimentally, unable to guess her mood from those large blank eyes.

She took his hands and put them against her waist which was naked when she lifted the shirt she wore. Her skin was hot and dry, quivering against his own trembling hands. Then he knew that the need she had spoken of on the phone was not for words or reassurance or searching of the heart but the same need as his own.

If Mr Casaubon had been capable of inspiring the slightest sentimentality, Wexford reflected, it would have been impossible to witness Monkey's extravagant care of him without disgust. But the old man—his real name would have to be ferreted out from some file or other—was so obviously a villain and a parasite who took every advantage of his age and an infirmity that was probably assumed that Wexford could only chuckle sardonically to himself as he watched Monkey settle him into one of Ruby Branch's armchairs and place a cushion behind his head. No doubt it was obvious to the receiver of these attentions as it was to the chief inspector that Monkey was merely cosseting the goose that would lay a golden egg. Presumably Mr Casaubon had already come to some financial agreement with his partner or impresario and knew there was no question of affection or reverence for old age in all this fussing with cushions. Humming with contentment in the fashion of an aged purring cat, he allowed Monkey to pour him a treble whisky, but when the water jug appeared the hum rose a semitone and a gnarled purple hand was placed over the glass.

Monkey drew the curtains and placed a table lamp on the end of the mantelpiece so that its radiance fell like a spotlight on the bunchy rag-bag figure of Mr Casaubon, and Wexford was aware of the dramatic effect. It was almost as if Monkey's protégé was one of those character actors who delight to appear solo on the London stage and for two hours or more entertain an audience to a monologue or to readings from some great novelist or diarist. And Mr Casaubon's repetitive nodding and humming rather enhanced this impression. Wexford felt that at any moment the play would begin, a witticism would issue from those claret-coloured lips or the humming would give place to a speech from *Our Mutual Friend*. But because he knew that this was all fantasy, deliberately achieved by that crafty little con-man Monkey Matthews, he said sharply: 'Get on with it, can't you?'

Mr Casaubon broke the silence he had maintained since leaving the Piebald Pony. 'Monk can do the talking,' he said. 'He's got more the gift of the gab than me.'

Monkey smiled appreciatively at this flattery and lit a cigarette. 'Me and Mr Casaubon,' he began, 'made each other's acquaintance up north about twelve months back.' In Walton gaol, Wexford thought, but he didn't say it aloud. 'So when Mr Casaubon was glancing through his morning paper the other day and saw about Mr Ivor Swan and him living in Kingsmarkham and all that, his thoughts naturally flew to me.'

'Yes, yes, I get all that. In plain English he saw the chance to make a little packet and thought you could help him to it. God knows why he didn't come straight to us instead of getting involved with a shark like you. Your gift of the gab, I suppose.' A thought struck Wexford. 'Knowing you, I wonder you didn't try putting the black on Swan first.'

'If you're going to insult me,' said Monkey, snorting out smoke indignantly, 'we may as well have done, and me and

116

my friend'll go to Mr Griswold. I'm doing this as a favour to you, like to advance you in your profession.'

Mr Casaubon nodded sagely and made a noise like a bluebottle drowsing over a joint of beef. But Monkey was seriously put out. Temporarily forgetting the respect due to age and golden geese, he snapped in the tone usually reserved for Mrs Branch, 'Give over that buzzing, will you? You're getting senile. Now you can see,' he said to Wexford, 'why the silly old git needs me to prop him up.'

'Go on, Monkey. I won't interrupt again.'

'To get to the guts of the business,' said Monkey, 'Mr Casaubon told me—and showed me his paper to prove it—that fourteen years back your Ivor Bloody Swan—listening, are you? Ready for a shock?—your Ivor Swan killed a kid. Or, to put it more accurate, caused her death by drowning her in a lake. There, I thought that'd make you sit up.'

Rather than sitting up, Wexford had slumped into his chair. 'Sorry, Monkey,' he said, 'but that's not possible. Mr Swan hasn't a stain on his character.'

'Hasn't paid the penalty, you mean. I'm telling you, this is fact, it's gospel. Mr Casaubon's own niece, his sister's girl, was a witness. Swan drowned the kid and he was up in court, but the judge acquitted him for lack of evidence.'

'He can't have been more than nineteen or twenty,' Wexford said ruminatively. 'Look here, I'll have to know more than that. What's this paper you keep on about?'

'Give it here, mate,' said Monkey.

Mr Casaubon fumbled among his layers of clothing, finally bringing out from some deep recess beneath mackintosh, coat and matted wool a very dirty envelope inside which was a single sheet of paper. He held it lovingly for a moment and then handed it to his go-between who passed it on to Wexford.

The paper was a letter with neither address nor date.

'Before you read it,' said Monkey, 'you'd best know that this young lady as wrote it was chambermaid in this hotel in the Lake District. She had a very good position, lot of girls under her. I don't know exactly what she was but she was the head one.'

'You make her sound like the madame in a brothel,' said Wexford nastily, and cut short Monkey's expostulation with a quick, 'Shut up and let me read.'

The letter had been written by a semi-literate person. It was ill-spelt, almost totally lacking in punctuation. While Mr Casaubon hummed with the complacency of a man showing off to an acquaintance the prize-winning essay of some young relative, Wexford read the following.

'Dear Uncle Charly.

'We have had a fine old fuss up hear that you will want to know of there is a young Colledge feller staying in the Hotel and what do you think he as done he as drowned a little girl swimmin in the Lake in the morning befor her Mum and Dad was up and they have had him up in Court for it Lily that you have herd me speak of had to go to the Court and tell what she new and she tell me the Judge give it to him hot and strong but could not put him away on account of Nobody saw him do the deed the young fellers name is IVOR LIONEL FAIRFAX SWAN i got it down on paper when Lily said it gettin it from the Judge on account i new you would wish to know it in ful.

'Well Uncle that it all for now i will keep in touch as ever hoping the news may be of use and that your Leg is better Your Affect. Neice

'Elsie'

The pair of them were staring eagerly at him now. Wexford read the letter again—the lack of commas and stops made it difficult to follow—and then he said to Mr Casaubon, 'What made you keep this for fourteen years? You didn't know Swan, did you? Why keep this letter in particular?'

Mr Casaubon made no reply. He smiled vaguely as people do when addressed in a foreign language and then he held out his glass to Monkey, who promptly refilled it and, once more taking on the task of interpreter, said, 'He kept all her letters. Very devoted to Elsie is Mr Casaubon, being as he never had no kiddies of his own.'

'I see,' said Wexford, and suddenly he did. He felt his features mould themselves into a scowl of rage as the whole racket worked by Mr Casaubon and his niece grew clear to him. Without looking again at the letter he recalled certain significant phrases. 'A fine old fuss that you will want to know of' and 'hoping the news may be of use' sprang to mind. A chambermaid, he thought, a chiel among us taking notes . . . How many adulterous wives had Elsie spotted? Into how many bedrooms had she blundered by the merest chance? How many homosexual intrigues had she discovered when homosexual practice was still a crime? Not to mention the other secrets to which she would have had access, the papers and letters left in drawers, the whispered confidences between women, freely given at night after one gin too many. The information about Swan, Wexford was sure, was just one of many such pieces of news retailed to Uncle Charly in the knowledge that he would use them for the extortion of money of which Elsie, in due course, would claim her share. A clever racket, though one which, to look at him now, had not finally worked to Mr Casaubon's advantage.

'Where was this Elsie working at the time?' he snapped.

'He don't remember that,' said Monkey. 'Somewhere up in the Lakes. She had a lot of jobs one way and another.'

'Oh, no. It was all one way and a dirty way at that. Where is she now?'

'South Africa,' mumbled Mr Casaubon, showing his first sign of nervousness. 'Married a rich yid and went out to the Cape.'

'You can hang on to the letter.' Monkey smiled ingratiatingly. 'You'll want to do a bit of checking up. I mean, when all's said and done, we're only a couple of ignorant fellers, let's face it, and we wouldn't know how to go about getting hold of this judge and all that.' He edged his chair towards Wexford's. 'All we want is our rightful dues for setting you on the track. We don't ask for no more than the reward, we don't want no thanks nor nothing. . . .' His voice faltered and Wexford's baleful face finally silenced him. He drew in a deep lungful of smoke and appeared to decide that at last it was time to offer hospitality to his other guest. 'Have a drop of Scotch before you go?'

'I wouldn't dream of it,' Wexford said pleasantly. He eyed Mr Casaubon. 'When I drink I'm choosey about my company.'

14

NERVOUS bliss, Wexford decided, best described Inspec-
Burden's current state of mind. He was preoccupied,
often to be found idle and staring distantly into space, jumping out of his skin over nothing, but at least it was a change
from that bleak irritable misery everyone had come to
associate with him. Very likely the cause of the change was a
woman, and Wexford, encountering his friend and assistant
in the lift on the following morning, remembered Dr Crocker's
words.

'How's Miss Woodville these days?'

He was rewarded, and somewhat gratified, by the uneven
burning blush that spread across Burden's face. It confirmed
his suspicion that recently there had been something going
on between those two and something a good deal more exciting than discussions about whether young Pat ought to have a
new blazer for the autumn term.

'My wife,' he went on, pressing his point home, 'was only
saying yesterday what a tower of strength Miss Woodville has
been to you.' When this evoked no response, he added, 'All
the better when the tower of strength has an uncommonly
pretty face, eh?'

Burden looked through him so intensely that Wexford
suddenly felt quite transparent. The lift halted.

'I'll be in my office if you want me.'

Wexford shrugged. Two can play at that game, he thought.
You won't get any more friendly overtures from me, my lad.
Stiff-necked prude. What did he care about Burden's dreary
love life, anyway? He had other things on his mind and
because of them he hadn't slept much. Most of the night he
had lain awake thinking about that letter and Monkey
Matthews and the old villain who was Monkey's guest, and
he had pondered on what it all meant.

Elsie was as sharp as a needle but bone ignorant. To a woman like her any J.P. was a judge and she wouldn't know the difference between assizes and a magistrates' court. Was it possible that all those years ago the young Swan had appeared before a *magistrate,* charged with murder or manslaughter, and the case been dismissed? And if that was so had the facts of that hearing somehow escaped being included in Wexford's dossier of Swan?

Night is a time for conjecture, dreams, mad conclusions; morning a time for action. The hotel had been somewhere in the Lake District and as soon as he was inside his office Wexford put through calls to the Cumberland and Westmorland police. Next he did a little research into the antecedents of Mr Casaubon, working on the assumption that he had been in Walton at the same time as Monkey, and this conclusion and the investigations it led to proved fruitful.

His name was Charles Albert Catch and he had been born in Limehouse in 1897. Pleased to discover that all his guesswork had been correct, Wexford learned that Catch had served three terms of imprisonment for demanding money with menaces but since reaching the age of sixty-five had fallen on evil days. His last conviction was for throwing a brick through the window of a police station, a ploy to secure —as it had done—a bed and shelter for the blackmailer who had become an impoverished vagrant.

Wexford wasted no sympathy on Charly Catch but he did wonder why Elsie's information had led her uncle to take no steps against Swan at the time. Because there really was no evidence? Because Swan had been innocent with nothing to hide or be ashamed of? Time would show. There was no point in further conjecture, no point in taking any steps in the matter until something came in from the Lakes.

With Martin and Bryant to keep watch from a discreet distance, he sent Polly Davis, red-wigged, off to her assignation at Saltram House. It was raining again and Polly got soaked to the skin, but nobody brought John Lawrence to the park of Saltram House or to the Italian garden. Determined not to speculate any further on the subject of Swan, Wexford racked his brains instead about the caller with the shrill voice, but still he was unable to identify that voice or to

121

remember any more about it but that he had heard it somewhere before.

Holding her in his arms in the dark, Burden said, 'I want you to tell me that I've made you happier, that things aren't so bad because I love you.'

Perhaps she was giving one of her wan smiles. He could see nothing of her face but a pale glow. The room smelt of the scent which she used to use when she was married and had, at any rate, a little money. Her clothes were impregnated with it, a stale musty sweetness. He thought that tomorrow he would buy her a bottle of scent.

'Gemma, you know I can't stay the night. I only wish to God I could, but I promised and . . .'

'Of course you must go,' she said. 'If I were going to my —to my children, nothing would keep me. Dear kind Mike, I won't keep you from your *children*.'

'You'll sleep?'

'I shall take a couple of those things Dr Lomax gave me.'

A little chill touched his warm body. Wasn't satisfied love the best soporific? How happy it would have made him to know that his love-making alone could send her into sweet sleep, that thoughts of him would drive away every dread. Always the child, he thought, always the boy who had secured for himself all his mother's care and passion. And he imagined the miracle happening and the lost dead boy, restored to life and to home, running into the darkened bedroom now, bringing his own light with him, throwing himself into his mother's arms. He saw how she would forget her lover, forget that he had ever existed, in a little world made just for a woman and a child.

He got up and dressed. He kissed her in a way that was meant to be tender only but became passionate because he couldn't help himself. And he was rewarded with a kiss from her as long and desirous as his own. With that he had to be satisfied; with that and with the crumpled chiffon scarf he picked up as he left the room.

If only he would find his bungalow empty, he mused as he drove towards it. Just for tonight, he told himself guiltily. If only he could go into emptiness and solicitude, free of Grace's

122

gentle brisk demands and Pat's castles in the air and John's mathematics. But if he were going home to an empty house he wouldn't be going home at all.

Grace had said she wanted to discuss something with him. The prospect was so dreary and so tedious that he forebore speculating about it. Why endure an agony twice over? He held the scented chiffon against his face for comfort before entering the house but instead of comfort it brought him only longing.

His son was hunched over the table, ineptly grasping a compass. 'Old Mint Face,' he said when he saw his father, 'told us that "mathema" means knowledge and "pathema" means suffering, so I said they ought to call it pathematics.'

Grace laughed a little too shrilly. She was flushed, Burden noticed, as if with excitement or perhaps trepidation. He sat down at the table, neatly drew the diagram for John and sent him off to bed. 'May as well have an early night myself,' he said hopefully.

'Spare me just ten minutes, Mike. I want—there's something I want to say to you. I've had a letter from a friend of mine, a girl—a woman—I trained with.' Grace sounded extremely nervous now, so unlike herself that Burden felt a small disquiet. She was holding the letter and seemed about to show it to him, but she changed her mind and stood clutching it. 'She's come into some money and she wants to start a nursing home and she . . .' The words tumbled out in a rush, '. . . she wants me to come in with her.'

Burden was beginning on a bored, 'Oh, yes, that's nice,' when suddenly he did a double-take and what she was actually saying came home to him. The shock was too great for thought or politeness or caution. 'What about the children?' he said.

She didn't answer that directly. She sat down heavily like a tired old woman. 'How long did you think I would stay with them?'

'I don't know.' He made a helpless gesture with his hands. 'Till they're able to look after themselves, I suppose.'

'And when will that be?' She was hot now and angry, her nervousness swamped by indignation. 'When Pat's seventeen, eighteen? I'll be forty.'

'Forty's not old,' said her brother-in-law feebly.

'Maybe not for a woman with a profession, a career she's always worked at. If I stay here for another six years I won't have any career, I'd be lucky to get a job as a staff nurse in a country hospital.'

'But the children,' he said again.

'Send them to boarding school,' she said in a hard voice. 'Physically, they'll be just as well looked after there as here, and as for the other side of their lives—what good do I do them alone? Pat's coming to an age when she'll turn against her mother or any mother substitute. John's never cared much for me. If you don't like the idea of boarding school, get a transfer and go to Eastbourne. You could all live there with Mother.'

'You've sprung this on me, all right, haven't you, Grace?'

She was almost in tears. 'I only had Mary's letter yesterday. I wanted to talk to you yesterday, I begged you to come home.'

'My God,' he said, 'what a thing to happen. I thought you liked it here, I thought you loved the kids.'

'No, you didn't,' she said fiercely, and her face was suddenly Jean's, passionate and indignant, during one of their rare quarrels. 'You never thought about me at all. You—you asked me to come and help you and when I came you turned me into a sort of house-mother and you were the lofty superintendent who condescended to visit the poor orphans a couple of times a week.'

He wasn't going to answer that. He knew it was true. 'You must do as you please, of course,' he said.

'It isn't what I please, it's what you've driven me to. Oh, Mike, it could have been so different! Don't you see? If you'd been with us and pulled your weight and made me feel we were doing something worth while *together*. Even now if you . . . I'm trying to say . . . Mike, this is very hard for me. If I thought you might come in time to . . . Mike, won't you help me?'

She had turned to him and put out her hands, not impulsively and yearningly as Gemma did, but with a kind of modest diffidence, as if she were ashamed. He remembered what Wexford had said to him that morning in the lift and he recoiled away from her. That it was almost Jean's face look-ing at him, Jean's voice pleading with him, about to say things which to his old-fashioned mind no woman should ever say to a man, only made things worse.

'No, no, no!' he said, not shouting but whispering the words with a kind of hiss.

He had never seen a woman blush so fierily. Her face was crimson, and then the colour receded, leaving it chalk white. She got up and walked away, scuttling rather, for on a sudden she had lost all her precise controlled gracefulness. She left him and closed the door without another word.

That night he slept very badly. Three hundred nights had been insufficient to teach him how to sleep without a woman and, after them, two of bliss had brought back with savagery all the loneliness of a single bed. Like a green adolescent he held, pressed against his face so that he could smell it, the scarf of the woman he loved. He lay like that for hours, listening through the wall to the muffled crying of the woman he had rejected.

15

THE lock of hair did not belong to Stella Rivers either. Enough of her own blonde curls remained on what remained of her for them to make comparison. 'A bracelet of bright hair about the bone,' Wexford thought, shuddering.

That proved nothing, of course. It was only to be expected, it was known, that the fur man—Wexford thought of his correspondent and his caller as the 'fur man' now—was a liar. There was nothing for him to do but wait for news from the Lakes, and his temper grew sour. Burden had been unbearable for the last couple of days, hardly answering when you spoke to him and not to be found when most he was wanted. The rain fell unceasingly too. Everyone in the police station was irritable and the men, depressed by the weather, snapped at each other like wet, ill-tempered dogs. The black-and-white foyer floor was blotched all day by muddy footmarks and trickles from sodden raincapes.

Marching briskly past the desk to avoid an encounter with Harry Wild, Wexford almost crashed into a red-faced Sergeant Martin who was waiting for the lift.

'I don't know what the world's coming to, sir, I really don't. That young Peach, usually won't say boo to a goose, flares up at me because I tell him he should be wearing a stouter pair of boots. Mind your own business, he has the nerve to say to me. What's up, sir? What have I said?'

'You've solved something for me,' Wexford said, and then more soberly, because this was only the beginning of an investigation, not a solution: 'Sergeant, the night we were searching for John Lawrence you told a man in the search party to put on thicker shoes—you must have a thing about it—and he too told you to mind your own business. Remember?'

'I can't say I do, sir.'

'I spoke to him too,' Wexford said wonderingly. 'He tried to stroke the dogs.' Fur, he thought, fur and rabbits. He had tried to stroke the alsatian, his hand seemingly impelled towards that soft thick coat. 'God, I can't remember what he looked like! But I remember that voice. That voice! Sergeant, the man you spoke to, the man who tried to stroke the dogs, is the writer of those letters.'

'I just don't recall him, sir.'

'Never mind. It should be easy to find him now.'

But it wasn't.

Wexford went first to Mr Crantock, the husband of Gemma Lawrence's neighbour, who was head cashier at the Kingsmarkham branch of Lloyd's Bank. Certain that this man would know every member of the search parties by sight if not by name, Wexford was disappointed to learn that not every searcher had been drawn from the three streets, Fontaine Road, Wincanton Road and Chiltern Avenue.

'There were a lot of chaps I'd never seen before,' said Crantock. 'Heaven knows where they came from or how they got to know the kid was missing that early. But we were glad of anyone we could get, weren't we? I remember there was one character came on a bike.'

'News of that kind travels fast,' Wexford said. 'It's a mystery how it does, but people get to know of things before there's time for them to be on television or radio or in the papers.'

'You could try Dr Lomax. He led one of the parties until he had to go back on a call. Doctors always know everybody, don't they?'

The supplier of Gemma Lawrence's sleeping pills practised from his own home, a Victorian Gothic house of considerable dimensions that was superior to its neighbours in Chiltern Avenue. Wexford arrived in time to catch the doctor at the end of his afternoon surgery.

Lomax was a busy harassed little man who spoke with a shrill voice, but it wasn't the shrillness Wexford was listening for and, besides, the doctor had a faint Scottish accent. It seemed that he too was unlikely to be of much help.

'Mr Crantock, Mr Rushworth, Mr Dean . . .' He enumerated a long list of men, counting them on his fingers, though

127

of what use this was Wexford didn't know, as the search parties had never been counted. Lomax, however seemed certain when he reached the end of his list that there had been three strangers, one the cyclist.

'How they even knew about it beats me,' he said, echoing Crantock. 'I only knew myself because my wife came in and told me while I was holding surgery. She acts as my nurse, you see, and she'd overheard someone talking in the street while she was helping an elderly patient out of a car. She came straight in here and told me and when my last patient had gone I went outside to see what I could do and saw all your cars.'

'What time would that have been?'

'When my wife told me or when I went outside? It would have been something after six when I went out, but my wife told me at twenty past five. I can be sure of that because the old lady she helped from the car always comes at five twenty on the dot on Thursdays. Why?'

'Were you alone when your wife told you?'

'No, of course not. I had a patient with me.'

Wexford's interest quickened. 'Did your wife come up to you and whisper the news? Or did she say it aloud so that the patient could have heard?'

'She said it aloud,' said Lomax rather stiffly. 'Why not? I told you she acts as my nurse.'

'You will remember who the patient was, naturally, Doctor?'

'I don't know about naturally. I have a great many patients.' Lomax reflected in silence for a moment. 'It wasn't Mrs Ross, the old lady. She was still in the waiting room. It must have been either Mrs Foster or Miss Garrett. My wife will know, she has a better memory than I.'

Mrs Lomax was called in.

'It was Mrs Foster. She's got four children of her own and I remember she was very upset.'

'But her husband didn't come in the search party,' said Lomax, who seemed now to be following Wexford's own line of reasoning. 'I don't know him, he's not my patient, but he couldn't have. Mrs Foster had just been telling me he'd broken one of his big toes.'

128

Except to say in an embarrassed low tone, 'Of course, I'll stay till you've made other arrangements,' Grace had scarcely spoken to Burden since telling him of her plans. At table—the only time they were together—they kept up a thin polite pretence of conversation for the sake of the children. Burden spent his evenings and his nights with Gemma.

He had told her, but no one else, that Grace was deserting him, and wondered, not understanding at all, when her great wistful eyes widened and she said how lucky he was to have his children all to himself with no one to come between or try to share their love. Then she fell into one of her terrible storms of weeping, beating with her hands on the dusty old furniture, sobbing until her eyes were swollen and half-closed.

Afterwards she let him make love to her, but 'let' was the wrong word. In bed with him she seemed briefly to forget that she was a mother and bereaved and became a young sensual girl. He knew that sex was a forgetting for her, a therapy—she had said as much—but he told himself that no woman could show so much passion if her involvement was solely physical. Women, he had always believed, were not made that way. And when she told him sweetly and almost shyly that she loved him, when she hadn't mentioned John for two hours, his happiness was boundless, all his load of cares nothing.

He had had a wonderful idea. He thought he had found the solution to the sorrows of both of them. She wanted a child and be a mother for his children. Why shouldn't he marry her? He could give her another child, he thought, proud in his virility, in the potency that gave her so much pleasure. She might even be pregnant already, he had done nothing to avoid it. Had she? He was afraid to ask her, afraid to speak of any of this yet. But he turned to her, made strong and urgent by his dreams, anxious for quick possession. Even now they might be making a child, the two of them. He hoped for it, for then she would have to marry him. . . .

The Fosters lived in Sparta Grove, a stone's throw from the Piebald Pony, in a little house that was one of a row of twelve.

129

'I didn't tell a soul about that poor kid,' said Mrs Foster to Wexford, 'except my husband. He was sitting in a deck-chair, resting his poor toe, and I rushed out to tell him the good news.'

'The *good* news?'

'Oh dear, what must you think of me! I don't mean the poor little boy. I did mention that, but only in passing. No, I wanted to tell him what the doctor said. Poor man, he'd been going up the wall and so had I, for that matter. My husband, I mean not the doctor. We thought we was going to have another one you see, thought I'd fallen again and me with four already. But the doctor said it was the onset of the change. The relief! You've no idea. I give the kids their tea and then my husband took me up the Pony to celebrate. I did mention the poor little boy when we was in there. I mean, you like to have a bit of a natter, don't you, especially when you're on top of the world. But it was well gone seven before we got there, that I do know.'

It had looked like a promising lead, had proved a dead end.

It was still half-light and Sparta Grove full of children, playing on the pavements. No one seemed to be supervising them, no one peeping from behind a curtain to keep an eye on that angelic-looking boy with the golden curls or guarding the coffee-skinned, sloe-eyed girl on her tricycle. No doubt the mothers were there, though, observing while themselves remaining unobserved.

The Pony was opening and, as sure as the sun rises, Monkey Matthews, supporting Charly Catch alias Mr Casaubon, appeared from the direction of Charteris Road. Wexford hurried off before they spotted him.

Find the three strangers in the search party was next morning's order of the day, made the more urgent by the printed letter which awaited Wexford among his mail. It was repetitious and Wexford hardly glanced at it, for awaiting him also was a report compiled and signed by an Inspector Daneforth of the Westmorland Constabulary.

Strict orders having been given that he was not to be disturbed, Wexford read:

'On August 5th, 1957, the body of a child, Bridget Melinda Scott, aged 11, was recovered from Fieldenwater lake, Westmorland. The child was found to have met her death by drowning and on August 9th an inquest was held by the Mid-Westmorland Coroner, Dr Augustine Forbes.'

An inquest. Of course! Why hadn't he thought of that? Elsie would call an inquest a court and a coroner a judge. Vaguely disheartened, Wexford read on.

'Evidence was given by:

'1) Lilian Potts, chambermaid, employed at the Lakeside Hotel where Bridget Scott with her parents, Mr and Mrs Ralph Scott, was a guest. Miss Potts told the coroner that she had met Bridget in one of the first floor passages of the hotel at 8 a.m. on the morning of August 5th. Bridget had said she was going swimming in the lake and was wearing a bathing coatume with a beach robe over it. She was alone. Miss Potts advised her not to go out of her depth. Bridget made no reply and Miss Potts saw her go down the stairs.

'2) Ralph Edward Scott, plumbing engineer, of 28 Barrington Gardens, Colchester, Essex. Mr Scott said he was the father of Bridget Scott. He and his wife and daughter had been spending a fortnight's holiday at the Lakeside Hotel, Fieldenwater. By August 5th they had been there for ten days. Bridget was a keen swimmer and used to swim in the lake regularly before breakfast. On August 5th, before he and his wife were up, Bridget came into their bedroom to say she was going for a swim. He warned her to stay close to the shore. He never saw her alive again.

'3) Ada Margaret Patten, widow, aged 72, of 4 Blenheim Cottages, Water Street, Fieldenwater Village. She said she had been exercising her dog, as was her habit, at 8.15 a.m. on the north shore of Fieldenwater, the opposite shore to that on which the hotel is situated. She heard a cry for help and noticed that there was a bather in difficulties. Herself unable to swim, Mrs Patten observed two men bathing at the eastern end of the lake and another man fishing from a rowing boat a short distance from the bather who had called for help. Asked by the coroner to explain what she meant by a short distance, Mrs Patten said she would calculate the distance was about twenty yards. Mrs Patten was carrying

131

a walking stick which she waved in the direction of the boat. She also tried to attract the attention of the other two bathers. The men at the eastern end of the lake eventually heard her and began to swim northwards. Her shouts had no apparent effect on the fisherman in the boat. Finally, she saw the boat moving towards the distressed swimmer but before it reached that part of the lake the swimmer had disappeared. She did not understand how the boatman could have failed to hear her as sound carries over water. She had often been in boats on the lake herself and knew that sounds from the shore were clearly audible in its centre.

'4) George Baleham, agricultural worker, of 7, Bulmer Way, New Estate, Fieldenwater Village. Mr Baleham told the coroner that he and his brother had gone for a swim in Fieldenwater at 7.30 a.m. on August 5th. He saw a child enter the lake from the Lakeside Hotel towards 8.10. Five minutes later he heard cries from across the water and heard Mrs Patten shouting. Immediately he and his brother began swimming towards the child who was two hundred yards from them. There was a boat in the vicinity of the child and he saw a man fishing from it. He shouted to the man in the boat, "There's a kid drowning. You are nearer than us," but the boat did not move. Mr Baleham said the boat did not begin to move until he was ten yards from it. By this time the child had disappeared. In his opinion, the man in the boat could easily have reached the child before she sank. From where he was he could not have failed to see the child or hear her cries.

'5) Ivor Lionel Fairfax Swan . . .'

Here it was then, what he had been waiting for. The name in cold type gave Wexford a strange little cold thrill. He felt like a man who for months has stalked a particular stag and now, groping through the brush and undergrowth of a bleak moor, sees his quarry standing aloof and unsuspecting, near him, oh, so near! on a crag. Stealthily and silently he reaches for his gun.

'5) Ivor Lionel Fairfax Swan, student, aged 19, of Carien Hall, Carien Magna, Bedfordshire, and Christ's College, Oxford. Mr Swan said he was on holiday at the Lakeside Hotel with two friends. Bridget Scott had occasionally spoken

132

to him in the hotel lounge and on the lake beach. Apart from that he did not know her and had never spoken to her parents. He enjoyed fishing and sometimes hired a boat to take out on to the lake in the early morning.

'On August 5th he took the boat out at 7 a.m. He was alone on the lake. He noticed two men swimming from the eastern shore at about 7.40, then, soon after eight, Bridget Scott came down the steps from the hotel and entered the water. He did not know whether she was a strong swimmer or not. He knew very little about her.

'She called something out to him but he did not answer. He thought she would make a nuisance of herself and disturb the fish. Some minutes later he heard her call again and again he took no notice. Several times in the previous week she had done things to draw his attention to herself and he thought it wiser not to encourage her. He heard Mrs Patten shouting, but thought she was calling her dog.

'Very soon after that two swimmers attracted his attention and then he saw that Bridget was in genuine difficulty. At once he began to draw in his line and make towards where he had last seen her. By then she had disappeared.

'In answer to the coroner's questions, Mr Swan said he had not thought of diving overboard and swimming. His line was an expensive one and he did not wish to spoil it. He could not dive and was not a strong swimmer. Up until the moment Bridget sank he had never believed her to be in genuine distress. No, he would not say he disliked the child. He had hardly known her. It was true he had not liked her attempts to intrude on himself and his friends. He was sorry she was dead and wished now that he had made efforts to save her. He was, however, sure in his own mind, that under the circumstances, he had acted as would any other man in his position.

'6) Bernard Varney Frensham, aged 19, student, of 16 Paisley Court, London, S.W.7 and Christ's College, Oxford. Mr Frensham said he was a friend of Mr Swan and had been on holiday with him and his (Mr Frensham's) fianceé at the Lakeside Hotel. Bridget Scott had taken an immediate liking to Mr Swan, a "crush" he supposed it would be called, and had tended to pester him. He said he had never been in a

133

boat on Fieldenwater. Fishing did not interest him. When asked by the coroner if Mr Swan was a good swimmer, Mr Frensham said, 'Must I answer that?' Dr Forbes insisted and Mr Frensham said he did not know anything about Mr Swan's style as a swimmer. He had never swum for his college. Pressed further, Mr Frensham said that he had once been shown a life-saving certificate with Mr Swan's name on it.

At this point there was a note explaining that medical and police evidence had been omitted. The report ended:

'The coroner commended Mr George Baleham and Mr Arthur Baleham for their prompt action in attempting to save the child.

'He then reprimanded Mr Swan. He said this was the worst case of callousness towards a child who was obviously drowning that he had ever come across. He took a serious view of what he could only call deliberate and cowardly lying on Mr Swan's part. Far from being an indifferent swimmer, he was an expert at life-saving. There was no doubt in his mind that Mr Swan had refused to listen to the child because he believed, or said he believed, she was pestering him. If he had jumped overboard when he first heard her cry out, Bridget Scott would be alive today. He could not be excused on the ground of his youth as he was a man of intelligence, an Oxford undergraduate and a man of privileged background. The coroner said he was only sorry the law permitted him to take no further steps. He then expressed sympathy for Mr and Mrs Scott.

'A verdict was returned of death by misadventure.'

16

WHEN giving Burden a résumé of Swan's life, Wexford had remarked on the series of disasters he had left in his wake. Here, then, was another instance of that catastrophe-causing faculty of his, that gift, or propensity, of leaving a trail of trouble and distress and disturbance. A true catalyst was Swan, Wexford reflected, a possessor of the power to hurt who yet did—nothing.

It wasn't difficult to picture that morning on the lake, Swan's line cast, the sun shining on the flat brown water, and Swan off in one of his daydreams that nothing must be allowed to disturb. Had he even caught a fish? Did he ever actually *do* anything? Shoot a rabbit? Choose a dog? Buy a pony?

And that was the crux of it. Clearly, Swan had let a child die. But the operative word there was 'let'. Would he actively force death on a child? Had he the nerve, the impulse, the *energy*?

Wexford would have liked to chew the whole thing over with Burden. They were illuminating and fruitful, those long discussions of theirs, examining motive, analysing character. But Burden was no longer fit to participate in such conversations. As soon expect percipience and intelligent speculation from Martin as from him. Each day he seemed to go a little more downhill, to grow more irritable and more distracted until Wexford began to wonder with dread how long it could go on. At present he daily covered up for Burden, did his work, smoothed his path. There was a limit to that, for soon the crack-up would come, the error that couldn't be overlooked or the hysterical scene in public. And then what? The embarrassed request for Burden's resignation before he was forced out?

Wexford shook himself out of these miserable reflections to concentrate on the report. One mystery, at any rate, was cleared up. He need no longer wonder why Swan had baulked at attending an inquest, particularly an inquest on another dead little girl.

The next step was to find Frensham, and this proved easy. Fourteen years had changed him from an undergraduate into a stock jobber, moved him from his parents' flat but not from Kensington, and maintained him in his bachelor state. What had happened to that fiancée who had accompanied him on that Lake holiday?

Hardly a question which need concern him, Wexford decided. He made the requisite polite phone call to the Metropolitan Police and then prepared to set off for London. In the foyer he met Burden.

'Any lead on the missing men from the search party?'

Burden lifted troubled eyes and muttered, 'Martin's got it in hand, hasn't he?'

Wexford went out into the rain, not looking back.

He alighted at Gloucester Road Tube station, got lost, and had to ask a policeman the way to Veronica Grove. At last he found it, a narrow little tree-lined lane which threaded its way from Stanhope Gardens down behind Queen's Gate. Water dripped softly from the branches overhead, and, except that the trees were planes and not oaks, he felt that he might have been at home in Kingsmarkham. The environs of the Piebald Pony were much more his idea of what London should be.

Meditating on such anomalies, he came within a few minutes to Bernard Frensham's house. It was tiny, a mews cottage, with neat but empty window boxes, and it looked very modest unless you happened to know that such properties were sold for twenty-five thousand pounds.

A manservant, small, lithe and dark, admitted him and showed him into the single living room the house contained. It was, however, a large room on three different levels and the furnishing gave an impression of varying textures, satiny polish, smooth velvet, delicate filigree work and highlighted china, rather than of solid masses. Much money had been

136

spent on it. The years Swan has wasted had been turned to good account by his friend.

Frensham, who had risen from his chair at the far end of the room when Wexford entered it, had received prior warning of his coming. And 'warning' rather than 'notice' seemed the appropriate word, for it was very apparent that he had been drinking. Because the coming interview caused him disquiet? Wexford was forced to suppose so. A stock jobber could hardly be so successful as Frensham surely was if seven o'clock always saw him as drunk as he was tonight.

Not that he didn't hold it well. It was only the brandy smell and the strangeness of Frensham's eyes that told Wexford of his condition.

He was thirty-three and he looked forty, the black hair already thinning and the face marked with dark patches. On the other hand, Swan, his contemporary, looked twenty-seven. Slothfulness and placidity preserve youth; hard work and anxiety accelerate its passing.

Frensham wore a beautiful suit of charcoal grey with a coppery sheen to it, a black-and-copper tie, and, on the little finger of his left hand, an opal ring. What an impression of civilised distinction the man would have made, Wexford thought, but for the brandy on his breath which struck you full-blast in the face.

'Let me give you a drink, Chief Inspector.'

Wexford would have refused, was on the point of refusing, but there was so much subdued urgency in Frensham's added, 'Please do,' that he felt bound to consent.

Frensham opened the door and called a name that sounded like 'Haysus'. Brandy was brought and various other bottles and decanters. When the manservant had gone, Frensham said, 'Odd, aren't they, the Spanish? Calling a boy Jesus.' He gave a short disconcerting giggle. 'Most inappropriate, I can tell you. His parents are Maria and Joseph, or so he says.'

Taking a gulp of his drink, he pursued this theme, but Wexford decided he wouldn't be sidetracked by Iberian nomenclature. It was impossible not to feel that Frensham was trying to postpone their discussion for as long as possible.

'May we talk about Mr Ivor Swan, sir?'

Frensham left the subject of Spanish names abruptly and said in a clipped voice, 'I haven't seen Ivor for years, not since we both came down from Oxford.'

'That doesn't matter. I have. Perhaps you can't remember much about him?'

'I remember all right,' said Frensham. 'I shall never forget.' He got up and walked across the room. At first Wexford thought he had gone to fetch a photograph or some document and then he realised that Frensham was in the grip of a powerful emotion. His back was towards the chief inspector and for some minutes he didn't move. Wexford sat watching him in silence. He wasn't easily embarrassed, but he wasn't prepared for Frensham's next words either. Wheeling round suddenly, staring oddly at Wexford, he said, 'Has he vine leaves in his hair?'

'I beg your pardon?'

'You have never seen or read *Hedda Gabler*? It doesn't matter. It's the kind of question I feel natural to ask about Ivor.' The man was very drunk, with the intoxication that rids the tongue of inhibition without slurring speech. He came back to his chair and rested his elbows against the back of it. 'Ivor was remarkably beautiful then, a pale golden-brown Antinous. I was very fond of him. No, that isn't true. I loved him with—with all my heart. He was very lazy and—well, tranquil. He never seemed to know what the time was or to take any account of time at all.' Frensham spoke as if he had forgotten Wexford was there or forgotten what he was. He reached for his brandy standing up. 'That kind of indifference to time, that sublime idleness, is very attractive. I often think it was this quality in her, rather than her religious zeal, that made Christ praise Mary and condemn Martha, the bustling busy worker.'

Wexford had not come to hear about the character of Ivor Swan, which he thought he already understood, but he was no more willing to interrupt Frensham in the midst of his discourse than a spiritualist would have been to cut short the outpourings of a medium in a trance. He felt somehow, as might the spiritualist also, that it would be dangerous to do so.

'He was always pursued by droves of girls,' Frensham went

138

on. 'Some of them were beautiful and all of them were intelligent. I am speaking, of course, of Oxford girls. He slept with some of them but he never took them out, not even for a drink. He couldn't be bothered. He used to say he didn't like clever women because they tried to make him talk.

'Once I told him the sort of woman he would marry, a feather-brained idiot who would adore him and fuss about him and demand only his presence. He wouldn't marry her, she would marry him, drag him to the altar against all odds. I saw in the paper he is married. Is she like that?'

'Yes, she is,' said Wexford. 'Exactly like that.'

Frensham sat down heavily. He looked ravaged now, as if overcome by painful memories. Wexford wondered if he and Swan had really been lovers, but decided against it. The willingness would have been there on Frensham's part all right, but Swan just wouldn't have been 'bothered'.

'I never married,' said Frensham. 'I was engaged to that girl, Adelaide Turner, but it never came to anything. I remember Ivor didn't want her to go on holiday with us and I didn't either, not really, not by then. He said she would get in the way.' He refilled his glass and said, 'I can't stop drinking, I'm afraid. I don't drink much usually but once I start I can't stop. I promise you I won't make a fool of myself.'

Some would say he was doing that already. Wexford was less harsh. He felt sorry for Frensham, sorrier when he said suddenly:

'I don't know whether I'm giving you a true picture of Ivor's character or not. You see, although I haven't seen him for twelve years, I dream about him a great deal, as much as three times a week. It must sound very silly, I haven't ever told anyone before. I mention it now because I don't know any more what is the real Ivor and the Ivor my own dreams have created. The two images are so confused they have run into each other and become one.'

Wexford said gently, 'Tell me about the holiday. Tell me about Bridget Scott.'

'She was only eleven,' Frensham said, and his voice was saner and more even when he wasn't speaking of Swan. 'But she looked much older, at least fourteen. It sounds very absurd to say she fell in love with him at first sight, but she did.

139

And, of course, at that age she hadn't learned to hide her feelings. She used to pester Ivor all the time, ask him to go swimming with her, wanted him to sit next to her in the lounge. She even asked her mother in our hearing if he could go up and say good night to her when she was in bed.'

'And how did Swan deal with all that?'

'Simply by taking no notice. He treated Adelaide in the same way. He used to answer Adelaide if she spoke to him, but most of the time he didn't speak to Bridget at all. He said she got in the way, and once, I remember, he told her so.'

Frensham leaned back and gave a heavy sigh. His eyes closed momentarily and he opened them as if with a great effort. 'The coroner,' he said, 'was an old man like a vulture. I didn't want to betray Ivor. They made me tell them about his swimming. I hadn't any choice.' The heavy lids fell again. 'I felt like Judas,' he said.

'What happened that morning when Bridget was drowned?'

Still Frensham kept his eyes closed and now his speech had begun to thicken. 'I never went out fishing with Ivor. I've never been an early riser. Ivor was. You'd think a man like —a man like him, would go to bed late and get up late. Ivor always used to be up by six. He'd sleep in the day, of course, if he got the chance. He could sleep anywhere. It was the early morning he liked and the countryside, the peace of it and the light.' Frensham made a funny little noise like a sob. 'He used to quote those lines of W. H. Davies. "What is this life, if full of care, we have no time to stand and stare?" '

'Go on about that morning.'

Frensham sat up, and half-toppled forward, resting his elbows on his knees, his chin in his hands. 'I don't know. I wasn't there. I woke up to hear people shouting in the corridor outside my room, running up and down and shouting. You can imagine. I went outside. The mother was there, screaming, and that poor old man, Scott.'

'Old? Bridget's father?'

'Not really old, I suppose. About sixty. The mother was younger. They had older children, someone told me. Does it matter? I found Ivor in the dining room, drinking coffee.

He was very white. He said, "It was nothing to do with me. Why involve me?" and that was all he ever said about it.'

'You mean he never again mentioned the subject of Bridget Scott's drowning to you? Not when you both had to attend the inquest?'

'He didn't like it because we had to stay on over the end of our holiday,' remembered Frensham, and now a glaze had come across his eyes. Weariness? Tears? Or only the effect of the drink? 'After—after the inquest he wouldn't let me speak of it. I don't know what he felt.' Very softly now, Frensham said, 'It may have been callousness or that he was upset or just wanted to forget. There wasn't much about the inquest in the daily papers and when we went up no one knew until —until Adelaide told them.'

'Why do you think he let her drown?' said Wexford.

'She got in his way,' said Frensham, and then he began to cry weakly. 'When people annoyed him or began to—to bore him he just—just—just . . .' There was a sob between each word. '. . . Just—ignored—them—pretended—they— weren't — there — didn't — talk — didn't—see—them—did that—to—me—after—later . . .' He threw out a hand and the brandy glass went over, spreading a stain across the thick pale carpet.

Wexford opened the door and called, 'Here, Jesus, or whatever your name is, your master wants you. You'd better get him to bed.'

The man came in, sidling and smiling. He put his arms under Frensham's shoulders and whispered to him. Frensham lifted his head and said to Wexford in a normal clear tone, 'Vine leaves in his hair . . .' Then he closed his eyes and slid into unconsciousness.

17

FRIDAY'S edition of the *Kingsmarkham Courier* carried on its front page a double-column spread asking for the three missing men from the search party to come forward. Much good that would do, Wexford thought, as he read it. Hadn't it occurred to Martin, when he asked Harry Wild for publicity, that an appeal of this kind would fetch forth only the innocents? And where was Burden in all this, Burden who was supposed to rule the place in Wexford's absence, yet who seemed as much surprised by the newspaper appeal as he was?

When he got back from London he had phoned Burden's house. He needed to discuss that interview with someone and he thought too that this might be a way of reawakening Burden's interest. But Grace Woodville had told him her brother-in-law was out, she didn't know where.

'I think he may just be sitting somewhere in his car, brooding about Jean and—and everything.'

'He's supposed to leave a number where he can be found.'

'Cheriton Forest doesn't have a number,' said Grace.

On Saturday afternoon two men walked into Kingsmarkham police station to say that they had read the *Courier* and believed they were two of the three missing men. They were brothers, Thomas and William Thetford, who lived in adjoining houses in Bury Lane, a half-slum, half-country road on the far side of Stowerton, not far from Sparta Grove. News of John Lawrence's disappearance had been brought to them by William's wife who cleaned for Mrs Dean and who had reached home at five-thirty. The Thetford brothers were on shift work, had both finished for that day. Guessing a search party might be got up—hoping for a bit of excitement to brighten up their day, Wexford thought—they had got into William's car and driven to Fontaine Road.

Neither man had a squeaky voice or even a voice Wexford could remember hearing before. They denied having passed the news on to anyone and said they had discussed it only with each other. Wexford supposed that routine demanded an interview with Mrs Thetford. Monday would be time enough for that.

'Golf in the morning?' said Dr Crocker, bouncing in after the Thetfords had gone.

'Can't. I'm going to Colchester.'

'Whatever for?' Crocker said crossly, and then, without waiting for an answer, 'I wanted to have a little chat with you about Mike.'

'I'd really rather you didn't. I'd rather you saw him. You're his doctor.'

'I think he's found a better doctor than I,' said Crocker slyly. 'I saw his car again last night.'

'Don't tell me. In Cheriton Forest. And he was in it, brooding.'

'It wasn't and he wasn't. It was parked at the bottom of Chiltern Avenue at midnight.'

'You're ubiquitous, you are,' Wexford grumbled. 'You're like the Holy Ghost.'

'It was at the bottom of *Chiltern Avenue*, next to *Fontaine Road* at *midnight*. Come on, Reg. I knew you were thick round the middle but not . . .' The doctor tapped his head, '. . . not up here.'

'That's not possible,' said Wexford sharply. His voice faltered. 'I mean . . . Mike wouldn't . . . I don't want to talk about it.' And he cast upon the doctor a fierce glare. 'If I don't know about it,' he said with none of his usual logic, 'it isn't happening.'

'I know it would be like a miracle,' said Gemma, 'but if—if John is ever found and comes back to me, I shall sell this house, even if I only get what the land's worth, and go back to London. I could live in one room, I shouldn't mind. I hate it here. I hate being in here and I hate going out and seeing them all look at me.'

143

'You talk like a child,' said Burden. 'Why talk about what you know can't happen? I asked you to marry me.'

She got up, still without answering, and began to dress, but not in the clothes she had taken off when she and Burden had come into the bedroom. He watched her hungrily, but puzzled as he always was by nearly every facet of her behaviour. She had pulled over her head a long black dress, very sleek and tight. Burden didn't know whether it was old, a garment of her aunt's, or the latest fashion. You couldn't tell these days. Over her shoulders and around her waist she wrapped a long scarf of orange and blue and green, so stiff and encrusted with embroidery that it crackled as she handled it.

'We used to dress up a lot, John and I,' she said, 'dress up and be characters from the *Red Fairy Book*. He would have grown up to be a great actor.' Now she was hanging jewellery all over herself, long strings of beads draped from her neck and wound about her arms. 'That sometimes happens when one of your parents, or both of them, has been a second-rate artist. Mozart's father was a minor musician.' She swayed in the soft red light, extending her arms. There was a ring on every finger to weigh down her thin hands. She shook down her hair and it fell in a flood of fire, the light catching it as it caught all the stones in the cheap rings and made them flash.

Burden was dazzled and fascinated and appalled. She danced across the room, drawing out the scarf and holding it above her head. The jewels rang like little bells. Then she stopped, gave a short abrupt laugh, and ran to him, kneeling at his feet.

' "I will dance for you, Tetrarch." ' she said. ' "I am awaiting until my slaves bring perfumes to me and the seven veils and take off my sandals." '

Wexford would have recognised the words of Salome. To Burden they were just another instance of her eccentricity. Very distressed and embarrassed, he said, 'Oh, Gemma . . . !'

In the same voice she said, 'I will marry you if . . . if life is to go on like this with nothing, I'll marry you.'

'Stop play-acting.'

She got up. 'I wasn't acting.'

'I wish you'd take those things off,' he said.

'You take them off.'

Her huge staring eyes made him shiver. He reached out both hands and lifted the bunch of chains from her neck, not speaking, hardly breathing. She lifted her right arm, curving it in a slow sweep and then holding it poised. Very slowly he slid the bracelets down over her wrist and let them fall, pulled the rings from her fingers one by one. All the time they stared into each other's eyes. He thought that he had never in his life done anything as exciting, as overpoweringly erotic, as this stripping a woman of cheap glittering jewellery, although in doing so he had not once touched her skin.

Never . . . He hadn't even dreamed that such a thing might be possible for him. She stretched out her left arm and he made no other move towards her until the last ring had joined the others in a heap on the floor.

It wasn't until he awoke in the night that he realised fully what had happened, that he had proposed and been accepted. He told himself that he ought to be elated, in a seventh heaven of happiness, for he had got what he wanted and there would be no more agony or struggling or loneliness or dying small daily deaths.

The room was too dark for him to see anything at all, but he knew exactly what the first light would show him here and downstairs. Yesterday it hadn't mattered much, the mess and the chaos, but it mattered now. He tried to see her installed in his own house as its mistress, caring for his children and cooking meals, tending on them all as Grace did, but it was impossible to conjure up such a picture, he hadn't enough imagination. What if Wexford were to call one night for a chat and a drink as he sometimes did and Gemma appear in her strange dress and her shawl and her long beads? And would she expect him to have her friends there, those itinerant sub-actors with their drugs? And his children, his Pat . . . !

But all that would change, he told himself, once they were married. She would settle down and be a housewife. Perhaps he could persuade her to have that mane of hair cut, that hair which, at one and the same time, was so beautiful and so evocative of desire and yet so unbecoming in a policeman's wife. They would have a child of their own, she would make new suitable friends, she would change . . .

He did not allow himself to dwell on the notion that such changes as he envisaged would destroy her personality and dull all the strangeness that had first attracted him, but it touched the edges of his mind. He pushed it away almost angrily. Why make difficulties where none existed? Why seek always to find flaws in perfect happiness?

Gemma and he would have love, a nightly orgy for two, an endless honeymoon. He turned towards her, pressing his lips against the mass of hair of which he planned to deprive her. Within minutes he was asleep and dreaming that he had found her child, restoring him to her and seeing her, by that gift, transformed into everything he wanted her to be.

'Kingsmarkham?' said Mrs Scott, smiling comfortably at Wexford. 'Oh, yes, we know Kingsmarkham, don't we, dear?' Expressionless, her husband gave a tiny nod. 'We've got a niece lives in ever such a nice little house near Kingsmarkham, built back in the seventeen hundreds, it was, and we used to go there regularly for our holidays right up till this year. But now . . .'

Wexford, who while she was speaking had been taking stock of the room and looking particularly at the framed photographs of those older Scott children who had survived, middle-aged now and with teenage children of their own, followed her gaze towards their progenitor.

No need to ask why they wouldn't go back to Kingsmarkham or to question the implication that they would take no more holidays. Scott was a little old man, nearing eighty, whose face was badly twisted, especially about the mouth. Two sticks hung from the wings of his chair. Wexford supposed that he was unable to walk without their aid and, from his silence, was beginning to suppose that Ralph Scott had also lost the power of speech. It was something of a shock when the distorted mouth opened and a harsh voice said:

'What about a cup of tea, Ena?'

'I'll have it ready in a jiffy, dear.'

146

Mrs Scott jumped up and mouthed something to Wexford, indicating that he should join her in the kitchen. This was a sterile-looking place full of gadgets, and it was modern enough to gladden the heart of any house-proud woman, but Mrs Scott seemed to think it needed apology.

'Mr Scott had a stroke back in the winter,' she said as she plugged in an electric kettle, 'and it's really aged him. He's not at all the man he was. That's why we moved out here from Colchester. But if he was himself I'd have had everything automatic here, he'd have done the lot himself, not left it to those builders. I wish you could have seen my house in the town. The central heating was *too* hot. You had to have the windows open night and day. Mr Scott did all that himself. Of course, him being in the trade all his life, there's nothing he doesn't know about heating and pipes and all that.' She stopped, stared at the kettle which was making whining noises, and said in a voice that seemed to be suppressing something explosive, 'We saw in the papers about that man Swan and you digging all that up again about his little girl. It made Mr Scott ill, just seeing his name.'

'The child died back in the winter.'

'Mr Scott never saw the papers then. He was too ill. We never knew Swan lived near our niece. We wouldn't have gone if we had. Well, he was living there the last time we went but we didn't know.' She sat down on a plastic-upholstered contemporary version of a settle and sighed. 'It's preyed on Mr Scott's mind all these years, poor little Bridget. I reckon it would have killed him to have come face to face with that Swan.'

'Mrs Scott, I'm sorry to have to ask you, but in your opinion, is it possible he let your daughter drown? I mean, is it possible he knew she was drowning and let it happen?'

She was silent. Wexford saw an old grief cross her face, travel into her eyes and pass away. The kettle boiled with a blast and switched itself off.

Mrs Scott got up and began making the tea. She was quite collected, sorrowful but with an old dry sadness. The fingers on the kettle handle, the hand on the teapot, were quite steady. A great grief had come to her, the only grief, Aristotle

147

says, which is insupportable, but she had borne it, had gone on making tea, gone on exulting in central heating. So would it be one day for Mrs Lawrence, Wexford mused. Aristotle didn't know everything, didn't know perhaps that time heals all pain, grinds all things to dust and leaves only a little occasional melancholy.

'Mr Scott loved her best,' Bridget's mother said at last. 'It's been different for me. I had my sons. You know how it is for a man and his little girl, his youngest.'

Wexford nodded, thinking of his Sheila, his ewe lamb, the apple of his eye.

'I never took on about it like he did. Women are stronger, I always say. They get to accept things. But I was in a bad way at the time. She was my only girl, you see, and I had her late in life. In fact, we never would have had another one, only Mr Scott was mad on getting a girl.' She looked as if she were trying to remember, not the facts, but the emotions of the time, trying and failing. 'It was a mistake going to that hotel,' she said. 'Boarding houses were more in our line. But Mr Scott was doing so well and it wasn't for me to argue when he said he was as good as the next man and why not a hotel when we could afford it? It made me feel uncomfortable, I can tell you, when I saw the class of people we had to mix with, Oxford boys and a barrister and a Sir. Of course, Bridget didn't know any different, they were just people to her and she took a fancy to that Swan. If I've wished it once I've wished it a thousand times that she'd never set eyes on him.

'Once we were in the lounge and she was hanging about him—I couldn't stop her. I did try—and he gave her such a push, not saying anything, you know, not talking to her, that she fell over and hurt her arm. Mr Scott went right over and had a go at him, told him he was a snob and Bridget was as good as him any day. I'll never forget what he said. "I don't care whose daughter she is," he said. 'I don't care if her father's a duke or a dustman. I don't want her around. She gets in my way." But that didn't stop Bridget. She wouldn't leave him alone. I've often thought since then that Bridget swam out to that boat so as she could be alone with him and no one else there.'

Mrs Scott picked up her tray, but made no other move to return to the sitting room. She seemed to be listening and then she said:

'She couldn't swim very far. We'd told her over and over again not to go out too far. Swan knew, he'd heard us. He let her drown because he just didn't *care*, and if that's killing, he killed her. She was only a child. Of course he killed her.'

'A strong accusation to make, Mrs Scott.'

'It's no more than the coroner said. When I saw in the paper about his own little girl I didn't feel sorry for him, I didn't think he'd got his deserts. He's done the same to her, I thought.'

'The circumstances were hardly the same,' said Wexford. 'Stella Rivers died from suffocation.'

'I know. I read about it. I'm not saying he did it deliberately any more than I'm saying he actually pushed Bridget under the water. It's my belief she got in his way too—stands to reason she would, a stepdaughter and him newly married—and maybe she said something he didn't like or got too fond of him like Bridget, so he got hold of her, squeezed her neck or something and—and she died. We'd better to go back to Mr Scott now.'

He was sitting as they had left him, his almost sightless eyes still staring. His wife put a teacup into his hands and stirred the tea for him.

'There you are, dear. Sorry I was so long. Would you like a bit of cake if I cut it up small?'

Mr Scott made no reply. He was concentrating on Wexford and the chief inspector realised that no explanation of his visit had been given to the old man. True, there had been a passing reference to Kingsmarkham and a niece, but Wexford had not been identified by name or rank.

Perhaps it was the look in his wife's eyes or perhaps something that he had overheard while they were in the kitchen that made him say suddenly in his harsh monotone:

'You a policeman?'

Wexford hesitated. Scott was a very sick man. It was possible that the only real contact he had ever had with the police was when his beloved daughter died. Would it be wise

149

or kind or even necessary to bring memories back to that exhausted, fuddled brain?

Before he could make up his mind, Mrs Scott said brightly. 'Oh, no dear. Whatever gave you that idea? This gentleman's just a friend of Eileen's from over Kingsmarkham way.'

'That's right,' said Wexford heartily.

The old man's hand trembled and the cup rattled in its saucer. 'Shan't go there any more, not in my state. Shan't last much longer.'

'What a way to talk!' Mrs Scott's brisk manner did little to cover her distress. 'Why, you're almost your old self again.' She mouthed incomprehensible things to Wexford and followed them up with a louder, 'You should have seen him last March, a couple of weeks after he had that stroke. More dead than alive he was, worse than a new-born baby. And look at him now.'

But Wexford could hardly bear to look. As he left them, he reflected that the interview hadn't been entirely fruitless. At least it would spur him on to take Crocker's tablets with renewed zeal.

18

THE impressions Swan made on other people had subtly altered Wexford's own image of him, investing him with a callous coldness and a magnetic beauty, making him godlike in appearance and power, so that when he came face to face with the man himself once more he felt a sense of letdown and almost of shock. For Swan was just Swan, still the idle good-looking young man leading his slow aimless existence. It was strange to reflect that the mere mention of his name might be enough to kill Mr Scott and that, incubuslike, he lived a separate life as the haunter of Frensham's dreams.

'Does Roz have to know about this?' he asked, and went on when Wexford looked surprised, 'I'd more or less forgotten it myself, except that going to that inquest brought it back. Do we have to talk about it?'

'I'm afraid we do.'

Swan shrugged. 'We won't be overheard. Roz is out and I got rid of Gudrun.' Wexford's face showed the absurd effect this had on him and Swan gave a low ironical laugh. 'Told her to go, sacked her, I mean. What did you think I'd done? Made away with her? In your eyes my path is strewn with corpses, isn't it? Roz and I love to be alone and Gudrun got in our way, that's all.'

That phrase again. 'She got in his way . . .' Wexford was beginning to get the shivers every time he heard it.

'D'you want a drink? It'll have to be something out of a bottle. Making tea and coffee is Roz's province and, anyway, I don't know where she keeps the things.'

'I don't want a drink. I want to hear about Bridget Scott.'

'Oh God, it was such a hell of a long time ago, ancient history. I suppose you've already had a splendid selection of biassed accounts.' Swan sat down and rested his chin in his hands. 'I don't know what you want me to say. I went to this hotel with another man and a girl. If you'll give me a minute I'll try and remember their names.'

'Bernard Frensham and Adelaide Turner.' Poor Frensham, Wexford thought. Swan lived on in his dreams but he had no reciprocal place in Swan's memory.

'Why ask me if you've already talked to them?'

'I want your version.'

'Of what happened on the lake? All right. I did let her drown, but I didn't know she was drowning.' Swan's face was petulant. In the November light, fitful and fading, he might have been nineteen again, but Wexford could see no shadow of vine leaves in his hair. 'She plagued the life out of me,' he said, the sullen look deepening. 'She hung about me and tried to get me to go swimming and walking with me and she staged scenes to attract my attention.'

'What sort of scenes?'

'Once she was out in a rowing boat and I was swimming and she started shouting she'd dropped her purse overboard and would I dive for it. I didn't but what's-his-name—Frensham—did and after we'd all been messing about for about ten minutes she produced it from the bottom of the boat. It was all a ploy. Then she came into my room once in the afternoon when I was trying to sleep and said if I wouldn't speak to her she'd scream and when people came she'd tell them I'd done something to her. A kid of eleven!'

'So that when you heard her cry for help you thought it was another ruse to attract your attention?'

'Of course I did. That other time when she'd threatened to scream, I said, "Scream away". I can't be taken in by that kind of thing. Out in the boat, I *knew* she was putting on an act. I couldn't believe it when they said she'd drowned.'

'Were you sorry?'

'I was a bit shattered,' said Swan. 'It made an impression on me, but it wasn't my fault. For quite a long time after that I didn't like having kids of that age around me. I don't now, come to that.'

Had he realised what he had said? 'Stella was just that age when you first saw her, Mr Swan,' said Wexford.

But Swan seemed unaware of the innuendo. He went on to

make matters worse. 'She used to try the same things on, as a matter of fact, always trying to get attention.' The petulance returned, making him almost ugly. 'Could she have a dog? Could she have a horse? Always trying to involve me. I sometimes think . . .' He directed at Wexford a gaze full of fierce dislike. 'I sometimes think the whole world is trying to get between me and what I want.'

'And that is?'

'To be left alone with Rosalind,' said Swan simply. 'I don't want children. All this has made me loathe children. I want to be in the country with Roz, just the two of us, in peace. She's the only person I've ever known who wants me for what I am. She hasn't made an image of me that's got to be lived up to, she doesn't want to jolly me along and encourage me. She loves *me*, she really knows me and I'm first with her, the centre of her universe. Once she'd seen me she didn't even care about Stella any more. We only kept her with us because I said we ought, that Roz might regret it later if she didn't. And she's jealous. Some men wouldn't like that, but I do. It gives me a wonderful feeling of happiness and security when Roz says if I so much as looked at another woman she'd do that woman the worst injury in her power. You don't know what that means to me.'

I wonder what it means to me? Wexford thought. He said nothing but continued to keep his eyes fixed on Swan who suddenly flushed. 'I haven't talked so much to anyone for years,' he said, 'except to Roz. That's her coming in now. You won't say anything about . . . ? If she began suspecting me I don't know what I'd do.'

It was the sound of a car Swan had heard, the Ford shooting brake crunching on the gravel outside Hall Farm.

'I was under the impression you couldn't drive a car, Mrs Swan,' he said as she came in.

'Were you? I let my licence lapse while I was out in the East but I took a new test last month.'

She had been shopping. In London perhaps, at any rate in some more sophisticated place than Kingsmarkham. Her packages were wrapped in black paper lettered with white, scarlet printed with gold. But she hadn't been buying for herself.

153

'A tie for you, my lover. Look at the label.' Swan looked and so did Wexford. The label said Jacques Fath. 'And some Russian cigarettes and a book and . . . It doesn't look very much now I've got it all home. Oh, how I wish we were rich!'

'So that you could spend it all on me?' said Swan.

'Who else? Did you remember to ring the electric people, darling?'

'I never got around to it,' said Swan. 'It went right out of my head.'

'Never mind, my lover. I'll see to it. Now I'm going to make you some nice tea. Were you lonely without me?'

'Yes, I was. Very.'

She had hardly noticed Wexford. He was investigating the murder of her only child but she had hardly noticed him. Her eyes, her attention, were solely for her husband. It was he who, now there was someone to prepare it, rather grudgingly suggested that Wexford might care to stay and share their tea.

'No, thank you,' said the chief inspector. 'I wouldn't want to be in your way.'

The lock of hair had belonged neither to John Lawrence nor to Stella Rivers, but it was a child's hair. Someone had cut it from a child's head. That meant whoever had written the letters had access to a golden-headed child. And more than just access. No one could go up to a child in the street and chop off a piece of his or her hair without getting into trouble. Technically, it would be assault. Therefore, the letter-writer, the 'fur man', must be in such close association with a golden-headed child as to be able to cut off a lock of its hair either while it was asleep or with its permission.

But how far did that get him? Wexford pondered. He couldn't interview every golden-haired child in Sussex. He couldn't even ask for such children to come forward, for the person 'in close association'—father? uncle?—would prevent the one significant child from answering his appeal.

Although it wasn't the prescribed time, Wexford swallowed two of his blood-pressure tablets, washing them down with the dregs of his coffee. He'd need them if he was going

154

to spend the rest of the day scouring Stowerton. Mrs Thetford first, to see if there was any chance she had broadcast the news of John's disappearance around the town. Then perhaps Rushworth. Sit down with Rushworth for hours if necessary, make him remember, make him describe his fellow searchers, get to the bottom of it *today*.

The climate in which Burden and his sister-in-law now lived wasn't conducive to confidences. It was nearly a week since she had smiled at him or said any more than 'Colder today' or 'Pass the butter, please'. But he would have to tell her about his forthcoming marriage, and tell the children too, perhaps even ask their permission.

He thought his opportunity had come when, thawing a little, Grace said, 'Aren't you having next weekend off?'

Guardedly, he said, 'Supposed to be. We're very busy.'

'Mother's asked all four of us down for the weekend.'

'I don't think . . .' Burden began. 'I mean, I couldn't manage it. Look here, Grace, there's something . . .'

Grace jumped up. 'There's always something. Don't bother to make excuses. I'll go alone with the children, if you've no objection.'

'Of course I've no objection,' said Burden, and he went off to work, or what would have been work if he had been able to concentrate.

He had half-promised to have his lunch in Fontaine Road. Bread and cheese, he supposed it would be, in that loathsome kitchen. Much as he longed to be with Gemma in the night, the meals she prepared had no attraction for him. The police-station canteen was almost preferable. And suddenly it occurred to him that soon every meal he ate at home would be prepared by Gemma.

Wexford had gone out somewhere. Time was when the chief inspector would never have gone out without leaving a message for him, but all that was changed now. He had changed it and the change in him had lost him Wexford's esteem.

Descending in the lift, he hoped he wouldn't encounter Wexford, and when the door opened he saw that there was no one in the foyer but Camb and Harry Wild, who these days

155

had become almost a fixture, as much a part of the furnishings as the counter and the little red chairs. Burden treated him like a chair, accepting his presence but otherwise ignoring him. He was nearly at the swing doors when they burst open and Wexford appeared.

Except when he was with Gemma, muttering had become Burden's normal mode of speech. He muttered a greeting and would have gone on his way. Wexford stopped him with the 'Mr Burden!' he habitually used in the presence of such as Camb and Wild.

'Sir?' said Burden with equal formality.

Speaking in a lower tone, Wexford said, 'I've spent the morning with that fellow Rushworth, but I couldn't get a thing out of him. Strikes me as a bit of a fool.'

With an effort, Burden tried to fix his mind on Rushworth. 'I don't know,' he said. 'I wouldn't have considered him as a possible suspect myself, but he does wear a duffel coat and there was that business when he nearly frightened the wits out of the Crantock girl.'

'*He did what?*'

The words had been spoken in a sharp hiss. 'I told you,' Burden said. 'It was in my report.' Hesitating, muttering again, he recounted to the chief inspector his experience of the encounter in Chiltern Avenue. 'I must have told you,' he faltered. 'I'm sure I . . .'

Wexford forgot about Wild and Camb. 'You never did!' he shouted. 'You never made any bloody report. D'you mean to tell me now—*now*—that Rushworth molested a child?'

Burden had no words. He felt his face grow crimson. It was true—he remembered now—he had made no report, the whole thing had vanished from his mind. Love and involvement had driven it away, for that night, while Stowerton was wrapped in mist, had been his first night with Gemma.

Things might have come to a head then between him and Wexford but for the intervention of Harry Wild. Insensitive to atmosphere, quite incapable of ever supposing himself to be *de trop*, Wild turned round and said loudly:

'D'you mean to tell me you've got Bob Rushworth lined up for this job?'

'I don't mean to tell you anything,' Wexford snapped.

156

'There's no need to be like that. Don't you want any help in your enquiries?'

'What do you know about it?'

'Well, I do know Rushworth,' said Wild, pushing himself between the two policemen. 'And I know he's a nasty customer. Friend of mine rents a cottage from him down in Mill Lane, but Rushworth keeps a key to it and pops in and out just whenever the fancy takes him. He went through all my friend's private papers one day without so much as by your leave and his boy goes in and takes apples out of the garden, pinched a pint of milk once. I could tell you things about Bob Rushworth as'd make . . .'

'I think you've told me enough, Harry,' said Wexford. Without extending the usual invitation to lunch, without even looking at Burden again, he swung out of the police station the way he had come.

Because he was sure that if he went to the Carousel Burden would only follow him and ruin his lunch with mealy-mouthed excuses. Wexford drove home and surprised his wife, who seldom saw him between nine and six, with a peremptory demand for food. He couldn't remember when he had last been in such a bad temper. Angry-looking black veins were standing out on his temples and this alarmed him so that he took two anti-coagulant tablets with the beer Mrs Wexford produced off the ice. Burden ought to know better than to upset him like that. Fine thing if he ended up like poor old Scott.

Somewhat calmer by three o'clock, he drove off to see Mrs Thetford. According to a neighbour, she was out at her job of cleaning for Mrs Dean. Wexford hung about till she got back and saw no reason to refuse her offer of a cup of tea and a piece of fruit cake. The Rushworths were both out all day, anyway, and he wanted to see them together rather than endure another interview with Rushworth in his estate agent's office, their conversation constantly interrupted by phone calls from clients.

But tea and cake were all he got out of Mrs Thetford. She repeated the story he had already heard from her husband. Mrs Dean had given her the news about John Lawrence at five o'clock but she declared she had passed it on to no one except her husband and her brother-in-law.

He drove slowly up the lane and entered Sparta Grove. Lomax's patient, Mrs Foster, was his only hope now. She must have told someone what she had overheard at the doctor's. Or been overheard herself? It was a possibility, perhaps the only one remaining. Number 14 was her house. Wexford parked outside it and then he saw the boy. He was swinging on the gate of the house next door, number 16, and his rather long hair was bright gold.

By now all the children were home from school and Sparta Grove was full of them. Wexford beckoned to a girl of about twelve and she approached the car suspiciously.

'I'm not supposed to talk to strange men.'

'Very proper,' said Wexford. 'I'm a policeman.'

'You don't look like one. Show me your warrant card.'

'By gum, you'll go far if you don't come to a bad end.' He produced his card and the child scrutinised it with huge delight. 'Satisfied?'

'Mmm.' She grinned. 'I learnt how to do that off the telly.'

'Very educational, the telly. I wonder they bother to keep the schools open. You see that boy with the fair hair? Where does he live?'

'Where he is. That house he's on the gate of.'

Ungrammatical but explanatory. 'You needn't tell him I was asking.' Wexford produced a coin which he knew he wouldn't get back out of expenses.

'What shall I say, then?'

'Come, come. You're a resourceful girl. Say I was a strange man.'

Now was not the time. He must wait until all the children were in bed. When the Piebald Pony opened he went into the saloon bar and ordered sandwiches and half a bitter. Any minute now, he thought, Monkey and Mr Casaubon would come in. Delighted to see him in their local, they would try to ascertain how near they were to getting their hands on that two thousand, and it would give him much pleasure to tell them they had never been farther from it. He would even be indiscreet and reveal his innermost conviction, that Swan was guiltless of any crime but that of indifference.

But nobody came. It was seven when Wexford left the

158

Piebald Pony and walked three-quarters of the length of quiet, dimly-lit Sparta Grove.

He tapped on the door of number 16. No lights showed. Every one of those children must now be safely in bed. In this house the golden-headed boy would be sleeping. From the look of the place—no blue-white glow of a television screen showed behind the drawn curtains—his parents had gone out and left him alone. Wexford had a low opinion of parents who did that, especially now, especially here. He knocked again, harder this time.

To a sensitive astute person an empty house has a different feel from a house which simply appears to be empty but which, in reality, contains someone who is unwilling to answer a door. Wexford sensed that there was life somewhere in that darkness, conscious tingling life, not just a sleeping child. Someone was there, a tense someone, listening to the sound of the knocker and hoping the knocks would cease and the caller go away. He made his way carefully through the side entrance and round to the back. The Fosters' house next door was well lit but all the doors and windows were shut. A yellow radiance from Mrs Foster's kitchen showed him that number 16 was a well-kept house, its path swept and its back doorstep polished red. The little boy's tricycle and a man's bike leaned against the wall and both were covered by a ·sheet of transparent plastic.

He hammered on the back door with his fist. Silence. Then he tried the handle very stealthily, but the door was locked. No getting in here without a warrant, he thought, and there was no hope of getting one on the meagre evidence he had.

Treading softly, he began to move round to the back of the house, feeling moist turf under his feet. Then, suddenly, a flare of light caught him from behind and he heard Mrs Foster say, as audibly as if she were standing beside his ear, 'You won't forget to put the bin out, will you, dear? We don't want to miss the dustmen two weeks running.'

Just as he thought. Every word spoken in the garden of number 14 could be heard in this garden. Mrs Foster hadn't seen him. He waited until she had retreated into her kitchen before moving on.

Then he saw it, a thin shaft of light, narrower than the beam from a pencil torch stretching across the grass from a french window. Tiptoeing, he approached the source of this light, a tiny gap between drawn curtains.

It was difficult to see anything at all. Then he saw that right in the middle of the window the edge of the curtain had been caught up on a bolt. He squatted down but still he couldn't see in. There was nothing for it but to lie down flat. Thank God there was no one to see him or observe how hard he found it to perform what should have been one of man's most natural actions.

Flat on his belly now, he got one eye up against the un-curtained triangle. The room unfolded itself before him. It was small and neat and conventionally furnished by a house-proud wife with a red three-piece suite, a nest of tables, wax gladioli and carnations whose petals were wiped each day with a damp cloth.

The man who sat writing at a desk was quite relaxed now and intent on his task. The importunate caller had gone away at last and left him to the special peace and privacy he de-manded. It would show in his face, Wexford thought, that concentration, that terrible solitary egotism, but he couldn't see his face, only the bare legs and feet, and sense the man's rapt absorption. He suspected that under the fur coat he wore he was quite naked.

Wexford watched him for some minutes, watched him pause occasionally in his writing and pass the thick furry sleeve across nose and mouth. It made him shiver, for he knew he was eavesdropping on something more private than secret speech or love-making or the confessional. This man was not alone with himself, but alone with his other self, a separate personality which perhaps no one else had ever seen until now.

To witness this phenomenon, this intense private fantasis-ing in a room which epitomised conformity, seemed to Wex-ford an outrageous intrusion. Then he remembered those fruitless trysts in the forest and Gemma Lawrence's hope and despair. Anger drove out shame. He pulled himself on to his feet and rapped hard on the glass.

19

IN his anxiety to reach the lift, Burden shoved Harry Wild out of the way.

'Manners,' said the reporter. 'There's no need to push. I've a right to come in here and ask questions if I . . .'

The sliding door cut off the rest of his remarks which would perhaps have been to the effect that, but for his modesty and fondness for the quiet life, he would have been exercising his rights in loftier portals than those of Kingsmarkham police station. Burden didn't want to hear. He only wanted Harry's statement, that they had found the boy, confirmed or denied.

'What's this about a special court?' he demanded, bursting into Wexford's office.

The chief inspector looked tired this morning. When he was tired his skin took on a grey mattness and his eyes looked smaller than ever, but still steel-bright, under the puffy lids.

'Last night,' he said. 'I found our letter-writer, a certain Arnold Charles Bishop.'

'But not the boy?' Burden said breathlessly.

'Of course not the boy.' Burden didn't like it when Wexford sneered like that. His eyes seemed to be drilling two neat holes into the inspector's already aching head. 'He's never even seen the boy. I found him at his home in Sparta Grove where he was occupied in writing another letter to me. His wife was out at her evening class, his children were in bed. Oh, yes, he has children, two boys. It was from the head of one of them that he cut the hair while the kid was asleep.'

'Oh God,' said Burden.

'He's a fur fetishist. Want me to read his statement?'

Burden nodded.

' "I have never seen John Lawrence or his mother. I did not take him away from the care of his mother, his legal

161

guardian. On October 16, at about 6 p.m., I overheard my neighbour, Mrs Foster, tell her husband that John Lawrence was missing and that search parties would probably be arranged. I went to Fontaine Road on my bicycle and joined one of these search parties.

' "On three subsequent occasions in October and November I wrote three letters to Chief Inspector Wexford. I did not sign them. I made one telephone call to him. I do not know why I did these things. Something came over me and I had to do them. I am a happily married man with two children of my own. I would never harm a child and I do not own a car. When I wrote about the rabbits I did this because I like fur. I have three fur coats but my wife does not know this. She knows nothing of what I have done. When she goes out and the children are asleep I often put one of my coats on and feel the fur.

' "I read in the paper that Mrs Lawrence had red hair and John Lawrence fair hair. I cut a piece of hair from the head of my son Raymond and sent it to the police. I cannot explain why I did this or any of it except by saying that I had to do it." '

Burden said hoarsely, 'The maximum he can get is six months for obstructing the police.'

'Well, what would you charge him with? Mental torture? The man's sick. I was angry too last night, but not any more. Unless you're a brute or a moron you can't be angry with a man who's going through life with a sickness as grotesque as Bishop's.'

Burden muttered something about it being all right for those who weren't personally involved, but Wexford ignored it. 'Coming over to the court in about half an hour?'

'To go through all that muck again?'

'A great deal of our work consists of muck, as you call it. Clearing muck, cleaning up, learning what muck is and where it lives.' Wexford rose and leaned heavily on his desk. 'If you don't come, what are you going to do? Sit here mooning all day? Delegating? Passing the buck? Mike, I have to say this. It's time I said it. I'm tired. I'm trying to solve this case all on my own because I can't count on you any more. I can't talk to you. We used to thrash things out together, sift

162

the muck, if you like. Talking to you now—well, its like trying to have a rational conversation with a zombie.'

Burden looked up at him. For a moment Wexford thought he wasn't going to answer or defend himself. He just stared, a dead empty stare, as if he had been interrogated for many days and many sleepless nights and could no longer sort out the painful twisted threads that contributed to his unhappiness. But he knew, for all that, that the time for fobbing Wexford off was long gone by, and he brought it all out in a series of clipped sentences.

'Grace is leaving me. I don't know what to do about the kids. My personal life's a mess. I can't do my job.' A cry he hadn't meant to utter broke out. 'Why did she have to die?' And then, because he couldn't help himself, because tears which no one must see were burning his eyelids, he sank his head into his hands.

The room was very still. Soon I must lift my head, Burden thought, and take away my hands and see his derision. He didn't move except to press his fingers harder against his eyes. Then he felt Wexford's heavy hand on his shoulder.

'Mike, my dear old friend ...'

An emotional scene between two normally unemotional men usually has its aftermath of deep miserable embarrassment. When Burden had recovered he felt very embarrassed, but Wexford neither blustered heartily nor made one of those maladroit efforts to change the subject.

'You're due to be off this weekend, aren't you, Mike?'

'How can I take time off now?'

'Don't be a bloody fool. You're worse than useless the state you're in. Make it a long weekend, starting on Thursday.'

'Grace is taking the children down to Eastbourne ...'

'Go with them. See if you can't make her change her mind about leaving. There are ways, Mike, aren't there? And now —my God, look at the time!—I'll be late for the court if I don't get cracking.'

Burden opened the window and stood by it, letting the thin morning mist cool his face. It seemed to him that with the arrest of Bishop their last hope—or his last fear?—of find-

163

ing John Lawrence had gone. He wouldn't disturb Gemma with it and she had never read the local papers. The mist, floating white and translucent, washed him gently and calmed him. He thought of the mist by the seaside and the long bare beaches, deserted in November. Once there, he would tell the children and Grace and his mother-in-law about Gemma, that he was to be married again.

He wondered why the idea of this chilled him more than the cold touch of the autumnal air. Because she was the strangest successor to Jean he could have picked in all his world? In the past he had marvelled at men who, in their selflessness or their temporary infatuation, marry crippled or blind women. Wasn't he contemplating doing just that, marrying a woman who was crippled in her heart and her personality? And that was the only way he knew her. How would she be if her deformity were healed?

Ludicrously, monstrous, to think of Gemma as deformed. Tenderly and with an ache of longing, he recalled her beauty and their lovemaking. Then, closing the window sharply, he knew he wouldn't be going down to Eastbourne with Grace.

Bishop was remanded for a medical report. The head-shrinkers would get to work on him, Wexford thought. Maybe that would do some good, more likely it wouldn't. If he had had any faith in psychiatrists he would have recommended Burden to attend one. Still, their recent confrontation had done something to clear the air. Wexford felt the better for it and he hoped Burden did too. Now, at any rate, he was out on his own. Single-handed he must find the children's killer—or fall back on the Yard.

The events of the past twenty-four hours had distracted his mind from Mr and Mrs Rushworth. Now he considered them again. Rushworth was in the habit of wearing a duffel coat, Rushworth was suspected of molesting a child, but surely, if he had been the loiterer in the swings field, Mrs Mitchell would have recognised him as one of her neighbours? Moreover, at the time of John's disappearance, every man within a quarter-mile radius of Fontaine Road had been closely investigated, Rushworth included.

Wexford delved once more among the reports. On the afternoon of October 16th Rushworth claimed to have been in Sewingbury where he had a date to show a client over a house. The client, Wexford saw, hadn't turned up. Back in February Rushworth hadn't even been questioned. Why should he have been? Nothing pointed to a connection between him and Stella Rivers and no one knew then that he was the owner of the rented cottage in Mill Lane. At the time the ownership of that cottage had seemed irrelevant.

He wouldn't see Rushworth yet. First he needed enlightenment as to the man's character and veracity.

'To get away from this house!' Gemma said. 'Just to get away for a little while.' She put her arms round Burden's neck and clung to him. 'Where shall we go?'

'You decide.'

'I'd like London. You can lose yourself there, be just one in a lovely enormous crowd. And there are lights all night and things going on and . . .' She paused, biting her lip, perhaps at the look of horror on Burden's face. 'No, you'd hate it. We aren't much alike, are we, Mike?'

He didn't answer that. He wasn't going to admit it aloud. 'Why not somewhere on the coast?' he said.

'The sea?' She had been an actress, if not a very successful one, and she put all the loneliness and depth and vastness of the sea into those two words. He wondered why she had shivered. Then she said, 'I don't mind if you'd like to. But not to a big resort where you might see—well, families, people with—with children.'

'I thought of Eastover. It's November, so there won't be children.'

'All right.' She didn't point out to him that he had asked her to decide. 'We'll go to Eastover.' Her lips trembled. 'It'll be fun,' she said.

'Everyone will think I've gone to Eastbourne with Grace and the children. I'd rather it was that way.'

'So that they can't get hold of you?' She nodded with a kind of sage innocence. 'I see. You remind me of Leonie. She always tells people she's going to one place when really she's going somewhere else so that she won't be badgered with letters and phone calls.'

'It wasn't that,' Burden said. 'It's just—well, I don't want anyone . . . Not until we're married, Gemma.'

She smiled, wide-eyed and uncomprehending. He saw that she really didn't understand him at all, his need to be respectable, to put a good face on things. They didn't speak the same language.

It was Wednesday afternoon, and Mrs Mitchell, that creature of routine, was cleaning her landing window. While she talked she clutched a pink duster in one hand and a bottle of pink cleaning fluid in the other and, because she refused to sit down, Wexford couldn't either.

'Of course I should have known if it was Mr Rushworth,' she said. 'Why, his own little boy, his Andrew, was playing there with the others. Besides, Mr Rushworth's quite a big man and the man I saw was little, very small-made. I told the other officer what little hands he had. Mr Rushworth wouldn't pick leaves.'

'How many children has he?'

'Four. There's Paul—he's fifteen—and two little girls and Andrew. I'm not saying they're my idea of good parents, mind. Those children are allowed to do just what they please, and Mrs Rushworth didn't take a blind bit of notice when I warned her about that man, but do a thing like that . . . ! No, you've got the wrong end of the stick there.'

Perhaps he had. Wexford left Mrs Mitchell to her window-cleaning and crossed the swings field. The year was far too advanced now for any children to play there and there would be no more freak summers. The roundabout looked as if it had never spun on its scarlet axis and mould had begun to grow on the seesaw. Hardly a leaf remained on the trees, oak and ash and sycamore, which grew between the field and Mill Lane. He touched the lower branches and fancied that here and there he could see where a twig had been snapped off. Then, in a more ungainly fashion, he was sure, than the leaf-picker and his young companion, he scrambled down the bank.

Briskly he walked the length of the lane, telling himself it was as much for his health's sake as for duty. He hadn't expected to find anyone at home in the rented cottage but

Harry Wild's friend was off work with a cold. Leaving again after a quarter of an hour, Wexford was afraid his visit had only served to raise the man's temperature, so heated had he been on the subject of Rushworth, a far from ideal landlord. Unless the tenant's account was exaggerated, it appeared that the whole Rushworth family was in the habit of entering the cottage, helping themselves to garden produce and occasionally removing small pieces of furniture for which they substituted pencilled notes of explanation. They had retained a key of their own and the tenant paid so low a rent that he was afraid to expostulate. At any rate, Wexford now knew the identity of the boy who had been seen leaving the cottage that February afternoon. Beyond a doubt, it had been Paul Rushworth.

The day had been dull and overcast and now evening was closing in, although it was scarcely five. Wexford felt a first few drops of rain. On just such a day and at much this time Stella had followed the road he was taking, quickening her steps perhaps, wishing she had more to protect her than a thin riding jacket. Or had she even come so far back towards Stowerton? Had her journey—and her life—taken her no further than the cottage he had just left?

He had immersed himself so much in Stella, mentally transmuting his own elderly, male and stout body into the slight form of a twelve-year-old girl, that when he heard the sounds ahead of him he stepped back on to the grass verge and listened with a kind of hope.

The sounds were of horse's hooves. A horse was coming round the bend in the lane.

He was Stella, not old Reg Wexford. He was alone and a bit frightened and it was beginning to rain, but Swan was coming . . . On a *horse*? One horse for two people? Why not in a car?

The horse and its rider came into sight. Wexford shook himself back into himself and called out. 'Good afternoon, Mrs Fenn.'

The riding instructress reined in the big grey. 'Isn't he lovely?' she said. 'I wish he was mine, but I've got to take him back to Miss Williams at Equita. We've had such a nice afternoon out, haven't we, Silver?' She patted the animal's neck. 'You haven't—er—caught anyone yet? The man who killed poor Stella Swan?'

Wexford shook his head.

'Stella *Rivers*, I should say. I don't know why I find it so confusing. After all, I've got two names myself and half my friends call me Margaret and half by my second name. I ought not to get mixed up. Must be getting old.'

Wexford felt no inclination for gallantry and simply asked if she had ever seen Rushworth in the grounds of Saltram House.

'Bob Rushworth? Now you come to mention it, he and his wife were up here a lot last winter and she actually asked me if I thought it would be all right for them to take one of the statues away with them. The one that was lying down in the grass, you know.'

'You said nothing about this before.'

'Well, of *course* not,' said Mrs Fenn, bending over to coo into the horse's ear. 'I *know* the Rushworths, I've known them for years. Paul calls me auntie. I suppose they wanted the statue for their garden. It's not my place to say whether you can have it or you can't, I said.' She edged herself more comfortably into the saddle. 'If you'll excuse me I must be on my way. Silver's very highly bred and he gets nervous when it's dark.' The horse lifted its head and emitted a loud whinny of agreement. 'Never mind, darling,' said Mrs Fenn. 'Soon be home with Mother.'

Wexford went on. The rain was falling thinly but steadily. He passed Saltram Lodge and entered that part of the lane which was most thickly overshadowed by trees. They thinned out after two or three hundred yards to disclose the celebrated view of the great house.

The parkland looked grey and the house itself, looming through mist, a black skeleton with empty eye-sockets. Wexford was glad he had never known the place or been in the habit of visiting it. To him it had become a graveyard.

20

HE hadn't been able to bring himself to book a double room for Mr and Mrs Burden. One day Gemma would be Mrs Burden and then it would be different. In the meantime the name was Jean's. Jean held the title like a champion whose honours cannot be taken from her by death.

Their hotel was Eastover village pub which had been extended since the war to accommodate half a dozen guests, and they had been given rooms side by side, both overlooking the wide grey sea. It was too cold for bathing, but there are always children on beaches. While Gemma unpacked, Burden watched the children, five of them, brought down there to play by their parents. The tide was far out and the beach a silvery ochre, the sand packed too tight and flattened too firmly by the sea to show footprints from this distance. The man and the woman walked far apart from each other, seeming entirely detached. Married for many years, Burden supposed—the eldest girl looked at least twelve—they had no need of contact or of reassurance. The children, running from one to the other, then wheeling towards the sea, were evidence enough of love. He saw the parents, separated now by a wide drift of shells and pebbles, glance casually at each other and in that glance he read a secret language of mutual trust and hope and profound understanding.

One day it would be like that for him and Gemma. They would bring their children, his and *theirs*, to such a beach as this and walk with them between the water and the sky and remember their nights and days and look forward to the night. He turned quickly to tell her what he was thinking but suddenly it came to him that he mustn't tell her, he couldn't because to do so would be to draw her attention to the children.

'What is it, Mike?'

'Nothing. I only wanted to say that I love you.'

He closed the window and drew the curtains, but in the half-dark he could still see the children. He took her in his arms and closed his eyes and still he could see them. Then he made love to her violently and passionately to exorcise the children and, in particular, the little fair-haired boy whom he had never seen but who was more real to him than those he had watched on the seashore.

The weekenders' cottage was very ancient, built before the Civil War, before the departure of the *Mayflower*, perhaps even before the last of the Tudors. Rushworth's was newer, though still old, belonging, Wexford decided, to the same period as that of Saltram House and its lodge, about 1750. In Burden's absence he was spending much of his time in Mill Lane, viewing the three little houses, sometimes entering their gardens and walking thoughtfully around them.

Once he walked from Rushworth's cottage to the fountains at Saltram House and back again, timing himself. It took him half an hour. Then he did it again, pausing this time to play-act the lifting of the cistern slab and the insertion of a body. Forty minutes.

He drove to Sewingbury and saw the woman who had a date to meet Rushworth on that October afternoon and heard from her that she had been unable to keep the appointment. What of that other afternoon in February?

One evening he made his way to Fontaine Road in search of the Crantocks and on an impulse knocked first at number 61. He had nothing to say to Mrs Lawrence, no good news, but he was curious to see this forlorn woman people said was beautiful and he knew from past experience that his very presence, stolid and fatherly, could sometimes be a comfort. No one answered his knock and this time he sensed quite a different atmosphere from that he had felt outside Bishop's door. Nobody answered because there was nobody there to hear.

For some moments he stood thoughtfully in the quiet street, and then, discomfited now for personal reasons, he went next door to the Crantocks.

'If you wanted Gemma,' said Mrs Crantock, 'she's away, gone down to the South Coast for the weekend.'

'I really want to talk to you and your husband. About a man called Rushworth and your daughter.'

'Oh, that? Your inspector kindly saw her home. We *were* grateful. Mind you, there was nothing in it. I know they say Mr Rushworth chases the girls, but I expect that's just gossip, and they don't mean *little* girls. My daughter's only fourteen.'

Crantock came into the hall to see who had called. He recognised Wexford immediately and shook hands. 'As a matter of fact,' he said, 'Rushworth came round the next day to apologise. He said he'd only called out to Janet because he'd heard we'd got a piano we wanted to get rid of.' Crannock grinned and turned up his eyes. 'I told him *sell*, not get rid of, so, of course, he wasn't interested.'

'Silly of Janet, really,' said his wife, 'to have got so worked up.'

'I don't know.' Crantock had stopped smiling. 'We're all on edge, especially kids who are old enough to understand.' He looked deep into Wexford's eyes. 'And people with kids,' he added.

Wexford walked into Chiltern Avenue by way of the shrub-shadowed alley. There he had to use his torch and as he went he thought, not by any means for the first time, on his great good fortune in having been born a man, and a big man at that, instead of a woman. Only in daylight and fine weather could a woman have walked there without fear, without turning her head and feeling her heart-beats quicken. No wonder Janet Crantock had been frightened. And then he thought of John Lawrence whose youth had given him a woman's vulnerability and who would never grow up to be a man.

In the evenings when the tide was far out they walked along the sands in the dark or sat on the rocks at the entrance to a cave they had found. The rain held off, but it was November and cold at night. The first time they went there they wore thick coats but the heavy clothing separated and isolated them, so after that Burden brought the car rug. They

171

cocooned themselves in it, their bodies pressed together, their hands tightly clasped, the thick woollen folds enclosing them and keeping out the salty sea wind. When he was alone with her in the darkness on the seashore he was very happy.

Even at this time of the year Eastbourne would be crowded and she was afraid of people. So they avoided the big resort and even the next village, Chine Warren. Gemma had visited the place before and wanted to walk there, but Burden prevented her. It was from there, he believed, that the children came. He tried all the time to keep children out of her sight. Sometimes, pitying her for her sorrow yet jealous of the cause of it, he found himself wishing a modern Pied Piper would come and whistle away all the little children of Sussex so that they might not be there to laugh and play and torment her and deprive him of joy.

'Would it be a quick death, the sea?' she said.

He shivered, watching the running tide. 'I don't know. Nobody who has died in it has ever been able to tell us.'

'I think it would be quick.' Her voice was a child's, gravely considering. 'Cold and clean and quick.'

In the afternoons Burden made love to her—he had never been more conscious of and more satisfied with his manhood than when he saw how his love comforted her—and afterwards, while she slept, he walked down to the shore or over the cliff to Chine Warren. There was still a little warmth left in the sunshine and the children came to build sandcastles. He had discovered that they were not a family, the couple not husband and wife, but that four of the children belonged to the man and the other one to the woman. How teasing and deceptive were first impressions! He looked back now with self-disgust on his romancing, his sentimental notion that this pair, known to each other perhaps only by sight, had an idyllic marriage. Illusion and disillusion, he reflected, what life is and what we think it is. Why, from this distance he couldn't even tell if the solitary child were a boy or a girl, for it was capped and trousered and booted like all the children.

The woman kept stooping down to collect shells and once she stumbled. When she stood up again he noticed that she dragged her leg and he wondered if he should go down the seaweedy steps and cross the sands to offer her his help. But

172

perhaps that would mean bringing her back to the hotel while he fetched his car, and the sound of the child's voice would awaken Gemma. . . .

They rounded the foot of the cliff, going towards Chine Warren. Receding fast, the tide seemed to be drawing the sea back into the heart of the red sunset, a November sunset which is the most lovely of the whole year.

Now the great wide sweep of beach was deserted, but its young visitors had left evidence behind them. As sure as he could be that he was unobserved, Burden walked down the steps, pretending to stroll casually. The two sandcastles stood proudly erect, as if confident of their endurance until the sea conquered them, rushing them away when it returned at midnight. He hesitated, the rational sensible man momentarily intervening, and then he kicked over their turrets and stamped on their battlements until the sand they were made of was as flat as the surrounding shore.

Once more the beach belonged to him and Gemma. John or his deputies, his representatives, should not take her away from him. He was a man and any day a match for a lost dead child.

Rushworth came to the door in his duffel coat.

'Oh, it's you,' he said. 'I was just going to take the dog out.'

'Postpone it for half an hour, will you?'

Not very willingly, Rushworth took off his coat, hung up the lead and led Wexford into a living room amid the cries of the disappointed terrier. Two teenage children were watching television, a girl of about eight sat at the table doing a jigsaw puzzle, and on the floor, lying on his stomach, was the most junior member of the family, Andrew, who had been John Lawrence's friend.

'I'd like to talk to you alone,' said Wexford.

It was a biggish house with what Rushworth, in one of his house agent's blurbs, would perhaps have described as three reception rooms. That evening none was fit for the reception of anyone except possibly a second-hand-furniture dealer. The Rushworths were apparently acquisitive creatures, snappers up of anything they could get for nothing, and Wexford, seating himself in this morning room-cum-study-cum-library, observed a set of Dickens he had surely last seen in Pomfret Grange before the Rogerses sold out and two stone urns whose design seemed very much in keeping with the other garden ornaments of Saltram House.

'I've racked my brains and I can't tell you another thing about the fellows in that search party.'

'I've not come about that,' said Wexford. 'Did you pinch those urns from Saltram House?'

' "Pinch" is a bit strong,' said Rushworth, turning red. 'They were lying about and no one wanted them.'

'You had your eye on one of the statues too, didn't you?'

'What's this got to do with John Lawrence?'

Wexford shrugged. 'I don't know. It might have something to do with Stella Rivers. To put it in a nutshell, I'm here to know where you were and what you were doing on February 25th.'

'How can I remember that far back? I know what it is, it's Margaret Fenn putting you up to all this. Just because I complained my girl wasn't doing as well as she should at her riding lessons.' Rushworth opened the door and shouted, 'Eileen!'

When she wasn't at work, typing specifications for her husband, Mrs Rushworth managed this sprawling household single-handed and it showed. She looked dowdy and harassed and her skirt hem was coming down at the back. Perhaps there was some foundation in the gossip that her husband chased the girls.

'Where were you that Thursday?' she enquired of him. 'In the office, I suppose. I know where I was. I got it all sorted out in my mind when there was all that fuss about Stella Rivers being missing. It was half-term and I'd taken Andrew to work with me. He came with me in the car to pick Linda up from Equita and—oh, yes—Paul—that's my eldest—he came too and dropped off at the cottage. There was a little table there we thought we might as well have here. But we didn't see Stella. I didn't even know her by sight.'

'Your husband was in the office when you got back?'

'Oh, yes. He waited for me to get back before he went out in the car.'

174

'What kind of a car, Mr Rushworth?'

'Jaguar. Maroon colour. Your people have already been all over my car on account of its being a Jaguar and a kind of red colour. Look, we didn't know Stella Rivers. As far as we know, we'd never even seen her. Until she disappeared I'd only heard of her through Margaret always going on about how marvellous she was on a horse.'

Wexford favoured them with a hard, unsympathetic stare. He was thinking deeply, fitting in puzzle pieces, casting aside irrelevancies.

'You,' he said to Rushworth, 'were at work when Stella disappeared. When John disappeared you were in Sewingbury waiting for a client who never turned up.' He turned to Mrs Rushworth. 'You were at work when John disappeared. When Stella vanished you were driving back from Equita along Mill Lane. Did you pass anyone?'

'Nobody,' said Mrs Rushworth firmly. 'Paul was still in the cottage. I know that—he'd put a light on—and, well, I'd better be quite frank with you. He'd actually been in Margaret Fenn's place too. I'm sure he had because the front door was open, just a little bit ajar. I know he shouldn't, though she does always leave her back door unlocked and when he was little she used to say he could let himself in and see her whenever he liked. Of course, it's different now he's so old, and I've told him again and again . . .'

'Never mind,' Wexford said suddenly. 'It doesn't matter.'

'If you wanted to talk to Paul . . . I mean, if it would clear the air . . . ?'

'I don't want to see him.' Wexford got up abruptly. He didn't want to see anyone at all. He knew the answer. It had begun to come to him when Rushworth called out to his wife and now nothing remained but to sit down somewhere in utter silence and work it all out.

21

'OUR last day,' said Burden. 'Where would you like to go? Shall we have a quiet drive somewhere and lunch in a pub?'

'I don't mind. Anything you say.' She took his hand, held it against her face for a moment, and burst out, as if she had kept the words inside her, burning and corroding for many hours, 'I've got a dreadful feeling, a sort of premonition, that when we get back we'll hear that they've found him.'

'John?'

'And—and the man who killed him,' she whispered.

'They'd let us know.'

'They don't know where we are, Mike. No one knows.'

Slowly and evenly he said, 'It will be better for you when you know it for sure. Terrible pain is better than terrible anxiety.' But was it? Was it better for him to know that Jean was dead than to fear she would die? Terrible anxiety always contains terrible hope. 'Better for you,' he said firmly. 'And then, when it's behind you, you can start your new life.'

'Let's go,' she said. 'Let's go out.'

It was Saturday and still no one had been charged.

'There's an uneasy sort of lull about this place,' said Harry Wild to Camb. 'Quite a contrast to all the activity of yore.'

'My what?' said Camb.

'Your nothing. *Yore.* Days gone by.'

'No good asking me. Nobody ever tells me anything.'

'Life,' said Wild, 'is passing us by, old man. Trouble with us is we've not been ambitious. We've been content to sport with Amaryllis in the shade.'

Camb looked shocked. 'Speak for yourself,' he said, and then, softening, 'Shall I see if there's any tea going?'

176

Late in the afternoon Dr Crocker breezed into Wexford's office. 'Very quiet, aren't we? I hope that means you'll be free for golf in the morning.'

'Don't feel like golf,' said Wexford. 'Can't, anyway.'

'Surely you're not going to Colchester *again*?'

'I've been. I went this morning. Scott's dead.'

The doctor pranced over to the window and opened it. 'You need some fresh air in here. Who's Scott?'

'You ought to know. He was your patient. He had a stroke and now he's had another. Want to hear about it?'

'Why would I? People are always having strokes. I've just come from an old boy down in Charteris Road who's had one. Why would I want to know about this Scott?' He came closer to Wexford and bent critically over him. 'Reg?' he said. 'Are you all right? My God, I'm more concerned that you *shouldn't* have one. You look rotten.'

'It *is* rotten. But not for me. For me it's just a problem.' Wexford got up suddenly. 'Let's go down the Olive.'

There was no one else in the lush, rather over-decorated cocktail bar.

'I'd like a double Scotch.'

'And you shall have one,' said Crocker. 'For once I'll go so far as to prescribe it.'

Briefly Wexford thought of that other humbler hostelry where Monkey and Mr Casaubon had both disgusted him and whetted his appetite. He pushed them from his mind as the doctor returned with their drinks.

'Thanks. I wish your tablets came in such a palatable form. Cheers.'

'Good health,' said Crocker meaningfully.

Wexford leaned back against the red-velvet upholstery of the settle. 'All the time,' he began, 'I thought it must be Swan, although there didn't seem to be any motive. And then, when I got all that stuff from Monkey and Mr Casaubon and the more accurate stuff about the inquest, I thought I could see a motive, simply that Swan got rid of people who got in his way. That would imply madness, of course. So what? The world is full of ordinary people with lunacy underlying their ordinariness. Look at Bishop.'

'What inquest?' Crocker asked.

Wexford explained. 'But I was looking at it from the wrong way round,' he said, 'and it took me a long time to look at it the right way.'

'Let's have the right way, then.'

'First things first. When a child disappears one of the first things we consider is that he or she was picked up by a car. Another disservice done to the world by the inventor of the internal-combustion engine, or did kids once get abducted in carriages? But I mustn't digress. Now we knew it was very unlikely Stella accepted a lift in a car because she had *already refused the lift we knew had been offered to her.* Therefore it was probable that she was either met and taken somewhere by someone she knew, such as her mother, her stepfather or Mrs Fenn, or that she went into one of the houses in Mill Lane.'

The doctor sipped his sherry austerely. 'There are only three,' he said.

'Four, if you count Saltram House. Swan had no real alibi. He could have ridden to Mill Lane, taken Stella into the grounds of Saltram House on some pretext, and killed her. Mrs Swan had no alibi. Contrary to my former belief, she *can* drive. She could have driven to Mill Lane. Monstrous as it is to think of a woman killing her own child, I had to consider Rosalind Swan. She worships her husband obsessively. Was it possible, in her mind, that Stella, who also worshipped Swan—little girls seem to—would in a few years' time grow into a rival?'

'And Mrs Fenn?'

'Tidying up at Equita, she *said*. We had only her word for it. But even my inventive mind, twisted mind, if you like, couldn't see a motive there. Finally, I dismissed all those theories and considered the four houses.' Wexford lowered his voice slightly as a man and a girl entered the bar. 'Stella left Equita at twenty-five minutes to five. The first house she passed was the weekenders' cottage, but it was a Thursday and the cottage was empty. Besides, it dated from about 1550.'

Crocker looked astonished. 'What's that got to do with it?'

'You'll see in a minute. She went on and it began to rain.

178

At twenty to five the Forby bank manager stopped and offered her a lift. She refused. For once it would have been wise for a child to have accepted a lift from a strange man.' The newcomers had found seats by a far window and Wexford resumed his normal voice. 'The next cottage she came to is owned, though not occupied, by a man called Robert Rushworth who lives in Chiltern Avenue. Now Rushworth interested me very much. He knew John Lawrence, he wears a duffel coat, he has been suspected, perhaps with foundation, perhaps not, of molesting a child. His wife, though warned by Mrs Mitchell that a man had been seen observing the children in the swings field, did not inform the police. On the afternoon of February 25th he could have been in Mill Lane. His wife and his eldest son certainly were. All the family were in the habit of going into their cottage just when it pleased them—and Mrs Rushworth's Christian name is Eileen.'

The doctor stared blankly. 'I don't follow any of this. So what if her name is Eileen?'

'Last Sunday,' Wexford went on, 'I went down to Colchester to see Mr and Mrs Scott, the parents of Bridget Scott. At that time I had no suspicion at all of Rushworth. I simply had a forlorn hope that one or both of the Scotts might be able to give me a little more insight into the character of Ivor Swan. But Scott, as you know, is—was, I should say—a very sick man.'

'*I* should know?'

'Of course you should know,' said Wexford severely. 'Really, you're very slow.' Having for once the whip hand over his friend was cheering Wexford up. It was a pleasant change to see Crocker at a disadvantage. 'I was afraid to question Scott. I was uncertain what might be the effect of alarming him. Besides, for my purposes, it seemed adequate to work on his wife. She told me nothing which increased my knowledge of Swan, but, unwittingly, she gave me four pieces of information that helped me solve this case.' He cleared his throat. 'Firstly, she told me that she and her husband had been in the habit of staying for holidays with a relative who lived near Kingsmarkham and that they had stayed there for the last time last winter; secondly, that the relative lived in an eighteenth-century house; thirdly, that in March, *a fort-night after he had been taken ill,* her husband was a very sick man indeed; fourthly, that the relative's name was Eileen. Now, sometime in March might well be a fortnight after February 25th.' He paused significantly for all this to sink in.

The doctor put his head on one side. At last he said, 'I'm beginning to get this clear. My God, you'd hardly believe it, but people are a funny lot. It was with the Rushworths that the Scotts were staying, Eileen Rushworth was the relative. Scott somehow induced Rushworth to make away with Stella in revenge for what Swan had done to his own child. Offered him money, maybe. What a ghastly thing!'

Wexford sighed. It was at times like this that he most missed Burden, or Burden as he used to be. 'I think we'll have another drink,' he said. 'My round.'

'You don't have to act as if I was a complete fool,' said the doctor huffily. 'I'm not trained to make this sort of diagnosis.' As Wexford got up, he snapped vindictively, 'Orange juice for you, that's an order.'

With a glass of lager, not orange juice, before him, Wexford said, 'You're worse than Dr Watson, you are. And while we're on the subject, though I've the utmost respect for Sir Arthur, life isn't much like Sherlock Holmes stories and I don't believe it ever was. People don't nurse revenge for years and years nor do they find it possible to bribe more or less respectable estate agents, fathers of families, into doing murder for them.'

'But you said,' Crocker retorted, 'that the Scotts were staying with the Rushworths in their cottage.'

'No, I didn't. Use your head. How could they have been staying in a house that was let to another tenant? All that made me consider that house was that it dated from about 1750. I had forgotten all about the Scotts' relative being called Eileen—it was only mentioned in passing—but when I heard Rushworth call his wife Eileen, then I knew. After that I only had to do some simple checking.'

'I am so entirely in the dark,' said Crocker, 'that I don't know what to say.'

For a moment Wexford savoured the experience of seeing the doctor at a loss. Then he said, 'Eileen is a fairly common name. Why should Mrs Rushworth be its only possessor in the district? At that point I remembered that someone else had told me she had two Christian names, was called by the first by half people she knew and by the second by the rest. I didn't care to enquire of her personally. I checked with Somerset House. And there I found that Mrs Margaret *Eileen* Fenn was the daughter of one James Collins and his wife Eileen Collins, *née* Scott.

'Beyond a doubt, it was with Mrs Fenn that the Scotts had been staying in February, at Saltram Lodge which is also an eighteenth-century house. They stayed with her, and on February 25th, after saying good-bye to Mrs Fenn before she left for work at Equita, they too left by taxi to catch the three-forty-five train from Stowerton to Victoria.'

Crocker held up his hand to halt Wexford. 'I remember now. Of course I do. It was poor old Scott who had that stroke on the platform. I happened to be in the station, booking a seat, and they sent for me. But it wasn't at a quarter to four, Reg. More like six o'clock.'

'Exactly. Mr and Mrs Scott didn't catch the three-forty-five. When they got to the station Scott realised they had left one of their suitcases behind at Mrs Fenn's. You ought to know that. It was you who told me.'

'So I did.'

'Scott was a strong, hale man at that time. Or so he thought. There wasn't a taxi about—mind you I'm guessing this bit —and he decided to walk back to Mill Lane. It took him about three quarters of an hour. But that wouldn't have worried him. There wasn't another train that stopped at Stowerton till six-twenty-six. He had no difficulty in getting into the house, for Mrs Fenn always leaves her back door unlocked. Perhaps he made himself a cup of tea, perhaps he merely rested. We shall never know. We must now go back to Stella Rivers.'

'She called at Saltram Lodge?'

'Of course. It was the obvious place. She too knew about the unlocked back door and that Mrs Fenn, her friend and teacher, had a phone. It was raining, it was growing dark.

181

She went into the kitchen and immediately encountered Scott.'

'And Scott recognised her?'

'As Stella Rivers. Not knowing what her correct name was, Mrs Fenn spoke of her sometimes as Rivers, sometimes as Swan. And she would have spoken of her to Scott, her uncle, and pointed her out, for she was proud of Stella.

'As soon as she had got over her surprise at finding someone in the house, Stella must have asked to use the phone. What words did she use? Something like this, I fancy: "I'd like to phone my father"—she referred to Swan as her father —"Mr Swann of Hall Farm. When he comes, we'll drive you back to Stowerton." Now Scott hated the very name of Swan. He had never forgotten and he had always dreaded a chance meeting with him. He must then have checked with Stella that it was Ivor Swan to whom she referred and then he realised that here he was, face to face with the daughter—or so he thought—of the man who had left his own child to die when she was at the same age as this child.'

22

WHEN they came back to Eastover from their drive the sun
hadset, leaving long fiery streaks to split the purple
clouds and stain the sea with coppery gold. Burden pulled the
car into an empty parking place on the cliff-top and they sat
in silence, looking at the sea and the sky and at a solitary
trawler, a little moving smudge on the horizon.

Gemma had withdrawn more and more into herself as the
days had passed by and sometimes Burden felt that it was
a shadow who walked with him, went out with him in the car
and lay beside him at night. She hardly spoke. It was as if
she had become bereavement incarnate or, worse than that, a
dying woman. He knew she wanted to die, although she had
not directly told him so. The night before he had found her
lying in the bath in water that had grown cold, her eyes
closed and her head slipping down into the water, and, although she denied it, he knew she had taken sleeping tablets
half an hour before. And today, while they were on the
downs, he had only just succeeded in preventing her from
crossing the road in the path of an oncoming car.

Tomorrow they must go home. Within a month they would
be married and before that he would have to apply for a
transfer to one of the Metropolitan divisions. That meant
finding new schools for the children, a new house. What kind
of a house would he find in London for the price he would
get for his Sussex bungalow? But it must be done. The mean,
indefensible thought that at any rate he would only have two
children to support and not three, that in her state his wife
would not vex him with riotous parties or fill the place with
her friends, brought a blush of shame to his face.

He glanced tentatively at Gemma, but she was staring out

to sea. Then he too followed her gaze and saw that the beach was no longer deserted. Quickly he started the car, reversed across the turf and turned towards the road that led inland. He didn't look at her again, but he knew that she was weeping, the tears falling unchecked down those thin pale cheeks.

'Scott's first thought,' said Wexford after a pause, 'was probably just to leave her to it, flee back the way he had come away from these Swans. They say murder victims—but this wasn't really murder—are self-selected. Did Stella point out that it was pouring with rain, that he could have a lift? Did she say, "I'll just phone. He'll be here in a quarter of an hour"? Scott remembered it all then. He had never forgotten it. He must stop her using that phone and he got hold of her. No doubt she cried out. How he must have hated her, thinking he knew what she meant to the man he hated. I think it was this which gave him strength and made him hold her too tight, press his strong old hands too hard about her neck . . .'

The doctor said nothing, only staring the more intently at Wexford.

'It takes half an hour to walk from Rushworth's cottage to Saltram House and back again,' the chief inspector resumed. 'Less than that from Saltram Lodge. And Scott would have known about the fountains and the cisterns. He would have been interested in them. He was a plumbing engineer. He carried the dead child up to the Italian garden and put her in the cistern. Then he went back to the lodge and fetched his case. A passing motorist gave him a lift back to Stowerton. We may imagine what sort of a state he was in.'

'We know,' said Crocker quietly, 'he had a stroke.'

'Mrs Fenn knew nothing of it, nor did his wife. Last Wednesday he had another stroke and that killed him. I think— I'm afraid—that it was seeing me and guessing what I was that really killed him. His wife didn't understand the words he spoke to her before he died. She thought he was wandering in his mind. She told me what they were. "I held her too tight. I thought of my Bridget." '

'But what the hell are you going to do? You can't charge a dead man.'

'That's in Griswold's hands,' said Wexford. 'Some non-committal paragraph for the press, I suppose. The Swans have been told and Swan's uncle, Group Captain what's-his-name. Not that he'll need to pay up. We shan't be arresting anyone.'

The doctor looked thoughtful. 'You haven't said a word about John Lawrence.'

'Because I haven't a word to say,' said Wexford.

Their hotel had no rear entrance, so it was necessary to come at last out of the hinterland on to Eastover's little esplanade. Burden had been hoping with all his heart that by now, in the dusk, the beach would be empty of children, but the pair who had brought tears to Gemma's eyes were still there, the child that ran up and down at the water's edge and the woman who walked with him, trailing from one hand a long ribbon of seaweed. But for the slight limp, Burden wouldn't have recognised her, in her trousers and hooded coat, as the woman he had seen before, or indeed as a woman at all. Inanely, he tried to direct Gemma's gaze inland towards a cottage she had seen a dozen times before.

She obeyed him—she was always acquiescent, anxious to please—but no sooner had she looked than she turned again to face the sea. Her arm was touching his and he felt her shiver.

'Stop the car,' she said.

'But there's nothing to see . . .'

'Stop the car!'

She never commanded. He had never heard her speak like that before. 'What, here?' he said. 'Let's get back. You'll only get cold.'

'Please stop the car, Mike.'

He couldn't blind her, shelter her, for ever. He parked the car behind a red Jaguar that was the only other vehicle on the sea front. Before he had switched off the ignition she had got the door open, slammed it behind her and was off down the steps.

It was absurd to remember what she had said about the sea, about a quick death, but he remembered it. He jumped from the car and followed her, striding at first, then running.

185

Her bright hair, sunset red, streamed behind her. Their footsteps made a hard slapping sound on the sand and the woman turned to face them, standing stock still, the streamer of seaweed in her hand whirling suddenly in the wind like a dancer's scarf.

'Gemma! Gemma!' Burden called, but the wind took his words or else she was determined not to hear them. She seemed bent only on reaching the sea which curled and creamed at the child's feet. And now the child, who had been splashing in shallow foam to the top of his boots, also turned to stare, as children will when adults behave alarmingly.

She was going to throw herself into the sea. Ignoring the woman, Burden pounded after her and then he stopped suddenly as if, unseeing, he had flung himself against a solid wall. He was no more than ten feet from her. Wide-eyed, the child approached her. Without seeming to slacken her speed at all, without hesitation, she ran into the water and, in the water, fell on to her knees.

The little waves flowed over her feet, her legs, her dress. He saw it seep up, drenching her to the waist. He heard her cry out—miles away, he thought, that cry could have been heard—but he could not tell whether it brought him happiness or grief.

'John, John, my John!'

She threw out her arms and the child went into them. Still kneeling in the water, she held him in a close embrace, her mouth pressed hard against his bright golden hair.

Burden and the woman looked at each other without speaking. He knew at once who she was. That face had looked at him before from his daughter's scrapbook. But it was very ravaged now and very aged, the black hair under the hood chopped off raggedly as if, with the ruin of her career, she had submitted to and accelerated the ruin of her looks.

Her hands were tiny. It seemed that she collected specimens, botanical and marine, but now she dropped the ribbon of weed. Close to, Burden thought, no one could mistake her for a man—but at a distance? It occurred to him that from far away even a middle-aged woman might look like a youth if she were slight and had the litheness of a dancer.

186

What more natural than that she should want John, the child of her old lover who had never been able to give her a child? And she had been ill, mentally ill, he remembered. John would have gone with her, quite willingly, no doubt, recalling her as his father's friend, persuaded perhaps that his mother had temporarily committed him to her care. And to the seaside. What child doesn't want to go to the seaside?

But something would happen now. As soon as she got over her first joy, Gemma would tear this woman to pieces. It wasn't as if this was the first outrage Leonie West had committed against her. Hadn't she, when Gemma was only a few months married, virtually stolen her husband from her? And now, a more monstrous iniquity, she had stolen her child.

He watched her rise slowly out of the water and, still keeping hold of John's hand, begin to cross the strip of sand that separated her from Leonie West.

The dancer stood her ground, but she lifted her head with a kind of pathetic boldness and clenched the little hands Mrs Mitchell had seen picking leaves. Burden took a step forward and found his lost voice.

'Now listen, Gemma. The best thing is . . .'

What had he meant to say? That the best thing was for them all to keep calm, to discuss it rationally? He stared. Never would he have believed—had he ever really known her? —that she would do this, the best thing of all, the thing that, in his estimation, almost made a saint of her.

Her dress was soaked. Oddly, Burden thought of a picture he had once seen, an artist's impression of the sea giving up its dead. With a soft, tender glance at the boy, she dropped his hand and lifted Leonie West's instead. Speechless, the other woman looked at her, and then Gemma, hesitating only for a moment, took her into her arms.

23

'IT would never have worked, Mike. You know that as well as I do. I'm not conventional enough for you, not respectable, not good enough if you like.'

'I think you are too good for me,' said Burden.

'I did say once that John—if John was ever found I wouldn't marry you. I don't think you quite understood. It will be better for both of us if I do what we're planning and go and live with Leonie. She's so lonely, Mike, and I'm so dreadfully sorry for her. That way I can have London and my friends and she can have a share in John.'

They were sitting in the lounge of the hotel where they had stayed together. Burden thought she had never been so beautiful, her white skin glowing from her inner joy, her hair mantling her shoulders. And never so alien in the golden dress Leonie West had lent her because her own was ruined by salt water. Her face was sweeter and gentler than ever.

'But I love you,' he said.

'Dear Mike, are you sure you don't just love going to bed with me? Does that shock you?'

It did, but not so much, not nearly so much, as once it would have. She had taught him a multitude of things. She had given him his sentimental education.

'We can still be loving friends,' she said. 'You can come to me at Leonie's. You can meet all my friends. We can sometimes go away together and I'll be so different now I am happy. You'll see.'

He did see. He almost shuddered. Go to her with her child there? Explain somehow to his own children that he had a—a mistress?

'It would never work,' he said clearly and firmly. 'I can see it wouldn't.'

She looked at him very tenderly. ' "You'll court more women",' she said, half-singing, ' "and I'll couch with more men ..." '

He knew his Shakespeare no better than he knew his Proust. They went out on to the sea front where Leonie West was waiting with John in her red car.

'Come and say hallo to him,' said Gemma.

But Burden shook his head. No doubt it was better this way, no doubt he would one day be grateful to the child who had robbed him of his happiness and his love. But not now, not yet. One does not say hallo to an enemy and a thief.

She lingered under the esplanade lights, turning towards him and then back again to where John was. Torn two ways, they called it, he thought, but there was little doubt who had won this tug of war. That light in her eyes had never been there when they looked at him, was not there now, died as soon as she ceased to face the car. She was parting from him not with regret, not with pain, but with *politeness*.

Always considerate, always ready to respect another person's conventions—for they were in a public place and people were passing—she held out her hand to him. He took it, and then, no longer caring for those passers-by, forgetting his cherished respectability, he pulled her to him there in the open street and kissed her for the last time.

When the red car had gone he leant on the rail and looked at the sea and knew that it was better this way, knew too, because he had been through something like it before, that he would not go on wanting to die.

Wexford was genial and sly and almost godlike. 'What a fortunate coincidence that you happened to be in Eastbourne with Miss Woodville and happened to go to Eastover and happened—Good God, what a lot of happenings!—to meet Mrs Lawrence.' He added more gravely, 'On the whole, you have done well, Mike.'

Burden said nothing. He didn't think it necessary to point out that it was Gemma who had found the lost boy and not he.

Quietly, Wexford closed the door of his office and for a few moments regarded Burden in silence. Then he said, 'But

189

I don't much care for coincidences or for melodrama, come to that. I don't think they're in your line, do you?'

'Perhaps not, sir.'

'Are you going to go on doing well, Mike? I have to ask, I have to know. I have to know where to find you when you're needed and, when I find you, that you'll be your old self. Are you going to come back and work with me and—well, to put it bluntly—pull yourself together?'

Burden said slowly, remembering what he had once said to Gemma, 'Work is the best thing, isn't it?'

'I think it is.'

'But it has to be real work, heart and soul in it, not just coming in every day more or less automatically and hoping everyone will admire you for being such a martyr to duty. I've thought about it a lot, sir, I've decided to count my blessings and . . .'

'That's fine,' Wexford cut off his words. 'Don't be too sanctimonious about it, though, will you? That's hard to live with. I can see you've changed and I'm not going to enquire too closely into who or what has brought that change about. One good thing, I'm pretty sure I'm going to find that the quality of your mercy is a lot less strained than it used to be. And now let's go home.'

Half-way down the lift, he went on, 'You say Mrs Lawrence doesn't want this woman charged? That's all very well, but what about all our work, all the expenditure? Griswold will do his nut. He may insist on charging her. But if she's really a bit cuckoo . . . My God, one culprit dead and the other crazy!'

The lift opened, and there, inevitably, was Harry Wild.

'I have nothing for you,' Wexford said coldly.

'Nothing for me!' Wild said wrathfully to Camb. 'I know for a fact that . . .'

'There was quite a to-do in Pump Lane,' said Camb, opening his book. 'One police van and two fire engines arrived at five p.m. yesterday—Sunday, that was—to remove a cat from an elm tree . . .' Wild's infuriated glance cut him short. He cleared his throat and said soothingly, 'Let's see if there's any tea going.'

On the station forecourt Wexford said, 'I nearly forgot to

tell you. Swan's uncle's going to pay out the reward.'

Burden stared. 'But it was offered for information leading to an arrest.'

'No, it wasn't. That's what I thought till I checked. It was offered for information leading to a *discovery*. The Group Captain's a just man, and not the sort of just man I mean when I talk about his nephew. That's two thousand smackers for Charly Catch, or would be if he wasn't a very sick old man.' Absently, Wexford felt in his pocket for his blood-pressure tablets. 'When Crocker arrived in Charteris Road last night there was a solicitor at his bedside and Monkey keeping well in the background because a beneficiary can't also be a witness. I must work out sometime,' said the chief inspector, 'just how many king-size fags you could buy with all that boodle.'

'Are you all right, Mike?' said Grace. 'I mean, are you feeling all right? You've been home every night this week on the dot of six.'

Burden smiled. 'Let's say I've come to my senses. I find it a bit hard to put my feelings into words, but I suppose I've just realised how lucky I am to have my kids and what hell it would be to lose them.'

She didn't answer but went to the window and drew the curtains to shut out the night. With her back to him she said abruptly, 'I'm not going in for that nursing-home thing.'

'Now, look here . . .' He got up, went over to her and took her almost roughly by the arm. 'You're not to sacrifice yourself on my account. I won't have it.'

'My dear Mike!' Suddenly he saw that she was not troubled or conscience-stricken but happy. 'I'm not sacrificing myself. I . . .' She hesitated, remembering perhaps how in the past he would never talk to her, never speak of anything but the most mundane household arrangements.

'Tell me,' he said with a new fierce intensity.

She looked astonished. 'Well . . . Well, I met a man while we were in Eastbourne, a man I used to know years ago. I—I was in love with him. We quarrelled . . . Oh, it was so silly! And now—now he wants to begin again and come here and take me out and—and I think, Mike, I think . . .' She stopped

191

and then said with the cold defiance he had taught her, 'You wouldn't be interested.'

'Oh, Grace,' he said, 'if only you knew!'

She was staring at him now as if he were a stranger, but a stranger she had begun to like and would want to know better. 'Knew what?' she said.

For a moment he didn't answer. He was thinking that if only he had the sense to realise it now, he had found his listener, his one friend who would understand, because of her experience of many sides of life, the simple daily joy his marriage had been to him and understand too the blaze of glory, the little summer, he had found with Gemma.

'I want to talk too,' he said. 'I've got to tell someone. If I listen to you, will you listen to me?'

She nodded wonderingly. He thought how pretty she was, how like Jean, and that, because she was like Jean, she would make a wonderful wife for this man who loved her. And because there could now be no misunderstanding between them he hugged her briefly and rested his cheek against hers.

He felt her happiness in the warmth with which she returned the hug and it infected him, almost making him happy too. Would it last? Was he finally finding a sense of proportion? He couldn't tell, not yet. But his own boy and girl were safe, sleeping behind those closed doors, he could work again, and he had a friend who was waiting now, still tightly clasping his hands, to hear what he had to tell.

Grace led him back to the fire, sat down beside him and said, as if already she half understood, 'It'll be all right, Mike.' She leaned towards him, her face serious and intent. 'Let's talk,' she said.

MURDER BEING
ONCE DONE

For Frits and Nelly Twiss

The chapter heading quotations are taken from
Sir Thomas More's *Utopia* in the Ralph Robinson
translation of 1551

1

*The sick ... they see to with great affection, and let
nothing at all pass concerning either physic or good
diet whereby they may be restored to their health.*

WHEN Wexford came downstairs in the morning his nephew
had already left for work and the women, with the
fiendish gusto of amateur dieticians, were preparing a con-
valescent's breakfast. It had been like that every day since he
arrived in London. They kept him in bed till ten; they ran
his bath for him; one of them waited for him at the foot of
the stairs, holding out a hand in case he fell, a lunatic smile
of encouragement on her face.

The other—this morning it was his nephew's wife, Denise—
presided over the meagre spread on the dining-room table.
Wexford viewed it grimly: two circular biscuits apparently
composed of sawdust and glue, a pat of unsaturated fat, half a
sugarless grapefruit, black coffee and, crowning horror, a glass
of wobbly pallid substance he took to be yoghurt. His own
wife, trotting behind him from her post as staircase attendant,
proffered two white pills and a glass of water.

'This diet,' he said, 'is going to be the death of me.'

'Oh, it's not so bad. Imagine if you were diabetic as well.'

'Who,' quoted Wexford, 'can hold a fire in his hand by
thinking on the frosty Caucasus?'

He swallowed the pills and, having shown his contempt for
the yoghurt by covering it with his napkin, began to eat sour
grapefruit under their solicitous eyes.

7

'Where are you going for your walk this morning, Uncle Reg?'

He had been to look at Carlyle's house; he had explored the King's Road, eyeing with equal amazement the shops and the people who shopped in them; he had stood at the entrance to Stamford Bridge football ground and actually seen Alan Hudson; he had traversed every exquisite little Chelsea square, admired the grandeur of The Boltons and the quaint corners of Walham Green; on aching feet he had tramped through the Chenil Galleries and the antique market. They liked him to walk. In the afternoons they encouraged him to go with them in taxis and tube trains to the Natural History Museum and Brompton Oratory and Harrods. As long as he didn't think too much or tax his brain by asking a lot of questions, or stay up late or try to go into pubs, they jollied him along with a kind of humouring indulgence.

'Where am I going this morning?' he said. 'Maybe down to the Embankment.'

'Oh, yes, do. What a good idea!'

'I thought I'd have a look at that statue.'

'St Thomas More,' said Denise, who was a Catholic.

'Sir Thomas,' said Wexford, who wasn't.

'St Thomas, Uncle Reg.' Denise whisked away the unsaturated fat before Wexford could eat too much of it. 'And this afternoon, if it isn't too cold, we'll all go and look at Peter Pan in Kensington Gardens.'

But it was cold, bitingly cold and rather foggy. He was glad of the scarf his wife had wrapped round his neck, although he would have preferred her not to have gazed so piteously into his eyes while doing so, as if she feared the next time she saw him he would be on a mortuary slab. He didn't feel ill, only bored. There weren't even very many people about this morning to divert him with their flowing hair, beads, medieval ironmongery, flower-painted boots and shaggy coats matching shaggy Afghan hounds. The teeming young, who usually drifted past him incuriously, were this morning congregated in the little cafés with names like Friendly Frodo and The Love Conception.

Theresa Street, where his nephew's house was, lay on the borders of fashionable Chelsea, outside them if you hold that the King's Road ends at Beaufort Street. Wexford was beginning to pick up these bits of with-it lore. He had to have something to keep his mind going. He crossed the King's Road by the World's End and made his way towards the river.

It was lead-coloured this morning, the 29th of February. Fog robbed the Embankment of colour and even the Albert Bridge, whose blue and white slenderness he liked, had lost its Wedgwood look and loomed out of the mist as a sepia skeleton. He walked down the bridge and then back and across the road, blinking his eye and rubbing it. There was nothing in his eye but the small blind spot, no immovable grain of dust. It only felt that way and always would now, he supposed.

The seated statue which confronted him returned his gaze with darkling kindliness. It seemed preoccupied with affairs of state, affairs of grace and matters utopian. What with his eye and the fog, he had to approach more closely to be sure that it was, in fact, a coloured statue, not naked bronze or stone, but tinted black and gold.

He had never seen it before, but he had, of course, seen pictures of the philosopher, statesman and martyr, notably the Holbein drawing of Sir Thomas and his family. Until now, however, the close resemblance of the reproduced face to a known and living face had not struck him. Only replace that saintly gravity with an impish gleam, he thought, those mild resigned lips with the curve of irony, and it was Dr Crocker to the life.

Feeling like Ahab in Naboth's vineyard, Wexford addressed the statue aloud.

'Hast thou found me, O mine enemy?'

Sir Thomas continued to reflect on an ideal state or perhaps on the perils of Reformation. His face, possibly by a trick of the drifting mist, seemed to have grown even more grave, not to say comminatory. Now it wore precisely the expression Crocker's had worn that Sunday in Kingsmarkham when he had diagnosed a thrombosis in his friend's eye.

'God knows, Reg, I warned you often enough. I told you to lose weight, I told you to take things easier, and how many times have I told you to stay off the booze?'

'All right. What now? Will I have another?'

'If you do, it may be your brain the clot touches, not your eye. You'd better get away somewhere for a complete rest. I suggest a month away.'

'I can't go away for a month!'

'Why not? Nobody's indispensable.'

'Oh, yes, they are. What about Winston Churchill? What about Nelson?'

'The trouble with you, apart from high blood pressure, is delusions of grandeur. Take Dora away to the seaside.'

'In *February*? Anyway, I hate the sea. And I can't go away to the country. I live in the country.'

The doctor took his sphygmomanometer out of his bag and, silently rolling up Wexford's sleeve, bound the instrument to his arm. 'Perhaps the best thing,' said Crocker, without revealing his findings, 'will be to send you to my brother's health farm in Norfolk.'

'God! What would I do with myself all day?'

'By the time,' said Crocker dreamily, 'you've had nothing but orange juice and sauna baths for three days you won't have the strength to do anything. The last patient I sent there was too weak to lift the phone and call his wife. He'd only been married a month and he was very much in love.'

Wexford gave the doctor a lowering cowed glance. 'May God protect me from my friends. I'll tell you what, I'll go to London. How would that do? My nephew's always asking us. You know the one I mean, my sister's boy, Howard, the superintendent with the Met. He's got a house in Chelsea.'

'All right. But no late nights, Reg. No participation in

10

swinging London. No alcohol. I'm giving you a diet sheet one thousand calories a day. It sounds a lot, but, believe me, it ain't.'

'It's starvation,' said Wexford to the statue.

He had started to shiver, standing there and brooding. Time to get back for the pre-lunch rest and glass of tomato juice they made him have. One thing, he wasn't joining any Peter Pan expedition afterwards. He didn't believe in fairies and one statue a day was enough. A bus ride, maybe. But not on that one he could see trundling up Cremorne Road and ultimately bound for Kenbourne Vale. Howard had made it quite plain in his negative gracious way that that was one district of London in which his uncle wouldn't be welcome.

'And don't get any ideas about talking shop with that nephew of yours,' had been Crocker's parting words. 'You've got to get away from all that for a bit. Where did you say his manor is, Kenbourne Vale?'

Wexford nodded. 'Tough sort of place, I'm told.'

'They don't come any tougher. I trained there at St Biddulph's.' As always when speaking to the green rustic of his years in the metropolis, Crocker wore his Mr Worldly Wiseman expression and his voice became gently patronising. 'There's an enormous cemetery, bigger than Kensal Green and more bizarre than Brompton, with vast tombs and a few minor royals buried there, and the geriatric wards of the hospital overlook the cemetery just to show the poor old things what their next stop'll be. Apart from that, the place is miles of mouldering terraces containing two classes of persons: *Threepenny Opera* crooks and the undeserving poor.'

'I daresay,' said Wexford, getting his own back, 'it's changed in the intervening thirty years.'

'Nothing to interest you, anyway,' the doctor snapped. 'I don't want you poking your nose into Kenbourne Vale's crime, so you can turn a deaf ear to your nephew's invitations.'

Invitations! Wexford laughed bitterly to himself. Much chance he had of turning a deaf ear when Howard, in the ten

11

days since his uncle's arrival, hadn't spoken a single word even to indicate that he was a policeman, let alone suggested a visit to the Yard or an introduction to his inspector. Not that he was neglectful. Howard was courtesy itself, the most considerate of hosts, and, when it came to conversation, quite deferential in matters, for instance, of literature, in spite of his Cambridge First. Only on the subject nearest to his uncle's heart (and, presumably, to his own) was he discouragingly silent.

It was obvious why. Detective superintendents, holding high office in a London crime squad, are above talking shop with detective chief inspectors from Sussex. Men who have inherited houses in Chelsea will not condescend very far with men who occupy three-bedroom villas in the provinces. It was the way of the world.

Howard was a snob. A kind, attentive thoughtful snob, but a snob just the same. And that was why, that above all, Wexford wished he had gone to the seaside or the health farm. As he turned into Theresa Street he wondered if he could stand another evening in Denise's elegant drawing room, the women chatting clothes and cooking, while he and Howard exchanged small talk on the weather and the sights of London, interspersed with bits of Eliot.

'You must try and see some City churches while you're here.'

'St Magnus Martyr, white and gold?'

'St Mary Woolnoth, who tolls the hours with a dead sound on the final stroke of nine!'

Nearly another fortnight of it.

They wouldn't go to Peter Pan without him. Some other day, they said, resigning themselves without too much anguish to attending Harvey Nichols' fashion show instead. He swallowed his pills, ate his poached fish and fruit salad, and watched them leave the house, each suitably attired as befitted thirty years and fifty-five, Denise in purple velvet, feathers and a picture hat, Dora in the ranch mink he had bought her for their silver wedding. They got on fine, those two. As well as their joint determination to treat him like a retarded six-year-old with a congenital disease, they seemed to have every female taste in common.

Everybody got on fine but him: Crocker with his twenty-eight-inch waistline; Mike Burden in Kingsmarkham police station getting the feel of his, Wexford's, mantle on his shoulders and liking it; Howard departing every day for his secret hush-hush job which might have been in Whitehall rather than Kenbourne Vale nick, for all he told his uncle to the contrary.

Self-pity never got anyone anywhere. He mustn't look on it as a holiday but as a rest cure. It was time to forget all those pleasant visions he had had in the train to Victoria, the pictures of himself helping Howard with his enquiries, even giving—he blushed to recall it—a few little words of advice. Crocker had been right. He did have delusions of grandeur.

They had been knocked on the head here all right. The house itself was enough to cut any provincial down to size. It wasn't a big house, but then, nor is the Taj Mahal very big. What worried him and made him tread like a cat burglar were the exquisite appointments of the place: the fragile furniture, the pieces of Chinese porcelain balanced on tiny tables, the screens he was always nearly knocking over, Denise's flower arrangements. Weird, exotic, heterogeneous, they troubled him as almost daily a fresh confection appeared. He could never be sure whether a rosebud was intended to lie in that negligent fashion on the marble surface of a table or whether it had been inadvertently dislodged from its fellows in the majolica bowl by his own clumsy hand.

The temperature of the house, as he put it to himself, exaggerating slightly, was that of a Greek beach at noon in August. If you had the figure for it you could have gone about quite happily in a bikini. He wondered why Denise, who had, didn't. And how did the flowers survive, the daffodils ill-at-ease among avocado-pear plants?

When he had had his hour's rest with his feet up he took

13

the two library tickets Denise had left him and walked down to Manresa Road. Anything to get out of that house. The beautiful, warm, dull silence of it depressed him.

Why shouldn't he go home?

Dora could stay on if she liked. He thought of home with an ache in his belly that was only partly due to hunger. Home. The green Sussex meadows, the pine forest, the High Street full of people he knew and who knew him, the police station and Mike glad to see him back; his own house, cold as an English house should be except in front of the one great roaring fire; proper food and proper bread and in the fridge the secret beer cans.

Might as well get out a couple of books, though. Something to read in the train, and he could send them back to Denise by post. He chose a novel, and then, because he now felt he knew the old boy and had actually had a sort of conversation with him, More's *Utopia*. After that he had nothing at all to do so he sat down for a long while in the library, not even opening the books but thinking about home.

It was nearly five when he left. He bought an evening paper more from habit than from any desire to read it. Suddenly he found he was tired with the staggering weariness of someone who had nothing to do but must somehow fill the hours between getting up and bedtime.

A long way back to Theresa Street on foot, too long. He hailed a taxi, sank into its seat and unfolded his paper.

From the middle of the front page the bony, almost cadaverous, face of his nephew stared back at him.

2

*They set up a pillar of stone with the dead man's
titles therein engraved.*

THE women were still out. Fighting the soporific heat which
had met him with a tropical blast as he entered the house,
Wexford sat down, found his new glasses, and read the
caption under the photograph. 'Detective Superintendent
Howard Fortune, Kenbourne Vale C.I.D. chief, who is in
charge of the case, arriving at Kenbourne Vale Cemetery where
the girl's body was found.'

The cameraman had caught Howard leaving his car, and it
was a full-face shot. Beneath it was another picture, macabre,
compelling the eye. Wexford, refusing to be drawn, turned his
attention to the newspaper's account of the case, its lead story.
He read it slowly.

'The body of a girl was this morning discovered in a vault
at Kenbourne Vale Cemetery, West London. It was later
identified as that of Miss Loveday Morgan, aged about 20, of
Garmisch Terrace, W.15.

'The discovery was made by Mr Edwin Tripper, of Kenbourne Lane, a cemetery attendant, when he went to give the
vault its monthly inspection. Detective Superintendent Fortune
said "This is definitely a case of foul play. I can say no more
at present."

'Mr Tripper told me, "The vault is the property of the
Monfort family who were once important people in Ken-

15

bourne. A sum of money has been set aside under a trust to keep the vault cared for but the lock on the vault door was broken many years ago.

' "This morning I went as I always do on the last Tuesday in the month to sweep out the vault and put flowers on the coffin of Mrs Viola Montfort. The door was tightly closed and jammed. I had to use tools to force it. When I got it open I went down the steps and saw the body of this girl lying between the coffins of Mrs Viola Montfort and Captain James Monfort.

' "It gave me a terrible shock. It was the last place you would expect to find a corpse".'

Wexford chuckled a little at that, but the photograph of the vault chilled him again. It was a monstrous mausoleum, erected apparently at the height of the Gothic revival. On its roof lay two vast slaughtered lions with, rampant and triumphant above them, the statue of a warrior, the whole executed in black iron. Perhaps one of the Montforts had been a big-game hunter. Beneath this set-piece, the door, worked all over with heroic frescoes, stood half open, disclosing impenetrable blackness. Ilexes, those trees beloved of cemetery architects, lowered their dusty evergreen over the vault and shrouded the warrior's head.

It was a good photograph. Both photographs were good, the one of Howard showing in his eyes that perspicacity and passionate determination every good police officer should have but which Wexford had never seen in his nephew. And never would either, he thought, laying down the paper with a sigh. He hadn't the heart to read the rest of the story. What was the betting Howard would come in for his dinner, kiss his wife, enquire what his aunt had bought and ask solicitously after his uncle's health as if nothing had happened? If anyone could ignore that evening paper, he would. It would be surreptitiously whisked away and the *status quo* would just go on and on.

But now it would be worse. Howard wouldn't really be able to pretend any longer and his continuing silence would prove what Wexford guessed already, that he thought his uncle an

16

old has-been, maybe just fit to catch a country shop-lifter or root out a band of thugs with a cock-fighting hide-out on the South Downs.

He must have fallen asleep and slept for a long time. When he awoke the paper had gone and Dora was sitting opposite him with his dinner on a tray, cold chicken, and more of those bloody biscuits and junket and two white pills.

'Where's Howard?'

'He's only just got in, darling. When he's finished his dinner he'll come in here and have his coffee with you.'

And talk about the weather?

It was, in fact, the weather on which he began.

'Most unfortunate we're having this cold spell just now, Reg.' He never called his uncle uncle and it might have caused raised eyebrows if he had, for Howard Fortune, at thirty-six, looked forty-five. People were inclined to deplore the age gap between him and his wife, not guessing it was only six years. He was exceptionally tall, extravagantly thin and his lean bony face was wrinkled, but when he smiled it became charming and almost good-looking. You could see they were uncle and nephew. The Wexford face was there, the same bone construction, though in the case of the younger man the bones were almost fleshless and in the older obscured under pouches and heavy jowls. Howard smiled now as he poured Wexford's coffee and placed it beside him.

'I see you've got *Utopia* there.'

It was not quite the remark expected of a man who has spent his day in the preliminary enquiries into murder. But Howard, in any case, didn't look the part. His silver-grey suit and lemon Beale and Inman shirt were certainly the garments he had put on that morning but they appeared as if fresh from the hands of a valet. His thin smooth fingers, handling the leather binding of More's classic, looked as if they had never handled anything harsher than old books. Having placed a cushion behind his uncle's head, he began to discourse on *Utopia*, on the 1551 Ralph Robinson translation, on More's

17

friendship with Erasmus, occasionally pausing to insert such deferential courtesies as, 'which, of course, you already know, Reg'. He talked of other ideal societies in literature, of Andreae's *Christianopolis*, of Campanella's *City of the Sun* and of Butler's *Erewhon*. He talked pleasantly and with erudition and sometimes he broke off to allow a comment from Wexford, but Wexford said nothing.

He was boiling with anger. The man was not merely a snob, he was monstrously cruel, a sadist. To sit there lecturing like a professor on idealist philosophy when his heart must be full of its opposite, when he knew his uncle had brought in not only *Utopia* but that Dystopia on which the newspaper had enlarged. And this was the same little boy whom he, Wexford, had taught to take fingerprints!

The telephone rang and, out in the hall, Denise answered it, but Wexford could see Howard was alert for the call. He watched his nephew's face sharpen and when Denise came in to tell her husband it was for him, he saw a silent signal pass between them, a miniscule shake of the head on Howard's part indicating that the call and all it implied must be kept secret from their guest. Of course, it was one of Howard's subordinates phoning to tell him of a new development. In spite of his mortification, Wexford was hungry to know what that development could be. He listened to the murmur of Howard's voice from the hall, but he couldn't distinguish the words. It was all he could do not to open the door, and then, when Howard returned, ask him baldly. But he knew what the answer would be.

'You don't want to bother your head with all that.'

He didn't wait for Howard to come back. He took *Utopia* and made for the stairs, calling a curt good night to Denise and nodding to his nephew as he passed him. Bed was the best place for an old fogey like him. He got between the sheets and put on his glasses. Then he opened the book. His eyes felt gravelly but surely it wasn't his eye playing him a trick like that . . .? He stared and slammed the book shut.

It was in Latin.

He dreamed a lot that night. He dreamed that Howard had relented and personally driven him to Kenbourne Vale Cemetery to view with him the Montfort vault, and when he awoke it seemed impossible to him that he could go home without ever having actually seen it. The murder would, for a short space, be a topic of conversation even in Kingsmarkham. How was he going to explain to Mike that he had been excluded from all concern in it? That he had stayed with the man in charge of the case and yet learned no more than the average newspaper reader? By lying? By saying he wasn't interested? His temperament revolted from that. By telling the truth, then, that Howard had refused to confide in him.

At ten he came downstairs to the usual pantomime. Shredded wheat and orange juice and Denise waiting at the bottom of the stairs today. Otherwise it was the same as all the other mornings.

Without his having told her, Dora had discovered *Utopia* was in Latin and the two of them were already planning to get him an English translation. Denise's sister-in-law worked in a bookshop and would get him a paperback; to make assurance doubly sure, she would herself go into the library and order the Ralph Robinson.

'You needn't go to all that trouble for me,' said Wexford.

'Where are you going for your walk this morning, Uncle Reg?'

'Victoria,' he said, not adding that he was going to enquire about trains and listening in silence while they gasped about walking that distance.

Of course, he wouldn't walk. There was probably a bus. The eleven, he thought, there were always dozens of elevens except when you wanted one. Today the eleven and the twenty-two seemed to be on strike, while buses going to Kenbourne Vale charged in packs across the King's Road and up Gunter Grove.

He had a terrible urge just to see that cemetery. Howard's men would have finished with it by now, and anyone could go into cemeteries if he wanted to. Then, when he got home, he could at least describe the vault to Mike and say it was unfortunate he had to leave just at that point. Victoria station could wait. Why not phone, anyway?

The next bus said Kenbourne Lane station on its front. Wexford didn't like to ask for the cemetery in case the smiling West Indian conductor took him for another ghoulish sightseer—he was unsure of himself in London, a little of his decisive identity lost—so he said, 'All the way, please,' and settled back into his seat to pretend he was complying with that piece of hackneyed advice to tourists that the best way to see London is from the top of a bus.

Its route was up to Holland Park Avenue and then along Ladbroke Grove. Once the bus had turned into Elgin Crescent, Wexford lost his bearings. He wondered how he would know they had left North Kensington, or Notting Hill or wherever it was and entered Kenbourne Vale. The neighbourhood already fitted Crocker's description of miles of mouldering terraces, but thirty years had passed and there were tower blocks and council estates as well.

Then he saw a sign: *London Borough of Kenbourne. Copeland Hill*. All the plaques with street names on them, Copeland Terrace, Heidelberg Road, Bournemouth Grove, bore the postal direction West Fifteen.

Must be nearly there. His humiliation was giving way to excitement. The bus had lumbered round a kind of circus and entered Kenbourne Lane, a wide treeless thoroughfare, inclining upwards, a street of Asiatic food shops, squat Edwardian pubs, pawnbrokers' and small tobacconists'. He was wondering how he would find the cemetery when, as the bus came over the crown of the hill, there rose to the left of him an enormous pillared portico of yellow sandstone. Wrought-iron gates, as huge as the gates to some oriental walled city, stood open, dwarfing the workman who was touching up the black paint on their posts.

Wexford rang the bell and got off when the bus pulled in to a request stop. In this exposed place the sharp wind caught him and he turned up the collar of his coat. The heavy leaden sky looked full of snow. There were no sightseers about, no police cars, and neither the workman nor some sort of attendant —Mr Tripper, perhaps?—who stood at the entrance to a lodge, said a word to him as he passed under the archway.

As soon as he was inside the cemetery, he remembered what Crocker had said about it being huge and bizarre. This was not an exaggeration, but the doctor had omitted to say that it was also, perhaps because of its size and because of staff shortages, hideously neglected. Wexford stood still and took in the sprawling wild panorama.

Immediately in front of him was one of those buildings all large cemeteries boast and whose use is in doubt. It was neither a chapel nor a crematorium, but it possibly housed offices for the staff and lavatories for the mourners. The style was that of St Peter's in Rome. Not, of course, so large, but large enough. Unluckily for the inhabitants of Kenbourne Vale, its architect had been no Bernini: the dome was too small, the pillars too thick and the whole edifice executed in the same yellow sandstone as the portico.

Of this material also were the two colonnades which branched out of the right-hand side of the St Peter's building like encircling arms and met some hundred yards distant at an arch which supported a winged victory. Between them and the outer walls, above which could be seen St Biddulph's Hospital, were deep strips of wilderness, a jungle of shrubs and trees, showing here and there protruding from the mass the weather-torn peaks of tombs.

In the space between the colonnades some attempt had been made to tidy the place. The shaggy grass was chopped off, the bushes pruned, to reveal grime-encrusted monuments, angels with swords, gun-carriages, broken columns, weeping Niobes, Egyptian obelisks and, immediately beside St Peter's, two tombs the size of small houses. Training his eyes, Wexford saw that one was that of the Princess Adelberta of Mecklenburgh-Strelitz, and the other of His Serene Highness the Grand Duke Waldemar of Retz.

The place was ridiculous, a grandiose necropolis, devouring land which might better have served Kenbourne Vale's homeless. It was also profoundly sinister. It was awe-inspiring. Never before, not in any mortuary or house of murder, had Wexford so tellingly felt the oppressive chill of death. The winged victory held back her plunging horses against a sky that was almost black, and under the arches of the colonnades lay wells of gloom. He felt that not for anything would he have walked between those arches and the pillars which fronted them to read the bronze plaques on their damp yellow walls. Not for renewed health and youth would he have spent a night in that place.

He had mounted the steps to view the cemetery and he had viewed it. Enough was enough. Luckily, the Montfort vault must lie between the wall and the colonnade. He guessed that because only there grew the ilexes, and he was foolishly relieved to know that he would not have to explore the inner area where the most monstrous and folly-like tombs stood and where the winged victory dominated everything like some sinister fallen angel.

But as soon as he had descended the steps and taken a path which led to the right-hand side of the cemetery he found that the depths were no less unpleasant than the heights. True, the winged victory and the colonnades were made invisible by the trees, but these in themselves, crowded together, untended and almost all of evergreen varieties, held their own kind of menace. They made the path very dark. Their trunks were hidden to shoulder height by ivy and thick brambly shrubs, and among these shrubs began to appear first the outlines of gravestones and then, as the path ran parallel with the outer wall, the shapes of larger and larger tombs.

Wexford tried to chuckle at some of the pompous inscriptions but his laughter stuck in his throat. The absurd was overpowered by the sinister, by the figures in bronze and sculped stone which, made furtive and hideous by encroaching moss and decades of fallen grime, lurked among the trailing tendrils and even, as the wind rustled between leathery leaves and broken masonary, seemed to move. Overhead, he could see only a narrow corridor of sky and that stormy, black and Turneresque. He walked on, looking straight ahead of him down the defile.

Just when he was beginning to feel that he had had about as much of this as flesh and blood could stand, he came upon the Montfort vault. It was the size of a small cottage and much nastier in reality than in the photograph. The cameraman had not been able to capture the mouldy smell that breathed out of the half-open door or render the peculiarly unpleasant effect of sour green moss creeping across the warrior's face and the paws of the dead lions.

Nor had the inscription appeared in the paper. It was unlike any other Wexford had seen in the cemetery, bearing no information about the dead who lay in the vault. The copper plate had turned bright green with verdigris, but the lettering, of some untarnishable metal—gold leaf?—stood out clear and stark.

'He who asks questions is a fool.
He who answers them is a greater fool.
What is truth? What man decides it shall be.
What is beauty? Beauty is in the eye of man.
What are right and wrong? Today one thing, another tomorrow.
Death only is real.
The last of the Montforts bids you read and pass on Without comment.'

This epitaph—if epitaph it could be called—so interested Wexford that he took a scrap of paper and a pencil from his pocket and copied it down. Then he pushed open the door, expecting a creak, but there was no sound at all. Perhaps Mr Tripper had oiled the hinges. A creak would somehow have been reassuring. He realised suddenly that some of the awe and the disquiet he felt was due to the profound silence. Since entering the cemetery he had heard nothing but the crepitation of dead leaves beneath his feet and the rustle of the wind.

Inside the vault it was not quite dark. Utter darkness would have been less unpleasant. A little greyish light fell on to the flight of steps from a narrow vitrine in the rear wall. He went down the steps and found himself in a chamber about twelve feet square. The dead Montforts lay not in the coffins mentioned by Mr Tripper but in stone sarcophagi which rested on shelves. In the centre of the chamber was a marble basin absurdly like a birdbath and containing a dribble of water. He couldn't imagine what purpose it served. He approached the sarcophagi and saw that there were two rows of them with a narrow space between. It must have been there in that trough, on the damp stone floor, that Loveday Morgan's body had been found.

He shivered a little. The vault smelt of decay. Not surely of the dead Montforts, passed long ago to dust, but of rotted grave flowers and stagnant water and unventilated age. A nasty place. She had been twenty, he thought, and he hoped she had died quickly and not in here. What are right and wrong? Today one thing, another tomorrow. Death only is real.

He turned back towards the steps and, as he did so, he heard a sound above him, a footfall on the overgrown gravel path. Some attendant, no doubt. He set his foot on the bottom stair, looking up at the rectangle of dingy light between door and frame. And then, as he was about to speak and declare his presence, there appeared in the aperture, gaunt and severe, the face of his nephew.

3

*You conceive in your mind either none at all or else
a very false image and similitude of this thing.*

EVERYONE is familiar with the sensation of wanting the
earth to swallow him when he is caught in embarrassing
circumstances. And what more appropriate plot of earth than
this, thought Wexford, aghast. These acres, choked with the
dead, might surely receive one more. There was, however,
nothing for it but to mount the stairs and face the music.

Howard, peering down into semi-darkness, had not at first
recognised the intruder. When he did, when Wexford, awkwardly brushing cobwebs from his coat, emerged on to the
path, his face registered simple blank astonishment.

'Good God. Reg,' he said.

He looked his uncle up and down, then stared into the vault,
as if he thought himself the victim of some monstrous delu-
sion. Either this was not Wexford, but some Kenbournite disguised to resemble him, or else this was not Kenbourne Vale
cemetery. It took him a few moments to recover and then he
said:

'I thought you wanted a holiday from all this sort of thing.'

It was stupid to stand there like a schoolboy. In general,
embarrassment was foreign to Wexford and he brimmed over
with self-confidence. Now he told himself that he was catching
criminals when this man was chewing on a teething ring and
he said rather coldly, 'Did you? I can't imagine why.' Never

25

apologise, never explain. 'Don't let me keep you from your work. I've a bus to catch.'

Howard's eyes narrowed. 'No,' he said, 'you're not going like that.' He always spoke quietly, in measured tones. 'I won't have that. If you wanted to see the vault, why didn't you say last night? I'd have brought you with me this morning. If you wanted the inside stuff on the case, you only had to ask.'

Absurd as it was, undignified, to stand arguing in the bitter cold among toppled gravestones, Wexford couldn't leave it like that. All his resentment had boiled to the surface.

'Ask?' he shouted. 'Ask you when you've made a point of excluding me from everything to do with your work? When you and Denise have conspired to keep quiet about it like a couple of parents turning off the television in front of the child when the sexy play starts? I know when I'm not wanted. *Ask!*'

Howard's face had fallen glumly at the beginning of this speech, but now a faint smile twitched his lips. He felt in the pocket of his coat while Wexford leaned against the vault, his arms folded defiantly.

'Here, read that. It came two days before you did.' Reassured by the evidence he had produced, Howard spoke firmly now. 'Read it, Reg.'

Suspiciously Wexford took the letter. Without his glasses he could only just read it, but he could make out enough. The signature, 'Leonard Crocker', leered blackly at him. '. . . I am confident I can rely on your good sense . . . Your uncle, a close friend of mine and my patient . . . Nothing he wants more than to get completely away from everything connected with police work . . . Better not let him come into any contact with . . .'

'We thought we were acting for the best, Reg.'

'Close friend!' Wexford exploded. 'What business has he got interfering with me?' Usually litter-conscious, he forgot his principles and, screwing the letter into a ball, hurled it among the bushes and the crumbling masonry.

Howard burst out laughing. 'I spoke to my own doctor

26

about it,' he said, 'telling him what had been the matter with you and he said—you know how diplomatic they are—he said there were two opinions about it but he couldn't see that you'd come to any harm indulging—er, your usual tastes. Still, Denise insisted we abide by what your own doctor said. And we did think it was your wish.'

'I took you for a snob,' said his uncle. 'Rank and all that.'

'Did you? That never struck me.' Howard bit his lip. 'You don't know how I've longed for a real talk instead of literary chit-chat, especially now when I'm short of men and up to my eyes in it.' Frowning, still concerned, he said, 'You must be frozen. Here comes my sergeant, so we can get away from all these storeyed urns and animated busts.'

A thickset man of about forty was approaching them from the direction of St Peter's. He wore the cheerful and practical air of someone totally insensitive to atmosphere, to that of the cemetery and that which subsisted between the two other men. Howard introduced him as Sergeant Clements and presented the chief inspector without saying that Wexford was his uncle or attempting to account for his sudden and surely astonishing appearance at the scene of a crime.

In such august company the sergeant knew better than to ask questions, or perhaps he had read the Montfort injunction.

'Very pleased to meet you, sir.'

'My uncle,' said Howard, relenting a little, 'is on holiday. He comes from Sussex.'

'I daresay it's a change, sir. No green fields and cows and what-not round here.' He gave Wexford a respectful and somewhat indulgent smile before turning to the superintendent. 'I've had another talk with Tripper, sir, but I've got nothing more out of him.'

'Right. We'll go back to the car. Mr Wexford will be lunching with me, and over lunch I'm going to try to persuade him to give us the benefit of his brains.'

'We can certainly use them,' said the sergeant, and he fell back to allow the others to precede him out of the cemetery.

The Grand Duke was a little old pub Howard took him to on the corner of a mews in Kenbourne Lane.

'I didn't know there were places like this left in London,' Wexford said, appreciating the linenfold panelling, the settles and the old mullioned glass in the windows. It was like home, the kind of inn to be found in Pomfret or Stowerton.

'There aren't around here. Kenbourne's no Utopia. Would you believe, looking out of the window, that in an unpublished poem, Hood wrote:

> ' "O, to ride on the crest of a laden wain
>   Between primrose banks in Kenbourne Lane"?'

'What will you eat, Reg?'

'I'm not supposed to eat anything much.'

'Surely a little cold duck and some salad? The food's very good here.'

Wexford felt almost dizzy, but he mustn't allow himself to break out entirely. It was a triumph of communication over misunderstanding that he was here with Howard at all and about to get his teeth into some real police work again without getting them into duck as well. The spread on the food counter looked mouth-wateringly enticing. He chose the least calorific, thin sliced red beef and *ratatouille froide,* and settled back with a sigh of contentment. Even the tall glass of apple juice which Howard presented to him with the assurance that it was made out of Cox's Oranges from Suffolk couldn't cloud his pleasure.

Ever since his arrival in London he had felt that partial loss of identity which is common to everybody on holiday except the most seasoned of travellers. But instead of returning to him as he grew accustomed to the city, this ego of his, this essential Wexfordness, had seemed to continue its seeping away, until at last in the cemetery he had briefly but almost entirely lost his hold on it. That had been a frightening moment. Now, however, he felt more himself than he had done for days. This was like being with Mike at the Olive and Dove where, on so many satisfactory occasions, they had thrashed

28

out some case over lunch, but now Howard was the instructor and he in Mike's role. He found he didn't mind this at all. He could even look with equanimity at Howard's lunch: a huge plateful of steak-and-kidney pudding, Jersey new potatoes and courgettes *au gratin*.

For the first five minutes they ate and drank and talked a little more about this misunderstanding of theirs, and then Howard, opening their discussion in the clearest and most direct way, pushed a snapshot across the table.

'This is the only photograph we have of her. Other may come to light, of course. It was in her handbag. Not very usual that, to carry photographs of oneself about on one. Perhaps she had some sentimental reason for it. Where and when it was taken we don't know.'

The snapshot was too pale and muzzy for reproduction in a newspaper. It showed a thin fair girl in a cotton frock and heavy unsuitable shoes. Her face was a pale blob and even her own mother, as Wexford put it to himself, wouldn't have recognised her. In the background were some dusty-looking shrubs, a section of wall with coping along the top of it and something that looked like a clothes post.

He handed it back and asked, 'Is Garmisch Terrace near here?'

'The backs of the houses overlook the cemetery but on the opposite side to where we were. It's a beastly place. Monstrous houses put up around 1870 for city merchants who couldn't run to fifteen hundred a year for a palace in Queen's Gate. They're mostly let off into rooms now, or flatlets as they're euphemistically called. She had a room. She'd lived there for about two months.'

'What did she do for a living?'

'She worked as a receptionist in a television rental place. The shop is called Sytansound and it's in Lammas Grove. That's the street which runs off to the left at Kenbourne Circus and also skirts the cemetery. Apparently she went to work by taking a short-cut through the cemetery. Why do you look like that?'

'I was thinking of passing through that place every day.'

'The local people are used to it. They don't notice it any more. You'd be surprised in the summer how many young housewives you see in there taking their babies for an afternoon's airing.'

Wexford said, 'When and how did she die?'

'Probably last Friday. I haven't had a full medical report yet, but she was strangled with her own silk scarf.'

'Last Friday and no one reported her missing?'

Howard shrugged. 'In Garmisch Terrace, Reg? Loveday Morgan wasn't living at home with her parents in some select suburb. They come and they go in Garmisch Terrace, they mind their own business, they don't ask questions. Wait till you hear Sergeant Clements on that subject.'

'How about boy friends?'

'She didn't have any, as far as we know. The body was identified by a girl called Peggy Pope who's the housekeeper at 22 Garmisch Terrace and she says Loveday had no friends. She came to Kenbourne Vale in January, but where she came from nobody seems to know. When she applied for the room she gave Mrs Pope an address in Fulham. We've checked on that. The street she named and the house she named are there all right but she never lived there. The owners of the house are a young married couple who have never let rooms. So we don't yet know where she came from and in a way we don't really know who she was.'

Having built up the suspense in a way Wexford recognised, for it was the way he had himself used on countless occasions, Howard went away to fetch cheese and biscuits. He returned with more apple juice for his uncle, who was feeling so contented that he drank it obediently.

'She lived in Garmisch Terrace by herself, very quietly,' Howard went on, 'and last Friday, February 25th, she went to work as usual, returning, as she occasionally did, during her lunchtime break. Mrs Pope supposed that she had gone back to work in the afternoon, but in fact, she didn't. She telephoned the manager of Sytansound to say she was sick and that was the last anyone heard of her.' He paused. 'She may have gone straight into the cemetery; she may not. The cemetery gates are closed each day at six, and on Fridays they were closed at that time as usual. Clements sometimes cuts through on his way home. He did that on Friday, spoke to Tripper, and Tripper closed the gates behind him at six sharp. Needless to say, Clements saw nothing out of the way. His route took him nowhere near the Montfort vault.'

Wexford recognised this short pause as the cue for him to ask an intelligent question, and he asked one. 'How did you know who she was?'

'Her handbag was beside her in the vault, brimming with information. Her address was on a bill from a dry cleaner's and this snapshot was there too. Besides that, there was a sheet of notepaper with two telephone numbers on it.'

Wexford raised an enquiring eyebrow.

'You rang those numbers, of course?'

'Of course. That was among the first things we did. One was that of an hotel in Bayswater, a perfectly respectable, rather large, hotel. They told us they had advertised in a newspaper a vacancy for a receptionist and Loveday Morgan had replied to the advertisement. By phone. She didn't sound the sort of girl they wanted—too shy and awkward, they said— and she hadn't the necessary experience for the job.

'The other number was that of a West End company called Notbourne Properties who are particularly well known in Notting Hill and Kenbourne Vale. Hence their name. They also had advertised a job, this time for a telephone girl. Loveday applied and actually got as far as an interview. That interview was at the end of the week before last, but they didn't intend to take her on. Apparently, she was badly dressed and, anyway, she wasn't familiar with the particular phone system they use.'

'She wanted to change her job? Does anyone know why?'

'More money, I imagine. We may be able to get some more information about that and her general circumstances from this Mrs Pope.'

31

'That's the woman who identified her? The housekeeper?'

'Yes. Shall we wait and have coffee or would you like to go straight round to Garmisch Terrace?'

'Skip the coffee,' said Wexford.

4

*A little farther beyond that all things begin by little
and little to wax pleasant; the air soft, temperate and
gentle covered with green grass.*

GARMISCH TERRACE was straight and grey and forbidding, a canyon whose sides were six-storey houses. All the
houses were alike, all joined together, flat-fronted but for
their protruding pillared porches, and, like the cemetery
building, their proportions were somehow wrong. It had been
an unhappy period for architecture, the time when they were
built, a period in which those designers who had not adopted
the new Gothic, were attempting to improve on the Georgian.

This would have mattered less if some effort had been made
to maintain these houses, but Wexford, looking at them with
a sinking heart, could not see a single freshly painted façade.
Their plaster was cracked and their pillars streaked where
water had run through dust. Rubbish clogged the basement
areas and these were separated from the pavement by broken
railings patched with wire netting. Instead of trees, parking
meters stood in a grey row, an avenue of them leading up the
cul-de-sac to where it ended in a red-brick church.

There were few people about, a turbaned Sikh lugging his
dustbin up area steps, an old woman wheeling a pram filled
apparently with jumble-sale spoils, a pregnant black girl
whose kingfisher-blue raincoat provided the only colour in the

33

street. The wind blew paper out of the Sikh's dustbin, whirling sheets of newsprint up into the grey sky. It teased at the girls woolly hair which, in a pathetic attempt to be accepted, to be in fashion, she was trying to grow long. Wexford wondered sadly about these coloured people who must have looked to a promised land and had found instead the bitter indecency of Garmisch Terrace.

'Would anyone live here from choice?' he said to Sergeant Clements, who, while Howard studied a report in the car, had attached himself to him as mentor, guide, and possibly protector.

'You may well ask, sir,' said the sergeant approvingly. His manner was not quite that of the schoolmaster addressing a promising pupil. Wexford's rank and age were recognised and respected, but he was made aware of the age-old advantage of the townsman over the greenhorn from the country. Clements' plump face, a face which seemed not to have changed much since he was a fat-cheeked, rosebud-mouthed schoolboy, wore an expression both smug and discontented. 'They like it, you see,' he explained. 'They like muck and living four to a room and chucking their gash about and prowling all night and sleeping all day.' He scowled at a young man and woman who, arm in arm, crossed the road and sat down on the pavement outside the church where they began to eat crisps out of a bag. 'They like dropping in on their friends at midnight and dossing down on the floor among the fag-ends because the last bus has gone. Ask 'em and most of 'em don't know where they live, here this week, there the next, catch as catch can and then move on. They don't live like you or me sir. They live like those little furry moles you have down in the country, always burrowing about in the dark.'

Wexford recognised in the sergeant a type of policeman which is all too common. Policemen see so much of the seamy side of life and, lacking the social worker's particular kind of training, many of them become crudely cynical instead of learning a merciful outlook. His own Mike Burden came dangerously near sometimes to being such a one, but his intelligence saved him. Wexford didn't think much of the sergeant's intelligence, although he couldn't help rather liking him.

'Poverty and misery aren't encouragements to an orderly life,' he said, smiling to take the sting out of the admonition.

Clements didn't take this as a rebuke but shook his head at so much innocence.

'I was referring to the *young*, sir, the young layabouts like that pair over there. But you'll learn. A couple of weeks in Kenbourne Vale and you'll get your eyes opened. Why, when I first came here I thought hash was mutton stew and S.T.D. a dialling system.'

Perfectly aware of the significance of these terms, Wexford said nothing, but glanced towards the car. He was beginning to feel chilly and at a nod from Howard he moved under the porch of number 22. That a lecture, contrasting the manners of modern youth with the zeal, ambition and impeccable morality of Clements' contemporaries in his own young days, was imminent he felt sure, and he hoped to avoid. But the sergeant followed him, stamping his feet on the dirty step, and launched into the very diatribe Wexford most feared. For a couple of minutes he let him have his head and then he interrupted.

'About Loveday Morgan ...'

'So-called,' said Clements darkly. 'That wasn't her real name. Now, I ask you, is it likely to be? We checked her at Somerset House. Plenty of Morgan girls but no Loveday Morgan. She just called herself that. Why? You may well ask. Girls call themselves all sorts of things these days. Now, let me give you an illustration of what I mean ...'

But before he could, Howard had joined them and silenced him with an unusually cold look. There was a row of bells beside the front door with numbers instead of nameplates.

'The housekeeper lives in the basement,' said Howard, 'so we may as well try Flat One.' He rang the bell and a voice snapped what sounded like 'Teal' out of the entry phone.

'I beg your pardon?'

'This is Ivan Teal. Flat One. Who are you?'

'Detective Superintendent Fortune. I want Mrs Pope.'

'Ah,' said the voice. 'You want Flat Fifteen. The thing that works the door is broken. I'll come down.'

'Flats!' said the sergeant while they waited. 'That's a laugh. They aren't any of 'em flats. They're rooms with a tap and a gas meter, but our girl was paying seven quid a week for hers and there are only two loos in the whole dump. What a world!' He patted Wexford's shoulder. 'Brace yourself for what's coming now, sir. Whoever this Teal is he won't look human.'

But he did. The only shock Wexford felt was in confronting a man nearly as old as himself, a shortish, well-muscled man with thick grey hair worn rather long.

'Sorry to keep you waiting,' he said. 'It's a long way down.' He stared at the three men, unsmiling, insolent in a calculating way. It was a look Wexford had often seen on faces before, but they had almost always been young faces. Teal had, moreover, a smooth upper-class accent. He wore a spotlessly clean white sweater and smelt of Faberge's Aphrodisia. 'I suppose we're all going to be persecuted now.'

'We don't persecute people, Mr Teal.'

'No? You've changed then. You used to persecute me.'

Assuming that Howard had given him *carte blanche* to question possible witnesses if he chose, Wexford said, 'Did you know Loveday Morgan?'

'I know everybody here,' Teal said, 'the oldest inhabitants and the ships that pass in the night. I who have sat by Thebes below the wall . . .' He grinned suddenly. 'Flat One if you want me.'

He led them to the basement stairs and went off without saying any more.

'A curious old queen,' said Howard. 'Fifteen years in this hole . . . God! Come on, it's down here.'

The stairs were narrow and carpeted in a thin much-worn haircord. They led down to a largish lofty hall, long ago

36

painted dark crimson, but this paint was peeling away, leaving white islands shaped like fantastic continents, so that the walls might have been maps of some other unknown world, a charted Utopia. Furniture, that looked too big to go up those stairs although it must have come down them, a sideboard, a huge bookcase crammed with dusty volumes, filled most of the floor space. There were three closed doors, each with an overflowing dustbin on its threshold, and the place smelt of decaying rubbish.

Wexford had never seen anything like this before, but the interior of Flat Fifteen was less unfamiliar. It reminded him of certain Kingsmarkham cottages he had been in. Here was the same squalor that is always present when edibles and wash-ables are thrown into juxtaposition, opened cans among dirty socks, and here in one of those battered prams was a baby with a food-stained face such as town and country alike pro-duce. It was deplorable, of course, that this young girl and her child should have to live in a subterranean cavern, perpetually in artificial light; on the other hand, daylight would have revealed even more awfully the broken armchairs and the appalling carpet. In a way, this was a work of art, so care-fully had some female relative of the landlord's repaired it. Wexford couldn't tell whether it was a blue carpet mended with crimson or a piece of red weaving incorporating patches of blue Axminster. The whole of it was coated with stains, ground-in food and the housekeeper's hair combings.

She alone of the room's contents could have stood up to the searching light of day. Her clothes were awful, as dirty and dilapidated as the chair coverings, and dust clung to her greasy black hair, but she was beautiful. She was easily the most beautiful woman he had seen since he came to London. Hers was the loveliness of those film stars he remembered from his youth in the days before actresses looked like ordinary women. In her exquisite face he saw something of a Carole Lombard, something of a Loretta Young. Sullen and dirty though she was, he could not take his eyes off her.

Howard and Clements seemed totally unaffected. No doubt

they were too young to have his memories. Perhaps they were too efficient to be swayed by beauty. And the girl's manner didn't match her looks. She sat on the arm of a chair, biting her nails and staring at them with a sulky frown.

'Just a few questions, please, Mrs Pope,' said Howard.

'Miss Pope. I'm not married.' Her voice was rough and low. 'What d'you want to know? I can't spare very long. I've got the bins to take up if Johnny doesn't come back.'

'Johnny?'

'My friend that I live with.' She cocked a thumb in the direction of the baby and said, 'Her father. He said he'd come back and help me when he'd got his Social Security, but he always makes himself bloody scarce on bin day. God, I don't know why I don't meet up with any ordinary people, nothing but layabouts.'

'Loveday Morgan wasn't a layabout.'

'She had a job, if that's what you mean.' The baby had begun to grizzle. Peggy Pope picked up a dummy from the floor, wiped it on her cardigan and thrust it into the child's mouth. 'God knows how she kept it, she was so *thick*. She couldn't make her meter work and had to come to me to know where to buy a light bulb. When she first came here I even had to show her how to make a phone call. Oh, they all impose on me, but never the way she did. And then she had the nerve to try and get Johnny away from me.'

'Really?' said Howard encouragingly. 'I think you should tell us that, Mrs Pope.'

'*Miss* Pope. Look, I've got to get the bins up. Anyway, there wasn't anything in it, not on Johnny's side. Loveday was so bloody obvious about it, always coming down here to chat him up when I was out, and it got worse the last couple of weeks. I'd come back and find her sitting here, staring at Johnny, or making out she was fond of the baby. I asked him what she was up to. What d'you talk about, for God's sake? I said. Nothing, he said. She'd hardly opened her mouth. She was such a bloody miserable sort of girl.' Peggy Pope sighed as if she, the soul of wit and gaiety, had a right to similarly exuberant companions.

'Do you know why she was miserable?'

'It's money with most of them. That's all they talk about, as though I was rolling in it. She asked me if I could find her a cheaper room, but I said, No, I couldn't. We don't have any flats less than seven a week. I thought she was going to cry. Christ, I thought, why don't you grow up?'

Howard said, 'May we come to last Friday, Mrs Pope?'

'*Miss* Pope. When I want to be *Mrs* I'll find a man who's got a job and can get me something better than a hole in the ground to live in, I can tell you. I don't know anything about last Friday. I saw her come in about ten past one and go off again about ten to two. Oh, and she made a phone call. I don't know any more about it.'

Wexford caught Howard's eye and leant forward. 'Miss Pope,' he said, 'we want you to tell us about that in much greater detail. Tell us exactly what you were doing, where you saw her, what she said, everything.'

'O.K., I'll try.' Peggy Pope pulled her thumbnail out of her mouth and looked at it with distaste. 'But when I've done you'll have to let me get shifting those bins.'

The room was rather cold. She kicked down the upper switch on an electric fire and a second bar began to heat. It was evidently seldom used, for as it glowed red a smell of burning dust came from it.

'It was just after one, maybe ten past,' she began. 'Johnny was out somewhere as usual, looking for work, he said, but I reckon he was in the Grand Duke. I was in the hall giving it a bit of a sweep up and Loveday came in. She said hallo or something, and I said hallo, and she went straight upstairs. I was getting out the vacuum when she came down again and said had I got change for ten pence because she wanted two pence to make a phone call. She must have known I don't carry money about when I'm cleaning the place, but, anyway, I said I'd see and I came down here and got my bag. I

39

hadn't got change, but I'd got one two-pence piece so I gave her that and she went into the phone box.'

'Where's that?'

'Under the stairs. You passed it when you came down.'

'Do you know whom she was phoning?'

She warmed her bitten fingers at the fire and creased her beautiful face into a ferocious scowl. 'How would I? There's a door on the box. She didn't say I'm going to give my mother a tinkle or ring my boy friend, if that's what you mean. Loveday never said much. I'll give her that, she wasn't talkative. Well, she came out and went upstairs again and then I went down to see if the baby was O.K., and when I came up with the pram to take the washing to the launderette she was just going out through the front door, all got up in a green trouser suit. I noticed because it was the only decent thing she had. She didn't say anything. And now can I get on with my work?'

Howard nodded, and he and Clements, thanking her briefly, made for the stairs. Wexford lingered. He watched the girl—she was round-shouldered and rather thin—lift one of the smelly bins and then he said, 'I'll give you a hand.'

She seemed astonished. The world she lived in had unfitted her for accepting help graciously, and she shrugged, making her mouth into an ugly shape.

'They should employ a man to do this.'

'Maybe, but they don't. What man would practically run this dump and do all the dirty work for eight quid a week and that room? Would *you*?'

'Not if I could help it. Can't you get a better job?'

'Look, chum, there's the kid. I've got to have a job where I can look after her. Don't you worry yourself about me. Some day my prince will come and then I'll be off out of here, leaving the bins to Johnny.' She smiled for the first time, a transcending, glorious smile, evoking for him old dark cinemas and shining screens. 'Thanks very much. That's the lot.'

'You're welcome,' said Wexford.

The unaccustomed effort had brought the blood beating to his head. It had been a silly thing to do and the pounding inside his temples unnerved him. Howard and the sergeant were nowhere to be seen, so, to clear his head while he waited for them, he walked down to the open end of Garmisch Terrace. A thin drizzle had begun to fall. He found himself in something which at home would have passed for a high street. It was a shabby shopping centre with, sandwiched between a pub and a hairdresser's, a little cheap boutique called *Loveday*. So that was where she had found the name. She had possessed some other, duller perhaps but identifying, distressing even, which she had wished to conceal. . . .

'Been having a breath of fresh air, sir?' said the sergeant when he rejoined them. 'Or what passes for it round here. By gum, but those bins stank to high heaven!'

Howard grinned. 'We'll take the sergeant back to the station and then I want to show you something different. You mustn't run away with the idea that the whole of Kenbourne is like these rat holes.'

They dropped Clements at the police station, a blackened pile in Kenbourne Vale High Street whose blue lamp swung from the centre of an arch above an imposing flight of steps. Then Howard, driving the car himself, swung into a hinterland of slums, winding streets with corner shops and pubs and patches of waste ground, once green centres of garden squares, but now wired-in like hard tennis courts and littered with broken bicycles and oil-drums.

'Clements lives up there.' Howard pointed upwards, apparently through the roof of the car, and, twisting round to peer out of the window, Wexford saw a tower block of flats, a dizzy thirty storeys. 'Quite a view, I believe. He can see the river and a good deal of the Thames Estuary on a clear day.'

Now the towers grew thickly around them, a copse of monoliths sprouting out of a shabby and battered jungle. Wexford was wondering if this was the contrast he had expected to admire when a bend in the road brought them suddenly to a clear open space. The change was almost shocking. A second before he had been in one of the drabbest regions he had ever set eyes on, and now, as if a scene had been rapidly shifted on a stage, he saw a green triangle, plane trees, a scattering of Georgian houses. Such, he supposed, was London, ever variable, constantly surprising.

Howard pulled up in front of the largest of these houses, cream-painted, with long gleaming windows and fluted columns supporting the porch canopy. There were flower-beds and on each side of the house carefully planned layouts of cypresses and pruned kanzans. A notice fixed to the wall read: *Vale Park. Strictly Private. Parking for Residents only. By order of Notbourne Properties Ltd.*

'The old Montfort house,' said Howard, 'owned by the company to whom Loveday applied for a job.'

'The paths of glory,' said his uncle, 'lead but to the grave. What became of the Montforts, apart from the grave?'

'I don't know. The man to tell you would be Stephen Dearborn, the chairman of Notbourne Properties. He's supposed to be a great authority on Kenbourne Vale and its history. The company have bought up a lot of places in Kenbourne and they've done a good job smartening them up.'

It was unfortunate, Wexford thought, that they hadn't operated on Kenbourne Vale police station. It was in acute need of renovation, of pale paint to modify the gloom of bottle-green walls, mahogany woodwork and dark passages. One of these vaulted corridors led to Howard's own office, a vast chamber with a plum-red carpet, metal filing cabinets and a view of a brewery. The single bright feature of the room was human and female, a girl with a copper beech hair and surely the longest legs in London.

She looked up from the file she was studying as they entered and said, 'Mrs Fortune's been on the phone for you, sir. She said please would you call her back as it's very urgent.'

'Urgent, Pamela? What's wrong?' Howard moved to the phone.

'Apparently your . . .' The girl hesitated. 'Your uncle that's

42

staying with you is missing. He went out five hours ago and he hasn't come back. Mrs Fortune sounded very worried.'

'My God,' said Wexford. 'I was going to Victoria station. I shall be in terribly deep water.'

'You and me both,' said Howard, and then they began to laugh.

5

They gladly hear also the young men, yea, ana purposely provoke them to talk . . .

'AUNT DORA,' said Denise icily, 'is lying down. When her headache is better we're going over to my brother's to play bridge.'

Wexford made a further attempt to placate her. 'I'm very sorry about all this, my dear. I didn't mean to upset you, but it went right out of my head.'

'Please don't worry about me. It's Aunt Dora who's upset.'

'Men must work and women must weep,' said Howard rather unkindly. 'Now, where's my dinner and his snack?'

'I'm afraid I didn't prepare anything special for Uncle Reg. You see, we thought that since he seems to be disregarding all his doctor's warnings . . .'

'You'd punish him by giving him a proper meal? Poor old Reg. It looks as if we shall have to deal with you as More dealt with the children in Utopia, by letting them stand and be fed from the master's plate.'

Dora's manner, when she came down, was injured and distrait, but the chief inspector had been married for thirty years and had seldom permitted petticoat government.

Observing the determined gleam in his eye, she contented herself with a piteous, 'Oh, darling, how *could* you?' before sallying forth to her bridge game.

44

'Let's go into my study,' Howard said when they had finished their pilaf. 'I want to talk to you about that phone call.'

The study was a lot pleasanter than Howard's office in Kenbourne Vale and its appointments less vulnerable than those in the feminine-dominated part of the house. Wexford took his seat by a window through which could be seen, by way of a narrow opening between house backs, the flash of lights passing eternally down the King's Road. He was not yet used to living in a place where it never grew dark and where all night the sky held a plum-red glow.

'You look much better, Reg,' Howard said, smiling. 'May I say that ten years have fallen away from you in the space of one afternoon?'

'I daresay. One doesn't like to take a back seat, to live vicariously.' Wexford sighed. 'The tragedy of growing old is not that one is old but that one is young.'

'I've always thought *Dorian Gray* a very silly book and that epigram one of its few redeeming features. *And* it comes nearly on the last page.'

'Literary chit-chat, Howard?'

His nephew laughed. 'Not another word,' he said. 'Now that phone call Loveday made from Garmisch Terrace . . .'

'It was to Sytansound, wasn't it? You said she phoned Sytansound to say she was sick.'

'So she did, but that call was made at two o'clock and the one from Garmisch Terrace at one-fifteen. Whom did she phone?'

'Her mother? An old aunt? A girl friend? Perhaps she was replying to one of those advertisements.' When Howard shook his head at that, Wexford said, 'You're sure the call to Sytansound wasn't made earlier?'

'The manager took it, a man called Gold, and he's positive Loveday didn't phone before two. She was due back at two and he was beginning to wonder where she was when the phone rang.'

'She made one call from home but the other from a call box outside? Why?'

'Oh, surely because she had no more change. Don't you remember the Pope woman said Loveday asked her for change but all she had was one two-pence piece? Loveday must have got change outside, bought some cigarettes or a bar of chocolate and then gone into a phone box.'

'Yes, the first call was the decisive one, the important one On the outcome of that depended whether she returned to work or not. It was made to her killer.' Wexford rubbed his eye, caught himself doing it and relaxed. It was easy to relax now that he was being admitted to the secret sanctum of Howard's house and, better than that, the sanctum of his thoughts. 'Tell me about the Sytansound people,' he said.

Believing that the passing lights troubled his uncle, Howard drew the curtains and began. 'Gold is a man of sixty,' he said. 'He has a flat over the shop and he was in the shop all Friday afternoon. At five-thirty he switched the phone over to the answering service and went upstairs where he remained all the evening. That's well corroborated. Also at Sytansound are two reps and two engineers. The two reps and one of the engineers are married and live out of Kenbourne. The other is a boy of twenty-one. Their movements are being checked, but, if we're assuming that whoever received that phone call is Loveday's killer, it wasn't any of the older ones. They were all in the Lammas Arms from one till ten to two and none left the table to take a phone call. The twenty-one-year-old was putting a new valve in a television set at a house in Copeland Road. It may be worth checking as to whether anyone phoned that house while he was there, although it seems unlikely. As far as we know, Loveday had hardly ever spoken to the reps and the engineers. Listen, this is from Gold's statement.'

Howard had brought his briefcase into the study with him. He opened it and sorted out one sheet of paper from a small stack. ' "She was very quiet and polite. She was popular with the customers because she was always polite and patient. You would not call her the kind of girl who would ever stick up for herself. She was old-fashioned. When she first came she

46

wore no make-up and I had to ask her to." Apparently, he also asked her to turn her skirts up a bit and not to wear the same clothes every day.'

'What wages did he pay her?'

'Twelve pounds a week. Not much, was it, when you remember she was paying seven for her room? But the job was quite unskilled. All she had to do was show people two or three types of television set and ask for their names and addresses. The reps deal with the rental forms and take the money.'

Wexford bit his lip. It troubled him to think of this quiet polite girl, a child to him, living among the Peggy Popes of this world and paying more than half her wages for a room in Garmisch Terrace. He wondered how she had filled her evenings when, after walking from work through the gloomy defiles of the cemetery, she let herself into a cell perhaps twelve feet by twelve, a private vault for the living. No friends, no money to spend, no kind lover, no nice clothes . . .

'What was in her room?' he asked.

'Very little. A couple of sweaters, a pair of jeans, one dress, a topcoat. I don't think I've ever been in a room occupied by a girl and found so little evidence that a girl had ever occupied it. What little sticks of make-up she had were in her handbag. There was a cake of soap in the room, a bottle of shampoo, two or three women's magazines and a Bible.'

'A *Bible*?'

Howard shrugged. 'It may not have been hers, Reg. There was no name in it and the room was furnished—so-called, as Clements would say. It's possible the Bible was left behind by a previous tenant or that it just drifted there from some hoard of old books. There was a bookcase in the basement, if you noticed. Peggy Pope didn't know if it was hers or whose it was.'

'Will you try to find her parents?'

'We *are* trying. Of course, we haven't a proper photograph but all the newspapers have carried detailed descriptions. They must show themselves in the next couple of days if they're still alive, and why shouldn't they be? They wouldn't have to be more than in their forties.'

Wexford said carefully, 'Would you mind if tomorrow I sort of poke about a bit at Garmisch Terrace, talk to people and so on?'

'Poke about all you like,' Howard said affectionately. 'I need your help, Reg.'

Wexford was up by seven-thirty, bent on leaving by car with Howard, and this defiance sent both women into a flurry. Dora had only just come downstairs and there had been no time to prepare a special breakfast for him.

'Just boil me an egg, my dear,' he said airily to Denise, 'and I'll have a cup of coffee.'

'If you hadn't worried us nearly to death yesterday, we'd have gone out and bought you some of that Austrian cereal with the dried fruit and the extra vitimins.'

Wexford shuddered and helped himself surreptitiously to a slice of white bread.

'Your pills,' said his wife, trying to sound cold. 'Oh, Reg,' she wailed suddenly, 'carry them with you and please, please, don't forget to take them!'

'I won't,' said Wexford, pocketing the bottle.

The rush-hour traffic was heavy and nearly forty minutes elapsed before Howard dropped him outside 22 Garmisch Terrace. The pavements were wet and darkly glittering. As he slammed the car door, he saw a black-caped figure come out of the church and scurry off towards the shops.

The only living creature visible, apart from a cat peering through a grating into sewer depths, was a young man who sat on the top step of number 22, reading a copy of *The Stage*.

'The entry phone doesn't work,' he said as Wexford approached.

'I know.'

'I'll let you in if you like,' said the young man with the lazy indifference of the Frog Footman. He looked, if no means

48

of entering had been available, capable of sitting there until tomorrow. But he had a key, or said he had, and he proceeded to search for it through the pockets of a smelly Afghan jacket. In fashionable usage, Wexford decided, he would be termed one of the Beautiful People, and if like went to like, this must be Johnny.

'I believe you were friendly with the dead girl,' he said.

'Don't know about friendly. I sort of knew her. You the police?'

Wexford nodded. 'You're called Johnny. What's your other name?'

'Lamont.' Johnny wasn't disposed to be talkative. He found his key and let them into the hall where he stood gazing rather moodily at the chief inspector, a lock of dark chestnut hair falling over his brow. He was certainly very handsome with the look of an unkempt and undernourished Byron.

'Who was she friendly with in this house?'

'Don't know,' said Johnny. 'She said she hadn't any friends.' He seemed even more gloomy and indifferent than Peggy Pope and a good deal less communicative. 'She never spoke to anyone here but Peggy and me.' With a kind of lugubrious satisfaction he added: 'No one here can tell you anything. Besides, they'll all be at work by now.' He shrugged heavily, stuffed his magazine into his pocket and shambled off towards the basement stairs.

Wexford took the upward flight. Johnny had been correct in his assumption that most of the tenants would be out at work. He had expected the door of Loveday's room to be sealed up, but it stood ajar. Two plain-clothes men and one in uniform stood by the small sash window talking in low voices. Wexford paused and looked curiously into the room. It was very small and very bare, containing only a narrow bed, a chest of drawers and a bentwood chair. One corner, curtained off with a strip of thin yellow cretonne, provided storage space for clothes. The view from the window was of a plain and uncompromising brick wall, the side evidently of a deep well between this house and the one next door. The well acted as a sounding box, and the cooing of a pigeon perched somewhere higher up came to Wexford's ears as a raucous and hollow bray.

One of the men, seeing him and taking him for a sightseer, stepped briskly over and slammed the door. He went on up. On the third floor he found two tenants at home, an Indian whose room smelt of curry and joss-sticks and a girl who said she worked in a nightclub. Neither had ever spoken to Loveday Morgan but they remembered her as self-effacing, quiet and sad. Somewhat breathless by now, he reached the top of the fourth flight, where he encountered Peggy Pope, a pile of bedlinen in her arms, talking to a girl with a plain but vivacious face.

'Oh, it's you,' said Peggy. 'Who let you in?'

'Your friend Johnny.'

'Oh God, he's supposed to be down the Labour. He'll just lie about in bed now till the pubs open. I don't know what's got into him lately, he's going to pieces.'

The other girl giggled.

'Did you know Loveday Morgan?' Wexford asked her sharply.

'I said hallo to her once or twice. She wasn't my sort. The only time I really talked to her was to ask her to a party I was giving. That's right, isn't it, Peggy?'

'I reckon.' Peggy turned dourly to Wexford. 'She has a party every Saturday night and a bloody awful row they make. Sets my kid off screaming half the night.'

'Come off it, Peggy. You know you and Johnny have a great time at my parties.'

'Did Loveday accept your invitation?' Wexford asked.

'Of course not. She looked quite shocked like as if I'd asked her to an orgy. Mind you, she was very nice about it. She said not to worry about the noise. She liked to hear people enjoying themselves, but I thought, well, you're more like an old aunt than a kid of twenty.'

'She'd got no life in her at all,' said Peggy with a heavy sigh.

50

At the top of the last flight Wexford had much the same sensation as he had received when coming from the dingy wastes of Kenbourne into the light and space which surrounded the Montfort house. The arch at the head of the stairs had been filled in with a glass door set in a frame of polished wood and from this frame, hooked to white trellis, hung a display of house plants. These were so well arranged and well tended as to have satisfied even Denise.

The air smelt cleaner, fresher. Wexford stood still for a moment, getting his breath back, and then he put his finger to the bell above a small plaque which read: *'Chez* Teal.'

6

There be divers kinds of religion not only in sundry parts of the island, but also in divers places of every city

'I THOUGHT you'd turn up sooner or later,' said Ivan Teal. The look he gave Wexford was not the insolent stare of the previous day, but slightly mocking, containing a kind of intense inner amusement. 'Come in. You seem rather out of breath. Perhaps you've been afraid to breathe in case you might inhale something nasty? The stairs do smell, don't they? There must be some very unusual germs lurking in those cracks. I'm sure they'd be a source of fascination to a bacteriologist.' He closed the door and continued to talk in the same light indulgent tone. 'You may wonder why I live here. In point of fact, it has its advantages. The view, for instance, and I have plenty of space for a low rent. Besides, I'm sure you'll agree I've made the flat rather nice.'

It would have seemed nice in any surroundings. Here it was like a jewel in a pigsty. Apart from being spotlessly clean, the flat was decorated with an artist's taste in intense clear colours, the carpets deep, the walls hung here and there with abstract paintings. Wexford walked ahead of Teal into a long lounge running the length of the back of the house. The small sash windows had been removed and replaced by a fifteen-foot-long sheet of plate glass through which could be seen, starkly and almost indecently, the full windswept panorama of Kenbourne Cemetery. He stepped back, disconcerted, and saw

Teal's lips twitch.

'Our guest thinks we have an unhealthy taste for the macabre,' he said. 'Perhaps, child, we should get some pretty little lace curtains.'

Wexford had been so drawn to the window that he had not noticed the boy who knelt on the floor beside a wall-length well-stocked bookcase. As Teal addressed him, he got up and stood awkwardly, fidgeting with the girdle of his towelling dressing gown. He was perhaps twenty-two, slim, fair, with huge rather dull eyes.

'Let me introduce Philip Chell, the other consenting adult in this establishment.' Teal's twitching mouth broke into a grin. 'You've no idea what a pleasure it is to say that openly to a policeman.'

'Oh, Ivan!' said the boy.

'Oh, *Ivan*!' Teal mocked. 'There's nothing to be afraid of. We're doing nothing wrong. At your age you can surely hardly remember when it *was* wrong.' Still smiling, but rather less pleasantly, he said to Wexford, 'Unlike me who have suffered much from policemen.' He shrugged in the boy's direction. 'We must let bygones be bygones and give him some coffee. Go and get it, child.'

Philip Chell went with a sulky flounce.

Teal stared out at the cemetery, his head slightly on one side. 'I'm badly hung-up about it, aren't I? Shall I tell you a joke? It's quite proper, though you might not think so from the way it starts.' He turned his pale grey insolent eyes full on Wexford's face. 'Three men, an Englishman, a Frenchman and a Russian. Each tells the others what gives him the greatest pleasure. The Englishman says cricket on the village green on a fine Saturday afternoon in June. A bowl of bouillabaisse made by *une vraie Marseillaise*, says the Frenchman. It is night, says the Russian, I am in my flat. There comes a knock at my door the secret police are outside, soft hats, raincoats concealing guns. And my greatest pleasure comes when they ask for Ivan Ivanovitch and I can tell them that Ivan Ivanovitch lives next door.'

Wexford laughed.

'But you see, my friend, I wasn't able to say that, for Ivan lived here. And on two occasions I had to go with them.' His voice changed and he said lightly. 'Now my pleasure is to have policemen in for coffee. You know, one advantage the straight has over the gay is that he has a woman in the house and women are better at chores. That boy's hopeless. Make yourself at home while I go and rescue him.'

The bookshelves contained Proust, Gide and Wilde, as he might have expected, and a lot more he didn't expect. If Teal had read all these books Teal was well read. He reached for a calf-bound volume and, as he did so, its owner's voice said at his elbow:

'John Addington Symonds? Isn't he rather old-hat? Poor fellow. Swinburne called him Mr Soddington Symonds, you know.'

'I didn't know,' said Wexford, laughing, 'and I don't want Symonds. I see you've Robinson's translation of *Utopia*.'

'Borrow it.' Teal took the book down and handed it to Wexford. 'Do you take cream with your coffee? No? My friend has retired to the bedroom. I think he's afraid I'm going to make all sorts of revelations to you.'

'I hope you are, Mr Teal, though not of a kind that would embarrass Mr Chell. I want you to talk to me about Loveday Morgan.'

Teal placed himself on the window-seat, resting one arm along the sill. Sitting down, Wexford couldn't see the cemetery. Teal's face, one of those polished brown faces, both youthless and ageless, was framed against the milky sky. 'I knew her only very slightly,' he said. 'She was a strange repressed child. She had that look about her of a person who had been brought up by strict old-fashioned parents. Once or twice on Sunday mornings I saw her go off to church, go creeping off as if she were doing something both wrong and irresistible.'

'To *church*?' Suddenly he remembered the Bible. It had been hers then, after all.

'Why not?' exclaimed Teal, his voice loud and impatient.

'Some people still go to church even in these enlightened times.'

'Which church?'

'That one up at the end of the street, of course. I wouldn't have known she was going to church if she'd been trotting off to St Paul's, would I?'

'You needn't get so heated,' Wexford said mildly. 'Is that place C. of E.? No, I shouldn't think so.'

'They call themselves the Children of the Revelation. They're rather like Exclusives or Plymouth Bretheren. There's this chapel—temple, they call it—and another one up north somewhere and one in South London. Surely you as a policeman remember the fuss a year or two back when one of their ministers was up in court for some sort of indecency. Poor sod. It was in all the papers.' He added reflectively, 'It always is.'

'Was Loveday a—er, Child of the Revelation?'

'Hardly. She worked in a television shop, and to them television, newspapers and films are synonymous with sin. She probably went there because it was the nearest church and she wanted some comfort. I never discussed it with her.'

'What did you discuss with her, Mr Teal?'

'I'm coming to that. More coffee?' He refilled Wexford's cup and stretched out his legs, yawning. 'She was a quiet, sad sort of a girl as I daresay you've gathered. I don't think I'd ever seen her smile or look cheerful until one day about a fortnight ago. It was February the 14th, if that's any help to you. I remember'—he smiled sourly—'because that idiot child Philip had seen fit to send me a Valentine and we had a row about it. Sentimental nonsense! Well, instead of going out with him as we'd arranged, I was going for a quiet drink on my own to the Queen's Arms when I met Loveday coming along Queen's Lane—that's the street at the bottom here, in case you didn't know—looking as if she'd come into a fortune. It was just before six and she was on her way home from work. I'd never seen her looking the way she looked that evening. She was almost laughing, like a child laughs, you know, from joy.'

Wexford nodded. 'Go on.'

'She almost bumped into me. She didn't know where she was going. I asked her if she was all right and she stopped smiling and gave me a rather a stunned look. For a moment I thought she was going to faint. "Are you all right?" I said again. "I don't know," she said. "I feel funny. I don't know what I feel, Mr Teal. I'd like to sit down." Anyway, the upshot of it was I took her into the Queen's Arms and bought her a brandy. She was rather reluctant about that, but she didn't seem to have much resistance left. I don't think she'd ever had brandy before. The colour came back into her face, what colour she ever had, and I thought she'd open her heart to me.'

'But she didn't?'

'No. She looked as if she wanted to. She couldn't. Years of repression had made it impossible for her to confide in anyone. Instead she began asking me about Johnny and Peggy Pope. Were they trustworthy? Did I think Johnny would stay with Peggy? I couldn't tell her. They've only been here four months, not much longer than Loveday herself. I asked her in what way trustworthy, but she only said, "I don't know." Then I brought her back here and the only other time I ever spoke to her was last week when she asked me about Johnny and Peggy again. She wanted to know if they were very poor.'

'Strange question. She couldn't have helped them financially.'

'Certainly not. She hadn't any money.'

'What does Lamont do for a living?'

'Peggy told me he's a bricklayer by trade but that kind of work spoils the hands, if you please, and our Johnny has ambitions to act. He did a bit of modelling once and since then he's had some very grandiose ideas about his future. He's scared Peggy'll leave him and take the baby, but not scared enough apparently to settle down to a job of work. I imagine Loveday was a bit in love with him but he wouldn't have looked at her. Peggy's quite dazzlingly beautiful, don't you think, in spite of the dirt?'

56

Wexford agreed, thanking Teal for the coffee and the information, although it had let in little daylight.

The bedroom door moved slightly as they came out into the hall.

'She had no friends, no callers?' Wexford asked.

'I wouldn't know.' Teal eyed the door narrowly, then flung it open. 'Come out of there, child! There's no need to eavesdrop.'

'I wasn't eavesdropping, Ivan.' In the interim the boy had dressed himself in a scarlet sweater and velvet trousers. He looked pretty and he smelt of toilet water. 'I *do* live here,' he said sulkily. 'You shouldn't shut me up.'

'Perhaps Mr Chell can help us.' Wexford did his best not to laugh.

'As a matter of fact, maybe I can.' Chell turned a coquettish shoulder in Teal's direction and gave the chief inspector a winning smile. 'I saw a girl looking for Loveday.'

'When was that, Mr Chell?'

'Oh, I don't know. Not very long ago. She was young. She came in a car, a red Mini. I was going out and this girl was standing on the step, looking at the bells. She said she'd rung at Flat Eight but the young lady seemed to be out. Funny thing for one girl to say about another, wasn't it? The young lady? Then Loveday came along the street and said hallo to her and took her upstairs with her.'

Teal looked piqued. He seemed put out because Chell had told Wexford so much and he had told him so little. 'Well, describe this girl, child,' he said pettishly. 'Describe her. You see, Mr Wexford, that here we have a close observer who looks quite through the deeds of men.'

Wexford ignored him. 'What was she like?'

'Not exactly "with it", if you know what I mean.' The boy giggled. 'She'd got short hair and she was wearing a sort of dark blue coat Oh, and *gloves*,' he added as if these last were part of some almost unheard-of tribal paraphernalia.

'A full and detailed portrait,' sneered Teal. 'Never mind what colour her eyes were or if she were five feet or six feet tall. She wore *gloves*. Now all you have to do is find a conventional young lady who wears gloves and there's your murderer. Hey presto! Run along, now, back to your mirror. Be good, sweet child, and let who will be clever!'

It wasn't until Wexford was out in the street that he realised he had left *Utopia* lying on Teal's table. Let it stay there. He didn't relish the thought of climbing all those stairs again to fetch it and perhaps intruding into the monumental row he guessed had broken out between the two men. Instead, he walked to the limit of the cul-de-sac where two stumpy stone posts sprouted out of the pavement and eyed the strange ugly church.

Like Peggy Pope's clothes, every item which went to make up this unprepossessing whole seemed chosen with a deliberate eye to the hideous. What manner of man, or group of men, he asked himself, had designed this building and seen it as fit for the worship of their God? It was hard to say when it had been built. There was no trace of the Classical or the Gothic in its architecture, no analogy with any familiar style of construction. It was squat, shabby and mean. Perhaps in some seamy depths at its rear there were windows, but here at the front there was only a single circle of red glass not much bigger than a bicycle wheel, set under a rounded gable of port-coloured brick. Scattered over the whole façade was a noughts and crosses pattern of black and ochre bricks among the red.

The door was small and such as might have been attached to a garden shed. Wexford tried it but it was locked. He stooped down to read the granite tablet by this door: *Temple of the Revelation. The Elect shall be Saved.*

The hand which descended with a sharp blow on his shoulder made him wheel round.

'Go away,' said the bearded man in black. 'No trespassers here.'

'Kindly take your hand off my coat,' Wexford snapped.

Perhaps unused to any kind of challenge, the man did as he was told. He glared at Wexford, his eyes pale and fanatical. 'I don't know you.'

'That doesn't give you the right to assault me. I know you. You're the minister of this lot.'

'The Shepherd. What do you want?'

'I'm a police officer investigating the murder of Miss Loveday Morgan.'

The Shepherd thrust his hands inside his black cloak. 'Murder? I know nothing of murder. We don't read newspapers. We keep ourselves apart.'

'Very Christian, I'm sure,' said Wexford. 'This girl came to your church. You knew her.'

'No.' The Shepherd shook his head vehemently. He looked angry and affronted. 'I have been away ill and someone else was in charge of my flock. Maybe she slipped in past him. Maybe, in his ignorance, he took her for one of the five hundred.'

'The five hundred?'

'Such is our number, the number of the elect on the face of the Earth. We make no converts. To be one of the Children you must be born to parents who are both Children, and thus the number swells and with death declines. Five hundred,' he said adding less loftily, 'give or take a little.' Gathering the heavy dull folds of his robe around him,' he muttered, 'I have work to do. Good day to you,' and marched off towards Queen's Lane.

Wexford made his way to the northern gate of the cemetery. The ground at this end was devoted to Catholic graves. A funeral had evidently taken place on the previous day and the flowers brought by mourners were wilting in the March wind. He took an unfamiliar path which led him between tombs whose occupants had been of the Greek Orthodox faith, and he noted an epitaph on a Russian princess. Her name and patronymic reminded him of Tolstoy's novels with their lists of *dramatis personae*, and he was trying to decipher the Cyrillic script when a shadow fell across the tomb and a voice said:

'Tatiana Alexandrovna Kratov.'

For the second time that day he had been surprised while

59

reading an inscription. Who was it now? Another churlish priest, bent on correcting him and reproving his ignorance? This time he turned round slowly to meet the eyes of a big man in a sheepskin jacket who stood, smiling cheerfully at him, his hands in his pockets.

'Do you know who she was?' Wexford asked, 'and how she came to be buried here?'

The man nodded. 'There's not much I don't know about this cemetery,' he said, 'or Kenbourne itself, for that matter.' A kind of boyish enthusiasm took the arrogance from his next words. 'I'm an expert on Kenbourne Vale, a walking mine of information.' He tapped the side of his head. 'There are unwritten history and geography books in here.'

'Then you must be . . .' What was the name Howard had given him? 'You're Notbourne Properties,' he said absurdly.

'The chairman.' Wexford's hand was taken in a strong grip. 'Stephen Dearborn. How do you do?'

7

*He thinketh himself so wise that he will not allow
another man's counsel.*

THEY had emerged into a windswept clearing, and now that
he examined him more closely, Wexford saw that his new
acquaintance was a man of substance. Dearborn's suit had
come from a price range to which Wexford could never aspire,
his shoes looked hand-made, and the strap of his watch was
a broad band of gold links.'

'You're a stranger here, are you?' Dearborn asked him.

'I'm on holiday.'

'And you thought you'd like to visit the scene of a recent
crime?'

Dearborn's voice was still friendly and pleasant, but Wexford thought he detected in it that note of distaste that was
sometimes present in his own when he spoke to ghoulish
sightseers. 'I know about the murder, of course,' he said, 'but
the cemetery is fascinating enough in itself.'

'You wouldn't agree with those people who are in favour
of deconsecrating the place and using it for building land?'

'I didn't know there was any such move on foot.' Wexford
saw that now the other man was frowning. 'You're opposed
to building?' he asked. 'To renovating the place?'

'Not at all,' Dearborn said energetically. 'I've been largely
responsible for improving Kenbourne Vale. I don't know how
much of the district you've seen, but the conversions in Cope-

61

land Square, for instance, they're my work. And the old Montfort house. My company's aim is to retrieve as much as possible of the Georgian and early Victorian from the wanton demolition that goes on. What I don't want to see is every place of interest like this cemetery levelled to make . . .' He spread out his arms and went on more hotly, '. . . characterless concrete jungles!'

'You live in Kenbourne Vale?' Wexford asked as together they followed the path to St Peter's and the main gates.

'I was born here. I love every inch of the place, but I live in Chelsea. Laysbrook Place. Kenbourne Vale wouldn't suit my wife. It will one day when I've done with it. I want to make this the new Hampstead, the successor to fashionable Chelsea. And I can, I can!' Again Dearborn swept out an arm, striking an ilex branch and sending dust-filled raindrops flying. 'I want to show people what's really here, hidden under the muck of a century, the beautiful façades, the grand squares. I'd show you over the cemetery now, only I don't suppose you've got the time and—well, it rather . . . I don't feel . . .'

'The murder,' said Wexford intuitively, 'has temporarily spoiled it for you?'

'In a way, yes. Yes, it has.' He gave Wexford a look of approval. 'Clever of you to guess that. You see, the odd thing is that that very girl came to me for a job. I interviewed her myself. Putting her body in that tomb seemed a sort of desecration to me.' He shrugged. 'Let's not talk about it. What d'you think of this building, now?' he went on, pointing towards the sandstone dome. 'Eighteen-fifty-five and not a trace of the Gothic, but by then they had lost the art of emulating the Classical and were experimenting with Byzantine. Look at the length of those columns . . .' Laying a large hand on Wexford's arm, he plunged into a lecture on architectural styles, laced with obscure terms and words which to Wexford were almost meaningless. His listener's faint bewilderment communicated itself to him and he stopped suddenly, saying, 'I'm boring you.'

'No, you're not. It's just that I'm afraid I'm rather ignorant. I find the district fascinating.'

'Do you?' The chairman of Notbourne Properties was evidently unused to an appreciative audience. 'I'll tell you what,' he said eagerly. 'Why don't you drop round and see us one night? Laysbrook House. I could show you maps of this place as it was a hundred and fifty years ago. I've got deeds of some of these old houses that would really interest you. What do you think?'

'I'd like that very much.'

'Let's see. It's Thursday now. Why not Saturday night? Come about half-past eight and we'll have a drink and go over the maps together. Now, can I give you a lift anywhere?'

But Wexford refused this invitation. The man had been kind and expansive to him. To confess now that he was a police-man, bound for Kenbourne Vale police station, might make Dearborn see him in the guise of a spy.

Instead of returning to the station, however, he turned east-wards along Lammas Grove in search of Sytansound. The police car parked outside told him where it was before he could read the shop sign. Sergeant Clements was at the wheel. He welcomed the chief inspector with a cheery, 'Had your lunch yet, sir?'

'I thought I might try your canteen,' Wexford said, getting in beside him. 'Would you recommend it?'

'I usually pop home if I can. I only live round the corner. I like to see the boy when I get the chance. He's in bed by the time I get home at night.'

'Your son?'

Clement's didn't reply at once. He was watching a boy un-load something from a Sytansound van, but it seemed to Wex-ford that this was a simulated preoccupation, and he re-peated his question. The sergeant turned back to face him. The strong colour in his cheeks had deepened to crimson and he cleared his throat.

'As a matter of fact,' he said, 'we're adopting him. We've

63

got him on three months probation, but the mother's signed the consent and we're due to get the order next week, a week tomorrow.' He slid his hands slowly around the wheel. 'If the mother changed her mind now I reckon it'd about kill my wife.'

Embarrassment and uncertainty had been transferred from one to the other, but there was nothing that Wexford could do about it now. 'Surely, if she's consented . . . ?'

'Well, sir, yes. That's what I keep telling my wife. We're ninety-nine per cent there. It's all been done through the proper channels, but natural mothers have been known to change their minds at the last minute and the court will always go with the mother even if she's given her consent in writing.'

'Do you know the mother?'

'No, sir. And she doesn't know us. We're just a serial number to her. It's done through what's called a guardian *ad litem*, she's a probation officer really. When the time comes the wife and I will go along to the court and the wife'll sit there with the boy on her lap—nice touch that, isn't it?—and the order'll be made and then—then he'll be ours for ever. Just as if he was our own.' Clements' voice grew thick and his lips trembled. 'But you can't help having just that one per cent chance in mind that something may go wrong.'

Wexford was beginning to feel sorry that he had ever opened the subject. The steering wheel which Clements' hands had gripped was wet with sweat and he could see a pulse drumming in his left temple. When he had spoken those last words he had looked near to actual tears.

'I take it Mr Fortune's inside the shop?' he said in an effort to change the subject. 'Who's the boy with the van?'

'That's Brian Gregson, sir. You've heard of him, I daresay. The one with the good friends all burning to give him an alibi.' Clements was calmer now as his attention was diverted from his personal problems back to the case. 'He's one of Sytansound's engineers, the only young unmarried one.'

Wexford remembered now that Howard had mentioned Gregson, but only in passing and not by name. 'What's this about an alibi?' he asked. 'And why should he need one?'

'He's just about the only man who ever associated with Loveday Morgan so-called. Tripper—that's the cemetery bloke— saw him giving her a lift home one night in his van. And one of the reps says Gregson used to chat her up in the shop sometimes.'

'A bit thin, isn't it?' Wexford objected.

'Well, his alibi for that Friday night is thin, too, sir. He *says* he was in the Psyche Club in Notting Hill—that's a sort of drinking place, sir. God knows what else goes on there—and four villains say he was with them there from seven till eleven. But three of them have got form. You couldn't trust them an inch. Look at him, sir. Wouldn't you reckon he'd got something to hide?'

He was a slight fair youth who seemed younger than the twenty-one years Howard had attributed to him and whose thin schoolboy arms looked too frail to support the boxes he was carrying from the van into the shop. Wexford thought he had the air of someone who believes that if he bustles away at his job, giving the impression of a rapt involvement, he may pass unnoticed and escape the interference of authority. Whether or not this was the hope that spurred him to trot in and out so busily with his loads, his work was destined to be interrupted. As he again approached the rear of the van, determinedly keeping his eyes from wandering towards the police car, a ginger-headed, sharp-faced man came out of Sytansound, beckoned to him and called out:

'Gregson! Here a minute!'

'That's Inspector Baker, sir,' said Clements. 'He'll put him through the mill all right, tell him a thing or two like his father should have done years ago.'

Wexford sighed to himself, for he sensed what was coming and knew that, short of getting out of the car, he was powerless to stop it.

'Vicious, like all the young today,' said Clements. 'Take these girls that have illegits, they've got no more idea of their responsibilities than—than rabbits.' He brought this last word

65

out on a note of triumphant serendipity, perhaps believing that the chief inspector with his rustic background would be familiar with the behaviour of small mammals.

'They can't look after them,' he went on. 'You should have seen our boy when he first came to us, thin, white, his nose always running. I don't believe he'd been out in the fresh air since he was born. It isn't fair!' Clements' voice rose passionately. 'They don't want them, they'd have abortions only they leave it too late, while a decent, clean-living woman, a religious woman, like my wife has miscarriage after miscarriage and eats her heart out for years. I'd jail the lot of them, I'd . . .'

'Come now, Sergeant . . .' Wexford hardly knew what to say to calm him. He sought about in his mind for consoling platitudes, but before he could utter a single one the car door had opened and Howard was introducing him to Inspector Baker.

It was apparent from the moment that they sat down in the Grand Duke that Inspector Baker was one of those men who, like certain eager philosophers and scientists, form a theory and then force the facts to fit it. Anything which disturbs the pattern, however relevant, must be rejected, while insignificant data are grossly magnified. Wexford reflected on this in silence, saying nothing, for the inspector's conclusions had not been addressed to him. After the obligatory handshake and the mutterings of a few insincere words, Baker had done his best to exclude him from the discussion, adroitly managing to seat him at the foot of their table while he and Howard faced each other at the opposite end.

Clearly Gregson was Baker's candidate for the Morgan murder, an assumption he based on the man's record—a single conviction for robbery—the man's friends, and what he called the man's friendship with Loveday.

'He hung around her in the shop, sir. He gave her lifts in that van of his.'

'We know he gave her *a* lift,' said Howard.

66

Baker had a harsh unpleasant voice, the bad grammar of his childhood's cockney all vanished now, but the intonation remaining. He made everything he said sound bitter. 'We can't expect to find witnesses to every time they were together. They were the only young people in that shop. You can't tell me a girl like Morgan wouldn't have encouraged his attentions.'

Wexford looked down at his plate. He never liked to hear women referred to by their surnames without Christian name or style, not even when they were prostitutes, not even when they were criminals. Loveday had been neither. He glanced up as Howard said, 'What about the motive?'

Baker shrugged. 'Morgan encouraged him and then gave him the cold shoulder.'

Wexford hadn't meant to interrupt, but he couldn't help himself. 'In a *cemetery*?'

The inspector acted exactly like a Victorian parent whose discourse at the luncheon table had been interrupted by a child, one of those beings who were to be seen but not heard. But he looked as if he would have preferred not to see Wexford as well. He turned on him a reproving and penetrating stare, and asked him to repeat what he had said.

Wexford did so. 'Do people want to make love in cemeteries?'

For a moment it seemed as if Baker was going to do a Clements and say that 'they' would do anything anywhere. He appeared displeased by Wexford's mention of love-making, but he didn't refer to it directly. 'No doubt you have a better suggestion,' he said.

'Well, I have some questions,' Wexford said tentatively. 'I understand that the cemetery closes at six. What was Gregson doing all the afternoon?'

Howard, who seemed distressed by Baker's attitude, making up for it by a particularly delicate courtesy to his uncle, attending to his wants at the table and refilling his glass from the bottle of apple juice, said quickly, 'He was with Mrs Kirby in Copeland Road until about one-thirty, then back at Sytansound. After that he went to a house in Monmouth Street—

that's near Vale Park, Reg—and then he had a long repair job in Queen's Lane that took him until five-thirty, after which he went home to his parents' house in Shepherd's Bush.'

'Then I don't quite see . . .'

Baker had been crumbling a roll of bread into pellets with the air of a man preoccupied by his own thoughts. He raised his head and said in a way that is usually described as patient but in fact is a scarcely disguised exasperation, 'That the cemetery closes at six doesn't mean that no one can get in or out. There are breaches in the walls, quite a bad one at the end of Lammas Road, and vandals are always making them worse. The whole damned place ought to be ploughed up and built on.' Having given vent to his statement, utterly in opposition to Stephen Dearborn's views, he sipped his gin and gave a little cough. 'But that's by the way. You must admit, Mr Wexford, that you don't know this district like we do, and a morning's sightseeing isn't going to teach it to you.'

'Come, Michael,' Howard said uneasily. 'Mr. Wexford's anxious to learn. That's why he asked.'

Wexford was distressed to hear that his new acquaintance—his antagonist rather—shared Burden's Christian name. It reminded him bitterly how different his own inspector's response would have been. But he said nothing. Baker hardly seemed to have noticed Howard's mild reproof beyond giving a faint shrug. 'Gregson could have got in and out of the cemetery,' he said, 'as easily as you can swallow whatever that stuff is in your glass there.'

Wexford took a sip of the 'stuff' and tried again, determined not to let Howard see him show signs of offence. 'Have you a medical report yet?'

'We'll come to that in a minute. Gregson met her in Queen's Lane at half past five and they went to a secluded spot in the cemetery. She became frightened, screamed perhaps, and he strangled her to silence her.'

Why hadn't they gone to her room? Wexford asked himself. Why not to her room in that house where no questions were asked? And why had she taken the afternoon off if she didn't

68

intend to meet Gregson until after work? These were questions he might ask Howard when they were alone together but not now. He saw that Baker was a man whose idea of a discussion was that he should be invited to state his views while the other so-called participants admired, agreed and encouraged him. Having given his own limited reconstruction of the case, he had turned to Howard once more and was attempting to discuss with him in an almost inaudible tone the findings of the medical report.

But Howard was determined not to exclude his uncle. Aware that Wexford had a small reputation as an investigator into quirks of character, he pressed Wexford to tell them about his morning's work.

'She was a very innocent girl,' Wexford began. He felt he was on safe ground here, for Baker could hardly claim to be as conversant with the personality of the dead girl as he was with the geography of Kenbourne Vale. 'She was very shy,' he said, 'afraid to go to parties, and very likely she'd only once in her life been into a public house.' He was pleased to see a smile of what might have been approval on Baker's face. It encouraged him to be bolder, to ask a question which might seem to reflect on the inspector's theory. 'Would a girl like that lead a man on, go alone with a comparative stranger into a lonely place? She'd be too frightened.'

Baker went on smiling tightly.

'There was another point that struck me ...'

'Let's have it, Reg. It may be helpful.'

'Tuesday was February the 29th. I've been wondering if he put her in the Montfort vault because he knew it was only visited on the last Tuesday of the month and that Tuesday, he thought, had already gone by.'

Baker looked incredulous, but Howard's eyes narrowed. 'You mean he *forgot* that this year, Leap Year, there was an extra Tuesday in the month?'

'It's a possibility, isn't it? I don't think a boy like Gregson would know about the vault and the trust. I was thinking that the man who killed her did know and that he might have put her in there because Loveday knew something he didn't want revealed before a few weeks had passed by.'

'Interesting,' said Howard. 'How does that strike you, Michael?'

The man who was not Burden, who shared with Burden only a Christian name and a certain sharp-featured fairness, raised his eyebrows and drawled, 'To your—er, uncle's other point, sir?' It was clever the hesitation he managed before saying 'uncle's', just sufficiently emphasising the nepotism. But he had gone a little too far. His remark brought a frown to Howard's usually gentle face and set him tapping his fingers against his wineglass. And Baker understood that he was admonished. He shrugged, smiled and spoke with cool courtesy.

'You called Morgan innocent and shy, Mr Wexford, but I'm sure you know how deceptive appearances can be. Post-mortem findings, on the other hand, aren't deceptive. Would it surprise you to hear that, according to the medical report, she gave birth to a child during the past year?'

8

Away they trudge, I say, out of their known and accustomed houses, finding no place to rest in.

AFTER Howard's kindness and the cheerful, matter-of-fact welcome he had received from other members of Howard's force, Wexford felt Baker's antagonism almost painfully. He was curiously disheartened. His first day here—his first day anywhere, come to that—as a private investigator had begun so promisingly. Baker's intervention had been like a dark cloud putting out the sun.

He knew that if he had been fit and quite well, if his confidence hadn't been shaken by his tough old body suddenly betraying him, he would have taken this small reverse in his stride. He wasn't, after all, a child to be put off playing his favourite game because another stronger and healthier child had come along and tried to show him how the bricks ought to be stacked. But now within himself he felt almost childlike, his bold adult identity once more disturbed. And when he looked back on his morning's work, it seemed amateurish. The appalling thought that Howard had sent him off on a little hunt of his own simply to occupy him and keep him happy couldn't be resisted.

Nor was he much comforted by the private office which Howard had set aside for his use and to which Detective Constable Dinehart had just conducted him. Like all the rooms Wexford had seen in this police station, it was dark, gloomy and with an enormously high ceiling. This one had a bit of

71

greyish carpet, chairs covered in slippery brown leather, and the view from the window was a full frontal one of Kenbourne gasworks. He couldn't help thinking nostalgically of his own office in Kingsmarkham which was bright and modern, and, looking at the pitch pine, pitted monstrosity in front of him, of his beloved rosewood desk, damson-red and always laden with his own particular clutter.

Sitting down, he asked himself sharply what was the matter with him. Howard's house was too grand for him, this place too shabby. What did he expect? That London would be a Utopian Kingsmarkham and that all these London coppers were going to roll out the red carpet for him?

He stared at the gasometer, wondering how he was going to pass the afternoon. 'Poke about all you like,' Howard had said, but where was he to poke about and how much authority had he got? He was considering whether it would be pushing or against protocol for him to seek Howard out when his nephew tapped on the door and came in.

Howard looked tired. His was a face which easily showed wear and tear. The grey eyes had lost their brightness and the skin under them was puffy.

'How d'you like your office?'

'It's fine, thanks.'

'Horrible outlook, I'm afraid, but it's either that or the brewery or the bus station. I want to apologise for Baker.'

'Come off it, Howard,' said Wexford.

'No. His treatment of you was rude but not indefensible. One has to make allowances for Baker. He's been under a good deal of strain lately. He married a girl half his age. She became pregnant, which made him very happy until she told him the child was another man's and she was leaving him for that other man. Since then he's lost his confidence, distrusts people and is chronically afraid of not being up to the job.'

'I see. It's a nasty story.'

They were both silent for a moment. Wexford found himself hoping desperately that Howard wouldn't go away again, leaving him alone with the gasworks and his depressing thoughts. To keep him there a little longer, he said, 'About this child of Loveday Morgan's . . .'

'That's really why I came to talk to you,' Howard said. 'I don't know what to think. I don't even know if it's significant in this case, and I need to talk it over with someone. With you.'

Wexford felt himself relax with relief. His nephew sounded sincere. Perhaps, after all . . . 'The child may be with his or her grandparents,' he said, and as he spoke he felt the case beginning to drive self-pitying thoughts from his mind. 'You've still heard nothing of them?'

'We're doing everything possible to trace them. For one thing, they'll have to be found before she can be buried, but I'm beginning to think they must be dead. Oh, I know that these days girls are always having differences with their parents and leaving home, but often that only makes the parents more anxious about them. What sort of people who have a missing, or at least absent, blonde twenty-year-old daughter, could read all the newspaper stories there have been these past few days and not get in touch with us?'

'Very simple unimaginative people, perhaps, Howard. Or people who just don't connect their daughter with Loveday Morgan because that isn't her real name and they don't know that their daughter was living in Kenbourne Vale.'

Howard shrugged. 'It's as if she dropped out of the blue, Reg, arrived in Kenbourne Vale two months ago without a history. Let me put you a bit more fully into the picture. Now, as you know, although we don't have absolute cards of identity as certain European nationals do, everyone has a medical card and a National Insurance number. There was no medical card in Loveday Morgan's room and she was on none of the local doctor's lists. It's inconceivable that she should have been the private patient of any doctor, but maybe she was so healthy that she didn't need medical attention. But she had a *child*, Reg. Where? Who attended her at the birth?

'When she first went to Sytansound, Gold asked her for her National Insurance card. She told him she hadn't got one and

73

he sent her along to the Social Security people to get a card which she did in the name of Loveday Morgan.'

'Stop a minute, Howard,' said his uncle. 'That means that she had never worked before. A working-class girl of twenty who had never worked . . .'

'She may, of course, have worked before and had a card in her real name. They don't ask for your birth certificate, you know, only your name and where you were born and so on. I really don't think there's anything to stop anyone from getting half a dozen cards and fraudulently claiming sickness benefit and unemployment money, only that one day they'd catch up with you. Of couse, there are certain jobs you can do where you needn't have a card at all. Most charwomen don't. Prostitutes don't. Nor do those who make their living by crime or drug pushing. But surely Loveday Morgan wasn't any of those things?'

Wexford shook his head. 'She seems the last girl in the world who would have had an illegitimate child.'

'You know what they say, it's the good girls who have the babies. Now, as well as her parents, we're trying to trace her child. It isn't fostered in Kenbourne Vale, we've established that. It could be anywhere. D'you know what I find hardest of all to understand, Reg?'

Wexford looked enquiring.

'I can see that she might have had reasons for wanting to cover her tracks, for wanting to be anonymous. She may, for instance, have had possessive parents who tried to deny her a life of her own. She may have been hiding from some man who threatened her—a point that, I must remember that. But what I can't fathom at all is why she had apparently been *doing this for years*. It almost looks as if years ago she avoided going to a doctor or getting a National Insurance card so that one day, *now*, when she came to die by violence, she would appear to have had a life of no more than two months duration, to have dropped from another planet.'

'What about this Fulham address?' Wexford asked.

'The one she gave Peggy Pope? It's a house in Belgrade

74

Road, as I told you, but she was never there.'

'The owners of the house ... ?'

'I suppose they could be lying, playing some deep game of their own, but all the neighbours aren't. I expect Loveday went along Belgrade Road in a bus one day and the name stuck in her mind. I realise, of course, that when you give a false address, unless you simply make up a name, the address you give is that of a street you've either seen or heard of in some connection that causes it to remain in your memory. But the mind is so complex, Reg, and she isn't alive to be psychoanalysed. If she were, we wouldn't be doing this, talking this way.'

'I was thinking that she might have known someone in this Belgrade Road.'

'You mean we ought to do a house to house on the chance of that?'

'Well, *I* could,' said Wexford.

He weighed himself before he went to bed and found that he had lost five pounds. But instead of being cheered by this in the morning he awoke depressed. It was raining. Like a humble trainee, he was going to have to plod round Fulham in the rain. And where, anyway, *was* Fulham?

Denise had stuck a rather alarming flower arrangement on the landing, a confection which was to floral decoration as Dali is to painting. A branch of holly grabbed him as he started to go downstairs and when he freed himself his hand came into disagreeable contact with a spider plant.

'Where's Fulham?' he asked as he ate his sugarless grapefruit. 'Not miles away I hope.'

Denise said, 'It's just down the road.' She added mournfully, 'Some people call *this* Fulham.'

She didn't ask why he wanted to know. She and Dora thought he was going for his favourite Embankment walk, not understanding that he hated the river when it was shivering and prickly with rain. By now it was falling steadily, not country rain which washes and freshens and brings with it a green scent, but London rain, dirty and soot-smelling. He went westwards, crossed Stamford Bridge and past the gates to the football ground. By the station, fans were buying Chelsea scarves and badges in the sports souvenir shops. Young couples stared disconsolately at secondhand furniture, battered three-piece suites growing damp on the pavement. In North End Road traffic crawled between the stalls, splashing shoppers. But it was more the sort of thing he was used to, a bit like Stowerton really. Here was none of the jaded and somehow sinister sophistication of Kenbourne Vale. The side streets looked suburban. They had gardens and whole families lived in them. Housewives shopped here with proper shopping baskets and almost everyone he passed seemed to belong to an order of society with which he was familiar.

He laughed at himself for being like a conventional old fuddy-duddy, and then he saw Belgrade Road ahead of him, debouching at a right angle from the main street. The houses were three storeys tall, sixty or seventy years old, terraced. At the end, as in Garmisch Terrace, was a church, but grey and spired and as a church should be. He furled the umbrella he was carrying and began on his house to house.

There were a hundred and two houses in Belgrade Road. He went first to the one where Loveday said she had lived, a cared-for house which had recently been painted. Even the brickwork had been painted, and it was a curious colour to choose for an English house in a grimy street, a bright rose-pink. Number seventy. It had a name too, Rosebank, printed in white on pink, the sign swinging in the rain. Had she chosen it for the number? For the name? Had she even seen it?

A couple lived there, Howard had said, and it was a young woman who answered his ring. It made him feel rather awkward asking about a girl with fair hair, quiet and reserved, a girl who might have had a baby with her, for this woman was also a blonde and she carried a young child supported on her hip.

'They came and asked me before,' she said. 'I told them we never let rooms or a flat.' She added proudly, 'We live in the *whole* house.'

76

He tried the immediate neighbours, worked back to the main street from which this one turned, then up towards the church, down the other side. A lot of people in Belgrade Road let rooms and he talked to half a dozen landladies who sent him off to other landladies. At one point he thought he was getting somewhere. A West Indian hospital orderly who worked nights but showed no dismay at being awakened from his sleep, remembered young Mrs Maitland who had lived on the top floor of number 59 and whose husband had abandoned her and her baby in December. She had moved away a couple of weeks later.

Wexford went back to 59 where he had previously met with ungraciousness on the part of the owner, and met this time with pugnacity. 'I told you my daughter was living here. How many more times, I should like to know? Will you go away and let me get on with my cooking? She left in December and she's living up Shepherd's Bush way. I saw her last night and she wasn't dead then. Does that satisfy you?'

Disheartened, he went on. There was no point in giving her name. He was sure she hadn't called herself Loveday Morgan until she went to live in Garmisch Terrace. All he could do was repeat the description and enquire about anyone known to have moved away at the end of the previous year. The rain fell more heavily. What a stupid invention an umbrella was, almost useless for a job like this! But he put it up again, tilting it backwards while he stood under the dripping porches.

Facing the rose-pink house and on the corner of the only side street to run out of Belgrade Road was a little shop, a general store, very like those to be found in the villages near Kingsmarkham. Wexford marvelled to see such a place here, only a hundred yards from a big shopping centre, and marvelled still more to see that it was doing a thriving trade. There was just one assistant serving the queue, a shabby little woman with a mole on the side of her nose, and he made his enquiries of her briefly, anxious not to keep her from her work. She had a curious flat voice, free from cockney, and she was patient with him, but neither she nor the woman shopper behind him

77

—a resident of the side street—could recall anyone answering his description who had moved away in December.

About twenty houses remained to be visited. He visited them all, feeling very cold now and wondering how he was going to explain to Dora that he had got soaked to the skin. Between them all they were turning him into a hypochondriac, he thought, and he began to feel nervous, asking himself what all this tramping about and getting wet might be doing to his health. Crocker would have a fit if he could see him now, water running from his hair down the back of his neck as he emerged from the last house. Well, Crocker didn't know everything, and for the rest of the day and all tomorrow until the evening he would take it easy.

He paused and, turning back, surveyed the whole length of the street once more. Through the falling silvery rain, under the massy clouds which were streaming across the sky from behind the grey church spire, Belgrade Road looked utterly commonplace. Nothing but the church and the pink house distinguished it from a sister street which ran from the main highway in the opposite direction, and this latter was, if anything, more interesting and memorable. Buses used it and on a sunny day both sides of it would catch the full sun for hours. Why, then had Loveday Morgan chosen Belgrade Road?

He tried to imagine himself giving a false address in London. What street would *he* choose? Not one that he had stayed in or knew well, for that might lead to discovery. Say Lammas Grove, West Fifteen? Number 43, for instance. Immediately he asked himself why, and reasoned that he had picked the street because he had sat outside Sytansound there with Sergeant Clements, the number was just a number that had come to him. . . .

So that was how it was done. That was the way Howard had inferred that it was done, and he had been right again. Obviously, then, it was hopeless to try to trace Loveday by these means. He must approach the matter from other angles.

9

*In them they have . . . all manner of fruit, herbs and
flowers, so pleasant, so well furnished, and so finely
kept, that I never saw thing more fruitful nor better
trimmed in any place.*

GOING out in the evening was one of the excesses on
which Crocker had placed a strict ban. If Wexford's
faith in the doctor had been shaken, his wife's had not. She
could only be consoled by his promise to take a taxi to Laysbrook Place, to abstain from strong drink and not to stay out
too long.

He was looking forward to this visit. A little judicious
questioning might elicit from Dearborn more information
about the cemetery. Was it, for instance, as easy to get in and
out after the gates were closed as Baker had insisted? Before
Tripper and his fellows went home at night did they make
any sort of search of the place? Or must Loveday have been
killed before six? If this was so, Gregson, occupied at work,
would be exonerated. And might Dearborn not also know
something of Loveday herself? He had interviewed her. It was
possible that, at that interview, she had told him something
of her past history.

Laysbrook Place was one of those country corners of
London in which the air smells sweeter, birds sometimes sing
and other trees grow apart from planes. An arch, hung with
a brown creeper Wexford thought was wistaria, concealed most
of the little street from Laysbrook Square. He walked under
it, light falling about him from two lamps on brackets, and

saw ahead of him a single house such as might have stood in Kingsmarkham High Street. It wasn't an old house but old bricks and timber had been used in its construction, and it was like no London house Wexford had seen. For one thing, it was rather low and sprawling with gables and lattice windows; for another, it had a real garden with apple trees in it and shrubs that were probably lilac. Now, in early March, forsythia blazed yellow and luminous through the lamplit dark and, as he opened the gate, he saw snowdrops in drifts as thick and white as real snow.

The front door opened before he reached it and Stephen Dearborn came down the steps.

'What a lovely place,' Wexford said.

'You'd agree with my wife, then, that it's an improvement on Kenbourne?'

Wexford smiled, sighing a little to himself, for he had been so piercingly reminded of the country. He was suddenly conscious of the peace and the silence. Not even in Howard's house had he been able to escape from the ceaseless sound of traffic, but there was nothing more to be heard than a faint throbbing, what Londoners call the 'hum', ever present in the city and its suburbs but sometimes so remote as to seem like a sound in one's own head.

'My wife's upstairs with our daughter,' Dearborn said. 'She wouldn't go to sleep and it's no good my staying with her. I just want to cuddle her and play with her all the time.'

It was warm inside but airy, enough heat turned on to take off the March chill without making one gasp. The house was very obviously the residence of a rich man, but Wexford couldn't see any sign of pretentiousness or evidence that money had been spent with an eye to impress. It wasn't even very tidy. There was a scattering of crumbs under a tea-table and an ivory teething ring lay on a blanket in the middle of the carpet.

'What will you drink?'

Wexford was getting tired of drawing attention to his illness and his diet. 'Have you any beer?' he asked.

'Sure we have. I couldn't get through the weekend without it after all those shorts I have to consume the rest of the time. I drink it from the can, as a matter of fact.' Dearborn gave a sudden boyish smile. 'We'd better have glasses or my wife will kill me after you've gone.'

The beer was kept in a refrigerator with a wood veneered door which Wexford had at first glance taken for a glass cabinet. 'My favourite toy,' said Dearborn. 'When Alexandra gets a bit older I shall always keep it full of ice cream and cans of coke.' Still smiling, he filled their glasses. 'I've come to fatherhood rather late in life, Mr Wexford—I was forty-three last Tuesday—and my wife says it's made me soppy. I'd like to get the moon and stars for my daughter, but, as this is impossible, she shall have all the good things of this world instead.'

'You're not afraid of spoiling her?'

'I'm afraid of many things, Mr Wexford.' The smile died away and he became intensely serious. 'Of being too indulgent and too possessive among other things. I tell myself that she's not mine, that she belongs to herself. It's not easy being a parent.'

'No, it's not easy. And it's as well people don't know it, for if they did, maybe they wouldn't dare have children.'

Dearborn shook his head. 'I could never feel like that. I'm a fortunate man. I've been lucky in marriage. And you know what they say, happy is the man who can make a living from his hobby. But, for all that, I didn't know what real happiness was till I got Alexandra. If I lost her I'd—I'd kill myself.'

'Oh, come, you mustn't say that.'

'It's true. I mean it. You don't believe me?'

But Wexford, who had many times heard men make similar threats without taking them very seriously, did believe him. There was a kind of earnest desperation in the man's whole manner, and he was relieved when the tension was slackened by the entry of Mrs Dearborn.

She told him she was glad to see him. 'As long as you don't

encourage Stephen to cart us all off to some slum,' she said. 'He gets tired of places he can't improve.'

'It would be hard to improve on Laysbrook House,' said Wexford politely.

She was not at all beautiful and she had made no attempt to look younger than her forty years. Her walnut-brown hair was threaded with grey, her neck ringed with lines. He wondered what constituted her appeal. Was it the willowy ease with which she moved—for she was very slim—or the play of her long fine hands or her extreme femininity? The last, he thought. Her nails were varnished, her skirt short, she was even now taking a cigarette from a cedarwood box, but for all that she had all the old-fashioned womanly grace of a lady out of one of Trollope's novels, a squire's lady, a chatelaine.

That Dearborn was in love with her was immediately apparent from the way his eyes followed her to her chair and lingered on her, watching her settle herself and smooth her skirt over her crossed legs. It was almost as if those briefly caressing hands had for a moment become his own and, vicariously, he felt under them the smoothness of silk and flesh.

Wexford was wondering how to broach the subject of Kenbourne cemetery when Dearborn announced that it was time to get the maps out.

'Dull for you, darling,' he said. 'You've heard it all so many times before.'

'I can bear it. I shall knit.'

'Yes, do. I like to see you knitting. It's a funny thing, Mr Wexford, the qualities women think will attract us and the qualities which really do. I could watch Miss World doing a striptease and it would leave me cold, but let me see a woman in a clean white apron rolling pastry and I'd be in love with her before she could close the kitchen door.'

Mrs Dearborn laughed. 'That's true,' she said. 'You were.'

So that's the way they came together, Wexford thought. It really happened and not too long ago either. It must have been like a Dutch interior, the man visiting the house as a guest for the first time, the kitchen door half open and behind it this brown-haired woman with the sweet face looking up, startled from her cooking, shy at being caught in her apron and with flour on her arms.

Mrs Dearborn seemed to sense what was going on in his mind, for her eyes met his fleetingly and she pursed her lips, suppressing a smile. Then she lifted from a bag a mass of wool and half-completed work, as white and fluffy as flour, and began to knit.

To watch her was curiously soothing. Every harassed businessman, he thought, should have a tank of tropical fish at one end of his office and a woman knitting at the other. Tired now, he could have watched her all the evening, but he had to turn his attention to the maps, photographs and the old deeds which Dearborn had brought into the room and spread in front of them.

The enthusiasm of the crusader had taken hold of Dearborn and as he talked a light came into his eyes. This was Kenbourne as it had been in the time of the fourth George; here had stood the manor house which a royal duke had rented for his actress mistress; on the south side of Lammas Grove had stood a row of magnificent elms. Why shouldn't the land be cleared and fresh trees planted? Why not make all this waste stretch here into playing fields? There was no need for Wexford to ask about the cemetery. Before he could interrupt he was told its acreage, the history of every interesting person buried there, and informed that the state of the walls on the eastern side was so bad that soon vandals would be able to enter and plunder at will.

A point to Baker. Wexford tried to relax and make himself receptive, but he felt overwhelmed. He was experiencing a sensation he had often had before when lectured by someone with an obsession. It is all too much. It should be done in easy stages, but the obsessed cannot see this. Night and day he has lived with his passion and when he comes to enlighten the tyro, he is unable, because he has not been trained in teaching, to sketch in a simple background, awaken terest and postpone the complex details until another occasion. Unrelated facts, historical anecdotes, instances of iconoclasm came tumbling from Dearborn's lips. He found maps to confirm this, deeds to verify that, until Wexford's head began to spin.

It was a relief when the time came for his glass to be refilled and he could lean back briefly to exchange a smile with Mrs Dearborn. But when he looked in her direction, expecting to be calmed by the sight of those rhythmically moving fingers, he saw that her work lay in her lap, her eyes were fixed in a dead stare on a distant part of the room, and she was compulsively picking at the piping on the arm of her chair.

The piping had been so badly frayed that the cord beneath was fully exposed on both arms. This was not the result of one evening of nervous tension but surely of many. And when he glanced at the other five or six chairs in the room and at the sofa, he saw that all, though otherwise immaculate, were in the same state. Loops of cord showed on every arm, protruding from feathery rags.

The sight upset him, for it seemed to destroy the picture he had of this couple's serene happiness. He felt a sudden tension. At the drinks tray Dearborn stood watching his wife, his face compassionate yet very slightly exasperated.

No one spoke. Into the silence the telephone rang shatteringly, making them jump but none of them as violently as Mrs Dearborn. She was out of her chair on the second ring, her sharp 'I'll get it!' almost a cry. Her grace had gone. She was like a medium who, awakened from a strange and transcending communion, must gather together the threads that hold her to reality and, in gathering them, suffers intolerable mental stress.

The telephone was at the far end of the room, on a table under the point on which Mrs Dearborn's eyes had long been fixed. She took the receiver and said hallo, clearing her throat so that she could repeat the word in a voice above a whisper. That she wanted the call and was not afraid of it was apparent; that the wrong person had called showed in the sudden sagging of her shoulders.

'That's all right,' she said into the mouthpiece, and then to her husband, 'Only a wrong number.'

'We get so many,' Dearborn said, as if apologising for a fault of his own. 'You're tired, Melanie. Let me give you a drink.'

'Yes,' she said. 'Yes, thanks.' She pushed a lock of hair from her forehead and Wexford saw how thin her wrists were. 'It's my daughter,' she said, the good hostess who knows that there must be no subterfuge before guests. 'I get so worried about her. Children arc an anxiety these days, aren't they? You never know what trouble they may be in. But I won't bore you.' She took the whisky her husband handed her. 'Thank you, darling.' She sighed.

Husband and wife stood facing each other, hands briefly locked. Wexford was even more in the dark than before. What had she meant about her daughter, about not knowing what trouble she might be in? A baby young enough to use a teething ring, a baby its mother had left upstairs an hour before, was surely peacefully sleeping in its cot. Unless she was expecting a doctor to phone her because the child had been ill ...

He drank his second glass of beer with a feeling of guilt. The unfamiliar alcohol made him feel lethargic and light-headed and he was glad when Dearborn packed up his papers and said that was enough for one night.

'You must come again. Or, better than that, I'll take you on a tour round some of the places we've talked about. I take Alexandra to Kenbourne Vale.' He spoke quite seriously. 'She's not really old enough yet to understand, but you can see in her eyes she's beginning to take an interest. She's a very intelligent child. Are you in London for long?'

'Only till next Saturday, I'm afraid. Then it's back to Sussex and work.'

'What sort of work?' Mrs Dearborn asked.

'I'm a policeman.'

'How interesting. Not an ordinary policeman, I'm sure.'

'A detective chief inspector.'

Her face sharpened. She looked at her husband, then away. Dearborn might have been expected to refer to the murder, but he didn't. 'That puts paid to our tour,' he said. 'You're going home and I've got an architect's convention in Yorkshire at the end of next week. Next time you come to London, maybe?'

Wexford nodded, but all further conversation was cut short by a wailing cry from upstairs. The adored, troublesome, precocious, super-intelligent infant was once more awake.

Melanie Dearborn, who had been so electrified by the telephone bell, behaved now like a woman who had reared six children. With a 'That's Alexandra off again,' she rose casually from her chair. It was Dearborn who made the fuss. Was the child ill? Should they call a doctor? He hadn't liked the rash on her face, although his wife had said it was only teething.

Wexford took advantage of this small crisis to leave them, furnishing them with Howard's telephone number and thanking them for a pleasant evening. Mrs Dearborn saw him out. Her husband was already upstairs, calling to the baby that Daddy was coming, that Daddy would make everything all right.

10

For as love is oftentimes won with beauty, so it is not kept, preserved and continued but by virtue and obedience.

WHILE Wexford was with the Dearborns and Howard at home playing bridge a burglary took place in Kenbourne Vale. It was one of a series, all break-ins involving the theft of silver or jewellery and cash and all occurring on Friday or Saturday nights.

'Your friend's answerable for some of this,' said Howard on Monday morning.'

'Dearborn?' Wexford queried.

'Kenbourne's coming up, you see, Reg. I'm all for improving the place, converting some of these old slums and so on, but there's no doubt that when you bring money in you bring crime too. Ten years ago there was scarcely a Kenbournite, excepting the shopkeepers, with anything worth pinching. Now, in the better parts, we've got company directors with heirlooms and safes a child could open. None of the break-ins have been in places owned by Notbourne Properties yet, but unless I'm much mistaken they'll go for Vale Park next.'

'Any idea who "they" are?'

'One always has. You know that,' Howard said bitterly. 'I spent most of yesterday questioning a man called Winter who has, of course, a beautiful unbreakable alibi. And who do you think is supplying it for him? None other than our old friend Harry Slade.'

Wexford looked puzzled. 'Not an old friend of mine.'

'Sorry, Reg. Haven't we put you in the picture? Harry Slade is one of the men who says Gregson was with him in the Psyche Club on the night of Friday, February 25th. He hasn't got a record but I'm beginning to think he's a professional alibi provider.'

'But surely . . . ?'

'Surely his word counts for nothing? Not to a judge, Reg. Here's a blameless citizen, a milkman of all things, pure as the goods he purveys, who says Winter spent Saturday night with himself, his dear old mother and his typist fiancée, playing Monopoly—again of all things—in mother's flat.'

'At least it gives you another lever against Gregson,' Wexford said as Baker entered the room. He spoke placatingly, for he pitied any man who feared he was losing his grip, but Baker eyed him with frosty politeness. He had the face of a cheetah, Wexford thought, all nose and little sharp mouth, the forehead receding and the gingery hair growing down his cheeks in sideburns.

'If you're going to Sytansound now, Michael,' said Howard, 'you might take my uncle with you.'

'Nothing would please me more, sir,' said Baker, 'but I'm taking Sergeant Nolan as it is, and I've promised to show young Dinehart the ropes. Won't it be rather using a sledgehammer to swat a fly?'

Wexford found it hard to keep his temper, to smile and pretend for Howard's benefit that he was happy to be the onlooker who is said to see most of the game. He reminded himself of Baker's unhappy history, the cruel young wife and the child who was not his. *Tout comprendre, c'est tout pardonner.* But what was he going to do with himself for the rest of the day? Gossip with Howard and distract him from his work? Potter about Kenbourne? He was beginning to understand just what Howard's kind act of opting him on to his force in an honorary capacity amounted to. He did no harm, he appeared to amuse himself, he supplied ideas for experts to demolish; he was like, he thought, a workman whose usefulness is at end, who should really be made redundant, but for whom a kindly boss finds a job which could more efficiently be done by a computer if it even needed to be done at all.

He might as well go home and take Dora to the pictures. In the entrance hall he met Sergeant Clements.

'Have a good weekend, sir?'

'Very pleasant, thank you. How's that boy of yours?'

'He's grand, sir. Had the wife up in the night, the little beggar, yelling his head off, but when she went in to him all he wanted was to play. The way he laughs! He's starting to crawl. He'll walk before he's a year old.'

These fathers! 'What are you going to call him?'

'Well, sir, I think his mother must have been one of the romantic kind, fond of fancy names. She called him Barnabas, but the wife and I, we like something plainer, so we've settled for James after my old dad. As soon as we've got that adoption order out of the way we'll have a proper christening.'

'Only four days to go, isn't it?'

Clements nodded. His cheerfulness had suddenly evaporated at the reminder of the short time—the agonisingly short, agonisingly long time—which separated probationary fatherhood from the real thing. Or denied him fatherhood altogether? Looking at the man's red weathered face which, for all his vaunted worldly wisdom, remained immature and schoolboyish, Wexford thought of the coming Friday with a small shiver of dread. Suppose this young woman, this romantic girl who had named her child fancifully, changed her mind again and came into the court to claim him? What would life be like then for Clements and his good patient wife, alone and desolate on top of their tower? It was fine and just, this law which gave prime consideration to the natural mother and her child, but it was a cruel law for the sterile who waited and longed and prayed.

'You've shown such an interest in our boy, sir,' Clements

89

said, smiling again, 'that the wife and I were wondering if you'd come along one day and have a bite of lunch with us and—well, see young James. Say tomorrow or Wednesday? We'd take it as an honour.'

Wexford was touched. 'Tomorrow will be fine,' he said, reflecting that it would be a way of passing the time. On an impulse, he patted the sergeant's shoulder.

Denise and Dora had just finished their lunch. Neither expressed surprise at seeing him or shock that he was still alive. There was a look in his wife's eyes that he had not seen there for many years.

'What have you been up to, Uncle Reg?' asked Denise, for the first time in their acquaintance eyeing him as a man rather than as an ancient invalid.

'Me?' said Wexford ungrammatically. 'What d'you mean?' It was odd, he thought, how guilty the innocent can be made to feel. Certainly the telegram: Fly at once, all is discovered, would send half the population packing their bags and making for the nearest airport. 'What d'you mean, "up to"?'

'Well, a woman's been phoning for you, a Melanie something. I didn't catch the last name. She said, could you go round and see her and in the daytime, please, *when her husband is out.* You're to phone her back and she says you know the number.'

Wexford was puzzled, but he burst out laughing just the same.

'Who is she, Reg?' said Dora, not quite believing she was deceived, but not entirely happy either.

'Melanie?' he said airily. 'Oh, *Melanie* Just a woman I'm having a red-hot affair with. You know all those times you thought I was over at Kenbourne with Howard? Well, actually I was with her. There's many a good tune played on an old fiddle, my dear.' He stopped, caught his wife's eye. It was admonitory, yet faintly distressed. 'Dora!' he said. 'Look at me. Look at *me.* What woman in her right mind would want *me?*'

'I would.'

'Oh, *you*.' He was oddly moved. He kissed her lightly. 'That's the blindness of love,' he said. 'Excuse me. I'll just give my mistress a tinkle.'

Dearborn was in the phone book, Stephen T., with some letters after it that Wexford thought indicated architectural qualifications. He dialled and Melanie Dearborn answered on the second ring. Did she always? Had she been sitting by the phone to jump out of her skin when it rang?

'I'm very sorry to trouble you Mr Wexford. I—I . . . Would it be a great imposition to ask you if you could come over here and see me?'

'Now, Mrs Dearborn?'

'Well, yes, please. Now.'

'Can you give me some idea what it's about?'

'May I leave that until I see you?'

Much intrigued, Wexford said, 'Give me ten minutes,' and rang off. He explained to Denise and Dora, or rather gave them what explanation he could, for he had no more idea than they as to why Melanie Dearborn wanted to see him in her husband's absence. Could it be that she was genuinely worried about Dearborn's obsession with the transformation of Kenbourne Vale because his passion led him to neglect her or his business? Or was it anxiety over some aspect of Alexandra's welfare that distressed her? Neither of these answers seemed probable.

'The library have got your book in, Uncle Reg,' said Denise. 'You can call in for it on your way back.'

As he picked up the blue card and left the house, he came to the conclusion that Mrs Dearborn had sent for him because he was a policeman.

The cab came to a halt at a double white line, and on the major road a red Mini passed them, coming from the direction of Laysbrook Square. Wexford caught only a quick glimpse of its driver, a young woman in a dark coat. Her gloved hands rang a bell in his mind but summoned nothing from its recesses, and he forgot the gloved girl when the taxi brought him under the mews arch and he saw Melanie Dearborn waiting for him on the steps of Laysbrook House.

Wexford achieved a calm and, he hoped, reassuring smile for her, but she did not smile back. She clasped his hand in both hers and began to let forth a stream of apologies for disturbing someone who was only a slight acquaintance.

His guess had been right. 'It's because you're a policeman,' she said when they were inside. 'Or rather, because you're a detective, but not exactly working at the moment, if you know what I mean.'

Wexford didn't.

'You can tell me what I ought to do,' she said, dropping into a chair and immediately applying both hands to the piping cords.

'I'm not so sure of that,' he demurred. She was such a nice woman and so obviously distressed that he allowed himself advice that should only have come from an intimate friend. 'Try to relax,' he said. 'Your hands . . . Let me give you a cigarette.'

She nodded, pulling her hands away from the chair arms and clutching one in the other. 'You're a soothing sort of person, aren't you?' she said as he lit her cigarette. 'I feel a bit better.'

'That's good. What's it all about?'

'My daughter,' said Melanie Dearborn. 'She's missing. I don't know where she is. Ought I to report her as a missing person?'

Wexford stared. 'The *baby*? You mean someone has taken the *baby*?'

'Oh, no, no, of course not! Alexandra is upstairs. I mean my elder daughter, Louise. She's twenty-one.' It was pathetic the way she waited shyly for the gallant thing to be said. Wexford couldn't say it. Today Mrs Dearborn looked amply old enough to be the mother of a grown-up daughter. But Dearborn—was he the father? He could have sworn this pair hadn't been married more than three or four years. 'She's not Stephen's,' said Mrs Dearborn. 'I was married before. I was only nineteen when Louise was born and my first husband died when she was ten.'

'What makes you think she's missing? Does she usually live here?'

'No. She never has. She and Stephen don't get on, but I don't really know why not. They used to and it was actually through Isa—she calls herself that—that I first met Stephen. I suppose she resented my marrying again.'

An old story. The mother and daughter close, the interloping lover who leaves the daughter out in the cold.

'We got married three years ago,' she said. 'Isa was still at school, waiting to do her A Levels. She already had a provisional place at Cambridge, but when she heard we were going to get married she threw all that up and went off to share a flat with another girl.' Mrs Dearborn's fingers had returned to the compulsive fraying of the cords while her cigarette burnt itself out on the rim of the ashtray. 'She has an allowance under her father's will, a thousand a year. I don't know if she ever worked.'

'You never hear from her?'

'Oh, yes, we made up our quarrel in a sort of way. We were never like we used to be. She was always reserved and she became terribly secretive. I suppose that was my fault. I don't want to go in for a display of self-pity, Mr Wexford, but I had rather a lot to bear in my first marriage and then widowhood wasn't easy. I rather taught Isa to keep—well, a stiff upper lip, and not show her feelings.'

Wexford nodded. 'But she kept in touch with you by phone or by letter?'

'She'd phone me from time to time but she would never come here and she refused to tell me where she was living after she had left the flat she shared with the other girl. She phoned from call boxes. It made me very unhappy and Stephen saw it and then—then he got some private detective to find out where she was. Oh, it was so terrible! Isa swore she'd never speak to me again. She said I'd ruined her life. After that I tried not to let Stephen know I was worried about her and that's why I asked you to come here while—while he was out.'

'When did you last hear from her?'

She crushed out the smouldering cigarette stub and lit another. 'I'd better tell you a bit more about it all. After Stephen ran her to earth like that she phoned me to tell me I'd ruined her life, I didn't hear a word for months. Then, about a year ago, she started phoning quite regularly again, but she wouldn't say where she was living and she always sounded unhappy.'

'You must have commented on that?'

'Of course I did. She'd always said, "Oh, it's nothing. The world's not a very jolly place, is it? You taught me that and it's true." Mr Wexford, you don't know her. You don't know how impossible it is to question her. She just says, "Let's leave that, shall we?" I wanted her to come and see me at Christmas to tell her about . . .'

He raised his eyebrows a fraction. 'Excuse me, if I don't tell you what that something was. It can't have anything to do with Isa being missing. Anyway, I begged her to come and she did come. She came on Boxing Day. That was the first time I'd seen my daughter for nearly three years. And after that she came again, two or three times, but always when Stephen was out.'

'She saw him on Boxing Day'?

Melanie Dearborn shook her head. 'No, he spent the day with his mother. She's in a nursing home. Isa looked very thin and pale. It frightened me. She was never vivacious, if you know what I mean, but all the life seemed to have gone out of her. But she began to phone me regularly, about once a week. The last time I heard from her—that was what you wanted to know, wasn't it?—the last time was Friday a week ago. Friday, February 25th.'

Wexford felt the blood go from his face. He hoped it didn't show. 'She phoned you last Friday week?'

'Yes, at lunchtime. She knows Stephen's never in for lunch and she always phoned at about one-fifteen.'

11

*Other rocks there be lying hid under the water, which
therefore be dangerous.*

WEXFORD sat quite still. He knew that her observant eyes
would detect any unease that he might show. He could
hear a clock ticking in the room, a sound he had not previously noticed Mrs Dearborn's fingers made a rending noise
as they tore another half-inch of piping out of the chair. Picking feverishly, she went on talking.

'Isa sounded tremendously happy. There was a note in her
voice I hadn't heard there since she was a little girl. She
actually asked me how I was and how Alexandra was. Then
she said she thought she'd soon have some news that would
please me. Of course I asked her what news and she said she
thought that could wait for a week or two, but she'd phone
me again in a few days. Well, I couldn't bear to leave things
like that, and I was begging her to tell me when the pips went
on the phone. I said to give me her number and I'd call her
back, but before she could they'd cut us off.'

It all fitted. It fitted horribly. 'She didn't phone you again?'
he said, knowing what the answer would be.

'No, it was a terrible let-down. I went almost mad with—
well, curiosity, I suppose you'd call it and I forgot all about
not chasing her and I tried to phone Stephen to get him to
find her again if he could. . . . But he was out all that afternoon and when he did come home I'd cooled off and I
thought I'd just wait until she phoned again. But she hasn't
phoned since.'

'What are you afraid of?'

'Of her happiness.' She laughed a little shrilly. 'Doesn't that sound absurd? I keep asking myself if happiness hasn't made her do something reckless, take some awful risk.' With a shiver, she said. 'What shall I do? Tell me what to do.'

Come to Kenbourne Vale with me and identify a body. He couldn't say that. If this had been Kingsmarkham and he in charge of the Morgan case, he would have said something like that but in the gentlest possible, the most roundabout way. He wasn't in Kingsmarkham and before he did anything he would have to talk to Howard, perhaps find out more before he did even that.

Melanie Dearborn had suffered a lot in her forty years. If his present assumption was correct, all the pain she had ever been through would be nothing compared with the anguish she was going to have to bear. He wouldn't wish it on his worst enemy. And this woman wasn't that. He liked her; he liked her femininity and her concern and her good manners.

What harm would it do to comfort her and let things slide for a bit? He had no duty here. He was on holiday.

'It's only just over a week, Mrs Dearborn,' he said. 'Remember there was a time when you didn't hear from Isa for months.'

'That's true.'

'If I may, I'll call on you again on Wednesday and if you still haven't heard by then, we'll report your daughter as a missing person.'

'You really think I'm making a mountain out of a molehill?'

'I do,' he lied. So what? He could be wrong, couldn't he? Isa—what was her other name?—could be alive and well and junketing about Europe with some boy for all he knew. Something like this had happened to him once before. He had *known* the girl was dead, all the evidence had pointed to it, and then she had turned up, all tanned and smiling from a holiday in Italy with a poet.'

'What's your daughter's surname?' he asked.

'Sampson,' said Mrs Dearborn. 'Louise Sampson, or Isa or Lulu or whatever she's calling herself at present.'

Or Loveday? Don't, he wanted to cry—he who had always rejoiced at positive identifications—don't make the thing worse for me, more definite.

'I must go.'

'How?' she asked. 'Taxi? Bus?'

'One of those,' he smiled.

'Let me drive you. You've been so kind, giving up your holiday time to me, and I've got to go shopping.'

They argued. Mrs Dearborn won. She went upstairs to fetch the baby and when she reappeared at the head of the stairs, Wexford went up to help her with the carry cot. Her head resting on a pale pink pillow, the child Alexandra stared up at him with large, calm blue eyes. She was rather a fat baby, exquisitely clean and dressed in an expensive-looking, one-piece garment of pink angora.

Mrs Dearborn tucked a white fur rug round her. 'My husband's latest extravagance,' she said. 'He buys presents for this child practically every day. She's got far more clothes than I have.'

'Hallo,' said Wexford to the baby. 'Hallo, Alexandra.' She behaved after the manner of her kind by first wrinkling her face threateningly, then allowing it to dissolve into a delightful smile of friendliness and trust. 'She's beautiful,' he said sincerely.

Mrs Dearborn made no reply to this. She was groping under coats on the hallstand. 'I'm looking for a scarf,' she said half to him, half to herself, 'a blue silk one I'm rather fond of. Heaven knows where it's got to. Come to think of it, I haven't seen it for weeks. I wonder if Stephen could have given it to the cleaning woman I had before this one? When she left he insisted on giving her masses of clothes. He's such an impulsive man.' The baby began to whimper. 'Oh, Alexandra, don't *start*. She's like a dog,' said Mrs Dearborn rather crossly, 'Once she knows she's going out she won't let you rest till you're up and away. I may as well borrow Stephen's coat. My fur's at the cleaners and it's so cold, isn't it?'

She enveloped herself in Dearborn's sheepskin jacket which was much too big for her and they ran to the car through a sudden downpour. Child and cot were dumped on the back seat as if they were luggage to be safely stowed and then forgotten. Wexford was rather surprised. He had judged Mrs Dearborn as a strongly maternal woman, wrapped up in her husband and her daughters. She wasn't too old to have a baby, but perhaps she was too old to enjoy caring for one. And yet she was no older than the sergeant's wife who even enjoyed playing with her baby when he woke her in the night. It must be her worry over Louise which all-consuming, withdrew her from the rest of her family.

'Tell me the name of the friend Isa shared a flat with,' he said.

'Verity Bate. They were at school together and Verity went to train as a teacher at St Mark and St John.'

'I take it that that's in London?'

'We're not half a mile from it now,' said Mrs Dearborn. 'It's quite near where you're staying, in King's Road. I'll show you. She'll be in her last year now, but I don't know if she's still in the flat. It's near Holland Park and I did try ringing the number, but I didn't get any reply.'

By now they had crossed the King's Road and were going nothwards. On the back seat Alexandra was making soft gurgling sounds. Wexford looked over his shoulder and saw that she was watching the rain slapping against the window, reaching out a fat hand as if she thought she could catch the bright glittering drops. They came into the Fulham Road by way of Sydney Street, and when they had passed the cinema and entered that part of the road which is as narrow as a country lane, Mrs Dearborn asked him if he would mind a few minutes delay.

'I always buy my bread and cakes here,' she said. 'Could you bear if if I left you with Alexandra?'

Wexford said he could bear it very happily. She parked the car by a meter in Gilston Road, exclaiming with satisfaction because its last occupant had left ten minutes still to run, and walked off to the cake shop without a parting word to the baby. Wexford turned to talk to her. She didn't seem at all put out at being left alone with a stranger, but put up her hands to explore his face. The rain drummed on the car roof and Alexandra laughed, kicking off the white rug.

Playing with the baby passed the time so pleasantly that Wexford almost forgot Mrs Dearborn and he was surprised when he saw that ten minutes had gone by. Alexandra had temporarily lost interest in him and was chewing her rug. He looked out of the window and saw Mrs Dearborn, deep in conversation with another woman under whose umbrella they were both sheltering. She caught his eye, mouthed, 'Just coming,' and then the two women approached the car.

Mrs Dearborn seemed to be pointing out the baby to her friend, if friend she was. From what he could see of her through the streaming rain as she pressed her face against the rear window, Wexford thought her an unlikely sort of acquaintance for a company chairman's wife. Her umbrella was a man's, of cheap uncompromising black, her shabby coat black, and underneath it she wore what looked like an overall. An old felt hat, jammed hard down on her head, partly hid her face but couldn't conceal the disfiguring mole between cheek and left nostril. He fancied he had seen her somewhere before.

Just as he was wondering how long they could bear standing there and gossiping in a downpour which had become a tempest, the woman in black moved off and Mrs Dearborn jumped into the car, slicking back her wet hair with her wet hands.

'I'm so sorry to have kept you. You must be wishing you'd taken that taxi. But you know how it is when you run into people and there's a very . . .' She stopped quite suddenly. 'Now, let's get you home,' she said.

'You were going to show me St Mark and St John.'

99

'Oh, yes. Can you see that sort of round building right down there to the left? Just before you get to Stamford Bridge? That's St Mark's library. The college grounds go right through to the King's Road. Are you going to talk to Verity?'

'I expect so,' Wexford said. 'At any rate, she can tell me where Isa went after she left her.'

'I can do that,' Melanie Dearborn said quickly. 'Don't forget that's where Stephen found her. It's in Earls Court. I'll write down the phone number. I'd phone it myself, I'd try to talk to Verity, only . . .' She hesitated and added rather sadly, 'None of her friends would tell *me* anything.'

Outside the house in Theresa Street they stopped and Mrs Dearborn wrote the number down for him. For half an hour her thoughts had been distracted from her daughter, but now he noticed that the hand which held the pen was shaking. She looked up at him, nervous again, her brow furrowed with anxiety.

'Are you really going to try and trace her for me? I'm a bit —I remember what happened when Stephen . . .'

'I'll be discreet,' Wexford promised, and then he said good-bye, adding that he would see her without fail on Wednesday.

The house was empty. Denise had left him a note, propped against a crystal vase of freesias, to say that they had gone out to buy a blackberry poncho. He wasn't sure whether this was something to wear or something to eat.

He phoned the Holland Park number, but no one answered. Now for girl number two, the witness perhaps to Dearborn's clumsy and tactless trapping.

A young man's voice said hallo.

'Who occupied the flat before you?' Wexford asked when he had explained who he was.

'Don't know. I've been here four years.'

'Four years? Louise Sampson was living there a couple of years ago.'

'That's right. With me. Lulu and I lived here together for— Oh, four or five months.'

'I see.' This little piece of information was doubtless one which Dearborn had thought it wise to keep from his wife. 'Can I come and see you, Mr . . . ?'

'Adams. You can come if you like. Not today, though. Say tomorrow, about seven?'

Wexford put the phone down and looked at his watch. Just gone five. The rain had dwindled to drizzle. What time did these college classes end for the day? With any luck, Verity Bate might just be leaving now or, better still, living in hall for her final year.

He found the big gates of the college its students call Marjohn's without difficulty. There were a few boys and girls about on the forecourt, embryo teachers, who gave him the kind of glances his generation—but not he—reserved for them, the looks which ask, Why are you wearing those curious clothes, that hairstyle, that outlandish air? He was convinced that no one in the King's Road wore his kind of clothes or was as old as he. He went rather tentatively into the porter's lodge and asked where he could find Miss Verity Bate.

'You've just missed her. She came in to see if there were any letters for her and then she went off home. Are you her dad?'

Wexford felt rather flattered. Suppose he had been asked if he were the girl's grandfather? 'I'll leave a note for her,' he said.

Before he went any further he really ought to tell Howard. His nephew had a force at his command, a force who could trace Louise Sampson in a matter of hours, match her with Loveday Morgan, or else show the two girls to be—two girls. But how much more satisfying it would be if he on his own could present Howard with a *fait accompli*, the checking and tracing all done. . . .

12

The truth shall sooner come to light . . . whiles he helpeth and beareth out simple wits against the false and malicious circumventions of crafty children.

'ANOTHER one of your women on the phone,' said Denise rather nastily.

Wexford was just finishing his breakfast. He felt relieved that Howard, who had gone to the study to fetch his briefcase, and Dora, who was making beds, hadn't heard the remark. He went to the phone and a girl's voice, breathless with curiosity, said this was Verity Bate.

It was only eight-fifteen. 'You didn't waste any time, Miss Bate.'

'I had to go back to Marjohn's last evening to fetch something and I saw your message.' The girl went on smugly, 'I realised it must be very important and, as I've got a social conscience, I felt I should get in touch with you as soon as possible.'

Couldn't wait to know what it's all about, more like, thought Wexford. 'I'm trying to trace someone you used to know.'

'Really? Who? I mean, who can you possibly . . . ?'

'When and where can we meet, Miss Bate?'

'Well, I've got this class till eleven-thirty. I *wish* you'd tell me who it is.' She didn't express any doubts as to his identity, his authority. He might have been a criminal lunatic bent on decoying her away. 'You could come to my flat . . . No, I've got a better idea. I'll meet you at a quarter to twelve in Violet's Voice, that's a coffee place opposite Marjohn's.'

Howard made no comment, asked no questions, when he said he wouldn't be in until after his lunch with Sergeant and Mrs Clements. Perhaps he was glad to be relieved of his uncle's company for the morning or perhaps he guessed that Wexford was pursuing a private line of enquiry, in current parlance, doing his own thing.

He got to Violet's Voice ten minutes before time. It was a small dark café, almost empty. The ceiling, floor and furniture were all of the same deep purple, the walls painted in drug-vision swirls of violet and lavender and silver and black. Wexford sat down and ordered tea which was brought in a glass with lemon and mint floating about in it. From the window he could see St Mark's gates, and before he had begun to drink his tea he saw a diminutive girl with long red hair come out of these gates and cross the road. She was early too.

She came unhesitatingly up to his table and said loudly, 'It's about Lou Sampson, isn't it? I've thought and thought and it must be Lou.'

He got to his feet. 'Miss Bate? Sit down and let me get you something to drink. What makes you so sure it's Louise?'

'She *would* disappear. I mean, if there's anyone I know who'd be likely to get in trouble or have the police looking for her, it's Lou.' Verity Bate sat down and stuck her elbows on the table. 'Thanks, I'll have a coffee.' She had an aggressive, rather theatrical manner, her voice pitched so that everyone in the café could hear her. 'I haven't the faintest idea where Lou is, and I wouldn't tell you if I had. I suppose it's Mrs Sampson tracking her down again. Mrs Dearborn, I should say. One thing about that woman, she never gives up.'

'You don't like Mrs Dearborn?'

The girl was very young, very strict and very intolerant. 'I don't like deceit. If my mother did to me what she did to Lou I'd never speak to her again.'

'I'd like to hear about that,' said Wexford.

'I'm going to tell you. It's no secret, anyway.' Verity Bate was silent for a moment and then she said very seriously, 'You do understand, don't you, that even if I knew where Lou was, I wouldn't tell you? I don't know, but if I did I wouldn't tell you!'

Equally seriously, Wexford said, 'I appreciate that, Miss Bate. Your principles do you credit. Let me get this quite straight. You don't know where Louise is, you've no idea, and you won't tell me because it's against your principles.'

She looked at him uncertainly. 'That's right. I wouldn't help Mrs Samp—Dearborn or *him*.'

'Mr Dearborn?'

Her white skin took a flush easily and now it burned fiery red, earnest and indignant. 'He was my dad's best friend. They were in partnership. Nobody ought ever to *speak to him again*. Don't you think the world would be a lot better place if we just refused to speak to people who behave badly? Then they'd learn bloody awful behaviour doesn't pay because society won't tolerate it. Don't you agree with me?'

She was more like fifteen than twenty-one. 'We all behave badly, Miss Bate.'

'Oh, you're just like my father! You're resigned. It's because you old people compromise that we're in the mess we're —well, in. Now I say that we ought to stop sending people to prison for stealing things and start sending people to prison who destroy other people's lives. Like Stephen Bloody Dearborn.'

Wexford sighed. What a little talker she was! 'He seems quite a pleasant man to me,' he said. 'I gather Louise didn't like him much, though.'

'*Like him*?' Verity Bate pushed back her hair and thrust her face forward until little sharp nose and large blue eyes were perhaps six inches from him. 'Like him? You don't know anything, do you? Lou worshipped that man. She was just so crazy about Stephen Dearborn it wasn't true!'

This statement had the effect on him she had evidently hoped for. He was profoundly surprised, and yet, when he considered it, he wondered why he hadn't arrived at the truth himself. That it was the truth, he had no doubt. No normal clever girl leaves school at a crucial stage in her school career, throws up a university place and cuts herself off almost entirely from her mother just because her mother has made a proper and entirely suitable marriage with a man to whom the girl herself has introduced her.

'She was in love with him?' he asked.

Of course she was!' Verity Bate shook her head until her face was entirely canopied in red hair, but whether this was in continuing wonder at her own revelation or at Wexford's obtuseness, he couldn't tell. The hair flew back, driven by a sharp toss. 'I'd better tell you the whole story and mine will be an unbiassed account, at any rate. It's no use you talking to Stephen Dearborn, he's such a liar. He'd only say he never thought of Lou in that way because that's what he said to my dad. Ooh, he's *disgusting*!'

'This—er, unbiassed account of yours, Miss Bate?'

'Yes, well, we were at school together, Lou and I, in Wimbledon. That's where my parents live, and Lou and Mrs Sampson lived in the next street. Stephen Dearborn was living up in ghastly Kenbourne Vale and Dad used to bring him home sometimes on account of him being what dad called a poor lonely widower.'

'He was married before, then?'

'His wife died and their baby died. That was all centuries ago. Stephen was supposed to be fond of kids and he used to take me out. Tower of London, Changing of the Guard, that sort of crap. Oh, and he dragged me around Kenbourne Vale too, showing me a lot of boring old architecture. It's a wonder I didn't catch something awful in that slum. When I got friendly with Lou, he took us both.'

'How old were you?'

'Sixteen, seventeen. I had to call him Uncle Steve. It makes me feel sick when I think of it, physically sick.' Her mouth turned down at the corners. 'Lou's not like me, you know. She keeps everything below surface, but it's all there, emotion welling and churning like a . . .' The childish voice dropped thrillingly. '. . . a cauldron! Anyway, we all went out together but I was the odd one. Stephen and Lou—well, it was like in the days when people had chaperones. I was their chaperone. And then one night when she was staying at my place she told me she was in love with him and did I think he loved her? It gave me quite a shock, Lou telling me anything about her personal life. I didn't know what to say, I didn't understand it. I mean, she was seventeen—maybe eighteen by then—and he was middle-aged. You can't imagine a girl of eighteen falling for a man of forty, can you?'

'It happens.'

'I think it's urky,' said Miss Bate with what looked like a genuine shudder. 'The next thing was she asked him back to her place. To meet,' she added darkly, 'her mother.'

Wexford had almost forgotten that the purpose of this talk had been to discover Louise Sampson's whereabouts. He was seeing the little cameo again, the stranger entering the house alone—because an unmannerly girl had left him to introduce himself—then, searching for the girl's mother, had come upon a half-open door and seen in a kitchen a woman in a white apron engaged in an age-old feminine task. The girl's strident voice jerked him out of his daydream.

'Lou and I were due to sit for our A's, but the week before they started Lou didn't come to school. I phoned her place and her mother said she wasn't well. Then one night my dad came in and said to Mummy, "What d'you think, Steve's going to marry the Sampson girl." Of course, I thought he meant Lou, but he didn't. Fancy calling a woman of thirty-seven a girl! Lou never took her A's. She was really ill, she had a sort of nervous breakdown '

'A case of *filia pulchra, mater pulchrior*,' said Wexford.

'I wouldn't know. I never did Latin. They sent Lou down to her grandmother and then they got married. I left school and started at Marjohn's and Daddy said he'd pay half the rent of a flat for me if I could find another girl to share and I was sort of looking for someone when Lou rang up from this grandmother's and said she'd never go to those two in Chelsea, and could she share with me?'

'How long did that last?'

'About a year. Lou was more shut in than ever. She was heartbroken. Her bloody mother used to phone and pretend to me it was all rubbish about Lou fancying Stephen. Anyway, Lou got fed up being hunted and she went off to share with someone in Battersea. I'm not telling you the address, mind you.'

'I wouldn't dream of asking you, Miss Bate.'

'After that we sort of lost touch.'

'You couldn't bear to see so much suffering, was that it?'

'Exactly.' She seemed relieved at so pat a solution which perhaps avoided for her the necessity of explaining that she hadn't bothered to phone and never wrote letters. 'Louise Sampson,' she said dramatically, 'went out of my life. Perhaps she's found happiness, perhaps not. I shall never know.' She lifted her chin and stared intensely in the direction of the coffee machine, showing to Wexford a delicate and faintly quivering profile. He wondered if she had attended all or some of the films shown at the Garbo season, a recent offering, according to Denise, of the Classic Cinema up the road. 'That's all I can tell you,' she said, 'but if I knew any more I wouldn't reveal a single word.'

Surely the sergeant's wife didn't go to all this trouble, a full dinner service, linen napkins, side plates and all, when her husband popped home alone for a bite to eat? Wexford was sure she didn't but he behaved as if all this ceremony was normal and even forgot his diet.

He was aware that further pomp was to attach to the entry of the child, delayed until after their coffee, not only for the sake of suspense but to prove Mrs Clements' ability to be a gracious hostess though a mother. It was touching, he thought, the way she kept stoically to the theme of their conversation—

inevitably, with her husband taking part, the general decadence of modern life—while listening surreptitiously for a squeak from the next room. At last, when Clements and Wexford had left the table and were standing at the picture window, contemplating Kenbourne Vale from twelve floors up, she reentered the room with the baby in her arms.

'He's got two teeth,' she said, 'and not a bit of trouble cutting them.'

'A fine boy,' said Wexford. He took the child from her and talked to him as he had talked to Alexandra Dearborn, but James responded less happily and his shining dark eyes grew uneasy. An adopted child, Wexford thought, might well show signs of insecurity, handled as he must have been since leaving his true mother by stranger after stranger. 'He's a credit to you,' he said, and then to his shame he found his voice thick with an unlooked-for emotion. It was out of his power to say more.

But he had said enough, or his expression had told what he couldn't say. Mrs Clements beamed. 'I've waited fifteen years for this.'

Wexford handed the boy back. 'And now you've got fifteen years of hard labour.'

'Years and years of happiness, Mr Wexford.' The smile died. Her full, rather dull, face seemed on an instant to grow thinner. 'If—if they'll let me keep him.'

'She's signed an affidavit, hasn't she?' said the sergeant fiercely. 'She's promised to give him up.'

His wife gave him a wifely look, part compassion, part gentle reproof. 'You know you're as worried about it as I am, dear. He was more worried than me at first, Mr Wexford. He wanted to—well, find out who she was and give her some money. To sort of buy James, you see.'

'I don't know much about adoption,' said Wexford, 'but surely it's illegal for money to pass in the course of these transactions?'

'Of course it is,' said Clements huffily. He looked put out. 'I wasn't serious.' His next words rather belied this remark.

108

'I've always been a saver, I daresay I could have raised quite a bit one way and another, but I . . . You don't think I meant it, sir?'

Wexford smiled. 'It would be a bit too risky, wouldn't it?'

'Breaking the law, you mean, sir? You'd keep the child but you'd always have the fear of being found out hanging over you.'

Clements was never very quick on the uptake, Wexford thought. He said, 'But would you have the child?

'Of course you would, sir. You'd have brought it from the natural mother, in a manner of speaking, thought it doesn't sound very nice put that way. You'd offer her a thousand pounds, say, not to oppose the making of the order.'

'And suppose she took the money and agreed and opposed the order just the same? What redress would you have? None at all. You couldn't ask her to sign an agreement or enter into a contract as any such transaction in matters of adoption would be illegal.'

'I never thought of that. An unscrupulous sort of girl might even engineer it so that she could get hold of money to support her child.'

'She might indeed,' said Wexford.

13

But in Utopia every man is a cunning lawyer . . .

SHE too had had a baby . . . During the past year Loveday Morgan had had a baby. If Loveday Morgan was Louise Sampson, Louise had had that baby. A good reason, added to the other good reasons, for not letting her mother see her until Christmas when she might have been fully recovered from the child's birth.

Now that birth must have been registered, but not, apparently to a mother called Morgan. Surely Louise wouldn't have dared register the child in a false name? The penalties for making false registrations were stated clearly enough, Wexford knew, in every registrar's office. They were more than sufficient to daunt a young girl. She would have registered it in her own name.

This, then, was what he just had to check on before he went any further. This might mean he need go no further. But his plan was doomed to postponement, for he was no sooner in his own office when Howard phoned through to request his presence at a house in Copland Road.

'Mrs Kirby?' Wexford said. 'Who's she?'

'Gregson was mending her television at lunchtime on February 25th. She's just phoned to say she's remembered something we ought to know.'

'You won't want me.'

But Howard did. He was very pressing. When Wexford

110

joined him at the car and noted the sullen presence of Inspector Baker, he saw it all. Tactful pressure had been brought to bear on Baker to include the chief inspector in this visit. A king-size sledge-hammer, indeed, to swat a fly, unless the fly itself had suddenly developed into a far larger insect. Evidently Baker didn't like it and not on these grounds alone. He gave Wexford a cold penetrating stare.

And Wexford himself was annoyed. He would have been far happier making his own private researches. Howard had arranged it to avoid hurting his uncle and Wexford was there to avoid hurting his nephew, but all they had succeeded in doing was to upset Baker thoroughly. The nape of his neck, prickly with ginger bristles, had crimsoned with anger.

Wexford wondered about his private life, the solitary existence he must lead somewhere, perhaps in a trim suburb in a neat semi-detached which he had furnished for the young wife who had deserted him. He could hardly imagine a greater humiliation for a middle-aged man than that which Baker had suffered. It would dig into the very roots of his manhood and shake what should, at his age, have been a well-adjusted personality.

He was sitting beside the driver, Wexford in the back with his nephew, and since they had left the station no one had uttered a word. Now Howard, trying to ease the tension, asked Baker when he would be moving from Wimbledon into the new flat he was buying in north-west London.

'Next month, I hope, sir,' Baker said shortly. He didn't turn his head and again the dark flush had appeared on his neck.

The mention of Wimbledon reminded Wexford of Verity Bate who had said that her parents and, at one time, the Sampsons had lived in that suburb. So it was there that the inspector's trouble had come upon him. Not discouraged, Howard pressed the point, but Wexford had the impression that Baker only replied because Howard was his superior officer. And when the superintendent spoke next of the week, terminating on February 27th, that Baker had taken off to

111

consult with solicitor's and arrange with decorators, Baker's shrug was almost rude.

'I'm afraid you're one of those people who never take a proper holiday, Michael,' Howard said pleasantly. 'Even when you were supposed to be off you were hanging about Kenbourne Vale nearly every day. Is it such an attractive place?'

'Filthy hole,' Baker said abruptly. 'How anyone could live here beats me.'

From the tensing of the driver's shoulders, Wexford guessed that he was one of those who did. Here was another instance of the inspector putting people's backs up, literally this time. A gloomy silence fell. Howard deliberately avoided catching his uncle's eye and Wexford, embarrassed, looked out of the window.

It was a damp, raw day, and although it was still early afternoon, lights showed here and there behind long sash windows, making pale bright rectangles in the grey façades. The air itself seemed grey, not dense enough for fog but laden with a damp which blackened the pavements. Kenbourne Vale wore the colours of a snail shell, glimmering faintly in a snail's pallid, dull hues, under the ashen sky which seemed to have dropped and to lie low and sombrely over it. Church spires, a stadium, sprawling factories loomed before the car, took solid shape and then dissolved again as they passed. Only the new office blocks, strident columns of light, had a positive reality in the thickening gloom.

They entered Copeland Hill, that district which, nearly a week before, had been Wexford's gateway to his nephew's manor. Much had happened since then. He asked himself how he would have felt on that bus last week if he had known that today he would be riding in a police car with Howard, honorary yet treated by Howard with honour, to interrogate an important witness. The thought cheered him and, viewing Copeland Road with quickening interest, he resolved not to let Baker deter him or damp his ardour.

This was one of the streets which Dearborn had his eye on, and Wexford saw that a whole section of the left-hand terrace

112

was undergoing renovation. Scaffolding covered it and men were painting the broad lofty expanse a rich cream colour so that the moulding above the windows was revealed as swags, bunches of grapes and lovers' knots. New railings of curled wrought iron rested against the scaffolding, ready to be fixed to the balconies.

The effect of this half-completed conversion was to make the neighbouring houses look even shabbier than they would otherwise have done. But neither the scars of decay nor the unmistakable signs that each was inhabited by a score of ill-assorted tenants rather than one prosperous family could quite ruin their stateliness. Garmisch Terrace was mean now and had been mean in the spirit of its conception; this place had a strange indestructible beauty because, like an old woman who had once been a pretty girl, its bones were good.

Mrs Kirby who occupied part of the ground floor of a house whose plaster front was scored all over with long river-like cracks, had also once been pretty in the Yorkshire of her girlhood. Her accent marked her as a native of the East Riding, and Wexford wondered what combination of circumstances had brought her to Kenbourne Vale. She was about sixty now. Apparently she owned a lease of the whole house, but lived in only three rooms of it which she kept as neat and sparkling as a pin.

He marvelled at her ordinariness. This place seemed curious to him, the broad street, the mansions like ornamented and windowed cliffs fascinating and wonderful, and he thought they must seem so to her too with her background. What did she think of the people in their exotic clothes, the black faces, the defiant boys and girls who lived in the warren above her head? She conducted her life as if she still lived in some Yorkshire cottage, it seemed, from the description she gave them in minute detail of the way she had spent February 25th. An early riser, she had got up at seven, cleaned the flat, chatted over the fence to a neighbour. Loquaciously, she took the three policemen round the shops with her, listed the dishes prepared for her lunch and came finally, while Baker tapped an impatient foot, to the arrival of Gregson sharp at twelve-thirty.

'Aye, it were half past twelve when he come. I know that on account of that's when I have my bit of dinner and I thought to myself, some folks have no consideration. I said to him, How long will you be? and he said half-an-hour so I put my plate in t'oven, not liking to have folks watch me eating.'

'When did the phone call come?' Howard asked.

'Must have been after one.' She pronounced the last word to rhyme with 'on'. 'Aye, because I recall thinking, you're taking a long half hour, lad. I heard t'phone ring and I answered it and this girl says, Can I speak to Mr Gregson. It's t'shop.'

'You're sure that's what was said, "the shop"?'

'Nay, I can't be sure. Might have been Sytansound or whatever they call theirselves. I called t'young lad and he talked to her, just said yes and no and good-bye. Then he finished t'job and off he went.'

'Be more precise about the time of the call, Mrs Kirby.'

She enjoyed being precise. Wexford could see, and see Howard also saw, that to her precision and accuracy were not the same thing. Her eyes flickered doubtfully. She wanted to impress, to earn praise, even if she did so through a precise inaccuracy.'

Baker said, 'If you thought it had been a long half hour Mrs Kirby, it must have been a while after one. Five or ten minutes.'

Wexford longed for the power to say like a judge to counsel, 'Don't lead, Mr Baker.'

The leading had done its work. 'Aye, about ten past,' said Mrs Kirby, and hopefully, 'Near a quarter past.'

Baker smiled in silent triumph. Smile on, thought Wexford. Loveday didn't phone Gregson, she phoned her mother. He spoke at last. Howard's encouraging glance permitted him a question. 'Did you recognise the girl's voice?'

'Nay, why would I?'

'Well, presumably you phoned the shop yourself to tell them your set wanted attention.'

114

'Aye, I did, and I phoned them last back end too, but I never talked to any girls. It was always that manager, that Gold.'

'Let him lie his way out of this one,' said Baker as they trooped into Sytansound where, on a dozen lambent screens, goblin puppets cavorted for the entertainment of the under-fives. Behind the desk which had been Loveday's was a fifty-year-old lady in boots and knee-breeches who swam out to them, followed by fat lumbering Gold.

'There wasn't any girl in the shop after ten to one on that Friday,' said Gold, unhappy at these frequent visits from the law.

'Where is he?' said Baker.

'Out the back with the van.'

A high brick wall made the van park gloomy. Behind it, Wexford knew, was the cemetery. He could see the trees over the top of it. You couldn't get away from that cemetery in Kenbourne Vale; it was the heart and soul of the place.

Gregson had heard them coming. He was leaning against the wall, his arms folded, waiting for them. The pose was defiant, but his face was frightened.

'He doesn't talk, you know,' Howard said conversationally to his uncle as Baker approached the boy. 'I mean, he literally doesn't open his mouth. He told Baker he didn't go out with the girl and where he was on Friday night, and since then he just won't talk.'

'The best defence. I wonder who taught him that?'

'I wish I knew. I only hope his mentor isn't giving lessons to all the villains in Kenbourne.'

Gregson had let his arms fall to his sides because Baker told him to and moved a few inches from the wall. He answered the inspector's questions only with shrugs. In his thin denim jacket he looked cold and pinched and very young.

'We're going to have a talk, my lad,' said Baker. 'Down at the station.'

Gregson shrugged.

At the police station they took him into an interview room. Wexford went upstairs and contemplated his gasworks. The gasometer had deflated quite a lot to reveal behind it a canning factory, a church and a building that was probably Kenbourne town hall. He thought about girls who were fond of romantic names, about babies who didn't look like their parents and then about Peggy Pope and her lover. He came to no conclusions.

His phone rang. Howard's voice said, 'Gregson's scared stiff of us. How about you having a go at him?'

'Why should he talk to me?'

'I don't know, but it can't do any harm.'

It didn't do any good either. Gregson chain-smoked. He made no answers to any of Wexford's questions. Wexford asked him if he knew what sort of a man Harry Slade was, that his word couldn't be relied on (not quite true, this), if he was aware of the implication of the phone call he had received at Mrs Kirby's. Gregson said nothing. It was, in its way, an admirable performance. Real hardened criminals, twice Gregson's age, couldn't have kept it up.

Wexford tried bullying, although it went against the grain with him. He stood over the boy and bawled questions into his ear. Gregson smelt of the sweat of fear but still he didn't speak. His cigarettes were all gone and he held his hands clenched on the table in front of him.

The stuff of martyrs, Wexford thought. In Sir Thomas's day they would have put him to the rack and the thumbscrew. He cooled his voice and went back once more to the telephone call. Who was the girl? He knew there was no girl in the shop at that time, didn't he? At that precise time Loveday Morgan had made a call. The call was to him, wasn't it?

Wexford leant across the table. He fixed his eyes on Gregson, forcing the boy to look at him, and then, shockingly, Gregson spoke. It was the first time Wexford had heard his voice, a thin cockney whine. 'I want a solicitor,' he said.

Wexford went outside, called in D.C. Dinehart, and told Howard what had happened.

'That's bloody marvellous,' said Baker. 'That's all we need.'

'If he wants a solicitor he'll have to have one,' said Howard. 'Someone's been showing him the ropes all right.'

'Mr. Wexford perhaps.' Baker could hardly conceal his rage. 'Telling him his rights, no doubt.'

Taking a leaf out of Gregson's book, Wexford said nothing. They went back into the interview room and Howard asked the boy which solicitor he wanted.

'I haven't got one,' said Gregson. 'You can bring me the phone book.'

14

If any man had rather bestow this time upon his own occupation, he is not letted or prohibited.

IT was half past six before Wexford got away. Howard was still closeted with a certain Mr de Traynor who smoothly and sympathetically referred to Gregson as 'my youthful client here.' Gregson had picked him out of the phone book because he liked the sound of his name.

There was more than a name to Mr de Traynor. His silky eyebrows almost disappeared into his silky hair when he heard that as yet no charges had been made against Gregson, that, in fact, no one was quite ready to charge him, and he settled down to teach Howard about the law.

'Am I to understand that my youthful client here has actually been detained for no less than three hours . . . ?'

Avoiding Baker, Wexford slipped out by a back way he had discovered which led him into a paved alley. On one side of it was a building that looked like a section house, on the other rows of newly-built garages used for housing police cars and vans. It was all on a much grander scale than anything in Kingsmarkham, and a few days before it would have had an oppressive, even deterrent, effect on him. But now neither the size of the place nor Baker's unjust attitude troubled him much. Human nature was the same here as in the country, and it was by studying human nature and patterns of behaviour rather than relying solely on circumstantial evidence that he had had his successes in the past. He told himself as he walked briskly in the direction of Kenbourne Lane that he had the edge on Baker, for he had never and would never compose a solution to a mystery and then manipulate facts and human nature to fit it. Pity, though, that he had missed his chance of going to Somerset House.

Rather than rely on finding a bus that would take him to Earls Court, Wexford made for a tube station he had seen from the police car. It wasn't called Kenbourne Vale but Elm Green. Something to do with those famous, long-felled trees about which Dearborn had discoursed? There were no elms now, only a wide grey pavement full of people scurrying towards the station under fluorescent lights, and inside a maze of long tiled passages.

When he came to change at Notting Hill Gate he got into the wrong train. Half an hour had passed before he finally alighted at Earls Court and by then he was fighting claustrophobia, the blood pounding in his head. How did Londoners stick it?

Nevern Gardens turned out to be another of those huge squares, tall houses glaring at each other across rows of parking meters and plane trees with branches like waving threads. He found Lewis Adams on the third floor of one of these houses, in an absurdly narrow, absurdly long, room with a tiny kitchen opening out of it, and he wondered why it was this curious shape until he realised it was a walled-off segment of a huge room, perhaps now divided into five or six shoe boxes like this one.

Adams was eating his evening meal, a Chinese concoction of beansprouts and bamboo shoots and little red bones heaped on a soup plate and balanced on his knees. On the table in front of him was a glass of water, a bottle of soy sauce and a plate of pancakes which resembled chunks of pink foam rubber.

But if his eating arrangements were Bohemian, the room he had shared with Louise Sampson was not. A well-vacuumed red carpet covered the floor, cared-for paperbacks filled the

119

bookshelves, a large television set faced the twin armchairs and the window overlooked the tops of plane trees.

'You'd better ask me questions,' said Adams. 'I don't know what it is you want.' He spoke economically. His voice was cultured and controlled with the tone of a budding barrister or a medical student preparing to sit for triumphant finals. But he looked too young for that, as young as Gregson and not unlike him. Smallish and neat, he had fair-brown hair which stopped short at the lobes of his ears. He would tell exactly what he wanted to tell, no more and no less, Wexford thought. There would be no reiteration here of grandiloquent principles, no juvenile drama.

'Where did you meet her?' he asked.

'She came into the restaurant where I was a waiter.' Adams didn't give a deprecating smile or apologise for his past (perhaps present) humble calling. He finished his beansprouts and set the plate to one side. 'We talked. She said she was sharing with a girl in Battersea, but she wasn't comfortable because they only had one room and the girl had her boy friend there at nights. I asked if she'd like to share with me.' Still without smiling, he added, 'I was finding the rent a bit much.'

'She agreed?'

'The same day. She collected her stuff and moved in that night.'

Wexford was rather shocked. Did they really go on like that these days? 'A bit cold-blooded, wasn't it?'

'Cold-blooded?' Adams hadn't understood and when he did he was more shocked than Wexford had been. His face went cold with disgust. 'You're not suggesting she slept with me, are you? *Are you*?' He shook his head, tapping one finger against his brow. 'I don't understand your generation. You accuse us of being promiscuous and casual and so on, but you're the ones with the unclean minds. I honestly don't care if you believe this or not, but Lulu lived here with me for four months and we were never lovers. Never. I suppose you're going to ask why not. The answer is that these days, whatever happened in your time, you can sleep in the same room as a girl and not want to make love to her because you're not frustrated. No one any longer has the power to force you into an unnatural celibacy, you're free to have the girls you do want. We didn't attract each other, that's all, and we weren't in the position of having to make do with any port in a storm.' He held up one hand. 'I'm not queer. I had girl friends. I went to their places. No doubt Lulu saw her boy friends at theirs.'

'I believe you, Mr Adams.'

At last he smiled. Wexford saw that delivering his little lecture had relaxed him and he wasn't surprised when he said, 'Don't call me that. My name's Lewis. People used to call us Lew and Lulu.'

'Did Lulu work?'

'She had some money of her own, but she worked sometimes. She used to go out cleaning. Why not? You *are* conventional. It's well paid around here and what you get you keep. No cards, no stamps, no tax.'

'What was she like, what sort of a girl?'

'I was fond of her,' said Adams. 'She was quiet and sensible and reserved. I like that. You get sick of the sound and the fury, you know. Her stepfather,' he added, 'was a great guy for sound and fury.'

'He came here?'

'She'd been here four months.' Adams took a drink from the glass of water on his dinner tray. 'She opened the door and when she let him in I heard her give a sort of cry—I was out in the kitchen through there—and say, "Stephen, darling Stephen, I knew you'd come for me one day".' He shook his head disapprovingly both, Wexford thought, at the hysterical utterance itself and at hearing it on his own lips. 'It wasn't like her, losing control. I was shattered.'

'But he'd only come to find out where she was?'

'He explained that. You know all those endless explanations people go in for. I didn't care for him, a big showy man, an extrovert. Lulu didn't say much. She told me afterwards that when she saw him she really believed he wanted her at last

121

and the shock of knowing he didn't for·the second time was too much for her. He thought what you thought, that I was her lover. He made a fuss about that. I didn't deny anything or defend myself. Why should I? Then there was a very nasty scene which is best forgotten and he went.'

'What was the scene about?'

Adams had now adopted a manner rather at odds with his youthful appearance. It was as if the young barrister had become an elderly and successful counsel who, conducting an unsavoury case, reveals because he must for his client's sake the bare facts, while taking pains to omit and make it clear that he is omitting all the nauseating details.

'How can knowing that possibly help you?'

'Anything about Louise might help. I can't make you tell me, but I think you should.'

Adams shrugged. 'I suppose you know your own business best. This stepfather—I don't know his name, I'm afraid, Stephen Something—was telling Lulu in a very tactless way how happy he and her mother were when Lulu said, "You're very fond of children, aren't you, Stephen?" And he said he was and he hoped to have some of his own. Lulu suddenly became rather like a powerhouse. I don't want to dramatise things, but she gave the impression of very strong pressure holding down an irrepressible force.'

Powerhouses, Wexford thought, cauldrons . . . A frightening sort of girl, intimidating as are all those passionate and turbulent creatures with no outlet for their fevers. 'She said something to him?'

'Oh, yes. I said it was nasty. She said, "Not with my mother you won't, Stephen. Surely she didn't forget to tell you she had a hysterectomy when I was fifteen?"' Adams' face creased with distaste. 'I left them then and went out into the kitchen. The stepfather screamed and shouted at her and Lulu did some screaming too. She didn't tell me what they said and a week later she left.'

'Where did she go?'

'She wouldn't tell me. We weren't on very good terms when

we parted. Pity, because we'd always trusted each other. Lulu didn't trust me any more. I'd told her off for shouting at this Stephen. She thought I was sympathising with her parents and that I'd tell them where she was if she told me.'

'You must have some idea,' Wexford protested.

'From various things she said, I think she went to Notting Hill. Possibly to a boy friend.'

'His name?'

'There was someone who used to phone her. Somebody called John. He used to ask for her and say, This is John.'

In the morning he asked to see everything Loveday Morgan had worn on the day of her death, and they showed him bra and tights from a chain store, black shoes, black plastic handbag, lemon acrilan sweater and sage green trouser suit. He saw too the contents of that handbag and every personal article found in her room.

'No cheque book?'

'She wouldn't have had one, sir,' said Sergeant Clements, putting on the indulgent look he kept for this naive old copper who thought every female corpse had been of the landed gentry. 'She hadn't any money, bar her wages.'

'I wonder what's become of the child's birth certificate?'

'With Grandma,' said Clements firmly. 'Grandma's blind or in the laughing house or she'd have come forward by now. Any thing else you want to see, sir?'

'The scarf she was killed with.'

Clements brought it in on a kind of tray.

'She's supposed to have been wearing this?' Wexford queried. 'It's a very expensive scarf. Not for a girl earning twelve pounds a week.'

'They have their funny extravagances, sir. She'd go without her dinners three or four days and then blue a pound on a scarf.'

Slowly Wexford handled the square of silk, exposing the label. 'This is a Gucci scarf, Sergeant. It didn't cost a pound. It cost eight or nine times that.'

Clements' mouth fell open. Who connected with this case, Wexford thought, but Mrs Dearborn would have an expensive silk scarf? Hadn't she been hunting for this very scarf before she went out on Monday afternoon? She hadn't been able to find it because her daughter had borrowed it, without saying anything in the way daughters do, on her last visit to Laysbrook House.

15

The sage gravity and reverence of the elders should
keep the youngers from wanton licence of words and
behaviour.

HOWARD was taking part in a top-level conference at Scotland Yard, discussing no doubt what the next move should be now that Gregson had made his escape under the protection of the ingenious Mr de Traynor. No matter how omnipotent Howard might appear to be, Wexford knew he was in fact answerable always to the head of his Divisional Crime Squad, a commander who very likely knew nothing of a country chief inspector's arrival on the scene.

The gasworks loured at him through a veil of drizzle. He paced up and down, fretting, waiting for Pamela to phone through and say when Howard would be back. He had to talk to Howard before going to Laysbrook House, and he half hoped he wouldn't have to go at all. His wishes in the matter of Louise Sampson were curiously divided. He liked Mrs Dearborn and the humane man in him wanted to see her come out of the mortuary weeping with relief instead of white with shock. But he was a policeman too, whose pride in his abilities had recently suffered blows. Considerable experience and hard work had gone into matching the missing girl with the dead. He knew his desire was base, but he admitted to himself that he would feel a thrill of pride if he vindicated himself in Baker's view and saw Howard's eyes narrow with

admiration. And she had, after all, to be someone's daughter
. . .

He jumped the way Melanie Dearborn jumped when the phone rang, but instead of Pamela's, the voice was a man's and one couldn't remember having heard before.

'It's Philip Chell.'

Wexford took a few seconds to remember who this was. 'Oh, yes, Mr Chell?'

'Ivan said to tell you he's got something for you.'

That bloody *Utopia*, Wexford thought. But it wasn't.

'It's something he's found out. He says, d'you want him to come to you or will you come here?'

'What's it about?' Wexford asked impatiently.

'Don't know. He wouldn't say.' The voice became aggrieved. 'He never tells me anything.'

'Will tomorrow morning do? About ten at your place?'

'Make it eleven,' said Chell. 'If he knows we've got a visitor he'll have me up at the crack of dawn.'

Pamela put her head round the door. 'Mr Fortune will be free at twelve, sir.'

An hour to wait. Why shouldn't he go to Garmisch Terrace during that hour instead of waiting until tomorrow? Whatever Teal had to tell him might provide another link between Loveday and Louise. He took his hand from the mouthpiece and said, 'How about if I were to . . . ?' but Chell had rang off.

The front door was open and he walked straight in. For once the hall was crowded. Chell, in fetching denim and knee-boots, was leaning against the banisters reading a picture postcard and giggling with pleasure. Peggy sat on one corner of the large hall table among newspapers and milk bottles, holding forth shrilly to the Indian and the party-giving girl, while Lamont, the baby in his arms, stood disconsolately by.

Wexford gave them a general good morning and went up to Chell, who, when he saw who it was, switched off his preoccupied smile like someone snapping off a light.

'Ivan's gone out for the day,' he said. He gave the post-card a last fond look and slipped it into his pocket. 'I can't tell you anything. All I know is Ivan was going through his cuttings when he suddenly said, "My God," and he must get hold of you.'

'What cuttings?'

'He's a designer, isn't he? I thought you knew. Well, people write about him in the papers and when they do he cuts the bit out and pastes it in his book.'

Aware that Peggy had fallen silent and that by now everyone was listening avidly, Wexford said in a lower tone, 'Could we go up and have a look at this book?'

'No, we could *not*. Really, whatever next? Ivan would *kill* me. He was perfectly horrid to me before he went out just because I'd left last night's washing up. I can't help it if I have these frighful migraines, can I?'

The party girl giggled.

'I feel very depressed,' said Chell. 'I'm going to draw out my whole month's allowance and buy some clothes to cheer myself up.' He stuck up his chin and marched out, banging the front door resoundingly behind him.

'All right for some,' said Peggy, passing a dirty hand across her face and leaving black streaks on her beautiful brow. 'Nice to be a kept man, isn't it, Johnny?'

'I look after her, don't I?' Lamont muttered, giving the baby a squeeze to indicate to whom he was referring. 'I've done everything for her practically since she was born.'

'Except when you're down the pub.'

'Three bloody hours at lunchtime! And you go out leaving me stuck with her every evening. I'm going back to bed.' He hoisted the baby on to his shoulder and made for the base-ment stairs, giving Peggy a backward glance which, it seemed to Wexford, contained more of hurt love than resentment.

'Look, Mr What's-your-name,' said Peggy, 'when are you lot going to open up Loveday's room so as we can re-let it? The landlords have lost fourteen quid already and it's keeping them awake at nights.'

127

'Is there someone wanting to rent it?'

'Yeah, her.' Peggy pointed to the party girl who nodded. 'Funny, isn't it? Big laugh. A guy like you would pay seven quid a week *not* to live in it.'

'It's two pounds a week less than what I'm paying,' said the other girl.

'Well, I'm not discussing the landlords' business in public,' said Peggy huffily. She jumped down from the table and tucked a milk bottle under each arm. 'You'd better come with me down to the hole in the ground.'

Wexford followed her, murmuring vainly that the matter wasn't in his hands. In the basement room Lamont was lying on the bed, staring at the ceiling. Peggy took no notice of him. She began to rummage among letters on the mantelpiece.

'I'm looking for a bit of paper,' she said, 'so you can write down who they have to contact about getting the room back.'

'Will this do?' 'This' was a sheet of paper he had picked up from the top of an untidy pile on the foot of the bed. As he held it out to her he saw that it was an estate agent's specification of a house in Brixton, offered for sale at four thousand, nine hundred and ninety-nine pounds.

'No, it won't do!' said Lamont, rousing himself and seizing the paper which he screwed up and hurled into a sooty cavern behind the electric fire.

Peggy laughed unpleasantly at him. 'You said you were going to chuck that out—God, it must be the weekend before last. Why don't you clear up the place instead of slopping about on the bed all day? It's time you got up, anyway, if that guy's going to phone you about that TV work. Did you give him the number of the Grand Duke?'

Lamont nodded. He slid off the bed, sidled up to Peggy and put his arm round her.

'Oh, you're hopeless,' she said, but she didn't push him away. 'Here,' she said to Wexford, 'you can write the number down on the back of this envelope.'

Wexford wrote down the number of the police station and of

128

Howard's extension and, glancing at his watch, saw that the hour was up.

The superintendent had spread before him photographs of the carefully restored and made-up face of Loveday Morgan, taken after death. The eyes were blue, the hair light blonde, the mouth and cheeks pink. But to anyone who has seen the dead, this was the modern version of a death mask, a soulless painted shell.

' "Life and these lips have long been separated",' Wexford quoted 'You wouldn't show these to her *mother*?'

'We haven't found a mother to show them to.'

'I have,' said Wexford and he explained.

Howard listened, nodding in slightly hesitant agreement. 'She'd better be brought here,' he said. 'We'll need her to identify the body. It'll be best if you go for her and take Clements and maybe a W.P.C. with you. I think you should go now, Reg.'

'I?' Wexford stared at him. 'You don't expect me to go there and . . . ?'

He felt like Hassan who can just bear the idea of the lovers being tortured to death out of his sight, but revolts in horror when Haroun Al Raschid tells him they must be tortured in his house with him as an onlooker.

Howard was no oriental sadist. He looked distressed, his thin face rather wan. 'Of course, I can't give you orders. You're just my uncle, but . . .'

'But me no buts,' said Wexford, 'and uncle me no uncles. I'll go.'

He phoned her first. He had promised to phone her. A thin hope, a thin dread, made him ask, 'You haven't heard from Louise?' He looked at his watch. Just after one, the time she would hear if she was going to.

'Not a word,' she said.

Break it gently, prepare the ground. 'I think I may . . .' Made cowardly by her anxious gasp, he said, 'There are some people I'd like you to talk to. May I come over straight away?'

'Baker said we'd never identify her,' said Howard. 'This'll shake him. Don't look so miserable, Reg. She has to be someone's child.'

Clements drove. They went through Hyde Park where the daffodils were coming out.

'Bit early, isn't it?' Wexford asked out of a dry throat.

'They do things to the bulbs, sir. Treat 'em so that they bloom before their natural time.' Clements always knew everything, Wexford thought crossly, and made all the facts he imparted sound unpleasant. 'I don't know why they can't leave things alone instead of all this going against nature. The next thing they'll be treating cuckoos and importing them in December.'

In the King's Road all the traffic lights turned red as the car approached them. It made the going slow and by the time Clements turned in under the arch to Laysbrook Place, Wexford felt as sick as he had done thirty years before on the day he took his inspector's exams. The brickwork of Laysbrook House was a pale amber in the sun, it's trees still silver-grey and untouched by the greening mist of spring. But the forsythia was a dazzling gold and the little silvery clusters he had noticed among the snowdrops now showed themselves as bushes of daphne, rose pink bouquets dotted all over the lawn. It was all very quiet, very still. The house basked in the thin diffident sunlight and the air had a fresh scent, free from the fumes of diesel to which Wexford had grown accustomed.

A young, rather smart, cleaning woman let him in and said, 'She told me you were coming. You're to go in and make yourself at home. She's upstairs with the baby, but she'll be down in a tick.' Was this the new char who stole things, who might have—but had not—made off with a Gucci scarf? The police car caught her eye and she gaped. 'What about them?'

'They'll stay there,' said Wexford, and he went into the room where Dearborn had shown him the maps and his wife had opened her heart.

16

I know how difficult and hardly I myself would have believed another man telling the same, if I had not presently seen it with mine own eyes.

H E didn't sit down but paced about the room, hoping that she wouldn't keep him waiting for long. And then, suddenly in the midst of his anxiety for her, it occured to him that once the girl was positively identified, the case would be solved. Things didn't simply look black for Stephen Dearborn. Louise Sampson had been murdered and who could her murderer be but Dearborn, her stepfather?

The motive now. He had better get that clear in his mind. And there was plenty of motive. Since he had talked to Verity Bate he had never doubted the sincerity of Louise's love for Dearborn, but he had supposed that Dearborn had been speaking the truth when he told Mr Bate that he hadn't returned it. Perhaps, on the other hand, he *had* originally been in love with Louise or had at least some strong sensual feeling towards her, a feeling which had lost some of its force when he met the mother. Of course, it was the reverse of the usual pattern, this preference of a man for an older woman over a young girl, but Wexford didn't find it hard to imagine. Anyway, a man could love two women at once. Suppose Dearborn had married the mother because she was more completely to his taste, while retaining the daughter as a mistress he couldn't bring himself to relinquish? Or their affair could

131

have started after Dearborn found her at Adams' flat, by which time he might have been growing weary of his wife.

In that case Dearborn was almost certainly the father of her child. Wexford sat down heavily when it occurred to him that the child could be Alexandra. Until now he hadn't thought much about Louise's announcement, reported by Adams, that her mother couldn't have children. After all, Louise had said she was only fifteen at the time. She could have got it wrong and have taken some minor surgery for the far more serious and final operation. If she had been speaking the truth, Melanie Dearborn couldn't be Alexandra's mother. But Dearborn could have brought home his own child—his and Louise's—to be adopted by himself and Louise's mother. And Melanie wouldn't have to know whose it was, only that it was a child whom Dearborn had adopted through a 'third party'. You didn't have to adopt through a society.

Alexandra, an adopted child . . . Or rather, adopted by one of her parents. That would account for the mother's indifference and the father's—the real father—passionate obsession.

But where was she all this time? Why didn't she come down? He heard her footsteps moving briskly overhead but he heard no other sound. Louise could have threatened Dearborn, especially if he had begun to cool off her, with exposure to her mother of their affair and then of the identity of the child. A very real threat, Wexford thought. Louise hadn't just been young and his mistress, but his stepdaughter as well. Melanie would surely have left him if she had found out. A strong motive for murder.

That was a clever explanation he had come up with for his office number having been found in Louise's handbag. How much more likely, though, that she had it there because she phoned him at work habitually! Perhaps it was he whom she had phoned on February 25th . . . But no, it couldn't be, for on that day, at that time she had phoned her mother.

There was, of course, a good deal more to be worked out. Probably Mrs Dearborn could help him if only she would come down. He felt a return of anguish for her, deepened now by his strong suspicion of her husband's guilt. The footsteps stopped and Alexandra began to cry, but the sounds were those of a baby who is peevish rather than distressed. He looked at his watch and saw that he had been there for nearly a quarter of an hour. Perhaps he should find the cleaning woman and ask her to ...

The door swung open and Mrs Dearborn walked in. She was more smartly dressed than on the previous occasions when he had seen her, her hair was brushed and lacquered and her face carefully made up. The baby was in her arms.

'Oh, Mr Wexford, I'm terribly sorry to have kept you waiting.' She freed one hand and held it out to him. 'My poor little girl is having such trouble with her teeth. I was trying to get changed and comfort her at the same time. I see you've brought reinforcements,' she said, and joked, 'Don't worry, I'd have come quietly.'

Have come? Did she mean she couldn't come? He wished she didn't look so happy and carefree, cradling the baby and stroking her head with a tenderness he had thought she lacked. 'Mrs. Dearborn,' he began, 'I want you to ...'

'Sit down, Mr Wexford. You can sit down for a moment, can't you?'

Uneasily he lowered himself on to the edge of one of the mutilated chairs. It is hard enough to break bad news to anyone at any time, but to break it to someone as cheerful and pleased with life as Melanie Dearborn looked now ... ? 'We really shouldn't delay,' he said. 'The car's waiting and...'

'But we don't have to go anywhere. It's *all right*. My daughter phoned me. She phoned me as soon as you rang off.'

His stomach seemed to turn over, the way it sometimes did when he was in a lift, and a faint sweat broke out in the palms of his hands. He couldn't speak. He could only stare stupidly at her. She smiled at him triumphantly, her head a little on one side. Some of her joy at last communicated itself to

133

Alexandra, who stopped crying, rolled over on to her back on the sofa cushion and gave a crow of laughter.

'Are you sure?' he said, and his voice was a croak. 'Sure it was your daughter?'

'Of course I'm sure! You'll see her if you wait a while. She's coming this afternoon. Isn't it marvellous? Isn't it?'

'Marvellous,' he said.

'The phone rang and I thought it was you, calling back for something or other.' She spoke quickly, chattily, quite unaware of the shock she had given him. 'I picked it up and I heard the pips. As soon as I heard them I *knew*. Then she said, "Hallo, Mummy." Oh, it was wonderful! I tried to get in touch with you but you'd already left. I just sat down and ate an enormous lunch—I haven't been able to eat properly for days—and then I went upstairs and got all dressed up. I don't know why.'

Wexford gave her a stiff, sickly smile. Alexandra laughed at him, kicking her legs in the air.

'Will you stay and see her?'

'No. I don't think anyone would doubt your word on this, Mrs Dearborn. I'll go and tell the sergeant not to wait, and then if you'd just give me a few details . . .'

Clements was treating the policewoman to one of his lectures, waving his hands as he pontificated on change and decay, Utopias and Dystopias, past glory and contemporary decadence. Wexford put his head through the car window.

'Tell Mr Fortune it's no dice. The girl's turned up.'

'Oh, great!' said the policewoman sincerely.

Clements wagged his head up and down with a kind of grim gratification. He started the car. 'She'll have a tale to tell, you can bet on that, and bring home a load of trouble for mother to sort out.'

'Give it a rest, can't you?' Wexford said savagely, knowing he shouldn't speak like that to a man who had been kind to him and hospitable and who liked him, but he hadn't been able to help himself. He saw Clements' face go red and truculent with hurt and then he went back into the house.

Alexandra was chewing voraciously at her teething ring while her mother fetched smoked salmon and a bottle of asti spumante out of her husband's fancy dining refrigerator, setting it all on a tray. Killing the fatted calf, he thought. Thou art ever my daughter and all that I have is thine . . .

'Where had she been? What was all that disappearing act about?'

'She's going to get married. It's this boy, John. I suppose she's been living with him.' Mrs Dearborn sighed. 'They've had their ups and downs, but it sounds as if they really love each other. He's married but separated from his wife—awful, isn't it, to be married and separated before you're twenty-five? He's getting a divorce under the new act. Isa knew that last time she phoned but she wouldn't tell me until he'd got his decree in case something went wrong. That's Isa all over always cautious, always secretive. She sounds so happy now.'

He smiled stiffly. She probably thought he disapproved. Let her. The realisation that he had been hopelessly wrong, the shock of it, was only just beginning to hit him where it hurt. An awful desire to run away had seized him, to run to Victoria and get on a train and go home. He couldn't remember ever having made such a monumental howler before and the memory of how he had talked so eagerly to Howard, had nearly convinced him, made him go hot all over.

And now, as he looked back, he saw that although certain circumstances in the lives of the two girls had seemed alike or coincidental, Loveday had never really matched Louise. He asked himself whether a wealthy girl brought up like Louise would have shown horror when asked to a party or baulked at being taken into a pub; if such a girl would have scuttled off for comfort to a non-denominational church; if Louise, who had been Dearborn's friend before he was her mother's, would have needed to carry his office number in her handbag, a number she must long have known by heart. He knew it was all impossible. Why hadn't he known before? Because he had so desperately wanted to prove his abilities, and in order to do so had sacrificed probability to wild speculation. He had been

135

guilty of the very sin he had laid at Baker's door, that of formulating a theory and forcing the facts to fit it. Fame had been more important to him than truth.

'Good-bye, Mrs Dearborn,' he said, and he added hollowly, 'I'm very glad for you.'

She shook hands with him on the doorstep but she didn't look at him. She was looking past him towards the arch. And she hadn't long to wait. As Wexford crossed Laysbrook Square, he saw the girl coming from the King's Road direction, saw her disappear under the shadows of the arch, a slim fair girl but otherwise quite unlike Howard's photograph of the dead.

Angrily cursing himself for an idiot, he walked for miles about Chelsea. Soon he would have to face Howard. By now Clements would have told him and he would be reflecting how unwise he had been to let family feeling and sentimentality persuade him into seeking his uncle's help. Baker would be told and Baker would shake his head, inwardly derisive.

At last he went home to Theresa Street, hoping there would be no one there, but both women were at home and a third with them, Denise's sister-in-law, who asked after his health, told him he could expect nothing else at his age, and assured him she could get any number of copies of *Utopia* he might desire from her bookshop.

'We all make mistakes, Reg,' said Howard gently when they sat down to dinner. 'And, Reg . . . ? We're not all competing for some sort of national forensics certificate, you know. It's just a job.'

'How many times have I said that, or something very like it, to my own men?' Wexford sighed and managed a grin. 'You can laugh if you like, but last week I really had some sort of idea that I was going to step in and solve the baffling case that eluded the lot of you. An elderly Lord Peter Wimsey. You were going to sit back and gasp in admiration while I expounded.'

136

'I daresay real life and real police work aren't like that.'
He might have added, Wexford thought, that his uncle had,
however, given them some useful tips. But he hadn't really,
so Howard couldn't. Instead he said almost as generously,
'I'd have felt the same if I'd come down to your manor.'

'It's odd, though, how convinced I was about that girl.'

'And you convinced me, but Baker would never go along
with it. I know you don't like him and I admit he's a peculiar
character, but the fact is he seldom does make mistakes. Even
when his wife went off and there was that business about the
unborn child, he went emotionally to pieces but his work
didn't suffer. If he says Gregson's guilty—and he's got a bee
in his bonnet about it—the probability is Gregson *is* guilty.'

Wexford said rather sourly, 'He doesn't seem to be getting
very far with proving it.'

'He's a lot further than he was. He's breaking up that
Psyche club alibi. Two of the men who were there with Harry
Slade have cracked and admitted they never saw Gregson
after eight o'clock. And another thing. Slade's girl friend—
remember the one he was supposed to be playing Monopoly
with last Saturday?—she's got a record. Baker's having another go at Gregson now without, we hope, the damping presence of Mr de Traynor.'

Wexford took two of his tablets and noticed how far the
level in the bottle had gone down. No one could say he had
failed there, at any rate.

'I don't think I'll come in with you tomorrow, Howard,'
he said. 'We're off on Saturday and there'll be the packing
and...'

'Come off it. Dora will do all that.' Howard surveyed his
uncle's burly figure. 'Besides, the only thing you could pack
is a punch.'

Wexford thought of Lamont. Had he avoided seeking a
further interview with him because he was physically afraid?
Perhaps. Suddenly he realised how deeply his illness had de-
moralised him. Fear of getting tired, fear of getting wet, fear
of being hurt—all these fears had contributed to his failure.

137

Wasn't it really fear of over-exerting himself that had made him waste the morning at Garmisch Terrace rather than go to Somerset House where a quick examination of records would have prevented today's *faux pas*? Kenbourne Vale police station was no place for him and Howard, for all his kindness, knew it.

'Well, I seem to have time on my hands for once, Reg. May as well catch up on my reading and dip into those Russian short stories my sister-in-law brought round. Curious stuff, but interesting, don't you find? One of these days I'd like your opinion . . .'

Literary chit-chat.

Four short stories and two hours later, Howard got up to answer the phone. Gregson had confessed, Wexford thought. The relentless Baker, Baker with the bee in his bonnet, had finally broken him.

But when Howard came back into the room, he could see from his nephew's face that it wasn't going to be as simple as that.

Howard didn't look at all pleased. 'Gregson's bolted,' he said. 'Baker was having a go at him in that Psyche Club, Gregson apparently doing his customary dumb act, when suddenly he found his fists if not his tongue, clouted Baker one and made a getaway in a stolen car. Baker fell off the bar stool and cut his head open on, of all things, a glass of advocaat.'

'Oh, poor Mr Baker!' said Denise, coming in from the kitchen with a white urn full of African violets.

'You weren't supposed to be listening. Here, let me take that thing, or give it to Reg. It's too heavy for you.'

'Gregson shouldn't take you too long to find,' said Wexford.

'God, no. He'll be under lock and key by morning.'

'Will you have to go over to Kenbourne, darling?' asked Denise, still hugging the urn.

'Not me. I'm going to bed. My days of running round in

138

squad cars chasing little villains are over. Will you mind that thing?'

Each put out his arms to grasp the urn which looked as if it weighed half a hundredweight. It was partly the idea that Howard had already got hold of it, partly a sudden terror of the effect on him of supporting so heavy a weight, that made Wexford draw back at the last moment. The urn crashed on to the carpet with a ponderous juddering thud, sending earth and broken leaves and pink and mauve petals flying against the walls and the pale hitherto immaculate Wilton.

Denise screamed so loudly that Wexford didn't hear Howard's hollow groan. Muttering apologies—although all apologies were inadequate—falling to his knees among the mess, he tried to scoop earth up in his hands and only made matters worse.

'At least the vase thing isn't broken,' he said stupidly.

'Never mind the bloody vase,' said Howard. 'What about me?' He had collapsed into a chair and was nursing his right foot. 'That landed fair and square on my toes.'

Denise had burst into tears. She sat in the middle of the wreckage and cried.

'I'm terribly sorry,' said Wexford miserably. 'I'd like to ... I mean, is there anything I can ... ?'

'Just leave it,' said Denise, drying her eyes. 'I'll see to it. Leave it to me. You go to bed, Uncle Reg.'

Ever polite, although he was white with pain, Howard said, 'Forget it. You couldn't help it, Reg. You're not fit enough to cope with things like that yet. No wonder you dropped it. God, my foot! I hope nothing's broken.'

He got his shoe off and limped towards the door. Denise fetched a dustpan and brush and began rescuing those of her plants that were still intact while Dora, summoned from upstairs by the uproar, picked grains of soil from the wallpaper.

Watching them disconsolately, Wexford reflected on his nephew's last remarks and upon their double meaning.

139

17

*You must not forsake the ship in a tempest because
you cannot rule and keep down the winds.*

I N the morning Howard's foot was worse, but he refused to
see a doctor, saying that it was imperative he arrived on
time in Kenbourne Vale.

'But you won't be able to drive, darling.' Denise had
stayed up until the small hours cleaning the carpet and she
had an exhausted air. Transferring her gaze from a large in-
eradicable stain to her husband's swollen instep, she said,
'You can hardly put that foot to the ground.'

'Never mind. I'll phone for a driver.'

'Unless Uncle Reg would . . .'

They looked at Wexford, Howard doubtly, Denise as if she
considered that anyone fit enough to reject yoghurt in favour
of bacon and eggs was quite capable of driving a car through
the London rush hours. Wexford didn't want to go. He had
lost all interest in the Morgan case, and plain cowardice overcame him when he thought of meeting Baker and Clements,
both of whom would know of his exploded theory. Why had
he ever been so stupid as to go and poke about in the Montfort vault in the first place? Let Howard send for a driver.

He was going to plead a pain in his eye—and for the first
time in days he could feel it aching and pricking again—when
Dora said unexpectedly, 'Of course Reg will take you, dear.
It's the least he can do after dropping that thing on your

foot. He can come straight back and have a rest, can't you, darling?'

'Give me the keys,' said Wexford resignedly. 'I hope you realise I've never driven in London traffic.'

But it wasn't as bad as he had feared, and concentrating on being one of the honking, thrusting herd, charging wild beasts which made Kingsmarkham motorists seem like sheep, made him forget his eye and, briefly, that stronger trepidation. They arrived to find Gregson safe in a cell, having been discovered taking refuge at his sister's house in Sunbury. Howard, sure of him now on the grounds of assault on a police officer and of taking and driving away a vehicle without its owner's consent—offences which even Mr de Traynor couldn't dispute—limped off to talk to him. Wexford decided to make his escape and get home before the threatening rain began and he made for that semi-secret exit into the mews. It had occurred to him happily by this time that if Howard's injury was insufficient to keep him from work, Baker's wouldn't be, so he was much disconcerted when, marching confidently down one of the bottle-green caverns, he came face to face with the inspector, his head swathed in bandages.

There was nothing for it but to stop and ask him how he was feeling.'

'I'll survive,' Baker said curtly.

The only polite answer one can make to this churlish response is a muttered, 'I hope so.' Wexford made it, added that he was glad things were no worse and moved on. Baker gave a dry cough.

'Oh, Mr Wexford . . . ? Still got a few days of your holiday left, haven't you?'

This sounded like the first move towards a truce. Wexford's spirits were so low that he was grateful for any show of cordiality. 'Yes, I'm in London till Saturday.'

'You want to try and take in Billingsgate, then. Plenty of red herrings there, and you'll find the wild geese at Smithfield.'

141

Like a goose himself, Baker cackled at his joke. His laughter with an accompanying patronising pat on the shoulder didn't rob the remark of insult. It simply made it impossible for Wexford to take offence. Immensely pleased with himself, the inspector went into the lift and clanged the doors behind him. Wexford went down the stairs. No point now in avoiding the front entrance.

Suddenly it seemed even more futile to avoid Clements. There, at least, the deference due to rank would forbid any witticisms of the nature Baker had indulged in. Wexford came down the last flight and caught sight of his own reflection in a window which the brick wall behind it had transformed into a huge and gloomy mirror. He saw a big elderly man, a wrinkled man in a wrinkled raincoat, whose face in which some had discerned wisdom and wit, now showed in every line the frustrated petulance of a spoiled child and, at the same time, the bitterness of age. He straightened his shoulders and stopped frowning. What was the matter with him to let a small reverse get him down? And how could he stoop to comfort himself with his rank? Not only must he not avoid Clements, but must seek him out to apologise for his behaviour of the previous day and—this was even more imperative—say good-bye. Had he really thought of quitting Kenbourne Vale for ever without taking a formal leave of the kind sergeant?

The big outer hall was deserted but for the two uniformed men who presided over a long counter and dealt with enquiries. One of them courteously offered to see if the sergeant was in the building, and Wexford sat down in an uncomfortable black leather armchair to wait for him. It was still only ten o'clock. Rain had begun to splash lightly against the arched windows which flanked the entrance. Perhaps the meteorological office had been right in its forecast of a deep depression settling over South-East England. If the weather had been more promising, he might have telephoned Stephen Dearborn and reminded him of the tour he had suggested. It would be doing the man a favour rather than asking for one, and Wexford felt he owed Dearborn something. Not, in this case, an apology—for you cannot apologise to a man for suspecting him of murder—but a friendly gesture to make up for harbouring such absurd and unfounded suspicions. Wexford was well aware of the guilt one can feel for even thinking ill of a man, although those thoughts have never found verbal expression.

He wasn't sure whether it was this reminder of his folly that made him go hot and red in the face or Clements' sudden appearance at his elbow. He rose to his feet, forgetting self-pity and self-recrimination. In a couple of hours Clements would be eating his lunch with his wife and James, his last lunch with James as a probationary father. Or his last lunch with James?

'Sergeant, I want to apologise for the way I spoke to you.'

'That's all right, sir. I'd forgotten all about it.'

Of course he had. He had other things on his mind. Wexford said gently and earnestly, 'Tomorrow's the great day, isn't it?'

As soon as he had spoken he wished he hadn't brought the subject up. Until this moment he had never quite realised the tension under which Clements lived and worked, the strain which daily grew more agonising. It showed now in the mammoth effort he made to keep his face ordinary and civilised and receptive, even stretching his mouth into a rictus smile. Wexford saw that he couldn't speak, that anxiety, invading every corner of his mind and his thoughts, had at last dried up that tide of moralising and censorious criticism. He was empty now of everything but the animal need to hold on to its young.

They stared at each other, Wexford growing embarrassed, the sergeant, all garrulity gone, dumb with panic and the dread of tomorrow. At last he spoke in a thick dry voice.

'I'm taking the morning off. Maybe the whole day.' He paused, swallowed. 'Depends on . . . My wife . . . On what they . . .'

'We shan't meet again, then.' Wexford held out his hand and Clements took it, giving it a hard painful squeeze as if it were a lifeline. 'Good-bye, Sergeant, and all the very best for tomorrow.'

'Good-bye,' said Clements. He dropped Wexford's hand and went out into the rain, not even bothering to turn up his coat collar. A passing car splashed him but he didn't seem to notice. Small incidents such as this, which would once have inspired a diatribe against modern manners, no longer had the power to prick the surface of his mind.

Wexford stood on the steps and watched him go. It was time for him to go too, to leave Kenbourne Vale and Loveday Morgan and forget them if he could. Strange how absorbed he had been in trying to discover who she was, tramping around Fulham, weaving fantasies. Now as he looked back on the past week, he realised that he was no nearer knowing who she was or who had killed her or why than he had been when Howard had found him in the vault. It seemed to him that he had had a few sensible ideas, firm conclusions, which even that howler of his couldn't shake, but they had grown vague now and he had almost forgotten what they were.

Water which had gathered on the blue glass panels of the lamp above his head trickled down and dripped on him. He moved slowly down the steps and as he did so water hit him from another angle. A wave of it splashed against his trouser legs and he glanced up, affronted. The taxi, cause of the offence, had drawn up a few yards from him and directly in front of the police station. Its rear door opened and a vision in a purple silk suit with a white orchid in its buttonhole descended on to the wet pavement.

'What a day for the Honourable Diana's wedding,' said Ivan Teal when he had paid the taxi driver. 'And she such a sunny-natured girl. Where are the flunkeys rushing to meet me with umbrellas?'

'This isn't the Dorchester,' said Wexford.

'Don't I know it! I have some experience of police stations, principally West End Central. Were you on your way to see me?'

144

'See *you*?' In Wexford's present state of mind, Garmisch Terrace and the case seemed a world away. 'Was I supposed to be seeing you?'

'Of course you were. I told Philip to say ten. He knew I had this wedding at St George's. The bride's gown is one of mine so I must be in at the kill. When you didn't turn up I came to you. The wedding's at half eleven.'

'Oh, that,' said Wexford, recalling how Chell had side-tracked him with his talk of newspaper cuttings. 'It doesn't matter now. Don't you waste your time.'

Teal stared at him. His hair was carefully waved and gusts of Aphrodisia came from it and his suit. 'You mean you've found out who she was?' he said.

Wexford almost asked who. Then he remembered that to some people Loveday Morgan's death was important and he said, 'If you've got some information you'd better see Superintendent Fortune or Inspector Baker.'

'I want to see you.'

'It was never my case. I'm here on holiday and I'm going home on Saturday. You're getting rather wet, you know.'

'This tussore isn't exactly drip-dry,' said Teal, moving under the arch from which the blue lamp hung. 'I wish I'd gone straight to Hanover Square,' he grumbled. 'It's always hell getting a taxi in Kenbourne. Can you see if that one down there has got his light up?'

Wexford didn't bother to look. 'You said you wanted to see the superintendent.'

'You said that. I'm not over-fond of policemen. Remember? You're different. If I can't talk to you I'll be on my way.' Teal flung out a purple silk arm. 'Taxi!' he shouted.

The cab was going the wrong way. It waited for some lights to go green and, in defiance of regulations, began to make a U-turn. Behind it, looming scarlet through the downpour, appeared the bus that went to Chelsea.

'It was nice meeting you,' said Teal, going down the steps. 'Never thought I'd say that to a ...'

The taxi drew up, the bus went by. 'You'd better come in a

minute,' said Wexford with a sigh. 'I can spare half an hour.'

Teal was never amiable for more than a few minutes.

'I can't spare that long myself,' he said with a return to asperity. 'Really, you're very inconsistent. What a ghastly place! No wonder policemen have a grudge against humanity. What's this? Some sort of annexe to the morgue?'

'An interview room.' Wexford watched him dust the seat of a chair before sitting on it. He supposed he ought to feel flattered. However highly one values one's profession, it is always a compliment to be told that one is better, more human, more sympathetic, less conventional, than the common run. But boredom with the whole business made him almost impervious to flattery.

'Comfy?' he said sarcastically.

'Oh, don't come that!' snapped Teal. 'Not you. You're not one of these flatfeet who think that because one's gay, one's got the mentality of a finicky schoolgirl. I'm going to a wedding and I don't want to muck up my clothes any more than you would.'

Wexford looked at him with positive dislike. 'Well, Mr Teal, what is it you want to tell me?'

'That minister we were talking about—remember? His name is Morgan.'

18

*The priests whom they find exceeding vicious livers,
them they excommunicate from having any interest
in divine matters.*

IT was like giving up smoking, thought Wexford, who had
given it up with some difficulty years before. The bloody
things made you ill, you resisted them, they even bored you,
but only let someone produce one—or, worse, light it under
your nose—and you were hooked again, yearning, longing to
get back to the old habit. Teal had done that to him, although
he hadn't lighted it yet. Wexford tried to suppress the excitement he felt, the hateful irritating excitement, and said:

'What minister?'

Maddeningly, Teal began to digress. 'Of course it's hind-
sight,' he said, 'but there was something funny about her
voice. I noticed it at the time and yet I didn't, if you know
what I mean. She didn't have any accent.'

'I don't have any accent,' said Wexford rashly.

Teal laughed at that. 'You mean you think you don't. You
can't hear that faint Sussex burr any more than I can hear
the rag-trade camp in my voice unless I listen for it. Just think
about it for a moment. Johnny talks R.A.D.A., Peggy South
London, Phil suppressed cockney with a gay veneer, your
superintendent pure Trinity. One doesn't have to be a Henry
Higgins to sort all that out. Everyone has an accent that he's
got from his parents or his school or his university or the
society he moves in. Loveday didn't have any at all.'

147

'What's that go to do with some minister?'

'I'm coming to that. I've thought about it a lot. I've asked myself who are these rare creatures that speak unaccented English. One example would be servants of the old school. I should think that when there was a whole servant class they all talked like that—flat, plain English without any inflexion or intonation. Their parents brought them up to it, having been servants themselves and knowing that cockney wouldn't be acceptable in a housemaid. Who else? Children brought up in institutions, maybe. People who spent years of their lives in hospitals and perhaps people who have spent all their lives in closed communities.'

Wexford was growing very impatient. 'Brought up in an institution . . . ?'

'Oh, come *on*. You're the detective. Don't you remember my telling you how she went to the temple of the Children of the Revelation?'

'She can't have been one of them. She worked in a television shop. They don't have television or read newspapers.'

'There you have it, the reason why her parents haven't got in touch. Didn't it occur to you? Anyway, her father couldn't have got in touch. He's that Morgan who was their minister and got put inside. He's in prison.'

There was a dramatic pause. Wexford had thought he could never care about this case again, never experience for a second time the thrill and the dread of the hunter with his quarry in sight. Now he felt the tingle of adrenalin in his blood, a shiver travel up his spine.

'I keep this book of press cuttings,' Teal went on. 'That is, I collect newspapers that have bits about me in them, but often I don't cut the bits out for a year or so and the papers accumulate. Well, a couple of nights ago, having time to kill, I started on my cuttings and on the back of a photograph of one of my gowns there was a story about this Morgan appearing in a magistrates' court.'

'You have the cutting with you?'

148

'Do me a favour, I'm on my way to a very fashionable wedding. As Wilde says . . .' Here Teal wriggled affectedly—purposely to annoy, Wexford thought—and said in a camp falsetto, 'A well-made dress has no pockets.' He chuckled at the chief inspector's discomfiture. 'Anyway, I stuck it in my book, court proceedings side downwards, of course. You can do some work now.'

'When did these proceedings take place, Mr Teal?' Wexford asked, keeping his temper.

'Last March. He was charged with bigamy, indecent assault on *five* women—the courage the man must have had! —and having had carnal knowledge of a fourteen-year-old girl. I don't know what that means precisely, but I expect you do. He was committed for trial to the Surrey Assizes.' Teal looked at his watch. 'My God, I mustn't be late and find myself in a rear pew. I want to get a good look at the Honourable Diana in all my glory.'

'Mr Teal, you've been very helpful. I'm grateful. There's just one other thing. You said Loveday asked you if Johnny and Peggy were trustworthy. What did she want to entrust to them?'

'To him, you mean. Herself, I suppose, if she was in love with him.'

Wexford looked doubtful. 'A woman of fifty might feel that way, but I don't think a young girl would. I'm asking myself what precious thing she had to entrust to anyone.'

'Then you mûst go on asking yourself, Mr Wexford, because I do have to go now.'

'Yes, of course. Thanks for coming.'

The interview room became a drab little hole again after Teal had gone. Wexford went out into the corridor and began to mount the stairs. It struck him suddenly that he could climb stairs now without getting short of breath.

It was a piece of luck really getting that information from Teal, for passing it on immediately would vindicate him in the eyes of Howard and Baker. Not that he had done anything but listen and that reluctantly. Never mind. He would tell them simply what Teal had told him and leave them to follow it up. Unless . . . Unless he delayed passing it on for half an hour, and used that half-hour to do a little research of his own in the police station library.

If they had one. At the top of the stairs he encountered someone he thought was Sergeant Nolan and asked him. They had. Down one floor, sir, and third door on your right.

In the library he found Pamela and D.C. Dinehart, each occupied with a newspaper file, and wearing on their young faces the serious and absorbed expressions of students in the British Museum. Both looked up to nod and then took no further notice of him. It took him no more than ten minutes to find what he wanted, the proceedings against Morgan in the Assize court.

The *News of the World* had dealt with the case lubriciously, yet with its customary manner of righteous outrage; *The People* had seen in it occasion for a venomous article on corruption among ministers of religion; *The Observer*, its nose in the air had tucked it away under a story about a blackmailed county councillor. For facts and photographs he selected *The Sunday Times* and the *Sunday Express*.

Alexander William Morgan had been separated from his wife for some years before the commission of the offences, he lodging next door to his church in Artois Road, Camberwell, she remaining in the erstwhile matrimonial home in nearby Ivy Street. Apparently, the rift had taken place when Morgan received a call and became shepherd of the Camberwell Temple. He had tried, very gradually, to infuse into the bitter and life-denying creed of the Children of the Revelation a certain liberalism, although, due to the opposition of diehard elders, had got no further than to make a few of them believe that television and radio enjoyed in the privacy of their own homes was no sin.

In sexual matters he had been more successful. Indeed, his success had been startling. A stream of young women had given evidence, including a Miss Hannah Peters whom he had married (gone through a form of marriage was the charge) in a ceremony of his own devising at which he had been both bride-groom and officiating priest. The other girls, even the fourteen-year-old, regarded themselves as his wives under the curious philosophy he had propounded to them. He had treated them affectionately. They said they had expected, as a result of what he had told them and by reason of his relationship with them, to inherit a more blissful form of eternal life than the less favoured Children. It was only when he made advances to older women that his propensities had come to light. Morgan had been sent to prison for three years, still protesting that he was responsible for conferring on these women a peculiar grace.

Wexford noted down the names of all the women witnesses. Then he studied the photographs, but only one of them caught his eye, a picture of the temple itself in Artois Road. He glanced up and, seeing that Pamela had finished her researches, beckoned her over.

'Are you going back to Mr Fortune's office?'

She nodded.

'He has a snapshot of Loveday Morgan . . .'

'Yes, sir, I know the one you mean.'

'I wonder if you mind asking him if he'd have it sent along to me here?'

That was that, then. It was the only way. Howard would, of course, come back with the snapshot himself, note from the newspaper stories that Morgan had two daughters, and the case would pass out of his, Wexford's, hands. He felt rather flat, for he had found her in such an undramatic way.

While her waited for Howard to appear, he looked at the other photographs, round-faced, bespectacled Morgan, forty six years old, a suburban satyr; Morgan with his wife and two fat little girls, either of whom might have been Loveday in childhood; Hannah Peters, plain, smiling, a bride among the handmaidens with an Alice band holding back her frizzy hair.

He smelt Pamela's floral perfume and looked round to find her at his elbow.

151

'Mr Fortune has gone to court, Mr Wexford, and he's left a message to say he's going straight on to St Biddulph's Hospital to get his foot X-rayed.'

'But you've brought the snapshot,' Wexford said slowly.

'It was on his desk, sir, and since you wanted it, I'm sure he wouldn't . . .'

'Thank you very much, Pamela,' said Wexford.

His hand was trembling oddly as he took it from her and placed it beside the *Sunday Express* photograph of Morgan's temple in Artois Road. Yes, it was as he had thought. The newspaper picture showed the whole church, the snapshot only a corner of it, but in both were the same dusty shrubs nudging a brickwall, the same ridge of coping, and what had seemed in the snapshot to be a wooden post was now revealed as a segment of a door.

There was no girl in the newspaper shot, Morgan, Wexford was sure, had posed the girl—his daughter? one of his 'brides'?—in front of the temple and taken the photograph himself. He returned the snapshot to Pamela and left the library, deep in thought.

What now? Follow Pamela and leave a message for Howard, his reasonable self told him. Or see Baker. The inspector would soon be back from the court. Wexford revolted from the idea of confiding in him and seeing that sharp mouth curl in a will-nothing-teach-the-old-fuddy-duddy expression.

He had been wrong last time. This time he knew he couldn't be. No one would have known of his folly if he hadn't alerted Howard before he had proof. It wouldn't matter if he failed this time, for no one would know except himself. They would think he had gone off on some sightseeing tour of his own, to Smithfield or Billingsgate perhaps, taking Baker's advice.

He could be what retired policemen sometimes become, a private detective. That thought had a bitter taste about it and he put it from him. Not retired, not old, but free to pursue a line of his own, bound to no one. No driver to take him, no

152

sergeant to accompany him, no chief to refer back to. And he wasn't going to withhold vital information for long, for, if he had got nowhere by tonight, he would just tell Howard and leave it at that.

It was just eleven-thirty. The rain fell steadily. Obviously, it was going to be one of those days when the rain never lets up. He had left his umbrella in Theresa Street. With unusual extravagance he bought a new one and then he walked jauntily, like a young man, towards Elm Green tube station.

19

But if the inhabitants . . . will not dwell with them to be ordered by their laws, then they drive them out of those bounds which they have limited and appointed out for themselves.

IT was a bit like Kenbourne Vale, the district of South London that was neither Camberwell nor Kennington but a dismal area lying between them called Wilman Park. The resemblance lay in the slummy greyness of the place, the absence of trees, rather than in the houses, for those in Wilman Park were small and tightly packed in streets standing at true right angles to each other. Wexford supposed that the third temple of the Children of the Revelation was probably situated in a similar district of some industrial city in the north of England. Strange sects do not abound among the rich who have their heaven here and need not rely on future bliss.

He found Artois Road which bisected Wilman Park and walked briskly along it between the puddles, passing women coming back from the shops before they shut for early closing. They were mothers and daughters mostly, with the daughter's children shielded from the rain in hooded prams. He recognised it as the working-class pattern, mother and daughter going everywhere together, shopping together, not divided by the girl's marriage. Somewhere here there might be a mother who walked alone because her daughter had been divided from her. Or were the Children excluded from such patterns, as they seemed to be excluded from everything, making their own customs and denying society?

The temple was so small and the rain so torrential that he almost went by without seeing it. He retraced his steps and contemplated it, glad of his umbrella. It was recognisable as the sister, if not the twin, of the one in Garmisch Terrace. The circle of red glass was smaller, the gable shallower, the garden-shed door painted a sticky green, but an identical plaque, signifying the nature of the place, had been cemented into the brickwork which in this case was a plain dull red. The shrubs, against which Loveday had posed, were now a leafless tangle, dripping water on to the pavement.

As in Garmisch Terrace, the temple was the connecting link between two rows of houses, squat mean houses here of yellow brick with stone bays. In one of its immediate neighbours Morgan had been a lodger. In which? Newspapers give the names of streets where defendents and witnesses live, not their house numbers. But it wasn't difficult to guess. One of the houses had daffodils coming into bud in a window box, a television aerial on its roof, red and yellow curtains; the other squatted, its windows blanked out with dark green blinds, behind a tiny front garden whose soil was hidden beneath a layer of concrete.

One of the blinds lifted an inch when he banged on the door —there was no bell, no knocker, only a letter box—but it fell again instantly. The activities of private detectives are limited. They cannot demand entrance or get warrants. He knocked again, and this time there was no movement at the window. He could hear nothing from inside the house, but he sensed hostility as if the people within were ill-wishing him. Strange. Even if they had something to hide, they couldn't know who he was. He might be the gasman, he might be delivering something. A voice behind him made him turn round. A postman with parcels coming out of a red van.

'You won't get in there, mate. They never let no one in.'

'Why not, for God's sake?'

'That's it,' said the postman, grinning. 'For God's sake.

155

They're too religious, see, to talk to the likes of you or me. They call themselves Children of the Revelation. A lot of them live around here, and they won't none of them let no one into their houses.'

'What, not even open their doors?'

'Some do that,' the postman admitted, 'but you can't get inside.'

'Can you tell me where the others live?'

'One lot at 56 and another lot at 92. The 56 lot, they'll *speak* to you, I'll give them that.'

So the refusal to admit him on the part of the occupants of the house next to the temple held no particularly sinister implication. He went to number 56, another grim little house with weeds instead of concrete in its front garden, and the door was answered rather reluctantly by an elderly man in a shiny black suit.

'I'm sorry. I know it's raining, but I can't let you in. What do you want?' His was a flat, cold voice, almost mechanical. Words were necessary for the business of living, Wexford thought, not to grace life, not to be chosen with care for smoothing the path, expressing feelings, pleasing the listener. He remembered what Teal had said.

'I'm writing a book on Christian sects,' he lied unblushingly. 'I wondered if you could give me . . . ?'

In the same dull monotone the man reeled off a list of dates, named the three temples and told Wexford that there were five hundred of the elect on the face of the earth.

'And your Shepherd?' Wexford interrupted him.

'He has a room in the house next to the temple, but they won't open the door to you there.' He gave a sigh as of one who had striven in vain against the temptations of the world. 'They have kept to a purer and straighter way then I. I married *out*.'

'How about number 92?' Wexford began. He got no further for the door was firmly closed in his face. There was nothing for it but to go to Ivy Street, and if that failed, begin a house-to-house in search of the 'brides'.

He had a sandwich in a pub and, feeling almost as guilty as a Child of the Revelation who had opened the door to one of God's rejects, a pint of bitter. Then he phoned Dora to stop her worrying, telling her he was off on a tour with Dearborn and didn't know when he would be home. The rain had slackened slightly. He asked the barman the way to Ivy Street and set off into the back doubles of Artois Road.

The house was a little detached villa with gnomes and an overflowing birdbath in its front garden. It looked shut up. No one answered when he rang the bell and he turned away to come face to face once more with the helpful postman.

'Mrs Morgan's away. Her married daughter's ill and she's gone to look after the son-in-law. Half a tick, while I take this parcel next door.'

Having decided to pump him, Wexford waited impatiently for the postman to return. What he called 'half a tick' became ten minutes' chat with the recipient of the parcel, but at last he came back, whistling cheerfully.

'What about the other daughter?'

'Got a day off from work. I saw her go out half an hour back.'

'I see.' Another disappointment, if you could call finding someone's daughter alive instead of dead a disappointment. 'Did you know Morgan?'

'Not to say know,' said the postman. 'I know *of* him. I used to see him about.'

'Did you ever see him about with a girl?'

The postman laughed. He didn't seem to want to know who Wexford was or why he was asking. 'Morgan was a dark horse,' he said. 'Most of Revelationers didn't know what he was up to till it all came out. Except the girls, that is. One or two of them called themselves Mrs Morgan, had letters addressed to them as Mrs Morgan, as bold as brass.'

'Can you remember which ones?'

'I remember Hannah Peters all right. She was the one as he went through a form of marriage with. That's how his little games came to light. Young Hannah got a letter addressed to

157

Mrs Morgan, her dad got suspicious and then the bomb went up. A lot of other women started complaining. Mind you, his wife had chucked him out years ago but they're not divorced. She says she'll never divorce him. A very vindictive woman is Mrs Morgan and you can't blame her.'

'Can you tell me where Miss Peters lives?'

'Work on a paper, do you?'

'Something like that,' said Wexford.

'I only ask,' said the postman, 'because it seems hard on a feller your age, especially in this weather. Wear the old ones out first, eh?'

Wexford swallowed his humiliation as best he could and managed an unamused grin. The postman gave him the address. 'I daresay she'll be at work now?' he said.

'Not her. The Revelationers don't let their daughters go to work, but I don't reckon you'll see her. They won't let you in.'

But they might open the door. Hannah herself might do that. What he needed now was a piece of luck, one of those near-miracles that had sometimes come his way in the past, clearing and illuminating the path he must follow. And he thought it had happened when, turning into Stockholm Street, he saw the frizzy-haired girl of the newspaper photograph come out of the corner house where the Peters family lived.

She held a letter in her hand which she thrust into the pocket of her long dark raincoat to protect it from the rain, and she paused on the step, darting quick glances about her. Timidly, she came out into the street. It was only a shabby back street where she had probably lived all her life and but for him it was deserted, but she peered about and hesitated as if she were a schoolgirl, separated from her party and lost in a foreign city. Then she walked rapidly towards a pillar box, her head down, keeping custody of her eyes like a nun.

Wexford followed her, and suddenly he felt shy himself. He had an idea, although it was without foundation, that the letter was for Morgan. She started violently when he spoke to her, gasped and put her hand up to cover her mouth.

'Miss Peters, I'm a policeman. I'm only talking to you in

158

the street because I was afraid I wouldn't be admitted to your home.'

Where did they go to school, these girls? Or did the Revelationers run special schools for their children? Did they never meet outsiders? He wondered if he was the first outsider she had spoken to since she had passed through the terror of the court, an experience which must have been torture to her, enough to shake her reason. Spoken? Was she going to speak now?

She had a plain, unformed face, half-covered still by her hand. No make-up, no rings on her hand. Her body was flat under the stiff heavy coat.

'Miss Peters . . .' Rapidly and rather awkwardly, for she gave him no help, he told her what he wanted and why he was there, accosting her in the rain. He didn't think she was frightened of him, but perhaps she was frightened of God. She scanned the street, her hand now a fist tapping her chin, but before she spoke to him she looked down at her feet. She wouldn't meet his eyes.

'Father would turn me out if he saw me. He was going to turn me out after . . . after . . . Mother made him let me stay.'

The strangest thing in all this strangeness, Wexford thought, was that she should have wanted to stay. But perhaps it wasn't so strange. Hatch out a wild bird, rear it in a cage, and when you set it free it will perish or be destroyed by its fellows. Easing his umbrella over her so that they were both sheltered by it, he began talking to her soothingly, apologising, explaining how important it was for him to know. But all the time he was thinking of the word which lay outside her experience, of the girls like Louise Sampson and Verity Bate who snapped their fingers at their parents, who lived where they liked and with whom they liked, to whom a tyrannical father, wielding real power, was a fictional monster they read about in books written in the distant past. It was almost unbelievable that such opposites as they and Hannah Peters could co-exist in the same city and the same century.

159

Without looking up, she said, 'I never heard of a girl called Loveday.' She shivered. 'She didn't have to go to the court. What was her real name?'

Wexford shook his head, feeling paralysed by her dull slow voice, her ox-like acceptance of oppression.

'Perhaps she left your congregation in the past twelve months?'

'Mary went away to be a teacher, and Sarah went and Rachel. Edna married out. They all went away.' She didn't speak wistfully but as of some dire enormity. 'My father will punish me if I don't go home now.'

'Their addresses?' he pleaded.

'Oh, no. No, no. Mary was at the court.' It cost her something to say that, he thought. Mary too, had been one of Morgan's brides. She struggled with an emotion no one had ever taught her existed or could be controlled. There were tears on her face or perhaps just rain. 'You must go to the Shepherd,' she said, and ducked out from under the umbrella.

'They won't let me into the house!'

She called back to him something about a prayer meeting that night. Then she ran home through the rain, the caged creature escaping from predators and the humane that would set it free. Back to the cage, the safety of a living death.

Wexford had been shaken by the interview. Hannah Peters bore no physical resemblance to Loveday Morgan, and yet he felt that it was to the latter he had been talking. Here, alive and in a different skin, was the dead girl, the shy, frightened, badly-dressed girl who didn't know how to make friends and was scarcely fit to be employed. At last she had been revealed to him, the cemetery walker, the Bible reader. Teal had known her and had seen her rare, wondering smile; Lamont had sat with her, witness her tortured silences; with a shrug, Dearborn had dismissed her ugly gaucheness. And now he too had seen her, or seen perhaps her ghost.

The street was empty again, the ghost gone. But she had left him a message. He must take the only way open to him now of catching her people outside their prisons.

160

20

*In dim and doubtful light they be gathered together,
and more earnestly fixed on religion and devotion.*

DARKNESS came early after that day of torrents. Sitting
in a lorry driver's retreat, his raincoat steaming in the
red glow of an electric fire, Wexford watched the fluorescent
lamps come on in Artois Road. The wet pavements threw back
scarlet and blue and orange reflections of neon overhead. The
sky was red and vaporous, any stars which might have been
up there quenched by the glare. He wondered when the
prayer meeting would begin. Surely not before seven? Hungry
in spite of tea and a doughnut, he ordered a labourer's meal,
a forbidden sinful meal of sausages and chips and fried eggs.

According to Crocker and Dora and their gloomy disciples,
he ought to have been dead by now, for he had broken all
their rules. He had worked when he should have rested, eaten
saturated fats when he should have fasted, gone out at night,
worried and today forgotten all about his pills. Why not break
one more and he hanged for a sheep?

The ultimate forbidden fruit would be to go back into that
pub he had visited at lunchtime and drink spirits. He found it
and had a double Scotch. Far from laying him out, it filled
him with well-being, and he made up his mind then and there
to defy them all. No one but a fool follows a regimen that
debilitates him while moderate indulgence makes him feel
good.

While he had been drinking the rain had stopped. He sniffed

161

the smell of London after rain, smoky, gaseous, with here and there other scents infiltrating, the odour of frying food and stranger oriental platters, the whiff of a French cigarette. They faded as he walked into the residential depths of Artois Road where the blue-white lamps looked too smart for this hinterland. Another light glowed ahead of him, a round red light like a Cyclops eye, and he saw that he was too late. The prayer meeting had begun. He stood outside the temple and heard the voices of the Children, intoning together sometimes, then one single voice raised in spontaneous praise or perhaps commination. How many hours before they came out? And would they talk to him when they did?

The house where the Shepherd lodged, where Morgan had lodged, looked entirely deserted now, no slits of lights showing at the edges of the blinds. The concrete garden lay under a sheet of water which was black because it had no light to mirror. There were perhaps fifty houses like this one in Wilman Park, vaults for the living. Rachel and Mary and Sarah had gone away . . . He hoped that now they wore scent and false eyelashes and feathers and flowers and sat on steps with their boy friends eating crisps out of paper bags.

Morgan must have met his brides somewhere and not under this severe roof. Did he walk with them, sneak off for clandestine love in the *temple*? Wexford wrinkled his nose in distaste. If he had some neighbour would surely have seen him, perhaps even seen him promenading with the chosen one of the moment.

The house next door showed plenty of light and the curtains weren't even drawn. He rang a bell that chimed, but when she came to admit him his heart sank. She smiled enquiringly. Her eyes were blue and vacant and she supported herself on a white stick.

She was a very old woman, not far off eighty, and she had just enough sight left, he guessed, to make out the shape of him on her doorstep. He didn't want to alarm her, so he explained who he was and why he was there before beginning to retreat. She was no use to him, although he couldn't put it so bluntly. Her blindness disqualified her.

'I was just going to make a cup of tea,' she said. 'Would you like one? My husband was in the force. You'll have heard of him. Wally Lyle.'

Wexford shook his head, then remembered she couldn't see. 'I'm a stranger in these parts,' he said. 'I won't keep you, Mrs Lyle. Perhaps you could just tell me the name of the people next door?'

'Vickers,' she said, and she chuckled. 'You won't get inside there. The only person she ever lets in is the electric meter man. They haven't got no gas.' Her cheerfulness moved him. Here she was, alone, blind, very old, but she could still joke, still find some zest in living. When she said, 'You may as well have that tea. I know how it is on the beat all day,' he agreed on an impulse. She couldn't see that he wasn't in uniform. She wanted a chat about her husband and old times. Why not? He had to pass the time somehow until the temple disgorged its throng.

All the lights were on in the hall and the little rooms. Light must help her, he decided, watching her edge her way to the brighter lamp of the kitchen like a moth. But it was he who finally made the tea and carried their two cups into the front room. All the while she kept close beside him, and when he went to sit by the window, waiting for the temple door to open and send a shaft of light out on to the pavement, she came and sat next to him, hooking her stick over the arm of her chair.

The little pokey living room was crammed with furniture, loaded down with ornaments. He wondered that she could move among all this bric-à-brac without hurting herself or knocking things over, and he recalled his own clumsiness in Howard's house. While she told him anecdotes of her husband's career, he observed the dexterity with which she handled her teacup, and he marvelled.

'How long have you lived here, Mrs Lyle?' he asked gently.

'Forty years. Them Vickerses were here before we come.'

163

'They're quite an elderly couple, then?'

'Not this lot. His mum and dad. I call this one *young* Vickers.' She peered into Wexford's face. 'I daresay he'd be old to you—about fifty he is, but a chip off the old block.'

'And you've never been into their house?'

She liked to talk about the dead Wally Lyle and she returned to him. 'My husband tried to get in there once, years and years ago. Young Vickers and his sister were schoolkids then, and the school sent round this doctor on account of Rebecca—that was the sister—having scarlet fever. They wouldn't have no doctor, you see. Revelationers don't believe in doctors, let their kids die rather than have the doctor.'

'So your husband was called in on account of being a policeman?' Wexford was interested in spite of the irrelevance of all this. 'Did he make them admit the doctor?'

Mrs Lyle laughed shrilly. 'Not likely. He banged and banged in the door till old Vickers come out, and old Vickers cursed him. It made your blood run cold to hear it. My husband said he'd never have nothing to do with them again and he never did.'

'And that was the only contact you ever had with them?'

She looked a little sheepish. 'The only contact *he* did. I never let on to him how I helped Rebecca run away and get married. He'd have given it to me hot and strong, being as he was in the force.'

Rebecca, a girl who had run away . . .

He spoke rather sharply. 'When was that, Mrs Lyle?'

She dashed his faint hope. 'Must be thirty years. It's her brother as lives there now. He got married and had kids and they've all gone now too. God knows where.'

She sighed and fell silent. Wexford watched the dark pavement, growing impatient. Mrs Lyle finished her tea and set the cup down correctly in its saucer. Her blue, filmed eyes were turned on his face now and he sensed that she wanted to make some sort of confession to him.

'What I did,' she said, and her expression was sly, almost naughty, 'I often thought maybe it was against the law, but I

164

never dared ask my husband, never breathed a word about it.'

'What did you do?' Wexford put laughter and encouragement into his voice, for it was no use showing them on his face.

'Won't do no harm telling you after all these years.' She grinned, enjoying herself. 'Rebecca wanted to get married to a fellow she'd met, fellow called Foster who wasn't one of *them*, and her dad he put his foot down and they shut her up in there. Just a prisoner she was, shut up in her bedroom. She used to write notes and throw them to me out of the window. I could see to read in them days. I was all for putting a spoke in the wheel of them Revelationers and I had young Foster in here, jollying him along, and one day when they was all in church we got a ladder and stuck it up at the window and down she come. Like a play it was.'

The orchard walls are high and hard to climb and the place death, considering who thou art, if any of my kinsmen find thee here . . . 'It must have been,' he said.

'I often have a good laugh about it to this day. Mind you, it'd have been better if I'd ever found out what they thought about it but I never did. I'd like to have seen old Vickers' face when he knew the bird had flown. Rebecca got married and she wrote to me, telling me bits of news, but that's stopped now. No good getting letters when you can't read them and you've no one to read them to you, is it?' Mrs Lyle laughed merrily at the doleful situation she had described. 'Vickers—the son, that is—he got married and they had kids but they've all gone off one by one. Couldn't stand it at home. And now there's just the two of them alone in there. Young Vickers—I call him that but he must be all of fifty—he never speaks to me. I reckon he knows what I did for Rebecca. I often have a good laugh when I think of her and that ladder and young Foster like a blessed Romeo. A bit of luck for her that was, catching him. She was nothing to look at and she had a great big mole on the side of her nose . . .'

The temple door must have opened, for a pale stream of

light seeped out across the wet stones and people began to appear on the pavement. Wexford, who had been waiting for this to happen, ignored it and turned to face Mrs Lyle, although he knew she couldn't see him.

'A mole in the side of her nose?'

'Stuck there between her nose and her cheek like.' Mrs Lyle jabbed a finger at her own apple complexion. 'My husband used to say she could have had that seen to, only seeing they didn't believe in doctors . . .'

'Where did she go?'

'South-west Ten her address was. I've got letters about somewhere. You'll have to look for them yourself. But I'll tell you one thing, Rebecca won't get you in that house next door. It'd take one of them bulldozers to do that.'

Wexford stood in the bay window and watched the congregation disperse. The women wore dull fashionless, rather than old-fashioned, coats and hats in black or grey or fawn, the men, even the young men, black suits topped by dark raincoats. Among them, like a crow, moved the Shepherd in his black robe, shaking hands, murmuring farewells until all but two were gone. This pair, evidently a married couple, stood arm-in-arm, waiting for him. Then the three of them filed slowly into the house next door. Briefly Wexford caught a glimpse of them mirrored darkly in the pool of water, three strange people crossing the Styx into their own underworld. The front door shut with a slam.

'You looking at young Vickers?' said Mrs Lyle who had the hypersensitivity of the blind. 'I wish my grandson was here to blow him a raspberry. All the kids round here do that, and good luck to them.'

'Better look for those letters now, Mrs Lyle.'

They went upstairs, the old woman leading the way. She took him into her bedroom which had the jumble sale look of rooms occupied by old people and in which they have grown old. Apart from the usual furniture there were work-boxes, wooden and wicker, stacked one on top of the other,

166

trunks under the bed and trunks covered with dust sheets which were themselves piled with old magazines and old albums. Two of those miniature chests of drawers, dear to the hearts of the Victorians, stood on the massive tallboy, and above them on the wall was a what-not, crammed full of letters and papers and little boxes and old pens and jars of hairpins.

'It might be in here,' said Mrs Lyle, 'or it might be in the other rooms.'

Wexford looked into the other rooms. None of them was exactly untidy. Nor were they rooms for people to live in. They were the repositories for the results of sixty years of hoarding, and it was apparent to his practised eye that some crazy filing system had been employed in the days when Mrs Lyle still had her sight.

She seemed to sense that he was taken aback. A note came into her voice that was not quite malice but faintly revengeful. She said, 'You've got a long job.' She meant, 'You can see and I can't, so you get on with it.'

He got on with it, beginning in her bedroom. Perhaps it was the smell of these souvenirs, merely musty to him but evocative to her of the occasions they commemorated, which made her face go strange and dreamy, though not unhappy, her hand shake a little as she touched the cards and photographs he lifted from the drawers. He fetched the old brass bedlamp and put it on the tallboy to give him light, and in its yellow radiance, moted with dust, he explored the archives of Mrs Lyle's long life.

She had been a great correspondent and she had kept every letter, every birthday and Christmas card she had ever received. Some male relative had been a philatelist so she had kept the envelopes too, but the collector had never come for his stamps which had accumulated in their thousands on envelopes and scraps torn from envelopes. The late policeman's love letters were there, bound in ribbon from a wedding cake, pieces of ancient and petrified icing still adhering to it. Every year he had sent her a Valentine. He found five in the tallboy, and then he began on the workboxes, seven more in there.

'I never throw anything away,' said Mrs Lyle happily.

He didn't say the cruel thing aloud, but he asked it of himself. Why didn't she? Why did she keep these cards, these cake boxes, these locks of babies' hair, these greetings telegrams and these reams of newspaper cuttings? She was blind; she would never be able to see any of them again. But he knew she kept them for another reason. What matter if she never again read the policeman's writing or looked at his picture and those of her posterity? They were the bricks of her identity, the fabric of the walls which kept it safe and the windows through which, though sightless, it could still look out upon its world. His own identity had been too precariously shaken in recent weeks for him to reproach someone who hoarded and harvested and stored to preserve her own.

And he could see. His eye didn't hurt him at all. Even in this dull and dusty light he could read the spidery writing and distinguish the faces in the cloudy sepia photographs. By now he felt that he could have written Mrs Lyle's biography. It was all here, every day of her life, keeping her alive and a unique personality, waiting to be burned by a grandson when she needed it no longer.

They moved on into the next room. Wexford didn't know what time it was; he was afraid to look at his watch. There must be easier ways of finding Rebecca Foster. If only he could remember where it was that he had seen her for the first time . . .

He wished he had begun in the smallest bedroom, for it was there that he found it. He unstrapped a suitcase, unlocked it, opened it. The case contained only letters, some still in their envelopes, some loose, their sheets scattered and mixed with others. And here it was at last. '36, Biretta St., S.W.10. June 26th, 1954. Dear May, Sorry to hear you are having trouble with your eyes . . .'

'Well, that didn't take too long, did it?' said Mrs Lyle. 'I hope you've put all my things back right, not mixed up. I like to know where they are. If you've done, I'll see you off the premises and then I think I'll get to bed.'

168

21

He made the proverb true, which saith: He that
shooteth oft, at last shall hit the mark.

HIS last day. He didn't think of it as the last day of his
holiday but as his last opportunity to solve this case. And
it was the first time he had really known what it is to be set a
deadline. In the past, of course, at Kingsmarkham, the chief
constable had pressed him and there had sometimes been
threats of calling in the Yard, but no one had ever said, You
have twenty-four hours. After that time has elapsed, the case
will be taken out of your hands. No one was saying it now
except himself.

Howard had ceased to regard him as being involved in it.
Come to that, he had never said, This is your case. Solve it
for me. How could he, in his position? All he had asked for
were his uncle's ideas and his uncle's advice, and with Wexford's failure he had given up asking even that. Not that he
gave any sign of being disappointed, but he pinned his faith
now to Baker and it was of Baker that he had talked the
night before.

Wexford had been too tired to take much of it in, gathering
only that Gregson had been remanded in custody on a charge
of assaulting a police officer. Baker still thought of him as his
prime suspect, but just the same he was pursuing other lines.
The scarf was interesting him at the moment and he was much
concerned about an interview he had had with one of the

169

tenants of Garmisch Terrace. Wexford couldn't summon up energy to ask questions, and Howard too was tired, his foot paining him, and he let his uncle go off to bed, wishing him good night with the optimistic assurance that the case might well be solved before the Wexfords left on the Saturday.

It might well, Wexford reflected on the morning of his last day, but not by Baker.

The women had long given up waiting at the foot of the stairs for him and with regard to breakfast he took pot luck. He felt perfectly well. Yesterday's exercise had taken off more weight while the meals had added none, and even doubtful solicitous Dora had to admit that his holiday had done its good work. It was hard for him to realise that this Friday was just the last day of their holiday for her, a time for packing and going out to buy last-minute gifts. Her only concern was whether or not she had remembered the order for milk to be left on Saturday, and would their little corner shop keep a loaf of bread for her?

'What did you say?' said her husband.

'The bread, Reg. I said I hoped Dixons would keep me a loaf of bread.'

'You said the corner shop . . .' That was where he had seen her! Not, of course, at Dixons down the road from him in Kingsmarkham, but at a little place that might have been its twin opposite a rose-pink house in Fulham. All those hours wasted, rummaging through the storeplace of a life! 'Pity you didn't mention it before,' he said abruptly.

They looked at him as if he were mad, but Denise often did that. 'How are you going to amuse yourself today, Uncle Reg?'

'I shall be all right.'

'Going to see St Thomas for the last time?'

'*Sir* Thomas.' He smiled at her, liking her scented prettiness, glad that he would soon be away from her speckless housekeeping and her dangerous plants. 'Don't you worry about me. I've got things to do. Howard get off all right?'

'Someone came to drive him.'

He waited until they had left the house to buy toys for his grandchildren, and then he walked down past the back way into St Mark and St John, catching sight of a red head by the gates that probably belonged to Verity Bate. She reminded him of his previous failure. He wouldn't fail again, not this time. Everything was falling beautifully into place. He even knew just why Loveday had picked on Belgrade Road and that colourful house opposite the shop as an address to give Peggy Pope. It was straight there that he was going. Why bother with Biretta Street which lay far off his course in the river-bound peninsula that is Chelsea but looks like Wilman Park or Kenbourne Vale?

The shop was ahead of him now, price reductions scrawled on its window, vegetables outside in boxes, a mongrel dog tied up to a lamp standard. He went inside. The shop was full of people, a long queue of women with long shopping lists. Two assistants were serving, a young girl and a woman with a pink wen pushing her nose slightly askew.

There was nothing for it but to wait until the place emptied, if it ever did on a Friday when shoppers stocked up with weekend provisions. He paced up and down the street, time passing with maddening slowness. Years and years ago, when he was young, he had felt like this, arriving too early for a date with a girl, killing time. The cold mist made him shiver and his fingers felt numb. Pity he hadn't thought of putting gloves on. Gloves . . . In all these enquiries of his he mustn't forget the girl with the gloves.

When he went back for the fourth time to the shop door, all but one of the queue had gone and this last one was being served by the girl. His woman, his longed-for date, had gone to the window and was stacking soap packets in a pyramid.

'Mrs Foster?' he said, his throat dry.

She stepped back, surprised, and nodded. The mole, which might once have marred a pretty face, was now only an ugly feature among general worn ugliness. She looked about fifty. Ah, the orchard walls are high and hard to climb . . .

'I'm a police officer. I should like to talk to you.'

171

When she spoke he heard the voice of a Child of the Revelation, accentless, dull, economical.

'What about?' she said.

'Your niece,' said Wexford. 'Your brother's daughter.

She didn't argue or expostulate but told the girl to see to the shop and led him into a small room at the rear.

'I've been talking to Mrs Lyle,' he said.

The blood poured into her face and she pressed her ill-kept hands together. It was impossible to imagine her as the young girl, the Juliet, who had climbed down a ladder into her lover's arms. 'Mrs Lyle . . . Does she still live down there? Next door to my brother?'

'She's blind now. She knew nothing, only your address.'

'Blind,' said Mrs Foster. 'Blind. And I'm a widow and Rachel . . .' To his horror she began to cry. She cried as if she were ashamed of her tears, scrubbing them away as they fell. 'The world's all wrong,' she said. 'It ought to be changed.'

'Maybe. Tell me about Rachel.'

'I promised her . . .'

'Your promises mean nothing now, Mrs Foster. Rachel is dead.' He had broken it without preamble but he regretted nothing, for he could tell that her niece had very little to do with her grief. She had been crying for herself, perhaps a little for Mrs Lyle. Who had ever shed a tear for Loveday Morgan?'

'Dead,' she said as she had said 'blind'. 'How, dead?'

He explained and all the time he was speaking her face was stony. 'Now it's your turn,' he said.

'She came to my house in July, last July.' The voice grated on him. It was even, monotonous, without rise or fall. 'My brother turned her out when he found she was expecting. She was small and she didn't eat much and she didn't show till nearly the end. My brother told her to get out.'

He had guessed but he could hardly believe it. In these days? In London in the nineteen seventies? Although she had

172

emancipated herself from her upbringing, Mrs Foster had about her something Victorian, and it was a Victorian situation, chronicled in a thousand novels, that she was describing.

'You can't credit it?' she said. 'You don't know what the Children are. She came to me because there was no one else. She'd never heard of people, societies, that look after girls like her. I'd have thought she was simple if I hadn't been like that myself once.'

'The baby?'

'She hadn't seen a doctor. I told her to go and see one. She wouldn't. She'd never been to a doctor in her life. The Children don't have doctors. She wouldn't go to the Assistance. I kept her. I had this job and two jobs cleaning. What else could I do? One day I got home from work and she'd had the baby all by herself in my bedroom.'

'Without any assistance?'

Mrs. Foster nodded. 'I made her have a doctor then. I sent for my own. He was very angry with me but what could I do? He sent in the midwife every day and I registered the baby in Chelsea, up in the King's Road.'

'Morgan was the father?'

'Yes. She said she was his wife and when he came out of prison they'd be married properly. I knew that wasn't true. He had a wife living. We looked after the baby between us and when she got work, cleaning work, sometimes I'd take it with me or she'd take it with her.'

'And then?'

Mrs Foster hesitated. The girl in the shop called her and she said, 'I'm coming. I'm coming in a minute.' She turned tiredly to Wexford. 'It was adopted. Rachel loved it, but she agreed. She knew it wasn't possible for us to keep it all on our own. We had to work, both of us, and women don't like it if you take a baby with you. But Rachel was no worker, anyway. She wasn't used to it. She was crazy about television. It was new to her, you see. All she wanted was to sit about all day, watching the television with the baby on her lap. She said she'd like to be somewhere where she could watch

173

it all day long. Then the baby went and being in my house without it got her down, so she left and got a room. I never heard from her. I thought maybe my brother had taken her back. All she'd been through hadn't stopped her wanting to be one of the Children . . .' Mrs Foster's voice tailed forlornly away.

'Who adopted the baby? Was it done through a society?'

'I can't tell you that. I promised. Rachel never knew. We thought it best she shouldn't know.'

'I must know.'

'Not through me. I promised.'

'Then I must go to the Children's Department,' said Wexford.

The phone book told him he would find it in Holland Park and he waited for a taxi to take him there. But he knew the answer already, the whole answer, and as he stood at the kerb he began carefully arranging mentally the complete sequence of events from Rachel Vickers' arrival in Biretta Street to her death as Loveday Morgan in Kenbourne Vale cemetery.

Poor Baker. Just for once he was to be cheated of his triumph, forestalled by the old fuddy-duddy from the country. Wexford felt gently amused to think of them all there in Kenbourne, pursuing lines which would lead to dead ends, running off at tangents, clinging obstinately to their need to pin it on a boy van driver. All there at the police station—except Sergeant Clements. And he would be in court, getting his order. Or perhaps, even at this moment, failing to get it?

Howard and Baker were at the Yard. Everyone knew Clements was taking the day off and why he was. Pamela told Wexford she didn't expect the superintendent to put in a further appearance that day.

The snapshot Pamela had found on Howard's desk was no longer there. Someone had taken it or put it away. Instead, Mrs Dearborn's blue scarf lay there, enclosed but not concealed by a case of clear plastic. It had the look of a prewrapped Christmas gift but for the neat official label stuck to the side of the case.

Wexford shrugged, thanked Pamela and went out. To get to Elm Green tube station he made a detour through the cemetery. In the gathering fog the winged victory was ghost-like and the black horses, half-veiled in vapour, seemed to plunge on the air itself without support, without anchorage. Beneath them the royal tombs had lost their solidity as had the still trees, spectres of trees rather, floating, rootless and grey. Water drops, condensed mist, clung to the thready brambles. Obelisks, broken columns, angels with swords, a hunter with two dead lions at his feet . . .

> 'He who asks questions is a fool.
> He who answers them is a greater fool . . .'

Wexford smiled.

22

The murder being once done, he is in less fear and more hope that the deed shall not be betrayed or known, seeing the party is now dead and rid out of the way, which only might have uttered and disclosed it.

A LAST day well spent. Wexford was a poor typist but he would have been glad of the use of a typewriter now. He had to write the whole thing out on sheet after sheet of Basildon Bond, using Dora's old fountain pen. It was after seven when he finished and then he went downstairs to wait for Howard.

His plan was to give Howard the report after dinner, and he envisaged their discussing it quietly in the study, but his nephew phoned to say he would be delayed and had replaced the receiver before Wexford had a chance to talk to him.

'You ought to go to bed, dear,' Dora said at ten.

'Why? So that I'll be strong enough to sit in the train? I've a good mind to stay up all night.'

He opened the book Denise had at last, in despair over his dilatoriness, fetched him from the library. 'To the Right Honourable and his Very Singular Good Master, Master William Cecil Esquire . . . Ralph Robinson wisheth continuance of good health with daily increase of virtue and honour.' That dedication, with different names substituted, might as well have served as an introduction to his own report as to Sir

176

Thomas's masterpiece. He had scarcely read the first paragraph when the phone rang again.

'He wants to talk to you, Uncle Reg. I said you were just off to bed.'

Wexford took the phone in a hand that trembled very slightly. 'Howard?'

Howard's voice was hard, a little disdainful. 'If you're on your way to bed it doesn't matter.'

'I'm not. I was waiting up for you.' Now that the time had come, Wexford found himself strangely reluctant, his voice uncertain. 'There are a few points . . . Well, I've written a sort of report . . . Would you care to . . . ? I mean, my conclusions . . .'

'Could be the same as ours,' Howard finished the sentence for him. 'The scarf? Yes, I thought so. Baker and I have just been to see a friend of yours and what we really need now is a little help from you. If you'll hold the line, I'll put Baker on.'

'Howard, wait. I could come over.'

'What, now? To Kenbourne Vale?'

Wexford decided to be firm, not to argue at all. He saw clearly and coldly that he was failing for the second time, but he wouldn't give in without some sort of fight, not let Baker steal his last faint thunder. 'I'll take a taxi,' he said.

The expected wail came from Dora. 'Oh, darling! At this hour?'

'I said I was going to stay up all night.'

What amazed him was that some of the shops were still open at ten minutes to midnight and people were still buying groceries for strange nocturnal feasts. In the launderettes the bluish-white lights were on and the machines continued to turn. His cab took him through North Kensington where the night people walked, chatting desultorily, strolling, as if it were day. In Kingsmarkham anybody still out would be hastening home to bed. Here the sky wore its red, starless glow, above the floating lights, the sleepless city. They came into Kenbourne Lane. The cemetery was like a pitch-black cloud, only visible because its mass was darker than the sky. Wexford felt the muscles of his chest contract as he realised they were nearly there. Soon he would be facing Baker. If only there might be a chance of Howard reading his report first . . .

He had had a foolish feeling that there might be a sort of reception committee awaiting him, but there was no one in the foyer but the officers on duty. And when he tried to treat the place as if it was more familiar with him than he with it, walking casually towards the lift, a sergeant called him back to ask his name and his business.

'Mr Wexford, is it? The superintendent is expecting you, sir.'

That was a little better. His spirits rose higher when he stepped out of the lift and saw Howard standing alone in the corridor outside his office.

'You've been very quick.'

'Howard, I just want to say . . .'

'You want to know about Gregson. I guessed you would and I meant to mention it on the phone. Where d'you think he was on the 25th? Doing that housebreaking job, of all things. The girl who phoned him at Mrs Kirby's was Harry Slade's girl friend to tell him the job was on and give him all the gen. Come on in now, and see Baker. Shall I send down for coffee?'

Wexford didn't answer him. He walked into the office, met Baker's eyes and silently drew his report out of his pocket. The handwritten sheets looked very amateurish, very rustic.

Howard said awkwardly, 'We really only wanted some inside information, Reg. A few questions we had to put to you . . .'

'It's all in there. It won't take you more than ten minutes to read the lot.'

Wexford knew he was being hypersensitive, but a man would have had to be totally without perception not to see that resigned and indulgent glance which passed between Baker and Howard. He sat down, sliding his arms out of his raincoat and letting it fall over the back of the chair. Then he stared at the uncurtained window, the thick red sky and the black bulk of the bottling plant. While Howard phoned to order coffee, Baker cast his eyes over, rather than read, the report.

It was ten pages long. He got to page five and then he said, 'All this stuff about the girl's background, it's very edifying, no doubt, but hardly . . .' He sought for a word. ' . . . Germane to this inquiry,' he said.

'Let me see.' Howard stood behind Baker, reading rapidly. 'You've put in a lot of work here, Reg. Congratulations. You seem to have reached the same conclusions as we have.'

'Taking all the evidence,' said Wexford, 'they are the only possible conclusions.'

Howard gave him a quick look. 'Yes, well . . . Maybe the best thing would be for you to sum up for us, Michael.'

The sheets of blue paper were growing rather crumpled now. Baker folded them and dropped them rather contemptuously on the desk top. But when he spoke it wasn't contemptuously. He cleared his throat and said in the uneasy tone of a man who is unaccustomed to graciousness, 'I owe you a bit of an apology, Mr Wexford. I shouldn't have said what I did about wild goose chases and red herrings and all that. But it did look like a red herring at first, didn't it?'

Wexford smiled. 'It looked like a needless complication.'

'Not needless at all,' Howard said. 'Without it we should never have traced the ownership of the scarf. Here's our coffee. Put it down there, Sergeant, thank you. Well, Michael?'

'For a time,' Baker began, 'we were completely put off the scent by the confusion between Rachel Vickers and Dearborn's own stepdaughter. We neglected to bear in mind the circumstantial evidence and we did not then, of course, know that his daughter Alexandra was not his own child.'

Wexford stirred his coffee, although it was black and sugarless. 'How do you know now?' he interrupted.

'Mrs Dearborn told us herself tonight. She was very frank, very open. When she realised the importance of the inquiry, she told us quite freely that Alexandra—named, she believed, after her natural father—is a child she and her husband had adopted privately. Two adoption societies had refused to con-

179

sider them on account of their age, and when the opportunity arose just before Christmas for them to take this baby they jumped at it. Dearborn acted very properly. He intended to adopt legally and through the proper channels. As soon as the child was received into his house in late December, he notified the Children's Department and the court of his intention to adopt. Did you want to say something, Mr Wexford?'

'Only that you make it sound very cold. He loves that child passionately.'

'I don't think we should allow our emotions to be involved. Naturally, the whole thing is painful. Let me resume. Mrs Dearborn has never met Rachel Vickers. All she knew about her came from the girl's aunt, her former charwoman, Mrs Foster, and from the guardian *ad litem.*'

'The girl with the gloves,' said Wexford.

Baker took no notice of this. 'The guardian and Mrs Foster knew the girl as Rachel Vickers, never as Loveday Morgan. Until February 14th, Dearborn also only knew the girl by her true name, he had never seen her and supposed everything would be plain sailing. On that day he came home and told his wife that while he had been showing Alexandra some property he intended to buy in Lammas Grove, Rachel Vickers came out of a shop and recognised her child.' Baker paused. 'I must admit I don't quite understand that, a man pointing out houses to a babe in arms, but I daresay it's irrelevant.' He glanced at Wexford and Wexford said nothing. 'According to Mrs Dearborn,' he went on, 'Rachel asked him if she might see Alexandra again and he agreed, though reluctantly, giving her his office phone number. Mrs Dearborn says—and I believe she is speaking the truth—that she knows of no more meetings between Rachel and her husband. As far as she knows, the girl showed no more interest in the child after that.'

'We, however,' put in Howard, 'have been told early in this inquiry that Rachel had an interview at Notbourne Properties sometime after February 14th, and I think we can conclude this interview had nothing to do with an application for a job. What are your views, Reg?'

'Dearborn,' said Wexford slowly, 'wanted to keep the child and Rachel, just as intensely, wanted her back. At that interview in his office she told him she would oppose the granting of his order and he took the highly illegal step of offering her five thousand pounds not to oppose it.'

'How can you possibly know that?'

Wexford shrugged. 'Finish reading my report and you'll know how. Without reading it, you can surely see that this is why Dearborn told his wife no more. He's unscrupulous but Mrs Dearborn isn't. She would never have gone along with him in any scheme to *buy* the child. When did they expect to get the order?'

'On March 24th,' said Baker with a certain triumph. 'If you don't know that, Mr Wexford, I don't see how . . . But let me get on with my ideas of what happened next. Rachel agreed to take the money—some money, we can't say how much—and promised to phone Dearborn to fix a date for this transaction. The date she chose was February 25th and she phoned Dearborn from Garmisch Terrace at one fifteen on that day. They met about an hour later in the cemetery.'

'You've identified the scarf as Mrs Dearborn's?'

'Certainly. That's why we went to see her in the first place. She told us she often wears her husband's sheepskin jacket and probably left the scarf in that jacket pocket. Dearborn met the girl as arranged, but when he was about to part with the money, thought how much easier it would be, how much safer he would be, to keep the money and kill the girl. He would never be sure otherwise that she wouldn't oppose the order just the same. So he strangled her with the scarf and put her body in the Montfort tomb.'

'You helped us again there, Reg,' said Howard. 'It was you who pointed out about its being Leap Year. Dearborn forgot that. He supposed that the last Tuesday of the month had gone by and that the tomb wouldn't be visited until *after* March 24th, by which time he would have his order.'

Wexford reached for his report, fingered it hesitantly and then laid it down again. 'He's confessed all this?' he asked. 'You've talked to him and . . . Have you charged him?'

'He's away from home,' said Baker. 'Up in the north somewhere at some architects' conference.'

'We wanted your *opinion*, Reg,' Howard said rather sharply. 'So much of this is conjecture. As you said yourself it's the only possible conclusion, but we thought you might have something more concrete for us.'

'I said that?'

'Well, surely. I understood you to . . . '

Wexford got up abruptly, pushing back his chair so that it almost fell over. He was suddenly frightened, but not of himself, not any more of failure. 'His wife will get in touch with him!'

'Of course she will. Let her. He's due back tomorrow morning.' Howard looked at his watch. 'This morning, rather. Once he knows he's in danger of not getting that order—his wife will tell him that the court will suspend all action until the matter is cleared up—he'll come hotfoot to us. My God, Reg, she doesn't know we suspect him of murder.'

'But he'll know by now he hasn't a hope in hell of remaining as Alexandra's father?' Wexford gripped the back of the chair. He was shivering. 'Will she have told him that?'

'Unless she's a far more phlegmatic woman than I take her to be, yes.'

He tried to stay calm. He knew his face had grown white, for he could feel the skin shrink and tremble. Baker's face was scornful and sour, Howard's entirely bewildered.

'You wanted my advice. It must be that because you don't want my opinion. My advice to you is to phone Dearborn's hotel now, at once.' Wexford sat down and turned his face to the wall.

'He's in his room,' said Baker, replacing the receiver. 'I don't see the need for all this melodrama. The man's in his room, asleep, but they've gone to check and they'll call us back. I suppose Mr Wexford's idea is they'll find a bundle of clothes under the sheets and the bird flown.'

Wexford didn't comment on that. His hands were clasped tightly together, the knuckles whitened by the strong pressure. He didn't relax them but he relaxed his voice, making conversation for the sake of it. 'What happened about Clements?' he asked, attempting to sound casual.

'He got his order,' Howard said. 'Phoned through to tell us. No difficulty at all.'

'I'll send his wife some flowers,' said Wexford. 'Remind me.' He helped himself to more coffee without bothering to ask permission, but his hand was unsteady and he slopped it on to the desk. Howard didn't say a word.

The phone gave the prefatory click that comes a split second before it rings. Before it rang Wexford had jumped and got the shock over. Three hands went out to the receiver, the other men infected by his dread. It was Howard who lifted it, Howard who said, 'I see. Yes. You've got a doctor? The local police?' He covered the mouthpiece with his hand. His thin face had grown very pale. 'There's a doctor staying in the hotel,' he said. 'He's with Dearborn now.'

'He tried to kill himself,' said Wexford and he said it not as a question but as a statement of fact.

'They think he's dead. They don't know. Some sort of overdose, it sounds like.'

Baker said, attempting a suitable dolefulness, 'Maybe it's the best thing. Horrible, of course, but when you think of the alternative, years inside. In his position I'd take the same way out.'

Howard was talking again, asking sharp questions into the phone. 'What position?' said Wexford. 'You don't still think he did it, do you?'

183

23

If by none of these means the matter go forward as they would have it, then they procure occasions of debate.

WEXFORD had seen many a dawn in Kingsmarkham, but never till now a London dawn. He parted the curtains at Howard's window and watched the indigo sky split and shred to show between the heavy clouds streaks of greenish light. A little wind, too slight to set the cemetery trees in motion, fluttered a flag on the roof of a distant building. Pigeons had began to coo, to take wing and wheel lazily against the façades of tower blocks which they, foolish creatures and slow to learn, still took for the cliffs of southern Italy from where the Romans had brought them two thousand years before. The roar of the traffic, half-silenced during the small dead hours, was rising again to its full daytime volume.

Apart from himself, the office was empty. As the great red ball of a sun began to rise, thrusting through reddish-black vapourish folds, the street lamps of Kenbourne Vale went out gradually. Wexford went across the room and snapped off the light switch. But no sooner had he found himself in the welcome, restful semi-darkness than the light came on again and Howard limped into the office with Melanie Dearborn.

Her face was haggard, the eye sockets purple with fatigue and fear. She wore trousers and a sweater and over them her husband's sheepskin coat. But for all her pain and her anxiety,

184

she hadn't forgotten her manners. Blinking a little against the light, she came up to Wexford and held out her hand. 'I'm so sorry,' she began, 'that we should meet again like this, that these terrible things . . .'

He shook his head, fetched a chair and helped her into it. Then he met Howard's eyes and Howard gave a tiny, almost imperceptible nod, pursing his lips.

'Your husband . . . ?'

'Is going to recover,' Howard answered for her. 'He's in hospital and he's very tired but he's conscious. He'll be all right.'

'Thank God,' Wexford said sincerely.

She looked up at him and managed a weak watery smile. 'Why was I so stupid as to phone him last night? I got in a panic, you see. I couldn't bear to think of him coming home and perhaps finding Alexandra gone. He told me all he'd done to keep her.'

Wexford sat down and drew his chair close to hers.

'What did he do, Mrs Dearborn?'

'I'm afraid to tell you,' she whispered. 'Because if it comes out . . . they may . . . I mean, they could take Alexandra away and not let us . . .'

Wexford looked at Howard, but Howard didn't move a muscle. 'It will be better to tell us,' he said. 'It's always better to tell the truth. And if the bribe wasn't taken . . .'

There was a discouraging cough from Howard and Melanie Dearborn gave a heavy sigh. She snuggled more deeply inside the coat as if, because it was her husband's and he had worn it, she had near to her a comforting part of himself. 'The bribe was offered,' she said.

'How much?' Howard asked gently but succintly.

'Five thousand pounds.'

Wexford nodded. 'She was to promise not to oppose the order in exchange for that?'

'She did promise. When she came to my husband's office. Then and there they made an appointment to meet in Kenbourne Vale cemetery on February 25th at two-fifteen.'

185

'Why did she change her mind?'

'She didn't exactly. According to Stephen, she was a very simple sort of girl. When he and she met that day she began to talk about how she was going to use the money and give it to someone to look after Alexandra while she was out at work. She didn't even have the sense to realise what she was saying. Stephen said, "But you won't have Alexandra. I'm giving you the money so that I can keep her." And then she put her hand over her mouth—you can imagine—and said, "Oh, Mr Dearborn, but I must keep her. She's all I've got in the world and you won't miss the money." She just didn't *see*.'

Wexford nodded but he said nothing. He had seen the girl, or her ghost, her counterpart, her *doppel-gänger*. Both had been brought up in a strict morality, but a morality which leaves out what ordinary human beings call ethics.

'Stephen was—well, appalled,' Mrs Dearborn went on. 'He said he'd give her more, anything she asked. He was prepared to go up to—oh, I don't know—fifty thousand, I expect. But she couldn't imagine that amount of money.'

'He didn't give her anything?'

'Of course he didn't. She was chattering on about how she'd give a thousand to someone to look after Alexandra and keep the four for the future, and he saw it wasn't any good and he just turned away and left her. He was very quiet and moody that night—I thought it was because he was tired of the way I fretted about Louise. By the middle of the next week he was on top of the world again. I know why that was now. He'd realised who the murdered girl was.'

Howard had listened to it all without intervening, but now he said in a steady cool voice, 'If you're going up to see your husband, Mrs Dearborn, we'd better see about transport for you.'

'Thank you. I'm afraid I'm giving everyone a great deal of trouble.' Melanie Dearborn hesitated and then said in a rush, 'What am I to say to him about—about Alexandra?'

'That depends on the outcome of this case and upon the court.'

'But we love her,' she pleaded. 'We can give her a good home. Stephen—he tried to *kill* himself. The bribe wasn't accepted. In the girl's mind it wasn't a bribe at all but a gift, just like the clothes we gave her aunt.'

'Well?' said Wexford to Howard after she had left them, casting over her shoulder a last imploring look.

'The court might, I suppose, see it in that light. But when the evidence given in Dearborn's prosecution . . .'

'What are you going to prosecute him for, Howard? Making a present of money to a poverty-stricken girl, his former servant's niece, so that she could raise a child he was fond of decently? And then withdrawing the offer because the chosen guardians weren't suitable in his eyes?'

'It wasn't like that, Reg, you're being Jesuitical. Dearborn killed her. The scarf was his wife's, in the pocket of that coat which they both wear. He had abundant motive which no one else had. And he had the special knowledge. He put her in a tomb he knew wouldn't be visited until after he had got his adoption order.'

'Knew?' said Wexford. 'He wouldn't have forgotten it was Leap Year. February 29th was his birthday.'

'I don't understand you, Mr Wexford,' said Baker who had just come in and had overheard his last words. 'According to your report you go along with our views entirely.'

'How do you know? You didn't bother to read to the end.'

Howard looked at his uncle, half-smiling as if he understood that this was triumph, this was the end he had asked for and more than Wexford had hoped to attain. He picked up the last two sheets of blue paper and, beckoning Baker to him, read them swiftly. 'We shouldn't be here,' he said when he had finished. 'We should be in Garmisch Terrace.'

'You should,' Wexford retorted. He looked at his watch and yawned. 'I've a train to catch at ten.'

Baker took a step towards him. He didn't hold out this hand or attempt to retract anything or even smile. He said, 'I don't know how Mr Fortune feels, but I'd take it as a personal

187

favour if you'd come with us.' And Wexford understood that this was a frank and full apology.

'There are other trains,' he said, and he put on his coat.

Early morning in Garmisch Terrace, a thin pale sunlight baring the houses in all their dilapidation. Someone had scrawled 'God is dead' on the temple wall, and the Shepherd was in the act of erasing it with a scrubbing brush and a bucket of water. Outside number 22, Peggy Pope, her hair tied up in a scarf, was loading small articles of furniture into a van.

'Going somewhere?' said Wexford.

She shrugged. 'Next week,' she said. 'I thought I owed it to the landlords to give them a week's notice.' Her face, unwashed, unpainted, rather greasy, had a curious spiritual beauty like a young saint's. 'I'm just getting shot of a few of my things.'

Wexford glanced at the driver. It was the Indian tenant. 'Off with him, are you?'

'I'm off *alone*, me and the kid, that is. He's just letting me have a loan of his van. I'm going home to my mother. Nowhere else *to* go, is there?' She thrust a battered record player into the van, wiped her hands on her jeans and went down the area steps. The three policemen followed her.

The stacks of old books were still there, the cumbersome shabby furniture. On the wall a little more paint had peeled away, enlarging the map of that unearthly, Utopian continent. Lamont was in bed, the baby lying restlessly in the crook of his arm.

Peggy showed none of the outraged propriety that might have been evinced by a respectable housewife under these circumstances. She wasn't a respectable housewife but a wandering girl about to leave her lover. Remembering perhaps how Wexford had once before assisted her in moving heavy objects, she seemed to take his presence as a sign that it was in this role that he had reappeared, and she thrust into his arms a shopping basket full of kitchen utensils. Wexford shook his head at her. He went over to the bed and stared at Lamont

188

who responded first by burying his head in the pillow, then by pulling himself slowly and despairingly into a sitting position.

Howard and Baker came closer to the bed, Peggy watched them. She knew now that something was wrong, that they were not merely here to ask questions. But she said nothing. She was leaving Garmisch Terrace and everything it contained, and perhaps she didn't care.

'Get up, Lamont,' said Baker. 'Get up and get dressed.'

Lamont didn't speak to him. Under the dirty sheet he was naked. His eyes had a naked empty look in them, expressing a total failure, an utter poverty, a lack of love, of possessions, of imagination. Thou art the thing itself, Wexford thought, unaccommodated man is no more than such a poor, bare animal as thou art . . . 'Come along, you know why we are here.'

'I never had the money,' Lamont whispered. He let the sheet drop, took the child in his arms and handed her to Peggy. It was the final renunciation. 'You'll have to look after her now,' he said. 'Just you. I did it for you and her. Would you have stayed if I'd got the money?'

'I don't know,' Peggy said, crying. 'I don't know.'

'I wish,' said Howard tiredly, 'I felt as well as you look. They say a change is as good as a rest, and you haven't had either, but you look fine.'

'I feel fine.' Wexford thought but he didn't say aloud, I'll be glad to get home just the same. 'It's good to be able to read again without feeling you're going to go blind.'

'Which reminds me,' said Howard, 'I've got something for you to read in the train. A parting gift. Pamela went out to the West-End and got it.'

A very handsome copy of *Utopia*, bound in amber calf, tooled in gold. 'So I've got it at last. Thanks very much. If we're going back to Chelsea now, d'you think we could make a detour for me to say good-bye to him?'

'Why not? And in the car, Reg, maybe you'll just clear up a few points for me.'

189

It was going to be a lovely day, the first really fine day of Wexford's holiday now that his holiday was over. He asked Howard to wind down the window so that he could feel the soft air on his face. 'After I made that first blunder,' he said, 'I realised Dearborn wouldn't have desecrated his cemetery, and then I remembered he'd told me February 29th was his birthday. A man doesn't forget when his own birthday is going to occur, especially when it only really occurs once in every four years. Lamont put her in the Montfort vault because it was outside it that he encountered her—and killed her.'

'What put you on to him in the first place?'

'The way Loveday—I think of her as Loveday, perhaps because she was trying to get out of her darkness into a kind of light—the way she went down to talk to him and wanted to *entrust* something to him. She had nothing to entrust but Alexandra. She approached him and not Peggy partly because she was afraid of Peggy and partly because it was Lamont who mostly cared for his own child.' They entered Hyde Park, a sea of precocious daffodils. Ten thousand saw I at a glance . . . 'She told him she was going to get five thousand pounds, and she must have convinced him in spite of the unlikelihood of it, for he consulted estate agents. I saw a specification he had there for a house costing just under five thousand.'

'She was only going to give him one thousand.'

'I know. I don't suppose he thought of resorting to violence then, but he meant to con the rest out of her.'

'So she phoned Dearborn,' said Howard as they drove past the museums, thronged with tourists this Saturday morning. 'She phoned him at one-fifteen on February 25th to make the appointment.'

'They'd already made it in his office. It was Lamont she phoned. He was in the Grand Duke and he always took his phone calls there. She told him the money was going to be handed over to her in the cemetery that afternoon. He must have waited for her and seen her part from Dearborn, concluding, of course, that she had got the money.'

'Then he waylaid her,' said Howard. 'He asked for his

190

thousand to start with, but she wouldn't give him even that. She had nothing to give.'

Wexford nodded. 'He desperately wanted to keep Peggy and his child. Nothing was to get in his way now. He strangled her with her own scarf.'

'No, Reg, I can't have that. It was Mrs. Dearborn's scarf.'

'It was once,' said Wexford. 'Dearborn gave it to Loveday's aunt.'

The river was rippling brown and gold, a big brother, dirtier and wider and stronger, of the Kingsbrook. Tonight, Wexford thought, when we've unpacked our bags and the grandchildren have been to get their presents, tonight I'll go down and look at my own river. He got out of the car and walked up to Sir Thomas. This morning the gold cap and the gold chain were almost too dazzling to look at.

Wexford turned to Howard who had limped after him. He tapped his pocket where the new book was. 'More than four hundred years since he wrote that,' he said, 'but I don't know that things have changed all that much for the better, not the way he must have hoped they would. It's a good job he doesn't know. He'd get up off that seat of his and go back to the Tower.'

'Aren't you going to read your new book?' asked Dora when they were in the train, and the outer suburbs, grey streets, red housing estates, white tower blocks, trees like numberless puffs of smoke in the gold mist, flowed past the window.

'In a minute,' said Wexford. 'What have you got there, more presents?'

'I nearly forgot. These two came for you this morning.'

Two parcels, a thick one and a thin one. Who could be sending him parcels? The handwriting on the brown paper wrappings meant nothing. He undid the string in the thin one and a copy of *Utopia* fell out, a paperback version, with a card enclosed, depicting a rabbit in rustic surroundings, and signed with love from Denise's sister-in-law. Wexford snorted.

'Are you all right, darling?' said anxious Dora.

'Of course I'm all right,' Wexford growled. 'Don't start that again.'

The other parcel also contained a book. He wasn't at all surprised to come upon another *Utopia*, second-hand this time but well preserved. The card had a violet border, the name on it printed in gold. 'You forgot this', Wexford read. 'Something to read in the train. You can keep it. One doesn't meet human policemen every day. I.M.T.'

Something to read in the train . . . Tiredness hit him like a physical blow, but he struggled to keep awake, clasping his three new books, staring out of the window. The green country was beginning now, fingers of it groping and inserting themselves into wedges of brick. Soon they would be travelling into the haunch of England, into the swelling downs. Now for *Utopia*, now at last.

Dora bent down and silently picked up the books from the carriage floor. Her husband was asleep.

A GUILTY THING
SURPRISED

For Michael Richards,
my cousin, with love

High instincts, before which our mortal nature
Did tremble like a guilty thing surprised;
    .... those first affections,
    Those shadowy recollections,
    Which, be they what they may,
Are yet the fountain light of all our day . . .

William Wordsworth

1

WHEN Quentin Nightingale left home for London each morning his wife was always still asleep. His housekeeper served him with breakfast, opened the front door for him and handed him his hat and his umbrella, while the *au pair* girl fetched his newspaper. Next to speed him on his way were the two gardeners, saluting him with a respectful 'Good morning, sir', then perhaps his brother-in-law, hurrying to the sequestered peace of his writer's haven in the Old House. Only Elizabeth was missing, but if Quentin minded he never showed it. He walked briskly and confidently towards his car like a happy man.

On this particular morning in early September everything was just as usual except that Quentin didn't need his umbrella. The gardens of Myfleet Manor lay half-veiled by a golden mist which promised a beautiful day. Quentin came down the stone steps from the front door and paused briefly in the shrubbery to remind Will Palmer that the incurved chrysanthemums they were nursing for Kingsmarkham flower show were due for a dose of liquid fertiliser. Then he followed the path to the courtyard between the old coach-houses, where his car, its windscreen newly polished by Sean Lovell, stood waiting.

Quentin was a little early. Instead of getting into his car, he strolled to the low wall and looked down over the Kingsbrook valley. The view never ceased to delight him.

Hardly another house was visible, only the meadows, green, and, those that had been newly shorn, pale gold; the river winding through its thin sleeve of willows; the low round hills each topped with its ring of trees, and there, to his left, on the other side of the road, the great fir forest. It covered a whole range of hills and this morning in the mist it looked like a dark velvet cloak flung carelessly across the landscape. Quentin was always thinking of metaphors for the forest, comparing it to something, romanticising it. Sometimes he thought of it not as a forest or a velvet cloak but as a recumbent animal, guarding the fields while it slept, and of those irradiating plantations as spread, powerful and protective paws.

He turned his gaze to his own parkland, then to the nearer grounds, the sleek misted lawns and the massed roses whose colours were made pallid by haze, and he was just considering whether he should take a rose, an Iceberg perhaps or a Super Star, when a finger touched his shoulder and a cool voice said :

> 'To her fair works did Nature link
> The human soul that through me ran;
> And much it grieved my heart to think
> What man has made of man.'

'Good morning, Denys,' Quentin said heartily. 'Not a very cheerful quotation to make on a lovely morning. Wordsworth, isn't it ?'

Denys Villiers nodded. 'If I'm not cheerful,' he said, 'it must be because term begins in two days' time and after that I shan't get any more work done till Christmas. By the way, I've something for you.' He opened his briefcase and brought out a book, new, glossy, evidently fresh from the binders. 'An advance copy,' he said. 'I thought you might like it.'

Quentin's face lit with pleasure. He read the title: *Wordsworth in Love*, by Denys Villiers, and then, with barely controlled excitement, he turned to the dedication. This he read aloud. ' "*For my brother-in-law, Quentin Nightingale, a true friend and patron.*" Ah, Denys, that's wonderful! Makes me feel like Southampton.'

Villiers gave one of his crooked, rare smiles. 'The only begetter of these ensuing essays, Mr Q.N. . . .' He frowned, as if at his own weakness. 'As long as you like it. Well, as I have work to do and so do you . . .'

'Yes, I must be off. Look after yourself, Denys. I shan't be able to wait to get home and start on this.' He tapped the book, patted Villiers' shoulder and turned away. Villiers pushed open the door in the Old House wall and entered the shady court where limes and cypresses grew and where the sun never penetrated. Still smiling, his present on the seat beside him, Quentin drove away to London.

Elizabeth Nightingale spent an hour preparing herself for the eyes of the world. The effect aimed at was one of simple youth, spotless, fresh, lightly painted, dressed with casual precision or perhaps precise casualness. People said she looked no more than twenty-five. Ah, said Elizabeth to her reflection, but they didn't know me when I was twenty-five! Sometimes she also said that nowadays it took her twice as long to look half as good.

Ever-democratic, she took her morning coffee with the staff in the kitchen. The two gardeners sat at either end of the table and Elizabeth sat opposite Katje Doorn. Mrs Cantrip drank her coffee standing up, issuing her orders.

'If you catch sight of that Alf Tawney, Will, mind you

tell him I've got a chicken ordered for tonight and I want it this morning, not five minutes before Madam's dinner-time. Take your elbows off the table, young Sean. If I've told you once, I've told you fifty times. Now, Catcher, when you've drunk your coffee you can take Mr Villiers' over to him. He'll think we're all dead and that's a fact. And, for pity's sake, turn off that radio. Madam doesn't want to listen to that racket, I'm sure.'

'Oh, but I like pop, Mrs Cantrip,' said Elizabeth.

Sean lifted his head. 'Only got to look at you,' he said, 'to see you're no square.'

Shocked, Mrs Cantrip said, 'That's no way to talk to Madam!'

'I take it as a great compliment,' said Elizabeth.

Sean's dark face flushed with pleasure and he smiled his pomegranate smile, showing even white teeth between red lips. Inspired by his employer's encouragement, he eyed first Mrs Cantrip and then Will Palmer. Katje was giggling, but he ignored her. 'You're all the same, you oldies,' he said, 'stuck in the same old groove.'

'Your groove's gardening and don't you forget it. You'll never be one of them singers.'

'And why not?' But Sean's aggressive mood had changed to despair. 'I'll have to get cracking, I'll just have to. I said to my old lady, Time's getting on, I'll be twenty-three come April. What would have happened if the Beatles had waited till they was twenty-three before making a start?'

'What would have happened?' said Mrs Cantrip. 'The world'd have been a quieter place and that's a fact.'

'Never mind, Sean,' said Elizabeth with her sweet smile. 'You know what I've promised. I won't forget.' And Sean nodded eagerly, watching Elizabeth with rapt eyes. 'Now, Will, there's a suit Mr Nightingale's finished with that

12

might fit you. While I'm in the giving vein, I've packed up a little parcel for your mother, Katje. Some of those biscuits she can't get in Holland. You'll find it on the hall table with a parcel of mine. Perhaps you'd take them to the post?'

'Madam,' said Mrs Cantrip when Elizabeth had gone, 'is an angel. It's a crying shame there aren't more like her about.'

Katje giggled.

The mist had lifted and the rooms of Myfleet Manor were full of light—strong, late summer sunlight that would show up the slightest vestige of dust. But Mrs Cantrip and Katje had been at work and there was no dust. Elizabeth walked from room to room across the thick smooth sun-bathed carpets, checking that the flowers in copper bowls and *famille rose* vases were still fresh, occasionally drawing a curtain to protect old delicate satin from the sun. From her bedroom window she watched Katje cross Myfleet village street, holding the two parcels, the one for Holland and the one for London in her plump pink hands. Elizabeth sighed. Almost any of her friends or her servants would have supposed she sighed because Katje had left both the gates—wrought-iron gates whose design was of wyverns rampant with snouts which should have met at the lock—wide open. On the bright white surface of the road Katje's shadow was black and bouncy, a little deformed by the bulges the parcels made.

Elizabeth went down and closed the gates. She got into the Lotus, driving first to Queens Waterford to discuss with Lady Larkin-Smith the arrangements for the country club dance, next to Pomfret to receive from Mrs Rogers the proceeds from the Cancer Relief collection, lastly to the hairdresser's in Kingsmarkham. She kept the windows of the car wide open, the top down, and her primrose pale hair streamed out behind her as she drove, like the thistle-down hair of a young girl.

At half past one Mrs Cantrip served luncheon in the dining room. Katje's status gave her the right to eat *en famille*, but in the absence of Quentin Nightingale she said little. The woman and the girl ate their asparagus, their ham and their blackberry shortcake, in a silence which Elizabeth occasionally broke to comment with pleasure on the food. When they had finished Katje said she would have preferred chipolata pudding.

'You must teach Mrs Cantrip to make it.'

'Perhaps I am teaching her this afternoon,' said Katje, who had difficulties with her present tense.

'What a good idea!'

'When you are tasting it perhaps you never wish black-berries again.' Katje poked about in her mouth, retrieving seeds from between her teeth.

'We shall have to see. I'm going up for my rest now. If anyone calls or telephones, remember, I'm not to be disturbed.'

'I am remembering,' said Katje.

'Were you thinking of going out tonight?'

'I meet a boy in Kingsmarkham and maybe we go to the movies.'

'Cinema or pictures, Katje,' said Elizabeth gently. 'You must only say movies when you're in the United States. You can take one of the cars if you like but I'd rather you didn't take the Lotus. Your mother wouldn't like to think of you driving a fast sports car.'

'I am taking the Mini, please?'

'That's right.'

Katje cleared the table and put the crockery in the dishwasher with the glass and the plates from Denys Villiers' luncheon tray. 'Now I am teaching you to make chipolata pudding,' she announced to Mrs Cantrip, who had been taking ten minutes off with a cup of tea and the *Daily Sketch*.

'And what might that be when it's at home? You know Madam never has no sausages in this house.'

'Is not sausages. Is cream and jelly and fruit. We have cream, yes? We have eggs? Come on now, Mrs Cantrip, dear.'

'There's no peace for the wicked and that's a fact,' said Mrs Cantrip, heaving herself out of her rocking chair. 'Though what's wrong with a good English dessert I never shall know. Mr Villiers ate up every scrap of his. Mind you, with all that book-writing he gets a hearty appetite.'

Katje fetched eggs and cream from the refrigerator. 'Often I am asking myself,' she said thoughtfully, 'why he is not working in his own home. When he has a wife too, is odd, very funny.'

'And might I ask what it's got to do with you, Catcher? The fact is Mr Villiers has always worked up there. It must be fourteen or fifteen years since Mr Nightingale had the Old House done up for Mr Villiers to work in. It's quiet, see? And Mr Nightingale's got a very soft spot for Mr Villiers.'

'A soft spot?'

'I don't know, these foreigners! I mean he likes him, he's fond of him. I reckon he's proud of having an author in the family. Switch the beater on, then.'

Tipping the cream into a bowl, Katje said, 'Mrs Nightingale is not liking him *at all*. Every day in the holidays he is working up there and never, not once, Mrs Nightingale is going to see him. Is funny not to like her own brother.'

15

'Maybe he's not easy to like,' said Mrs Cantrip. 'You can depend on it, if there's a quarrel—and I'm not saying there is, mind—it's not Madam's fault. He's got a very funny manner with him, has Mr Villiers. A nasty temper, like sarcastic. Between you and me, Catcher, I wouldn't be too happy if I had a boy at that school where he teaches. Now switch that thing off or the cream'll all be turned to butter.'

Elizabeth didn't appear for tea.

The sky was cloudless, like a Mediterranean sky, and the sun, at five, as hot as ever. Out in the grounds Will Palmer lit a bonfire down by the gate which led on to the Kingsmarkham road, fouling the warm, scented air with acrid smoke. He fed it with grass mowings and helped it occasionally with a drop of paraffin. Sweating and grumbling, Sean pushed the motor mower over the terraced lawns.

Mrs Cantrip laid the dining table and left a cold dinner on the trolley. Fair weather or foul, she always wore a hat when she went outside. She put it on now and went home to her cottage at the other end of the village.

In the Old House Denys Villiers typed three more sentences on Wordsworth and the emergence of nature as artistic inspiration, and then he too went home. He drove slowly and cautiously to his bungalow in Clusterwell, to be followed half an hour later by Katje Doorn, revving up the Mini and making it roar and squeal its way through the villages to Kingsmarkham.

Elizabeth lay on her bed with witch-hazel pads on her eyes, conserving her beauty. When she heard the Jaguar come in she began to dress for dinner.

She wore a pale green caftan with crystal embroidery at the neck and wrists.

'How's my beautiful wife?'

'I'm fine, darling. Had a good day?'

'Not so bad. London's like a hothouse. Can I get you a drink?'

'Just a small tomato juice,' said Elizabeth. Quentin poured it for her and for himself a double whisky. 'Thank you, darling. It *is* hot, isn't it?'

'Not so hot as in London.'

'No, I suppose not.'

'Not nearly so hot,' said Quentin firmly. He smiled; she smiled. Silence fell.

Quentin broke it. 'Katje not about?'

'She's taken the Mini into Kingsmarkham, darling.'

'All on our own then, are we? No one coming in for cocktails?'

'Not tonight. As you say, we're all on our own.'

Quentin sighed and smiled. 'Makes a pleasant change, really,' he said, 'to be on our own.'

Elizabeth made no reply. This time the silence was intense and of longer duration. Quentin stood by the window and looked at the garden.

'We may as well have dinner,' said Elizabeth at last.

In the dining room he opened a bottle of *Pouilly Fuissé.* Elizabeth took only one glass.

'Turning cooler at last,' said Quentin during the *vichy-soisse.* 'I suppose the nights will soon be drawing in.'

'I suppose they will.'

'Yes, no matter how hot it is at this time of the year, you always feel that faint nip in the air.' Elizabeth ate her cold chicken in silence. 'But it's been a good summer on the whole,' Quentin said desperately.

'On the whole.'

Presently they returned to the drawing room.

17

'What time is it?' asked Quentin from the french windows.

'Just on eight.'

'Really? I should have said it was much later.' He went out on to the terrace to look at his chrysanthemums. Elizabeth looked at *Queen* magazine, turning the pages indifferently. Quentin came back and sat looking at her. Then he said, 'I wonder if Denys and Georgina will look in?'

'I shouldn't think so.'

'I think I'll give Denys a ring and see if they'll come over for a hand of bridge. What do you think?'

'If you'd like it, darling.'

'No, no, it's up to you.'

'I really don't mind one way or the other, darling.'

'Well, I'll just give him a ring, then,' said Quentin, expelling pent-up breath in a long sigh.

The Villiers arrived and they played bridge till ten.

'We mustn't be too late, Georgina,' said Villiers, looking at his watch. 'I've got a couple of hours' work to put in at the school library before I go to bed.'

'What, again?' said Georgina.

'I told you earlier, I've got a reference to look up.'

His wife gave him a mutinous glare.

'Denys is dedicated to his work,' said Quentin, the peacemaker. He smiled kindly at Georgina as the women left the room. 'Talking of dedications,' he said to his brother-in-law, 'will you write in the book for me?'

Using a broken old ballpoint, Denys Villiers wrote on the flyleaf:

The thought of our past years in me doth breed
Perpetual benediction . . .

Quentin read it and a faint flush of pleasure coloured his cheeks. He laid his hand on Villiers' shoulder. 'Now write your name,' he said.

So Villiers wrote beneath the quotation : *Your brother, Denys Villiers.*

'It's not like you to be inaccurate. It ought to be "brother-in-law".'

'There's no need,' said Villiers sharply, shaking off the hand, 'for too much bloody accuracy.'

The women came back, Georgina fastening her large handbag.

'Thanks very much for letting me have this, Elizabeth,' said Georgina. 'It's awfully good of you.'

'You're more than welcome, my dear. I shall never use it again.' And Elizabeth kissed her affectionately.

'When you've finished billing and cooing,' said Denys Villiers unpleasantly, 'perhaps we can get a move on.'

'I think I'll go straight to bed,' said Quentin. 'I can't wait to start the new book. Are you going to sit up a bit longer?'

'It's such a fine evening,' said Elizabeth. 'I may have a walk in the grounds before I go to bed.'

'Wrap up warm, darling. I'll say good night, then.'

'Good night, darling.'

Elizabeth fetched herself a coat, a soft lightweight thing of deep green angora. In the moonlight it was the same colour as the cypresses that grew in the Italian garden. Late blooming roses, pink, apricot, lemon, all looked white tonight. She walked across the turf between the rosebeds, hexagonal, semicircular, rhomboid, then by the paved path between yew hedges to a door in the red brick wall. The smoke from Will's fire rose in a thin grey column.

Elizabeth unlocked the gate and let herself out on to the grass verge which, overhung by the Manor beeches, separated the wall from the Pomfret road. As car headlights flared, flowed past, she stepped back for a moment into the shadows of the garden. Katje in the Mini, coming home from Kingsmarkham. Once more the road was empty, lighted only by the moon. Elizabeth closed the gate behind her, crossed the road and began to walk away from it by a sandy path that led into Cheriton Forest.

When she was out of sight of the road she sat down on a log, waiting. Presently she lit a cigarette, the third of the five she would smoke that day.

The Nightingales slept in separate bedrooms on the first floor of Myfleet Manor and at the front of the house. Quentin undressed and got into bed quickly. He switched on his bedlamp and opened *Wordsworth in Love*.

First, as was his custom with Villiers' books, he studied with pride and pleasure the publisher's eulogy of the author and his works, and scrutinised his brother-in-law's portrait on the back of the jacket. Next he looked at all the illustrations in turn, the photographed paintings of Wordsworth, of his sister Dorothy, and of the 'mazy Forth' as seen from Stirling Castle. Then, finally, he began to read.

Quentin read like a scholar, religiously looking up every bibliographical reference and reading each footnote. He had just come to the poet's meeting with his French sweetheart when he heard footsteps on the stairs. Elizabeth in from her walk? But no . . .

The footsteps went on, up and up, until they sounded faintly above his head. Not Elizabeth, then, but Katje who slept on the top floor.

It was eleven-thirty and growing chilly. He had said

earlier that there was a nip in the air. Elizabeth would be cold out there in the garden. The sashes in his own windows and the casements up above rattled as the wind rose. Quentin laid aside his book, got up and looked out of the window.

The moon had disappeared behind a bank of cloud. He put on his dressing gown, opened the bedroom door and stood for a moment in perplexity before making for the stairs.

2

IT was Detective Inspector Michael Burden's day off. He lay in bed till nine. Then he got up, bathed, and began on the task to which he intended to devote this free day, painting the outside of his bungalow.

A great wind, offshoot of a Caribbean hurricane the Americans called Caroline, had arisen during the night. Burden needed to use no ladders; the eaves of his bungalow were too near the ground for that, but today he didn't even fancy ascending the steps. Certainly he wasn't going to allow his eleven-year-old son John, home for the school holidays and an enthusiastic helper, to go up them.

'You can do the front door, John,' he said, knowing that he was conferring a special favour. All painters, particularly amateurs, long for the moment when the top coat, an excitingly contrasting colour, is due to be applied to the front door.

'Blimey, can I?' said John.

'Don't say blimey. It means God blind me, and you know I don't like to hear you swear.'

John, who normally would have argued the point, trotted off to fetch from the garage a virgin pot of flamingo-pink paint. There he encountered his sister Pat, feeding lime leaves to a hawk-moth caterpillar imprisoned in a shoe box. He was about to say something calculated to aggravate, something on the lines of the folly of encouraging garden pests, when his mother called to him from the back door.

'John, tell Daddy he's wanted on the phone, will you?'

'Who wants him?'

Mrs Burden said in a voice of resigned despair, 'Can't you guess?'

John guessed. Carrying the tin of paint, he returned to his father, who had just put the first stroke of top coat on the picture-window frame.

'Cop shop on the phone for you,' he said.

Burden never swore, in front of his children or in their absence. Carefully he placed his brush in a jam jar of synthetic turps and entered the house.

His bungalow had seldom looked so attractive to him as it did this morning. Poole pottery vases filled with red dahlias (Bishop of Llandaff, very choice) graced the hall and living room; the new curtains were up; from the kitchen came the rich aroma of a steak-and-kidney pudding boiling for lunch. Burden sighed, then lifted the spotless polished receiver of the white telephone.

The voice of Detective Chief Inspector Wexford said nastily, 'You took your bloody time.'

'Sorry. I was painting.'

'Hard cheese, Picasso. You'll have to complete the masterpiece some other time. Duty calls.'

Burden knew better than to say it was his day off. 'What's up, sir?'

'Do you know a Mrs Elizabeth Nightingale?'

'By sight. Everyone knows her. Husband's a Lloyd's underwriter. Pots of money. What's she done?'

'Got herself murdered, that's what she's done.'

Burden broke his rule. 'Good God!' he said.

'I'm at Myfleet Manor. Get over here as soon as you can, Mike.'

23

'And I've made this great enormous pudding,' said Jean Burden. 'Try and get back for lunch.'

'Not a hope.' Burden changed his clothes, grabbed his car key. John was sitting on the garden wall, waiting for starter's orders. 'Better leave the front door for a day or two, John. Sorry about that.'

'I'd be O.K. on my own.'

'Don't argue, there's a good lad.' He fished in his pocket for a half-crown. 'You were saying something about a new transistor battery . . . Get yourself some sweets too.' He got into the car. 'Here, John—isn't a Mr Villiers that's brother to Mrs Nightingale a teacher at your school?'

'Old Roman Villa?' said John. 'I don't know whose brother he is. He teaches Latin and Greek. What d'you want to know for?'

'Oh, nothing,' said Burden.

It was a red-brick house, built during the reign of Queen Anne, and it had an air of crouching close above the road, its windows Argus eyes that gazed down over the village, its footings embowered in thick green shrubs which rustled in the wind. Burden parked his car behind the bigger official one Wexford had arrived in, pushed open the wyvern gates and mounted the steps to the front door. Detective Sergeant Martin opened it before he had a chance to ring the bell.

'Chief Inspector's in the—er, what they call the morning room, sir.'

The house was full of people and yet a thick breathless hush seemed to hang over it, the silence of the incredible, the silence of shock. Burden tapped on the morning-room door and went in.

It was a small elegant room, its panelling painted in cream and blue. A broad shelf followed the line of the

24

picture rail on which stood floral plates in blue Delft. There were water-colours too, delicate pictures of pastoral scenes—Myfleet Mill, Forby Church, the river bridge at Flagford.

Squeezed into a small chair upholstered in cream satin, Wexford looked even more mountainous than usual. His heavy face was grave but his eyes were alert and watchful, fixed on the woman who sat on the opposite side of the fireplace. Glancing at the neat white hair, the homely red face furrowed by tears and the trim blue nylon overall, Burden summed her up as a faithful servant, an old and devoted retainer.

'Come in,' said Wexford. 'Sit down. This is Mrs Cantrip. She has kept house for Mr and Mrs Nightingale since they were married sixteen years ago.'

'That's right, sir,' said Mrs Cantrip, putting a handkerchief up to her swollen eyes. 'And a lovelier person than Mrs Nightingale you couldn't wish to meet. Good as gold she was and the best I ever worked for. I often used to think, though it don't sound respectful, pity it's me and not her who might be wanting a reference one of these days. I could have painted it in glowing colours and that's a fact.'

Burden sat down gingerly on another satin chair. All the furnishings were spotless and exquisite from the gleaming china to the lady's firescreens, painted oval discs on long stems.

'I'm sure I don't know what you must think of us, sir,' said Mrs Cantrip, misinterpreting his expression. 'The place in the state it is, but nothing's been done this morning. Me and Catcher, we haven't felt up to lifting a duster. When they told me the news I felt so bad I don't know why I didn't pass clean out.' She turned to Wexford and sniffed back her tears. 'Well, sir, you said as you wanted to see everyone in the house, so I mustn't keep you now the other gentleman's come.' Counting on work-worn fingers, she said, 'There's old Will Palmer, him that found her poor dead body, and Sean Lovell and Catcher . . .'

'Who's Catcher?'

'The foreign girl, what they call an *au pair*, sir. You'll find her up in her room on the top floor. And then there's poor Mr Nightingale himself, locked in his study and won't open the door to no one.'

'I will see Mr Palmer first,' said Wexford.

'How long have you been here?' asked Burden. The sepulchral silence of the place made him feel that whispering was in order.

'Since seven-thirty,' said Wexford, keeping his own voice low as they followed Mrs Cantrip down a long passage and into the garden via the kitchen. 'Thank you, Mrs Cantrip. I think I can see Mr Palmer coming up to meet us.'

The grounds were being searched by men in uniform and men in plain clothes. Will Palmer, emerging from behind a macrocarpa hedge, stopped in the middle of the lawn, looking surly, as Constable Gates grubbed among the flower-pots in one of the greenhouses, and Constable Bryant, his shirt-sleeves rolled up, thrust his arms into the green depths of the lily pond.

'The body has been photographed and removed,' said Wexford. 'Someone hit her on the head. God knows what with. They're looking for the weapon now. There was a hell of a lot of blood.' He raised his voice. 'Mr Palmer! Will you come over here, please?'

He was a tall lean old man with hard fleshless features that the wind and weather had polished to the tint of rosewood. Dark red, too, was the bald spot on his crown, a daisy centre amid white petals.

'I reckoned you'd want a word with me,' he said with lugubrious importance. 'What's all this poking about in my garden in aid of?'

'We are searching,' said Wexford frankly, 'for the weapon that killed Mrs Nightingale.'

'Don't reckon you'll find it among my fuchsias.'

'That remains to be seen.' Wexford pointed in the direction of a thin column of smoke. 'How long has that bonfire been burning?'

'Since yesterday afternoon, governor.'

'I see. Where can we go and talk, Mr Palmer? How about the kitchen, or will Mrs Cantrip be there?'

'Like enough she will, governor, and she's got mighty long ears when she wants. We could go in the Italian garden, being as it's sheltered from the wind.'

They sat down on a long seat of metal scrollwork beside a formal pool whose waters were still muddy from the investigations of its bottom by Wexford's men. At the far end of this pool was an elaborate baroque structure with a niche in which stood a bronze boy pouring water from a flagon into a bowl. The whole garden measured perhaps thirty feet by twenty and it was surrounded by cypress trees which shivered in the wind.

'Well, it was like this,' said Palmer. 'That old wind come up in the night, making such a racket it was, it woke me up. Near enough about four-thirty. First thing I thought of was Mr Nightingale's chrysanths, them as we're getting ready for the flower show. They was standing out in the open in their pots, see, and I thought, That wind'll have them over, sure as Fate. So I got on my bike and I come up here, quick as I could.'

'What time did you get here, Mr Palmer?'

' 'Bout five.' Palmer spoke slowly and with relish. It was evident he was beginning to enjoy himself. 'Them

27

chrysanths was all standing up well to the wind but I put them in the greenhouse to be on the safe side. Then I saw something was up. I couldn't believe my eyes. One of them french windows was wide open. Burglars, I thought. They've had burglars. I didn't rightly know what to do for the best. Maybe it's just that old wind, I thought, and they've forgot to lock up. Still, I reckoned it was my duty to wake Mr Nightingale, so in I went and up the stairs and banged and banged on his bedroom door. Must be a real heavy sleeper, I thought to myself, and I took the liberty of going in to have a look.'

'He was there?'

'No, he weren't. His bed was empty. "Mr Nightingale," I said, "are you there, sir?" thinking he might be in his bathroom, the door being shut ...'

'But you didn't look?' Wexford interrupted as he paused for breath.

'I hope I know my place, sir. Besides ...' Palmer looked down at his darned and shiny trouser knees. 'Besides, for all they slept separate like, they was married and ...'

'You thought quite reasonably that he might have spent the night in Mrs Nightingale's room?'

'Well, governor, I did at that. I always have said the gentry have their funny ways as the likes of us don't understand.' Giving no sign of embarrassment at his perhaps inadvertent inclusion of Wexford and Burden among the hoi-polloi, Palmer went on, 'So, not getting no answer from Mr Nightingale, I took it upon myself to knock on Madam's door. Nobody come and I was beginning to get the wind up, I can tell you. A proper state I was in. Nothing else would have got me barging into a lady's bedroom, and me just a servant like and in me working things. Well, she wasn't there either and the bed not touched.'

'You didn't think of calling the *au pair* girl?'

'Never crossed my mind, governor. What could that Catcher do I couldn't do myself? I went round the grounds then and found the wall gate open. Best get on the phone to the police yourself, Will, I thought, but when I got back to the house Mr Nightingale was up and about. Been having a bath, he said, and when he'd dried himself and come out I was gone.'

'What happened next?' asked Burden.

Palmer scratched his head. 'Mr Nightingale said Madam must have met with an accident while she was out in the grounds, but I said I'd searched the grounds. Then,' he said, building up suspense like an experienced narrator, 'I thought of that open gate and that dark old forest and my heart turned over. "I reckon she went into the forest and come over bad," I said to poor Mr Nightingale, so we went into the forest, our hearts in our mouths like, and I went first and then I found her. Lying face down she was with blood all over her lovely golden hair. But you saw her, governor. You know.'

'Thank you, Mr Palmer. You've been very helpful.'

'I always try to do my duty, sir. Mr Nightingale's been real good to me and Madam too. There's some I could name as would take advantage, but not me. I reckon I belong to what they call the old school.'

Wexford glanced up and saw through the cypresses a figure leaning on a spade. 'Did Sean What's-his-name take advantage?' he asked softly.

'Lovell, governor, Sean Lovell. Well now, he did, in a manner of speaking. Folks don't know their place like what they did when I was young, and that Lovell—common as dirt he is. His mother's no better than she should be and I don't reckon he never had no father. Turn you up, it would, to see the inside of their cottage. But he

29

fancied himself Madam's equal, if you've ever heard the like. Elizabeth this and Elizabeth that, he says to me behind her back. Don't you let me hear you refer to Madam like that, I said, snubbing him proper.'

Burden said impatiently, 'How did he take advantage?'

'Fancies himself singing in one of them pop groups, he does. Madam was soft, you see, and she'd smile and listen ever so patient when he'd start his singing. Sang to her, he did . . .' Palmer mouthed disgustedly, showing foul broken teeth. 'When she'd got a window open he'd come up underneath and sing one of them rubbishy songs he'd got off the telly. Familiar, you wouldn't believe! I come on him one day standing with Madam down by the pond here, nattering to her nineteen to the dozen and his dirty paw on her arm. I could tell Madam didn't like it. She jumped proper and went all red when I shouted at him. "A diabolical liberty," I said to him when we was alone. "Elizabeth and me, we understand each other," he says. The nerve of it!' Palmer's old bones cracked as he got to his feet and scowled in Lovell's direction. 'All I can say is,' he said, 'I hope I'm gone before all this equality gets any worse than what it is.'

Skilful conversion and the use of room dividers had transformed the largest attic into an open-plan flat for the *au pair* girl. Sleek shelves of polished beech on which stood books and house plants divided the sitting room from the sleeping area. All the furniture was modern. Vermilion tweed covered the sofa and the two armchairs; the carpet was a sour smart green; the curtains red corded velvet.

'Speak good English, do you, Miss Doorn?' Wexford asked as she admitted them.

'Oh, no, I am very bad,' said the Dutch girl, giggling.

'Everybody tell me I am very very bad.' She smiled without shame.

She belonged, Wexford thought admiringly, to the classic Dutch type which, photographed in clogs and peasant dress among windmills and tulips, advertises the attractions of Holland on holiday posters. Her hair was pale gold and long, her eyes a bright frank blue and her skin as dazzling as any ivory tulip in the Keukenhof Gardens. When she laughed, and she seemed to be always laughing, her face lit up and glowed. She looked, Wexford thought, about twenty.

'How long,' he asked, 'have you been living here with Mr and Mrs Nightingale?'

'One year. Nearly one year and a half.'

'So you knew them well? You lived as one of the family?'

'There is no family,' said Katje, pushing out full pink lips in disgust. 'Just him and her.' She shrugged. 'And now she is dead.'

'Yes indeed. That is why I am here. No doubt, you were a good friend to Mrs Nightingale, like a grown-up daughter?'

Katje laughed. She curled her legs under her, bounced up and down. Then she covered her mouth, suppressing giggles, with one hand. 'Oh, I must not laugh when all is so sad! But it is so funny what you say. A daughter! Mrs Nightingale wouldn't like to hear that, I think. No, she think she is young girl, very young and pretty in little mini skirts and eye-liner on, so!'

Burden fixed her with a disapproving glare which she met with frank wide eyes. Persisting doggedly, Wexford said, 'Nevertheless, you were in her confidence?'

'Please?'

Burden came to his assistance. 'She talked to you about her life?' he said.

'Me? No, never, nothing. At lunch we sit so, she there, I here. How is your mother, Katje? Will it rain today? Now I lie down and have my little rest. But talk? No, we do not *talk*.'

'You must have been lonely.'

'Me?' The giggles broke out in fresh gusts. 'Perhaps I should be lonely . . .' She hesitated, struggling with her conditionals. 'Perhaps if I stay in all day with him and her and all evening too, then I am lonely. No, I have my friends in Kingsmarkham, many many friends, boys and girls. Why do I like to stay here with old people?'

'They were only in their forties,' said thirty-six-year-old Burden hotly.

'This,' said Katje calmly, 'is what I am saying to you. I am young, they old. Mr Nightingale, he make me laugh. He is a nice man and he say things to make me laugh, but he is old, old, older than my father in Gouda.'

Smug and secure in the unarguable possession of radiant youth, Katje smiled at Wexford, then let her eyes travel to Burden, where they lingered. She looked at him as if she were wondering whether he were obtainable. She giggled.

Blushing, Burden said sharply, 'What did you see when you came home last night?'

'Well, I am going to the movies with my friend who is a waiter at the Olive and Dove. First we see the movie, is Swedish film, very sexy, make me feel so hot, you understand?'

'Oh, yes,' said Burden, looking down.

'This is natural,' said Katje severely, 'when one is young.' She stretched her long stockingless legs and wriggled her toes in the white sandals. 'Afterwards I wish to go with my friend to his room but he will not because there is a manager at the hotel, a very unkind man, who is not letting him have girls. So we are sad and my friend takes me instead to the Carousel café. There we have coffee and one, two cakes.'

'What time was this?'

'It is a quarter to ten when we leave the movies. We are having our coffee and then we are sitting in the car, kissing and cuddling, but very sad because we cannot go to his room. My friend must rise very early in the morning, so he go back to the hotel and I go home. Now it is eleven, I think.'

'You saw Mrs Nightingale leave the Manor grounds?'

Katje poked a lock of hair into the corner of her mouth. 'Her I am seeing in the lights of the car, coming out of the gate near where the bonfire is burning. And she is seeing me too. This I know because she is closing the gate quick and hiding till I go by. Very funny, I think to myself. So I drive up along the road and I am leaving the car parked and walking back very soft, very secret, to see if she is coming out again.' Suddenly Katje sat up straight, shooting her legs out and displaying the tops of her thighs to the nervous Burden. 'She is coming out again!' she said triumphantly. 'I see her cross the road and go into the wood. And she is walking very quiet, looking like this over her shoulder.' Katje pantomimed it in a swift, curiously animal-like burlesque. 'Then I know what she is doing. Many many times have I too walked like this when I am going to meet my friend in the woods and the unkind man is not allowing us to go to his room. Over my shoulder I am looking to see that no one is following to spy what we do.'

'Yes, yes,' said Wexford gruffly. 'I understand all that.' He didn't dare look at Burden. It wouldn't altogether have surprised him if the inspector, like the man in *Bleak House*, had entirely disappeared, melting away by a process of spontaneous combustion. With more than an edge of irony to his voice, he said, 'You have been very frank with us, Miss Doorn.'

'I am good, yes?' said Katje with intense satisfaction. She chewed her hair enthusiastically. 'I tell you things that help? I am knowing all about talking with the police. When I am in Amsterdam with the provos the police are asking me many questions, so I am knowing all about police and not frightened *at all*.' She gave them a radiant smile which lingered and sparkled when it was turned on Burden. 'Now I think I am making you coffee and telling you how we throw the smoke bombs in Amsterdam while this old police chief is talking with poor Mr Nightingale.'

Burden had lost all his poise and while he stammered out something about having already had coffee, Wexford said smoothly, 'Some other time, thank you.' He didn't mind being called a police chief, but the adjective rankled. 'We shall want to talk to you again, Miss Doorn.'

'Yes, I think so too,' said Katje, giggling. Placidly she accepted the fact that most men, having once met her, would want to talk to her again. She curled up in her chair and watched them go, her eyes dancing.

'Now for Nightingale,' said Wexford as they descended the stairs. 'I've already had a few words with him but that was before I knew about these dawn ablutions of his. He'll have to come out of that study, Mike. I've sent Martin to swear a warrant to search this house.'

3

HE had the kind of looks women call distinguished. His hair was silver without a black strand and he wore a small silver moustache which gave him the look of an ambassador or a military man of high rank. Because of this rather premature silvering he looked no younger than his fifty years, although his tall figure was as slim as Sean Lovell's, his chin muscles firm and his skin unlined.

People expect a pretty woman to have a handsome husband or a rich one. Otherwise they feel the marriage is unaccountable, that she has thrown herself away. Elizabeth Nightingale had been more than usually pretty and her widower was more than usually rich besides being handsome enough to match her beauty. But this morning he looked almost ugly, his features haggard and drawn.

It had taken a good deal of persuasion and finally peremptory insistence to make him admit them to the study, but now he was inside, Wexford's anger dissolved into an impatient pity. Quentin Nightingale had been crying.

'I'm sorry, sir. I must question you just as I must question everyone else.'

'I realise that.' The voice was low, cultured and ragged. 'It was childish of me to lock myself in here. What do you want to ask me?'

35

'May we sit down?'

'Oh, please . . . I'm sorry. I should have . . .'

'I quite understand, Mr Nightingale.' Wexford sat down in a leather chair that resembled his own at the police station, and Burden chose the high wooden stool that stood by the bookcase. 'First of all, tell me about last evening. Did you and Mrs Nightingale spend it alone?'

'No. My brother-in-law and his wife came up to play bridge with us.' A little animation came into his voice as he said, 'He is the distinguished author of works on Wordsworth, you know.'

'Really?' said Wexford politely.

'They came at about eight-thirty and left at half past ten. My brother-in-law said he had some research to do at the school library before he went to bed.'

'I see. How did your wife seem last night?'

'My wife . . .' Quentin winced at the word and at having to repeat it himself. 'My wife was quite normal, gay and lovely as always.' His voice broke and he steadied it. 'A very gracious hostess. I remember she was particularly sweet to my sister-in-law. She gave her some present and Georgina was delighted. Elizabeth was the most generous of women.'

'What was this present, sir?'

'I don't know,' Quentin said, suddenly weary once more. 'I only heard Georgina thank her for it.'

Burden shifted on his stool. 'Why did your wife go into the forest, Mr Nightingale?'

'I don't know that either. My God, I wish I did. She often went for a walk in the grounds. In the late evening, I mean. I never dreamt she would go into the forest.'

'You were a happily married couple, sir?'

'Certainly we were. Ideally happy. Ask any of our

friends. Oh God, would I be like this, the way I am, if we hadn't been happy?'

'Please don't distress yourself, Mr Nightingale,' Wexford said gently. 'Now I want you to answer very carefully. You're aware that Palmer came into your bedroom just after five this morning but couldn't find you? Would you mind telling me where you were?'

A dark ashamed flush coloured Quentin's face. He put his hands up to his cheeks as if he thought their cold touch would drive the blood away. 'I was in the bath,' he said stiffly.

'A curious time to take a bath.'

'Occasionally we all do curious things, Chief Inspector. I awoke early on account of the wind. I couldn't get to sleep again, so I had a bath.'

'Very well, Mr Nightingale. I should like to search this house now, if you please.'

'As you like,' said Quentin. He looked like a condemned man who has received a reprieve but knows it is only a temporary stay of execution. Fingering a paperweight of dark blue stone threaded with silver, he said, 'You'll be careful, won't you?'

'We aren't vandals,' said Wexford sharply, then relenting slightly, 'Afterwards you won't know we've passed this way.'

As country houses go, Myfleet Manor wasn't large, but it wasn't, to use Burden's own phrase, a council maisonette either. Altogether there were fifteen rooms, each furnished with taste and apparently with love, nearly every one a museum of *objets d'art*. Nothing was out of place, no carpet stained or cushion crumpled. Clearly no child and certainly no dog had ever been permitted to run wild here. Only the petals fallen from flower arrangements told of half a day's neglect.

And yet, despite the dahlia-filled vases and the pale sunbeams that the wind blew flickeringly across satin and polished wood, the place had a cold sepulchral air. It was, as Wexford remarked, ascending the staircase, rather like being in church.

The life of the Manor, its pulse and the sole source of its laughter, was up above them in the *au pair* girl's flat. Glancing up the topmost flight rather wistfully, Wexford entered Quentin's bedroom, Burden following close behind.

The bed had been made. Beside it on a low table lay a book which Wexford glanced at, making no comment. He opened drawers and scanned the well-stocked wardrobe while Burden went into the bathroom.

'The bath towel's still wet, sir,' he called. 'It's on a hot rail, though, and . . .' Wexford tramped across to the bathroom where he found Burden looking at his watch. 'It wouldn't take seven hours to dry, would it?'

Wexford shook his head. 'He's either had two baths,' he said, 'or just one and that at nine or ten this morning.'

'You mean the first one was a real cleaning-up operation? In that case there ought to be blood on the towel or somewhere, and there isn't.'

'We'll check the laundry with Mrs Cantrip. Let's go next door.'

The dead woman's bedroom was papered in lilac and silver, a pattern of rosebuds and blown roses which was repeated identically in the satin of the curtains. Between the two windows stood a triple-mirrored dressing table, its legs skirted in white tulle. The bed was white too, huge and smooth, flanked on either side by white fur rugs like patches of snow on the emerald field of carpet.

While Burden searched the dressing table and lifted the

lid of a writing desk, Wexford examined the wardrobe. Mrs Nightingale had possessed enough clothes to stock a boutique, the only difference between this rack and a boutique's being that these garments were all of one size, a young girl's size twelve, and they had all belonged to one woman.

'No diary,' said Burden, busy at the desk. 'A couple of receipted dressmaker's bills from a shop in Bruton Street, London, a place called Tanya Tye. The bills she's paid were for a hundred and fifty-odd and two hundred pounds, and there's a third one outstanding for another ninety-five. No interest there, I think.'

Wexford moved on to the dressing table. He lifted from its surface jars of cream, bottles of lotion, lastly a flagon of liquid whose declared purpose was to lift and brace facial muscles. 'Made out of a cow's digestive juices,' he said expressionlessly. 'Or so they tell me.' His face softened and grew sad. ' "Why such high cost," ' he quoted, ' "having so short a lease, dost thou upon thy fading mansion spend?" '

'Pardon?'

'Just a sonnet that came into my head.'

'Oh, yes?' said Burden. 'Personally, I was thinking what a waste of money when you've got to get old anyway. I don't suppose she went to all this trouble for her husband, do you?'

'No, there was another man.'

Burden nodded. 'The man she went to meet last night, presumably,' he said. 'What's your theory, sir? That Nightingale suspected, followed her into the forest and killed her? Burnt his clothes on Palmer's fire?'

'I haven't got a theory,' said Wexford.

They descended slowly. The staircase was long and shallow with a wide landing halfway down. Here a

39

window whose crimson velvet curtains matched the Etoile de Hollande roses in a copper bowl on its sill, gave on to the garden. The wind was still fresh and skittish, sending the hedges rippling like green rivers.

'There's a candidate for the third side of our triangle,' said Wexford, pointing down at the hothouse.

'Sean Lovell?' Burden's intense disapproval of this suggestion, with all its attendant implications, showed in an angry frown. 'The gardener's boy? Why, he can't be more than twenty and she . . . I never heard of such a thing!'

'Oh, rubbish,' said Wexford. 'Of course you've heard of it. Even you must have heard of Lady Chatterley, if you haven't read it.'

'Well, a book,' said Burden, relieved that the chief inspector had chosen a literary rather than a real-life instance of what he considered a monstrous perversion. 'Cold in here, isn't it? I suppose it must be the wind.'

'We'll go and have a warm in the hothouse.'

Sean Lovell opened the door for them and they stepped into steamy tropical heat. Pale orchids, green and lemony pink, hung from the roof in moss-lined baskets, and on the shelves stood cacti with succulent lily-shaped flowers. Scented steam had condensed on the cold glass and there was a constant soft dripping sound.

The perfume, the heat and the colours suited Sean's rather exotic looks. Although probably an inheritance from gypsy forbears, his jet-black hair and golden skin suggested Italian or Greek descent. Instead of jeans and sweater he should have worn a corsair's shirt and breeches, Wexford thought, with a red scarf round his head and gold hoops in his ears.

'She was a nice lady, a real lady,' Sean said gruffly. Viciously he snapped a fat leaf from a xygocactus.

'Always on the look-out for what she could do for you. And she has to go and get herself murdered. It's like what my old lady says, it's always the good as dies young.'

'Mrs Nightingale wasn't that young, Lovell.'

A brilliant seeping of colour came into the olive-gold cheeks. ' 'Bout thirty, that's all she was.' He bit his lip. 'You can't call that old.'

Wexford let it pass. Elizabeth Nightingale had tried so hard with her creams and her muscle bracer that it seemed ungenerous, now that she was dead, to disillusion her admirers.

'I'd like to know your movements last night. What time d'you knock off here and where did you go?'

Sean said sullenly, 'I knock off at five. I went home to my tea. I live alone in the village with my old lady. I had my tea and I watched telly all evening.'

'Don't you have a girl friend?'

Instead of answering directly, Sean said, 'You seen the girls round here?' He gave Wexford a shifty look that gave him the appearance of a Greek pirate. 'Some evenings I watch telly and some I go into town and play the juke box at the Carousel. What else is there to do in a dump like this?'

'Don't ask me, Lovell. I'm asking the questions. You watched television right up to the time you went to bed?'

'That's what I did. Never went out again. You can ask my old lady.'

'Tell me what programmes you saw.'

'There was Pop Panel, then the Hollywood musical till ten.'

'You went to bed at ten?'

'I don't remember. I can't remember what I saw and when I went to bed. How can I? I reckon we went on with our viewing after that. Yeah, it was Sammy Davis

Junior, that's what it was.' The dark face lit suddenly with an almost religious awe. 'My God, I'd like to be like him. I'd like to *be* him.' Chilled by Wexford's eyes, he shifted his own and said rapidly, 'I've got to go now. I've got to get on with my work. Old Will'll be after me.'

He sidled past Wexford, roughly bruising cactus spikes as he made his escape. Suddenly in the doorway Mrs Cantrip loomed.

'Your dinner's ready in the kitchen, Sean. I've been looking all over for you. Get cracking, do, or it'll be stone cold.' Thankfully Sean marched out of the hothouse and, when no one called him back, made for the kitchen at a run.

'Odd, that,' said Wexford. 'Sammy Davis was booked to appear on television last night, but the programme was cancelled at the last moment. They put on an old film instead.' He patted Burden's shoulder. 'Off you go to lunch now, Mike. I'll join you when I can.'

He watched Burden go, and then, almost running himself, he caught up with Mrs Cantrip. 'Is there anyone else living in this house or employed here that I haven't yet seen?'

'No, sir.' Her look told him that she was still bemused with shock, the reins of the household as yet unsteady in her hands. 'Would you be wanting a bite to eat?' she asked tremulously. 'You and the other police gentlemen?'

'No, thank you.' Wexford put a firm hand under her elbow as she tripped at the terrace steps. 'You can tell me one thing, though. Who were Mrs Nightingale's friends? Who came visiting to the Manor?'

She seemed pleased at this tribute to her dignity as a valued and confidential servant. 'Mrs Nightingale was never one of them as gossips, sir, or passes the day on the telephone. The ladies she saw was to do with business, like, arranging bazaars and gymkhanas, if you know what I mean. Then . . .' Her voice took on a sad importance, 'Then there was *their* friends as came here to dine, Sir George and Lady Larkin-Smith, and Mr and Mrs Primero, and all the county folks, sir.'

'Gentlemen friends? Please don't be offended, Mrs Cantrip. These days a lady can have men friends without there being anything—er, wrong.'

Mrs Cantrip shook her head vigorously. 'Her friends was their friends, sir,' she said, adding with a shade of sarcasm, 'Would there be anything else you wanted to know?'

'There is just one thing. A question of laundry. Whose job is it to change the linen in this house, the—er, sheets and towels?'

'Mine, sir,' said Mrs Cantrip, surprised.

'And did you remove any damp towels from Mr Nightingale's bedroom this morning?'

'No, sir, definitely not. I wasn't looking for work this morning and that's a fact.' Mrs Cantrip gave a virtuous lift of her chin. 'Besides, it's not the day for that,' she said. 'I change the sheets Monday mornings, and the towels Mondays and Thursdays. Always have done, year in and year out since I've been here.'

'Suppose someone else were to have . . . ?' Wexford began carefully.

'They couldn't have,' said Mrs Cantrip sharply. 'The soiled linen's kept in a bin in the back kitchen and no one's been near it today. I can vouch for that. Now, if you'll excuse me, sir, I've got my lunch to serve. I'm sure I don't know if Mr Nightingale's feeling up to a snack but there's the tray to go over to Mr Villiers as usual . . . Oh, my dear God! Mr Villiers! I'd forgot all about Mr Villiers.'

Wexford stared at her. 'D'you mean to say Mr

Nightingale's brother-in-law lives in this house?'

'Not to say "lives", sir,' said Mrs Cantrip, still wide-eyed, a red hand frozen to her cheek. 'He comes up every day to do his writing in the Old House. And, oh, sir, I don't reckon no one's told him!'

'Mr Villiers must have seen all our comings and goings.

'He wouldn't, sir. You can't see a thing from the Old House on account of all them trees, no more than you can see it from the outside. I'll have to go and tell him. All I can say is, thank God they wasn't close. He won't take it hard, there's one blessing.'

She trotted off at a half-run. Wexford watched her disappear under an arch in the hedge, an arch overhung with the leaves of lime trees turning gold. Above these all that showed of the Old House was a shallow roof against the white-spotted blue sky.

He allowed her five minutes and then he followed the path she had taken. It led him into a little paved court in the centre of which was a small square pond. Carp swam in the dark clear water under the flat shining rafts of lily leaves.

The court was heavily shaded by the trees which surrounded it. Their roots had sapped strength from the narrow borders, for nothing grew in them but a few attenuated and flowerless plants stretching desperately in the hope of reaching the sun. Mrs Cantrip must have entered the ancient house—to Wexford it appeared at least four hundred years old—by a black oak door which stood ajar. By the step stood a boot-scraper, a cock with spread wings made of black metal. Looking up past creeper-grown lattice windows, Wexford noticed its fellow, a crowing chanticleer on the weather vane.

As he entered the Old House, he became aware that the wind had dropped.

4

THE place in which Wexford found himself was evidently used as a storeroom. Birch logs were stacked against the walls in pyramids; racks above them awaited the Manor harvest of apples and pears. It was all very clean and orderly.

Since there was no other room down here and no sign of Denys Villiers' occupation, Wexford ascended the stairs. They were of black oak let into a kind of steeply sloping tunnel in the thick wall. From behind the single door at the top he heard low voices. He knocked. Mrs Cantrip opened the door a crack and whispered:

'I've broke the news. Will you be wanting me any more?'

'No, thank you, Mrs Cantrip.'

She came out, her face very red. A shaft of sunlight stabbed the shadows of the lower room as she let herself out. Wexford hesitated and then he went into Villiers' writing room.

The classics master remained sitting at his desk but he turned a grave cold face towards Wexford and said, 'Good morning, Chief Inspector. What can I do for you?'

'This is a bad business, Mr Villiers. I won't keep you long. Just a few questions, if you please.'

'Certainly. Won't you sit down?'

A large, somewhat chilly room, darkly panelled. The windows were small and obscured by clustering leaves.

There was a square of carpet on the floor. The furniture, a horsehair sofa, two Victorian armchairs with leather seats, a gateleg table, had apparently been rejected from the Manor proper. Villiers' desk was a mass of papers, open works of reference, tins of paper clips, ballpoint pens and empty cigarette packets. At one end stood a stack of new books, all identical to each other and to the one Wexford had seen on Nightingale's bedside table: *Wordsworth in Love*, by Denys Villiers, author of *Wordsworth at Grasmere* and *Anything to Show More Fair*.

Before sitting down, Wexford picked up the topmost of these books just as he had picked up the one in the bedroom, but this time, instead of quickly scanning the text, he turned it over to eye the portrait of Villiers on the back of its jacket. It was a flattering photograph or else taken long ago.

The man who faced him, coldly watching this brief perusal, seemed in his late forties. He had once, Wexford thought, been fair and handsome, strikingly like his dead sister, but time or perhaps illness had taken all that away. Yes, illness probably. Men dying of cancer looked like Villiers. In their faces Wexford had seen that same dusty parched look, yellowish-grey drawn features, blue eyes bleached a haggard grey. He was painfully thin, his mouth bloodless.

'I realise this must have been a great shock to you,' Wexford began. 'It seems unfortunate that no one broke the news to you earlier.'

Villiers' thin colourless eyebrows rose a fraction. His expression was unpleasant, supercilious. 'Frankly,' he said, 'it makes very little difference. My sister and I weren't particularly attached to each other.'

'May I ask why not?'

'You may and I've no objection to answering you. The

46

reason was that we had nothing in common. My sister was an empty-headed frivolous woman and I—well, I am not an empty-headed frivolous man.' Villiers glanced down at his typewriter. 'Still, I hardly think it would be tactful for me to do any more work today, do you?'

'I believe you and your wife spent last evening at the Manor, Mr Villiers?'

'That is so. We played bridge. At ten-thirty we left, drove home and went to bed.' Villiers' voice was clipped and sharp with an edge of temper to it, a temper that could be quickly aroused. He coughed and pressed his hand to his chest. 'I have a bungalow near Clusterwell. It took me about ten minutes to drive there from the Manor last night. My wife and I went straight to bed.'

Very tidy and brief, thought Wexford. It might all have been rehearsed beforehand. 'How did your sister seem last night, sir? Normal? Or did she appear excited?'

Villiers sighed. More from boredom than sorrow, Wexford decided. 'She was just as she always was, Chief Inspector, the gracious lady of the Manor whom everyone loved. Her bridge was always appalling, and last night it was neither more nor less appalling than usual.'

'You knew she went for nocturnal walks in the forest?'

'I knew she went for nocturnal walks in the *grounds*. Presumably it was because she was foolish enough to venture further that she met the end she did.'

'Is that why,' asked Wexford, 'you weren't surprised to hear of her death?'

'On the contrary, I was very surprised. Naturally, I was shocked. But now that I've considered it, no, I'm not very surprised any more. Women on their own in lonely places do get murdered. Or so I'm told. I never read the newspapers. Matters of that kind don't interest me.'

'You've certainly made it clear that you disliked your

47

sister.' Wexford glanced about the large quiet room. 'Strange, under the circumstances, that you should have been among those who accepted her bounty.'

'I accepted my brother-in-law's, Chief Inspector.' White with anger or with some other emotion Wexford couldn't analyse, Villiers sprang out of his chair. 'Good morning to you.' He opened the door and the dark stair well yawned ahead of him.

Wexford got up to leave. Halfway across the room he stopped and looked at Villiers, suddenly puzzled. It was impossible to believe the man could look worse, more ill, more corpselike, than when he had first seen him. But now as he stood in the doorway, one thin arm outflung, all vestige of colour, yellow-greyish pigment as it was, had drained from his skin.

Alarmed, Wexford started forward. Villiers gave a strange little gasp and fainted into his arms.

'Here we are, then,' said Crocker, who was the police doctor and Wexford's friend. 'Elizabeth Nightingale was a well-nourished and extremely well-preserved woman of about forty.'

'Forty-one,' said Wexford, taking off his raincoat and hanging it on the peg behind his office door. A couple of rounds of beef sandwiches and a flask of coffee, sent down from the canteen, awaited him on the corner of his desk. He sat down in the big swivel chair and, after looking distastefully at the topmost sandwich which was beginning to curl at the edges, started on it with a sigh.

'Death,' said the doctor, 'resulted from a fractured skull and multiple injuries to the brain. At least a dozen blows were struck by a not very blunt metal instrument. I don't mean an axe or a knife, but something with sharper edges to it, for instance, than a lead pipe or a poker. Death

48

occurred—well, you know how hard it is to estimate—say after eleven p.m. and before one a.m.'

Burden was sitting against the wall. Above his head hung the official map of the Kingsmarkham district on which the dark mass of Cheriton Forest showed like the silhouette of a crouching cat. 'Nothing's come of our search of the grounds and the forest so far,' he said. 'What sort of a weapon had you in mind?'

'Not my job, Mike old boy,' said Crocker, moving to the window and staring down at the High Street below. Possibly he found this familiar sight boring, for he breathed heavily on the pane and began to draw on the breath film a pattern that might have been a pot plant or a diagram of the human respiratory system. 'I just wouldn't have a clue. Could be a metal vase or even a cooking utensil. Or a fancy ashtray or fire-tongs or a tankard.'

'You think?' said Wexford, munching scornfully. 'A fellow goes into a wood to murder a woman armed with an egg-whisk, does he, or a saucepan? A bloke sees his wife carrying on with another man so he whips out the carved silver vase he happens to have in his pocket and bops her over the head with it?'

'You don't mean to say,' said the doctor, shocked, 'that you've got that pillar of society Quentin Nightingale lined up for this job?'

'He's human, isn't he? He has his passions. Frankly, I'd rather plump for that brother of hers, that Villiers. Only he looks too ill to lift a knife and fork, let alone hit anyone with a frying pan.' Wexford finished his sandwiches and replaced the cap on the thermos flask. Then he swivelled round and gazed thoughtfully at the doctor. 'I've been talking to Villiers,' he said. 'He impressed me as a very sick man, among other things. Yellow skin, tremb-

49

ling hands, the lot. Just now, when I was leaving, he fainted dead away. For a minute I thought he was dead, but he came to all right and I got him over to the Manor.'

'He's a patient of mine,' said Crocker, rubbing out his drawing with the heel of his hand and revealing to Wexford his favourite view of ancient housetops and old Sussex trees. 'The Nightingales go privately to some big nob but Villiers has been on my list for years.'

'And you,' said Wexford sardonically, 'being a true priest of the medical confessional, are going to keep whatever's wrong with him locked up in your hippocratic bosom?'

'Well, I would if there was anything to lock. Only it so happens that he's as fit as you are.' Crocker eyed Wexford's bulk, the purple veins prominent on his forehead. 'Fitter,' he said critically.

With an effort Wexford drew in the muscles of his abdomen and sat up straighter. 'Ain't that amazement?' he said. 'I thought it was cancer, but it must be some inner torment feeding on his damask cheek. Like guilt. How old is he?'

'Now look . . .' said the doctor, fidgeting in his seat.

'Go on, strain yourself. A man's age isn't something he confides to his quack behind the aseptic green shades of the consulting room.'

'He's thirty-eight.'

'*Thirty-eight!* He looks ten years older and damn' ill with it. By God, Mike here is a stripling compared to him.'

Two sets of ageing eyes focussed speculatively on Burden, who looked modestly away, not without a certain air of preening himself. The doctor said rather pettishly, 'I don't know why you keep on about him looking ill. He works himself too hard, that's all. Anyway, he doesn't look that ill or that old.'

'He did today,' said Wexford.

'Shock,' said the doctor. 'What d'you expect when a man hears his sister's been murdered?'

'Just that, except that he evidently hated her guts. You should have heard the generous fraternal things he said about her. As nasty a piece of work as I've come across for a long time is Mr Villiers. Come on, Mike, we're going to call on some ladies who will melt and tell all under the effect of your sexy and—may I say?—youthful charm.'

They all went down together in the lift and the doctor left them at the station steps. The wind had dropped entirely but the High Street was still littered by the debris the gale had left in its wake, broken twigs, a tiny empty chaffinch nest blown from the crown of a tall tree, here and there a tile from an ancient roof.

Bryant drove them out of town by the Pomfret road, soon taking the left-hand fork for Myfleet. Their route led them past Kingsmarkham Boys' Grammar School, more properly known as the King Edward the Sixth Foundation for the Sons of Yeomen, Burgesses and Those of the Better Sort. The sons were at present home for the summer holidays and the brown-brick Tudor building bore a lonelier, more orderly, aspect than in term-time. A large new wing—a monstrosity, the reactionaries called it —had been added to the rear and the left side of the old school five years before, for the yeomen and burgesses, if not the better sort, had recently increased in alarming numbers.

The school had a dignity and grace about it, common to large buildings of its vintage, and most Kingsmarkham parents sought places there for their sons, setting aside with contempt the educational and environmental advantages of Stowerton Comprehensive. Who wanted a magnificent steel and glass science lab, a trampoline room or a swimming pool of Olympic standard, when they could instead boast to their acquaintance of historic portals and worn stone steps trodden (though on one single occasion) by the feet of Henry the Eighth's son? Besides, if your boy was at what everyone called the 'King's' school you could quite convincingly pretend to those not in the know that he attended a public school and conceal the fact that the State paid.

Burden, whose son had been admitted there one year before on passing a complex and subtle equivalent of the Eleven-plus, now said:

'That's where Villiers teaches.'

'Latin and Greek are his subjects, aren't they?'

Burden nodded. 'He takes John for Latin. I reckon he teaches Greek to the older ones. John says he works there a lot after school hours, doing something in the library. That's the library there in the new wing.'

'Research for his books?'

'Well, it's a marvellous library. Not that I know much about these things, but I went round it on Open Day and it impressed me no end.'

'John like him, does he?'

'You know what these boys are, sir,' said Burden. 'Those little devils in John's class call him Old Roman Villa. Good disciplinarian, I'd say.' And the father who had that morning mollified his own son with a gratuitous half-crown added severely: 'You have to be tough when you're dealing with these young lads, if you ask me.'

Grinning to himself, Wexford changed the subject. 'There are three main questions I'd like the answers to,' he said. 'Why was Quentin Nightingale taking a bath at five in the morning? Or, conversely, why does he pretend he was? Why did Sean Lovell tell me he was watching a

52

programme on the television last night that was, in fact, cancelled at the last moment? Why did Elizabeth Nightingale get on well with everyone except her only brother?'

'Why, for that matter, sir, did she have no intimate friends?'

'Perhaps she did. We shall have to find out. Mike, we're coming into Clusterwell. D'you happen to know which belongs to Villiers?'

Burden sat up straighter and turned his eyes to the window. 'It's outside the village, on the Myfleet side. Not yet, wait a minute. . . . Slow down, will you, Bryant? That's it, sir, standing by itself.'

Frowning a little, Wexford scanned the isolated bungalow. It was a squat, double-fronted place with two low gables under which were bay windows.

'Needs a coat of paint,' said Burden, contrasting it unfavourably with his own attractive, soon to be completely redecorated home. 'Shabby-looking dump. You'd think he could afford a decent garage.'

The front garden was a mass of Michaelmas daisies, all one colour. At one side a long drive of cracked and pitted concrete led to a prefabricated asbestos garage with a roof of tarred felt.

A black Morris Minor stood on this drive just in front of the asbestos doors and someone had very recently cleaned it, for there were damp patches on its bodywork and a small pool of water lay in a pothole under its rear bumper.

'That's odd,' said Wexford. 'Your sister is murdered, you pass out when you hear the news, and yet a couple of hours later you're lively enough to give your car a wash and brush-up.'

53

'It isn't his car,' Burden objected. 'He drives an Anglia. That belongs to his wife.'

'Where's his, then?'

'Still up at the Manor, I suppose, or in that revolting apology for a garage.'

'I wouldn't have said it was muddy in the forest last night, would you?'

'Tacky,' said Burden. 'We had rain at the weekend if you remember.'

'Drive on, Bryant. We'll leave the Villiers in undisturbed domestic bliss a little longer.'

The first person they saw when they parked in Myfleet village was Katje Doorn, coming out of the general store with a bag of fruit and a bottle of shampoo. She giggled happily at them.

'Do you happen to know which is the Lovells' cottage, Miss Doorn?' Burden asked her stiffly.

'Yes, look, it is that one.' She pointed, clutching the cringing inspector's arm and, as Wexford put it later, almost engulfing him in delectable curves. 'The most dirty in all the village.' As representative of perhaps the most house-proud nation on earth, she shuddered and, for the first time in their short acquaintance, lost her amiable expression. 'They are living there like pigs, I think. His mother is a very nasty dirty woman, all fat.' And, some six inches from her own rich contours, she described in the air a huge cello shape.

Wexford smiled at her. 'Will the fat lady be at home, do you know?'

Katje ignored the smile. She was looking at Burden. 'Maybe,' she said, shrugging. 'I know nothing of what these pig people do. You are liking a nice cup of tea? I think you are working very hard and would like some tea with me while your chief is in the nasty dirty cottage.'

'Oh, no—no, thank you,' said Burden, appalled.

'Perhaps tomorrow, then,' said Katje, sucking her hair. 'All evenings I am free and tomorrow my friend must work late, serving drinks for the dance. Mind you are not forgetting.' She wagged her finger at him. 'Now I say good-bye. Do not be catching anything nasty in that very dirty place.'

She tripped, straight-backed, yellow hair bobbing, across the road and up to the Manor gate. There she stopped and waved to them, her round breasts rising under the pink fluffy sweater.

Wexford waved back, turned away, laughing. 'Odds my little life, I think she means to tangle your eyes too!'

'A ghastly young female,' said Burden coldly.

'I think she's charming.'

'Good heavens, if I thought my daughter . . . !'

'For God's sake, Mike. I'm a married man, too, and a faithful husband.' His grin dying now, Wexford patted his large belly. 'Don't have much chance to be otherwise, do I? But sometimes . . .' He sighed. 'God, what wouldn't I give to be thirty again! Don't look at me like that, you cold fish. Here we are at this very nasty dirty place and let's hope we catch nothing more from our afternoon's work than a *nostalgie de boue.*'

'A what?' said Burden, trying to open the front gate without getting his hand stung by the nettles that thrust their leaves through it.

'It is just,' said Wexford with a rueful smile, 'a long name for a kind of chronic plague.' He laughed at Burden's incredulous suspicious face. 'Don't worry, Mike, it's not infectious and it only attacks the old.'

5

Nᴏᴛ only the front gate, but the front door too, was overgrown with nettles and their antidote, the dock. Before they had a chance to lift the knocker a grey lace curtain, re-perforated with larger holes, was lifted at a lattice window and a face appeared.

'I don't know what you want but you'll have to go round the back.'

The side gate fell over as they pushed it. With a shrug, Wexford laid it down flat on a luxuriant bed of weeds. The back garden was a squalid blot on a fair landscape, the magnificence of the forest showing up, like a stain on black velvet, these twenty square yards of waist-high grass, dandelions, tumbled corrugated iron and broken chicken coops. A reasonably shipshape shed filled one of the farthest corners, its footings hidden under heaps of rags, green glass bottles and a mattress which looked as if it had been used for bayonet practice. Among the weeds an enamel chamber-pot and several battered saucepans could be discerned. Wexford noticed that a gate in the back fence led directly into the forest.

The back door opened suddenly and the woman who had spoken to them from the window put her head out.

'What d'you want?'

'Mrs Lovell?'

'That's right. What d'you *want*?'

'A word with you, if you please,' Wexford said smoothly. 'We're police officers.'

56

She gave them a narrow suspicious glance. 'About her over at the house, is it? You'd better come in. His lordship said there was police about.'

'His lordship?' queried Burden. Had the exalted circles in which they found themselves even more exalted people, in fact titled personages, on their perimeters?

'My son, my Sean,' said Mrs Lovell, disillusioning him. 'Come on. You can go in the lounge, if you like. In here.'

This room, euphemistically named, was slightly less dirty than the kitchen, but it too smelt of greens, a chronic gas leak, faintly of gin. It was furnished with a new bright pink suite, already soiled, and a heterogeneous assortment of ancient cottage pieces and modern gimcrack. The Queen smiled aloofly from a calendar, pinned to the wall between newspaper cut-outs of the Rolling Stones and a large framed oil of a Roman lady stabbing herself.

In feature she wasn't unlike Mrs Lovell, while unable to compare with her in amplitude. There was a strong flavour of the gypsy in Mrs Lovell's still-handsome face, the aquiline nose, full curved lips and black eyes. Medusa hair, black and tangled, fell to her shoulders. Her embonpoint didn't extend to her face. The impression was that fat had crept upwards to cease at the neck, deterred perhaps by the threat implicit in that strong unwrinkled chin.

Her body was enormous, but not without a coarse attraction, the fat distributed hugely in the right places. The bosom of a Mother Earth goddess, sixty inches round yet discernibly cloven, matched in girth immense hips. Like Katje, Mrs Lovell lacked inhibition and when she sat down her already low-cut blouse strained a further two inches down, corresponding to the ascent above her knees of a tight black skirt. Feeling that where feminine flesh was concerned, enough was enough for one afternoon—

besides, in this case, the flesh could have done with a bath
—Wexford looked away.

'We're just making routine enquiries, Mrs Lovell,' he
said. 'Would you mind telling me how your son spent last
evening?'

'Had his tea,' she said. 'Then he sat about watching the
TV. His lordship's keen on the TV, and why not, being
as he pays the licence?'

'Why not indeed? But he didn't watch it after nine-
thirty, did he?'

Mrs Lovell looked from Wexford to Burden. It was
transparent she was deciding whether to lie or tell the
truth, perhaps only because telling the truth is always
easier. Everything about her appearance and that of the
cottage testified to a gross laziness, a deadly sloth. At last
she said economically, 'He went out.'

'Where did he go?'

'I never asked him. I don't interfere with his ways . . .'
She picked at a ragged thumbnail. '. . . and he don't with
mine. Never have. Maybe he went down the shed. Spends
a lot of time down the shed, he does.'

'Doing what, Mrs Lovell?'

'His lordship's got his records down there.'

'Surely he can play his records in the house?' said
Burden.

'Can if he wants.' Mrs Lovell chewed a hangnail. 'Don't
matter to me one way or another. I don't interfere with
him and he don't with me.'

'What time did he come in?'

'I never heard him. My gentleman friend come in about
seven. Sean and him, they don't hit it off all that grand.
I reckon that was why his lordship took himself off down
the shed. He hadn't come in when my friend went, half

ten that'd have been—but there, like I say, I don't interfere with him and he don't . . .'

'Yes, yes, I see. Sean was very fond of Mrs Nightingale,
I believe?'

'You can believe what you like.' Mrs Lovell gave a huge
yawn, revealing fine sharp teeth. 'Live and let live, that's
my motto. Her up at the Manor, she believed in interfering with folks, making them better themselves. Gave
his lordship some funny ideas.' She stretched her arms
above her head, yawned again and swung her legs up on
to the sofa. Wexford thought of a fat cushiony cat, purring and preening itself, unconscious of the squalor in
which it lived.

'What sort of ideas?' he asked.

' 'Bout getting into show business, singing, all that. I
never took no notice. Maybe she fancied him. I never
asked.'

'Would you have any objection if we searched this
house?'

For the first time she smiled, showing an unsuspected
ironic humour. 'Search all you like,' she said. 'Rather you
than me.'

'A depressing experience,' said Wexford as they
returned to the car. Bryant, rather pale, followed at a
distance.

'Never in all my years of C.I.D. work have I come
across anything like it,' Burden exploded. 'I itch all over.'
He wriggled inside his clothes, scratching his head.

'Well, your young lady friend did warn you.'

Burden ignored this. 'Those beds!' he said. 'That
kitchen!'

'More than I'd bargained for, I admit,' Wexford agreed.
The only clean place was that shed. Odd that, Mike. A

rug on the floor, couple of decent chairs, a record-player. Could be a love-nest.'

Burden shuddered. 'No one's ever going to make me believe a lady like Mrs Nightingale would have assignations there.'

'Perhaps not,' Wexford said reluctantly. 'On the practical side, we didn't unearth much, did we? One brass candlestick and a metal hot-water bottle. They hadn't got blood on them and they hadn't been cleaned, by God, in the last fifty years. And the clothes she said "his lordship" wore last night were almost natty. But what was he doing, Mike? Bryant checked on the pub and he wasn't there. The last bus out of Myfleet goes at nine-twenty, so he wasn't on that. A boy like Sean Lovell doesn't traipse about admiring the beauties of nature. He gets too much of that all day long.'

'Nobody,' Burden persisted doggedly, 'is going to make me believe there was anything between him and Mrs Nightingale. That mother of his is no more than the village trollop, if you ask me. "I don't interfere with him" indeed. That's just another way of saying you've always neglected your child. I know you think I'm old-fashioned, sir, and a puritan, but I don't know what women are coming to these days. Dirty, feckless or immoral, or the whole lot together. First there's this Mrs Nightingale with her face-lifting and her secret meetings, then there's that Dutch girl boasting of the way she carries on, and as for Mrs Lovell . . .'

'I thought you'd feel that way,' said Wexford with a kindly smile, 'and that's why I'm laying on something respectable for you. We are going to call on a virtuous wife, Mrs Georgina Villiers, who will tell us, I hope, without fainting or assuring us of her broken-hearted devotion to Mrs Nightingale's memory, just who her friends were and what her nasty brother did to make them loathe each other.'

'My husband's gone back to the Manor,' said Georgina Villiers. 'He won't be long.'

'We should like to talk to you.'

'Oh, would you?' Mrs Villiers looked surprised and rather frightened, as if few people had ever wanted to talk exclusively to her. 'Well, all right.'

She led them by way of a porridge-papered hall into a porridge-papered living room. It was as untidy and characterless as its owner, who stood awkwardly before saying in the abrupt voice of a charmless woman, 'Well, sit down.'

'We shan't keep you long, Mrs Villiers. How is your husband after this morning's shock?'

'Oh, that. He's all right now.' Suddenly she became aware that her visitors wouldn't sit down before she did and, with a slight nervous laugh, she crossed the room and perched herself on the arm of a chair. 'Oh, dear. I'd better close the front door. Excuse me, I'll just do that.' Wexford noticed that for so thin and slight a woman she had a strong athletic stride. Her legs, stockingless, were well muscled, tanned a reddish brown.

'Well, what did you want to ask me?' Her voice had a brusque barking note, as if she were used to command but not always to having her commands obeyed. Hundreds of dark brown freckles peppered her skin, the white vulnerable skin of the auburn-haired. She seemed in her late twenties, a woman who didn't know how to make herself pretty but who tried. The edelweiss brooch on her blouse collar, the slide in her hair, showed that she tried. 'My husband—you really should talk to my husband. He won't be long.' She eyed the clock rather wildly. 'Quen—

my brother-in-law, that is—wouldn't keep him long. Anyway, what did you want to ask me?'

'First of all, Mrs Villiers,' said Burden, 'did you and your husband come straight back here after your visit to the Manor last night?'

'Oh, yes.'

'What did you do when you got home?'

'We went to bed. We both went straight to bed.'

'You had been driving the car I saw outside?' Wexford put in.

Georgina Villers shook her head so violently that her hair flew out, disclosing unsuitable pendant ear-rings. 'We went in Denys's car. We've got two cars. When we got married last year I had a car and he had a car. Only old cars, but we kept them both. They aren't worth much, you see.' She managed a feverish, very bright smile. 'He's out in his car now.'

'And yours, I see,' said Wexford in a pleasant fatherly voice, 'has just been cleaned. Always clean your car on a Wednesday, do you, Mrs Villiers? I expect you're like my wife, a special time of the week for every little chore, eh? That way nothing gets left.'

'No, I'm afraid not. I'm not methodical.' She blinked at him, puzzled by the turn the conversation had taken. 'I ought to be, I know. Denys would like it if . . . Why do you ask?'

'I'll tell you, Mrs Villiers. If you were very methodical and always worked to a routine you'd be conditioned to it, and then I could understand that even the violent death of your sister-in-law might not make you deviate from that routine. But since you aren't methodical and only, I assume, clean your car when you feel like it or when it needs it, why did you choose today of all days?'

She blushed deeply. A fear that was almost anguis

showed in her eyes and she blinked again, bringing her hands together and then clasping them. 'I don't know what you mean. I don't understand.'

'Don't distress yourself. Perhaps you cleaned the car *because* you were upset. Was that it?' She was very slow on the uptake, Wexford thought, too frightened or too obtuse to see the loophole he was offering her. He offered it more explicitly. 'I suppose you took the very sensible attitude that when one is unhappy or worried, work is the best thing to take one's mind off one's troubles?'

Relieved at last, she nodded. 'Yes, that was it.' Immediately she undid the small good her agreement had done her. 'I wasn't very upset, not really. I mean, she wasn't *my* sister.'

'That's true,' said Wexford. He drew his chair closer towards her and their eyes met, hers held by his like the eyes of a rabbit mesmerised by headlights. Suddenly Burden was excluded and the two of them were alone. 'She was your husband's sister, of course, just a sister-in-law.' Her face sharpened and hardened. 'They didn't like each other much, did they?'

'No, they didn't.' She hesitated very briefly, sliding as if involuntarily from the arm to the seat of the chair, but not taking her eyes from Wexford's face. 'They didn't get on at all,' she said. 'If you must know, Denys couldn't stand her.'

'Strange, Mrs Nightingale seemed to get on with everyone else.'

'Did she? Oh, with the county people, you mean.' She gave a deep quiet sigh and then spoke in a level rapid voice, 'Elizabeth didn't have any real friends. My husband, he thinks she was killed by a maniac, one of those men who attack women. I expect that's what it was. She

63

must have been mad, going into the forest at night. Really she was asking for it.'

'Perhaps,' Wexford said. He smiled genially to help the atmosphere relax. Georgina Villiers was calmer now. She unclasped her hands and looked down at them, breathing shallowly. 'Do you know why your husband didn't get on with his sister?'

'Well, they hadn't anything in common.'

And what, Wexford asked himself, does a woman like you, dull and characterless and conventional, have in common with an intellectual like Villiers, a teacher of classics, an authority on Wordsworth?

'I suppose,' she said, 'he thought her rather silly and extravagant.'

'And was she, Mrs Villiers?'

'Well, she had a lot of money, didn't she? He hadn't any other reason for not liking her, if that's what you mean. She and Quen were very ordinary people really. Not the sort of people I've been used to, of course. I never associated with people like that before I was married.'

'You got on well with them?'

'Quen was always kind.' Georgina Villiers twisted her wedding ring, moving it up and down her finger. 'He liked me for my husband's sake, you see. He and my husband are *great* friends.' She looked down, nervously biting her lip. 'But I think he got to like me for myself. Anyway,' she said, suddenly shrill and cross, 'why should I care? A man's wife ought to come first. He ought to think more of her than of outsiders, not go and do his work in somebody else's house.'

'You felt that Mr Nightingale had too great an influence over your husband?'

'I don't care,' said Georgina, 'for any outside interference.' She pulled at the ear-rings, slightly releasing the

64

screw of one of them. 'I was a teacher of physical education,' she said proudly, 'before I was married, but I've given it up for good. Don't you think a woman ought to stay at home and look after her husband? That's best for people like us, have a real home and family without too much outside interest.'

Frowning at Burden who was nodding his head approvingly, Wexford said, 'Would you object if we searched this house?'

Georgina hesitated, then shook her head.

The bungalow had another reception room and two bedrooms, the smaller of which was unfurnished and uncarpeted.

'I wonder what he does with his money?' Wexford whispered. 'He's got a good job and he writes those books.'

Burden shrugged. 'Maybe he's extravagant like his sister,' he said. 'He'll be different now. He's got a good wife.'

'Oh, my God!'

Searching the sparsely filled cupboards, Burden said stiffly, 'Well, I think it makes a nice change, talking to an ordinary decent woman.'

'Perhaps she is ordinary and decent. She's dull enough, God knows. There's nothing here, no blood, nothing that could conceivably have been used as a weapon.' They moved on into the kitchen where Wexford lifted the lid of the old-fashioned coke boiler. 'Blazing away merrily,' he said. 'They could have burnt practically anything on here and she's had hours to do it in.'

Georgina was waiting for them in the living room, sitting apathetically, staring at the wall.

'I can't think why my husband's so long. You'd think that today he'd want to be here with me. You'd think . . .' Suddenly she froze, listening intently. 'Here he is now.'

She leapt from her chair and rushed into the hall, slamming the door behind her. Listening with half an ear to the whispered conversation between husband and wife, Burden said, 'She's certainly a mass of nerves. It's almost as if she expected us to find something. I wonder if . . .'

'Sssh!' said Wexford sharply.

Denys Villiers walked into the room, talking over his shoulder to his wife. 'I can't be in two places at once, Georgina. Quen's in a bad way. I left him with Lionel Marriott.'

Burden's eyes met Wexford's. The chief inspector got up, his eyebrows raised in pleased astonishment.

'Did I hear you mention the name Lionel Marriott?'

'I expect so, if you were listening,' said Villiers rudely. He still looked a good deal more than thirty-eight, but less ill than in the Old House that morning. 'Why, d'you know him?'

'He teaches,' said Wexford, 'at the same school as you do. As a matter of fact, his nephew is married to my elder daughter.'

Villiers gave him an offensive glance. 'Remarkable,' he said, his tone clearly implying that Marriott, a cultured person and colleague of his own, had distinctly lowered himself in being associated by marriage with the chief inspector's family.

Wexford swallowed his wrath. 'Is he a friend of your brother-in-law's?'

'He hangs about the Manor from time to time.' Coldly Villiers disengaged his arm from his wife's grasp and slumped into an armchair. He closed his eyes in despair or perhaps simply exasperation. 'I want a drink,' he said, and as Georgina hovered over him, her ear-rings bobbing, 'There's a half-bottle of gin somewhere. Go and find it, will you?'

6

IT was a great piece of luck, Wexford thought as he strolled down Kingsmarkham High Street at sunset, that by serendipity he had lighted on one of Quentin Nightingale's cronies and that the crony was Lionel Marriott. Indeed, had he been allowed to select from all his vast acquaintance in the town one single person to enlighten him on the Nightingales' affairs, Marriott would have been that one. But it had never crossed his mind to connect Marriott with the Manor, although perhaps it should have done, for what great house in the whole neighbourhood was closed to him? What person with any pretension to culture or taste wasn't on hob-nobbing terms with him? Who but a recluse could deny familiarity with Kingsmarkham's most hospitable citizen and most fluent gossip?

Wexford had met him half a dozen times and this was enough for Marriott to count him one of his intimates and to avail himself of a rare privilege. Few people in Kingsmarkham knew the chief inspector's Christian name and still fewer used it. Marriott had done so since their first meeting and required in exchange that Wexford should call him Lionel.

His own life was an open book. You might not want to turn its pages, but if you hung back, Marriott himself turned them for you, as anxious to enlighten you as to his own affairs as to those of his huge circle of friends.

He was about Wexford's own age, but spry and wiry, and he had been married once to a dull little woman who had conveniently died just as Marriott's boredom with matrimony was reaching its zenith. Marriott always spoke of her as 'my poor wife' and told stories about her that were in very bad taste but at which you couldn't help laughing, for his narrative gift and art of skilful digression was such as to reveal the funny side of every aspect of the human predicament. Afterwards you salved your conscience with the thought that the lady was better dead than married to Marriott, who could never for long be attached to just one person and 'all the rest', as Shelley puts it, 'though fair and wise, commend to cold oblivion'.

For 'cold oblivion' or, at any rate, loneliness, seemed to be Marriott's great dread. Why else did he fill his house with people every night? Why else teach English literature at the King's School by day when he had a private income, sufficient even for his needs, his generosity and his hospitality?

Since his wife's death he hadn't been celibate and each time Wexford had encountered him it had been in the company of one of a succession of attractive well-dressed women in their forties. Very probably, he thought, as he entered the High Street alley that led down to Marriott's house, the current companion would be there now, arranging Marriott's flowers, listening to his anecdotes, preparing canapés for the inevitable ensuing cocktail party.

His house was at the end of a Georgian terrace of which all but this first one had been converted into shops or flats or storeplaces. By contrast to their sad and dilapidated appearance, his looked positively over-decorated with its brilliant white paint, renewed every two years, its jolly little window boxes on each sill, and the six curly balconies which sprouted on its façade.

Those not in the know would have supposed it to be owned by a spinster of independent means and a fussy inclination towards horticulture. Smiling to himself, Wexford climbed the steps to the front door, ducking his head to avoid catching it on a hanging basket full of Technicolor lobelias and fire-engine geraniums. For once the alley wasn't chock-a-block with the cars of Marriott's visitors. But it was early still, not yet seven o'clock.

It was Marriott himself who came to the door, natty in a red-velvet jacket and bootlace tie, a can of asparagus tips in one hand.

'Dear old boy, what a lovely surprise! I was only saying five minutes ago how miserable I was because you'd utterly deserted me, and here you are. The answer to a sinner's prayer. Wouldn't it be lovely, I was saying, if dear old Reg Wexford were to turn up tonight?'

Wexford belonged to the generation and social stratum that feels almost faint to hear Christian names on the lips of mere acquaintances and he winced, but even he couldn't deny that whatever Marriott's faults, no one could make you feel as welcome as he did.

'I was passing,' he said, 'and anyway I want to talk to you.'

'And I've been longing to talk to you, so that makes two of us. Come in, come in. Don't stand there. You'll stay for my party, won't you? Just a little celebration, a few old friends who are dying to meet the great chief inspector after all the lovely things I've told them about you.'

Wexford found himself swept into the hall, propelled towards Marriott's drawing room. 'What are you celebrating?' He took a deep breath and brought out the first name. 'What is there to celebrate, Lionel?'

'Perhaps "celebrate" was the wrong word, dear old boy. This part is more in the nature of an "I, who am about to die, salute you" gathering, if you take my meaning.' He peered up into Wexford's face. 'I see you don't. Well, no, a busy man like you would hardly realise that this is the last night of the holidays and it's back to the spotty devils tomorrow.'

'Of course,' Wexford said. He remembered now that Marriott always gave an end-of-the-holidays party and that he always referred to his pupils at the King's School as the 'spotty devils'. 'I won't stay, though. I'm afraid I'm being a nuisance, interrupting you when you're preparing for a party.'

'Not a bit! You don't know how overjoyed I am to see you, but I see from your icy looks that you disapprove.' Marriott threw out his short arms dramatically. 'Tell me, what have I done? What have I said?'

Entering the drawing room, Wexford saw a bar improvised in one corner, and through the arch that led into the dining room, a table loaded with food, roast fowls, cold joints, a whole salmon, arranged among carelessly scattered white roses. 'I see,' he said, 'that I was wrong in supposing you to have been a close friend of Elizabeth Nightingale.'

Marriott's mobile face fell, becoming suddenly but perhaps not sincerely, lugubrious. 'I know, I know. I should be in mourning, sackcloth and ashes, no less. Believe me, Reg, I wear the ashes in my heart. But suppose I were to put all these dear people off and fling the baked meats to the Pomfret broiler-pig farm, what good would it do? Would it bring her back? Would it wipe one tear from Quentin's cheek?'

'I suppose not.'

'Dear Reg, I can't bear your censure. Let me give you

70

a drink. A whisky, a pernod, a champagne cocktail? And a little slice of cold duck to go with it?'

Overwhelmed as usual, Wexford sat down. 'Just a small whisky, then, but nothing to eat.'

'I'm an outcast, I suppose. You won't eat my salt.' Marriott trotted towards the bar, shaking his head. He began pouring huge measures of Vat 69 into cut-glass tumblers. Wexford knew it would be useless to demur. He eyed the room with an inward grin. Although he knew many of the antiques were almost priceless, the chandeliers unique and the décor the envy of every person of taste in the town, Marriott's drawing room always suggested to him a mixture of the Wallace Collection and an Italian restaurant in the Old Brompton Road. The walls were covered by bottle-green paper embossed with emerald fur and hung with gilt-framed brothel mirrors. On every table stood an assortment of carriage clocks, snuff-boxes and useless little bits of Crown Derby. You would be afraid to move except that you knew that whatever damage you did Marriott would only smile and tell you it didn't matter at all, so much more precious was your company, including your clumsiness, than any inanimate object.

The clatter of heels from the kitchen region told him there was a third person in the house, and as he took his triple whisky, the woman appeared carrying a tray loaded with more food. She was a tall blonde of about forty-five with charm bracelets on both wrists which rang like bells as she moved.

'This is Hypatia, my amanuensis,' said Marriott, seizing her arm. 'You've no idea the funny looks I get when I introduce her like that. But then people are so illiterate, aren't they? This is Chief Inspector Wexford, my dear, the guardian of our peace.'

Unmoved by Marriott's remarks, Hypatia extended a large calm hand.

'She won't interfere with us,' said Marriott as if she wasn't there. 'She's just going to have a bath and make herself more beautiful than ever. Run along, Patty, darling.'

'If you're sure that's enough nosh,' said Hypatia.

'Quite sure. We don't want any bilious attacks like last time, do we? Now then, Reg, do your grand inquisitor stuff. I'm desolated that this isn't a social call, but I don't delude myself.' Marriott raised his glass. 'Here's to kindness!'

'Er—cheers,' said Wexford. He waited until the woman had gone and sounds had reached him of water gurgling through the pipes. Then he said, 'I want to know about the Nightingales, anything you can tell me.' He grinned. 'I know you won't let yourself be inhibited by any foolish scruples like good taste or not speaking ill of the dead.'

'I was very fond of Elizabeth,' said Marriott in a slightly offended tone. 'We'd known each other all our lives. We were infants together, in a manner of speaking.'

'A manner of stretching, more like,' said Wexford nastily. 'She could have given you a good fifteen years, so don't kid yourself.'

Marriott sniffed. 'It's easy to see you got out of bed the wrong side this morning.'

'I don't know about the wrong side. I got out of it a damn' sight too early. So you've known her since *she* was born, have you? Where was that?'

'Here, of course. Didn't you know she and Denys were born here?'

'I hardly know a thing about them.'

'Oh, that's what I like. Total ignorance. As I say to the spotty devils, blessed are they who hunger and thirst after enlightenment, for they shall be filled, even if I have to knock it into 'em with a slipper. Well, they were born here all right, in a nasty little damp house down by Kingsbrook Lock. Their mother came from London, quite a good family, but their father was Kingsmarkham born and bred. He was a clerk in the council offices.'

'Not well-off, then?'

'Poor as church mice, my dear. Elizabeth and Denys went to the council school, as it then was, and no doubt he would have gone on wasting his sweetness on the desert air but for the bomb.'

'What bomb?' enquired Wexford as the bathroom door slammed and something went glug in the water tank far above their heads.

'One of that stick of bombs a German plane let fly over here on its way to the coast. It was a direct hit and it took Villiers *père* and *mère* to Kingdom Come in one fell swoop.'

'Where were the children?'

'Denys was out fishing and Elizabeth had been sent to fetch him home. It was early evening, about seven. The Villiers children, Elizabeth and Denys, were fourteen and eleven respectively.'

'What became of them?'

'A rather peculiar and most unfair arrangement was made for them,' said Marriott. 'Denys went to his mother's brother and did very well for himself. This uncle was a barrister in a good way of doing and he sent Denys to some public school and then to Oxford. Poor Elizabeth was left behind with her aunt, her father's sister, who took her away from the High School here when she was fifteen and sent her to work at Moran's, the draper's.'

Wexford's face registered the astonishment Marriott had hoped for. 'Mrs Nightingale a draper's assistant?'

'I thought that would shake you. That old bitch Priscilla Larkin-Smith still goes about telling her mates about the days when Elizabeth Villiers used to fit her for her corsets.'

'How did she meet Nightingale?'

'Oh, that was a long time later,' said Marriott. 'Elizabeth wasn't at Moran's for long. She ran away to London and got a job, the clever little thing. Have some more Scotch, ducky?'

'No, really. You know, Lionel, if it wasn't for What's-her-name upstairs and her predecessors, one would suspect you of—how shall I put it?—a certain ambivalence. Sometimes you're too epicene for words.'

Marriott smirked at that, not displeased. 'I do camp it up rather, don't I? People are always telling me about it. Just a pose, I assure you. Do let me fill your glass.'

'Oh, all right.' The water was running out of the bath now and Hypatia's feet could be heard tapping on the upper floor. 'Did the brother and sister meet in London?'

Marriott lit a Russian cigarette and blew elegant smoke rings. 'That I wouldn't know.' He looked crestfallen. Wexford knew he hated to admit ignorance of any detail of a friend's private life. 'I didn't see either of them again until I heard Quentin had bought the Manor.' He recharged their glasses and came back to his chair. 'When we heard the Manor had new people in I naturally got my wife to call. You can imagine my joy when I heard who this Mrs Nightingale was.'

'I'm not sure that I can,' said Wexford, 'seeing she was a kid of fifteen and you around thirty when you last met.'

'How you do throw cold water on all one's impulsive little expressions! I mean, of course, that it was lovely to see someone I used to know, and anyway it was always a pleasure to be with Elizabeth. An absolute beauty, you see, and what style! I love those classic English blondes.'

'You ought to get married again,' said Wexford.

Marriott cast a shifty glance upwards and said epigrammatically, 'A man who marries again doesn't deserve to lose his first wife.'

'Sometimes,' said Wexford, 'you shock me. Talking of marriage, how did the Nightingales get on?'

'They were a very happy couple. If you and your wife never discuss anything but the weather, are waited on hand and foot, are childless and equally cold sexually, what is there to quarrel about?'

'It was like that, was it? And may I ask how you know they were sexually cold?'

Marriott shifted a little in his seat. 'Well, you've only got to look at Quentin and . . . You must allow for a little guesswork, Reg.'

'I'll do the guessing. Let's get back to those early days, fifteen, sixteen years ago. Was Villiers living here then?'

'No, he turned up a couple of years later. First day of the autumn term it was, and that makes it fourteen years ago almost to the day. We had a couple of newcomers to the staff, a science man and a second-string classics bloke. That was Denys. The Head introduced us veterans and, of course, I was thrilled to see Denys.'

'But naturally,' said Wexford.

Marriott gave him an injured look. 'I thought his behaviour very odd, most peculiar. But then Denys is odd, the complete misanthropist. "What a stroke of luck for you," I said, "knowing me. I can take you around and introduce you to anyone who is anyone." You'd have thought he'd have been overjoyed, but not a bit of it. He just gave me one of his sick looks, but I thought I'd better make allowances.'

'Allowances for what?'

'Well, he's a poet, as you know, and poets are curious creatures. There's no getting away from it. I see you didn't know. Oh, dear me, yes. Several very charming little verses of his had appeared in the *New Statesman* by that time, and I'd just read his collection of essays on the Lake Poets. Most scholarly. So, as I say, I made allowances. "Perhaps you're relying on your sister to give you the entrée," I said. "Don't forget she's new here herself." "My sister here?" he said, going quite white. "You don't mean you didn't know?" I said. "Christ," he said, "I thought this was the last place she'd want to show her face in." '

'But you made sure they got together?' said Wexford.

'Naturally, my dear. I had Denys and his wife up there the same evening.'

'His *wife*?' Wexford almost shouted. 'But he's only been married a year.'

'No need to blow your cool, dear old boy. His first wife. You weren't joking when you said you didn't know anything about these people, were you? His first wife, June, a most . . .'

'Look, don't let's get on to her yet,' groaned Wexford. 'Why was Villiers so upset when you said his sister was here?'

'I asked myself the same thing at the time, but we were all together quite a lot after that and it was plain they couldn't stand each other. Odd when you think how sweet Elizabeth was to everyone else. Frankly, Reg, she acted towards him as if he'd done her some injury, and as for him . . . The man's rudeness to her was beyond belief. But you mustn't lay too much stress on that. Denys is foul to everyone except Quentin. He's quite different with Quen and, of course, Quen adores him. But Elizabeth and Denys were never friends. As children they were always quarrelling. Even now I can remember Mrs Villiers and my poor wife discussing it, how trying it was, you know, and how helpless it made Mrs Villiers feel. But if you want to know why they carried on with this feud of theirs, I can't help you. Elizabeth never discussed her brother if she could help it, and if she didn't confide in me, whom did she confide in? We were very close friends, intimate, you might say.'

'Might I?' said Wexford thoughtfully. 'Might I indeed?' He fixed Marriott with a searching look and would have pursued this further but for the entry of Hypatia, bathed, perfumed and dressed in gold trousers and a black and gold tunic.

She had a cool smile for Wexford, a maternal one for Marriott. 'Still nattering? Pam and Ian are here, Leo. I've just seen their car turn into the alley.' She said pointedly to Wexford, 'Must you go?'

Wexford got up, shaking off Marriott's restraining hand. 'Will you be having another party tomorrow night, Lionel?'

'Really, Reg, I'm not a complete sybarite. Tomorrow night I'll be utterly prostrate after my tussles with the sons of yeomen, burgesses and those of the better sort. Spots before the eyes, no less.'

'In that case,' said Wexford, grinning, 'I'll pick you up from school and give you a lift home.'

'Lovely,' said Marriott, showing for the first time a vague uneasiness. He escorted Wexford to the door, let him out and admitted two bright elderly people. 'How marvellous to see you, my dears. You're looking good enough to eat, Pam darling. Now do let me . . .'

Wexford slipped quietly away.

7

THE Burden children were going back to school and from the bungalow bathroom came the sounds of retching. Pat was always sick on the first morning of term. Her parents stood in the kitchen listening to these sounds with the helpless misery of people who are just beginning to realise that their children are human beings as well as their children and that there is a point beyond which they cannot help them. This child would vomit on the first day of every term, before every interview for a job, probably too on her wedding morning.

'Oh, Mike,' said Jean Burden, 'ought we to send for Dr Crocker? Sometimes I even think about sending her to a psychiatrist.'

'When you know she'll be as right as rain as soon as she sets foot in the classroom? Keep a sense of proportion, love.'

'I just wish I could help her. We've never been nervy. I never thought I'd have a child who was a mass of nerves.'

'I'm not nervy,' said John, coming in with satchel and shining morning face. 'If I ever have kids and they go on like her I'll give them a right walloping.'

Burden looked at his son with distaste. His children, though only two years apart in age, brought up by loving and happily married parents in a solid middle-class background, had never got on. From quarrelling ever since

John was a toddler and Pat able only to scream at him from her pram they had progressed through physical fights to their current daily fripping.

He said severely: 'You're to stop speaking about your sister like that. I'm sick of telling you. Suppose,' he said, a thought coming to him from the case he was engaged on, 'suppose you and Pat were to be separated now and knew you wouldn't see each other again till you were grown up, how would you feel then? You'd be very sorry you were so unkind to her. You don't know how much you'd miss her.'

'I wouldn't miss her,' said John. 'I wish I was an only child.'

'I can't understand this dislike,' Burden said helplessly. 'It's not natural.' He put out his hand as his daughter, white-faced and with hanging head, came in under the shelter of her mother's arm. 'I'll drive you to school, sweetheart. I'll come right inside with you.'

'You never drive me to school,' said John. 'And I've got further to go, a dirty great mile to walk.'

'Don't say "dirty great",' said Burden mechanically, and then: 'I'll drive you both. But, for heaven's sake, don't quarrel in the car.'

The forecourt of the King's School was thronged with boys. Burden edged the car up the drive, sending the littlest ones, John's contemporaries, scuttling out of the way, squealing and whooping at the tops of their voices. Sixth-formers, draped against the wall in languid groups, their ignominious caps folded and tucked into their pockets, stared at him with lofty insolence. John jumped out of the car while it was still moving and was immediately absorbed by the whooping mob.

'You see, John isn't a bit worried,' Burden said encouragingly. 'You know you were both bored stiff being at home so long and he's glad to be back with his friends.'

'I hate him,' said Pat.

'That's no way to talk about your brother.' Burden reversed carefully and, making a three-point turn just inside the gates, came face to face with Denys Villiers. He nodded courteously, just raising his hand. Villiers looked through him, thrust his hands into his pockets, and marched in the direction of the new wing.

'Stop the car, Daddy,' Pat said as soon as they reached the open road. 'I'm going to be sick again.'

His children deposited, Burden drove down to the police station through the morning rush. He had been surprised to see Villiers, whom, he thought, tact if not grief would have kept from work for at least this week. A strange man, one who seemed to care nothing for public opinion. His behaviour in ignoring Burden, a policeman who had been in his house the day before and was, in any case, the parent of a King's pupil, had been— well, outrageous, Burden thought.

Aware that he was twenty minutes late, he leapt into the lift and arrived breathless in Wexford's office. The chief inspector, in an even more disgracefully shabby suit than usual, sat at his rosewood desk, leafing through stacks of papers. Standing behind him at the window was the doctor, breathing on the glass and drawing with one finger something that looked disturbingly like a plan of the alimentary canal. Burden had had enough of alimentary canals for one morning.

'Sorry I'm late,' he said. 'My girl Pat's always sick on the first day of term, so I hung about and drove her to school.' He nodded to the doctor. 'Jean wanted you called in.'

'But you wouldn't bother a busy man?' said Crocker

with a lazy grin. 'Pat'll grow out of it, you know. It's all part of the human predicament from which your kids aren't going to be absolved, hard cheese though that may be.'

Wexford looked up with a scowl. 'Spare us the philosophy, will you? I've got some lab reports here, Mike. The ash from the Manor bonfire shows distinctly that woollen cloth was burnt on it. No weapon has come to light, although our people went on combing the forest until it got dark last night and they're at it again now.'

'It could be anywhere,' Burden said hopelessly. 'In the river, chucked in someone's garden. We don't even know what it is.'

'No, but we're all going to have a hard think about that. First of all we have to decide if Mrs Nightingale's assailant planned this murder or if it was unpremeditated.'

Dr Crocker rubbed out his drawing with the heel of his hand. He sat down on one of Wexford's flimsy chairs. The chief inspector's was the only solid one in the room, a dark wood and leather throne, strong and ample enough to bear Wexford's weight. It creaked as Wexford leaned back, spreading his arms.

'Premeditated,' said the doctor, concentrating. 'Otherwise she wouldn't have been killed in that way in that place. The kind of thing she was killed with isn't the kind that people carry with them on country walks. Right?'

'You mean that if it was unpremeditated she could only have been killed by strangling, for instance?'

'Roughly speaking, yes. You don't have to bring the weapon with you in a planned murder if you know the means are going to be available. For example, Y intends to kill X in X's drawing room, but he doesn't take a weapon because he knows the poker will be where it always is, on the hearth. But in an open space there aren't going to be any means, so he arms himself before he starts. That's what your man did.'

'Does it have to be a man?' Wexford asked.

'A man or a very strong woman.'

'I agree with you. My own view is that it was planned, and that can still apply in a jealousy murder. The killer followed her, expecting to see what he did in fact see. He took the weapon with him, guessing what he was going to see and only waiting for confirmation. What do you think, Mike?'

'Unpremeditated,' said Burden coolly. 'Our murderer was carrying with him something that could be used as a murder weapon but had some other primary purpose. As in the case of a woman cutting bread. Her husband says something to her which drives her over the edge of reason and she makes for him with the bread knife. But the original purpose of having the knife in her hand was to cut bread.'

'I'm all for pre-cut loaves myself,' said the doctor facetiously.

A deepening frown was the only sign Wexford gave of having heard this. 'Well, if we play along for the moment with Mike's theory, what could he (or the very strong she) have been carrying? What do people carry when they go into a wood at night?'

'A walking stick,' said Burden promptly, 'with a metal tip.'

Crocker shook his head. 'Too thin. Not the kind of thing at all. A *shooting* stick possibly, but it seems farfetched. A golf club?'

Wexford glared at him derisively. 'Going to have a few drives among the trees, was he? Trying to get his handicap down? Oh, give me strength!'

'Well, it was moonlight,' said the doctor. 'Or it was till the wind came up. Metal heel of a shoe?'

'Then where's the dirt in the wound?'

'You're right. There wasn't any.'

Wexford shrugged and fell into moody silence. Equally silently, Burden eased the papers from under his hand and began reading them without expression. Suddenly Wexford swivelled the groaning chair round.

'You said something just now, something about light.'

'I did?'

Burden said in his prim official voice: 'Dr Crocker said that it had been moonlight until the wind came up.' He gave a barrister-like inclination of his neat head in the doctor's direction. Crocker raised his eyebrows.

'Oh, yes. I remember because I was out at Flagford, delivering a baby. There was a bright moon but the clouds were already coming up by eleven and by half past the moon had gone.'

A slow grin that had nothing to do with humour and a great deal to do with triumph spread across Wexford's face. 'So what would anyone take with him into the wood?'

'An umbrella,' said the doctor, but Burden said, his gravity giving way to excitement, 'A torch!'

'A torch?' said Quentin Nightingale. 'Those we have are kept in the garden room.' The skin under his eyes looked brown and crêpey, the result perhaps of a second sleepless night. His hands trembled nervously as he touched his forehead, fidgeted with his tie, finally putting them behind his back and clasping them lightly together. 'If you think . . .' he muttered. 'If you're hoping . . . Your people searched the house throughout yesterday. What can . . . ?' He seemed incapable of ending his sentences, but let them trail away on a note of despair.

'I'm pursuing a new line,' Wexford said briskly. 'Where is this garden room?'

'I'll take you there.'

As they re-entered the hall the front-door bell rang. Quentin stared at the door as if Nemesis itself awaited him on the other side of it, but he made no move, only nodding limply when Mrs Cantrip marched out from the kitchen.

'Whoever's that now?' she said with some exasperation. 'Are you at home to visitors, sir?' His apathy aroused her sympathy rather than impatience. 'For two pins I'd send them away with a flea in their ear.'

'You'd better see who it is,' said Quentin.

It was Georgina Villiers and Lionel Marriott. They made a strange couple, the tall raw-boned young woman incongruously bedizened with costume jewellery, and the little sharp-eyed man. Georgina's face registered a mixture of assorted emotions, hope, shyness, an intense curiosity. She carried a canvas hold-all with plastic straps and handles, more suitable for a hiker than a woman paying a morning call, and as she stepped over the threshold she broke into a disjointed stream of apology and explanation.

'I felt I had to come and see how you were bearing up, Quen. It's all so dreadful for you. . . . I've brought my own lunch so that Mrs Cantrip won't have to be bothered cooking for me. How are you? You do look bad. Well, of course it's the strain and everything. Oh dear, perhaps I shouldn't have come.'

Quentin's face, contorted in an effort to hide his anxiety, showed plainly that he agreed with her, but courtesy forbade his saying so. 'No, no. It was nice of you to take the trouble. Won't you come into the morning room?' He swallowed hard and half-turned to Wexford. 'Perhaps Mrs Cantrip can take you to where the torches are kept?' The hand he put up to his sister-in-law's shoulder to shepherd her along shook now with violent jerks that were painful to see. They moved slowly towards the room where Elizabeth Nightingale had sat in the mornings, Georgina still muttering apologies.

'One moment,' said Wexford, putting out an arm to prevent Marriott from following them. The morning-room door closed. 'What the hell are you doing here, anyway?' the chief inspector said wrathfully. 'I thought you were supposed to be at school?'

'I had a free period, my dear, and how use it better than by popping up here to console poor Quen?'

'Perhaps you can tell me how someone without a car "pops", as you put it, up to Myfleet from Kingsmarkham and back again in forty minutes?'

'Georgina,' said Marriott, unable to restrain a grin of triumph, 'gave me a lift. I was standing at the school gates lost in thought, wondering in fact how I was going to accomplish my popping, the Myfleet bus having just gone, when along she came, Manor-bound. Such a relief! We had a nice little chat, planning the things we were going to say to cheer Quen up.'

'Then you'd better go in and say them,' said Wexford, giving the little man a small shove. 'Say them and go. I'm just about to start another massive search of this place and I don't want a lot of cheerful nosy people interfering with my men. And don't forget,' he added, 'that we have a date at four o'clock.' He sighed, shaking his head. 'Now, Mrs Cantrip, for the garden room.'

'Just down this passage, sir, and mind the step. I'm sure you'll say it was wrong of me to listen but I couldn't help hearing what you said to that Mr Marriott. Just what he needs, I thought, always up here snooping. And as for that Mrs Villiers . . . Did you hear her say she'd brought her own lunch? A nasty packet of sandwiches, I daresay. As if I wouldn't have given her a nice lunch. She'd only got to ask like a lady.'

'Is this the place, Mrs Cantrip? It's very dark down here.'

'You can't tell me, sir. I'm always telling Mr Nightingale to have a light fixed up. There was quite a nasty accident five or six years back when that Twohey fell down the step and thought his leg was broken but it was only a sprained ankle. He'd been too free helping himself from Mr Nightingale's whisky bottle and that's a fact.'

'Who was Twohey?' asked Wexford, stepping back for Mrs Cantrip to open the door. 'A friend of the family?'

'Oh, no, sir, just a servant. Him and his wife used to work here, if you can call it work. It didn't lighten my load, I can tell you. I was never so relieved in all my life as when Mr Nightingale sacked them. This is the garden room, sir, and there's a bit more light, you'll be glad to see.'

The light came from a glazed door leading into the garden. His face impassive, Wexford looked slowly round the small uncarpeted room. Its walls were whitewashed and on one of them hung a couple of shotguns, while beneath golf clubs and walking sticks lay in a long rack. There were two tennis rackets in presses, a string bag of tennis balls and a chip basket and scissors for cutting flowers. His glance went up to a shelf above the rack on which stood an array of torches: a lantern with a red cone on its top of the kind that is used to warn motorists of the presence of a broken-down car, a bigger storm lantern, a pencil torch and a bicycle lamp.

'That's funny,' said Mrs Cantrip. 'There should be

another one, a great big silver-coloured one.' Suddenly she had become rather pale. 'A torch with a big head,' she said, 'a big head and a sort of long thick tube thing to hold it with. I reckon it'd be nine or ten inches long.'

'And it should be up there with the others?' Mrs Cantrip nodded, biting her lip. 'When did you last see it there?'

'Oh, it'd be two or three weeks back. You don't kind of clean a room like this, if you take my meaning, sir. There's like no dusting or polishing, you see. Young Sean gives it a sweep out every so often.'

'He does, does he?' Wexford pulled out from under the rack a short set of steps, mounted them and looked at the surface of the shelf. A thickish patina of dust lay on the unpainted wood. In the front, between the bicycle lamp and the storm lantern, was a dust-free circle some four inches in diameter.

He licked his finger and just touched the centre of this clean circle. Then he said, looking at his fingertip, 'That torch was taken down yesterday or the day before.' He wiped his finger on his handkerchief, observing that the linen was unmarked. His inspired guess had turned out to be well founded.

It was such a big house, he thought, as he emerged from the passage and stood once more in the hall, a big country house full of cupboards and hidey-holes. His men had been instructed to look for a weapon without being told what they should look for. Suppose they had seen the missing torch in Nightingale's bedroom, sticking out perhaps from the pocket of a raincoat, would any one of them have had the intelligence, the faculty of putting two and two together to make more than four, to note it and draw it to the attention of his superiors? Wexford doubted it. They would have to begin again, this time with a specific missing object in view.

He tapped on the morning-room door, then opened it. There was no one inside. Only a cigarette end still smouldering in a blue pottery ashtray showed that Marriott had been there, then had obeyed Wexford and gone.

Giving himself *carte blanche* to explore the house all he pleased, Wexford looked into the drawing room and the dining room, and found both empty. He mounted the stairs to the first landing, treading shed rose petals under foot, and peered out between the crimson velvet curtains. Georgina Villiers was standing on the lawn, munching sandwiches and talking to Will Palmer. There was no sign of Quentin Nightingale. Wexford went down again, entered the empty study and telephoned Burden, asking him to come up to the Manor with Loring and Bryant and Gates and anyone else he could get hold of. He put the receiver down and listened to the silence.

At first it seemed absolute. Then, from far above him, he made out faintly thin reedy music from a transistor, Katje's perhaps; the tiny muted clink of plates as Mrs Cantrip prepared lunch; then footsteps coming from he couldn't tell where but which brought Quentin Nightingale into the room.

'A torch is missing from the garden room,' Wexford said in a cool level voice. 'A big torch, shaped like this.' Using both hands, he drew it in the air. 'Have you seen it about lately?'

'It was there on Sunday. I went in to get my golf clubs and I noticed it was there.'

'It isn't there now. That torch killed your wife, Mr Nightingale.'

Quentin leaned against a bookcase and put his head in his hands. 'I don't honestly think,' he whispered, 'that I can take any more. Yesterday was the most ghastly day of my life.'

'I can understand that. I'm afraid I can't promise you today or tomorrow will be improvements.'

But Quentin seemed not to have heard him. 'I think I'm going mad,' he said. 'I must have been mad to do what I did. I'd give everything I've got to go back to Tuesday evening and start again.'

'Are you making me some sort of confession?' Wexford asked him sternly, getting up. 'Because, if so . . .'

'Not that sort of confession,' Quentin almost shouted. 'Something private, something . . .' He clenched his hands, threw up his head. 'Show me,' he said hoarsely, 'show me where you think this torch ought to be. I might be able . . . Just show me.'

'All right. I'll show you and then we'll have another little talk. But let me tell you one thing first. Nobody involved in a murder case has any private life. Please remember that.'

Quentin Nightingale made no reply, but he hunched his shoulders and again put that trembling hand to his forehead. Puzzled, Wexford speculated as to the nature of this acute anxiety that was turning the other man into a nervous wreck. Had he killed his wife? Or was this distress the result of some other act, something necessarily more venial, yet as productive of agonising guilt?

They walked down the dark passage, Wexford going first. Ahead of them a vertical slit of light showed the garden-room door slightly ajar.

'I closed that door,' Wexford said sharply and pushed it wide. On the high shelf where, half an hour before, there had been only a clean circular patch in the dust, stood a large chrome torch, up-ended.

8

THE torch had been scrubbed, probably immersed in water. Wexford held it gingerly in his handkerchief and unscrewed its base. The batteries had been removed but the glass and the bulb inside were unbroken. He noted that a few drops of water still clung to the interior of the tube that formed its handle.

Very slowly, he said, 'Only you, Mr Nightingale, knew that I came to this house this morning in search of a torch. Did you speak of it to any of your servants or to Mrs Villiers or Mr Marriott?'

White-faced, Quentin Nightingale shook his head.

'I believe,' Wexford said, 'that this torch was used to kill your wife. It wasn't here when I first visited the garden room; it is here now. Someone replaced it in the past half-hour. Come, let us go back to your study.'

The widower seemed unable to speak at all. He sank heavily into a chair and covered his face with his hands.

'Did you replace that torch, Mr Nightingale? Come, I want an answer. I shall sit here until I get one.' There was a tap at the door and Wexford opened it to admit Burden. A quick glance passed between them, Burden raised his eyebrows at the silent slumped figure, and then moved without speaking towards the wall shelves as if fascinated by the books they held. 'Pull yourself together, Mr Nightingale,' Wexford said. 'I'm waiting for an answer.' He would have liked to shake the man, stir him into some sort of response. 'Very well,' he said at last. 'Since I don't believe in wasting time and Inspector Burden looks as if he might appreciate a little entertainment, I'll tell you a story. You may find some parallels in it with your own conduct over the past days. Who knows?

'There was a country gentleman,' he began, 'who lived with his beautiful wife in a manor house. They were happy together, even if their marriage might have been said to have grown a little rusty and dull with the years.' Quentin moved a fraction at that, pushing his fingers hard into his white hair. 'One day,' Wexford said in the same pleasant conversational tone, 'he discovered that his wife was being unfaithful to him, meeting another man in the woods at night. So, consumed with jealousy, he followed her, taking a torch with him, for the moon had gone and the night was dark. He saw her with this man, kissing each other, and heard them making plans and giving promises. Perhaps they even abused him. When the man had left her and she was alone, the husband confronted her, she defied him, and he struck out at her with the torch, struck again and again in his jealous frenzy until he had beaten her to death. Did you say something, Mr Nightingale?'

Quentin's lips moved. He moistened them, struggled forward in his chair and managed a strangled, 'However . . . however it happened, it wasn't . . . it wasn't that way.'

'No? The husband didn't burn his bloodstained sweater on the still-smouldering bonfire? He didn't pace the garden for hours in his anguish, finally locking himself in his own bathroom to spend more hours cleansing every trace of his wife's blood from his person? Strange. We know he took a bath and that at what some would call an ungodly hour . . .'

'Stop!' Quentin cried, clutching the arms of his chair. 'None of this is true. It's a monstrous fabrication.' He swallowed, then cleared his throat. 'I didn't take a bath.'

'You told me you did,' retorted Wexford.

'Twice,' said Burden, the word dropping like a bead of cold water.

'I know. It was a lie.' A fiery blush coloured Quentin's face and he closed his eyes. 'Would you get me a drink, please? Whisky. It's in there.'

Burden looked at Wexford and Wexford nodded. The whisky was in a small cabinet under the window. Burden poured about an inch into a glass and put it into the shaking hand, closing the fingers around it. Quentin drank, the glass chattering against his teeth.

'I'll tell you where I was,' he said. Wexford noticed that he was at last making a determined effort to steady his voice. 'But you alone. I should like it if the inspector could leave us.'

And if he was about to confess to murder . . . ? Wexford didn't like it much. But he had to know. He made a quick decision. 'Will you wait outside, please, Inspector Burden?'

Obediently Burden went, without a backward glance. Quentin gave a heavy sigh. 'I don't know where to begin,' he said. 'I could just tell you baldly, but I need to justify myself. God, if you knew the remorse, the shame . . . I'm sorry. I am trying to get a grip on myself. Well, I . . . I must start somewhere.' He finished the last of his drink, putting off, Wexford thought, the evil moment as long as he could. Then he said: 'I want you to know that it was quite correct what you said about my wife and me, being happy together, I mean, but with our marriage grown dull with the years. That was true. I accepted it. I thought it inevitable with people who had been married as long

92

as we had, and who had no children. We never quarrelled. I think I should tell you now that if my wife had fallen in love with someone else I shouldn't have been angry. I shouldn't even have objected. I expect I would have been jealous, but I wouldn't have shown my jealousy by violence, God forbid!—or in any other way. I want to make that clear now.'

Wexford nodded noncommittally. The man's words were simple and frank, carrying, he thought, an unmistakable ring of truth.

'You said,' Quentin went on, 'that nobody involved in a murder case has any right to a private life. I'll have to tell you about my private life to make you understand why I did what I did.' He got up suddenly and walked swiftly to the bookshelves, pressing his hands flat against morocco and gilt bindings. Staring at the titles of the books but perhaps unseeing, he said, 'I used to go to her room once a fortnight, always on a Saturday night. She would push back the bedcovers and say, always the same, "This *is* nice, darling," and afterwards, when I left her to go back to my room, she'd say, "That was lovely, darling." She never called me by my name. Sometimes I think she forgot what it was.'

He stopped. Wexford wasn't the sort of policeman who says impatiently, 'Is all this really relevant, sir?' He said nothing, listening with a grave face.

'I was so bored,' Quentin said to the books. 'I was lonely. Sometimes I used to feel that I was married to a kind of beautiful animated statue, a doll that smiled and wore pretty clothes and even had a vocabulary of a certain limited kind.'

'And yet you were happy?' Wexford ventured quietly.

'Did I say that? Perhaps because everyone else said I was, I grew used to telling myself I must be.'

He moved away from the bookcase and began to pace the room. It seemed for a moment that he had changed the subject when he said, 'We used to keep servants, a proper staff, but Elizabeth gave them notice. Then we had a succession of *au pair* girls, two French and one German. I think Elizabeth made a point of choosing plain girls.' He swung round, faced Wexford and looked him straight in the eyes. 'Perhaps she thought Katje was plain. Fat and coarse was the way she once described her. I suppose—I suppose I was attracted to Katje from the start, but I never did anything about it. She was a young girl and I was—well, *in loco parentis*. I told myself I thought of her as a daughter. How we delude ourselves!' He turned away his face. 'It's almost impossible for me to find the words to tell you. I . . .'

'You slept with her?' Wexford said expressionlessly.

Quentin nodded.

'The night before last?'

'That wasn't the first time. Chief Inspector, in all the sixteen years we'd been married, I'd never been unfaithful to my wife. I'd had my opportunities. What man hasn't? I loved my wife. All those years I hoped for a sign of warmth, just one spontaneous sign that she recognised me as a human being. I never gave up hoping until Katje came. Then for the first time I saw a woman who was close to me, a woman living under my roof, behaving like a woman. Perhaps not as a woman should behave. She had boy friends all over the place and she used to tell me about them. Sometimes in the evenings Elizabeth would be out, walking in the grounds or gone early to bed, and Katje would come in from some date and she'd tell me about it, giggling and laughing, talking as if the best thing in the world was to take and give pleasure.

'One night, after one of these talks, I was lying in bed,

waiting for Elizabeth to come in. I said I'd given up hope but that isn't true. I always hoped. I never remember feeling such a depth of loneliness as I felt that night. I thought I'd give everything I possessed, this house, the fortune I've amassed, if she would just come into my room and sit on the bed and talk to me.'

Again he covered his face. When he took away his hands Wexford expected to see tears on his cheeks, for he had spoken that last sentence on a sob, but he was quite calm, even relieved, it appeared, at having so nearly got it all off his chest.

'Presently I heard her come upstairs,' he said. 'I willed her to come in. I exercised all the power of my will. God knows how I stopped myself crying out to her. Her bedroom door closed and I heard her begin to run a bath. In that moment I forgot who I was, my age, my position, my duty to my wife. I put on my dressing gown and went upstairs. I knew what I was going to say to Katje, that I smelt gas and thought it was coming from her room. Of course I couldn't smell gas. All that was coming from her room was the faint sound of music from her radio.

'I knocked and she called to me to come in. She was sitting up in bed, reading a magazine. I didn't have to say anything about gas. It sounds incredible but I didn't speak a word. She smiled at me and put out her arms . . .'

Abruptly he stopped speaking. Like an old-fashioned novel, Wexford thought. If it were written down, asterisks would come at this point. Quentin Nightingale's asterisks were a sudden burning flush that threw into sharpness the whiteness of his hair and his moustache, ageing him. Fumbling for words and getting no help from the chief inspector, he said :

'There were—well, other times. Not many. There was

95

the night before last. I went up to Katje at about a quarter past eleven. I didn't know whether Elizabeth had come in. I wasn't thinking about Elizabeth. Katje and I—well, I stayed with her all night. It was Palmer walking about on the floor below that awakened me. I sensed something was wrong, so I got up and dressed and found him on the terrace.'

'A pity you didn't tell us all this before,' Wexford said, frowning.

'Put yourself in my place. Would you have?'

Wexford shrugged. 'That's beside the point.' He was at a loss to account for his feelings. An alibi had been destroyed and a more convincing one had replaced it. Normally, when this occurred, he felt anger at the wasted time, relief at progress made. His present unease wasn't normal and briefly he questioned himself. Then he knew. He was allowing himself something indefensible, personal involvement. What he felt for Quentin Nightingale was envy. Stiffly he got up.

'This will have to be corroborated, Mr Nightingale,' he said in a cold hard voice.

Pale again, Quentin said, 'I realised you would want to ask Katje. It won't embarrass her. She's strange, unique. She's . . . Oh, I'm wasting your time. I'm sorry.'

Wexford went upstairs. When he reached the first floor he paused for a second outside the door of Quentin Nightingale's bedroom and then, as he turned towards the top flight and began to mount, he heard music coming from above. It gave substance, near-reality to the unpermitted dream his envy of Nightingale had evoked. A soft, throaty voice was singing the number one song in the pop charts, singing of love. A passionate longing, bitter and savage, to recapture for one hour the youth he had lost engulfed Wexford. And suddenly growing old seemed the only tragedy of life, the pain beside which every other pain dwindled into insignificance. Mature, wise, usually philosophical, he wanted to cry aloud, 'It isn't fair!'

He came to the door and rapped on it sharply. The music should have stopped. Instead the voice welled and trembled on a vibrant note and she came to the door and let him in.

Her pink dress had white frills like a nightgown, and like a nightgown it was cut low to show milk-white half-moons and shoulders where even the bones looked soft. She smiled at him, her sea-blue eyes full of laughter. Quentin Nightingale had had all this, easily, without argument. So had the waiter at the Olive and Dove. So had how many others?

For the first time in his career he understood what impelled those men he questioned and brought to court, the men who forgot for a while chivalry and social taboo and sexual restraint, the rapists, the violators. But here there would perhaps be no need for violence, need only for a smile and an outstretched hand. *Ca me donne tant de plaisir et vous si peu de peine*. Oh, how much pleasure! He followed her into the room, and out of the dressing-table mirror their reflections marched towards them.

A young girl with her father. No, her grandfather. She was one of those people who make other people look un-finished and ill-made. In a bitter flash of illumination, Wexford saw himself as a battered bundle of old clothes. Not even middle-aged. Elderly, a grandfather.

'Please sit down, Miss Doorn,' he said, surprised that his voice was steady and sane. 'And would you turn that radio off?'

She complied, still smiling.

He felt just the same about her. The longing—perhaps

97

only a longing for rejuvenation?—was still there, but as he had turned away from the mirror he had experienced that sensation which divides the sane man from the mad. Between fantasy and reality a great gulf is fixed. And that which seems possible, reasonable, felicitous, when conjured in the mind, dissolves like smoke in a fresh wind when its object is present in words and solid flesh. He had seen her for a brief moment as a lovely thing, but a thing only, without the power of discrimination, without rights, without intelligence. Now he saw her as a young girl who saw him as he was, an old man. Inwardly his whole body seemed to laugh harshly at itself.

'I have some questions to ask you,' he said. He wished the laughter would stop so that he could control himself and mould himself into the image he desired, something between God and a robot, tempered with avuncular geniality. 'About your relations with Mr Nightingale.' Pity they had to talk about sex. But if they hadn't, perhaps the fantasy would never have grown. 'What terms are you on with him?'

'Terms?'

'You know very well what I mean,' he growled at her.

She shrugged at that, threw out her hands. 'I work for him and I live here in his house.' She pulled at a strand of hair, considered it and then poked it into her mouth. 'He is very nice and kind. I like him much.'

'He's your lover, isn't he?'

She said cautiously, not embarrassed and not at all frightened, 'He has said this?'

'Yes.'

'Oh, poor Kventin! He does not want anyone to know *at all*, must be kept very secret thing. And now you have found it out.'

'I'm afraid I must ask you to tell me about it.'

Stubbornly she stuck out her lower lip and shook her head.

'Come now. He's told me himself. You wouldn't want him to go to prison, would you?'

She opened her mouth wide. 'This is true? In England you can go to prison because you are making love?'

'Of course not!' Wexford almost shouted. 'Now listen. Mr Nightingale will not go to prison if you tell me the truth. Just tell me everything that happened between you . . . No, no, not *everything*.' An incredulous smile had widened her eyes. 'Simply how it began and so on.'

'All right.' She giggled with pure pleasure. 'This is always nice, I think, to talk about love. I like to talk of this more than anything.' Wexford could feel his angry frown, artificially assumed, pushing all his features forward. 'It is four, five weeks ago. I am in my bed and there is a knock and it is Kventin. Perhaps he is going to say the radio is too loud or I put the car away wrong, but he is saying nothing because at once I know he is coming to make love. I can see this in his face. Always I can see it in faces.'

God Almighty! thought Wexford, his soul cringing.

'So I am thinking, Why not? I am thinking how he is kind with nice manners and thin straight body and I am forgetting he is older than my father in Holland. And also I know he is lonely man married to a frigid cold woman. So we are making love very soon and all is different, for when he is in my bed he is not old any more.'

She said this triumphantly, pointing to the bed. Her favourite subject had driven away her laughter and she spoke earnestly, with concentration. 'Much much better than my friend the waiter,' she said. 'For Kventin has much experience and is knowing exactly how . . .'

'Yes, yes, I can imagine,' Wexford cut in. He drew a

deep breath. 'Miss Doorn, please spare me the lecture on sexual technique. Let us have the facts. There were other occasions?'

'Please?'

Grinding his teeth, Wexford said, 'Mr Nightingale—er, made love to you at other times?'

'*Of course*. He is liking me as much as I am liking him. The next week and the next week and then the night before last.'

'Go on.'

'But I have told you. I go out with my friend and the unkind man will not let us go into the hotel. My friend want us to go in the car, but this I will not do. This is not nice. Kventin would not do this. I am coming back home and I am thinking perhaps Kventin come up and make love with me. And I am wishing and wishing when he knocks at the door and then I am happy. We are both very very happy.'

'How long did he stay with you?'

'All the night,' said Katje airily. 'I tell him that just before I come in I see Mrs Nightingale go into the wood and he is saying very very sadly, She does not want me, she has never wanted me. But I say, *I* want you, Kventin, and so he stay all the night. But he is going away very early in the morning because he is hearing the old gardener man walk about. So I lie in my bed alone, thinking perhaps I shall not see my friend the waiter any more, but go only with Kventin, and then I too am getting up to see why the old gardener man is in the house. There, now I have told it all!'

Wexford was silent for a moment. Then he said, 'At what time did you see Mrs Nightingale cross the road?'

'Two minutes after eleven,' said Katje promptly.

'And at what time did Mr Nightingale pay you this

nocturnal visit?' She looked at him, her blue eyes naive and enquiring. 'I mean, come to your room?'

'Fifteen minutes after eleven. I come in, I go straight to bed.'

'How can you be so sure of the time?'

'I am wearing my new watch and always I am looking at it.' She waved her left wrist at him. The watch had a dial two inches in diameter fastened to a wide strap of pink and purple patent leather. 'This my friend is giving me for my birthday and all the time I look at it.' She glanced up at him under long dark gold lashes. 'You are angry with me?'

'No, no, I'm not angry, Miss Doorn.'

'I am wishing that you will call me Katje, please.'

'All right, Katje,' said Wexford, far from displeased.

Suddenly correct and very Continental, she held out her hand to him. Her fingers were soft and warm. 'Because,' she said, 'you resemble my old uncle in Friesland who is sometimes kind and sometimes cross like you.' She wagged a forefinger at him.

God, he thought, still smarting from that last thrust, how pretty that mannerism is now and how dreadful it will be when she's forty. And will she still chew her hair? In such reflections a little comfort lies.

'Now,' she said, her head on one side, 'I think I will go down and dust Kventin's study.'

9

BURDEN listened with disdain and incredulity to Wexford's condensed and to some extent expurgated account of his two interviews. It aroused in him a cold angry disgust. Anyone who knew the chief inspector less well than he might imagine Wexford to be quite smitten by the charms—invisible to Burden—of that immoral Dutch girl.

'I cannot see,' he said, standing by the window in Wexford's office and disentangling a knot in the string of the venetian blind, 'why you suppose this story of theirs lets them out at all.' He straightened the string and wound it round its hooks in a figure of eight. Burden liked everything to be neat and shipshape even in someone else's domain. 'On the contrary, they could have been in it together. You've only got that girl's word that he—er, joined her at eleven-fifteen. It could have been later. Of course she'd back him up.'

'Oh? Why would she? Just what would she get out of being an accessory to the murder of her employer's wife?'

Burden stared at him. Really, the old man was almost simple at times.

'Get out of it? Marriage with Nightingale, of course.'

'Don't keep saying "of course". It's far from of course. And leave that blind alone. Sometimes I think you've got a compulsion complex, always tidying everything up. Listen to me, Mike. You've got to bring your ideas up to date a bit. You may be only thirty-six but you're so dead old-fashioned it isn't true. First of all I want you to know that I believe Nightingale. I believe his story because some instinct in me recognises the truth when I hear it. I don't believe he's capable of violence. If he thought his wife had a lover—if he cared, which is more to the point —he'd divorce her. Secondly, Katje Doorn isn't a kind of Lady Macbeth. She's a very contemporary young woman who is enjoying life enormously and not the least of what she enjoys is plenty of anxiety-free sex.'

Burden went pink at that and blinked his eyes. He tried to put on a sophisticated expression and failed.

'What reason have we to suppose she wants to marry Nightingale?' Wexford went on. 'He's an old man to her,' he said urbanely. 'She said as much. And for all her immorality, as you'd put it, she's a nice normal girl who'd recoil in horror from the thought of taking into her bed a man fresh from murdering his wife. Mike, we've got to change our whole pattern of thinking in these domestic murder cases. Times have changed. Young women don't look on marriage as the be-all and end-all of existence any more. Girls like Katje won't help kill a man's wife just so that he can make honest women of them. They don't think they're *dishonest* women just because they're not virgins. And as for Katje wanting him for his money, I don't think she's given much thought to money yet. That may come later. At present she's out for a good time without any worry.'

'I sometimes wonder,' said Burden like an old man, 'what the world is coming to.'

'Let the world look after itself. We'll concentrate on our own small corner of it. We made a pattern, Mike, and now we've destroyed it. What next? There are two lines to pursue, it seems to me. Who was Mrs Nightingale's lover? Who had access to that torch?'

'You've had a lab report on it?'

Wexford nodded. 'There were traces of blood in the threads of the base screw and the lamp screw, and under the switch. The blood was of the same group as Mrs Nightingale's and it's a rare group, AB Negative. There's no doubt the torch was the weapon.'

'Well, who did have access to it? Who could have replaced it this morning?'

Wexford counted them off on his fingers. 'Nightingale, Katje, Mrs Cantrip, Will Palmer, Sean Lovell, Georgina Villiers—oh, and Lionel Marriott. Quite a list. We might also include Villiers, as Georgina could have replaced it for him. Now what about Sean? He's confessed to an admiration for Mrs Nightingale. He's young and hot-headed, therefore jealous. It may not have been he she went to meet but he could have seen her with that person. His alibi is hopeless. He had access to the torch; his garden gives directly on to the forest.'

'She was old enough to be his mother,' said Burden.

Wexford laughed, a raucous bray. 'My God, Mike, you don't know what life's about, do you? It's because he was twenty and she forty that he *would* have an affair with her. Like . . .' He paused, then went on with apparent detachment, 'Like middle-aged men and young girls. It happens all the time. Didn't you ever fancy any of your mother's friends?'

'Certainly not!' said Burden, outraged. 'My mother's friends were like aunts to me. I called them all auntie. Still do, come to that. What's so funny?'

'You,' said Wexford, 'and if I didn't laugh I'd go round the twist.'

Burden was used to this but still he was very offended.

It seemed unfair to him, a sad sign of the times, that a man should be laughed at because he had high principles and a decent concept of what life should be. He gave a thin dry cough and said :

'I shall go and have another talk with your favourite suspect, young Lovell.'

'You do that.' Wexford looked at his watch. 'I have a date at four.' He grinned. 'A date with someone who is going to enlighten me further as to certain past histories.'

Wexford parked a hundred yards up the road from the school gates, well behind the cars of parents waiting for eleven-year-olds. A crocodile of cricketers in green-stained white came across from the playing fields as the clock on the school tower struck four. If they were punctual in nothing else, King's pupils were punctual in getting out of school. As the last chime died away, they poured through the gates, laughing, shoving each other, paying no attention to the kerb drill with which Wexford had used to believe they were thoroughly indoctrinated by the road safety officer. Only the supercilious sixth-formers walked sedately, lighting cigarettes when they reached the shadow of the overhanging trees.

Denys Villiers came out in his dark blue Anglia. He sounded his horn repetitively to clear boys out of the road, then, putting his head out of the window, shouted something Wexford couldn't catch. The tone of his voice was enough. Wexford had the notion that if the man had had a whip he would have used it. He turned his head and saw Marriott trotting out of the main gate. When the little man had passed the car he wound down the window and hissed :

' "A frightful fiend doth close behind you tread!" '

Marriott jumped, collected himself and smiled.

'A very overrated poem, I've always thought,' he said.

'I daresay. I didn't come here to discuss poetry. You were going to give me the slip, weren't you?'

Marriott came round the bonnet and got into the car.

'I must admit I was. I thought you'd give me a lecture for going up to the Manor this morning. Now please don't, there's a dear. I've had a most exhausting afternoon introducing *Paradise Lost* to the Lower Fifth and I really can't stand any more.'

' "The mind," ' quoted Wexford, ' "is in its own place and in itself can make a heaven of hell, a hell of heaven." '

'Yes, very clever. I'm different. Mine makes a hell of hell. Do let's rush, ducky, and get ourselves huge drinks. I suppose you'll want me to go on with the next instalment on the way.'

'I can't wait,' said Wexford, starting the car and moving out into the stream.

'Where had I got to?'

'Villiers' first wife.'

'June,' said Marriott. 'She didn't like me. Oh dear, no. She said I'd be more use teaching in a Borstal institution. The first time she went to the Manor d'you know what she said to Quentin? "I call it scandalous," she said, "two people living by themselves in this barrack. It ought to be converted into a mental hospital." Poor Quen didn't like that at all. His beloved house! But that was little June all over. She had a sociology degree and she'd been some kind of probation officer.

'She and Denys had a dreadful flat over the pet foods shop in Queen Street. You know the place I mean. I only went there once and that was enough. The stink of putrefying horseflesh, my dear, and June's funny friends all over the place. Crowds of them there every evening, all very earnest and wanting to put the world right. Banning the Bomb was the thing in those days, you know, and June used to hold meetings about it in their flat, that and famine relief before famine relief was even fashionable. She was the original demonstrator, was June. Whenever there's a rumpus in Grosvenor Square I look very closely at the pictures, I can tell you, because I'm positive I'm going to see her face there one of these days.'

'She's not dead, then?' Wexford said as they emerged into the High Street.

'Good God, no. Denys divorced her or she divorced him. I forget which. Heaven knows why they got married in the first place. They had nothing in common. She didn't like Quen and Elizabeth and she took a very dim view of Denys going up to the Manor so much. Associating with reactionary elements, she called it.'

'If he didn't care for his sister why did he go so much?'

'Well, you see, he and Quen got on together like a house on fire from the word go,' said Marriott as Wexford pulled into the centre of the road to take the right-hand turn. 'Quen was thrilled to bits finding he'd got an up-and-coming writer for a brother-in-law and I suppose he saw himself in the light of Denys's patron.' The car moved slowly down the alley and Wexford pulled up in front of the white flower-decked house. 'Anyway, Denys must have complained to him about how impossible it was to work in his home atmosphere, and Quen offered him the Old House to write in. Don't let's sit out here, Reg, I'm dying of thirst.'

The rooms where the party had been held still smelt strongly of cigar smoke. Someone had tidied up and washed all the dishes. Hypatia, probably, Wexford thought, as Marriott flung open all the windows.

'Now then, Reg, the cocktail hour, as they say. A little

early perhaps, but everything's early in the country, don't you find? What's it to be? Whisky? Gin?'

'I'd rather have a cup of tea,' said Wexford.

'Would you? How odd. All right, I'll put the kettle on. I must say, Hypatia has left everything very nice. I must remember to say a word when next I see her.'

Wexford followed him into the kitchen. 'She doesn't live here, then?'

'Oh, no. I shouldn't care for that at all.' Marriott wrinkled his nose distastefully. 'Once have them permanently in and you can't call your soul your own.' He gave Wexford a sidelong very sly look. 'Besides, there's safety in numbers.'

Wexford laughed. 'Quite a devil with the ladies, aren't you, Lionel?'

'I have my successes,' said Marriott modestly. He put three spoonfuls of Earl Grey into the teapot and poured the boiling water on daintily. 'Shall I go on with the story?'

'Please.'

'Well, as I said, June didn't at all care for Denys working at the Manor. He was up there most evenings nattering with Quen, you see, and every day in the holidays to work. She thought he ought to be out with her, waving banners and writing things on walls. So finally she walked out on him.'

'Leaving him to his *ménage à trois*?'

'What a funny way of putting it. Still, no doubt, there was a triangular element there, but not an isosceles triangle. Poor Elizabeth was definitely the unequal angle. It always used to fascinate me when I went up there to see Denys and Quen utterly immersed in each other, books, books, books, my dear, and a positively ringing exchange of Wordsworth quotes, the two of them groan-

108

ing that they had thoughts which do often lie too deep for tears. And all the time poor Elizabeth sat there reading *Vogue* and not a word to say for herself.'

'I daresay you found something to chat to her about,' said Wexford, drinking his tea. 'I never met anyone who knew so much about—what shall I say?—current trivia?'

'Really, Reg, you *are* unkind. I'll have you know, Elizabeth wasn't at all an empty-headed woman. Just as intelligent as Denys in her way.'

'That's not what he says, but let it pass.'

'Why are we sitting out here, anyway? I never could abide kitchens and I'm pining for my gin. Good, the cigar smoke's cleared.'

Marriott fetched his drink and pulled two chairs up to the open french windows. His small walled garden was full of butterflies, drinking from the buddleia flowers and sunning themselves with spread wings on the stones. Wexford sat where he could feel the warmth of the precious September sun that would soon be gone. It made him feel lazy and he told himself sternly to keep his mind alert.

'So Villiers spent a good deal of his time at the Manor, did he?' he said.

'Believe me, you couldn't set foot in the place without finding him there. And as if that wasn't enough to make him and Quen heartily sick of each other, he used to go away on holiday with them too.'

'That must have been hard on Mrs Nightingale, especially as they excluded her from their conversations. Just what were her interests, Lionel?'

Marriott bit his lip and seemed to cogitate. 'Let me see,' he said with the air of someone dredging in the depths. 'Well, she took an active part in county life, you know, organising things and sitting on committees. And she spent hours every day making herself look lovely. She did the flowers and a bit of gardening . . .'

'Is that so?' Wexford interrupted. 'In the hothouse maybe with young Sean Lovell?'

'What can you mean, dear old boy?'

'As one of Wordsworth's contemporaries put it:

' "What men call gallantry and gods adultery,
    Is much more common where the climate's sultry." '

Marriott smiled, opening his eyes wide. 'So that's the way the wind's blowing, is it?'

'Well, she wasn't having secret meetings in the forest with old Sir George Larkin-Smith, was she? Or the rector of Myfleet or Will Palmer? Unless it was you, Lionel.'

'I wondered when you were going to ask me that.' Marriott stretched languorously in the sunshine and laughed. 'But no, it wasn't. And if you're serious about this, Reg, Hypatia will tell you where I was. Mind you, I'm not saying I didn't wish I'd had the opportunity . . .'

'Maybe you even tried your chances?'

'Maybe I did.'

This time it was Wexford's turn to laugh. 'So we come back to Sean Lovell, don't we?'

'She was fond of Sean,' said Marriott. 'I met her once coming out of the record shop here in the High Street. She'd been buying the number one pop single in the charts. "I must keep up with my little song-bird," she said. "Really, he's the only true Nightingale in Myfleet." Quite witty, I thought. Elizabeth was no fool.'

'An extraordinary remark to make,' said Wexford.

'Oh, I don't know. You read too much into things, my dear. All you policemen are terribly salacious. Sean used to stand under Elizabeth's windows and serenade her. I suppose she was flattered and it made her feel young. It was a case of heroine worship on one side and a sort of flattered acceptance on the other.'

'Let's get back to Villiers,' said Wexford. 'But first how about another cup of tea for a poor old salacious policeman?'

Myfleet was a pretty village even on a winter's day. Now, bathed in mellow sunshine, it lay in its hollow beneath the forest like a sleeping beauty. This afternoon it seemed unpeopled; only the flowers in cottage gardens stood out in the open enjoying the sun.

Burden drove to the Kingsmarkham end of the village and decided to walk the rest of the way. It was a day made for strolling, for appreciating the scent of ripening fruit and admiring the great multi-petalled dahlias, raised for a flower show or a harvest festival.

But he had been wrong in thinking the village totally deserted. Now, as he approached the Manor, he noticed Mrs Lovell leaning over the gate of her disreputable cottage, talking to a swarthy man in a cap who carried two dead and bleeding rabbits over his arm. The shifty looks he was giving the Manor—though probably the natural accompaniment to his conversation, concerned as it must be with the only topic currently of interest in Myfleet—gave him the air of a poacher. Mrs Lovell encouraged him with peals of uninhibited ringing laughter.

He found Sean in the Old House, unloading apples from a basket on to one of the racks. They were pale red and gold, Beauty of Bath, their skins striped and shiny like old silk. The boy was whistling but he stopped abruptly when Burden came in.

'Come here often, do you?' Burden asked softly. 'Is this where you used to meet Mrs Nightingale?'

'*Me?*' He gave Burden a sullen glare, sat down on a stack of silver-birch logs and began to roll a cigarette. 'It'd be a help,' he said, 'if I knew what you was getting at. No, I don't come here often. Fact is I never set foot in here since April.' He cocked a thumb at the tunnel staircase. 'On account of *him* being up there.' Scowling, he lit his cigarette. 'Me and old Palmer, we've got strict orders not to come in here disturbing him, see?'

'You go into the garden room, though, don't you? You go to sweep it out. Ever borrowed a torch, Lovell, to light your way when you went to Mrs Nightingale in the forest?'

'Me?' Sean said again. 'Are you off your nut?' His cigarette had gone out. He re-lit it, blinking when the flame caught the ragged paper and flared. Perhaps it provided a flash of mental as well as physical illumination, for he said, 'You trying to make out I was carrying on with Mrs Nightingale? You *are* a nut and a dirty-minded nut at that.'

'All right, that'll do,' said Burden, mortally offended. The supreme injustice of the accusation wounded him more than the insolence. 'Come now,' he said, keeping his temper, 'you were on very friendly terms with her.'

'Look,' said Sean, 'if you must know, she was interested in helping me with my career.'

'Helping you do the *gardening*?'

The boy's face flushed deeply. Unknowingly, Burden had returned thrust for thrust. 'Gardening's not my career,' Sean said bitterly. 'That's just a stop-gap, just to fill in time till I get on with my real work.'

'And what might that be?'

'Music,' said Sean. 'The Scene. Up there in London.' Again he cocked a thumb, this time northwards. His face had grown rapt and, like Dick Whittington, he seemed to see a vision, a city paved with gold. 'I've got to get there.' His voice shook. 'I know it all, see, like it was recorded in my head. I could tell you the way all the charts were, right back for years. I could pass exams.' He clenched his hands and there shone in his eyes the fanaticism of the religious mystic. 'There's not one of them D.J.s knows half of what I do.' Suddenly he shouted at Burden, 'Take that grin off your face! You're just ignorant like the rest of them, like my old lady with her men and her booze. Mrs Nightingale was the only one as understood and she's dead.' He drew a dirty sleeve across his eyes, the artist *manqué* that the world persists in treating as an artisan.

Gentler this time, Burden said, 'What was Mrs Nightingale going to do for you?'

'There was this bloke in London she knew,' Sean said, muttering now. 'He was with the B.B.C. and she promised faithful she'd mention my name. Maybe for singing, maybe for a D.J. In a small way for a start.' he added humbly. 'You got to start in a small way.' He sighed. 'I don't know what'll happen to me now.'

'Best stick to your gardening, grow up a bit and get rid of some of these fancy ideas,' Burden said. Sean's glance of pure hatred riled him. 'Let's forget your ambitions for a moment, shall we? Why did you tell the chief inspector you were watching a television programme when that programme wasn't even shown?'

Sean looked peevish rather than frightened at being caught out in his lie. 'I had been watching the telly,' he said, 'but I got fed up. My old lady had got her bloke in for the evening, that Alf Tawney. Grinning at me, they was, and mocking me on account of me watching Pop Panel.' Sean clenched his fingers over an apple until his knuckles whitened. 'One fellow after another my mum's had ever since I was a kid and all they've ever wanted is to get me out of the way. I tell you, when I was about ten I saw my mum with one of them men of hers, kissing and pawing each other and I picked up the carving knife and went for her. I'd have killed her, I would, only the bloke got the knife away and hit me. I'd have killed her,' he said fiercely, and then something he saw in Burden's eyes silenced him. Awkwardly he said, 'I don't care any more, not about her, only I get—I get fed up.' His fingers relaxed and he dropped the apple into the rack. Burden saw that his nails had pierced the rosy skin, leaving deep juicy wounds.

He said smoothly, 'It seems to me you let your emotions get the better of you.'

'I said I was ten, didn't I? I'm not like that now. I wouldn't lay a finger on her whatever she did.'

'I take it,' said Burden, as Sean wiped his sticky hand on his jeans, 'I take it you're referring to your mother?'

'Who else'd I be referring to?'

Burden shrugged lightly. 'So you got "fed up" with your mother and Alf Tawney. Where did you go?'

'Down to my shed,' said Sean. 'I sat there all alone, thinking.' He sighed heavily, got up and, turning his back on Burden, resumed his unloading of the apples. 'Just thinking and—and listening.' The bright fruit, bruised by his hands, rolled into the rack. Very softly he began whistling again. His face had coloured as vivid a red as the apples. Getting up to leave, Burden wondered why.

'Denys always went on holiday with them,' said Marriott. 'With both of them, I mean. But two years ago he had to go with Elizabeth alone. Quen caught the measles, poor thing. So humiliating. Elizabeth told me she absolutely dreaded being stuck with Denys in Dubrovnik, but Quen said he'd never forgive them if they stayed at home on his account, so they had to put up with it.

'Well, they must have rowed the whole time because they both looked rotten when they got back and there was a distinct coldness between Denys and Quen all the following winter and Denys stopped going up to the Manor. Then, one day, in the June of the summer before last, I was up at the Manor when in walked Denys. "You are a stranger," Quen said, but I could tell he was overjoyed. "I only came," said Denys, "to tell you I can't go to Rome with you next month. I've promised the Head I'll be one of the escorts to the school party."

' "You?" I almost screamed. "You must be out of your mind." I mean, it's a joke at school, the lengths the staff go to get out of it. "You'd pass up lovely Rome," I said, "for the lousy old Costa Brava?" "I'm going," he said, "it's all fixed." You should have seen poor Quen's face. He did his best to work on Denys but it was no use. He was adamant.'

'What about this year, Lionel?'

'He was married by then, wasn't he? He met Georgina on the Costa Brava, but I'll come to that later. No, this year they went off to Bermuda by themselves, and I think that secretly they were only too glad to have got rid of old misery face. Elizabeth said as much to me when I went up there to witness her will and ...'

'Her what?' said Wexford slowly. 'Did you say her will?'

10

'WHY didn't I tell you that my wife had made a will? Frankly, Chief Inspector, because I'd forgotten all about it.' Quentin Nightingale had seemed bewildered at first, but now he smiled a slightly derisory smile as if at someone making a mountain out of a molehill. He had negotiated his own mountain and descended it with only a few bruises. Why bother him now with trivialities? 'I don't for a moment suppose it's legal. It was just a piece of nonsense my wife took into her head, you know.'

'No, I don't know,' said Wexford, refusing the offer of a leather chair and standing instead against the tall bookcase. 'I imagine that people in your position have their solicitors draw up their wills for them. Who is your solicitor, Mr Nightingale?'

'But no solicitor was involved. I told you it was just a piece of nonsense. Really, I can't think how you came to hear of it.' He paused expectantly, but when it became clear to him that Wexford didn't intend to enlighten him, he said, with an edge of impatience to his voice, 'I'd better tell you about it.'

'I wish you would,' said Wexford, leaning his head against the hard smooth bindings of Motley's *Rise of the Dutch Republic*.

'Well, it was last summer. My wife and I had decided on Bermuda for our holiday and naturally we intended to fly. Although my wife had flown before—when we went to America seven years ago—she didn't like flying and we usually went on holiday by sea and car.'

'She was afraid to fly?'

'Oh, come. "Afraid" is putting it too strongly.'

'If she made a will,' Wexford retorted, 'I suppose it was because she thought she might die. "Afraid" isn't too strong a word to use about the anticipation of death.'

'You're looking at it much too dramatically,' Quentin said with exasperation. 'She was a little anxious but she was quite prepared to joke about it. This will was a sort of joke. I told you I never took it seriously.'

He stopped talking and listened for a second. By straining his ears Wexford too could just hear the sound of Katje's radio from far above them. Then Quentin's eyes met his and the other man flushed slightly. He went on in quick impatient tones. 'One day she said she was making a will and I saw her scribbling something on a sheet of paper. I'm afraid I didn't even look at it. I took it for one of those romantic fads very feminine women go in for. I remember my mother,' he said, going off at a tangent, 'when my youngest sister was born, going and having her photograph taken to be a last memento for my father in case she died in childbirth, and writing farewell letters for all her other children. But of course she didn't die any more than Elizabeth . . .'

'But your wife did die, Mr Nightingale,' Wexford said quietly.

Quentin looked down and clasped his hands together. 'Yes . . . About this will, I took it for nonsense, as I've said. I doubt if it was even witnessed.'

'One person witnessed it, at any rate,' said Wexford. 'Lionel Marriott.'

Quentin raised his eyes and there was genuine surprise in them.

'Mr Nightingale, I can't just let this go by. What became of this piece of paper your wife was "scribbling" on?'

'She gave it to me and asked me to put it in my safe.'

'And did you?'

'Well, yes, I did. Elizabeth insisted on my doing so in her presence. Oh, it was very silly but I didn't want to distress her.'

'Is it still there?'

'I suppose so,' Quentin said wonderingly. 'I told you, I forgot all about it and I imagine Elizabeth did too when we got back safe and sound.'

Wexford said heavily, 'I'll trouble you to open that safe now, sir, if you please.'

Eyeing Wexford as if he thought he was dealing with a lunatic who needed to be humoured, Quentin lifted down from the study wall a small Stubbs oil of a phaeton and pair. Behind it, set into the wall, was a steel door. Murmuring the combination under his breath, Quentin opened it to reveal a space about the size of a large biscuit tin. The safe contained a neat stack of papers which Wexford supposed to be share certificates and personal documents, and several leather jewel boxes. Quentin took out a handful of papers. He leafed through them and then, his expression still amused and derisive, held out to Wexford a long brown envelope.

'It's in there,' he said.

'May I?' Wexford's tone left no room for refusal. He slit open the envelope and drew out a sheet of expensive blue writing paper headed with the Manor address. The paper was covered with a bold, rather masculine handwriting. Wexford turned it over, glanced at the foot of the reverse side and said in his strong official voice, 'This is a perfectly legal will, sir, none the less valid and binding because it was not made on a will form or in the presence of a lawyer.'

'Good heavens!' said Quentin. He sat down, leaving the safe door open.

'It is witnessed by—let me see—Myrtle Annie Cantrip and Lionel Hepburn Marriott and correctly signed by your wife. You'd find yourself up against a great deal of trouble if you tried to contest it.'

'But I don't want to contest it.'

'I think you'd better read it before you commit yourself, Mr Nightingale.'

'What does it say?' Quentin's face was now utterly bewildered, the smile wiped away. 'Will you read it me, Mr Wexford?'

'Very well.' At last Wexford sat down. He cleared his throat and read in the same expressionless voice:

' "This is the last will and testament of me, Elizabeth Frances Nightingale, born Villiers, being of sound mind. This is my last will and revokes all other wills made by me." ' Here Mrs Nightingale's knowledge of legal language had apparently dried up, for she continued in a more natural manner, interspersed, however, with occasional officialese. ' "I leave all my money, including the money my husband invested for me, to Sean Arthur Lovell, of 2 Church Cottages, Myfleet, in the county of Sussex, in the hope that he will use it in the furtherance of his ambition...." '

'Good heavens!' Quentin said again. 'Good heavens!'

' "... and all the personal jewellery I possess to my sister-in-law, Georgina Villiers, of 55 Kingsmarkham Road, Clusterwell ..." ' Here Wexford paused and raised his eyebrows. ' "... so that she may indulge her love of *adornment, although as a virtuous woman her price is above rubies." '*

'Elizabeth wrote that?' Quentin asked in a hollow voice.

'Yes, sir.'

They were both surprised, Wexford thought, but probably for different reasons. For his part he was astonished that the woman whom her brother had described as frivolous and empty-headed should have had the wit to compose it and the knowledge to give it that malevolent bite. Quentin's astonishment stemmed perhaps from the malevolence alone. He had gone pale.

'Is that all?' he asked.

'That's all. How much money did your wife leave, sir?'

'Oh, nothing to speak of.' Quentin forced a laugh. 'She was overdrawn, as a matter of fact, on her private account. There's about three hundred pounds that I invested for her years ago.'

'Mmhm. I'm sure you won't grudge that to young Lovell. Is something troubling you, sir?'

'No, well, I . . .'

'Mrs Villiers,' said Wexford thoughtfully, 'is a lady who seems fond of jewellery, as your wife—er, pointed out. Let us hope there are a few nice pieces for her.'

'A few nice pieces!' Quentin suddenly sprang to his feet. 'My wife's jewellery is in those boxes.' He plunged his hands into the safe. 'At a rough estimate,' he said, 'I'd value it at thirty thousand pounds.'

Wexford had seen too many precious stones to be dazzled by this small but brilliant collection. He was, in any case, not given to gasping, and his face was calm with a hint of taciturnity as he watched Quentin open the three boxes.

One was of white leather, one of green and the third of teak inlaid with onyx. Quentin had placed them on his writing desk and lifted the lids to disclose more boxes, tiny caskets for rings and ear-rings, longer cases for bracelets and necklaces.

Quentin took out one of the rings, a diamond half-hoop, set in platinum, and held it to the light.

'It was her engagement ring,' he said. 'She wore it sometimes, when,' he said, his voice growing hoarse, 'I particularly asked her to.' He looked at Wexford. 'Perhaps I could buy it from Georgina.'

'Your wife was fond of her?'

'I don't know,' Quentin said hopelessly, pushing the ring back into its velvet bed. 'I never thought much about it. She must have been . . . And yet she can't have been, can she? You couldn't be fond of someone and leave that cruel message for them. I don't understand it.'

'We know Mrs Nightingale had a strong dislike for her brother. Perhaps that dislike extended itself to his wife.'

Quentin closed the ring box. 'The idea seems to have got about,' he said carefully, 'that my wife and her brother were at daggers drawn.'

Wexford raised his eyebrows. 'It isn't true?'

'It seems strange for me, her husband, to say this, but really I don't know. Denys never found fault with her to me and as for Elizabeth . . . Well, she never tried to stop him coming to the house, although it's true she did sometimes say rather spiteful things to me about him when we were alone. And yet, you know, I used to see her look— well, almost compassionately at him when we were all three together. I never saw signs of any real hatred.'

'Perhaps you're not a man who probes much into other people's motives and emotions.'

'I can't be, can I?' Quentin said sadly. 'Otherwise I'd

have seen that Elizabeth didn't enjoy Georgina's company and I'd have . . . I'd have realised she was going secretly into the forest at night. No, I suppose Elizabeth and Denys did have a genuine dislike of each other and I hadn't the perception to see it. Or I didn't want to.' He spoke quietly now and with slight embarrassment. 'When you love people you want them to love each other and you convince yourself they do. I hate the idea of malicious stories going round that there was some sort of feud.'

There was a short silence and then Wexford said, 'Back to this will, sir. You evidently didn't know of your wife's friendship with Sean Lovell?'

'I knew she took a maternal interest in him. We had no children of our own. She asked me to get a friend of mine at the B.B.C. to hear him sing and I wasn't too keen, but I will now. It's the least thing—and the last thing—I can do for her.'

'Forgive me—you never suspected the interest might be more than maternal?'

Quentin screwed up his face in distaste, shaking his head violently. 'Oh God,' he said, 'there can't have been, but if there was . . . I've no right to sit in judgment, not while I and Katje . . . Mr Wexford, I don't understand all these undercurrents. I don't understand any of it.'

'Nor do I,' said Wexford grimly.

Meanwhile Burden was making discoveries of his own. Emerging from the Old House and from the gate to the courtyard which surrounded it, he encountered Mrs Cantrip coming from the kitchen garden with a bunch of parsley in her hand.

'Oh, you startled me, sir,' she said. 'You walk so soft. Would you like a cup of tea?'

'Getting a bit late for that, isn't it?' said Burden look-ing at his watch and seeing that it was half past five. 'When do you knock off, anyway?'

'Supposed to be at four and that's a fact, but we're all at sixes and sevens these days, don't know where we are. Come on, sir, do. It'll do you good and there's Will wait-ing to have a word with you.'

'What does he want me for?' Burden walked towards the house with her.

'He wouldn't say, sir. Something about a scarf, I reckon.'

In the kitchen Will Palmer sat at the table next to the man Burden had observed earlier talking over her gate to Mrs Lovell. They were drinking tea from cups of dark glazed earthenware. The other man's presence in the kitchen was explained by the two rabbits, four wood pigeons and a basket of eggs that filled a checkered counter top.

As soon as he saw Burden, Palmer got to his feet.

'Got something to show you, governor.'

'Well?' Burden took his teacup from Mrs Cantrip, removing it as far as possible from the dead game.

'This is it.' With an air of triumph, Palmer produced from under the table a wet polythene bag, its neck fastened with garden twine. Burden undid the string and pulled out a piece of material. It was dampish but not wet and it was still plainly recognisable as a silk scarf. The design on it was *art nouveau*, a stylised exquisite pattern of gold leaves on a primrose ground. Across the centre of the scarf was a long brown stain. Burden frowned.

'Where did you find this?'

'In a hole in the oak way down Cleever's Vale.'

'And where might Cleever's Vale be?'

123

Palmer's face registered a stunned astonishment. It was evidently inconceivable to him that anyone, especially a policeman, should be ignorant of something that to Myfleet was as much a part of the scene as the forest itself.

Mrs Cantrip said impatiently, 'It's part of the estate, sir, part of the park, the bit you come to first when you're coming this way from Kingsmarkham.'

'I was by way of clearing that old fungus from the oak,' Palmer said, recovering from his astonishment. 'Then I come on this hole, see? Likely an owl made it . . .'

'Squirrel,' said the other man laconically, wiping his mouth. His face was very dark with a good day's growth of beard.

'Or a squirrel, as I was going to say, Alf,' said Palmer, ruffled. 'An owl or a squirrel, it being over-large for a woodpecker.'

'Spare me the natural history.'

'All right, governor, no need to get sarky.' Palmer's expression gained a new importance as the door to the garden opened and Sean came in to take his place at the table. 'This hole would be about six feet up, I reckon,' Palmer continued. 'Level with the top of my head, it was.'

'Rot,' said the swarthy man.

Palmer glared at him, but, apparently deciding that the interjection referred to the cause of the hole rather than to the nonsensical content of his remarks, went on, 'This old fungus were all round the hole. What we call the Oyster Mushroom, sir, on account of his cap looks like an oyster, see? The Poor Man's Oyster we calls him in these parts and mighty good fried he is, I can tell you.'

'Stewed.'

'Or stewed, Alf,' said Palmer more graciously. 'To cut a

124

long story short, I stuck me hand in this hole and that's what I found, what's in that bag.'

'In the bag? Or did you put it in?'

'It wasn't in no bag, governor. Just rolled up and stuffed down the hole.'

'Have you ever seen it before?'

'Of course he has,' said Mrs Cantrip. 'It belonged to poor Mrs Nightingale. She used to wear it for a headscarf like when she went out walking.' She bent over the scarf and recoiled sharply. 'Would that be her blood, sir?'

'I'm afraid so.'

Sean Lovell jerked to his feet.

'Going to be sick!' he shouted. Moving faster than Burden would have believed possible in a woman of her age, Mrs Cantrip flung open the garden door.

'Not in my kitchen, you're not!'

With the unmoved scowl of the English rustic, the old gardener and the purveyor of game watched him stagger out, then listened with a quickened though still apathetic interest to the sounds of retching. Alf, hitherto monosyllabic, made what was for him a long speech.

'Old stomach complaint,' he said. 'No guts.' He laughed. 'Wants to be a bleeding pop singer. Mental, I reckon he is.'

Mrs Cantrip took his cup and saucer and put them in the dishwasher. When the man made no move to go, she said briskly, 'I'll say good night, then, Alf. And we don't want no more eggs till Monday.'

Leaving the Manor by the front and back doors respectively, Wexford and Burden encountered each other in the village street. There they exchanged news and were about to embark on one of their acrimonious but valuable

125

discussions when Mrs Cantrip, puffed with running, caught them up.

'Oh, sir,' she said to Burden, 'I *am* glad I caught you. I want to apologise, like, for the way those two went on, old Will and that Alf. Will's that talkative and as for Alf Tawney . . . He's not got the manners he was born with. Would I be in your way if I was to walk along with you a bit?'

'Not at all, Mrs Cantrip,' said Wexford graciously. He stopped by the official car and told Bryant to drive it back to the station. 'Who's Alf Tawney?'

'Just a fellow we get our veg and chickens and such from, sir. He lives in a caravan on his ground at Cluster-well.' Mrs Cantrip's face closed into a kind of prudish blankness, just as Burden's own sometimes did when a subject he would have described as 'suggestive' was about to be discussed. 'You wouldn't be interested in Alf,' she said primly.

'I don't know,' said Wexford. 'Anyone associated with Mrs Nightingale interests us, even if he only supplied her with vegetables.'

'Mrs Nightingale never associated with him, sir,' said Mrs Cantrip, shocked. 'If she'd ever heard of him it was only through that Sean.' She sighed, as if coming to a painful decision. 'Well, you may as well know, seeing as it's common gossip and the scandal of the village. Alf's carrying on with Sean's mother.'

'Dear me,' said Wexford. 'That's bad.'

'There's some as don't blame Alf, him being a widow man since his boy was twelve and what with no one to cook his meals and see to his things. It's her I blame. For, like the Bible says, sir, woman is a temptation to man and no two ways about it.'

'True,' said Wexford with feeling.

'Mind you, I don't care for that Sean myself, but there's none as 'd deny Mrs Lovell's neglected him shameful. You might say he's never had no proper mother.'

'And Mrs Nightingale never had a son.'

Mrs Cantrip turned her face up to him. Once more, as they approached ground she had decided must be forbidden, she looked guarded and resentful. 'That Sean wouldn't have dared think of Madam in that way,' she said. 'There *are* limits. Besides, Mrs Nightingale—well, she looked so young and lovely, sir. She didn't like people knowing her age. It went to my heart sometimes the way she wanted Sean and Catcher to feel she was the same age as what they were. And when Sean said—it wasn't respectful, sir, but he doesn't know no better—when he said she wasn't square and once when he said she was nicer to look at than any lady for miles round, she looked so pleased and happy.'

'He is a very handsome young man,' said Wexford.

'I can't see it myself, sir, but tastes differ. Well, here's where I live, so I'll say good night. And I hope you've taken no offence at the way them two went on, sir.'

They watched her go into the freshly painted white cottage whose patchwork-quilt garden was one of those Burden had earlier admired. She gathered into her arms a cushiony yellow cat which had strolled out to meet her, and closed the front door.

'The poor neglected boy,' said Wexford thoughtfully, 'inherits three hundred pounds under Mrs Nightingale's will. I wonder if he knows and if he thought it worth killing for? But we'll leave that for the moment and call on the principal beneficiary.'

'Sir?' Burden looked at him enquiringly.

'I'll tell you in the car.' Wexford grinned broadly.

'How beautiful on the mountain are the feet of him who bringeth good tidings!'

How would she receive the news? Wexford wondered. With surprised gratification? Or with fear that the will had been disclosed to official eyes? It might be that she was genuinely ignorant of its contents or even of its existence.

He told her baldly that Mrs Nightingale's will was in her favour and watched her reactions. They were disappointing. She shrugged her shoulders and said, 'That's a surprise. I had no idea.' As usual she wore the necklace, bracelets and ear-rings which were as indispensable to her as stockings and lipstick might be to another woman, and not even the faintest flash of concupiscence crossed her face to show that she would be glad to replace them with real stones. Her expression was apathetic and indifferent, almost sleepy, as if she had recently passed through some ordeal, so tumultuous that it had left her drained of all feeling.

'You didn't know she had made a will? Or you don't know what she's left you?'

'No to both,' said Georgina. She sat down on the arm of a chair. Her blouse was sleeveless and Wexford noticed the strong sinews of her shoulders and upper arms. Only once before had he seen such sinews on a woman's arms and that woman had been a female wrestler.

'You inherit all Mrs Nightingale's jewellery,' he said.

'I see. When you said the will was in my favour I thought it must be something like that. Elizabeth hadn't any money of her own and she always got through her allowance before the next was due. She was awfully extravagant.'

'Mrs Villiers, this puts a rather different complexion on

the circumstances of your sister-in-law's death.'

'Does it? I'm afraid I don't quite understand.'

'Let me explain then.' Wexford paused as the door opened and Denys Villiers came in, his recently published book open in his hand.

'Oh, there you are, Denys,' his wife said, getting up. Her voice was still dull and toneless as she said, 'Fancy, Elizabeth made a will and left me all those rings and necklaces of hers.'

Villiers put his thumb between the pages of his book to mark the place and looked with dry amusement into the stern faces of the two policemen. Then, without warning, he burst into a roar of hysterical laughter.

11

HER husband's laughter had a far more disturbing effect on Georgina than had Wexford's tidings. Something had been slumbering under her veil of apathy. The laughter brought it to life and it showed in her eyes and her trembling lips as raw terror.

'Don't, Denys, don't. Oh, stop!' She clutched his arm and shook it.

'May we share the joke, sir?' asked Wexford blandly.

Villiers stopped laughing as people can when their laughter doesn't stem from amusement but from some irony they have observed with admiration. He shrugged and then, his face going blank, opened his book once more and began to read where he had left off.

'Mrs Villiers,' said Wexford, 'I want to talk to you again about the events of Tuesday night.'

'But, why?' Her voice was barely under control. 'I thought it was all over. I was just beginning to stop thinking about it and now . . . Oh God, what shall I do?' She stood for a moment, staring wildly at them and then ran from the room.

Villiers smiled a little, apparently at something in his own book. Aware as he was of the huge vanity of writers, Wexford was nevertheless unable to understand how one of them could actually laugh at something he had written himself.

'I can see I shall have to read this book of yours.'

Villiers lifted his eyes and, again closing his book, kept his fingers inside it to mark the place. He took a copy of *Wordsworth in Love* from a stack on the window-sill and handed it to the chief inspector. 'You can have this if it interests you.' The weary grey eyes met Wexford's and held them.

'Thank you. It will interest me. I'm always willing to be enlightened. For one thing, I'm curious to discover why you've made yourself an authority on Wordsworth.'

'A matter of taste, Mr Wexford.'

'But there is always something to account for taste.'

Villiers shrugged impatiently. 'Well, you've brought us the news and we've had our little bit of literary chit-chat. Is there anything else?'

'Certainly there is. I am investigating a murder, Mr Villiers.'

'But not very fruitfully, if I may say so.' Villiers sat down astride a dining chair, his chest against its bars and his arms folded on the top of its back. The ashen face with its tracery of lines again gave Wexford the impression that this man was sick, was dying. 'And what's the point, anyway?' he said. 'Elizabeth is dead and cannot be resurrected. You find who killed her and put him in prison for twenty or thirty years. Who benefits? Who's the happier for it?'

'You're in favour of capital punishment perhaps? I'm surprised your first wife didn't convert you from that view.'

If Villiers was astonished that Wexford knew of his previous marriage he gave no sign of it. 'Capital punishment?' he said. 'No, I'm not in favour of it. I don't care much. I don't care about people being kept in prison

131

either except that my tax pays for their board.'

'It seems to me, sir, that you don't care much for anything.'

'That's so. So-called current affairs don't interest me and nor does current opinion. I don't like people and people don't like me. They're mostly fools,' said the misanthropist with a kind of bitter relish. 'I don't suffer fools gladly. Progress bores me and so does noise.' He added very quietly, 'I want to be left in peace to live in the past.'

'Then let's discuss the past,' said Wexford. 'The recent past. Tuesday night, for instance.'

Sitting opposite Burden in the living room, Georgina said fretfully, 'I told you about Tuesday night last time you were here. If you've got a bad memory you ought to have written it down.'

'Never mind my memory, Mrs Villiers. You just tell me again. You left the Manor at ten-thirty in your husband's car. Who was driving?'

'My husband was driving. He always drives when we're out together. I think the man should always drive, don't you?' She set her mouth stubbornly. 'The man should always be the dominant partner in a marriage so that his wife can look up to him. We,' she said in a loud defiant voice, 'are very happily married.'

'That's nice,' said Burden. 'What time did you reach home?'

'I *told* you. About twenty to eleven. We went in and we went straight to bed. And that's all.'

'No, it isn't all. No one comes home from an evening out and goes straight to bed. One of you must have put the car away. One of you must have locked up.'

'Oh, well, if *that's* what you want. My husband just left the car on the drive. Mine was in the garage.'

'Did you both go into the house together?'

'Of course.'

'Side by side? Squeezing through the door at the same time?'

'Don't be silly,' said Georgina petulantly. 'I went in first and then my husband followed about a minute later. He locked the car because it was going to be left on the drive all night. He always does that.'

'Very prudent. Since you're evidently so careful, you wouldn't have put the milk bottles out before you went to the Manor. Who did that when you got home? Who checked that all the windows were closed and the back door locked?'

She hesitated, looking at him sullenly. Her fingers played nervously with her beads. 'My husband always does that,' she said. 'I went to bed first.'

'How long did it take you to get to bed, Mrs Villiers? Ten minutes? A quarter of an hour? You didn't go to bed unwashed and in all your clothes.'

'Of *course* I didn't. I put the bedroom light on and undressed and went to the bathroom and then I went to bed. My husband came to bed. He always reads for about half an hour before we go to sleep.'

'Double bed, Mrs Villiers?'

'No, we have twin beds. But you needn't read anything into that. We're a very happy couple.'

'Yes, you told me before. Now, tell me, what time did you go to the Manor?'

'We got there at about half past eight.'

'I believe,' said Burden disarmingly, 'that you often went there to play bridge. How long did you usually stay there?'

'Sometimes till midnight in the holidays.'

133

'Tuesday night was still in the holidays, wasn't it? Why did you leave so early?'

'My husband,' said Georgina, putting as she always did a self-conscious pride of ownership into the word, 'my husband had some research to do down at the school and . . .' She clapped her hand over her mouth but too late to stifle a little sharp cry. 'When we got home,' she stammered, 'he changed his mind and . . . Oh, why won't you leave us alone? We could be happy if everyone would leave us alone!'

Burden's stare was hard and penetrating. He looked at her without blinking as she began to cry.

'I left the car on the drive,' said Villiers to Wexford. 'No, I didn't check the back door or the windows. That's my wife's province. I went straight to bed and straight to sleep.'

Burden came in. 'May I, sir?'

'Go ahead,' said Wexford.

'What about this research you were going to do down at the school, sir? The essential research that took you away from the Manor at ten-thirty?'

Villiers lit a cigarette. 'Don't you ever make excuses to get away from a boring host and hostess, Inspector?' he asked imperturbably. 'Don't you ever say you're expecting a phone call or you must get back to that boy of yours?'

Burden scowled at him, furious that John had been brought into this interrogation. It was humiliating to find that Villiers, who ostentatiously ignored him as a private person, should all the time have recognised him as a parent.

'So this was an empty excuse,' he said angrily. 'A deliberate lie.'

'Sometimes I do tell lies,' said Villiers, smoking with a kind of frivolous delicacy. 'I'm a good liar.'

'Strange for a man who declares himself indifferent to the opinions of others,' Wexford commented, and suddenly, meeting Villiers' arrogant eyes, a couplet came into his head. He quoted it, not only because it was apt but because he felt a pressing unquenchable need to show Villiers that he wasn't a moron, that he wasn't the flat-footed unlettered country policeman the writer thought him.

' "So much he soared beyond or sunk beneath
The men with whom he felt condemned to breathe." '

The effect was astonishing, not at all what he had expected. Villiers didn't move but his face became feverishly pale. Statue-still, he seemed to be waiting, and not, Wexford thought, for more words, but for action, for some decisive crucial move. And then, perhaps because no one moved but both policemen stood in bewilderment, Villiers laughed.

That laughter electrified Burden into rage.

'What *do* you want, Mr Villiers?' he almost shouted. 'What are you trying to prove? Why do you try to set yourself so much above everyone else?'

'Or beneath them, Mr Burden.' Villiers hadn't shifted his eyes from Wexford's face and now they were very wide and very opaque. 'Or sunk beneath them, remember. As to what I want, that's simple.' He got up, turned his back. 'I want to die,' he said.

'And what the hell,' said Wexford thoughtfully as they got back into the car, 'came over him when I quoted those lines?'

'Search me,' said Burden, the Philistine. He made an effort. 'Er—where do they come from? Wordsworth?'

'I don't think so. I don't know where they come from. They were just sort of floating about in my head.' Burden nodded indifferently. He was used to hearing lines that floated about in his superior's head. Tedious bookishness, that's what it was, and it rather embarrassed him. 'But I'd like to know,' said Wexford. 'It'd be a job tracing them, our England being a nest of singing birds.'

'We've got more important things to worry about,' Burden said impatiently. 'What's more to the point is, are we going to be able to find a witness to corroborate that he didn't go out again after he got home?'

'Or that she didn't.'

'Pity the place is so isolated.'

'Yes. We need to find someone who passed the place in a car. That can wait till the morning. You get that scarf sent over to the lab and then you can get off home to your painting. Manual work often helps the brain, Mike, and you can have a good think while you're wielding the brush.'

With a sigh of relief, Burden started the car. 'Which of those two have you in mind, anyway?'

'Mike, you'll say I'm jumping to conclusions, but I'm as near as dammit certain she did it. She's a strong healthy young woman, physically capable of felling another woman with a torch. It is she and not her husband who inherits. She was at the Manor when the torch was replaced. She knew the layout of the Manor grounds and she could have noticed the bonfire earlier in the evening. If she got blood on her clothes, she knew she could have burnt her outer clothes—say a sweater—on the fire.'

'All this,' said Burden, 'argues premeditation, that she

deliberately chose a torch of all things for her weapon.'

'Think about it. Try and see what you can make of it all. I'm going to pick up Lionel Marriott and take him to the Olive for a drink.'

12

THE new cocktail bar at the Olive and Dove was almost deserted, for by now most of its patrons had deserted it for the dining room, while the serious drinkers were in the public or the saloon. Wexford shepherded Marriott into a secluded corner and placed a large whisky in front of him. The bar communicated with the dining room by means of double glass doors, but Wexford had made sure the diners were out of Marriott's line of vision. He wanted their talk to be uninterrupted and Marriott removed from the temptation of waving to friends or sending smiling dumb-show messages to pretty women.

'Now,' he said, 'I want to hear about this holiday on the Costa Brava.'

'Holiday!' said Marriott, momentarily closing his eyes. 'Really, I'd rather spend a fortnight in a labour camp. The spotty devils are bad enough when you have to cart them up to London to the V. and A., but imagine two weeks cooped up with them in some torrid slum. They go mad, you know. None of the local girls is safe. They're all in an advanced state of satyriasis at the best of times, and once get them in the sun . . . ! And as for appalling infringement of the exchange regulations, you wouldn't believe the diabolical ingenuity of some of them. Every one an accomplished smuggler and his mother's milk scarce out of him.'

'All right, all right,' said Wexford, laughing. 'What about Villiers?'

'God knows how he found the time to go courting. You'd have thought every minute would have been taken up, what with having to be a Customs officer and a male nurse and a watch committee all rolled into one. Anyway, he met Georgina.'

'She was holidaying there too?'

'Only in the same sense that he was,' said Marriott, waving enthusiastically as a satin-gowned brunette swept past their table. Wistfully, he watched her disappear into the dining room. 'Georgina had gone with her own school party,' he said, 'a bunch of teenage nymphomaniacs, from what I heard. Denys and she encountered each other on one of their nightly rounds of the local taverns, picking their charges up off the floor, you know.'

'It really can't have been as bad as that, Lionel.'

'Perhaps I exaggerate a little,' said Marriott airily. 'Not that I heard any of this from Denys. He didn't even bother to send me a card. No, the first hint I got was on the day before he was due back. Elizabeth and Quen dropped in one evening. "We've got some good news for you," said Quen. "Denys has met a girl and they're going to be married." "Fast worker," I said, and then of course I had to say I was pleased, although I was thinking she must be out of her mind, poor thing. Let me get you another drink, Reg.'

'Tonight,' said Wexford firmly, 'I'm the host.' Once let Marriott get to the bar and he would be within range of the allurements of his friends. He asked for two more whiskies and, while he waited for them, he cast his eyes speculatively over the waiters in the dining room, wondering which of them was Quentin Nightingale's rival.

The tall one with acne? The thin youth with slicked-back black hair?

'They were married,' Marriott went on, 'from Georgina's home in Dorset. Quen went down for the wedding but Elizabeth couldn't. She had a migraine. Of course, even Denys couldn't very well bring a second bride home to a horsemeat shop, so Elizabeth asked them to stay at the Manor while they were looking for a house.'

'The Nightingales gave a dinner party for the bride. Everybody who was anybody was there. Old Priscilla and Sir George, the Rogerses from Pomfret, the Primeros from Forby and, of course, your humble servant.' Looking anything but humble, Marriott lowered his voice to a suspenseful whisper. 'Georgina was staying in the house but she was the last to arrive. Ah ha! I thought, making an entrance, the clever little thing. None of us had seen her, so naturally we sat with bated breath. All the women were got up to the nines. Elizabeth looked wonderful. White velvet, you know. It always does something for a woman. Believe it or not, I even saw Denys looking at her with a sort of grudging admiration.

'Then, just when we can contain our impatience no longer, in comes Georgina in Woolworth's pearls and a— well, we used to call them tub frocks, and this one had been in the tub a good many times, I can tell you. Did those women stare! Georgina wasn't a bit shy. In fact, she dominated the conversation at the table. We heard all about her little housewifely plans and how she was going to make a real home for Denys and how they were going to have six children. And possessive! My dear, she actually grumbled to Elizabeth because she hadn't been placed next to him.

'I must say Elizabeth was charming to her. She even complimented her on her dress and really tried to keep her the centre of attention. She was bubbling over with gaiety and she didn't look a day over twenty-five.'

'Georgina,' said Wexford, 'did she seem envious?'

'Of the *mise en scene*? If denigrating everything around one and trying to assume an ascendancy on the grounds of one's middle-class ideas is only a mask for envy, yes, I suppose she was envious. Of course, I've seen her dozens of times since then and all she can talk about is what a marvellous marriage she and Denys have and how they're all in all to each other.'

'And are they?'

'He's everything she wants,' said Marriott, 'although we see no sign of these six children, do we? As for him, I think he's as bored with his second marriage as he was with his first, but there's only one thing that interests Denys Villiers and that's his work. Once he and Georgina were settled in their bungalow, he was buzzing round the Manor again just like the old days.'

Wexford said slyly, 'You must have been buzzing too to have seen him there.'

For a moment Marriott looked a little foolish. Then he jumped up smartly. 'You'll excuse me one second while I pop into the dining room and have a word with . . .'

Wexford laughed. 'I'll excuse you altogether,' he said, 'for tonight.'

'You've been thinking,' said Dr Crocker on the following morning, 'that she was wearing that scarf when the deed was done. Well, she wasn't. It would have been saturated with blood if she had.'

'Perhaps it was round her neck or she was holding it in her hand.'

The doctor gave a derisive snort. 'And after she was dead she took it off and wiped her head with it? That's what it looks as if it was used for, to wipe blood off someone or something.'

Wexford folded the report and put it down on his blotter. 'You said you were out delivering a baby on Tuesday night,' he said. 'I don't suppose your route took you through Myfleet via Clusterwell?'

'Sure it did. Why?'

'You know Villiers' bungalow?'

'Of course I do. He's a patient of mine. I passed it at about eleven.'

'Did you notice the bungalow at all?' Wexford said more urgently. 'Were any lights on? Were the cars on the drive?'

The doctor's face fell. 'I didn't look. I was thinking about my patient and the possibility of the child being a breech presentation. Now, if I'd known . . .'

'That,' said Wexford irritably, 'is what they all say. Here's Mike now.'

Burden came in wearily. 'Three of us have done a house-to-house in Myfleet,' he said. 'I don't reckon any of them go out in the evenings. The whole place shuts up about nine and those that aren't in bed are in the pub. Nobody passed that way bar Katje Doorn. I've talked to her again and all she did was simper and tell me about a disgusting Swedish film. Though I did have the feeling she didn't want to discuss her drive.'

Wexford gave a slight embarrassed cough. 'Rubbish,' he said, listening to the bluster in his voice and trying to quell it. 'I tell you, that girl had nothing to do with Mrs Nightingale's death.'

'Perhaps not. But it's a bit funny, isn't it? She'll talk very freely about her goings-on with Nightingale and that waiter, but she shuts up like a clam when I try to get her to describe her drive home. And another thing, Nightingale's Mini was standing out by those stables and young Lovell was cleaning it, doing his best to get a scratch off the front bumper.'

'I don't know where all this is getting us, Mike. We aren't looking for a damaged car but for a witness who saw something when he passed Villiers' bungalow.'

'I like all the ends tidied,' said Burden. 'Anyway, I checked downstairs and no accident was reported on Tuesday night.'

'Then let's leave it, shall we?' said Wexford crossly. 'Get Martin to go over to Clusterwell and find out if anyone does any regular nightly dog walking. I may as well go myself,' he added. 'Spy out the land a bit. It's not possible *no one* used that road.'

The cottages of Clusterwell were scattered over a spider-shaped network of lanes. Sergeant Martin took the body of the spider, Wexford its legs. Recalling the painstaking routine work of his youth, he knocked on every door. But the inhabitants of Clusterwell took a perverse pride in their own peculiar brand of respectability. Like those of Myfleet, they stayed in at night. Virtue lay in bolting one's doors, drawing one's curtains and gathering round the television by nine o'clock. And, judging by the number of mongrels Wexford encountered in the lanes, their dogs exercised themselves.

A large black one, patrolling what looked like a field of allotments, growled at him as he approached the hedge. He decided to venture no nearer the caravan—in any case clearly deserted—which stood behind runner-bean vines and stacked chicken coops. Instead he stepped back to read the words on a shabby board mounted on poles: *A. Tawney. New-laid eggs, roasting chickens, veg.*

'Myfleet,' he said tersely to his driver.

Mrs Cantrip was in her rocking chair, engrossed in her

paper, a little flustered because he had caught her in idleness. Katje, who had shown him in, disappeared in the direction of the study.

'Alf Tawney, sir? If he's not out on his rounds, you'll likely find him over at Mrs Lovell's.'

'How does he travel to and fro?'

'On his bike, sir. He's got one of them big baskets on the handlebars of his bike.'

Wexford nodded. 'Does he stay at Mrs Lovell's all night?'

It was easy to shock Mrs Cantrip, who adhered to that school of thought which holds that fornication can only be committed between midnight and dawn. 'Oh no, sir,' she said, flushing and looking down. 'He's always gone by eleven. I reckon even Mrs Lovell's got some idea of what's right.'

The lovers were in the middle of their evening meal. A saucepan of baked beans stood in the middle of the clothless table.

Mrs Lovell re-seated herself. 'His lordship been up to something?' she asked, carving more bread and resting her gigantic bosom among the crumbs.

'My visit has nothing to do with Sean.' It was clear to Wexford that he was to be offered no tea, but a glance at the cracked cups and the scum-ringed milk bottle told him he wasn't missing anything. 'I hoped to have the pleasure of a little talk with Mr Tawney.'

'With Alf? What d'you want with Alf?'

Wexford eyed the purveyor of eggs and vegetables, wondering how to interrogate a man who apparently never opened his mouth. The small black eyes in the swarthy hatchet face stared expressionlessly back at him.

At last he said, 'Spend a good deal of time here with your friends, do you, Mr Tawney?'

Mrs Lovell gave a full-throated giggle. 'My Sean's no friend of his,' she said. 'It's me you come to see, don't you, Alf?'

'Um,' said Tawney lugubriously.

'And very nice too,' said Wexford. 'A man needs a little feminine company after a hard day's work.'

'And his hot meals. Wasting away Alf was till I got him coming here. You fancy a cream horn, Alf?'

'Um.'

'What time,' said Wexford, 'do you reckon on leaving Mrs Lovell's to go home?'

'Alf has to be up betimes,' said Mrs Lovell, looking more gypsy-ish than ever. 'He's always gone by a quarter to eleven.' She sighed and Wexford guessed that this early retreat had been a bone of contention between them in the past. With surprising intelligence, she said, 'You want to know if he saw anything the night her up at the Manor got killed?'

'Precisely. I want to know if Mr Tawney took a look at Mr Villiers' bungalow—you know the one I mean?— as he was cycling back to Clusterwell.'

'Don't know about look. He tried to knock them up, didn't you, Alf?'

'Um,' said Tawney. Very alert now, Wexford waited.

'Go on, Alf. The gentleman asked you a question.' A tremor disturbed Tawney's body as if, by unprecedented effort, he was trying to summon speech from the depths of his stomach. 'He was mad enough about it at the time,' said Mrs Lovell. 'Quite talkative for him. *Go on,* Alf.'

Tawney spoke.

' 'Twere no good,' he said. 'They was out and the place locked up.'

'Now let's get this straight,' said Wexford, guessing for all he was worth and mentally apologising to Burden. 'Mr Tawney was riding home when a car passed him and nearly knocked him off his bicycle.' Mrs Lovell's admiring grin told him he was guessing right. 'And he took the number of this car, intending to give it to the police so that the driver might be prosecuted.'

'He never took the number.' Mrs Lovell dipped into a paper bag for the last cream horn. 'He knew who it was. That foreign girl from the Manor.'

'Mr Tawney knocked at the bungalow because he wanted to use their phone?' Incredible to imagine Tawney explaining, apologising, dialling, explaining again.

'The place was all dark,' said Mrs Lovell with relish, the gypsy scaring children with her stories round the camp fire. 'Alf banged and banged, but no one come, did they?'

'Nope,' said Tawney.

Talk about hearsay evidence, thought Wexford. 'What time was it?'

'Alf left here half past ten. He'd been knocking a long time when the clock struck eleven, Clusterwell church clock. Go on, Alf, you tell him. You was there.'

Tawney swigged his last drop of tea, perhaps to lubricate his rarely used vocal cords. 'I banged and no one come.' He coughed horribly and Wexford looked away. 'He's out and she's out, I said to myself.'

'That's right, Alf.' Mrs Lovell beamed encouragement.

'Might have known. The garage doors was open.'

'And both cars was gone! So Alf give it up, and next morning—well, you cool off, don't you? You think to yourself, Why bother when there's no bones broken? Mind you, I'll let that little foreign bitch know what I know if I see her about the village.'

146

Poor Katje. Wexford wondered if he should drop her a gentle word of warning, closeted with her, calling her by her Christian name, even though that privilege had only been accorded him because he reminded her of some old uncle. Talk to her like an old Dutch uncle . . . ? He laughed to himself. Better forget it, stay securely tied to the mast while the siren sang for others.

In September even the best-kept gardens usually have a ripe wild look. This one was a barren island among the fields, a sterile characterless plot in which every unruly branch and every straggling stem had been docked. The grass was brown and closely shorn and there was nothing to provide shade.

Denys and Georgina Villiers sat in a pair of deckchairs, the uncomfortable cheap kind which have thin metal frames and economically small wooden arm-rests. Wexford observed them for a moment before making his presence known. The man who said he never read newspapers was reading one now, apparently oblivious of his wife. With neither book nor sewing to occupy her, she stared at him with the rapt attention of a cinema fanatic gazing at the screen.

Wexford coughed and immediately Georgina sprang to her feet. Villiers looked up and said with the icy unpleasantness he seemed always able to muster, 'Control yourself. Don't be so silly.'

Wexford walked up to them. Over Villiers' shoulder he looked at the newspaper and saw what he had been reading: a review of his own latest published work which occupied half a page. 'Mr Villiers,' he said roughly, 'why did you tell me you came straight home from the Manor on Tuesday night and went to bed? This house was empty and in darkness at eleven. Why didn't you tell me you went out again?'

'I forgot,' said Villiers calmly.

'You *forgot*? When I asked you most pointedly?'

'Nevertheless, I forgot.' Villiers' cold face showed neither fear nor embarrassment. The man had a curious strength, an iron self-control; he seemed unbreakable. Why then have this strange sensation that he had been irrevocably broken long ago and that his strength had never been quite strong enough?

'Come now, sir. You forgot you went out. Very well. Have you also forgotten where you went?'

'I went,' said Villiers, 'where I said I was going, to the school library to look up a reference.'

'What reference?'

With cool contempt, Villiers said, 'Would it mean anything to you if I told you?' He shrugged. 'All right. I was looking up the precise relationship of George Gordon Wordsworth to William Wordsworth.'

Somewhat to his own humiliation, Wexford found that it did indeed mean nothing. He swung round on Georgina who crouched in her deckchair, gooseflesh on her arms and tiny beads of sweat on her upper lip. For once she wore no jewellery. Did the cheap gaudy stuff no longer please her now that she would be able to adorn herself with real gems? Or had she ferreted out of Nightingale the scornful words in which her sister-in-law's bequest was couched?

'Did you accompany your husband to the school, Mrs Villiers?' He noted the faint shake of her head. 'Had you done so you would hardly have gone in two separate cars. But you went out. Where?'

Her voice came in a shrill squeak. 'I drove—I drove around the lanes.'

'May I ask why?'

Villiers answered for her. 'My wife,' he said silkily, 'was annoyed with me for going out. She did what she often does on such occasions, took her own car and went for a country drive.' He gave a waspish smile. 'To cool her temper,' he said.

'I'm not convinced of any of this,' said Wexford slowly. He glanced around the bare garden. 'I think we could all talk more frankly down at the police station.'

Georgina gave a wild cry and threw herself into her husband's arms. Wexford expected him to repudiate her but instead he held her with almost a lover's tenderness. Standing up now, he stroked her dry rough hair. 'As you like,' he said indifferently.

'No, no, no,' she sobbed into his shoulder. 'You must tell him. You tell him.'

He was going to lie again. Wexford was sure of it.

'What my wife wants me to tell you,' said Villiers, 'is that you've been a complete bloody fool.' He patted Georgina as one pats a dog and then he pushed her away. 'Let me give you a piece of advice, Chief Inspector. Next time you suspect anyone of murder for gain, you had better check up on the value of what they're gaining. I'm a good liar,' he said urbanely, 'but I'm not lying now. My sister's pieces of jewellery are all fakes. I'd be surprised if the whole lot would fetch more than fifty pounds. You had better look elsewhere, Mr Wexford. You know as well as I do that your absurd trumped-up case against my wife has nothing but motive to make it stand up, and where is your motive now?'

Gone with the sun, thought Wexford, watching it sink behind the misty fields. He was suddenly quite sure that this time Villiers hadn't been lying.

13

KATJE was nowhere to be seen and it was Quentin Nightingale himself who this time admitted Wexford to the Manor. But Wexford sensed her recent presence in the austere study. He felt that she had been standing here with Quentin, in his arms, kissing him, then running away when the bell rang.

Quentin himself had an abstracted air, the look of a lover dreaming of the past, impatient for the near future. Wexford's news jolted him into unwelcome reality.

'Every piece of jewellery Elizabeth had I bought for her,' he said. 'I've still got the receipts for most of it, if you'd care to see them.'

'Later. First I should like to see the stones themselves again.'

Quentin removed the Stubbs, opened the safe. Then he lifted the jewels from their boxes in handfuls, letting them fall through his fingers, as a child on its first visit to the seaside sifts shells and stones, its pleasure mixed with astonishment at the unknown.

He picked out from the heap his dead wife's engagement ring and took it to the window, but the growing dusk defeated him and, returning, he switched on the desk lamp.

'My glasses,' he said. 'Just by your elbow. Would you mind?'

Wexford handed them to him.

'This is a fake.' There was a small quiver in Quentin's voice. 'This isn't the ring I gave Elizabeth on our engagement.'

'How do you know?'

'Not because I'm an expert on precious stones. I shall have to find an expert to tell us for sure about the rest. Are there any to be found around here or should I get someone down from London?'

'We can find someone here. You haven't told me how you know that ring is false.'

Quentin said bitterly, 'When I bought it for her I had some words engraved inside it.' Taking the ring from him, Wexford knew he wasn't going to be told what those words had been. 'There's nothing inside this one.'

'No.'

Quentin sat down. With a rapid, almost reflex gesture, he pushed the sparkling heap away from him, knocking a rivière of diamonds—diamonds or paste?—on to the carpet. It lay like a glittering snake at Wexford's feet.

'I suppose,' Quentin said, 'that they're all copies. Perfect copies too, aren't they? All but one. Exquisite facsimiles of the real thing. Except one. She had the stone copied and the platinum copied but she didn't bother to have the words copied because they meant nothing to her. How utterly indifferent she must have been to me. . . .'

Was it this indifference, finally and irrevocably brought home to him, that made Quentin's mind up for him? Was it this knowledge that led him to take his new and perhaps reckless step? Much later, after the case was over, Wexford often asked himself these questions. But on the following morning, returning to the Manor from the jeweller's, he hadn't given them a moment's thought and the news came to him as a complete surprise.

Katje showed him into the drawing room and he was already unwrapping the brown paper from the jewel boxes as he followed her when he saw that Quentin wasn't alone. Denys Villiers was with him, standing by the french windows and holding both Quentin's hands in his. Wexford heard the tail end of what sounded like a speech.

'. . . Anyway, my best congratulations, Quen. I couldn't be more glad for you.' Then Villiers saw Wexford. He dropped his brother-in-law's hands and his face set arrogantly.

'May I know what ground there is for congratulation, sir?'

Villiers shrugged and turned his back, but Quentin, flushing, put out a hand to Katje and the girl ran to him.

'Perhaps I'm indiscreet to tell you, Chief Inspector. You might read so much into this.' Villiers made a faint derisive sound. 'I'd like it kept secret for the time being,' Quentin said. 'Katje and I are going to be married.'

Wexford put down his parcel. 'Indeed?' he said. They looked like father and daughter standing there. There was even a slight resemblance between them, the family likeness apparent between any two people belonging to the classic north European type. 'Then let me congratulate you also,' he said, and again he apologised silently to Burden, whose ideas had perhaps been not so old-fashioned after all.

'Naturally, we shall wait six months. A year might be more . . .'

'But I am not waiting a whole year, Kventin. Half a year perhaps. It is not fair if you are making me wait a whole year for my flat in London and my new fast sports car and my going all round the world for my honeymoon.'

So she was a gold-digger, after all. Wexford thought

152

sadly. He had been wrong. These days it seemed that he was always wrong.

'Now I should like to see you alone, sir,' he said.

'Yes, of course.'

Abruptly Villiers threw open the french windows and walked out of the room. Casting a dazzling smile over her shoulder, Katje followed him to pause on the lawn and survey everything around her with frank concupiscence.

'She'll go home to her parents until the wedding,' Quentin said, and earnestly, 'I want everything to be right. I want—what is it Antony says? "Read not my blemishes in the world's report. I have not kept my square." '

' "But that to come," ' Wexford capped it, ' "shall all be done by the rule." ' I daresay, he thought, I daresay. But what of 'that to come' for her? Such a long future, so much money, such idleness for temptations to gain ground in. She was the last for him and he perhaps only one of the first for her. Would they dine at the Olive sometimes and be served by a waiter who had once romped with this lady of the Manor in the coverts of Cheriton Forest? Poor Kventin, Wexford thought, aping her accent. He was no longer to be envied. It was a nice game he was playing, a game which had once seemed enticing to Wexford. But not any more, not on those terms, for it wasn't worth the exorbitant price of the candle.

'The jewellery,' he said laconically, 'is all fake. I took it to an old jeweller in Queen Street. He's helped me in the past and he's absolutely reliable. If he says it's fake, it's fake. She must have sold what you bought her and had exact copies made.'

'But why, Chief Inspector? I gave her all the money she could possibly have needed. If she wanted more she had only to ask. She knew that.'

'Would you have given her thirty thousand pounds?'

'I'm not a millionaire, Mr Wexford.' Quentin sighed, bit his lip. 'The jewellery was hers to do as she liked with. She chose to sell it. Perhaps it doesn't matter why.' He met Wexford's eyes pleadingly. 'I'd like to forget the whole thing.'

'It isn't as simple as that.' Wexford sat down, rather imperiously motioning his host to sit down too. 'Your wife sold her jewellery because she needed money. Now it's my turn to ask why. Why did she need money, Mr Nightingale, and what did she do with it? We know she spent it. Her bank account was overdrawn. Where did the money go?'

Quentin shrugged unhappily. 'She was generous. Perhaps she gave it to charity.'

'*Thirty thousand pounds?* And why keep it dark from you? No, Mr Nightingale, I think your wife was blackmailed.'

Quentin leaned forward, frowning his bewilderment. 'But that's impossible! People are only blackmailed when they've done something against the law. My wife was . . .' He waved a helpless hand, encompassing the room. Wexford understood what he was trying to put into words, that the woman who had reigned here had been entirely cushioned by her position and her wealth from the squalor of criminal temptation. We aren't of that class, his eyes said, of that seamy underworld. Haven't you realised yet that we are only a little lower than the angels?

'It need not necessarily have been some offence against the law,' said Wexford quietly, 'but against morality.'

Puzzled, Quentin seemed to consider. Then his brow cleared. 'You mean she might have been unfaithful to me and someone found it out?'

'Something of that kind, sir.'

'No, Mr Wexford, you're on the wrong track. I wasn't that kind of husband either. Whatever my wife had done I would have forgiven her, and she knew it. We discussed the subject soon after we were married, as young couples do. Elizabeth asked me for my views. It was an academic question, you understand, a matter of seeking to know me better. We were—we were very much in love in those days.'

'And what was your answer?'

'That if she ever came to me and told me she had— that there had been someone else, I would never blame her, certainly not divorce her. Not as long as she came to me and confided in me. I told her that I believed forgiveness to be a part of love, and that in such circumstances, when she was unhappy, she would need me most. And I would expect her to do the same by me if the need arose. I would never have divorced her. She was my wife, and even when we grew so terribly apart I still believed that marriage was for ever.'

A nice man, Wexford thought, his usual cynicism for a moment in abeyance, a kind and eminently civilised person. Cynicism returned. An ideal husband, or a man fate had designed for women to take for a ride? It was, he reflected, a good thing Quentin Nightingale had formed such admirable principles during his first marriage as he would certainly have to put them into practice during his second.

'There are some things,' he said, 'which cannot be forgiven.' Illustrations came into his mind, examples from his long experience of wrongdoers. There was the woman who had taken her husband back a dozen times after his terms of imprisonment for theft, but had refused ever to see him again when he had been convicted for indecent exposure. Or the man who had borne his wife's infidelity for twenty years but when she was caught shoplifting had repudiated her. 'You're an intelligent broad-minded man,' he said at last, 'but you're very conventional. I wonder if you really know yourself. You know what pleases you, but do you know what would disgust you?'

'Nothing Elizabeth could have done,' Quentin said obstinately.

'Perhaps not, but she believed it would have disgusted you, believed it so firmly that she was prepared to pay thirty thousand pounds to keep it from you.'

'If you say so,' Quentin said helplessly. 'Who could she ever have known that would extort money from her?'

'I was hoping you could tell me that. A servant?'

'Mrs Cantrip who has been devoted to us for sixteen years? Old Will who is respect itself? Sean who worshipped the very ground she walked on? You see yourself how absurd this is. Why should it be a servant, anyway?'

'It's more unlikely that it was one of her friends, isn't it, sir? A servant who lived in this house would have access to private papers, might have been an eye witness, might have discovered photographs.'

'Evidence of infidelity? I tell you, she *knew* I'd have understood. I'd have overlooked it, however much it hurt.'

Wexford stared at him, hardly able to contain his impatience. The man didn't know what life was. He spoke of infidelity as if it was always a straightforward and temporary preference for someone else, a matter of temptation, of love and of subsequent guilt. He was innocent. But Wexford wasn't. He had seen the letters even the most elevated and cultured lovers write to each other, the photographs elegant and fastidious women revel in posing for. Thirty thousand pounds might not be too great a price to pay to keep them from a husband's eye.

'You had a series of *au pair* girls, you told me.'

'Ordinary young girls,' Quentin said. 'Quite straight-forward and happy to be here. They adored Elizabeth.'

Just like Katje did?

'Before the girls came,' said Wexford, 'you had a married couple. What was the name again?'

'Twohey,' said Quentin Nightingale.

The small white cottage was being scoured from top to bottom. When Wexford arrived, Mrs Cantrip abandoned the cleaning that had necessarily to be done on a Saturday, and sat down with the ginger cat in her lap. The room smelt strongly of polish and mothballs.

'Twohey, sir?' she said. 'Mr Nightingale dismissed him for insolence. He never showed a proper respect, not from the start, and he never did a fair day's work, as far as I could see. Always hanging about where he wasn't sup-posed to be, snooping and listening, if you know what I mean.'

'And that was why he was sacked?'

The cat slithered to the floor and began sharpening its claws against a table leg. 'Stop that, Ginger,' said Mrs Cantrip. 'Well, things came to a head, sir, and that's a fact. A couple of weeks before he was sacked he got so disrespectful to Madam it was past bearing, and Madam always so gentle and never standing up for herself.' She picked up the cat and dropped it out of the window among the zinnias and dahlias. 'She caught him helping himself to Mr Nightingale's whisky, and when she spoke to him about it, he said, "There's plenty more where that came from," if you've ever heard the like.'

'And his wife?'

'She wasn't so bad. Under his thumb, if the truth were known. She took quite a fancy to me. Sent me a Christmas card two years running.'

'You know their address, then?' Wexford asked urgently.

'I never wrote back, sir,' said Mrs Cantrip, bristling a little with indignation. 'They weren't the kind of folks I'd care to associate with. I did notice the first one had a Newcastle postmark.'

'Did they continue in service?'

'That I wouldn't know, sir. Twohey was always bragging and boasting, and he did say he was sick of the life. Going to set himself up in a hardware business, he said, but Mrs Twohey said to me, out of his hearing like, that it was all castles in the air. Where would they get the capital, sir? They hadn't a penny to bless themselves and that's a fact.'

Having left Sergeant Martin to begin the search for Twohey, Wexford drove down Tabard Road and parked in front of a bungalow whose pink front door matched the geraniums in its garden. Two children sat on a ground-sheet on the lawn, but at opposite ends of it, as if they had put as much space between them as was consistent with their mother's rule about not sitting on damp grass. The boy was cleaning paint brushes, the girl transferring caterpillars from a glass jar into a collection of match-boxes.

Wexford greeted them cheerfully, then strolled up to their father who was painting his garage doors. He noted with an inward chuckle that Burden looked anything but pleased to see him.

'Carry on painting,' said Wexford. 'I like watching other people work. You needn't look so worried. I only want you to lend an ear while I talk.' And he told Burden about the jewellery and about Twohey.

Behind them the children, who had been silent since

Wexford's arrival, began a soft though fierce bickering.

'I was wondering if what this Twohey found out was the secret of Villiers' and Mrs Nightingale's intense dislike of each other. There's no doubt Nightingale is very attached to Villiers, and if he found out his wife had once done her brother some dreadful injury ...'

'But what dreadful injury, sir?' Burden dipped his brush into the paint, scraping the bottom of the tin. 'Look at my two,' he said bitterly. 'They really seem to hate each other and there's no cause for it, as far as I can see. They've been like cat and dog ever since John was a toddler and Pat in her pram.'

'It'll be different when they're grown up.'

'But will it? Why shouldn't the Villiers-Nightingale case be a parallel? Apparently you get these cases of brothers and sisters who are absolutely incompatible.'

'They were separated,' Wexford said. 'They never had a chance to adjust to each other in the late teens and early twenties. If you separated Pat and John, then they might turn out like Villiers and Elizabeth, because one or other of them might let an old grievance smoulder. Your two will grow more tolerant from daily contact.'

'I don't know,' said Burden. 'Sometimes I think of sending one of them away to boarding school.'

'But you can see that separation doesn't work, Mike.' Wexford sat down on the short stepladder. 'I wonder if it's possible that Twohey killed her himself? If it was he she met in the forest and he killed her when she told him her source of supply had come to an end?'

'Then how,' Burden objected, 'did he get hold of the torch? He was the last person to have access to the garden room at the Manor.'

'True. Now, let's see. Our case against Georgina falls to the ground because now we know Georgina had no motive. Villiers remains a possibility. He could have killed her because, her money having come to an end, she told him she would reveal everything to Nightingale. That bloody secret, whatever it was. Sean could have killed her because he saw her with another man.'

'No, sir. We know it was premeditated. The killer took the torch with him.' Burden placed his brush on his paint rag and turned the now empty tin upside down. 'John!' he called, then, 'John!' more loudly to make his voice heard above the quarrelling. 'Go into the shed, will you, and fetch me another tin of pink?'

'I can't. It's pitch dark in there and the bulb's gone.'

'Well, take a torch, then. Don't be so feeble, and leave your sister's things alone.'

'Encouraging garden pests,' said John scathingly. He got up with a sigh, trailed into the open garage and reached up for a torch which stood on a high shelf.

Wexford watched him, saying slowly, 'Of course. Why didn't I think of it before? We realised almost from the first that when you're going into a place that you know will be dark you take a torch with you. But you take your own torch, don't you? Everyone owns a torch. John knew exactly where his torch was and he fetched it as a matter of course. We've been daft, Mike. We thought of someone going to the Manor and taking the Nightingales' torch. But why should they? What possible purpose could there be in going out of your way in securing a weapon that was the property of the woman you intended to kill? Why not bring your own?'

'But the murderer didn't bring his own,' Burden objected. He struck his forehead with the flat of his hand, leaving a broad pink smear. 'No, I'm being stupid. You mean that, if we exclude Nightingale himself, the only possible person to have taken that torch into the wood was Elizabeth herself?'

'That's what I mean. And you know what else it means? No one would choose a torch as a murder weapon if there was anything else to hand. Therefore, *no one planned this murder.* The killer premeditated nothing. He (or she) was overcome by an impulse of the moment and struck Elizabeth Nightingale with the torch she herself had brought with her.'

Burden nodded gravely. 'She brought it,' he agreed, 'but someone else put it back.'

And, Wexford asked himself, how did Villiers know the jewels were fakes?

14

WEXFORD walked to church with his wife and left her at the gate. Without any religious feeling himself, he sometimes went to morning service to please her. Today his office called him as peremptorily as the church bells had called her, but with a silent beckoning finger.

Burden was already there, busy at the phone, setting in motion the search for Twohey.

'Born in Dublin about fifty years ago,' Wexford heard him say. 'Dark, Irish-looking, small eyes, cyst at the left corner of his mouth unless he's had it removed. One conviction, fraudulent conversion while he was a hotel manager in Manchester in 1954. That's right, could be in your Newcastle or Newcastle under Lyme. Keep in touch.' He put the receiver down and grinned wryly at his superior.

'You've been doing your homework,' Wexford said when Burden handed him a photograph of the man he had described. 'I thought I told you to take last evening off and finish your painting?'

'I have finished it. Anyway, I didn't do my homework last night, but I was up bright and early this morning. I've been having a conference with Mrs Cantrip.'

'Has she any idea how the money was paid over to Twohey?'

Burden closed the window. He didn't care for the sound of the bells. 'It was all news to her. I don't think she really took it in. Her Mrs Nightingale being blackmailed!'

'She'd never heard of such a thing,' said Wexford with a grin, 'and that's a fact?'

'Something like that. She's sure Twohey isn't in the neighbourhood because if he was his wife would have come to see her.'

Wexford shrugged. Burden had planted himself in the solidly built swivel chair, so there was no help for it but to settle for one of the flimsier seats. He glared at the inspector and said coldly, 'Why should he be in the neighbourhood?'

'Because maybe it was him,' Burden said ungrammatically, 'that Mrs Nightingale met in the forest.'

'It's blackmailers that get killed, not their victims.'

'Suppose she told him her source had dried up? He might have killed her in a rage. We know it wasn't premeditated, don't we? Thank goodness those bells have stopped.' He opened the window again, raising the blind so that the sun streamed into Wexford's eyes. Wexford shifted his chair irritably. 'Or Sean Lovell might have seen them together and mistaken the reason for their meeting and . . .'

'So you're coming round to young Lovell yourself now, are you?'

'I've felt differently about him since he told me he took a knife to his mother when he was a young lad and saw her with one of her men. Besides, there's the money he gets. I bet she told him she was leaving him all her money and she might not have said how much. He'd have thought it was a hell of a lot more than it was.'

'Come off it, Mike. He either killed her from jealousy or he killed her for gain. The two don't go together.' Wexford got up. 'Well, I'm off to stand Lionel Marriott a drink in the Olive.'

Burden picked up the phone once more. 'Very nice,' he said distantly. 'I'm sorry I'm too busy to join you.'

'Wait till you're asked,' Wexford snapped. Then he chuckled. ' "Blessed is he," Mike, "that sitteth not in the seat of the scornful." '

'Well, it's your seat, sir,' said Burden blandly.

It was funny the way Burden seemed to have taken over everything these days, Wexford thought as he hung over the Kingsbrook Bridge, waiting for the Olive and Dove to open and for Marriott to come. When he looked back on the past week's investigations it seemed to him that Burden had done most of the enquiries while he had sat listening to Marriott's stories. Perhaps he was exaggerating. But Burden was certainly proving to be right in his theories. About the lack of premeditation, for instance, and Katje wanting to marry Nightingale and Georgina Villiers being just a nice ordinary woman. Soon, no doubt, he would have a theory as to the secret and another to account for Sean's non-existent alibi. He dropped a chipping from the bridge parapet into the water. Our young men shall see visions, he thought, and our old men shall dream dreams. . . .

'A penny for your thoughts,' said Marriott, tapping him on the shoulder.

'I was thinking I'm getting old, Lionel.'

'But you're the same age as I am!'

'A little younger, I think,' said Wexford gently. 'It's just struck me, this case is full of people who are too old for other people. It reminds me that I'm older than the lot of them.' He looked up at the serene Sussex sky, cloudless and brilliant. 'An old man in a dry month,' he said. 'An old man on a dry case . . .'

'The Olive won't be dry,' said Marriott. 'Come on, Gerontius, let's have that drink.'

On sunny days the patrons of the Olive could have their drinks at tables in the garden. It was a dusty little garden, rather arid, but Wexford and Marriott, like most Englishmen, felt it almost a duty to sit outside when the sun shone, for fine weather came so seldom and lasted so short a time.

'But I've told you the whole story, Reg,' Marriott said. 'There isn't any more.'

'That from *you*?'

'I'm afraid so, unless you want me to embroider it with my own ideas.'

Wexford picked a leaf out of his drink and looked irritably up into the tree from which it had fallen. He said sharply, 'Do you think it possible that Villiers is homosexual?'

'Oh, my dear, I shouldn't think so.'

'And yet you say he had no women friends between his marriages.'

'He didn't have any men friends either.'

'No? What about Quentin Nightingale?'

'Quentin certainly isn't. I've a shrewd suspicion he's chasing that little Dutch girl. Gone overboard for her, if you ask me. I grant you Denys's feelings for his wives have only been lukewarm, but Quen was in love with Elizabeth when he met her and now he's in love again.'

Wexford wasn't going to betray Nightingale's confidence even by a nod of agreement. 'I wondered,' he said, 'if Elizabeth knew her brother was homosexual and hated him for it but was prepared to go to considerable lengths to keep it dark.'

'I don't see why she'd get murdered for that.'

Finishing his drink, Wexford decided not to breathe a

word to Marriott about the blackmail payments. 'No, it's more likely she was seen in the forest with a man and the person who saw her killed her.' He added thoughtfully, ' "My little songbird, the only true Nightingale in Myfleet." '

In an eager helpful voice, Marriott said, 'Perhaps he's Quen's natural child. Will Palmer's always going about saying "he never had no father". How about that?'

'What have you been reading?' Wexford snapped. 'Mrs Henry Wood? *The Marriage of Figaro?*'

'Sorry. It was just an idea.'

'And a very poor one. You may be a good teacher of English, Lionel, but you're a rotten detective.' Wexford smiled ruefully. 'Even worse than me,' he said, and he got up, wondering what Burden had found out in his absence.

Marriott remained sitting at the table for a moment but he caught Wexford up just as the chief inspector was crossing the bridge.

'I've remembered something,' he said, out of breath. 'Elizabeth used to send a hell of a lot of parcels. Smallish brown-paper parcels. Often, when I've been up there in the daytime, I've seen a parcel on the hall table, but there was always a letter or two waiting for the post on top of it. Any use to you?'

'I don't know, but thanks all the same.'

'You're welcome, my dear,' said Marriott, turning to leave him. He looked back over his shoulder and added rather wistfully, 'Don't drop me, Reg, now you've squeezed me dry.'

'Even a copper needs friends,' said Wexford, and then he walked back up the High Street to the police station.

Burden was sitting at the rosewood desk eating a sandwich lunch.

'Clear out of it,' said Wexford crossly. 'You're making crumbs on my blotter.'

'You always make crumbs.'

'Maybe, but it's my blotter and, incidentally, my office.'

'Sorry, sir,' said Burden virtuously. 'I thought you'd gone on a pub crawl.'

Wexford gave an ill-tempered snort. He blew away the crumbs and sat down with dignity. 'Any news?'

'Not yet. No dice from either of the Newcastles. I've been on to Dublin.'

'You're wrong about one thing, Mike. Twohey didn't meet Mrs Nightingale in any forest. She sent his money to him in parcels. I don't know to what address but we could try asking Katje.'

Burden compressed his lips into a thin line.

'You've had your lunch,' said Wexford, 'so I suggest you get over there now.'

Burden groaned. 'Do I have to?' he said in an almost schoolboy voice, in the voice of his son.

'Are you joking?' Wexford roared. 'Are you out of your mind? She won't eat you.'

'It's not being eaten that I'm scared of,' said Burden. He screwed up his lunch paper, dropped it in the basket and went out, giving Wexford a glance of mock dismay.

There was nothing more for him to do now, Wexford reflected, but wait. He sent Bryant to the canteen to fetch him some lunch and after he had eaten it a great weariness overcame him. He decided to read to keep himself awake and, since the only reading matter he had to hand apart from a heap of reports he knew by heart was the book Denys Villiers had given him, he read that. Or, to put it more accurately, he read the first three paragraphs, only to nod off and nearly jump out of his skin when the phone bell shrilled.

'Try hardware shops,' he told his caller tiredly. 'Especially those which have changed hands in the past four years. He may have changed his name.' With a spark of inspiration, he added, 'I'd be interested in any ironmonger's shop called Nightingale's or, say, the Manor Stores.'

He returned to page one of *Wordsworth in Love*, flicked on to a family tree. There, in strong black type, was the name, George Gordon Wordsworth. He had been, Wexford noted, the poet's own grandson. And this piece of information, already recorded in his newly published book, was what Villiers had led him to believe he had sought from the school library. The man had a weakness, then, the weakness of underrating his opponent.

It was nearly six before Burden got back.

'My God, you've been long enough.'

'She and Nightingale were out. Picnicking, I gather. I waited till they got back.'

'Could she remember the address on the parcels?'

'She says she only posted parcels of stuff Mrs Nightingale sent to Holland, except for last Tuesday, the day Mrs N. got killed. Then she posted two, one to her mother in Holland and another one. She never even looked at the address.'

Wexford shrugged. 'Well, it was worth a try, Mike. Sorry about your Sunday afternoon. I don't suppose you met with a fate worse than death, though, did you?'

'Nightingale was there all the time.'

'You make him sound,' said Wexford, 'like a nurse in a doctor's consulting room. Well, I'm going to Myfleet myself now just for another scout round that forest and maybe a talk with Mrs Cantrip. I'd advise you to go home. They can put through any calls that come in.'

It might take days, it might take weeks, but eventually Twohey would be found. And then, Wexford thought as he drove past the King's School, he would talk. He would sit in Wexford's office, staring at the expanse of pale blue sky through the picture window as hundreds of unscrupulous villains had sat and stared before him, but, unlike most of them, he would have no reason to hold his tongue. A long term of imprisonment awaited him whether he spoke or kept silent. Probably he would be glad to talk to revenge himself on the dead woman and all her family, for no more money would come his way from that source.

And what would he say? That Villiers' love for his brother-in-law was of a kind that their narrow society couldn't condone? That Elizabeth had had a series of lovers young enough to be her own children? Or that, long ago, Villiers and Elizabeth had been concerned together in a criminal conspiracy?

Suddenly Wexford remembered the bombed house in which their parents had died. They were only children then, but children had been known to commit murder . . . Two people buried under rubble but still alive, parents who were perhaps a stumbling block in the way of their children's ambition. Certainly Villiers had benefited greatly from their deaths. His sister hadn't. Did the clue lie there?

Twohey would know. It was terribly frustrating to Wexford to think that perhaps Twohey was the only person now alive who did know and that he was hidden away comfortably with his secret. And it might be days, it might be weeks. . . .

On to Myfleet. The church bells of Clusterwell were ringing for Evensong and, as soon as their chimes died away behind him, he heard those of Myfleet ahead, eight bells ringing great brazen changes through the evening air.

There was a note pinned to Mrs Cantrip's front door: *Gone to church. Back 7.30.* An invitation to burglars, Wexford thought, only he couldn't remember any burglary taking place in Myfleet for ten years. Its trees shrouded crimes of greater moment. He turned away, and the ginger cat, locked out among the flowers, rubbed itself against his legs.

Breathing in the scent of the pines that all day had been bathed in sunshine. Wexford entered the forest. The path he took was the path Elizabeth Nightingale had taken that night, and he followed it until he came to the clearing where Burden believed she had met Twohey and he believed—what?

Perhaps Burden was right again, after all. Those parcels might never have been posted but delivered by hand. She would hardly have carried such large sums of money loose in her handbag. Anyway, she hadn't had a handbag, only a coat and a torch . . . He stared at the lichened log where she had sat. The scrape marks of four shoes were still apparent on the dry sandy ground and in the whorls of pine needles four shifting feet had made.

If her companion was Twohey—observed perhaps by Sean who misunderstood the purpose of their meeting— how had Twohey come? Over the black wooded hill from Pomfret? Or by the path that skirted the Myfleet cottage gardens and came out eventually—where? Wexford decided to explore it.

The church bells had stopped and the place was utterly silent. He walked between the straight narrow pine trunks, looking up sometimes at the patches of pale silvery sky, and sometimes from side to side of him into the forest itself which was so dark and, up to head height, so sterile, that no birds sang there and the only visible life was that of the midges which danced in swarms.

It was on account of the midges that he was glad when the trees to the left of him petered out and he found himself walking against the cottage fences. Presently, ahead of him, he heard a whisper of music. It was a sentimental treacly melody that he soon defined as belonging to the pop or dance-music order, and it reminded Wexford of those soft and faintly erotic tunes which had floated down to him from Katje Doorn's transistor. Just as he was thinking how pleasant and undemanding it sounded on this peaceful summer evening, it ceased and was succeeded by an appalling cacophony, the furious result of several saxophones, organs, drums and electric guitars all being played at once.

Wexford put his head over the fence and stared into the square plot of land, part wilderness and part rubbish dump, which was the Lovells' back garden. From the open kitchen window some fifty feet of electric lead stretched to the shed from which the noise emanated. Wexford backed a little, covering his assaulted ears.

Then he took his hands down.

Inside the shed someone was speaking. The tone and timbre of the voice were unmistakable, its accent deliberately cultivated. Mid-Atlantic, Wexford decided.

With mounting curiosity, he listened.

Addressing his unseen, indeed non-existent, audience as 'guys and dolls', Sean Lovell, with smooth professional patter, made a short dismissive comment on the last piece of music and then, more enthusiastically, announced his next record. This time it was the effusion of a big band and it was even more discordant than the composition which had made Wexford cover his ears.

It stopped. Sean spoke again and, as he took in the full

implication of his words, a shaft of intense pity pierced Wexford. Perhaps, he thought, there are few things so sad as eavesdropping on a man alone with his daydreams, a man indulging his solitary, private and ridiculous vice.

'And now,' said the disembodied voice, 'what you've all been waiting for. You've come a long way tonight and I can promise you you're not going to be disappointed. Here he is, boys and girls. Let's have a big hand for your own Sean Lovell!'

Unaccompanied, he began to sing. Wexford walked away, very delicately and softly for such a big man, his feet scarcely causing a crackle on the needled forest floor.

He knew now what Sean had been doing that night, what he did every night and would perhaps do for years until some girl caught him and showed him how daydreams die and that life is digging a rich man's garden.

15

WEXFORD was so tired that he fell asleep as soon as his head was on the pillow. Like most people approaching that phase of life which succeeds middle age but is not yet old age, he was finding it more and more difficult to get a good night's sleep. Years ago, when he was still young, he had acquired the sensible habit of emptying his mind at night of all the speculations and worries which troubled him during the day, and of turning his thoughts to future domestic plans or back to pleasant memories. But his subconscious was outside his control and it often asserted itself in dreams of those daytime anxieties.

So it was that night. In his dream he was down by the Kingsbrook, the scene of many of his favourite walks, when he saw a boy fishing upstream. The boy was fair and thin with a strong-boned Anglo-Saxon face. Wexford went nearer to him, keeping in the shadow of the trees, for some inexplicable dream reason not wishing to be observed. It was pleasant and warm down by the river, a summer evening that, he felt, had succeeded a long hot day.

Presently he heard someone calling and he saw a girl come running over the brow of the hill. Her light, almost yellow, hair and the cast of her face told him she was the boy's sister, older than he, perhaps fourteen or fifteen. She had come to fetch him away, and he heard them break into bitter argument because the boy wanted to remain and go on fishing.

He knew he had to follow them across the meadows. They ran ahead of him, the girl's hair flying. Above him a plane zoomed over, and he saw the bombs dropping like heavy black feathers.

Something of the house still remained standing, bare windowless walls enclosing a smoking mass from which came the cries of those buried alive. The children were neither shocked nor frightened, for this was a nightmare where natural emotions are suspended. He watched, a detached observer, as the girl groped her way into the black inferno, the boy at her heels. Now he could see a long pale arm protrude from the rubble and hear a voice calling for help, for mercy. The children began shovelling with their bare hands and he came closer to help them. Then he saw that they were not uncovering the screaming faces but burying them deeper, laughing like demons as they worked furiously to finish what the bomb had begun, and he jerked awake as he shouted to them to stop.

Conscious now, he found himself sitting up, his shouts coming as half-choked snores. His wife, lying beside him, hadn't stirred. He rubbed his eyes and looked at the luminous hands of his watch. It was five past two.

If he awoke at that hour he knew he would never get to sleep again and his usual habit was to go downstairs, sit in an armchair and find something to read. The dream stayed with him, vivid and haunting, as he put on his dressing gown and made for the stairs. In the morning he would set in motion the research necessary to discover exactly what had happened that day the Villiers' home was destroyed. Now for something to read . . .

As a young man, when he had had more spare time and less responsibility, he had been a great reader, and literary criticism and writers' biographies had been among his favourite reading matter. Mrs Wexford couldn't understand this and he remembered how she had asked him why he wanted to read what someone else said about a book. Why not just read the book itself? And he hadn't quite known how to answer her, how in this field he couldn't trust his own judgment because he was only a policeman and he hadn't a university degree. Nor could he have told her that he needed instruction and knowledge because the purpose of education is to turn the soul's eye towards the light.

Thinking of this and of the pleasure he had had from such works, he turned his physical eye to *Wordsworth in Love* which he had left lying on the coffee table. After only four hours' sleep he was no longer tired and far more alert than when he had formerly tried to apply himself to this book. He might as well have another go at it. Pity it was about Wordsworth, though. Rather a dull poet, he thought. All that communing with nature and walking about in the Lake District. A bit tedious really. Now if only it had been about Lord Byron, say, that would have been a different matter, something to get his teeth into. There was an interesting character for you, a romantic larger-than-life man with his sizzling love affairs, his disastrous marriage, the scandal over Augusta Leigh. Still, it wasn't; it was about Wordsworth. Well, he would read it and maybe, even if it bored him, he would get some idea of the nature of the fascination the Lake poet had for Villiers, the obsession almost that had made him write God knew how many books about him.

He began to read and this time he found it easy and pleasant to follow. After a while he began to wish he had read more of Wordsworth's poetry. He had no idea the man had been in love with a French girl, had been involved in the Revolution and had narrowly missed losing his head. It was good, bracing stuff and Villiers wrote well.

At six he made himself a large pot of tea. He read on, utterly absorbed, and by now considerably excited. The room began to fill with light, and slowly, with the same gradual dawning, Wexford's mind was illuminated. He finished the last chapter and closed the book.

Sighing, he addressed himself coldly, 'You ignorant old fool!' Then he rubbed his stiff hands and said aloud, 'If only it had been Byron! My God, if only it had. I would have known the answer long ago.'

'The first Monday morning of term,' said John Burden, finishing his third slice of toast and marmalade, 'is worse than the first *day* of term.' And he added gloomily: 'Things really start getting serious.' He prodded his sister with a sticky finger. 'Isn't it time you started being sick?'

'I'm not going to be sick, you beast.'

'Why ever not? Today's worse than the first day, much, much worse. I bet you'll be ever so sick when you start at the High School. *If* you get there. You'll be too sick to do the exams.'

'I shan't!'

'Oh, yes, you will.'

'Be quiet, the pair of you,' said Burden. 'Sometimes I think there's more peace and quiet down at the nick.' He left the breakfast table and prepared to go there. 'You must be the most unnatural brother and sister in Sussex,' he said.

John looked pleased at being placed in this unique category. 'Can I have a lift, Dad? Old Roman Villa's taking us for Prayers and there'll be hell to pay if I'm late.'

'Don't say "hell to pay",' said Burden absently. 'Come on, then. I've got a busy day ahead of me.'

A day of hunting for a needle in a haystack, of running a predator to earth. He marched into the police station and met Sergeant Martin in the foyer.

'Anything turned up on Twohey yet?'

'No, sir, not as far as I know, but Mr Wexford's on to something. He said he wanted to see you as soon as you came in.'

Burden went up in the lift.

The chief inspector was sitting at his desk, impatiently drumming his fingers on the blotter. There were pouches under his eyes and he looked, Burden thought, very much the worse for wear. And yet, about his whole demeanour, there was an air of triumph, of momentous discovery that until this moment he had kept suppressed.

'You're late,' he snapped. 'I've had to go over and swear out the warrant myself.'

'What warrant? You mean you've found Twohey?'

'Twohey be damned,' said Wexford, jumping up and taking his raincoat from the stand. 'Hasn't it yet penetrated your dapper little skull that this is a *murder* hunt? We are going to Clusterwell to make an arrest.'

Obediently, Burden followed him from the room. Wexford didn't care for the lift and, since he had been trapped in it for two hours one afternoon, had tended to avoid it. But now he jumped in and pressed the button apparently without a qualm.

'Villiers' place?' Burden asked and, when Wexford nodded, 'Well, you won't find him there. He's taking school Prayers this morning.'

'How bloody unsuitable.' Wexford gave an explosive snort. The lift sank gently and the door slid open. 'We'll take one of the W.P.C.s with us, Mike.'

'Shall we indeed? When are you going to tell me who we're arresting and why?'

'In the car,' said Wexford. 'On the way.'

'And how you suddenly happened to see the light?'

Wexford smiled a smile full of triumph and renewed confidence. 'I couldn't sleep,' he said as they waited for the policewoman to join them. 'I couldn't sleep, so I read a book. I'm an ignorant old policeman, Mike. I don't read enough. I should have read this one when its author first gave it to me.'

'I didn't know it was a detective story, sir,' said Burden innocently.

'Don't be so bloody silly,' Wexford snapped. 'I don't mean the book outlines the murder plan. Anyway, there was no plan.'

'Of course not. It was unpremeditated.'

'Yes, you were right there and right about a lot of things,' Wexford said, adding in a sudden burst of confidence: 'I don't mind telling you, I began to think you were right in everything. I thought I was getting old, past it.'

'Oh, come, sir,' said Burden heartily. 'That's nonsense.'

'Yes, it is,' the chief inspector snapped. 'I've still got my eyesight, I've still got some intuition. Well, don't stand hanging about there all day. We've got to make an arrest.'

Someone else must have stood on the dais and commanded the boys to lift up their hearts and voices, for Denys Villiers was at home.

'I took the day off,' he said to Wexford. 'I'm not well.'

'You look ill, Mr Villiers,' said Wexford gravely and, meeting the man's eyes, 'You always look ill.'

'Do I? Yes, perhaps I do.'

'You don't seem curious about the purpose of our call.'

Villiers threw up his head. 'I'm not. I know why you've come.'

'I should like to see your wife.'

'I know that too. Do you imagine I think you've brought a policewoman for the sake of a little feminine company? You underrate your opponent, Mr Wexford.'

'You have always underrated yours.'

Villiers gave a slight painful smile. 'Yes, we have been a mutual denigration society.' He went to the bedroom door. 'Georgina!'

She came out, shoulders hunched, head bent. Wexford had only once before seen anyone come through a doorway like that, and then it had been a man, a father who for two days had kept his children at gunpoint in a room with him. At last he had been persuaded to drop his gun and come out, walk across the threshold to the waiting police and crumple into his wife's arms.

Georgina crumpled into her husband's.

He held her in a close embrace and he stroked her hair. Wexford heard her murmuring to him, begging him not to leave her. She wore no jewellery but her wedding and engagement rings.

It was so painful to watch that he couldn't bring himself to speak the words of the charge. He stood awkwardly, clearing his throat, giving a little cough like the sound he had made when she had locked herself in the bathroom. Suddenly she lifted her head and looked at them over her husband's shoulder. Tears were pouring down her freckled cheeks.

'Yes, I killed Elizabeth,' she said hoarsely. 'The torch was on the ground. I picked it up and killed her. I'm glad I did it.' Denys Villiers, still holding her, shivered violently. 'If I had known before, I would have killed her sooner. I killed her as soon as I knew.'

Very quietly Wexford spoke the words of the charge.

'I don't care what you take down in writing,' she said. 'I did it because I wanted to keep my husband. He's mine, he belongs to me. I never had anyone else to belong to me. She had everything but I only had him.'

Villiers listened with a still set face. 'May I go with her?' Wexford had never expected to hear him speak so humbly.

'Of course you may,' he said.

The policewoman took Georgina to the waiting car, an arm round her shoulders. The arm was only for support and to prevent her from stumbling, but it looked as if it had been placed there from kindness and a kind of sisterly regard. Burden followed them, walking with the slow stiff pace of a mourner at a funeral.

Villiers looked at Wexford and the chief inspector returned his gaze. 'She can't tell you very much,' said Villiers. 'I'm the only person living who knows it all.'

'Yes, Mr Villiers, we shall need to take a statement from you.'

'I've written something already. Other people talk or else shut it all up inside themselves, but writers write. I wrote this in the night. I haven't been able to sleep. I haven't slept at all.'

And the envelope was waiting on the hall table, propped against a vase. Taking it, Wexford saw that it was addressed to him and that there was a stamp on it.

'If you hadn't come this morning I should have posted it. I couldn't have borne the waiting any longer. Now you have it I think perhaps I shall sleep.'

'Shall we go, then?' said Wexford.

Burden drove with Villiers beside him. No one spoke. As they entered Kingsmarkham, Wexford slit open the envelope and glanced briefly at the first typewritten sheet.

Then the car swung on to the police station forecourt.

He got out and opened the nearside front door. But Villiers didn't move. Touching his shoulder to tell him they had arrived, Wexford saw with a sudden shaft of compassion, the first he had ever felt for the man, that Villiers was fast asleep.

For the attention of Chief Inspector Wexford

I cannot suppose that I am among your favourite authors, so I will keep this statement as brief as I can. I am writing it at night while my wife sleeps. Yes, she can sleep, the sleep of the innocent, just avenger.

When you quoted Byron to me I was sure that you knew why if you did not know how. But I have asked myself since then, did you know? Did you even know what you were saying? I stared at you. I waited for you to arrest my wife, and my face must have told you what I was afraid of : that you, to frighten me and to extract a confession from me, had quoted to me the words of a man all the world knows to have been his sister's lover.

I think I betrayed myself then. I certainly did so when I gave you my book to read. But then I thought you were too ignorant, too dull and plodding, to equate a short passage in my book with my own life. Now, as the dawn comes up and in its light I look at things coldly and dispassionately, as I remind myself of my provocative rudeness to you and your civilised forbearance, as I remember your percipience, I know that I was wrong. You will read and you will realise, 'Thou best philosopher, thou eye among the blind!'

Wordsworth wrote that, Mr Wexford. Wordsworth, as you now know, also loved his own sister, but being a disciple of duty (stern daughter of the voice of God), he left her. You will no longer need to ask what attracted me to Wordsworth, in what particular our affinity lay. For, although Dorothy appears in my book as the merest interlude between Annette and Mary, you will have noted the parallel; you will have realised what, when I was a young man, seeking a subject to which I might devote my life, drew me to this poet. That among other things, of course. I consider Wordsworth second only to Milton and can say with Coleridge, 'Wordsworth is a very great man, the only man to whom at all times and in all modes of excellence I feel myself inferior.'

I might, of course, have chosen Lord Byron. The obviousness of the choice repelled me. Besides, I did not want to waste my muse on one whom I consider superficial and grandiloquent, a swashbuckling pop star, simply because he had committed incest (very probably) with Augusta Leigh. But Byron, *because* he is better known now for his incest than his verse, affects me strangely, the very mention of his name, the quotation of his lines, sets my nerves on edge. You could say that I am allergic to him.

But I am forgetting my promise to be brief.

When we were children I did not love my sister. We were always quarrelling and our separation caused us no distress. We were glad to get shot of each other. I did not see her again until I was in my last year at Oxford.

Our meeting was at the twenty-first birthday party of a university acquaintance of mine. This man's father introduced me to his secretary, a girl called Elizabeth Langham. We went out together and soon we became lovers.

I told you I was a good liar but I am not lying now when I say that I had no idea who she really was or that I had ever seen her before the night of this party. Nine years had passed and we had altered. I asked her to marry me and then she had to tell me. For two months I had been my own sister's lover.

For years she had followed my fortunes, from envy and a sense of the unfairness of the arrangement that had been made for us. Having run away·to London with a man called Langham who had paid for her to take a secretarial course, she took a job with my friend's father, knowing that his son and I were at Oxford together. She went to the party, curious to see me; she came out with me with some unformed plan of revenge in her mind. But then the situation passed out of her control. In spite of what she knew, she had fallen in love with me. Did it trouble her? I don't think so. Long before this she had passed far beyond the confines of accepted morality, so that she saw this step only as something especially daring and defiant of society.

We parted, she to America with her employer, I to Oxford. I will not dwell on my feelings at this time. You are a sensitive man and perhaps you can imagine them for yourself.

I married as soon as I had my degree; not for love—I have never in my life been in love with anyone but Elizabeth—but for safety, for normality. The allowance my uncle had made me ceased when I was twenty-one, so, knowing that I could never make a living from writing poetry or from writing about it, I applied for a teaching job at the King's School.

Was I taking a risk in returning to Kingsmarkham? Elizabeth had told me she hated the place. I thought I had found the one town in the world my sister would be sure to avoid.

It was that egregious busyboy, Lionel Marriott, who

told me Elizabeth was here. I dreaded meeting her; I longed to see her. We met. She introduced me to her husband, the son of a millionaire who had been on holiday in America while she was working there. He had bought the Manor as a surprise for her, believing she would like to live near her childhood home.

We sat at table together with her husband and my wife. We made small talk. As soon as our chance came we saw each other alone, and that, Mr Wexford, was the second beginning.

Our love would have been impossible without the innocent acquiescence of Quentin Nightingale. If he had disliked me it would have been difficult for Elizabeth and me to have met and, since I could not have borne to live near her but separated from her, I should have been forced to change my job and move away. I wish with all my heart now that this had happened.

Women are tougher than we are, less scrupulous, less a prey to guilt. I suppose Elizabeth had been in love with Quentin when she married him and had meant to be an honest faithful wife. Immediately I re-entered her life she put all this behind her and began to use him as a tool. Her aim was to have me as her lover and at the same time to keep her position, her money and her reputation. She wanted the best of both worlds and she got them. Still, to shift the blame like this is useless. I was as guilty as she. The difference between us was that I had a conscience and she had none.

She worked on Quentin in devious and subtle ways. She told him, pretending that June was her source, that I was a difficult man with a disturbed personality. It would be a kindness on his part to befriend me. Characteristically, he reacted by offering me a room in the Old House for my exclusive use.

It was to seem as if all my invitations to the Manor came from Quentin, for Elizabeth and I must appear to dislike each other. Why? She said that if we showed even normal fraternal affection in public we should soon be betrayed into showing a deeper love than is permitted to brother and sister. I do not believe this was her true reason. Rather, I think, she loved intrigue for its own sake and our public indifference lent for her a spice to our private love.

And if I say that I loved Quentin too will you call this the vilest hypocrisy? Or has your experience taught you that it is often those whom we have betrayed and deceived and dishonoured that we love the best? For, in preventing them from discovering our betrayal, we learn how to protect them from other harm as well as this one, and the kind words we use initially to blind them become habitual and ultimately sincere. Yes, Mr Wexford, I loved Quentin, and Elizabeth, who discouraged all my friendships lest I should be driven to confide in a friend, allowed me this one, never understanding that of all mankind he was the man I longed to confess to, his the only forgiveness I should have valued.

I shall now come to Twohey.

He had been watching Elizabeth visit me at the Old House, and one day he saw me walk down the stairs with her and embrace her in the apple room. It was not a brother's embrace and Twohey, from outside the window, took a photograph. I paid him blackmail. When he had bled me white Elizabeth began selling her jewellery and having copies made.

You have not found Twohey yet, have you? Let me help you. Apart from saving Georgina as much suffering as I can, I have only one wish left and that is to see Twohey as wretched as he made Elizabeth and me. You will find his address on the dressmaker's bills in the writing desk in her bedroom. Tanya Tye is the name (more probably the alias) of the woman with whom he lives in a luxury flat over the shop in Bruton Street. It was all quite simple and very clever. Whenever Twohey wanted money he would send Elizabeth a bill from Tanya Tye and the money she was to pay was the sum on the bill *plus* one nought added to the figure. For example: if the bill was for a hundred and fifty pounds, Elizabeth was to send him fifteen hundred. She sent the money in brown paper parcels. The last one was posted by Katje the day before Elizabeth died. To show her he had received the money he sent her receipted bills.

Good hunting, Mr Wexford.

I suppose Marriott has enlightened you as to all the details of my surface life. You will know that the Nightingales and I always took our holidays together and that two years ago, because of Quentin's illness, Elizabeth and I went away alone. Marriott said we looked ill and careworn when we came home from Dubrovnik, but it never occurred to him that we were sick at heart, not because we had quarrelled but because we had been happy.

I wanted her to leave Quentin and come away with me. She refused. Had we set up house together years ago no one would have suspected that we were brother and sister. Now everyone knew it and the scandal would be monumental. That is what she said. But I knew her so well, *soror mea sponsor*. I knew that her money and her position meant as much to her as I did. She was used to her two worlds, her eggs in two baskets, and, leaving out her terror of Twohey, I think she was mostly happy.

I had come to the end. I was thirty-six and all my life

I had worked hard but I had nothing. The fruits of all my labours had gone to keep a Mayfair modiste's lover in luxury; I had no wife, no children, no friends and I lived in three rooms. True, I had Elizabeth, but for how long? The time would come when she, tranquillised by middle age, would sacrifice me to her other, safer world.

I decided to make a complete break, so I refused all Quentin's invitations to the Manor, his almost irresistible pleas. I thought I should be able to work. Instead I lay evening after evening on my bed, thinking, doing nothing, sometimes contemplating suicide. It was a dark night of the soul, comparable to the breakdown Wordsworth had when he had to leave France and leave Annette behind.

I no longer wanted Elizabeth. If I missed either of them it was Quentin that I missed. I went to the Manor at last and told them I would not go to Rome with them. I looked at Elizabeth and felt—nothing. It was incomprehensible to me that I had wasted the best of my life in loving her.

I went to Spain. Not the romantic, magic Spain of Madrid and the high sierras, but the sweltering Blackpool which is what we have made of the Costa Brava, and I went as escort to the school party. I suppose I told myself that to feel rage and exasperation and excruciating boredom would be better than to feel nothing at all.

Georgina was staying at the same hotel. I am no longer an attractive man, Mr Wexford, and I look much older than I am. I have no conversation, for I have talked my whole soul out to my sister. Long long ago I lost the technique of talking beguilingly to young women. I am better suited to a Trappist's cell than to caper nimbly in a lady's chamber. But Georgina fell in love with me, poor thing. It was quite a joke in that horrible hotel, Georgina's love.

I had had everything and, rich in gifts, had squandered

them all. She had never had anything. The youngest child of a large poor family, she told me that she had never possessed anything she could feel to be exclusively her own. No man had ever wanted her or even taken her out more than a couple of times. She was plain and shy and dull.

A poor ill-favoured thing, but mine own . . .

We were married. I brought Georgina to the Manor and to the disappointment in Quentin's eyes. Elizabeth suffered no disappointment. She was triumphant in her white velvet and her fake jewels. I looked at her, I looked at poor Georgina and I asked myself, as once again I fell in love with my sister, what have I done?

The third beginning and the last. . . .

I wanted to settle down. I wanted those children. If not six, I wanted some. But I did not listen to the stern daughter of God's voice, nor even to the shriller querulous voice of my wife, clamouring for me to be all in all to her, a compensation for long loneliness, a real husband who would cherish her. I listened to my sister.

So we come to the day of Elizabeth's death.

No, of course you did not believe me when I said I went down to the school library in the evenings to do research for my work. Only someone as innocent and as uninterested in literature as Georgina would believe that. My own works on Wordsworth are the only ones in the school library, apart from the Selincourt and Darbyshire collection edition and those volumes I have in my own house. I went to meet Elizabeth in the forest.

We had spent the afternoon of that day together, but that was not enough for us. The school holidays would soon be over and then . . . ? Weekly bridge parties? Literary discussions with Quentin, and Elizabeth a silent third? We were sick for each other. We arranged to meet in the forest at eleven.

I have said that Georgina accepted my excuses, but if she had, Elizabeth would be alive today. Georgina had begun to doubt me and to a woman as possessive as she, doubt calls for action.

We went to the Manor and played bridge. Just before we left Elizabeth gave Georgina a silk scarf. She used to give Georgina a lot of her cast-off clothing. I suppose it amused her to see my wife in handed-on finery, knowing that Georgina would look less well in it than she and that I would notice and make the obvious unjust comparison.

I drove Georgina home and went out again to meet Elizabeth. She came to the clearing in the wood just before eleven. We sat on a log, we smoked, we talked. Elizabeth had brought with her that torch from the garden room, for the moon had gone in and it was dark.

At about twenty past she said that we should go. Georgina's faint display of temper after our bridge game had made her nervous and she said to spend too long in the forest would be to tempt Providence.

It was my usual practice, after these meetings of ours, to wait by my car and watch her cross the road and gain the safety of the Manor grounds, so we walked to the car together with our arms round each other. As we went we saw the headlights of another car moving on the road, as if searching the fringe of the forest with its beams. It passed on and we forgot it.

When we came to my car Elizabeth said that she had forgotten her torch and must go back for it, in case someone should find it and know she had been there. I wanted to go with her, but she said she would be safe alone. What, after all, could happen to her? What indeed?

I took her in my arms and kissed her, just as I had

kissed her on the day Twohey was outside the window. Then I drove home. Georgina was not there when I got back; nor was her car. She came in at midnight, shivering in a thin shirt—for she had burnt her sweater on Palmer's bonfire—and in her hand she held a bloodstained torch wrapped up in newspaper.

She had followed me, Mr Wexford, and seen me kiss Elizabeth, so she waited by the log for Elizabeth to come back for the torch. What happened then I only know from what Georgina told me. She was so shocked by what she had seen, so horrified, that the balance of her mind, as coroners put it, was disturbed. She tried to express this to Elizabeth, but she was incoherent, she was hysterical, and Elizabeth laughed at her. What did she, Georgina, think she could do about it? she asked her. We would not, in the nature of things, be lovers for ever. Georgina must wait and one day I would return to her. Surely she would not risk the scandal that would arise if she made scenes or told anyone?

Elizabeth bent over to find the torch which she thought had fallen behind the log. It had not. Georgina was holding it and, while Elizabeth had her back to her, she raised it and struck my sister. Again and again until Elizabeth was dead.

Georgina was wearing the scarf herself. She pulled it off and wiped her own hands with it. Then she crossed the road, stuffed the scarf into a hollow tree and burnt her sweater on Palmer's bonfire.

Is that not nearly all? When Georgina came home and told me what she had done, I confessed the whole story to her. I told her about the blackmail and about the jewels.

I know what you are asking me. Why didn't I, as my sister's lover and dearest friend, immediately give my wife up to you? And you have provided your own answer, that I was afraid of the relationship becoming known. But it was not entirely that. I was almost stunned with horror, with grief, and yet even then I wanted to salvage my life. With Elizabeth gone, I might yet settle down, be peaceful, be happy, tell no more lies.

Man is a strange creature, Mr Wexford. He has lifted himself so far above his fellow animals that Darwin's Theory seems fantastic to him, a monstrous libel. And yet he still shares with them his strongest instinct, self-preservation. The whole world may lie in ruins about him, but still he looks for a corner to run into and clings to his hope that it can never, no matter what bombardment he has suffered, be too late.

At that moment I loathed Georgina. I could have beaten her to death. But I told myself that what had happened was my fault. I had done it. I did it when I went to that party so many years ago. So, instead of doing violence to her, I took her in my arms and smelt Elizabeth's blood in her hair and under her fingernails.

I washed the torch myself and threw away the wet batteries. I ran a bath for Georgina and told her to wash her hair. The skirt she had been wearing and her shirt I burned on the kitchen boiler.

I could not see why you should suspect Georgina, for she had no apparent motive, and that is why I grew hysterical when you brought us the news of the will. To arrest my wife and convict her for the wrong motive! That would have been the ultimate irony.

She was very nervous, very bad at countering your attacks. When we were alone she told me she would like to confess, for you or any right-thinking person would understand. I prevented her. I thought we still had a chance. Then you quoted Lara to me and I began to make notes in preparation for this statement.

It is all over now.

You will, I am sure, be gentle with Georgina, and I know that during her trial every newspaper reader in this country will be for her heart and soul, as well as those more significant arbiters, the judge and jury. She will go to prison for two or three years and then one day she will marry again, have the children she needs and the normal quiet life she wants. June re-married long ago. Soon Quentin will have his little Dutch girl as chatelaine of Myfleet and, if she is unfaithful to him, it will be a natural run-of-the-mill infidelity that my kind brother will bear with a perhaps not too painful fortitude. As for Elizabeth, she died at the height of her love and her triumph and just in time to avoid the bitterness of growing old.

Indeed, one might say with Wilde that the good ended happily and the bad unhappily, for that is the meaning of fiction. Perhaps it should also be the meaning of fact. In other words, I have my deserts. I have no idea what I shall do, but I think it unlikely that after the trial any authority will wish to employ me on its teaching staff.

I care very little about that. I think I can bear scandal without too much distress, and if people shun me I can do without people. The one person I cannot do without I shall never see again, and this thing which is unbearable I must bear. I shall never again kiss her in the dark forest or among the shadows of the Old House or see her dressed in white velvet or hear her name spoken with admiration. She is dead and her death is for me the ultimate irreparable mutilation.

Your inspector asked me what I wanted and nothing has happened to make me change my answer. I want to die.